S0-BAV-815

THE
KING

DAVID FEINTUCH

2003
50TH
ANNIVERSARY

ACE BOOKS, NEW YORK

THE KING

An Ace Book / published by arrangement with
the author

PRINTING HISTORY
Ace hardcover edition / August 2002
Ace mass-market edition / April 2003

Copyright © 2002 by David Feintuch.
Cover art by Christian McGrath.
Cover design by Pyrographx.

For information address: The Berkley Publishing Group,
a division of Penguin Putnam Inc.,
375 Hudson Street, New York, New York 10014.

Check out the ACE Science Fiction & Fantasy newsletter!

ISBN: 0-441-01037-7

ACE®
Ace Books are published by The Berkley Publishing Group,
a division of Penguin Putnam Inc.,
375 Hudson Street, New York, New York 10014.
ACE and the "A" design
are trademarks belonging to Penguin Putnam Inc.

PRINTED IN THE UNITED STATES OF AMERICA

10 9 8 7 6 5 4 3 2 1

PART ONE

---◆◆◆---

ONE

AS AUTUMN GAVE way to winter, we swept down from the hills, a thousand strong, driving Danzik's Norlanders from their barricades before dashing toward Stryx, royal seat of Caledon. Home, such as it was.

Captain Tursel urged our weary men to the coast road that ended in Stryx at Llewelyn's Keep, held in stubborn defiance of the Norlanders by my vassal Tantroth's Eiberians. Above that strongpoint lay Castle Stryx, still in the hands of my ruthless Uncle Margenthar.

In a shady grove at roadside, my mentor Rustin spoke with Earl Groenfil and my ward Anavar as the column trudged past. I spurred Ebon to their grazing, resting mounts. "Rust, the wagons are missing. They were supposed—"

"They're over the rise." Though there were but two years between us, my friend spoke soothingly, as if to a child. He jerked Ebon's reins from my chapped fingers, withstood my glare. "Take ease, Roddy. Trust in Captain Tursel."

I knew he was right; Tursel was an old campaigner loaned us by Uncle Raeth of Cumber for his experience. But Caledon was not a land of trust.

At last I took deep breath, and wisps of my frenzy melted, as mist before the sun. "As you say." I managed to make my tone civil. I owed him that.

Rust added reassuringly, "We'll be in Stryx by nightfall."

Groenfil's tone was dour. "Unless Tantroth betrays us."

I massaged my left cheek, and the scar that ran from eye to chin. I well understood Groenfil's unease. An hour past, Tantroth, Duke of Eiber, once my enemy, now my ally, had led his mounted guard along the coast road to Llewelyn's Keep, where we must follow. If he failed to open the gates to us, we'd be trapped in the old city's cobbled streets between the Keep and Danzik's Norlanders, who, ousted from the crossroads, swarmed like maddened bees about their winter camp.

I'd fretted over the possibility, but try as I might, I couldn't see how Tantroth could gain by betraying us to the foe. Only with our help might he dislodge King Hriskil's Norland regiments from Eiber, and regain his domain. Else, he was undone. And Hriskil surely would not reward Tantroth with Eiber merely for my capture; the duchy of Eiber abutted the Norlands. Through Eiber, Hriskil had access to the passes between our realms. Hriskil wanted its high valleys perhaps even more than he coveted Caledon itself.

Earl Groenfil looked about. "We're too slow; Danzik will regroup before our stragglers are past his camp."

I glanced at Rustin as if to say, "I told you so," but I forbore. "Give Tursel a hand, my lord, but don't quarrel with him."

"Aye, sire." The winds stirred, a sign of Earl Groenfil's displeasure. It was a Power of his House, as Caledon's Power was the Still I wielded.

"I could help too." Anavar looked hopeful. "Have I leave, sir?" At fifteen, he thought himself a man, and chafed at being ward of one only two years his senior. A year past, young Anavar had been an Eiberian noble, taken our prisoner during Tantroth's savage attack on Caledon. I'd made him my bondsman to save his life—Tursel would have cut his throat—but that was long past: now he enjoyed the rank of Baron of the Southern Reaches, an empty title admittedly, but he had grown to be my confidant and member of my inner circle.

Reluctantly, I nodded. I couldn't keep him in the warmth of my robe forever; to help him grow, I had to risk him.

As Anavar rode off, Rustin patted my knee in quiet approval. Though barely my elder, he was infinitely older in good humor, grace and sense. I'd come most reluctantly to rely on his guidance, even appointing him guardian of my person. My mother's early death had left me a very young king indeed, vulnerable to the maneuverings of my uncle Margenthar, who'd managed to be appointed regent. Time and again during my struggle for the crown, I'd proven, to my infinite dismay, that I wasn't quite ready to assume a man's station. Now Rustin bullied me unmercifully, and I was compelled by my oath to abide it.

TANTROTH OPENED THE sturdy Keep he'd captured, and bid us welcome.

Above us, accessed by the winding Castle Way, loomed

Castle Stryx, behind whose ramparts Mother had ruled and I had grown toward manhood. Now the castle was held by Margenthar, Duke of Stryx, whom I loathed. Uncle Mar had strangled my eight-year-old brother Pytor; now only my brother Elryc and I remained of the House of Caledon.

Together, castle and Keep presented a formidable defense. The road to the castle wended through the Keep: in one gate, out another. Over the years, detouring wagons had established the narrow Tradesman's Cut alongside the outer walls of the Keep, that brewers' wagons and tradesmen's carts might bypass the gates. But no army could mount assault on the castle without coming within deadly and continuous bowshot of the Keep.

Installed within this strongpoint, we immediately sent envoys up the steep hill to the castle.

Waiting for answer I paced the battlements of the Keep. I stalked to an arrow slit, peered through the slit to the coast road beyond. Still no sign of Danzik's Norlanders. "What word from Mar?" I rubbed my cold nose. If Margenthar wouldn't give up Castle Stryx, our position was precarious.

"You're king, Roddy. We'd tell you if he sent reply. Genard!" Rust snapped his fingers, and the stableboy leaped to his feet. "Find Rodrigo warm drink. No wine."

"I'm Lord Elryc's man." Genard was sullen. "Not yours."

Rust's tone had an edge. "I pray thee, Lord Elryc's man, find the king to drink!"

When Genard had gone Rustin unclenched his fingers, and I saw the effort his calm had cost.

"That lout maddens me," I said. Genard's irrepressible tongue could try the most patient of souls. Scarce thirteen, he deemed himself high enough to reproach his king. "He ought be thrashed."

Rustin's hand fell on my shoulder, as if to brush off the sting of his words. "You've fallen back to harsh ways. Yesterday, along the trail—"

"He wouldn't take Ebon to be fed."

"He's your brother's vassal, for good or ill. You had no right to order it." He regarded me until, shifting uncomfortably, I looked away. "Try to be kind, Roddy."

Hah. Easy for *him* to say; he wasn't king. Rubbing my scar, I stared at the sullen winter clouds.

The next morning, envoys descended the winding road

from Castle Stryx, with tidings too good to fathom. My uncle had bowed to the inevitable. He would surrender the castle, in return for safe conduct to his own holding at Verein.

FOR TWO WEEKS, while we set our defenses in order, I moodily paced the castle battlements.

We hadn't fought our way to Stryx, I argued, to hide behind its walls. Only by engaging the Norlanders might we dislodge them. If we didn't act now, winter's icy hand would stay us.

Rustin reluctantly agreed to a raid on the Norlander supply wagons.

We probed in strength, an elaborate way of saying we were too many to steal past Danzik's scouts, too few to mount a serious challenge to the sturdy breastworks he'd mounted around his camp.

As we crept through a grove of ash and beeches, an arrow whizzed past my head, buried itself in the bole of an aged beech tree. A few dead leaves drifted lazily to earth.

"*Will* you get down?" With a mighty tug on my jerkin, Rustin hauled me off my feet. "Idiot!"

Anavar favored him with a glance of reproach. After all, Rustin was berating his king.

"Withdraw, sire?" Tursel. We were pinned in the leafy grove, with no way out save that from which we came.

"Gather torches to light the arrows." Sourly, I eyed the Norlanders' wagons. At least we might burn their supplies, and leave Danzik's troops hungry and discomfited, facing winter in a hostile land.

It was a damp day; the pitch smoked and sputtered. A few of our arrows embedded themselves uselessly in the splintered rails of their wagons; none fell in the beds, where lay the sacks of grain, blankets, bundles of arrows and other implements of war.

"Rodrigo! M'lor!" Genard windmilled through the bushes to the hollow in which we crouched. "They attack the hors—"

Rustin clamped a hand over the boy's mouth. "Fool! You bellow the king's name? You'd tell the Norlanders he stands before them?"

Genard thrust away Rustin's palm. His voice dropped to little more than a whisper. "They're sneaking behind the pickets to cut the horses loose. Twenty men at least."

"I'll go. You three, and you." Tursel chose his men. "Move!"

"I'm sorry, Roddy. I mean, King. M'lor." Genard peered at our efforts. "Why do they shoot so low? Tell our archers the wagons won't burn unless they set the barrels afire, and the cloths. A few arrows in the side won't—"

I growled, "Silence him. Slit his throat. If that doesn't work—"

Mercifully, the boy subsided.

Three of the Norlanders' dozen wagons smoldered. One burst at last into a respectable blaze. Then another.

A runner scuttled to our forward line. "Tursel says we'd best withdraw. Our thirty men clashed with forty of theirs, and—"

"Fall back." In a rage, heedless of the risk of arrows, I stalked through the grove. My stride increased as I thought of Ebon, my treasured stallion. If he'd been hurt, or taken . . .

Kadar, chief of my bodyguards, scampered to keep pace. Earnest young soldiers, all of them, handpicked by Rustin. "Sire, let us lead."

"Bah." I thrust aside a low branch, was drenched by a torrent of droplets. "Imps take this weather! And Hriskil!" I wiped my brow with a damp sleeve.

Stiff fingers tweaked my ribs. "Patience, my prince."

I slapped away the offending hand. "And Rustin of the Keep!" But, quickly, I muttered a rite of propitiation.

Ahead, cries and shouts. I drew my sword. "To the horses!" My bodyguards drew steel, formed themselves around me. I would have none of it. I raced ahead, toward the thicket where we'd tied our mounts.

Before us, ever more Norlanders poured across a defile. They brandished short swords and heavy leather shields embellished with the half moon that their kind revered. They made for our pickets.

The handful of men we'd left to guard the horses were retreating, but so far in good order. I charged into the line. *"For Caledon!"* My bodyguards, caught unsuspecting, thundered after.

"For Rodrigo!"

The fury of our charge threw back Danzik's attackers. I wheeled, sprinted to the horses, tore loose Ebon's reins, threw myself in the saddle.

A squad of Norlander foot soldiers evaded our troop, raced toward us. I spurred Ebon, leaned low and whirled my sword. They dived to the soggy turf, all but one who was too slow. My sword sliced through his breastbone and was wrenched from my grasp. I whipped out my dagger, reined Ebon, wheeled to pursue our attackers. I plunged my blade into a fleeing foeman's shoulder.

Rustin, cursing mightily, galloped alongside. He caught my bridle. "Ride, Roddy! To Stryx!" His stallion Orwal's eyes were wild.

"We can't leave—"

"The horses are saved."

I risked a glance backward. In great haste, Tursel's men were cutting free our mounts. Anavar swarmed atop his mare, raced to the edge of the grove, beckoned me frantically.

Slowly, my battle fever ebbed. I spurred Ebon, to wait with Anavar by the safety of the road.

"RODDY, YOU'LL CATCH your death of cold." Rustin offered the cloak he'd brought.

A few miserable lights glimmered in the town far below the stony ramparts of the castle. Over the rushing sea beyond, the moon rode gallantly through mountains of cloud. I squinted, seeking the Norlanders' dark sails. It wouldn't be long before they loomed. Hriskil of the Norlands coveted both Caledon and Eiber, and his chieftain Danzik roamed both south and north of Stryx harbor. When the winter's snows melted to mist and the muddy roads dried, his hordes would break winter camp and march anew. Our recent foray had been but a pinprick, easily ignored.

I stared moodily over the dripping battlements. "I would be alone." Within the walls of Stryx I was secure, even in time of war. The castle was not so large I didn't know every soul within its ramparts.

As always, Rustin paid no heed. "Cover yourself, my prince." Gently, he draped the cloak over my damp shoulders.

"Thank you." My voice was remote.

"What troubles you?" He rested his lean form against an arrowguard.

"Where's Hriskil? Why doesn't he resupply Danzik?"

"Hriskil? In his palace, if he has the sense Lord of Nature

gave a pup." He drew his cloak tighter as if to make his point. "And Danzik will live off your peasants, if he must."

"Where, for that matter, is Uncle Mar?"

"Still in Verein, I imagine." Rustin hugged himself. "Come inside."

"After a while."

When winter drew nigh, Groenfil and Lady Soushire, two nobles who'd committed their houses to my cause, had returned to their domains. I had little more than the household guard with which to hold Stryx.

Rustin sighed, pulled his cloak tighter, prepared to wait the night.

Vexed, I rounded on him. "I ride with you, dine with you, tent with you. Am I to have no solitude?"

A light faded from Rustin's eyes. "As you decree, sire." He turned to go.

Now I'd wounded him. Imps and demons! "Stay." I curled my fingers around his shoulder. After a moment his ire faded, and he wrapped his arm around my waist.

So long I'd dreamed of becoming king of Caledon and of the pleasure it would bring. The sullen obeisance I'd force from cousin Bayard, the fine raiment I'd order, the dazzling banquets I'd set. I'd be the envy of my people and all the kingdoms round. Even Rust would stand in awe.

It hadn't worked out quite so. I'd come to my crown in betrayal and hurt, and bore a frightful scar from eye to chin that none but Rust could disregard. Worse, Stryx and all of Caledon were under siege. Even my Power couldn't overcome our peril.

Every land had its peculiar Power, each Power its own properties. The White Fruit of Chorr made whoever ingested it forever a devoted servant; through its use the King of the Chorr secured the loyalty of his courtiers. In the land of Parrad, trees were made to speak of what they'd seen. The Norlanders had their Rood, which augmented their already fearsome strength in battle; thank Lord of Nature, Hriskil himself wasn't outside our walls to wield it.

Powers followed crown and land. Within every kingdom it was so. Even our vassal earls had some small Powers; Earl Groenfil's rage summoned winds that felled great trees, and Uncle Raeth's unruly sensual passion snuffed out candles, to our mutual embarrassment.

Caledon's Power was the Still.

From time to time, I set my palms over a bowl of stillsilver, to consult my late mother, the queen, and my forebears, in their cold dusty gray cave. I paid a high price for my Power; the Still demanded that its wielder hold himself True, and virgin. The former requirement meant that to break any oath would cost my Power, and with it, the realm on which my grip was as yet frail. As to the latter, how could a young king who craved the station of manhood abide such restriction? In all the kingdom, only I was denied. Even my young ward Anavar was said to rut with camp women. Until recently my loneliness had led me, against my natural yearning for a woman's touch, to Rustin's embrace.

"You frown, my prince."

"I was thinking of Tresa." Uncle Raeth's granddaughter. I'd allowed myself to dream that perhaps, one day, the requirements of the Still set aside, I might frolic in the fields of her munificence. I had hope, until she saw my scarred face, and fled from my presence. Now, I would die rather than accept her pity.

"No doubt she's well. Three times she wrote, and you—"

"Let's not speak of it."

An uneasy silence.

"Come along, Roddy." Rust tugged me toward the imposing stone steps and the door of state that led to the donjon's great hall.

"I'd rather—"

"Now."

Meekly, I followed.

I was no longer a boy. At seventeen, I was master of myself and my kingdom. As Guardian of the King's Person, Rustin took unfair advantage of the license I'd freely and trustingly given; at times he ordered me about most imperiously. I found it easier to comply than to sunder our friendship. And, to tell truth, there were times I needed his counsel and even—though I might never admit it—his restraint. My temper was fearsome. Of late, since I'd begun to wield the Still, it seemed worse than ever.

The door to the Keep was guarded, within and without. The sentry bowed as he thrust it open before me. "King Rodrigo."

In the great hall, welcome warmth, and the glowing faces

of my nobles. Rust and I crossed to the vast fireplace, whose flames were so mighty they must be roaring through the chimney to the sky. "Are you heating the castle, or razing it?" My tone was sour.

At the table, nursing his mulled wine, Elryc stirred. "I had them throw on logs. My ague . . ."

I sighed. My brother's frail frame was always battered by one ailment or another. But he was wise beyond his twelve years, and counseled me well.

In the seasons since we'd wended our way home to Stryx and evicted my odious Uncle Margenthar, Elryc had shot up like a weed. A hint of hair darkened his lip, and his voice had plummeted from the upper registers. Soon, he too would lie with women, and we would grow apart.

"What news from Eiber, Roddy?" Elryc left his place at the table, stood warming himself at the furnace of a fire.

"Tantroth still holds his western hills. But the Norlanders have his Eiber Castle and all the lands to the sea." A log fell. Gloomily, I stared at the cascade of sparks. "When the weather breaks, we'll have to send more men."

"To Uncle Raeth first."

"It's the same." The lands of Raeth and Tantroth adjoined.

"It is not." Impatient, Elryc shook his head. "We can trust Raeth."

Raeth of Cumber, my father's uncle, was a canny old party, who like any lord schemed constantly to enlarge his domain. But we'd reached an understanding, he and I, that had deepened into mutual respect. And I knew that he had truly loved my late father. I said, "I promised Tantroth—"

"Send a token force. Give the bulk of your men to Raeth; they'll serve Tantroth as well in Cumber." True, if they'd draw the Norlanders' relentless hordes from Eiber. But Hriskil's troops were so many that our forces were a nuisance, a fly buzzing at a campfire.

"Sir, I wish you a good night." Anavar's Eiberian accent seemed thick tonight, but my landless young baron bowed with due courtesy. These days he showed me careful civility. Noble or not, he was my ward, and in recent weeks I'd beaten him twice for too haughty a mien. He, like Elryc, had grown, and was of that age I'd not long ago passed, in which one knew all there was to know. Rustin, of course, disapproved of my chastisement. I paid little heed; Rust disapproved of almost all my notions, and it gave me fervent satisfaction to set the boy right.

"Sleep well, Anavar." Self-consciously, I drew him into a moment's hug. He was my ward, and had no father near. And he'd ridden at my side in battle.

WET AND SHIVERING from my morning bath, I snapped my fingers. My servant handed me a thick cloth. I dried myself as quickly as I could, still shy that my body showed fewer signs of manhood than it ought. At seventeen, my chest was bare, and I passed razor over cheeks but once a fortnight, if that. If only my beard would grow; I'd look more manly, and it would help hide my hideous scar.

I shivered. My room had no fire. Nothing barred me from moving to Mother's old chamber where I could make myself warm, but I could not. A foolish hesitation, I knew, but how could I explain the usurpation, when I met her through the Still? If she took offense . . . Besides, I liked my familiar room.

"Wear these." Rustin thrust me breeches and shirt of his choosing.

I opened my mouth to object, but thought better of it. Rust amused himself making sure my jerkin matched my breeks; why deny him the pleasure? In truth, my sense of color and style was rudimentary. Someday, when I had time, I'd study the art he and others practiced with such ease.

"Why so fancy?" My jerkin was decorated with gold thread.

Rust pulled me onto a bench, dried my hair with rough affection. "Because you're king. And Freisart comes today."

I laced the jerkin. "He must be desperate for shelter." Poor Freisart of Kant, a distant relative, had long ago lost throne and castle. He spent his days wandering from noble to noble, pitied and disdained.

"Your hospitality is ample."

I snorted. Stryx was but a shadow of its former self. What riches Tantroth hadn't plundered in his occupation of the city, we'd lost to Uncle Mar during his regency.

I snapped my fingers to the servant. "Run tell cook I'll break fast in a moment. In the great hall."

"Hold, Roddy," said Rust, reaching for my hairbrush.

"But—"

His look had become grim. Taking the brush, I worked the tangles from my hair.

Rust was notorious for his moods. Usually amiable, at times his good cheer would shatter like an icicle dropped onto stone. Perhaps our return to Stryx caused him pain. The view of his father, Llewelyn's, Keep below would do him no good; Llewelyn had surrendered to Tantroth, without need, on Eiber's attack.

When I was presentable Rust laid down the brush, took my face between his hands, gently touched my forehead to his. "Now, you're handsome." He pulled me to the door.

On the way out, I caught a glimpse of myself in the silver mirror, and shuddered. Only in Rust's eye was I handsome. Though, were one to see only the right profile . . . Uncle Mar had ruined my looks forever, with his cruel knife, but before his ministrations . . . yes, I could have been called handsome.

"You still are."

I raced him down the stairs. "Are my thoughts so plain?"

"Every nuance. I despair of you in matters of state."

I snorted, knowing Rust but tweaked me. Though he thought me a callow boy in personal matters, his respect for my statecraft grew daily. Was it possible to be cleft in twain, a dunce in private matters and wise at public affairs? At times I felt so. Yet I was not such a dolt as to spurn his tutelage, even though more often than not I found it galling.

FREISART'S GREEN, BROWN-HEMMED robes were clean but threadbare. Round-faced, with weary bags under his eyes, he greeted me like a long-lost brother. It was his first visit in years; when last he'd come, Mother had received him in the great hall while I watched with the castle brats from the alcove.

"My brother, Elryc, his man Genard." 'Man' was stretching it; Genard, at thirteen, was younger than Anavar. A stableboy of the castle, he had vaulted to liegesman because of good service to Elryc. My struggle to keep his pride in check was constant. Among Freisart's sparse entourage were two bony ladies who shared a sour expression, introduced as royal cousins. Three servants. And a prosperous-looking fellow, meaty, with a thick red beard.

"Jestrel, my lord. A wondrously talented silversmith. He served my court in . . . past days."

"Welcome." I eyed him dubiously. I didn't mind providing for Freisart—well, I minded, but not all that much—but this fellow wasn't even nobility.

"My Lord King." Jestrel bowed low. "A pleasure. An honor." His eyes flickered to my scar, and away. "We've heard of your exploits."

"Have we?" My tone was barely civil. Who was he to praise me?

"Why, yes, my lord. Even in Ghanz they say—"

My breath hissed. "You come from Ghanz?" The principal city of the Norlanders, in the cool hills where Hriskil summered. Was he a spy, to ferret out our troop dispositions?

Freisart said gently, "We're welcomed in all quarters, Roddy, now we have no land. We're a threat to no one."

I flushed, for having made him speak of his shame. To ease the moment I said, "Tell me of Ghanz."

"High hills," said the exiled king. "A city surrounded by tall wood. Hriskil is a builder. No, an alterer. He enlarges, remodels, rebuilds palaces 'til his nobles go mad. Dust and mortar throughout. Draperies in storage. Cold meals always, because the kitchen's never quite finished."

"You came directly?"

"Why no, Rodrigo. Through Eiber, and Cumber, and the Sands."

Anavar said eagerly, "Cumber, my lord? How goes it with the Earl's granddaughter?"

My hand closed around the boy's nape. "Haven't you better to do than annoy King Freisart?"

A gulp. "Yes, sir. Pardon." To Freisart of Kant, he made a shamefaced bow. "Excuse me, I'm due at . . . I must go." He hurried off, his ears red.

Rust raised an eyebrow, but said naught.

"We dine at seventh hour, my lord king." I made a short bow, that of host to guest.

"IS TARANA DEAD or alive?" Hester peered at me through her better eye.

"Your sister's gone these four years." I slumped on her bench in the ancient stone-walled nursery, head on hands.

My old nurse sighed. "I was afraid so, but my mind gulls me." Her gnarled familiar hand stroked my neck. "You're almost grown, lad. Elena would be proud."

"She says she is."

"You tell her . . . ?"

"Every time." With each visit to the cave, I brought Mother Hester's words of endearment. The feeble old lioness had raised Mother in her day, before my brothers and me.

"Elryc is troubled," she said.

I searched her wrinkled face. "Is this more than a dream?"

"Think you I'm daft?" She waved a claw at my nose. "Yesterday, on this very bench."

"What about?"

"You." She sighed. "Be a good boy and heat the tea." Dutifully, I set the pot on the embers. "You make them cry, Roddy. Anavar and Genard."

I dismissed it. "Servants." Well, not Anavar, though he'd been bondsman before I'd freed him. As for Genard, he needed a good cry more often than he got one.

Her voice grated like glass on slate. "A churl's misery is as great as a lord's."

Rustin argued the same. In theory, I knew he was right, but . . .

"You humbled Anavar before Freisart." She eyed me accusingly. "Why, Roddy? Did I raise you to be cruel?"

I made a helpless gesture. "He inquired after Tresa. I couldn't allow it."

"Only to please you. Because you were too embarrassed to ask."

"I was not!"

"Bah. A moonstruck boy as king. You're head over heels in love, think you we're all blind? Wait a bit longer, there'll be naught but the roasting teapot."

"Imps take it!" I reached for the pot, came to my senses just in time. I wrapped my fingers in cloth, reached gingerly for the handle. Violent water sputtered into her cup. "There."

"How oft must Tresa say she's sorry?"

"I ought to go, Nurse. I promised Willem—"

"A coward to boot." Her tone was acid.

I sighed. Hester's vexation knew no bounds. "What would you I say?"

"That you'll ignore Tresa no longer. You shake your head? Ask Llewelyn's boy his mind. Rustin has sense, for a colt."

Resigned, I bowed to take my leave. She pulled me close, gave me a fierce hug that brought a sting to my eyes. "Send Elryc, when he has time."

"Yes, Nurse."

"And Pytor."

Pytor was dead. She herself had searched for him, unearthed his craftily hidden corpse, and in the doing unstaked the tent pegs of her mind.

JESTREL THE SILVERSMITH took a long draught of unwatered wine. "Yes, Cumber's a pretty town. Too pretty. I prefer the—shall I say austerity?—of the Sands."

Mother had taken me to visit, when I was twelve. I recalled grim cliffs, a drab joyless town. And of course the fine castle, strangely built, in which we were given grand welcome.

"Have you met the Warthen, my lord?"

"Only in formal greeting." I reddened. Mother had deemed me too young to sit through a long banquet; I'd been sent to eat with the servants and retainers. I remembered the Warthen of the Sands as a tall somber figure whose eyes bore a constant pain.

"He'd just done a Return," Jestrel said. "He was downright skeletal."

Elryc's face was flushed. Unobtrusively, I watered his wine. Genard looked annoyed, as if I'd usurped his function.

King Freisart swayed dreamily. "Oh, the Return I'd buy."

The Warthen's rites were a well-guarded mystery. Through them, the Warthen's petitioner could return to an event in his life, no matter how far in the past. Not merely return, but, reenact, and change what had been.

But the Return must be bought by suffering, moment by precious moment. And, aside from the Warthen himself, any wielder of the Power could only return to one event in his life. He might Return as often as he could abide, so long as he paid the cost. But once the event was chosen, he could return to no other.

It was suffering that made the Warthen's eyes dark pools. It was said that he and the wielder suffered equally, when he sold the return, though he sold it for a mighty price. The

Sands were a desolate place, bereft of rivers, watered by few springs. They sowed no grain, raised no sheep, grew no sweet olives. The wealth of the Sands came from the Return, and from those desperate enough to seek its use.

Once, when my tears of despair dampened his shoulder, Rust had stroked my jagged scar and whispered of the Return. The dream of restoring my face sustained me, on days the silver was too cruel. But the Warthen's fees were beyond my reach. That I was his liege lord mattered not a whit.

Freisart had not the coin to contemplate a Return, and never would.

Later, in bed, Rust asked, "How must it feel, at the moment of change?"

I frowned, uncomprehending.

"Say your wife lies with another. You buy a Return, and go back to prevent the act. Do you know, after? Does she?"

"I think . . . of *course* you do. Remember when Erastos didn't drown?" His queen had carried on for weeks, weeping and gnashing her teeth. Then she'd seized the treasury, rushed to the Warthen. A fortnight later, it was known that Erastos had set sail on a different ship, one that reached shore safely. No one had told us. We simply knew.

Rustin said sleepily, "You're right, but it feels . . . odd."

"So does that!" In the dark, I snatched away his hand. "I told you, Rust. No more."

A long silence.

With resolve, I made my tone gentle. "When we were boys, we played as boys. Now I would be a man."

"As I am not?"

"I didn't say that. I treasure your wisdom, your sympathy, your example. Your . . ." I forced the awkward word. ". . . love. But not in that manner. You told me you would abide my wish." I waited, but, hurt, he said naught. Embarrassed, I cast about for a new track. "We can't stay bottled in Stryx."

After a moment, Rustin sighed. "Not again, my prince."

"Again, and always. How will we eject Danzik, corked in our castle?"

"The Norlanders have only the coast road. They've moved against neither Verein nor Stryx. It's we who have Caledon. And now we hold the Keep . . ."

Llewelyn's Keep, at the foot of Castle Way, guarded the approach to Castle Stryx. That's why Llewelyn's betrayal the year previous had been such a blow. If Tantroth of Eiber hadn't renounced his own treason and made himself my ally, I'd never have regained it, or been able to eject Uncle Mar from Castle Stryx.

I said, "The Norlanders hold the coast road, and effectively the town; half our churls have fled, and the market is deserted. While we baste turkey for cousin Freisart, Danzik grinds Cumber to dust. And Tantroth, despite his wiles, fights for his life."

"In two full moons the roads will be passable."

"In two moons Cumber may fall."

"You're trembling, Roddy."

"I'm frustrated." After a moment I muttered, "No, not that way." I sighed, determined not to yield. I could consign Rust to a chamber of his own, but I, more than most, knew one hated to be alone.

Two

"SO YOU WERE but a gnat, and they swatted you away. What of it?" My grandfather Tryon glared across the firepit of the gray cave, as clearly as if he lived.

"The Norlanders chuckle over their campfires. We lost seven men trying—"

"Every bite hurts."

"Gnats don't bite, Grandsir." I paced the worn stone cave.

"But in time, in number, they drive you insane."

I rolled my eyes. Mother's hand flitted to my shoulder in a rare gesture of affection. I shivered. Would that during her lifetime . . .

"While we guard Stryx, Grandsir, he'll take Cumber."

"Let Cumber go. It's Eiber you must hold."

"Nonsense. I—"

A blast of white rage nearly knocked my feet from under me. "SAY YOU WE SPEAK NONSENSE?"

"No, Father Varon!"

In his dim corner Varon of the Steppe, my mother Elena's grandsire, first of our line, thrashed and rumbled. He'd gone far, since his death, and seldom returned save in fury. I bowed, the long, deep bow of obeisance. "Your pardon, sire. I meant no disrespect."

"DID YOU NOT?"

My tunic was clammy. "Perhaps a little, Lord. I'm young."

A grunt, of what might have been amusement. "Well said." A stirring. "Sit. Take warmth from the fire."

Obediently, I sat on crossed legs before the burning fagots. As always, their heat was cold as ice.

"Tell him, Tryon."

My grandfather hitched up his burial robe, squatted at my side. "Cumber is what you love, because it's yours. Yet before my brother Rouel's foolishness, Eiber too was part of Caledon."

"But, Grandsir—"

"It matters not. Look." Tryon seized a twig, drew a rough map in the dust. "Eiber's land runs to the sea. Cumber's doesn't."

I nodded.

"Though they both abut the Norlands. Now, from here, and here"—he jabbed at the dirt—"Hriskil may take sail between Eiber and Stryx, as he wills. Deny him Eiber and his journey is thrice as far."

A small waspish form peered over Tryon's shoulder, chanting. "Deny him Eiber. Deny him Eib—the long Norland border with Eiber is indefensible, and the boy's about to be thrown into the sea. What can he deny Hriskil?"

Tryon looked cross. "It was once your land too, Cayil of the Surk."

"Aye, ere you stole it." The little man's voice was petulant. In the cave of the Still dwelt not merely my ancestors, but all those who'd ruled Caledon.

"Don't start, this day," Tryon said heavily. "My point, youngsire, is this: with your force holding Eiber, Hriskil will attend to his borders, and no else."

"Nons—I mean, I don't follow. If we massed in Eiber, Hriskil would annihilate us. Surely you don't mean us to attack the Norlands?"

"Don't be a fool, lad." His tone was gruff. "A hare attack a panther? There are better forms of suicide."

"And Uncle Raeth? If he falls while I aid Tantroth?"

"Then he falls." Tryon's glowing eyes drew close. "Raeth isn't Caledon. You are."

RUSTIN SHEATHED HIS sword, unbolted the door. "You cried out."

I clenched and unclenched my aching fingers, and set aside the bowl of stillsilver. "He frightened me."

"Your grandfather?"

I nodded. "Hold me a moment." I clung to him, as a small child. More oft than not, sessions with the Still left me timid and shaky.

"You need a bath."

I sighed. "All right, Rust." I'd known Mother too well to fear her. But Tryon's eyes glowed, and Varon . . . no wonder I'd sweated through my tunic. I wondered if ever I would inspire dread in my successors.

What must it be like, to live in the cave? Was there consciousness, when the king did not visit? They spoke sometimes of old quarrels, and sometimes one or another of them was absent.

Late in the afternoon I had gloomy conclave with Willem of Alcazar, my chamberlain. Revenue had dwindled to a trickle, and we were hard pressed to feed troops and tradesmen. In Eiber, Tantroth would be even harder pressed; it was his bizarre custom to pay his soldiers with coin, like swordsmiths or coopers. True, it freed them to practice their art the year round, without concern for their crops. But who needed troops in the winter's ice?

As dusk approached, I took a long dreary walk with Anavar, from kitchens to stables to courtyard. Bundled in wool and cotton, my ward chattered like a youngsire released from his tutors. From time to time I grunted a response.

Master of my castle, I felt trapped within its walls. Little more than a year before, I'd been free to mount Ebon and canter down the hill whenever the whim struck me. Now, I dared not be caught abroad, lest Hriskil's sails sweep into the harbor and I be captured. Rust could go, or Willem, but the king must be held safe.

The courtyard was soggy, and my boots soon covered with mud. No matter; a servant would clean them, but it took the joy from walking. Then Anavar wanted to go down the hill to market, and I wouldn't hear of it; with youthful high spirits, he'd demanded what was forbidden me.

The rising wind chilled my bones. Muttering foul oaths, I stomped inside and made ready for dinner.

Over tough fowl and overcooked fish Freisart prattled interminably about the room arrangements of his palace in the Kingdom, now the Duchy, of Kant. If his story had a point, I failed to discern it. As host I couldn't very well get up and leave. Despite their squirming, I made Elryc and Anavar sit at table as long as I myself was forced to.

At last the meal was done. Freisart and his cousins tottered off for a postprandial stroll. I curled up on pillows before the fire, nursing a skin of wine. Genard and Elryc disappeared. In the far corner, a lutist strummed melancholy lays.

I dribbled wine down my chin. A fit end to a foul day.

"You could always go to bed." Rust's tone was dry.

"You could always hang yourself." I wasn't feeling magnanimous.

A studied silence. "My prince, I pray it's weeks of mud and sleet makes you so ungracious."

I rolled my eyes. "Again you upbraid me?"

A sigh. "Never I thought I'd see again the Roddy whose deportment was so loathsome. But day by day, you drive us to distraction."

"You're here by choice. If it's such an ordeal—"

The door crashed open. "Roddy, come quick!" Elryc panted for breath. "Freisart's fallen and won't rise!"

Flushed, I stumbled to my feet. "Where?"

"The anteroom upstairs!"

Freisart lay wheezing on the stone flag. His face was gray. "My chest . . . a knot."

"Call a physicker!"

A servant rushed off.

His voice was thin. "I so wanted to see Chorr again, in spring, when the blossoms—"

I knelt. "Shall we take you to chambers, my lord?"

"Yes, do tha—" His eyes rolled up, and he was dead.

Elryc dropped to his side, ran slender fingers over Freisart's frayed robe. "Who will mourn you, King?" His eyes glistened.

Absently, I kneaded Elryc's shoulders. "His day was past."

"He's dead, Roddy. Moments ago he was grousing about the stair. His worst worry was a cold bed, and porridge again to break fast. Now . . ."

"You barely knew him."

"We all barely knew him."

I touched the old king's flesh, still warm. "He isn't Mother. You need not grieve as for her."

Elryc buried his head in my chest.

Servants carried the old man's still form to his chamber. Respectfully, Elryc and I walked behind. Afterward I led him away. "You'll sleep tonight with Hester."

"I'm twelve, I don't need a . . ."

"Nonetheless." Firmly, I led him up the stair.

Docile, perhaps grateful, he let me deliver him to his old nurse.

Rustin was gentle as he helped me dress for bed. "At times you amaze me."

"How?"

He would say no more.

THE FUNERAL WAS delayed a day, while gardeners clawed at the stony earth. It rained most of the morn, making their toil sheer misery.

In normal times invitations would issue to all the nobles for days' ride around. But Groenfil and Soushire wouldn't leave their castles when Danzik's troops might lunge. And Raeth was far beyond Cumber, in his windswept winter camp.

After the rite, I paced the great hall, the passageways, the cellars. I startled a cook in the steamy kitchen, where for years I'd been made to take my meals. The barrel of apples was near empty. They were soft and starchy, no treat for a bored palate.

At last, in afternoon, the rain ceased. I thrust on my cloak, went to the stables to visit Ebon, fed him carrots and an apple from my pouch. He was less particular than I.

At the stable door, Anavar struggled into his outer jerkin. "May I walk with you, my lord?"

I gestured assent. We tromped through the muddy courtyard. Restless, I climbed the ramparts. The walls were manned, though our defenses were not at full alert. Thanks to our prominence on the hill, an enemy could be spotted hours before reaching us. We had more to fear from a saboteur with a torch than from troops at our battlements.

Far below was the harbor, lashed by gray waves. I tossed pebbles from the high wall to break the excruciating boredom.

We descended the narrow stone step. Anavar glanced longingly at the gate.

Again? My fists knotted. If he so much as breathed a word of . . .

I hesitated. Well, why not?

Anavar followed my gaze. His tone was eager. "May I, sir?"

"No." His face fell. I added, "Not without me."

He gaped.

"Raise your cloak." I thrust my own cloak around my ears. "Gateman, open." I pulled Anavar through.

The gatekeeper stammered, "My lord, what shall I—"

"Say naught."

I strode down the winding hill. Anavar, his eyes alight, trotted to keep pace. "Where do we—"

"To the market." And then perhaps the tavern.

A long walk, and soggy, but I reveled in it. If only I could have saddled Ebon, my day would have been perfect, but I could hardly ride my charger into my town and go unremarked.

At Llewelyn's Keep—we'd have to find a new name, soon or late—we detoured by the Tradesman's Cut that ran outside the ramparts. Sharp-eyed guards watched from the walls. The Keep, nowadays, was manned by soldiers from Stryx. No vestiges of Llewelyn's tenancy remained after his betrayal, making homecomings grim for poor Rustin.

As we strode along the coast road a freshening wind blew through my hair; I threw back my cloak. Anavar danced alongside like a marmot freed from his cage. He stooped for pebbles and twigs, tossed them at the rocky shore.

A brisk walk brought us to Potsellers' Way, the narrow alley that led to the market square. Most of the stalls were open, but trade was lethargic, the few shoppers listless and weary. As I hoped, with my hood obscuring my face, we went unrecognized.

Anavar stopped at the leatherer's stall, pawed through sheaths and bridles. "Might you increase my stipend, sir?"

"Again?" I knotted my fists. "What do you spend it on?"

"Trinkets, now and —"

"Women?" My tone was grim.

"No, my lord."

"Bah." He wouldn't tell me, even if it were so. "It's the third time this year you've asked."

He reddened. "I have no lands." No revenue from taxes, as a baron should.

"That's not my fault." If Anavar hadn't joined the war on Caledon, he wouldn't have been captured. I sighed. "Learn to live within your purse." How often had Chamberlain Willem told me the same, in my recent youth?

"Aye, my lord."

We walked on.

"What caught your eye at the leatherer?"

"The inlaid dagger sheath. It's a perfect fit for—"

"How much?"

"A silver and three coppers."

"Beyond reason." I examined a winter hat I didn't need. Then, with a sigh, I unknotted my purse, fished out a pair of silvers. "Well, get it. Don't gape, it's rude."

Anavar dashed to the stall, raced back with the sheath. He threw his arms around me in a joyous hug.

"Don't make a scene. I'm king."

"Nobody here knows." His eyes sparkled. "It's beautiful. See how the black threads make a horse? Look at—"

"All right." My tone was gruff. Perhaps at times I was harder on him than I might be.

His grin vanished. "Look!" He stared past my shoulder.

I whirled, hand on dagger. We'd left impulsively; my sword was left at home. What if assassins—

Nothing, save a parchment broadsheet pasted to the wall. A crude drawing. Squinting, I moved closer. A drawing of an old man. He lay flat on his back, his crown tumbled aside. Green slime oozed from his mouth. Nearby a boy gloated. He carried a bowl overflowing with an evil green substance. He, too, wore a crown.

I was a pillar of stone.

Anavar tugged at my sleeve. "Please, sir."

"Who made this?" I spun from one side to the other, but none looked my way. The hatter busied himself with his wares. I demanded, *"Who?"*

"Don't call attention, my lord. We left our swords—"

I tore down the broadsheet, surged toward the hatter. Anavar barred my way. I slapped him hard. An angry blotch sprang up on his cheek.

I thrust the broadsheet in the hatter's face. "How dare you allow this?"

"I didn't—"

"Traitor!" I threw down his table, dumping his stock of hats in the mud. "Mock me, would you?"

"Help! Fedor! Maron, Help!"

My foot lashed out in a wild kick. The leatherer's table went flying.

Peasant folk materialized from doorways, stalls, the road. Angry hands clawed at my cloak.

Anavar pulled loose his blade. "Stand clear! He's the king!" No one paid heed.

In the distance, a clatter of horses.

A swarthy fellow lunged. I kneed him, seized him by the shirt, threw him at a wall. An old woman kicked Anavar from behind. He stumbled, lost his dagger.

An elbow snaked around my neck. I stamped on a foot, drove backward with all my might. My assailant crashed into a furrier's stall. His grip eased. I broke free. I turned, smashed his mouth. My knuckles oozed blood.

A clamor rose. "Get him! Kill him!"

"Stand away!" The crack of a riding crop on a peasant's back. "No swords, unless they—Roddy, mount!" Rustin slapped Ebon's reins into my hand. A dozen guardsmen milled about.

Numbly, I swung into the saddle. "Easy, boy. Anavar?"

"Here, my lord." He clutched a guardsman's waist, riding behind.

"Move." Rustin lashed his gray.

"Did you see that sheet? They say I killed Freisart!" I reined in, dismounted to retrieve it for Rustin. "Here, look—"

From his saddle Rustin bent, seized my hair, pulled me to the tips of my toes. "Ride, King Rodrigo. This moment!"

Gasping at the sting of my scalp, I swarmed into the saddle. Rust lashed Ebon with his crop. My stallion bolted. I had all I could do to hang on.

We dashed along the coast road. The gates to the Keep were open. In moments we were out the upper end, cantering up the hill. As the horses tired, we slowed to a walk.

I hauled out the torn broadsheet, fuming. Who was responsible for this calumny? Uncle Mar, most likely. It had his touch.

Anavar rode head down, dejected. "I lost my dagger."

"So?"

"I've a beautiful new sheath, and no blade."

I snorted. I had worse to worry about. If Mar had his way, the whole world would think me a poisoner.

"Rust, how will we—"

He cocked a finger in my face. "We'll speak later." He spurred his gray to the head of our troop, his mouth set in a grim line.

The horses trod up the winding hill, a long slow walk that gave my ire time to cool. By the time the castle gates hove into view I was in good humor; we'd had our adventure, though it had come to a rather abrupt end.

I walked Ebon to the stable, handed the reins to a stableboy. "Rub him down, before he—"

Rust grasped my arm. "Do it yourself."

I met his eyes. They held a menace I didn't care to ponder. Sometimes he was beyond sense. "Very well." Sullenly, I yanked the reins from the boy's hand.

When Ebon was dry and brushed, watered and fed, I stalked to the donjon, ravenous with hunger, but pleased I hadn't taken out my growing fury on the mount I loved.

Before the day was out, I would put an end to Rust's dominance. When I'd sworn by the True to submit to his guidance, I'd been but a boy. Now I was near a man, yet he rebuked me before my subjects like—I couldn't think of the like. He'd even pulled my hair until I'd nearly squealed from the pain. How dare he treat so, the king of Caledon?

I swept the guard aside, hurled open the door to the Keep. It crashed into the stone wall. "Is dinner set? What's—"

My court was assembled in the great hall at a laden table. Freisart's women cousins, Jestrel, Chamberlain Willem. Elryc and his Genard, Anavar, gazing greedily at a roast. And a tall stranger in traveler's cloak.

"Who's this?"

"Banwarth of Harc, my lord." Rust's manners were impeccable. "Envoy of our liegesman Tantroth, with tidings of—"

"What news, Banwarth? How fares your master?"

"He's in his hills, sire." From the recesses of his cloak, he whipped out a scroll, liberally sealed with wax and imprints of Tantroth's ring of state. "He sends you word."

I cut myself a liberal slice of beef, waved my courtiers to begin. "Let's have it." I perched the scroll by my plate, eyed it dubiously. "When written?"

"I've been two weeks en route, sire." Eiber was only a day's sail, but Tantroth had lost his harbors. His runner had to thread his way past fortified points, patrols and scouts, with betrayal ever a risk. Tantroth's wax seals couldn't prevent unauthorized reading, though they would tell me whether the missive had been tampered with.

A plea for men and arms, no doubt. I busied myself with my meal. I'd waited two weeks for my duke's letter; a few moments more wouldn't matter, and I was famished. I piled steaming corn, juice of the meat, turnips, and thick hot bread onto my trencher, washed it down with copious draughts of dark wine.

When at last my hunger eased, I took the scroll, broke its seals, read laboriously.

"To our royal cousin and liege, Rodrigo of Caledon, we send greetings."

How like Tantroth, to deny my authority while acknowledging it. He called me liege while referring to himself as 'we', a royal prerogative.

No matter. Tantroth would serve me as long as it served himself, and no longer; we both knew as much.

"Hriskil himself occupies our dwelling in the Hadriads, according to reliable informants. Distressing, but a great opportunity. I know every nook, every cranny of the castle, and every rock in the foothills and streams. With your full support, and if we can lure him from . . ."

Full support, indeed. He'd have me strip Caledon bare to restore his duchy, which, when freed, he would promptly remove from my vassalage.

I glanced up, hoping to catch Rust's eye, but he was chatting amiably with Willem. Further down the table, Genard clowned with boys of his station. He'd taken a grease cloth, rolled it as if a scroll. He made a great show of breaking the seals. As he pretended to read, his brow knotted, and his lips moved laboriously with each word.

I threw down my letter. What was the world coming to, that a stableboy mock a king? Had I a blade handy, I'd gut him like . . . no, instead, I would give him his own. I splashed water into a bowl, waited impatiently for it to settle. It was high time I practiced the other attributes of my art. When the bowl was still, I cupped my hands atop its rim, closed my eyes, muttered familiar words of encant.

Slowly, the great hall faded. Over and again, I murmured the words of my Power. When the open mouth of the cave loomed, instead of entering as usual, I opened my hooded eyes, fixed them on Genard.

He read again from his pretended scroll, threw it down, fashioned the cloth into a sort of crown, plopped it on his head. He made elegant, exaggerated gestures toward his tablemates, as one noble greeting another.

Elryc nudged him sharply, but Genard paid no heed. He

climbed his bench, danced a clumsy jig. Conversation fell to a hush.

"Look, I'm a king!" Genard's voice was a strangled squawk. He leaped to the floor, began to dance and twirl, ever more foolishly.

Hands cupped over the bowl of still water, I watched his face grow red from exertion.

Genard capered around the hall, spinning, twitching, grinning like the oaf he was. His arms flapped. "I'm king!" His frenzied feet jerked and twisted ever faster. Sweat beaded his forehead, his cheeks. A great gaping grin, and behind it, eyes wide with terror. He stumbled, caught himself, began to hop maniacally from foot to foot.

A hand shot out, splashed a goblet of wine full in my face. I spluttered, wiped my burning eyes.

As my hands left the bowl Genard collapsed. He lay gasping, his face purple. His chest heaved. Elryc crouched, a protective hand on his shoulder.

"To your chamber, lord King!" Rustin's eyes blazed.

"He mocked me. Did you—"

Rust's stiffened palm lashed out. A thunderclap, that rocked my head. "This very instant!"

My hand shot to my blazing cheek. He raised his hand again. I flinched. His eyes were merciless. Mortified, I stumbled from my seat, rushed to the door.

"Sir, take your leave!"

"My lords, my ladies—I—please excuse—I must go!" I bolted to the stair, galloped up the steps to my bedchamber, trying to rub the sting from my cheek.

My fist hammered the feathered bed.

I loved Rustin as a brother, and I had lost him forever. I had no choice but to banish him from Stryx, from Caledon itself. If only . . . but no, he'd struck me in front of my court, my intimates. Before my brother. Even Genard. I stifled a sob.

On the stair, in the hall, unhurried footsteps. Behind me, the door closed. The bolt slid.

"Rodrigo."

A dread. Why didn't Rust call me Roddy, as always? Cautiously, I turned my head.

He lowered himself, to sit alongside me. For an instant his

hand flitted to my shoulder, but withdrew. His eyes were sorrowful. "There's evil in you, my prince."

"Rust, he mocked my reading. He sat there moving his lips, peering at a cloth, scratching his head . . ."

"Practice the skill, if you would not be mocked." He waved it away. "His misdeeds are not the issue."

It was a colloquy I mustn't allow. "I'm sending you away."

"I call you to your vow."

"Release me."

"I will not."

Astonished, I raised my head. "Rust . . ."

"I love your life more than my own. Know you that?"

In my throat, a lump. I could only nod.

"Yet I despise your cruelty, the power you flaunt, the hurt you willingly bestow." He tapped my chest with each word. "There . . . is . . . evil . . . within . . . you!"

"In front of everyone, you . . ." I couldn't even say it. "I banish you, Rust. From all of Caledon."

"Very well, my lord. Live without the Still."

"You can't—that's not your . . ." I swallowed. "Mother will understand. And Tryon."

"If you see them. Shall I pour stillsilver, that we learn who of us speaks truth?"

"I swore to let you guide me, as older brother, as a father. Not to strike me as—"

"As you strike Anavar?"

"He's a boy!"

"What are you?"

"Seventeen, and—"

"A child." Head in hands, he rocked. "A spiteful child, my prince. When you were crowned, I marveled at your wisdom, your gentle nobility, the courage that led Groenfil and Soushire and Cumber, all of Caledon, to your standard. You were a glory!"

I squirmed in the heat of his praise.

"But since the snows, what has befallen you? You beat Anavar, jeer at Genard, mock Willem, box Elryc's ears—"

"Once!"

"Shall I box yours, if once is but a trifle?"

"No!" I cupped palms over ears. In this mood, he was capable of anything.

"How *dare* you misuse your Power to avenge yourself on a helpless boy?"

"How dare you berate me? I'm king!"

"And a fool! You'd make an enemy for life, over a table jape!"

"You have no leave to censure me!"

His whole form smoldered. His fists knotted and unknotted. Then the heated coals burst into flame. He stood. "I'll leave, as you decree. Imps take your oath! Demons take the Still! You've no will to keep your word. See if you have power to rule Caledon." He strode to the door, unbolted it, hurled it open. "I bid you good-day!"

And he was gone.

From my high window, cursing, I watched him cross the dusk, to the stable. Long moments later, he cantered to the gate, bid the guardsman open.

Out the gate. I couldn't contain my glee.

Down the hill. A good riddance.

He was halfway to Stryx before I came to my senses.

I bounded down the stairs. "Guards! Saddle and mount! Stop him!" I thrust the sentry toward the stable. "Now, you fool! Tell Lord Rustin I'll keep my vow!"

Bootless, I danced from foot to foot. It took them forever to saddle their mounts, canter out the gate.

I rushed upstairs, thrust my head out the window. I couldn't see him, but perhaps, behind a bush, an overhang . . .

A dozen guardsmen raced down the hill, spears in their saddle grommets, swords bouncing. Lord of Nature, did I tell them not to hurt him? What if they . . . I bit my knuckle. Surely they knew.

Night was fallen. I paced my chamber, feverish and distraught. Elryc came, but in a frenzy I sent him away.

At the foot of the hill, Rust might turn left to town, or pass through the Keep to the northern coast road. If my guards missed his track . . .

It was only for the Still. Not for Rust himself. Without the Still I couldn't hold Caledon. I cared not a whit for my erstwhile friend, my mentor, my gentle confidant—

An anguished sound, akin to a sob.

I bit my knuckle, hurled myself onto the cushions. It wasn't Rustin whose absence cleaved my heart. It was the Still.

Truly.

"My Lord?" A voice in the hall, hushed.

"Send him in!"

"Sire, he's . . ." the guardsman hesitated. "We have him, at the edge of town. He refuses to come. We weren't sure if you wanted him . . . ah, by force."

"Tell him . . ." Best put it in writing. I searched for parchment, found none. Very well. My humiliation would be known to my guards, and the world. "Tell him I sincerely beg his pardon and ask that he resume his station. That I won't contest him again. That I beg his return, to teach me what he might."

The door closed.

For the Still.

It was for the Still.

THREE

"HAVE I LEAVE to go down?" My voice was hopeful.

"No."

It was the third day. I was imprisoned in my bedchamber. No lock secured the stout oaken door, no bars, no gaoler save myself and Rustin's iron word.

I squirmed. The vile things he'd said to me, while I'd laid sniveling on my bed. Step by remorseless step he'd made me acknowledge the impulsive, thoughtless cruelty I'd inflicted upon my household, my family, my ward Anavar. In a way I was glad of the respite from their sight; I knew not how to face them.

My dinners were the simple fare we fed our servants, but I didn't really mind. Though I missed the wine; Rustin forbade me even a drop. As punishment, he said, not that he thought me a drunkard.

Asking pardon of Anavar was excruciating, of Genard even more so. Rust had found some fault in my manner, shut out the stableboy, cuffed me lightly over and again until I pleaded desperately for a chance to make amends. It wasn't that his blows hurt. It was the disgust, the contempt with which he bestowed them. Had I truly earned such disfavor?

In my secret heart that no man must ever see, I feared it was so. All my life I'd toyed with a desire to hurt. Crowned, now that all bowed to me, temptation abounded. Especially when I was weak, after invoking the Still, it was so easy to order Anavar about, berate the servants, twit Genard, abuse the stablemen. Who could gainsay me?

I hunched on the bed. Better had Rust intervened earlier, before his temper had been well and truly ignited. A few sharp words . . . well, he'd said them, and I'd paid no heed. He ought have given warning, then, that he'd tolerate no more cruelty.

I'd had that, and ignored it.

An arm fell around me. "Why do you mope, youngsire?"

I swallowed. "How do I make myself better than I am?"

"Could this be remorse?" Rust raised my chin.

"Please don't laugh."

He rubbed my shoulders. "Welcome back, my prince. Now you're the Roddy I love."

"Do you really?" It was a whisper, scarce spoken.

"Always." He sat by my side, folded his legs. "Roddy, I think all men have a touch of evil. But in a king, it's a great hazard. You more than most must learn to control your darker nature."

"It comes on me without thought." I was earnest, a puppy seeking his master's approval. "That day in market, I bought Anavar a sheath he coveted. Then I slapped him."

"You did worse."

I searched my mind. "How?"

"You are king. We depend on your constancy." He slipped from the bed, knelt on the rush mat. "Tantroth's rider came with dispatches. I turned the castle on its head, searching for you, before learning you'd sworn the gateman to secrecy and stolen down the hill. Like a mere boy, but now you're king!"

I felt my ears redden.

"What must your people think? Then, to top all, you ran riot in the market. The hatter, the furrier . . . you destroyed their livelihood, yet without them you are naught."

"How so?"

"Think you that by grace of nobles alone you rule? The furrier, his sons, his nephews and neighbors man your ramparts, tromp alongside your wagons, guard your camp, cook your stew, sling your arrows. Lose their faith, Roddy, and you lose all." He offered me a cloth. "Wipe your eyes."

"Do you know I'm sorry?"

"Yes, my prince." He tousled my hair. "But it won't do. You must master your behavior, not regret it."

I craved absolution, and there was but one way to earn it. "What will you do to me?"

"Nothing. It's beyond that. I'd have you seek a ritemaster. There's a good one not far from Lady Soushire's court. We'll be there in a few weeks."

"For the Rite of Cleansing?"

"Expulsion."

I took shuddering breath. "Think you an imp has seized my soul?" I'd sworn by them often enough, and as any dolt knew, that summoned them.

"Perhaps."

I swallowed bile. "What if he can't—can't be—"

"I'll love you still."

Blindly, I groped, fell into his soothing embrace.

"There's one more thing," Rust said gently. He rummaged through a chest, dropped a handful of scrolls in my lap. "Practice reading. Put a finger to your lips, like so. Learn to keep your mouth still, and Genard won't mock."

Meekly, I complied.

ON THE SIXTH day, he let me downstairs, for an hour. I flung open the door, breathed in the chill wind with unfettered joy. "Have I leave to go out?"

"Not today."

I battled a gush of rage. I won, but it left me shaken. "As you say, sir."

Approvingly, he clapped me on the back. "Perhaps I was too hasty. Say hello to Ebon."

In a trice I was out the door, cloakless, careless, racing to the stable. I met old Griswold, under the hayloft, forking hay into a handcart.

"Do you ride today, my lord?"

I found a juicy apple I thought Ebon would like. "Rustin won't let me." Lord of Nature! I colored, aghast that I'd made so public an admission of my state.

Griswold seemed not to notice. "Genard's taken him for exercise each day."

"But he's Elryc's man now. Does he still work the stable?"

"No, and it's a pity. The new boy is . . ." he sighed. "He did it for Ebon. And just possibly for you."

"You . . . heard?"

"Yes." His visage was stony.

"I'm sorry."

"Your mother would be not proud."

"She turned away, when I told her." My voice was tremulous. Far more than Rustin's ire, that had pained me.

I fed Ebon, stroked him, crooned to him, and hurried back to the donjon, anxious not to breach my parole.

Rustin was deep in converse with Jestrel, the silversmith. On an open cloth before them lay a handful of extraordinary castings. A lovely dove, whose silver wings glistened. A castle, complete even unto the silver banner flying high from a turret.

". . . two days ride beyond the high passes."

Rustin said, "We were stopped at the pass."

"A gift to the guards . . ." Shrugging, Jestrel fingered a tiny silver squirrel. "It's expected." As I neared, he stood and bowed. "My lord, we were speaking of the Warthen." A hesitation. "Sire, is it meet that we leave your city? Now that King Freisart's gone . . . I don't speak for his cousins Bertholda and Rosalind, but surely your generosity must reach an end."

I'd been thinking as much, but his forthright manner swayed me. Before Rust could guide me I said, "You're welcome, until the roads dry. Entertain us with stories of your travels." He flushed with pleasure. "Beyond spring, I cannot promise you a bed. I may lose my own."

"Hriskil is a menace, yes." Jestrel pondered. "Always building. He's expanding the walls of Ghanz, even now. Lord of Nature knows why. The old walls were handsome enough, and it's not as if he fears attack." When the Ukras swarmed his eastern border, Hriskil had set the Rood over his troops, and the enemy lines had swirled in fear and confusion. Later, they'd made treaty.

THE SEVENTH DAY, Rust freed me from captivity, with a stern lecture that dampened my spirits for at least an hour.

A long, late, luxurious morning meal, then back up to my room to don my best garb, for the King's Justice. A formality, really, but one Mother had insisted on.

In Stryx, old Vessa had been Speaker of the City. I allowed him his office still, though it was much diminished now the town was impoverished. He was, in theory, spokesman and intermediary for the masses of townsmen who lived below our walls.

But any churl, aggrieved by judgment of the king's justiciar, could appeal past Vessa directly to the crown. In Mother's reign, that meant the queen herself. One day each fortnight was set aside for the purpose. She affirmed nearly all her officials' decrees, but on occasion her sense of justice was offended, and she reversed them, ignoring their pained protest.

I'd continued the practice. Few cases from outlying regions

were brought, now the Norlanders held much of the countryside. My petitioners came primarily from Stryx.

This day there were seven. Wearing a beautiful ermine robe
and my favorite coronet, I took my place on the simple
throne—nothing more than a raised chair, actually—at the far
end of the great hall. Willem, a participant in the mummery,
tapped his rod of office. "Let the petitioners approach!"

The first case involved an old woman who'd refused shelter to her grown son. The justiciar had ruled in his favor, rely-
ing on the well-settled rule that a parent's obligation never
ceased. I confirmed his decision. In the audience Rust raised
an eyebrow, but I ignored him. What if Mother had thrown me
out on my ear? Would I not have demanded her succor? At
any rate, it wasn't my role to make law. Not in this setting. Al-
though . . .

"I amend my ruling. Let the mother provide shelter, as if to
a youth. It is her obligation. But let her set likewise the
youth's hours, and his work, and she shall say yea or nay to
his drink." The assembly tittered. Encouraged, I added, "And
as to his consorting with women." A roar of laughter. The
son's fists knotted, and his brow was a thundercloud.

The next case involved three churls, a shared plowhorse,
and the hours of sowing each man's lot. I understood not a
word of it, and let the ruling stand.

They brought forward two bound boys, one about fourteen,
the other my age. Filthy clothes, the sour smell of an alehouse.
In the audience, a woman wailed; someone angrily hushed
her. Two rough-looking men thrust themselves forward to
stand with the youths, wringing their hats.

The criminals shuffled from foot to foot. The younger
seemed unconcerned. With a gap-toothed grin, he waved at
someone in the crowd until a guard cuffed him still.

Absently stroking my scar, I heard out the sordid tale. A
drunken spree. Chairs smashed at the tavern. Drinks unpaid.
The boys had fled into the alley.

I sighed. But there was more.

In the dead of night, they'd been caught stumbling about a
widow's shed, thrusting her squawking chickens into a bag.

Theft in the night. There was nothing for it. They would be
hanged. Two days prior, the justiciar had decreed so, as he
must.

"Who are these men?"

"One's the drayer, sire. He heard the commotion. He called yield, but they fled."

Worse and worse. Flight from capture. Another hanging offense.

"And the other?"

"A mother."

"Let her speak."

Her Soushire accent was so thick I could barely understand a word. I should save her boy. Tanner meant no harm. It was just a few chickens. When she was old, why would they support her. No, *who* would support her. On and on.

At last she wound down.

"Hang them." Someone in the hall, his voice a growl. Murmurs of agreement.

I saw no reason to intervene. Certainly Mother wouldn't have. One doesn't suppress lawless behavior with pardons. As to stealing, the law was inflexible, and rightly so, else every churl would have to guard his oxen the night long. Almost every session, some hapless soul was caught at market with a sack of pilfered goods. He danced in air, always.

A sneeze. The elder boy wiped his nose with his sleeve. "Pardon, my lord." His voice was meek.

I regarded him. His life in the balance, and he asked pardon for a sneeze?

"Come closer."

His bailiff gave slack to the rope round his neck; he shuffled near.

"Your name?"

"Bollert."

"What do you do?"

"Do?" He looked about, as if for answer. "Do?"

"Have you work?"

A light dawned. "Help with horses. At the inn, sometimes."

"Are you paid?"

"Stables." He would share the horses' warmth.

"Where's your father?"

A grin. "Dunno."

"Do you know him?"

A shake of the head.

Hopeless. I beckoned to the second lad. "You are . . ."

"Tanner, m'lord."

"You live . . . ?"

"By Shoemakers' Stair. That's my ma." He jerked a thumb toward the old woman from Soushire.

"She lets you run wild?"

"I'm too big for her to whip." A grin, that faded under my scowl.

"You'd rather be hanged?"

"It's law." For a moment he looked regretful. "Justiciar says . . ." Apparently he accepted his fate.

"Very well, take them—"

"Sir, may I speak?" Anavar. A deep bow. "I'd have them as bondsmen and make myself surety for their conduct."

"You know not our law. If they absconded—"

"I'd be imprisoned, 'til their debt was paid."

"And who would pay it? Your only income is my stipend, youngsire. The bail of a thief is three silvers, that's six in all. Have you such a sum?"

"No, my lord."

"Nor any chance of getting it." I tried to make my tone kind. "If you think you can wheedle me so high . . ."

He blushed. "I could try, sir."

"No." I stood, stretched. "I myself will stand surety. They'll be the king's bondsmen."

I stole a look at Rustin and warmed with satisfaction: his jaw was agape. "You two, come hither." They shuffled to the foot of my throne. "Will you be my bondsmen forevermore, or hang according to law? Be quick."

"Bondsman, m'lord." Tanner. He scratched his filthy blond hair.

"Go with him." Bollert, the elder, swallowed with relief.

"The king so orders. Willem, take them to the stable and have them washed. Burn those rags. Find them something that doesn't crawl."

Later in my room, I paced from window to washbasin. "The law would see them hanged, Rust. But that Tanner lad was barely older than Elryc. I couldn't allow it."

"I'm glad. But to make them—"

"It's how Anavar began." Before I'd freed him, and given him a barony.

"Anavar began as a noble." In Eiber, his own land.

"You'd rather I hanged them?"

"You could have flogged them and set them free."

"They'd have been back at next Justice, a fortnight hence."

"Roddy . . ." He lay on his back, hands behind head. "You've made yourself responsible for their lives. Avoid a noble gesture that you can't carry through."

"Who says I can't?"

"We'll see."

I FRETTED ABOUT the castle, anxious to be about the business of Caledon. Rustin, as always, deferred to me in matters of state, but kept me on a particularly short leash in personal affairs. If I was short-tempered with Elryc, he was short-tempered with me. When I chided Anavar's manners, Rust forced me thereafter into a more rarified realm of politeness from which I wasn't allowed to deviate a smidgeon. From time to time, fuming, I endured an afternoon exiled to my chamber, before I became resigned to his requirements.

His most exacting demand was that I practice weekly acts of kindness. I wasn't unwilling to be kind, but he refused to give me a clue as to what would satisfy. A purse from Chamberlain Willem's vault wouldn't do, I learned, when I was sent to bed without dinner. It must be a kindness that related to the recipient, that I'd thought of myself, and that came from me personally.

He drove me mad. It was all I could do to keep my oath.

A stroke of inspiration, while I was idly toying with my jeweled dagger, a parting gift from Lady Soushire. It was a beautiful piece of work, with a finely carved ebony haft. I presented it to Anavar, to replace the blade he'd lost defending me at the market. His eyes filled, and he threw his arms around me. What house had he been raised in, that he knew not proper respect for a king's majesty? I affected not to notice.

At least, Rust was pleased. He said so, thrice. Perhaps he thought me deaf. I smiled a lot that day, though not without a pang of regret for the loss of so exquisite a dagger.

The next week, I prevailed on Rust to escort me, with ten guardsmen and full regalia, to the market, where I gave a purse to the hatter, another to the furrier, and begged their forgiveness for wrecking their stalls. With each word the crowd swelled. As I left, I was actually cheered.

The thief Tanner was put in training as a room servant, to work about the castle.

Griswold seized on Bollert, who had some familiarity with horses, to replace Genard's unsatisfactory successor. Now, whenever I went to the stable to feed Ebon I was greeted by a grimy, brow-knuckling oaf who stared open-mouthed at my discourse with my handsome, snorting stallion. I grew adept at finding errands to divert him from our company.

"To RODRIGO, KING of Caledon and my liege lord, greetings, in the hope this missive from his cousin Tresa finds him well and content.

"I'm sorry you suffered so much dreary rain at winter's end. Still, I was delighted to have word from you at last. Is there other news?

"The Hadriad Mountains are cold and grim, and will see spring late, if ever. Grandfather Raeth made winter camp in the fortified town of Pezar, which guards the most convenient pass to Cumber, but now spring is near, he and old Baron Imbar are anxious to set out for Eiber. It is in the eastern hills—Eiber's east, our west—that he thinks Hriskil will be stopped, if at all.

"Twice, Tantroth made his way through the snows, to plan next spring's campaign. He is a difficult man, cruel and flinty, and his racking cough is no better.

"Grandfather is adamant that I soon leave Pezar for Cumber Town. He says he has need of me to manage his domain while he and Imbar are encamped in the hills. That may be so, but we both know he fears to see me captured, if his troops are overrun.

"In truth, Pezar is a rude garrison town, small, provincial and dirty, and I would be happily rid of it if Grandfather weren't here. I have a small, low-ceilinged chamber in a stone house that once was a miller's, and the hearth has a fitful draught.

"Until we meet in happier times, Tresa, daughter of Aptar and Stira, of the House of Cumber, salutes you."

SLOWLY THE DAYS lengthened. Newly tamed winds learned to caress rather than bite. Messages flew between Soushire, Groenfil and Stryx, as we planned our spring maneuvers.

We would gather our forces to strike at Danzik's camp, along the coast road south of Stryx. Those Norlanders were furthest from home, and must be supplied by ship or live off the land. If we could eliminate the threat from that quarter, Stryx itself might for the long term be defended; Llewelyn's Keep was a formidable obstacle to attack from the north. And from Stryx, we might eventually seize opportunity to free all Caledon.

We would first meet Earl Groenfil in the Southron hills, where Lady Soushire would join us. After wheeling to attack Danzik, we'd sweep on to haven at Castle Stryx, and organize to strike north past the Keep.

As unobtrusively as we could, we made ready for our journey from Stryx. We would be most vulnerable before our forces joined Groenfil and Soushire.

It was three days before our departure, and our nerves were taut.

Willem came to me, apologetic. He would deal with it himself, but after all, they were *my* bondsmen. Jestrel was *my* guest, and Tanner would say not a word, even when the silver dove was found rolled in his bedding.

"Have them brought before me." In moments they appeared in the great hall, Jestrel flushed and angry, the boy Tanner held firmly by the scruff of the neck.

"I'm sorry, my lord." The silversmith looked ill at ease. "I could tell the moment I went to my bedchamber. Pillows and cushions strewn about, my carrying cloths awry . . ."

"Who tended your room?"

"This lad, as always."

I rounded on Tanner. "What have you to say?" The obstinate young thief said not a word. "Answer!" He shrugged.

It enraged me beyond bearing. "Willem, take him to the courtyard! He's to be whipped!" Guardsmen hustled the youngster out the doors, hauled him along the cobbles. In moments they had the shirt and breeches off him, strung him kicking and protesting to a sturdy post. A delighted crowd gathered. I watched from the steps. Instead of using a cat, Willem raised high a riding crop, such as I might use to goad Ebon. He lashed it hard on the boy's bare back. Tanner danced in frenzied effort to relieve himself of the fearsome sting.

After a time I went inside, seated myself on my throne. In a few moments Willem returned, shoving the whimpering boy before him.

"Well, lad?"

No answer.

My voice was hard. "Again, Willem." This time they had to drag Tanner out the door, down the stone steps.

When they returned, tears coursed down the boy's face.

"Answer. You won't want a third lashing."

"Didn't do it." Tanner rocked in anguish.

"They found the dove in your bedroll."

"Didn't want to."

Why were his words muddled? Why couldn't he admit his thievery, like an honest churl? "Bind him! Call guards!" I was king; he wouldn't get away with it. "Take him to a quiet place, where none will hear." I'd flay the skin from his quivering body. I'd leave him screaming and bloody in the dirt. I'd . . . I took deep breath, appalled at what I heard in myself. "Summon Lord Rustin!"

I paced the hall, while none dared to speak. Rust appeared in the doorway. I almost cried with relief. I laid my hand on Rust's shoulder. "This boy . . ." For a moment, I bowed my forehead to his chest. "Forgive me."

"What did you do?"

"It's what I was about to do." Briefly, I explained.

Rust patted me absently on the shoulder. "There's a good lad. Go change your jerkin." More loudly, "The king will announce his mind. Tanner, to your quarters, and pray he's merciful. Sir Willem, return Jestrel's silver to him. My lords." A short bow. He followed me up the stairs.

"It was as you said, Rust!" I paced the bedchamber, the rank sweat of fear upon me. "I was evil. I'd have tortured him even to death. The thought of his blood excited me."

"But you caught yourself."

"This time." My voice wavered. "And not before I had him twice whipped. I can't be trusted. I can't even trust myself." I swallowed, paced with mounting frenzy. "Lord of Nature, Rust. What am I?"

"Honest."

"Hateful. Did Willem draw blood?"

"No more than a trickle. He's softhearted."

I hadn't remembered as much, when Mother had sent me to his strap.

Rust added, "Tanner has welts, but after all, he's a thief."

My eyes were tormented. "Rust, when I snarled at Elryc you snarled at me, and I hated it. When I chided Anavar's manners, you corrected mine, and I loathed it. But I haven't been harsh to Anavar since." I shuddered at the thought that followed. I'd prefer my evil. Would I not? Then, forced by some dread resolve within, "It's how I learn."

He tapped a warning finger between my eyes, making me blink. "I'll decide that. Not you."

"But—"

"Rodrigo."

"Yes, sir. You decide that." A short bow, as youngsire to elder. I'd tested Rust enough in recent days, and dared no further. Yet why did I feel none of the humiliation I ought?

"For today, it's enough that you caught yourself. I sentence you to the bath you know you need. Summon the room servant."

I did, and soon they were carrying water.

"Consider, Rodrigo. You made yourself responsible for a guttersnipe. I did warn you." Rust left me to my ablutions.

Four

I SHIVERED IN the predawn glimmer.

Captain Tursel cantered to the front of our line. "Ready, my lord."

"The wagons?"

"I supervised the loading myself."

Eighty-five horses, three hundred fifty troops. Piteously few, but all we could muster without stripping the castle walls. I glanced at the sky. The first light would paint the east as we negotiated our way down the steep hill. We'd be through Stryx town at dawn, while Danzik's Norlanders still slept in their camps, a few leagues south. Or so we hoped. The army of Caledon—or at least that portion of it led by the king—was in train to depart for the hills, where we'd rendezvous with Groenfil and Lady Soushire, to wheel and strike at Danzik's force along the coast.

"Proceed."

The huge gates swung open.

To my left, Anavar, proud of his place. To my right, Rustin, his eyes searching and vigilant. Immediately behind, the troops of my bodyguard, Kadar leading.

Ebon snorted and pranced. I soothed him, whispering his choicest cajolements. Behind us, the wagons rumbled.

We'd be at greatest risk descending Castle Way hill, and again at the southernmost reaches of Stryx, where the coast road met the meandering trail to the hills. The hill, because on it we couldn't maneuver. The crossroads, because we'd be closest to the Norlanders, who outnumbered us greatly.

Fear not the Norland camps, Mother had advised, ensconced in her distant cave. If we moved quickly, we'd pass before they were aroused. The Norlanders were most to be feared when King Hriskil carried the Rood; it cast fear and consternation upon his enemies, which was often enough to turn the tide of battle. But Hriskil was far to the north, harrying my ally Duke Tantroth of Eiber.

At the coast road, the gates to the Keep swung open. We assembled within its walls, waiting for the cumbersome wagons.

Within the dim-lit, shadowed Keep, Rustin sat like a statue, eyes locked on the dark brooding gate. Even I hesitated to speak to him. His father Llewelyn's treachery lay, as always, hard upon him, and his one-time home must recall excruciating memories. At length, I leaned across, patted his knee.

"It shall be yours. When you're ready, you shall be Householder of Stryx." I kept my voice low, so that he not be embarrassed by Anavar's hearing.

Somehow, it didn't seem enough.

At last the wagons creaked into position, and our line reassembled. Seventy of the Keep's defenders joined our ranks. As briskly as we could, we trotted through the gates and down the coast road, foot soldiers at the double march.

The blacksmith's boy gawked as we cantered past. When Tantroth had occupied the town, the smith forged steel for Eiber's army. Now it was returned to Caledon, he labored for me.

Mother hoped we might achieve surprise, but inwardly I girded myself for a skirmish. In Caledon no secret went unbetrayed. Surely our preparations had been observed. And if not, Hriskil was not without his spies in Soushire and Groenfil. If he fell on us, at road's end. . . . My jerkin began to dampen.

At my side, Anavar bounced on his saddle, his cheeks flushed. "Think you they'll be at the crossroad? Tursel says not. His scouts—"

"They'll be beyond the crossroad, concealed."

"I'll wager that Tursel's right, my lord. A silver?"

"Don't wager what you can't pay, youngsire."

He stiffened. "You accuse me of dishonor?"

"Have you a silver?"

"I will on seventh day." When he received his stipend.

"Bah. If you're killed by then, should I collect from your father in Eiber?"

His lips tightened.

Softly, Rustin nudged me.

I thrust away his hand. Then, after a few moments, "I'm sorry, Anavar. I've no reason to doubt your honor."

"Thank you, sir." A long pause. "Am I likely to be killed?"

"I hope not. Who else would anger me twice a day?"

The mischievous grin I'd sought. "Genard?"

I rolled my eyes. The former stableboy had accepted my apology willingly enough, but ever since I'd set him gamboling and gibbering he'd taken pains to avoid my company. He even took his meals in the kitchen with the housemen, to Elryc's dismay. I'd have to make greater amends.

I thought again of my brother, safe behind the castle walls. He'd begged to ride with us, but my refusal was set in stone. If I were taken, Elryc was the last of our line. He and Genard languished behind the battlements. My brother had come out of his sulk long enough to bestow on me a rib-creaking hug by way of good-bye.

We clattered past Potsellers' Way and the moribund tavern. As we passed the far harbor breakwater and the ruined lighthouse, Captain Tursel galloped back, wheeled alongside our column. "The crossroad's clear. But, make haste. The Norland camp's not an hour beyond. The noise of our passage . . ."

My heels tensed at the spurs. "At a gallop?"

"And leave our foot soldiers in our dust?" Tursel's eyes twinkled. "Steady, my lord. A canter will do."

I blushed. It was hateful to be a boy, at war.

We maneuvered through the crossroads in surprisingly good order, and turned away from Danzik's camp, toward the hills. Only two wagons got mired in the roiled sand, and a score of willing hands propelled them to firm ground. I darted Ebon back and forth, urging greater speed, helping clear the way, checking the progress of our soldiers, until Rustin caught my reins and led me protesting to the side of the road.

After a time Anavar joined us, and I occupied myself governing his behavior, his stance, his manner, until I caught him exchanging amused glances with Rust. Then I subsided into sulky silence that lasted almost an hour.

WE RODE WELL past dark, by torchlight. Hunger and dancing shadows left me dizzy. Grateful to make camp, I dismounted, ran into the bush, relieved myself of an endless stream.

My bondsmen were hard at work. As they ought to be, having spent the day at nothing more strenuous than walking alongside the wagons, or sneaking rides when their betters' eyes were elsewhere.

Bollert tended horses. Tanner helped raise tents, starting with mine, then busied himself at the cookfire. I'd left him to lick his wounds. Mother, I knew, would have had him hanged to set an example. Even now, she urged me to do so. But, thievery aside, he was a willing enough worker, once taught. I couldn't send him to guests' rooms, light-fingered; that meant I'd have to occupy him myself. Rustin was right; I had no business taking on such a burden.

Tursel set pickets and outriders, and urged me to bed. We'd have ample warning of attack, he said. Sleepily, I undressed, handing my garb to Tanner.

Rust was already beneath the covers. "Thank you for what you said." His voice was soft. "Consider it this week's kindness. Fold it, you loon. On the chair, where he'll have—" He sighed, as Tanner fumbled haplessly with my clothes. "Did you live in a barn?"

"Only a year, m'lord."

Instantly, Rust was out of bed. "I'm sorry, Tanner." He took the leggings from the abashed young bondsman, folded them. "Like so. They gave you a blanket? Good. Go now." He closed the flap.

Outside, fire painted fanciful pictures on the canvas.

Silence. Then Rust said, "if I touch you, you'll bolt from the tent." His tone became wistful. "Never have you feared me."

"I don't." My protest rang hollow.

We lay apart.

An hour passed. I had not a prayer of sleep. "Rust, I'm sorry I don't feel . . ." I could barely say it. "I know you covet me."

"As you say, my prince, that time is done."

"Can you abide it?"

A sigh. "I must, if I'm to be with you." Affably, he patted my flank. "Sleep, Rodrigo. I'll content myself with friendship."

SOUSHIRE WAS AT best a day's journey, even if the trail was un- contested. We rode in silence. It was a miserable day, gray, damp and aguey. The trees dripped. It was too warm for a cloak, but without it one's clothes would be soaked. We gnawed on cold rations for midday meal, and plodded on our way.

Tursel was cautious that we avoid Norland patrols. Three times we stopped, waited in the silent steaming wood while his scouts probed the valleys ahead.

It was dusk before we reached Lady Larissa's lands. We camped in a pasture rather than ride on and rouse her castle after dark.

IN A VAULTED receiving room of her keep, Lady Larissa of Soushire clasped pudgy hands over her ample stomach. "Your uncle asks only that we make common cause against—"

"I won't invite Duke Margenthar into our counsels." I shot a glance to Rust, to see if he disapproved my obstinacy, but his face showed nothing. He clasped his hands behind his back, wandered to the diamond-paned window of her hall. The Earl of Groenfil was on the march and would join us within hours.

She said, "Consider, sire. His holding of Verein is but a long day's ride from Stryx, and would provide the Norlanders a substantial base from which to assail your royal seat of power. When you spurn Margenthar—"

"Madam, he strangled my brother. What's more, he'd betray us on a whim. For the mere joy of it."

"Can you afford to choose your friends?"

I nodded, to concede the point. "If I tell him when and where we strike, what's to stop his selling the knowledge to the Norlanders?"

"Self-interest, I would think." She selected a dried plum, examined it, frowned, chose another. "What's to stop him giving Danzik the castle of Verein?"

I chewed my lip. The lady's questions meant she was in parlay with my uncle. It wasn't surprising, considering the proximity of their estates. But by bringing me Mar's proposal, she was willing that I know it. That *was* surprising.

I asked, "What does Groenfil think?"

"He says his brother-in-law Mar has a force that should be treated with care."

"Yes, Madam. What does he *think*?"

It was her turn to bow for a point scored. "That Mar is a snake, but a dangerous one, and Groenfil wouldn't have those words heard outside his chamber, lest they be told to Mar." She busied herself with the tray of fruits.

Without giving answer, I bade good night and retired to the quarters she'd prepared for my use.

Groenfil was yet to join us. The delay was maddening. By the time he did, it would be too late in the day to set forth. A bad omen; even were we to lunge for the coast on the morrow, Danzik's spies would give him an extra day's warning.

I sent a servant to request that a ritemaster be summoned.

Afterward, fretting over Lady Soushire's words, I paced our chamber, while Rust lounged by the window. Anavar sat crosslegged on the floor, cleaning his fingernails with his bejeweled dagger. I growled, "I won't have it, Rust. I've forgiven Tantroth his invasion. I'll ride with Uncle Raeth's Imbar, whom I detest. I'll make treaty with the Ukras, should it be possible. Anyone but Uncle Mar."

"All right."

"He ruined my face. He threatened to geld me. He took me captive under Tantroth's truce."

"Understood."

"I won't do it!"

Anavar grinned. "Calm yourself, sir. You fight shadows. None of us suggested you treat with Mar."

"He's stable dung. He's—"

Rust put an arm around my shoulder, lifted the ewer brimming with wash water over my head.

"Rust, don't!"

"You'll compose yourself?"

"Yes!" Rolling my eyes, I sank onto the bed. My unhinged guardian was capable of any affront.

THE AGED RITEMASTER was from a small village, a holding of Soushire. Perhaps Lady Larissa summoned him often; his cart was laden with his vessels and the implements of his rites. His name was Hembir.

We were taking a considerable risk; if word got out that the king might be possessed, my following would melt away. Furthermore, I had little doubt that Lady Soushire had a spyhole to our chamber; she'd have been foolish not to.

All that, I knew, but to share my body with an imp was unbearable. The mere thought gave me cold sweats.

Sworn to secrecy on the mightiest of oaths, Hembir was told what we wanted. We would perform the rite in my chamber, while waiting for Groenfil.

Even Anavar was banished from the room; ward or no, he'd been told nothing of what we contemplated. Only Rustin, I and Hembir remained.

After the ritual bath, I lay shivering on my bed, dressed only in white. Even my pant rope was banned as the wrong color.

"Ritemaster, if there's no imp . . . ?"

"The rite will do no harm."

"Will it hurt, if an imp is within?"

"It will not pain your body. But the essence of your being . . ." Hembir toyed with his white mustache. "My lord, it's best we begin."

Most rites were mumbo-jumbo, weren't they? The Rite of Mourning was useful, and that of confession, in which one's shameful secrets were banished to the breaking jar, but as for the rest . . .

Hembir wouldn't hurt me. If he did, Rustin would instantly put a stop to it, and to him. Why then, did acrid sweat trickle down my flanks? Why did my heart pound so hard the bed quivered on its ropes?

Hembir began his ritual. The taper was passed around the bed. Incense filled the room. *"Tombala, iskerd ot forra. Seti onis Rodrido asta! Tombala, iskerd ot forra . . ."* Hear, creature of night. Take thyself from Rodrigo. His chant was soft, yet compelling. The incense stung my eyes.

Nothing happened. After a time my heartbeat eased.

Seven times Hembir carried the candle around my still form. He upended a jar, took from it a damp cloth. Without warning he seized my robe, threw it open, drew a wet circle on my chest.

The candle guttered.

Hembir's eyes narrowed. "Something's there, my lord."

"Get it out!" Almost, I tore at my ribs.

Hembir relit the taper. I thrashed on the sweat-soaked bed.

"Seti onis Rodrido asta! Tombala iskerd ot forra."

All the times I'd spoken so foolishly: imps take this, demons take that. I'd opened myself to a vile creature of the night. From within, it watched my every move, heard my every thought.

"Don't weep, my prince. I am with thee."

"Rust, I'm so—"

From the depths of my chest, a horrid thump that raised me a handsbreadth off the bed, dropped me paralyzed. The room faded.

Rustin dived across the room.

Hembir rasped, "Don't touch him!"

"He's—"

With a gasp and a rattle, my breath renewed.

"SETI ONIS RODRIGO ASTA!" The ritemaster's face was damp with perspiration. He loomed over me, his mouth set in grim resolve.

From within, a swirling. I couldn't breathe, speak, swallow. My eyes bulged. The room faded to gray mist, not unlike that of Mother's cave.

"Tombala iskerd ot forra. Seti onis Rodrido asta!"

My heart thudded. A form surged from the core of my being, hurled itself at Hembir. The old man flew across the bedchamber, slammed into the far wall.

"GET THEE GONE, PUNY MANLING!" Varon of the Steppe, my great-grandsire. His eyes blazed. Abruptly he faded to smoke, disappeared.

Hembir lay dazed, his taper extinguished, his jar shattered.

On the bed, someone was mewling.

It was Rodrigo, the king.

FIVE

"WHERE AM I?"

It was evening, and I lay on a bedsheet. Gently, Rustin sponged me, with cloth from a basin.

"We're in—"

"Soushire." Memory sprang on me like a wolf in the night. I leaped from the bed. "Where's a silver?" I found it by the door. I stared at my image, searching for the crater in my chest that must be, for the sign I was not alone within.

Nothing. Only myself, trembling, scarred, nude.

Rustin brought a robe.

"Don't come near! I may hurt—"

He laid it across my shoulders, fastened the clasp.

"Take care, Rust. I don't know what I might—"

He kissed me on the forehead. "Come, my prince." He led me to the bed, guided my toes into a pair of breeks.

"You're not afraid?"

"No, Roddy."

"You saw him?"

"A shapeless form. After Hembir left, you thrashed about, muttering the name of Varon."

I stayed his hand from my lacings. "Rustin, if I beg a thing of you, will you do it? If I truly beg?"

"It's most likely." His smile was the glow of dawn.

"Kill me. Right now, while I have the courage. I don't want to—"

His palm stopped my mouth. "That you cannot ask."

"Everyone knows imps flee a corpse. Varon will too, and then—"

"You're not to speak of it, or I'll beat you." His mouth was tight. "I forbid it. What do you say to me?"

"All right, I'll—"

He slapped my mouth. "What do you say?"

"Yes, sir!" My voice caught. "I won't kill myself, or speak of it."

"Oh, Roddy!" He gathered me into a ferocious hug. I clung to him, seeking his strength.

After a time I wiped my nose, bent to finish the lacing.

"Besides, my prince, you have another course." He gestured to the ewer, and the empty bowl. "Go to them. Ask of it."

"Ask Varon?" My tone held horror.

"Why not?"

"What if he . . ." I ground to a halt. Why not? Never had he hurt me. Sometimes I even amused him. It seemed, on reflection, a far saner course than ending my life. A knot in my stomach began to ease. "I like the idea. Yes. Bring the ewer."

"After you've slept. You're weak as a kitten."

"Right now."

"It's been a trying day, my prince." His voice was exceedingly gentle. "My temper is near unraveled. Do as I say in this. I ask you with courtesy."

Headstrong I might be, but I was not an utter fool. "Yes, Rust. May I at least have to eat, and greet my Earl Groenfil?" I threw on a cloak, waited politely for his nod, hurried downstairs.

WE PLUNGED DOWN a ravine thick with undergrowth, our horses neighing and sliding on the wet earth. Earl Groenfil, his face dark, spat out orders, encouragements, warnings to his troops. Lady Soushire, more sedate, sat back on her white palfrey and let her men at arms struggle on their own. For my part, I relied on Tursel, who'd forgotten more of war than I'd ever learned.

Our trail was more downhill than not, and I'd had hope we'd reach the Norlanders' camp near Stryx before night made battle impossible. But the sultry wind had died, and the skies grown ominously dark with brooding clouds that foretold a spring storm. We'd conferred, decided to bow to the inevitable, and chosen a suitable clearing for our camp. Another day wasted.

Moreover, our early start from Soushire had made it impossible for me to lose myself in the Still before leaving; sometimes hours would pass before I could rouse myself from its mysteries. At least an early camp would give me opportunity to seek Mother's cave.

My tent was no more than half raised before the first

raindrops were upon us, scouts of a host to follow. The more advice I gave Bollert and Tanner, the more clumsy their work. My exhortations, my curses, seemed to have no effect.

The crash of thunder. Thick sheets of rain dropped onto the clearing. Sweating, Anavar wound tent ropes around the pounded stakes and pulled them tight. My tent was sway-backed, leaning as if too tired to stand, but erect. Hastily Anavar adjusted the flap, to deflect the pounding rain. Hunched atop Ebon, cloak over my head, I nodded grudging thanks.

Hair plastered to his scalp, Anavar grinned up at me. Water dripped from his nose. His clothes were beyond soaked, as if fished from a washing stream.

His eyes darted to his own tent, barely begun. Turning over the canvas, Bollert and Tanner dragged it carelessly through the mud.

The pounding rain had soaked his tent beyond salvage; it would need a thorough drying to be usable. Anavar shrugged, gave a rueful grimace.

I had little choice. "Sleep with us the night." I had to raise my voice over the slap of raindrops on the turf.

"Thank you!" He held my reins. "Would you I unsaddled Ebon?"

"You'll be soaked."

He laughed, and for a moment I felt the fool. I dismounted, raised my cloak, hurried into the tent.

Tanner rushed about, hauling chests and accoutrements into the soggy tent. I shivered. As lodging it would do, but barely. I wondered how Groenfil and Soushire fared in their tents across the clearing.

A campfire was out of the question; we'd have to make do with cold rations. I waited impatiently for Rust to appear; he'd gone off with Tursel to arrange the camp. Tanner dropped candlesticks, stepped on pillows, gawking at everything, though he'd seen it before.

Anavar swept aside the flap, bringing a bedroll, a bundle of clothes and a pungent aroma of damp horse. He made a face. "All of it wet. May I hang it from the poles?"

"For now."

In moments he had the royal tent looking like a wash-woman's hovel. He peeled off his jerkin, his leggings, padded to the pole, draped his fragrant garments with the others. He squealed with joy. "A dry blanket!" Eagerly he wrapped himself, vigorously pummeled his hair with a damp cloth. He flicked a thumb at Tanner. "Where will he stay?"

"Eh? Under a wagon, I suppose." It didn't matter.

I sent my bondsmen for our dinner.

Time at last to pour water into a bowl, wait for it to still, lay my hands across the top, murmur the familiar words. I closed my eyes. The cave grew more distinct.

"Oh, no!" A cry of dismay.

My eyes popped open.

Feverishly, Anavar scrambled about the tent. "I had it, I know I did!"

I glowered.

"My dagger, sir! I laid down my sheath; I'm sure the dagger was in it." He held up the empty sheath. "Perhaps in the mud . . ." Barefoot, he rushed out.

A moment later he was back, tracking mud. "Gone!"

"The jewelled dagger I gave you." The gift of Lady Soushire.

"I didn't mean . . . yes, my lord."

My eyes were glowing coals.

THE CAVE MOUTH widened. A deep breath, for courage.

I strode in.

As bare as the cavern always was, today it seemed . . . disorderly. Fagots were strewn about, the fire stones dislodged.

Mother rose from her place at the fire. "Rodrigo."

Varon was gone. I felt immense relief. I bowed, as I had in life. "Madam."

"What foolishness was that?" She gestured to a shattered stone. "Have you no sense?" She wrapped her fraying robe tighter against a chill only she could feel.

"Did I . . . ?"

"Like a great wind, that tears the summer earth as it fells trees and castles. Had you succeeded . . ."

"You'd be dead?"

"I'm already that. We'd be snuffed out, and you with us.

Oh, Roddy." She opened her arms to an embrace, and I fell into it. From the fire, Cayil and Tryon watched, impassive.

"I'm so sorry." I basked in the solace I'd not had in life. "I knew not what to do." Reluctantly, I held her shoulders at arm's length, told her of my fears, of the cruelty that overcame me despite my earnest intent.

Tryon beckoned me near; I squatted by his side. "Am I possessed, grandsir? Father Varon was within me, was he not? Are you all? Is that the Still?"

He patted me on the shoulder; almost, I crawled into his lap like a weary tyke. "Slow your questions, youngsire." He took a slender stick, nudged a coal, watched the point of the branch burst into flame. "No, we are not within you."

"But Varon—"

"You're not possessed, except by royalty that summons the Still. Your Hembir did much damage. Almost we were swept into the vortex. Only Father was strong enough to grasp the cave wall and bid you desist. You're—" A glance to Mother. "—augmented, shall we say? I never knew what to call it." As if with affection, his arm fell on my shoulder. "You didn't tell him, Elena?"

"He rarely listened. He was a difficult boy." Mother sounded cross.

"Roddy, within each wielder, the Still takes a prominent quality and redoubles it. Your Mother—don't blush, Elena—suffered from lust. It near drove her mad."

"It made me set down the Still before I should." Mother's tone held regret. "Before Margenthar was truly bound, or Eiber. But thought of your father plagued my every night."

"Cayil's failing was gluttony. He ate himself torpid."

"True." The waspish little man seemed embarrassed. "It was years after I set down my Power that I regained my form."

Tryon patted his own ample stomach, as if in sympathy. "It's not necessarily a vice, merely a quality that's strong in you. While you're possessed of the Still, it's intensified."

"As cruelty is strong in me." My tone was dull.

"I sent you to Willem oft enough," said Mother. "His strap curbed you. I hoped you'd outgrow spite, and petty—"

I covered my ears. "Stop, I beg you!"

"But it's true, Roddy."

"I know." I slumped on the cold dirt. "What's to become of me? I won't be a tyrant."

"You'll be what you must. It's for Caledon."

"Is it?" I hurled a stick at the fire. "Is it?"

I CURLED ON the damp cushions, legs drawn up, hands between. My cold dinner lay untouched. Relentless rain drummed a dirge on the sagging canvas.

Rustin threw open the flap, unclasped his sodden cloak, shook himself like a hound. "War is meant for high summer. You don't like dried fruit? I'll have it." He pulled up a stool, attacked my plate. A glance over his shoulder, to Anavar, huddled in the corner. "Why is he weeping?"

"He lost the blade with emeralds and garnets I gave him. All he could do was snivel. A year's stipend wouldn't buy—"

"What did you do?"

"I thrashed him." With a thick green shoot I'd made him cut.

Rust crossed the tent, jerked the blanket free of Anavar's grasp, inspected his stripes. Gently, he replaced the cover. His hand flitted to Anavar's nape.

I swallowed. I'd done it before visiting the cave. Perhaps now, I'd forbear.

Rustin knelt by my bed. "He was distressed, so you beat him."

"Rust—"

"You claim to rule Caledon, who can't rule yourself?"

"He'll learn to take care—"

He grasped my mouth, squeezed it so I gawped like a fish. "Roddy, I love you so dearly, and can't abide what you do!" His eyes filled.

I gulped.

"Anavar!" Rust snapped his fingers. The boy roused himself, hurried across the tent. Rust seized his anxious face, drew a blade, thrust it into my hand. "Don't stop with stripes. Cut him a scar like your own, if you'd embrace Mar's villainy!"

I dropped the dagger as if it were white hot.

Rust gave Anavar an absent pat, encouraged him back to his corner. "I'm sorry, Roddy. I can't bear your company tonight."

"Where will you sleep?" Anavar's soggy tent was abandoned; our troops had what miserable shelter scraps of canvas could provide.

"Here." He seized me, wrapped me in my blanket, propelled me to the flap, spun me around. "Alone." With his boot, a mighty kick to my rump. I landed on my face in the mud. The flap snapped shut.

I huddled under a dripping supply wagon, sneezing, shivering, hoarding my rage.

Anavar deserved what he'd got. Lose Lady Larissa's blade? I'd warrant he wouldn't be so clumsy again. His hapless pleas had fallen on deaf ears, as he received the king's justice.

Yet Anavar slept in warm comfort, while I, king of Caledon, crowned and acknowledged, victor over my erstwhile regent Margenthar, lay shivering in the mud, nursing a bruised rump. Were I the man I wanted to be, I'd avenge Rust's casual contempt. Kick the king? Fah! I was no boy, to be treated so. I would show them the might of Caledon. If Rust thought Genard had gibbered and pranced, wait 'til he beheld his own dance.

I searched for a still puddle, spotted it behind the wheel. Greedily, I crawled, heedless of the mud. I cupped eager hands over the water, mildly regretful it wasn't stillsilver. How he'd caper, if I had the full strength of my Power!

I shut my eyes, muttered the words of encant.

Compare me to Uncle Mar, would he? A vicious calumny. Margenthar was twisted, evil clear through. I'd show him. The caved shimmered into focus. I'd make Mar's cruelty seem mere child's—

By brute force, I wrenched my hands from the puddle. Aghast, I stared at my palms, as if theirs was the fault.

What had I done?

What had I become?

BY DAWN'S GRAY light I crept back to the tent. I hadn't slept a wink. The rain continued unabated. My every bone ached, and my nose ran.

Yet I felt strangely at peace.

I shook Rustin to wake him.

Groggy, he sat up, rubbed his eyes.

"Anavar, come hither." My tone was a command.

Sleepily, the boy roused himself.

I knelt by the bed. "Stay awake, Rust. Now do I, Rodrigo, King, in the presence of Anavar Baron of the Southern Reaches, appoint Rustin, son of Llewelyn and Lord of the Keep, as regent of the crown of Caledon and of my person, and decree that he shall hold said office until he himself declares it vacant, and that no man, including myself as king, may remove him or end the regency lacking his consent."

He gaped.

My voice trembled. "Rust, I would not be a villain."

"But you can't—"

"Now you're guardian *and* regent. I count on you to shield Caledon from my rage. I charge you with doing so. If you're wise, make me swear on the True I'll never use the Still to cause torment."

"You went to war to end a regency."

"Uncle Mar's. But I trust you more than myself. Be my regent until you're sure I'm the king we'd both see. Then release me." I felt noble, and proud, and would have continued so had I not suddenly sneezed all over him. "Pardon, my lord." I bowed my head.

He raised my chin. "Roddy, you ought not do this. Such power will tempt me."

"I must. There's much you don't know." I told him of my visit to the cave. "So I'm not possessed. I'm twisted, as in an ill-tempered silver. The wrong parts of me are magnified. Last night was the end." In a voice I could barely make heard, I told him of the puddle, and my intent. "So, it is done."

"Are you sure? Quite sure?"

"Anavar, find parchment, and one to act as scribe. Be quick."

"Hold." Rustin's voice was sharp.

"Whom shall I obey?" Anavar looked between us.

"If I'm regent, he has no say."

I said, "I would publish—"

"Be silent."

Fuming, I did as I was told.

"If this becomes known, Roddy, your cause is weakened. How if I be your regent, but in secret?"

"You can't act for the state if no one recogniz—"

"I can, through you."

"I'm willful. I might refuse."

"I'll bind you in vows by the True. You'll do as I say or lose all." An oath solemnly sworn would bind me by my Power itself.

I said dubiously, "I don't think I like it."

"I don't believe I gave you choice."

I surged to my feet, stomped to the tent pole, hammered it with my fist. Only when I'd struck several mighty blows did I heed the warning ache in my knuckles.

I wanted so badly to do right, and he made it so hard.

A deep breath. "Your pardon, sir. It will be as you say."

"Just a moment." Anavar. "I agreed to be *your* ward, not Lord Rustin's."

"How can I be your guardian? I'm not even my own."

"What matters that?"

"And your welts?"

"Last night I hated you until well past twelfth hour!" A sniffle. "But you treasured that blade; whenever I toyed with it your look had such longing . . . almost I gave it back. To lose it . . . how could I be such a clumsy fool? I cried half the night over that. My father would have beaten me, my Lord Treak would have, my Duke Tantroth. Why berate yourself over a whipping?"

"Because . . . I enjoyed it." Somehow, I met his gaze without flinching.

"What matter, if I deserved it?"

"When you're grown, perhaps you'll know." Lord of Nature save him from the bitter knowledge I'd gained.

Rust said, "I'll give you one last chance to withdraw, Roddy. It's a noble deed, but I won't hold you to—"

"No." Caledon deserved better than what I now was. The part of me that knew it was glad.

"So be it. Anavar speaks rightly; he's yours to govern. I'm not his master. But if you beat him, I'll likely do the same to you."

"I understand." Perhaps the threat would chain me. Somehow, I doubted it.

I STARED BALEFULLY at my muddy boots, trying not to disclose my fright.

It had been a busy morning. We'd broken fast with Groenfil and Lady Soushire, in his large, well-appointed tent. It wouldn't kill our men to walk in rain, we knew, and another day's delay could only give Danzik's Norlanders more warning. But we were tired, many of our men were soaked through, and the trail would be slippery and mud-logged. In what state would we reach Stryx to confront the Norlanders in their camps?

While we debated, rain drummed relentlessly on the canvas. We agreed to wait for the sun. That is, Lady Larissa and Groenfil agreed, and after catching Rustin's almost imperceptible nod, I concurred.

That done, Rustin had steered me back to my tent, sent Anavar away. He sat me down and begun devising oaths, to which I swore, one after another, on my honor, in the name of our house, by my crown, and by the True.

When he was done I was bound beyond all cavil. I had not the slightest doubt my Power would be forever lost were I to attempt to overthrow him. The careful wording was necessary, he'd said, because I was willful, clever and devious. "I'll help you as best I can. The day I'm sure of you, Roddy, is the day I'll resign. I swear it on my father's—I swear it."

"Thank you."

Despite his promise of good will, Rust could now bend me to his every whim, and I could do nothing, save abdicate.

As if to make the very point, my oaths of submission still echoing in my ears, he issued a series of stern edicts that bound my conduct as to grooming, bathing, manner, dress, and headlong speech. He'd even bade me clean my own boots. An affront, to a king. No, beyond that: an outrage. Almost, I'd summoned Tanner, given him the labor, but Lord of Nature knew how Rust would retaliate.

Now I sat chewing a fingernail, nursing rising panic at the impetuosity that had thrown away my hard-earned crown and made of me little more than Anavar: ward to an authoritarian despot.

And the boots awaited.

IT MUST BE the foul weather. Men fought over naught and were rebuked. Tanner's clumsy manner irritated me beyond reason, until I sent him away with harsh words. Rust found fault with my tone, my nervous pacing, the cleanliness of my boots.

It wasn't his reproof I found so galling, but my erstwhile willingness to submit to him. Was I so evil, that I needed such remaking? Rust sat me down, stroked me as Hester had when a skinned knee had been my catastrophe, until I calmed. Anavar did well to hide the contempt he surely must feel; I saw not the slightest sign of it. Else, despite Rust's admonition, I'd have lashed him to ribbons.

In the afternoon, despite the persistent drizzle, I had to leave the tent or go mad. Accompanied by my bodyguards I wandered our camp, visited with wet and miserable soldiers. I'd thought our damp and chill tent a burden of discomfort, but found their lean-tos and improvised tarpaulin shelters appalling.

Embarrassed, ashamed, I helped pass out rations, urged my bodyguards to strengthen some of the least adequate of the shelters, joked with the tired and cold guards set over the horses.

Halfway through my meander Rustin joined me, watched with silent approval that helped dispel the frigid wind.

On the way back we passed our supply wagons. Tanner lay curled under one of them, only his tousled blond hair visible from under his blanket. All his worldly belongings were in the ragged bundle beside. Bollert, the older boy, sat nearby, staring at nothing.

When they'd helped with my tent the night before, I hadn't for a moment thought of inviting them to share a corner. My mind was too full of myself, and rebuking Anavar.

I stood stock still, my thoughts awhirl.

"Roddy?"

I held up a hand. "Later." I walked on, to my tent.

Anavar was within. I handed him his cloak. "Find my guards. And collect Tanner, with his bundle." Walking with discomfort, Anavar did as bidden.

Rustin looked askance.

"By your leave, sir." My courteous tone reassured him, and he stood aside.

A few moments later my two bondservants shivered in my crowded tent, wrapped in their dirty blankets. The bodyguards looked about with interest.

I knelt, threw open Tanner's bundle of belongings. A grimy shirt, the only spare he'd been given. A few other old and discarded clothes. A child's rag doll, the arms long since torn off and lost. A few rounded stones and pebbles.

"Leave 'em 'lone!"

With a hiss, Anavar cuffed Tanner silent.

"I won't steal them." I replaced the stones, rolled up the bundle as best I could.

"My prince?"

"I'm sorry, Rust. I hoped—" I sighed. "Let him go. Summon Bollert."

Wiping his nose, the ragged youngster gathered his worldly possessions, edged to the flap.

"Just a moment." Rust's tone was curt. He herded Tanner inside. "Set down the bundle. Let's have your blanket." His nose wrinkling, he inspected the grimy bedrolls "Now, unclothe yourself."

"Rust?"

"The job's only half done." Perhaps Tanner was too slow for him. He hauled the youngster's jerkin over his arms.

Loincloth at his feet, Tanner laced his fingers to cover a small thatch of hair.

"What's this?" Anavar darted forward, pawed at a bulky bandage knotted around Tanner's leg. It fell open. A cloth dropped to the ground. Wincing from his aches, Anavar bent and unraveled it.

A bejewelled dagger tumbled out. Gingerly, his expression blissful, Anavar took it to his breast, hugged it.

All eyes turned to Tanner. He stood naked, grinning. Only a small sheen of sweat on his forehead hinted of anxiety.

I closed my eyes, recalling how I'd beaten Anavar for his carelessness, his negligence, when it was Tanner who'd stolen the blade.

The servant's penalty was clear. Yet having spared him once, I was loath to take his life. "Tie him to a wagon wheel. Have him flogged."

"No." Rustin was somber. "Hang him."

"As king, I commute—"

"Roddy." His voice was soft. "Shall we have private words?"

"No." I swallowed. "No, sir." But I couldn't let it be. "Tanner, what made you take it?"

"Hadda." He scratched himself.

"Why?"

He shrugged. "Hadda."

Rust thrust his clothes at him. "Get him out!"

My palms itched. "Tanner, explain. You know a thief is for hanging?"

Still clutching himself, he nodded.

"Dress yourself. Why do you do it?"

His lips tightened to a thin, bloodless line. "Gotta." He slipped on his loincloth.

"Why?"

"Can't say."

They dragged Tanner to a nearby beech. From the wagon, Bollert watched stolidly.

"Rust . . ." I rubbed my sweating palms.

"It must be done. Twice he's been caught."

"Something's wrong." My eyes searched the tent. I seized on the ewer, snatched it up, settled myself on the floor, the pitcher between my knees. "Rust, stop them."

"No, my prince."

"Just for a moment. Hurry, or I'll—I'll abdicate!" My voice trembled. "I need time!"

He studied my face, nodded. "All right." To the guards. "Hold!"

Feverishly, I waited for the water to still. I placed my throbbing palms over the pitcher, impatiently recited words of encant.

Nothing. I was too agitated, too eager. I forced a surface calm, fastened my eyes shut. Slowly, the cave mouth widened.

I opened my eyes. My hooded eyes sought Tanner. My mouth moved silently, as I repeated over and over the incantation of my Power.

Tanner began to sweat.

My palms fit tight to the ewer. Over and again, the words. Tanner shifted from foot to foot. "M'lord!"

My hooded eyes never left his.

"Please, I—don' make—oh!" He dripped perspiration. His fists clenched and unclenched.

"Roddy!"

"No, Rust. It isn't what you think." I lapsed silent.

Under the tree, Tanner danced a jig of anguish. His bound hands scrabbled at his back.

I wove it as strong as my ineptitude let me. Then I concentrated my whole being on the frantic boy. "Why?"

"M'lord—"

"WHY?"

"Made me. Gotta!"

"Who?"

"Oh, stop!" He stumbled about the tent in frenzy. "Can't say. Gotta do what—" A strangled sound. "Didn' mean take it. Bollert—" Desperately, he clapped hands over his mouth. One by one, jerking, scrabbling, his fingers pulled away. "Gotta, when Bollert say!"

"Why?"

"'Cause he . . . dunno!"

I bent to the ewer. My lips moved without cease.

From the tree, a howl. "Stop, king! Boller' made me! Was Boller'! Can't—ayee!"

"Enough, Roddy." A hand on my shoulder.

I peeled my hands from the ewer. Red indentations marked where they'd met the rim. Trembling, I reached for Rustin, pulled myself to my feet. I was so shaky I could barely stand.

Together we walked into the rain.

Bollert sat under the wagon, peeling bark from a dead twig.

"Seize him."

They brought him forth, stripped off his clothes.

Nothing.

In his bedroll, a shirt, a rude clay frog, chipped and battered. A tiny silver squirrel I'd seen before.

I drew him within a handbreadth. "How do you do it?"

"Dunno. Always could."

"Have they choice?"

Expressionless eyes met mine. My knees were weak. I felt a great yearning to kneel. I shivered. "Do it and I'll flay you."

Abruptly, the yearning was but a memory.

"How?"

"Gotta look at 'em."

Anavar ran to the tent, brought out a cloth, made of it a

hood. He slipped it over Bollert's head, fastened it with a tie from the wagon. Guardsmen bound his hands.

I said to Rust, "Release Tanner."

"Aye, my prince." He gestured it so. "Roddy . . . ?" His fingers flitted to the small of my back. "How did you know?"

"It felt wrong." As we strolled to the tent I clutched him for support. I was weak as a newborn calf. "And the Still called."

"Your Power does that?"

"Apparently. Thank you for listening, sir."

"At the moment, humility isn't called for." Rust closed the flap behind us.

I paced, disturbed beyond saying. "Bollert can't have a Power, he's a brat of the streets. Only royal houses manifest—"

"It would seem he does."

Anavar ducked through the flap. "He's secured."

Rust asked, "What's to be done with him?"

Anavar was grim. "I want him."

"You?" I gaped.

He loosened his belt rope, bared his welted thigh. "From you, or my father, I'll allow those, because I must. From him . . ." His tone hardened. "He's a churl, and gave me stripes!"

"It was I who—"

"Because of him!"

"Easy, lad."

"Don't 'easy' me, I'll—" He saw my visage, and gulped.

"How would you avenge yourself?"

"As I might." Eiberians practiced barbarous savagery on their Cumber prisoners. It wouldn't do to grant the boon he asked.

A soft sound. In the corner, a blanket moved. I threw it aside. Tanner lay weeping, knees drawn up to his chest. The gall of him, to hide in the royal tent. As I stood fuming, his hand shot out, wrapped itself desperately around my boot. "Please, lor'! No more!" He drew himself close, as a suppliant. "Won' take nothin'. Don' make me hurt."

I dropped to my knees, kneaded his shoulders. "It's done, boy. You need not fear."

He lapsed into uncontrollable sobs.

"It's me you serve, Tanner. Not Bollert." I looked helplessly at Rust. "What must I do?"

"Comfort him. Hang Bollert, as quickly as possible. He's a monster."

"A sport of nature. Or could it be he has royal blood?"

"Him?" Rust's tone dripped contempt.

"I'd be like him, raised in a stable."

Rust's whole mien softened. "Ahh. You understand at last."

Six

In the first light of day we rode down the still-soggy trail, Rust and I and Tursel. Alongside rumbled a wagon in which lay Bollert, bound and hooded. I would speak with Mother before deciding his fate. I gulped. Would it be possible?

Lady Soushire and the Earl of Groenfil, once antagonists, rode together chatting civilly. As always, Groenfil kept sharp eye on his troops' progress.

Because Tursel was close and no doubt watching, I did my best to quell my panic. From time to time Rust reached across to pat my knee.

What had I done?

In my tent the night before, as darkness had fallen, I'd sat again with the ewer. I had much to ask Mother. Wearily, I set my hands across the still water, murmured the usual words.

No cave. Only the lights that dance behind closed eyes.

Over and again I summoned my Power, and felt naught. At last, exhausted, I rose to pace the tent in growing agitation. Never, in the year I'd been visiting the cave, had it been denied me.

Anavar came in, saw my turmoil. I turned aside his inquiries with harsh words. A few moments later Rustin thrust through the flap. I flew to him in a panic.

Startled, he soothed me, bid me practice my art again. I did so, and caught not a glimmer of the cave. "What have I done, Rust? Did I gainsay the True?"

"Not that I—"

"I obeyed you as I pledged. My boots weren't that clean, I know, but—"

"Calm yourself, my prince."

"I'm calm. When I told Tursel I thought the rain would stop, could that be it? I wasn't sure it was true, I know—"

"Roddy." He hugged me, rocking.

For the second night, I slept not at all. Well before dawn I crept out of bed, poured water.

I didn't know how many times I chanted the words, in a whisper only I could hear. About me, the camp began to stir. Wagons were packed, tents and tarpaulins thrown down, cold bread and cheese handed the men.

I sat unmoving, feverishly repeating dead enchantments.

"Roddy, it's long time we struck the tent." Rust's cool hand soothed my damp shoulder.

"In a while."

"Now, my prince." Firmly, he pulled my cramped fingers from the useless ewer.

I looked up, eyes glistening. "I've lost the Still."

Whatever solace he'd offered left no memory. Now, hours later, I rode at his side, exhausted and disconsolate.

AT FIRST THE day was cloudy and grim. By afternoon, as we neared Stryx, a cautious sun broke through. Everyone's spirits lifted, except mine. Tanner trotted up, chest heaving from the run, to offer water fresh drawn from a stream. Gratefully, I drank.

Tursel's scouts cantered back to camp. In a moment the captain drew near. "Verein road's clear." Outlandish as it might be, I wouldn't have put it past Uncle Mar to attempt to bar our way at the cross.

At a fast march, we advanced toward the seacoast and Danzik's camp. Tursel's scouts buzzed like angry bees, probing hillsides and ravines, goat trails and the road ahead.

As the sun looked toward the western hills and debated its plunge for the night, Tursel called a brief halt. "Danzik's sallied from his camp. He's blocked the road."

For the first time, my spirits rose. I smiled at lord Groenfil. "Excellent. He had all winter to fortify his breastworks and abandons them."

"Aye, but he set his men here, and here." Tursel jabbed his sharp stick at a rude drawing in the dirt. "Where the road turns. On the one side, steep hills, which he occupies. On the other, a ravine. We won't be able to focus enough strength to—"

Groenfil asked, "What if we bypass the road? We'd come between him and Stryx."

"Our wagons need the road."

I mused. Rustin drew me aside. "Turn back, Roddy." His voice was quiet.

"Without a fight? It's taken us all spring to assemble—"

"We've lost surprise, they have the advantage of terrain."

"But Larissa and the earl are committed. Lord of Nature knows when again they would—Rust, is it your decision or mine?"

"Answer yourself."

I sighed, hating what I'd vowed. "Yours, sir."

"I agree. But the crown is yours, and the choice may gain or lose it. I would not take that from you. Decide."

I pondered.

"Rust, every day strengthens Danzik's grip on my lands. We're in the field, and . . ." I floundered. "I wish I could consult Mother."

Somberly, he nodded.

I took deep breath. "Time favors Hriskil, not us. I say proceed."

"As you wish, my prince."

We resumed our march. Tursel let the wagons fall back to the tail of our column, just before our rear guard.

Insisting I not lead our force to battle, Rust held Ebon's reins himself to make sure I obeyed. Anavar, with drawn sword, joined my tense bodyguards.

Across the road to Stryx, Danzik had mounted barricades of downed trees and stones. Behind them were his pikesmen. A few paces behind, massed ranks of archers.

Our men advanced behind wide sturdy shields that turned aside or absorbed most of the enemy's first volley. Inevitably, shafts slipped between, and some drove home. One by one, our men fell, and comrades dragged them behind the battle line.

"Roddy, this is madness!" Earl Groenfil's face was grim. A harsh breeze swept the treetops, harbinger of his ire.

Our assault dwindled to ignominious failure. Wind whistled, blowing mounds of dust to furious circles. Groenfil had lost only eight men, but anxiously, I scanned the thrashing treetops for falling limbs. I said hopefully, "If we attack with horse—"

"We lose horsemen, to no avail."

I patted Ebon's mane. "What would you, my lord earl?"

"In darkness, I'll lead a hundred horsemen on a circle, to the rear of their camp. You attack the road by last moonlight. Between us . . ."

"Rust?"

"We've few enough men, to split our force." Pacing, he considered. "Very well, I assent."

I said, "I'll lead the—"

"Perhaps." Rust's tone was curt. "Tursel, can we hold for the night, against attack?"

"Half a league back, there's land I could defend."

"Roddy, you've had no sleep. Help Anavar gather the boys and set your tent."

"After the earl and lady decide—"

Abruptly, he hauled me from my saddle. "You try me, sir!"

I clawed at his iron grip on my jerkin. "Yes, Rust. The tent. Right away. We'll raise it." I clamped my jaw, to still my babble.

Slowly, his fingers eased. "Thank you, my prince." An absent pat on the cheek.

Shamefaced, I beckoned to Anavar, cantered off to the supply wagons.

IN A CLEARING well behind our lines, Anavar scowled at the tent. "Too much work, and too few of us. By your leave, sir." He crossed to the wagon, cut Bollert's bonds, gave the stable-boy a ferocious kick. "Try your witchery and I'll roast your heart for supper!" He slapped a hammer in Bollert's hand, threw a tent peg at his feet.

After the tent, there were clothes chests to haul, stools to set, cushions to place. I was drenched with sweat, but we found a cold stream in which to frolic.

Afterward, rejuvenated by cool water, feeling magnanimous as I hadn't in many weeks, I invited the boys into my tent, even Bollert, who'd hammered tent pegs with unstinting will. I sorted through my dried foods, fed them an occasional delicacy. Toweled clean, Tanner was almost presentable.

"King." Bollert tapped me on the shoulder. I whirled, ready to strike him down for insolence, but his tone was submissive. "Let me live." It was a plea, not a demand.

"You're a thief." And something worse.

"Aye." Perhaps there was a hint of apology in his shrug.

"You'd have seen Tanner hanged."

"'Steada me." He picked at a toenail. "Wanna live. 'Sides, never . . ." He made an unmistakable back and forth motion with his hand. "Girl. Ain' fair to die 'fore that."

Anavar caught my hand before I could loose my dagger. "It's no jape, my lord. He means it."

I thought the blood would burst from my temple. I grated, "How do you know?"

"Look at him."

Bollert squirmed with embarrassment. He looked up, quickly dropped his eyes. If it was mummery, he ought to join a troupe and astound lords and ladies.

My ire fading, I peeled Anavar's fingers from my wrist. "Who are you to stay my hand?"

"Baron and privy councillor, sir."

I grunted. It was I who had made him so. "You owe Bollert no kindness."

"Nor will I give it." He settled himself more comfortably. "I spoke for your sake."

Rustin came to the tent not long after, and his astonishment at the sight of us far outvalued my wasted delicacies. Ending our evening, Anavar shooed the churls to the campfire, not neglecting to secure Bollert's hood and ropes, despite the older boy's anguished protests. With a regretful last look at our tent, my ward joined the others.

Yawning prodigiously, I sat again with a bowl of water. Stillsilver would have made the cavern more distinct, but it was costly stuff, and I preferred to safeguard it in Stryx.

I settled into the familiar incantations. At last, in the distance, the dim contour of a cave. Chant as I might, I could go no closer, achieve no greater clarity. Defeated, I gave it up and settled to bed. At least, after a fashion, I could see the cavern. The Still was not wholly lost. I drifted to sleep.

Moments later someone prodded me awake. I groaned. "What time . . ."

"Fourth hour," said Rustin. "The earl's men are gone these two hours. Here, wear these."

Feverishly, I dressed.

Outside, the camp was a beehive of quiet labor. Men rushed about striking tents, dousing campfires, sheathing arrows. Under his hood Bollert called plaintively to be let out to piss, but no one had the time.

Tanner brushed past, lugging my chest to the wagon. I stifled a yawn and asked Rust, "Where's Ebon?"

"Anavar saddles him for you. Be sure to thank him."

"Yes, sir." I was too weary to be other than meek.

Lady Soushire picked her way across the campground, leading her palfrey. "My lord Rodrigo."

"My lady." A short bow, of courtesy.

"How did you persuade me to accompany this excursion? I've never been so cold, so inconvenienced." Nonetheless, a small, grudging smile. "I wish you well, sire. I'll wait with the wagons, as before."

"Of course. Think you the earl's yet mounted his attack?"

She glanced at the waning moon. "Within the hour. He's a man of . . ." She blushed. "Great resolve."

"A match for yourself, then." I said it out of gallantry, but she seemed discomfited.

Groenfil was circling Danzik's barricades and creeping up from the rear; our task was to attack along the road where before we'd failed to breech the Norland defenses. If we made enough commotion, perhaps Groenfil's approach would go unnoticed until too late.

We organized for our march: spearmen at the lead, archers behind, horse at the rear, where they could charge into the fray at a critical moment. Rustin took me aside. "Ride where I ride. Don't show me that face; I won't see you killed by a stray spearthrust."

"I'm king, Rust. I have to show myself." I shifted my shield. Even Anavar was among the horsemen awaiting our charge.

"You gave me authority, my prince. I'll use it to preserve you. Ride behind me, I say."

Fuming, I complied. How could men follow a coward?

WE ADVANCED AT a furtive walk, an army of ghosts flitting through the ebbing night. Bobbing spears brushed aside drooping branches. Beards glistened in the last rays of moonlight. Fists clenched and unclenched on the hafts of swords. Eyes flickered to the gaze of companions, building and fastening resolve.

The last rise that concealed us was a hundred paces from the Norland barricade.

Rust bent low, soothing his gray gelding, his shield dangling.

Tursel's raised sword flashed down. At the peak of the hill, our men broke into a silent run.

For a moment, nothing but the thud of feet. Then, from the foe, shouts of warning. Behind the downed trees, torches bobbed. New flames spouted, as pitch sputtered and caught.

Full two hundred of our spearmen careened down the road. A mass of archers followed. An instant before the first spearmen reached the trees, our archers began dropping to one knee. Their loosed shafts whirred into the night.

Shouts, cries of pain.

Behind us, the rumble of massed horse.

Our spearmen clambered over the breastworks, jabbing fiercely. Some fell, kicking and twitching.

Swarms of arrows shot into the first of dawn.

Suddenly, as if recalled by an omnipotent hand, barbs whirred down from the sky, fell about us. As one, Rust and I raised our shields, huddled beneath.

A drumbeat of hooves. Our horsemen swept past, swords drawn. Their mounts raced with bulging eyes, bits between their teeth. I soothed Ebon with a hissed word. "Now, boy." I kicked. He shot toward the downed trees.

Waving his sword, Rustin raced after. I would pay a price for this.

On the whole, the enemy archers overshot; most of their arrows whizzed harmlessly overhead.

I thundered toward the Norland breastworks.

For once, we'd had the advantage of surprise; only a light guard had manned the hastily erected barricades. They'd given warning, but too late. Our initial charge had driven them off.

One by one, our horses leaped over the unmanned barrier and galloped down the road. Norland archers stood their ground, loosed a deadly volley, but broke and ran even as our men tumbled. I leaned forward on Ebon's neck and he sailed over a dead Norlander stretched over the barricade as if on a rack.

"Wait for me, Roddy!"

I slowed Ebon's gallop the merest trifle. In fifty paces, Rust was at my side.

Ahead, a shriek of agony. Wails, moans, cries.

The music of war.

The Norlanders were in full flight. Our spearmen, panting, caught one after another, burst through their spines with barbed points. Norland archers were particularly vulnerable, unprotected by pikemen. As I watched, a horseman galloped past. His sword sliced at an exposed neck. The Norlander fell, twitched once. Without a pause, our horseman raced on. It was Anavar.

A hundred paces down the road the Norlanders rallied to make a stand. A score of our horsemen milled about. One went down, an arrow in his breast.

"Don't, Roddy!"

"CALEDON!" I reared in my saddle. My voice was shrill. "For Caledon!"

"For the king!" Rustin could only support me.

"Charge!" Waving my sword, I flew past our disordered troops. A Norland pikeman set his haft in the hard dirt, aimed at Ebon's breast. I yanked Ebon to the right, desperately let fly my sword. It buried itself in the man's ribs. Swordless, I raced on, batted aside an archer with my shield.

Behind, the thunder of hooves.

"For Rodrigo!"

I reined in. Our horsemen had swept aside the Norland rally. As far as the eye could see, the road was ours.

DESPITE OUR DEAD and grievously wounded, we had almost a festive air as we jangled west along the trail toward the sea-coast road. We were in a great hurry, lest Danzik's force re-group. Somewhere between the turn in the road where we'd skirmished and the Norlander camp, we hoped to join with Earl Groenfil's horsemen, who'd attacked the Norland camp from the rear.

Anavar, flushed and proud, joined our circle and chattered of a stallion to succeed his rather gentle mare. At fifteen, he ought have one; I made a silent vow to see to it.

Only Rustin was grim and silent, his face a thundercloud. Aware of the cause, I knew better than to remonstrate.

Uncle Raeth of Cumber had trained Tursel well; despite the chaos of battle, the captain had reassembled our men in good order and refused them pause to loot the dead.

Notwithstanding our victory, we held our shields high. The forest was thick, and Norland stragglers might be lurking. My bodyguard Kadar and his troop surrounded me as we rode.

Abruptly we were on a downhill, the seacoast road before

us. To the south, our left, lay Danzik's main camp that we'd attacked so ignominiously a few weeks past. To the north, Stryx harbor, and beyond it, the Keep and Castle Way.

Our pace increased.

The clatter of horse came out of nowhere. Norland cavalry streamed from the wood onto the road ahead. As our spearmen fell into rank, a few turned tail and ran.

More horsemen poured onto the trail. My heart leapt. They wore the leathern jerkins of Groenfil's troop.

The milling Norsemen hesitated, plunged toward the seacoast road.

"Give chase!" I stood in my stirrups, and Ebon snorted. "Tursel, sound the advance!" I cupped my hands. "Tursel!"

A wave of acknowledgment. In a moment the horn sounded. As I dug in my spurs, fingers closed on my cloak, hauled me rearward. It was all I could do to stay in the saddle. Furious, I whirled. "Who dares . . . oh." I gulped.

"Dismount, sir!" Rustin, his eyes ablaze.

"They're in flight! Let me lead—"

"Am I your guardian? Am I regent?" He held out his hand for my reins. Reluctantly, I opened my fingers. As I dismounted he seized my upper arm, led me to the wood. Kadar and my guard followed.

"Tell them not to interfere."

"With what?"

"Still you defy me? Will you never cease?"

Stung, I turned to Kadar. "Wait over there. Do nothing, whatever Rustin . . . raise no hand to him."

Rust drew his blade, cut a shoot, began to strip the leaves.

I swallowed. "Not here, I beg you. Not in front of—"

For a moment, his labor ceased. "Roddy, when you give a command, do you expect the king to be obeyed?"

"Yes."

"Always, or when it's convenient?"

I felt my face redden. "Always."

"You've no right to rule, unless you'd do what you ask of others."

My mouth was dry.

"Bare your back, my prince."

Heartsick, trembling, I did so. Not knowing where else to put them, I set my cloak and jerkin on the grass.

He led me to a sapling. "Embrace the tree."

I wrapped my arms around the smooth wood, fighting a wave of fury.

Now do I appoint Rustin, son of Llewelyn and Lord of the Keep, as regent of the crown of Caledon and of my person.

It had been of my own free will. I closed my eyes.

The switch lashed my bare back until I was aflame with hornet stings. In moments he was done. It was his intent to castigate, not to wound me, and he didn't break skin. He dropped the switch.

I made myself face him. "I thank thee for thy care and—you're crying!"

"What of it?" He handed me my cloak.

"I'm sorry!" Almost, I dropped to my knees. "Rust, forgive me!"

"I had to do it, Roddy." His voice was anguished.

"I know, Rust, I'm willful." His caress brushed my back, and I yelped. I giggled, and it turned to tears. He held me tight, his hands well clear of my smarting flesh.

After a time he released me. Wiping my eyes, I growled at Kadar, "What are you gawking at? Have you never seen a lashing?"

"Yes, my lord. I mean, not—" Not of the king.

"Lord Rustin is my protector and has the right." I threw on my cloak, tried not to grit my teeth. There was no thought of wearing my jerkin this day. I untied Ebon, hesitated. "Do I ride behind you, Rust?" My tone was more than civil.

"Is there need?"

I sighed. "No, sir."

He motioned me to mount Ebon.

Together, almost amiably, we cantered after our troop.

FOR ONE SO portly, Lady Larissa of Soushire was astonishingly light on her feet; she trotted across the sodden clearing that had once been the Norland camp.

"A brilliant stroke." She beamed at the captured Norland wagons laden with supplies, the abandoned defensive earthworks, the stacks of unused arrows propped against a downed tree. Anavar dangled his legs off the backboard of a wagon, charged with guarding our newfound treasure against looting.

"Not my doing, my lady." A pang of regret, that it was so. "Earl Groenfil captured their camp."

"Of course, but after you drew them forth."

Wistfully, I considered donning the glory she proffered. No, what adulation I might have, I would earn. "It was he," I repeated.

"And Danzik, my lord?"

"Fled south, with a remnant of his men." Groenfil's horsemen were after him. But the bulk of the Norlanders had been herded between the coast road and the Keep. They'd made a hurried, halfhearted effort to loot the town, hindered by the relentless pursuit of Groenfil's horsemen. Now, most were surrendered and under guard. Our role was to guard their erstwhile camp, and the seacoast road, lest Danzik somehow slip past his pursuers and bolt north.

"What now, sire?"

"Is Tursel about?"

Anavar heard me, shook his head. "He's gone with Groenfil." The boy's tone was unhappy.

"What ails you?"

"I would ride with him, but . . ." A contemptuous thumb indicated the ignominy of the wagon.

For a moment, I let my annoyance show. Then I bowed pardon of Lady Larissa, approached the backboard. My tone was low. "I am king, and am forbidden the chase. Can you not bear likewise?"

He gulped. "Rustin?"

"Yes." I held his eye.

His voice was small. "Forgive me."

"Done." I clapped his knee.

For two hours I forced myself to make idle talk, with Anavar, with Lady Soushire, with Rust. My answers grew shorter, my pace more agitated. My cloak chafed my stinging back, but shame stopped me from taking it off, in front of all.

At last, the rumble of hoofbeats. I strode to the edge of the glade. A column of horse, led by Earl Groenfil. He raised his hand; they halted. He dismounted, tossing his reins to Tanner.

"My lord King." A short bow, almost of equals. His dark face lightened in a slow smile. "We have him! He'd have fought unto death, but he lost his sword when—"

"Danzik?" My voice shot into the upper registers.

"Aye. Tursel escorts him, under heavy guard."

I raced to the wagons. "Rust! Anavar!"

Anavar's grin was as wide as my own. "At last, my lord." I seized his hands, danced him across the clearing.

Rust eyed me. "One would think you were pleased."

"Would you I feigned despair? We have *Danzik*!"

He allowed himself a small smile. "Yes, it's worth a frolic. But he's not Hriskil."

"I know." For the merest moment, my joy was dampened. "But Rust, Stryx is freed!" We'd hoped, by our attack, to break Danzik's hold on the coast road, to force him southward into the marshes. But thanks to Groenfil's maneuver, the Norland camp was seized, Danzik's army broken, their commander taken. We'd bought not merely time, but sorely needed victory.

"What now, my prince?"

"On to Cumber?" I debated. "Or should we first force Uncle Mar from Verein?" Margenthar's holding was a mere day's ride from Stryx, and provided him secure base for a sudden lunge at my royal seat.

"May I speak?" Anavar waited for my nod. "I've explored your castle oft enough . . . where will you put Danzik?"

"In a—" I stopped. Stryx Castle had no cells, though rumor had it that in Grandfather Tryon's day the winecellar had served as a gaol. I shrugged. "In a bedchamber, I suppose. Under guard."

He snorted.

"What would you, then?"

"Finish what you start." Lest I failed to understand, Anavar drew a finger across his throat.

"This is Caledon. We're civilized." In Eiber, Anavar's land, attackers were put to death without mercy.

"He's your enemy."

I grasped his blouse. "As were you, youngsire. Had I your thirst of blood, you'd be bones under earth."

His hand closed over mine, without rancor. "I irk you, sir, but you've made Caledon my home. I'd see you keep it." His guileless eyes studied mine. "While you're in your donjon, Danzik is your prisoner. What when you take the field? Do you leave him at Stryx, that intrigue may swirl about his head? Do you haul him with you?"

"Bah. He's not yet in my hands, and you'd quarrel about his keep." I patted his hand, released him. "You mean well."

Rustin's eyes lit in approval, and I blushed. I hadn't meant to be kind, just . . . well, perhaps I had. Anavar was a good soul.

At last, Tursel rode into camp. Fully a hundred horse surrounded Danzik and his four countrymen. The Norland leader's hands were bound behind his back, and Tursel's most trusted men encircled him. Danzik sported a full beard and a bushy mustache. His hair was wild, and blood caked his scalp.

I held his reins. "You're Hriskil's deputy."

He stared at my scar. "Rez?"

I looked about.

Tursel translated, " 'King?' "

"Yes."

Gripping the saddle with his knees, Danzik leaned over, spat full in my face.

Rustin batted me aside, hauled Danzik from his mount. The two rolled on the turf. Anavar threw himself atop the pile, fists swinging.

I wiped spittle from my cheek. "Stop!" They paid no heed. I waded in, got a grip on Anavar's ear, twisted. He squawked. "Off, this instant! Rustin, you too!" I hauled Rust clear of the fray. In a moment Danzik lay alone in the dirt.

I helped Danzik rise. "My nobles scuffling like churls? Bah!" I raised a hand to slap Anavar, barely stopped myself. "Go sit on the wagon. I won't hear a word from you 'til day's end!"

If I'd expected gratitude from Danzik, I was mistaken. He made as if to spit again. I whipped out my dagger. "Don't try me, Norlander." He might not have understood my words, but my tone quelled him. "Kadar, put him in the saddle." I mounted my stallion, peered at the lonely coast road. The Keep guarded Stryx from the north, but southward the town gave way to wood and fields. Danzik and Hriskil had taken full advantage. "Captain Tursel, might we fortify this place?"

"We can build on their earthworks."

"Let it be done. Rust, I would go home."

"NEVER AGAIN, RUST!" We rode, at a walk, up the steep Castle Way.

"Danzik dishonored you."

"He dishonored Hriskil, and himself. You redeemed his worth."

"By striking him?"

"A bound man. You shamed me." My voice was hot. "I warn you, don't—"

"*You* warn me?"

"It's statecraft. I know whereof I speak." I nudged Ebon closer to Rust, gave his shoulder a squeeze. "I'm no dunce in this."

"Almost I believe you."

"Don't you see? When I kicked over tables in the market, what did I make of myself?"

"A churl."

"And when my guardian scuffles in the dirt?"

Rust's fists bunched. I was wary, lest he strike me. With great effort, he unknotted himself. Then, "You're right."

"Good. Talk to Anavar, will you?" I picked up my blouse. "He's furious that I tugged his ear."

"Why not beat him? It's been your way."

"Was it, today?" We'd spoken of Danzik's capture, and I'd made generous allowance for his youth.

"Sorry. I'm annoyed that you knew better than I. Yes, you were kind to Anavar."

"Nonetheless, cruelty comes easy to me. He meant no harm, yet . . ." I sighed. "I had to work at kindness."

Rust said, "You saw I was pleased with you?"

"Yes." I stretched, and winced. "I'm sore."

"Roddy, since I—since I took you to the trees . . . how shall I say it? You've acted a man."

"That's not the cause," I said quickly. He smiled, but it didn't relieve my trepidation. If he took it into his head that stripes lent me maturity . . .

He nodded assent. I spurred Ebon.

IN THE COURTYARD of Castle Stryx, Elryc hurled himself at me with unfeigned joy, while behind him, his liegesman Genard grinned like a simpleton.

"Easy, brother." I clapped his back, separated myself from his iron embrace. "It's been but five days."

"Forever." He pulled me to the ramparts, to watch the procession wind its way up the hill. "Truly, you have Danzik himself?"

"He rides between my guards." I pointed. "Don't get close; he spits."

Elryc clasped my hand. "I worried so. Twice I dreamed you were . . ." He swallowed. "Genard and I had the ritemaster do a propitiation."

A few paces away, the former stableboy pricked up his ears.

I lowered my voice. "I have much to tell you." I spoke of our fiasco with Lady Soushire's ritemaster, of Bollert's apparent Power, of my loss of the cave.

"Roddy . . ." Elryc puzzled through matters beyond his ken. "Who taught you to wield the Still to force truth from Tanner? Or how to plague Genard, that day at dinner?"

"It's—" I had not words. "It was there when I wanted the knowing."

"Is there else the Still allows you?"

"I don't know. I think not."

"I wish . . ."

"That you had use of it?"

Miserably, he nodded.

"It's a wonderful Power. Notice how attentive Tanner's become, ever since—"

"In the cave you speak with Mother."

I felt shabby, and callous. "Yes, Elryc. What would you I say on your behalf?"

"That I love her still."

"She knows, and loves you as much. Last year when Mar told me you were dead, she keened."

His eyes filled. Genard sidled close.

"It's all right, Gen." Elryc sniffled, and manfully took deep breath. He watched the horses' slow tread with bleak eyes.

I said, "Tonight I'll want your advice. We need to strike again, before our troop dissipates."

He nodded. "We'll talk after the banquet."

I raised an eyebrow.

"Surely you intend to fete Groenfil and Tursel? Make heroes of them, Roddy."

"I too was in the field." My tone was bitter.

"But you're king, and the king's praise has more worth than gold."

* * *

"DRESS YOURSELF. THEY'LL be waiting." Rustin paced my chamber.

"And hungry, no doubt." I'd roused the cooks, to set under way the banquet Elryc advised. "What's that confounded yowling?" I unbolted the door. Outside, Tanner napped on the bench. "Go stop that racket. Find the cause."

"Aye, King." He raced down the stairs.

Before I was done brushing my hair he was back. "It's Bollert. He doesn't want hooding."

"We can't let him dictate—" I rolled my eyes. "You're handsome enough, Rust. Leave it, and we'll visit Bollert before dinner."

The groomsman was confined in a sparse room of what had been Uncle Mar's wing. He cowered in a corner, his eyes wild, hands and feet bound. From the doorway, Tanner watched openmouthed.

"What is this uproar?" I stood, hands on hips.

"Please, King. Gotta see." A sheen of sweat gleamed. "Horrible, under hood. You don' know."

"Sorry." I motioned to the guard. "A kick or two in the stomach, if he starts that—"

"Please!" Bollert scrambled to his knees, wrists tight to his back. "Demons. In dark, imps. Feel 'em walking on me." He shuddered. "Beg you, King."

"If I let you look, you'll spell the guard to free you."

"Won't. Swear." His voice caught. "Don't put me in hood."

I frowned. Rustin was impassive. Tanner watched wide-eyed, mouth ajar.

"So be it. Use your Power on the guard, and I'll hang you." I went to my dinner.

"To RODRIGO, KING of Caledon and my liege lord, greetings from his cousin Tresa of Cumber.

"I cannot imagine why you apologize for a scroll in your own hand. We engage in no contest of scribes for the clearest lettering. Your script is legible, and crossed out words matter not a whit, nor your charming variance in spelling. The honor you do me by writing of your own person is one I treasure.

"May your union with Lord Groenfil and Lady Soushire be blessed by good fortune, though I fear this missive will not

reach you until the issue is decided. If Danzik may be turned aside, so you are free to aid your vassals of the north, I will rejoice no less than you. Grandfather is weary of war, though he would never say as much. I know it by the deepening lines on his forehead, the ever-rarer smile he bestows.

"As he threatened, he sent me to Cumber at first snowmelt, and I pass my days setting matters right in the town and castle. Tantroth did great harm in last year's siege, as you saw.

"That I may see you soon gladdens my heart. I will say this now, that it not poison our meeting: I truly regret the dismay that sent me fleeing at the sight of your grievous wound; I was overcome with horror that your mother's brother Margenthar could scar your beauty so terribly.

"If I allowed thee to think it was more, I pray thee, forgive me, in the generosity of thy soul.

"Looking forward to the day we may meet again, Tresa, daughter of Aptar and Stira, of the House of Cumber, salutes thee fondly."

RUST SET DOWN Tresa's scroll, made himself comfortable on the bedcushions. "No matter how you peer into that silver, your face is unchanged."

"When she first saw me . . ."

"She was shocked. Now she'll pay it as little heed as I."

I grimaced at my image. "I'm a ruin." The scar my uncle had inflicted ran its jagged course from eye to chin.

"You're what you always were. There's no shame in a scar."

"I hate it."

"If it troubles you so, buy a Return."

"The Warthen might demand half Soushire." That, beyond the pain I'd bear.

"Whatever the cost, pay it, if you're so troubled."

"Rust, you really think I might?" Even had I the cost, a Return was by no means certain. It wanted the Warthen's consent, and he could accomplish few Returns, lest he be worn beyond redemption.

"I think you ought, if you grimace at the sight of yourself."

I slumped on the bed, beside him. "It's partly that. And also . . ."

"You're afraid to meet her. Why?"

I shrugged. "Uncle Raeth holds our frontier. I can't afford to alienate—laugh again and I'll dump you on the floor!"

With effort, he twisted a smile into a frown, but it wouldn't stay transformed. "I'm sorry, Roddy." He didn't sound it.

"You've had Chela, and other girls. I'm as shy as—" I bit it off.

"As a virgin." His tone was gentle.

I stood, smoothed my jerkin. "Let's speak of other things."

"She's smitten with you, I think." Idly, he perused the scroll. "Did you reply?"

"This afternoon." Tongue between my teeth, cursing my errors and blotches.

"Between the two of you, they'll need widen the trail, to accommodate your couriers." Mischief, in his grin.

I loomed over him. "What penalty, if I strike the regent?"

"None, tonight."

Once more I examined my cheek in the silver. "Perhaps, while we're in Cumber, we ought send envoy to the Warthen."

SEVEN

THE RITUAL WORDS of encant mumbled, my palms pressed over the receptor, I dashed into the cave, shaky with relief. "Mother!"

"Ah. You're back." She rose from the fire.

"Why did you—why couldn't I—" I threw myself into her embrace.

"There, now." Awkwardly, as seldom in life, Elena Queen of Caledon comforted me.

After a time, I drew back. "What happened? Try as I might, I couldn't summon . . ."

"Of course not." Her tone was placid. "You wielded the Power."

"I've oft used it to visit you and Grandfather."

"Don't be silly." She drew me to the fire, made herself comfortable beyond the outermost stones. Across the firepit, shadowy figures perched. "From time to time you visit, but only twice have you *used* the Power."

"There's a difference?"

"Eleven years had you, when first I showed you the Vessels." Her tone was tart. "As was your way, you wouldn't listen. As you grew I explained over and again." A sigh, of exasperation. "Knowing a mind, forcing a will, these use the Power you must husband. Like a dammed stream, once opened, it wants time to refill. Why were you such a headstrong boy?"

"I had no wisdom."

"And now?" A deep voice, from the shadows.

"I would acquire it, Father Varon. If I might."

"Look you, youngsire." He cleared his throat. "The Still isn't to be wasted. What if you spend yourself making a stableboy dance, and Hriskil plants himself that day before your gate? Would you bid him wait a four-day, that you might restore yourself?"

"No, Grandsir."

"Well, then."

"Did I do ill, learning truth of my bondsmen?"

A rumble. "Who's to say good or ill? Spend your purse on silks or steel, whatever your need. Just know the cost."

"Grandsir, might a churl wield a Power?"

"Of course not."

"Yet I think it's so." Haltingly, I told him of Bollert.

"It cannot be. You dreamt it."

"I felt his compulsion."

"Only royal houses—"

From the far corner, a waspish voice. "Not so, Varon."

A withering blast. *"WHO INTRUDES?"*

"Save your fury." Cayil of the Surk, my predecessor whom Varon overthrew these ages past. "It awes the boy, but not Cayil."

"What say you, petty king?"

"Hah! Not so petty I couldn't hold you at bay ten years or more. Even your sappers couldn't—"

"By Lord of Nature, give it rest!"

Carefully, I retreated from the firepit.

Cayil snapped, "While you play at anger, your mewling son flees. Look!" A contemptuous gesture, toward me. "But you miss my gist."

A heavy breath, perhaps of resignation. "Which is?"

"I knew a churl who had Power. Rowlan, she was, a wash-girl. Saucy face, swaying hips . . ." Cayil's expression was dreamy. "And she could summon beasts. Horses, cats, wolves. Even birds heeded her call."

"Impossible."

Cayil's voice grew shrill. "Think you all wisdom came from the Steppe? That your brute spearmen knew all there was to fathom?"

"Churls have no Power. It's what separates—"

"This one did. Take it for truth. And Hastar told me of another."

I tugged at Mother's robe. "Hastar?"

A whisper. "Long before Cayil. He's seldom with us."

"Hmpff." Varon seemed nettled. "A sport of nature, your churl," he told me. "Kill him."

"I thought of it," I admitted. "But . . ."

"Don't let Power spread. It's an end to order."

"Yes, Grandsir. Oh! . . . We captured Danzik. What now?"

* * *

"WHAT OF CUMBER?" Elryc perched crosslegged on my rope bed.

I curled in a ball. It had been a long, eventful day, starting with the battle for the coast road. I was weary, and I hurt. Even the night candles seemed too much light, and I was dangerously close to weeping, as so often after using the Still. "We didn't speak of it tonight. His advice, before we took Danzik, was to ignore all else, and save Tantroth of Eiber."

In the corner, Anavar examined the stick he was whittling. "Better to save Raeth of Cumber."

Genard looked up from the string he'd wrapped around his fingers. "But you're Eiberian."

Elryc prodded him. "Shush, Gen. Let the nobles speak."

"Sorry, m'lor." Genard sounded abashed.

I glanced up in surprise. What magic did Elryc wield, that the stableboy deferred without cavil?

"I'm Eiberian born," said Anavar, "but pledged to Rodrigo and Caledon."

"But . . ." Reluctantly, Genard contained himself.

To be perverse, I told him, "Go on."

"Anavar, if the king rides to Cumber, Hriskil's free to attack Eiber. What of your family, your home?"

Succinctly put. I looked at Genard with new appraisal.

"My sister." Anavar's eyes were distant. "And father. They're at our holding, near Stoth. Hriskil is further west. If he attacks, they may die, but if Roddy sends men, will Tantroth use them against Hriskil, or to some devious end of his own devising?" He slashed viciously at his stick. "Besides, I can't be of two loyalties. I've chosen Rodrigo."

"Why?" Genard and I spoke as one.

"My lord Tantroth has no honor." He studied his stick. "And Roddy does."

My eyes stung. I blinked, to no avail.

"Why cry," asked Genard, "when he speaks well of you?"

Elryc nudged him hard.

"I'm not—if I am, it's the Still. It leaves me weak, and confused." With a prodigious yawn, I sat up, stripped off my blouse.

Elryc's breath caught. "Your back is raw."

"Rustin switched me." Somehow, I made it sound of little consequence.

My brother's hand caught mine, squeezed hard.

"It's all right, Elryc."

"I have salve," said Anavar. "I used it when you . . ." He rose, padded to his chamber.

Genard's eyes were wide. "You allow it, m'lor'?"

I sought dignity. "He makes me a better man."

Genard muttered something to Elryc.

"What was that?" I caught his wrist.

"I said, a pity he didn't do it before you made me dance." His gaze was defiant.

"Guttersnipe! Ignorant churl! Who cares what nonsense escapes your mouth? Out!"

"Come, Genard." Elryc rose from my bed. "I bid thee all good night." He guided his vassal to the hall.

At the door Anavar stood aside for them, knelt on my bed. He dabbed fingers in a pot of ointment. "By your leave, my lord." Gently, he spread soothing salve on my smarting back. His sturdy hands worked their massage, bringing the day's first peace. "Why do you weep, sir?"

"Because I'm everything I called Genard."

"I didn't hear."

"Good." My eyes stung. "Enough." I sat, wiped my eyes. "I have work to do."

"You need sleep."

"After this." Reluctantly, I made my way to Elryc's chamber, knocked softly.

Genard opened. His face went taut.

"Where's my brother?"

"He bids Nurse Hester good night."

Unbidden, I brushed past. "Sit with me." I slumped on the cushions of Elryc's bed, put my head in my hands. "What I said was false and vile. It's worse after I wield the Still, but the fault is mine. Cruelty lurks within me, awaiting escape."

"Fah." A snort of derision. "How like a lord, to make it sound noble. The truth is, you're small of spirit, and meanly made."

"Am I?" I tasted of it, with sinking heart. "I suppose so." I bowed my head. "Genard, I'm truly sorry. I wanted to hurt you, and snatched the first weapon at hand."

"Why take the trouble, m'lor'?" He sounded bitter. "What

glory in besting a guttersnipe, an ignorant churl? I'm all of that. Is it wrong that I'd be more?"

"No." My voice was subdued. "I give you leave to tell Rust. No doubt he'll beat me again."

He cried, "I don't want you beaten, I want you not to hate me!"

"I don't—"

The door swung open. Elryc's face was tight. "Leave him alone! You've no right, Roddy!"

"It's not what you—"

"This is my room. Have we nowhere to escape your foul—" He pursed his lips. "Go!"

"I'm sorry, Genard!" I fled to my chamber.

After a time, a knock.

"Enter." My voice was muffled.

"Elryc sent me, m'lor'." Tentatively, the stableboy approached my bed. "After I told him why you came. May I sit?"

I nodded, and felt the cushions shift.

"It plagues you," he said, "that I say what comes to me. It drove old Griswold mad, in the stable."

"As it does me, but you're good-hearted."

"Not so much. I jape at you."

I turned carefully, so as not to scrape my back. "Why do you love my brother?"

He licked dry lips. "I'm thirteen summers, almost fourteen."

I nodded.

"My whole life, he's the only person ever asked if I was hungry, or had thirst." He saw my puzzlement. "Griswold sent me to eat, when the work was done. And Cook gave me fruit, when I asked. But only Lor' Elryc cared to know."

"Is that so much?"

"When you've had no one."

I was quiet a while. Then, "When I wielded the Still against you, Rustin made me ask your pardon, so I did. Now I ask of my free will. Pardon me, Genard. Pardon my jeers, my curses, the compulsion I set on you." My voice was tremulous.

A long silence. "You said I could speak my mind?"

"Yes."

"I hate how you make me feel. You're noble; I'll never be. That's done. But a yeoman isn't dirt, and need not feel so."

I felt my ears heat.

"I don't pardon you, m'lor'. I've too much hate of you. But go four weeks without making me a worm, and I'll pardon you with all my heart."

I seized his hand, and held it.

Rustin found us thus, when at last he came to bed.

I GLARED AT Danzik, making little effort to hide my petulance. We would be a week, at least, augmenting and refitting our force before striking north of the Keep. We'd agreed to combine all the force the kingdom could muster; this very afternoon, as a year ago, I had set my standard fluttering in the earth and proclaimed proud words, summoning men of all Caledon. We'd dispatched criers to every town and village under our sway, and now were forced to await the results.

"Has he no civilized speech?" The Norlander had been brought to the great hall in chains; no harm in emphasizing to my court our accomplishment. Lady Soushire looked on in approval, beside Lord Groenfil.

Glowering, the Norland leader snarled more of his gibberish.

Rust's tone was dry. "No doubt in his country the Norland tongue is thought civilized."

Addressing Danzik, I spoke loudly and clearly. "Are you a noble?" If so, we owed him more courtesy than he'd received.

Among the courtiers, someone cleared his throat. "My lord?" Jestrel, the silversmith. "I have some Norland speech."

"Very well, ask this barbarian his station."

"Aye, my lord. Danzik, er vos lini rez?"

"Farang vos!"

"Er vos?" Jestrel's tone sharpened.

"Han." It sounded grudging.

"He says not, sire. At first he told me . . . ah, he didn't properly answer." Jestrel blushed.

"Hom ordin Norl verta Caledi rez!"

"Eh? What does he say?"

"That a Norland commoner ranks with a king of Caledon."

"Rust, I would teach him manners." My voice was ominous.

"But you won't."

I sighed. "No. What is Hriskil's intent? Will he land more troops?"

Jestrel mouthed more nonsense, and learned nothing.

I stirred impatiently. "Lady Larissa, my lord Earl, neither of you speak his tongue? I wish I weren't . . ." I remembered not to say more. I hated to be dependent on a commoner, not even of my court. Now Freisart was dead, who could say where Jestrel's true loyalty lay.

Well, I had nearly a ten-day to wait, before we could prepare the army for so long an expedition as to Cumber, and beyond to Eiber. Not much time, but . . . "Ask him if he would teach his language."

Jestrel did. "No, he says."

"Ask if he would teach a king. And earn the same food we eat, and a softer chamber."

Even I could grasp Danzik's vehement refusal.

"Imps take him, the stubborn . . . tell him he'll do his master no harm. I'd need the Norland speech to treat with Hriskil."

Danzik bit his lip. Suddenly, to my amazement, he nodded.

And so, grown and crowned, I was prenticed to a Norlander.

Rust was annoyed, but I'd acted in front of my court, and he was loath to overrule me. He insisted Danzik be kept in chains, and an armed guard with us always. To keep peace, I acquiesced.

Without much else to do, I devoted several hours a day to my task. The Norland language was cruel, and hard on the tongue.

Danzik started with common words: *soldier, churl, king.* Since he had no civilized speech, I often wasn't sure what he was teaching me. Genard, who insinuated himself into my lessons, came up with guesses as to the word Danzik meant, sometimes preposterous, more often quite correct. No matter how foolish Genard's speculation, I managed not to mock him, remembering our conversation in my bedchamber.

The stableboy wasn't a bad sort, really, when one got over his ways. As he'd said, his prime fault was blurting out whatever nonsense came to his head, no matter how disrespectful. Had I the managing of him, instead of Elryc, the quality would soon be whipped out of him, but I had to admit that once I became accustomed to his speech, the content at times held sense. Not that it would do to tell him so, lest he become even more presumptuous.

Danzik kept his bargain, though he didn't mellow a whit. I dared not draw too close, lest he let fly with a gob of spittle as before. In any event, Rust had assigned Kadar as his guard, with instructions to keep us separated by force, if necessary. After the bodyguard once grabbed my arm and yanked me back to my chair, I kept my distance and risked no further humiliation.

It wasn't fair, by any means. Did my regent have power to delegate his will? And to a commoner, a mere bodyguard? When I reproached Rust on the point, his manner became so frosty I dropped the matter entirely.

ELRYC DRANK OF his wine. His face was flushed. "You were mad, appointing a regent."

I snapped, "Twice you've seen my spite with Genard. Almost, I had Tanner flayed, before I caught myself. With the Still augmenting my nature, I'm beyond my own governing."

"I know you love Rustin, but—"

"I respect him."

"—but to put Caledon in his hands! Should not your council have say in such matters?"

"I had no time. I was crouched under a wagon, looking for still water to agonize Rust. It was that or abdicate."

A silence, while he contemplated the tile of his bedchamber. "Roddy?" His voice was hushed, amazed. "You really want to be a proper king."

Unable to speak, I nodded.

His frail hand sought my shoulder. "I'm glad." He sipped more wine.

After a time I said, "There's truth in your worry. Rust can be . . . imperious."

"He has power without check." Elryc sighed. "What does Mother think?"

I snorted. "That I'm a boy, and a regent is fit and proper." She'd been somewhat surprised and questioned me closely. In the end, she'd approved of my choice of Rustin. Her father, Tryon, had raised no objection. Cayil had growled that if Rustin grew too troublesome, I could kill him. They seemed not to mind that it would cost me the Still.

"Roddy, I don't like Jestrel."

"He asks too many questions."

"That's just curiosity. But he's mean to the servants."

I shrugged. Elryc was always fretting about servants. "He'll go his own way at Cumber." If Rust approved his sharing our journey. I'd forgotten to ask.

"Why would he ride to a siege?" Elryc's voice was dreamy, as he toyed with his goblet. "There are peaceful places to go."

"I doubt he'll tarry in Cumber." The Norlands were near, as was Eiber, and even the Ukra Steppe. One with Jestrel's talent could always find a home. Perhaps I ought to invite him stay with us, but I feared his refusal. A silversmith, above almost all men, avoided lawless lands, lest his wares be ransacked.

Elryc said, "You'll take me with you, this time."

"So an ague can—"

"Genard will look after me." He giggled.

"You've drunk too much—"

"Rodrigo! Rustin!" Anavar, skidding past Elryc's chamber on his way to mine.

I thrust open the door. "What is it?"

He was scarce of breath. "Lady Soushire's in her chamber, taken ill."

Cursing, I ran down the steps. Lady Soushire had been housed in Margenthar's opulent quarters, on the first floor.

At her door, a servant barred my way. "She has a flux. The physicker is with her."

"Get out of—" I pushed him aside, shouldered my way through to Larissa's outer room.

Earl Groenfil stopped his pacing. "She's gravely ill. It came on her just after she ate." Through the window, in the court-yard, wind whipped the bushes.

The physicker's boy rushed out of the inner chamber, sped out the door. In a moment, he was searching boxes in their cart.

I said lamely, "Is there anything I—"

"First Freisart, now Larissa." Groenfil's voice was hot. "What game play you?"

"How dare you!" My hand leapt to my dagger.

"If you covet a noble's lands, poisoner, hazard mine." The window crashed to shards, as the wind snapped its stay.

I whipped out my blade.

"No, my lord!" Anavar wrapped his arms around me, dragged me backward. I shook him loose.

Groenfil drew his sword.

"Hold, the lot of you!" Rustin, in a voice that would sunder steel. "Roddy, to your chamber."

"Rust, he called me a—"

"I heard." He shoved me rudely toward the stair. "How dare you draw steel on a vassal? And you!" He rounded on Groenfil. "Have you fact to voice a charge so foul?"

"She was well as I, before she ate of—"

"Have you cause to accuse your king?" Rustin's eyes gave me chill.

"No fact, save the obvious compar—"

"Roddy, begone. Anavar, take him upstairs." He swung back to Groenfil. "Obvious, is it? Not an hour after a meal, you know she was poisoned, and can name—"

"Sir, come." Anavar tugged at my sleeve.

"Wait."

"Now, before Rustin . . ." He leaned close to my ear. "Don't provoke him further, sir. For your sake."

I allowed myself to be dragged out, and took the stairs two at a time, to my chamber.

By the time Rustin joined me, Anavar had borne the full fury of my fulminations.

Rust threw off his cloak. "Anavar, out."

I said cautiously, "Please let him stay, sir. He's advised me well."

Rust raised an eyebrow. "Anavar, what did you advise our king?"

Anavar said only, "My speech is for Rodrigo to divulge, if he would."

"It's you I order."

"Without warrant."

"Please!" I stepped between them. "Rust, he advised that I be exceedingly polite, when you came."

A grudging smile. "And about Groenfil?"

"That I should have held my peace. And that the Earl was mad with worry."

"Yes. Do you know why?"

"He's grown a love for Lady Larissa, and she for him. How is she?"

"Still alive. The physicker won't say more."

I took deep breath. "How may I redeem our cause?"

"Wait 'til Groenfil calms. When he sees there's been no

poison—assuming that's so—he'll be mortified. You'll humbly beg his pardon and put him at disadvantage."

"Is it that easy?"

"I think . . ." Rustin laced his new shirt. "It was but a quarrel of the moment. Under all, he respects you and would have you as king."

"TO MY LORD Rodrigo, king of Caledon and my liege lord, fond greetings from his cousin Tresa of Cumber.

"Rodrigo, it's wonderful! Danzik himself in your hands . . . Hriskil must be livid. How did you ever do it?

"The moment the horseman rode through the gate, your missive tucked under his cloak, I tore the seals off and read it, there in the courtyard, the wind blowing my hair. Immediately I sent a courier to Grandfather; he needs all the good news he can get. Hriskil presses him hard, and may soon take Pezar.

"In the meanwhile, Duke Tantroth is beside himself to retake his citadel, and demands we loan him troops. He accuses Grandfather of 'improvident delay,' in a tone that suggests cowardice is the cause. Roddy, I hesitate to meddle in matters of state, but might you speak to him? Tantroth has a harsh manner that only sets Grandfather's teeth on edge, and Imbar's sarcastic commentary only inflames him further.

"Hriskil moves ever more troops through Eiber to our border. Tantroth mutters, in Grandfather's hearing, that you will abandon us both. My lord king, I know full well you will come when you can, and that you treasure Grandfather and Cumber. Pay no heed if you hear Tantroth's calumny repeated elsewhere; I tell you only that you may be forewarned.

"Thy cousin and friend, Tresa of the House of Cumber, scans the castle road, eagerly awaiting thy next writing."

ONCE LADY LARISSA was purged of the rotted meat that sickened her, two servants, and Jestrel the silversmith, her recovery was swift. Two days later, she was eating as before, with perhaps a bit extra to make up for lost bulk.

I took Groenfil aside, apologized profusely for daring to draw my blade, and gave him the very dagger as a present of exculpation. It was a nice touch, one Rustin hadn't thought of, and it softened the earl's visage. We agreed to put the matter behind us, and swore renewed oaths of trust.

Afterward, in the great hall, Jestrel's tone was meek, as befit one asking boon of a king. "Might I ride as far as Cumber?"

I had to take care in my reply. Daily, Rustin was growing more insistent on a regent's prerogative; any decisions I announced without consulting him, he claimed I barred him from making. Twice we'd debated the matter, with increasing heat, until I realized that by my vows I'd surrendered what weapons might sustain my end of the dispute.

"I can't guarantee passage." It wasn't truly an answer.

"Think you Hriskil will bar the way?"

The great hall was drafty, and I shivered. The season was inconstant, the sun sullen and elusive. "I imagine he will, yes. Is not our aim to seek each other out?" And if Hriskil had the sense Lord of Nature gave a cow, he'd block our path before we linked with Uncle Raeth of Cumber, and near doubled our force.

"Will you seek battle this side of Cumber Town?"

"I—" My mouth snapped shut. Jestrel had cause for concern that he might be swept up in battle without quarter. But Hriskil would pay well to know my intent. I managed an evasion, sent him on his way, promising I'd consider his request to ride with us.

I glanced at the hour candle. I was due at a lesson with Danzik. Inexplicably, Rust had insisted that, as far as punctuality, I treat Danzik with the courtesy due any tutor, though few other pedagogues were chained to the wall of their chamber. "Where's Genard?" I'd grown used to his company at my lessons.

"Here, m'lor'." He scurried down the hall in my train. "Rodd—M'lor', don't let him goad you."

"Is that an order?"

Genard reddened. "No, m'lor'. Sorry. It's just . . . why allow him the pleasure?"

Kadar swept open the door. I took my place at the opposite wall from Danzik; any closer and I risked Kadar's intervention.

"*Liste memor,*" I said carefully. *I'm ready to learn.*

Danzik grunted. His bedchamber was small but adequate,

and he'd been given a decent rope bed instead of the straw a prisoner might expect. "Rez."

"King." It was one of the first words he'd taught me.

"Mata."

"Mother."

"Modre."

"I have no idea."

"Kill," said Genard. "Murder."

Danzik pointed to the bed. "Camm," he said.

"Camm," I repeated dutifully. "Bed."

He walked as far as his chain would let him, and taught me the word for walking, then mimed running, and sitting. I struggled to memorize the harsh sounds.

Then, "Mata ke Rez Caledi er tupa."

Genard drew sharp breath.

I studied my fist, willing it to open. Then, casually, as if it were of no import, I translated. "The King of Caledon's mother is a whore. Ev Rez Caledi modre Danzik."

For the first time, a grin blossomed. "Mod*ra*," said Danzik.

"Modra." *Will murder.*

The rest of the lesson went without incident.

After, Genard and I climbed the steps to my chamber. "I thought you'd explode," he said.

"I have you to thank that I didn't."

He threw me a suspicious glance.

"I mean it. You warned me ahead of time. Thank you."

It left him muddled and confused. Massaging my scar, I hid a smile the rest of the way.

Eight

BY THEIR TWOS and threes, handfuls and scores, men gathered to the banner of Caledon, drawn by the silver pence for their enlistment, and perhaps even by loyalty to the crown. Castle and Keep grew crowded with newcomers, while Tursel and Groenfil struggled to set them in order.

South of Stryx, our new earthworks were garrisoned, though in truth if the Norlanders came in strength, they could simply flank the breastworks.

I was impatient to set forth, but an army didn't march by valor alone. I was beset by wagoners, purveyors of a breathtaking array of goods, coopers, armorers, arrow makers, blacksmiths, every trade known to the realm and some I'd never imagined. Questions abounded. Clothing, tents, spare parts for wagons, shoes, forage, provisions, harness, leather, wax, thread, needles . . . my head spun. I issued warrants, selected from what I was offered, relied on Tursel's experience to guide me. All the while, our treasury shrank.

At long last, we set forth. In doing so we left Castle Stryx and Llewelyn's Keep dangerously undermanned, but in conclave my nobles and I had decided, with Rustin's assent, that we were better carrying the war to Hriskil than cowering behind defensive positions.

Willem of Alcazar, Mother's chamberlain and mine, was put in charge of our defenses. No warrior he, but a sturdy, honest man, loyal to Mother and her house.

Reluctantly, I let my brother ride with us; he threatened outright rebellion if left behind. Were I to leave him, Elryc said, I had only to look at the edge of our camp to find him and Genard seeking shelter. That, unless I locked him in his chamber. That was too like Uncle Mar for my taste. Rustin left the decision to me, claiming he was more concerned I would squabble with Genard than whether Elryc himself was in our train.

For a day Rust and I weren't speaking, from the vehemence

of our argument over Danzik. I proposed we bring him along, now that he was making himself useful; Rustin wanted him safe in the castle.

I'd found for once in my life I was enjoying lessons. Daily, Danzik worked to goad me, with sentence after sentence of humiliations. "Caledon nobles are stupid." "In Stryx, the king eats excrement." "The scarred boy has a horse for a father." The latter took all my self-control, but I was able to smile, repeat the sentence in his speech and mine. After the lesson Genard said something mild to twit me, and it was all I could do not to strangle him.

Inflicting constant indignities softened Danzik's rage enough to permit him to teach me well, and I suspected he secretly enjoyed it. The more so when I made it my habit to start each lesson with a pungent insult I'd devised during the night, using words he'd taught me. The more foul my imprecations, the greater Danzik's respect grew, and after a few days we spoke almost as equals.

Alternating sulks and beseechments, I finally earned Rustin's consent to have the Norlander brought along.

Riding chained to a jouncing wagon must have been uncomfortable, but Danzik made no complaint. I'd offered him the choice of remaining in Stryx, knowing that without his cooperation I could learn nothing from him. When I told him we rode to confront his master, he was eager to go. No doubt he hoped a Norland raid on our wagons would free him.

We descended the hill of Castle Way, passed through the Keep, and emerged on the north coast road. On the plain outside the Keep we formed our line of march. I was content to let Groenfil and Tursel handle the details, especially after Rustin took me aside and warned me quite sharply not to interfere.

Jestrel the silversmith drove his wagon in our train. Elryc and Genard were on horse, together always. They rode with Anavar, just behind Rustin, Lord Groenfil, Lady Larissa and me, alongside the place Tursel would occupy if he wasn't constantly spurring up and down the line.

We made good time. We soon turned off the coast road, onto Searoad Track, winding its way up the hills toward Seawatch Rock. The famed landmark jutted from a range of the Caleds between the coast and my great-uncle's domain of

Cumber. At its base our path crossed Nordukes' Trek, which threaded through the high passes to Eiber and Cumber Trail.

We lodged for the night just past Seawatch Rock.

My tent sufficed for four; Anavar and Elryc were to share it with us, but Elryc was so crestfallen at Genard's absence that Anavar volunteered to sleep elsewhere, and I found myself sharing a roof with a stableboy. No matter; I was tired enough to drift quickly into sleep.

At dawn they struck the tent, while I leaned yawning against a tree. My bodyguards cantered up, leading Ebon. As I put a foot up to mount, a shadowy form hurtled under Ebon, wound itself around my legs.

Instantly Kadar's sword flashed.

"Please, King!" On his knees, my bondsman Bollert clasped me tight.

"Hold!" I raised a hand to Kadar, gripping the pommel to keep from toppling. "He means no harm." I untangled myself. "How'd you escape?" I'd left him bound, in a locked bed-chamber.

"He hooded me!" Bollert was clammy with sweat. "Soon as you left. Said wouldn' let demon look at 'im."

"Who?"

"Guard." The boy licked his lips. "Made me berserk. When I stopped screaming, asked for drink, and for jus' a moment, could see."

"You spelled him?"

"Hadda! Please, King. You said no hood." He bowed his head, brushed my boot with his forelock.

"You made him unchain you?"

"Made him think it, aye. Then ran. Gateman too."

"Why follow me, Bollert? Why not flee to the hills?"

He swallowed. "Made me bond man, you did. Gotta stay with. Beside, lookin' not always strong enough. Can't always get away. Don' want be hang for escape, and don' know no place but Stryx."

I pried loose his fingers, wiped my breeks. "Rust?"

"Didn't I tell you?" His tone was sour. "A noble gesture, but you saddled yourself with . . ."

"Since you won't decide, I will." I was scarce awake and heedless of his wrath. "Bollert, walk alongside Tanner. Be warned, you teeter on the gallows' edge. Run away, or set your compulsion on one of us, and you dance in air." I heaved myself into the saddle. "Where's Elryc? Ah, there you are; ride close."

I spurred, took my place in the line.

As we rode, the Earl of Groenfil spoke quietly with Lady Soushire. After a time, he came up alongside. "A word with you, sire."

I raised an eyebrow.

"That groomsman," said Groenfil. "The demon-friend."

I puzzled it out. "Bollert?"

"Why curse our trail, my lord? Put an end to him. Is he not thief and worse?"

Casually, Rust reached across, patted my knee. I allowed myself a breath or two, for diplomacy. "Bollert's an odd one, my lord, but more afraid of us than we are of him."

"Lord of Nature knows what's in his head. What if he spells Kadar to plunge a dagger into you?"

My bodyguard, riding close, started nervously.

Groenfil inclined his head, a short bow of civility. "I cast no aspersion, Kadar. The demon boy's a menace."

"Stop calling him that!"

"What else, sire? Is he royalty, to wield a Power? He's an affront to nobility. He's unnatural and shouldn't share our camp, especially with Lady Larissa present. If you won't slit his throat, bind him to a distant tree for the night."

"Is that your command?"

"No." His eyes held mine. "I seek no quarrel, my lord."

"That he has a Power is wonder indeed." I rode some paces, quiet. "Tell me, my lord Earl. When in your fury the winds howl, have you control of it?"

"Not a whit. As my rage quickens, the air stirs."

"Like Raeth's power with fire. He hasn't the willing use of it. I wield the Still by conscious thought."

"So I've heard."

"Bollert too controls his Power. It's what makes you fear him."

"I don't—yes, I suppose I do. With good cause."

I rode a long while, thinking. Then, "Bollert stays, but I'll keep him far from your tents."

When Groenfil had dropped back to his place behind us, Rust said softly, "Well done, Roddy."

"I expected you to intervene."

"You let Bollert stay; I'll not overrule you before others."

"Think you I'm wrong?"

"When Genard enraged you, you drew steel. When Groenfil spoke hotly you did the same. Yet for this thieving churl you have infinite patience. Has he put compulsion on you?"

"I think not, unless it's quite subtle."

"Yes, if it's subtle it would escape you."

My fierce protest died stillborn; I'd noticed the corners of his mouth twitch.

WE PASSED THROUGH Fort, while townsmen gaped. I'd issued strict orders to curtail looting—the men called it foraging—and hoped I'd be obeyed.

We were many, for Caledon, though the full Norland host would sweep us aside as riders would a barnyard of chickens. We must choose our ground carefully, defend tight passes, and maneuver so we never met the Norland foe in their full numbers.

Outside Fort an envoy caught us. A rider from Verein, with a proposal from Uncle Mar.

It brought the column to a halt, while Rust, Tursel, Groenfil and Lady Soushire conferred with me over a hasty campfire. Elryc and Anavar sat just behind me, offering whispered advice.

"I won't make cause with him." I hoped I sounded as stubborn as I felt.

"Near a thousand men, Roddy." Lady Soushire swallowed mushroom after mushroom, bathed in sweet garlic.

"Half of them mounted," added Tursel. "And only hours from joining us."

"You trust him?" Did only I know his perfidy?

"Margenthar says repulsing Hriskil comes before minor quarrels."

"Minor?" Elryc's voice was sharp. "He killed our brother, ruined Roddy's face, made alliance with Tantroth against us."

"Yes, of course." Groenfil sounded impatient. "He wanted the crown."

Anavar tugged at my sleeve. "Your uncle doesn't want a final answer. Just safe-conduct to parley."

I scrambled to my feet. "Lord Rustin, I would speak with you." I led him to the perspiring horses, and beyond. "They want this. They think I'm unreasonable."

"I'm glad you see it."

"Well?"

"Well what?"

I snarled, "You're regent; don't play with me! Decide!"

"Take ease, my prince."

"I loathe him utterly."

He said nothing.

"On the other hand," I said reluctantly, "we'll learn from what he wants. Or from what he won't say." At times I despised games of state.

"As he'll learn from your dismay, if you fail to hide it."

Despite a manful effort, my lip trembled. "Yes, I'm callow, and conceal naught. Go, then. Tell them your will, in my name." I bent to Ebon, laid my forehead on his flank.

An absent pat on my shoulder, as Rustin went off to the conclave.

I ASKED, "WELL?" We'd resumed our march.

"You gave him safe-conduct," Rust said. "With a guard of twenty to the edge of our column. But you won't break march for him; he can catch us on the road to Cumber if he wishes an audience."

"An audience." I tasted of it, decided I liked it. "Very well." I swatted away an annoying fly. "Must I set out a table and offer refreshment?"

"Cool wine, no more."

"King." Bollert, his face damp from the stride that kept pace with Ebon.

"Now what?"

"Didn't eat, last day. Running after wagons. Found you too late, this morning."

"So? Did I ask you to flee your confinement?" After a moment I relented. "Find the cookwagons. Tell them I said to give you fruit and bread."

He licked his lips. "Thanks to you." He dropped back.

"And a place to ride," I called after. "But only today."

After a while I found the silence irksome. "He's exhausted and starving. What would you have me do?"

"Mount him behind you," said Rustin, as if serious. "Let Ebon carry you both."

"A groomsman? A thief? Riding with the king of—imps

and demons take you!" I flicked my crop at his leg, hard enough to sting. "I hate it when you goad me."

"One would never know." Rubbing his leg, Rust guided his mount around a fallen branch. "Be sure to carry your crop, for Mar's goading."

A moment passed. "I'm sorry."

"You should be. Not for the sting, but the ease with which I change your mood."

"I'll try harder, Rust." I'd been doing so, with Genard. Had the boy's manner truly changed, or was it only that I saw him as irrepressible and good-hearted, where before he'd been a burr under my saddle?

"At Cumber you'll be faced with Lady Tresa." He eyed me. "I warn you now, my prince: she and Raeth are our allies in a desperate fight. Display your lovesick temper, and I'll deal with you severely."

I felt myself blush furiously. "You've no call to—"

"On our last visit, you rushed up and down stairs, muffed apologies, slammed doors, snapped boorish words, until I was ready to tear out my hair."

Behind me, Elryc giggled.

I said helplessly, "Please, Rust."

"I'll tell you the trick of it, Roddy. You haven't come to woo her. Simply speak to her as to me or Anavar. As a normal person talks to another. Not as a deranged monarch with delusions of infancy."

I yanked at the reins, hauled Ebon off the roadway and sat, head bowed, by the bole of a huge shade tree while the column plodded past.

At last, a stirring, and a quiet voice behind me. "I'm sorry. I jest of it, and hurt your sensibility. In truth, there's something comical in how you charge and shy away, backing and filling. Women are people like the rest of us. You need not be afraid of their converse."

"I'm not."

"Then we should rejoin our comrades." He picked up his reins and patted my knee as he passed.

"Rust, will I ever be a man?"

"You did a man's deed the day you appointed me regent. I'm proud of you."

*   *   *

UNCLE MAR RODE to us late in the afternoon, three leagues past Fort. I kept Anavar at my side, bade Groenfil and Soushire wait out of our hearing, knowing that Margenthar was expert at fomenting disunion.

When Mar dismounted, a hundred strides distant, Rust searched him, confiscating a small dagger as well as his sword, and then escorted him to the sunswept barley field where I stood.

Rustin made a formal bow, low and measured. "My King Rodrigo, thy vassal Margenthar, Duke of Stryx."

Uncle Mar bowed, the short, familiar bow of relatives.

I nodded the merest fraction, begrudging him even that. The coronet I'd donned made my scalp itch but for dignity's sake I dared not scratch.

"You look well, Rodrigo." His eyes flickered to my scar.

"State your business."

"Hriskil, my lord King." Mar stroked his graying beard. "He'll overwhelm you, and then we are lost."

"You'd save me?"

"I'd save Caledon, and if that requires saving you . . ."

Anavar gasped, but I'd known Mar all my life, and was used to worse. "What do you propose?"

"That my troops and I join you. That we give battle to Hriskil, or hold the Cumber passes, as you command."

"Such modesty, Uncle. I hardly know you."

"You've never known me." Uncle Mar opened the clasp on his cloak. "A warm day. I've wine in my saddlebags I might offer you."

Deftly done. "Anavar, fetch wine. Use the goblets in my chest." Then, to Mar, "I can't imagine why I'd want your troops among mine."

"They're yours, King Rodrigo." His eyes met mine, unflinching. "Shall I pretend I harbored no doubt of your ability? You were a callow child, and to a degree, still are. But . . ." He shrugged. "You're king, and wield the Still. I would safeguard Elena's kingdom."

"You would be a viper in our sheets. I'd know not when I'd be stung."

"Dramatic, Roddy." He clapped, as if complimenting a troupe of mummers. "How many does Hriskil have under arms? Do you know?"

"More than I care to—"

"Forty thousand, and more. Combined with Raeth of Cumber, you meet them with seven. I'd make it eight thousand, and that is few enough. A year ago Tantroth had twelve thousand, but his army is crushed. Count it fortunate if he meets you with three thousand men." His eyes were hard. "Will you cherish your grievance, or save your realm?"

I lifted my coronet and scratched my sweating scalp. "What of Verein, and Stryx?" I spoke to buy time, overwhelmed by his stark figures. Margenthar's accounting was no surprise. Yet on his lips, the numbers sounded grimmer than ever.

"I've stripped Verein, as you have Stryx. All the more reason to meet Hriskil far from home."

"Wine, my lord King." Anavar knelt with a tray, with a jug and two goblets. I poured blood-red wine, handed Uncle a glass.

Mar waited for me to drink, which I ought to do; it was the common courtesy of suspicious nobles. I made no move to raise my glass.

He rolled his eyes, as if in exasperation. "Your refinement leaves me speechless," he murmured, and took a deep draught. "Thank you. A moment's refreshment soothes the most difficult—uhhh!" His eyes widened, and he clutched his stomach.

Rustin bounded forward, but Uncle Mar straightened and handed him his glass. A grin of malice. "Roddy concerns himself for his safety, but look you, who's to secure mine, with poisoners about?"

My fists knotted, and I took deep breath. Anavar, still on his knees, stumbled, knocking me hard. Couldn't the Eiberian lout even . . . his eyes bored steadily into mine.

I swallowed, thankful of Anavar's silent counsel. "Your point is taken, Uncle. If you come among us, my hospitality will match your own." I drew my cloak about me, hoping the trembling of my legs didn't show. "I will consult my advisors. In three hours time you'll have answer."

UNCLE MAR DEPARTED with his outriders, and we wended our way toward Cumber. Now, with darkness upon us, Tursel paced off our camp in a green meadow by a chuckling stream.

I sat with water in a still bowl, recited the familiar words. In time, the cave grew from shadows.

"Mother? Grandsir?"

"They've gone for the nonce." Cayil of the Surk. A bow. "Join us, usurper of Caledon."

"Not I. Caledon's been our holding since my Great-grandsire Varon—"

"Oh, recite your pedigree, do." A sardonic grin that showed many teeth. "Persuade the last of the Surk you've right to claim his seat."

"When will Mother return?"

"Hours. Days. Eons." A shrug. "I'm here." He squinted at shadows across the chill fire. "Aresk, and Vaya too. Varon sleeps in the corner. What would you of Elena?"

I regarded him warily. "You'd aid me?"

"It's our purpose. From this side of the grave, all rulers are as one." He squatted, briskly rubbing his hands. "I've no love for your line, but you're Caledon."

"Well . . ." Dubious, I saw no other course. "You know of Elena's brother Mar?"

"Yes, get on with it." He nudged a fagot closer to the flames.

I told him Uncle's proposal.

He frowned. "A demon's choice. Cast him away and lose his strength. Invite him in and wait for his betrayal."

"Yes."

"Aresk, what say you?"

A slow rumble. "Does he fight?" It was as if the voice had forgotten speech.

I said, "Yes. He's pugnacious and devious."

"He's strength." Aresk said no more.

Cayil nodded. "Not eloquent, but Aresk makes his point. I agree. Let go your petty rage over a scar and save your realm."

"It's not pet—"

"Your imprisonment and the strangling of your brother, yes." Impatiently, he waved it away. "Would you see Hriskil among us after your death? He'll sit at your side if he takes Caledon."

A shudder creased my spine. "You'd forgive all Mar's done?"

"Eh? Of course not. Time was, I'd nail his skin to my gate. But now's no moment to be choosy. Elena would tell you like-wise."

I hugged myself. "She said as much, last year."

"So."

I said hesitantly, "Might I speak to Varon?"

"If you'd risk it. For a usurper, he has much anger. Varon?" Cayil's voice was timid. "Would you speak to the boy?"

Silence.

"Varon?" Cayil's voice was a touch louder.

A growl. "You wake me, to echo what he's heard?"

"So say you?"

"Bid him make peace with his uncle. Mar's thousand may prove the balance."

I waited, but Varon had no more to say.

At length, I left the cave, woke myself.

Groenfil, Soushire and Elryc stood patiently, waiting the end of my trance.

Shakily, I stood. My tone was stubborn. "I don't want Uncle Mar among us."

Groenfil said, "Your grievance is just, but—"

"It's more than that. Today, at our meet, he mocked me, called me poisoner before my vassals. A week in his company and our alliance would be imperiled; his tongue could cleave stone."

"Five hundred horse, four hundred archers, a hundred spearmen." Rustin chewed his knuckle. "Might they be dispersed among us, under our own officers?"

"They'd be so in name only," said Larissa. "We all know Mar."

"I thought you favored his proposal."

"I'm not a child." She glanced impatiently at the cookwagon, awaiting provender. "I'd endorse his aid, not his deportment."

"Roddy, let's walk." Rustin was being circumspect.

"Your pardon, my lords." I followed Rust from our gathering. When we were far enough I asked, "What's your decision?"

"We ought to have him."

I sighed. "Yes, sir."

"But we won't." He hooked thumbs in his belt rope. "There's genuine risk he'll turn on you. And that aside, he's too divisive. He'll have you on the edge of frenzy."

"If you really feel we ought join with him—"

"Have peace," he said. "We'll hold Caledon without the viper." He guided me back toward my gathering of nobles. "Announce your mind, great King, and await Mar."

Lady Larissa was unhappy, Groenfil less so. Captain Tursel, who'd joined our conclave, listened glumly and had little to say. Elryc was overjoyed that we would spurn our uncle.

Once more I drew Rustin aside. "Tomorrow we'll be in Cumber. If you meet Baron Imbar . . ." Uncle Raeth's confidant, once a valet, had coerced Rustin into his bed as the price of his favor, in my greatest hour of need.

"He's in Pezar, with Raeth." Rust turned back to the trail.

"So we assume. Soon or late, your paths will cross."

Rust was calm, betrayed only by his bunched fists. "Don't concern yourself."

I said gently, "As Mar grates on me, Imbar abrades your—"

"Be silent!" His eyes flashed steel. "Don't tread where you're not wanted."

I stopped short. "At times you're hateful."

"My lord King!" A soldier rushed up, flushed of face. "The Duke of Stryx." He pointed down the road. "He comes alone."

"I'll escort him." Rust strode off. "Let the hateful greet the hateful."

I donned my coronet. Fretting, I paced the trail. A hundred paces distant, outside our rear guard, Rustin stalked to Margenthar. My uncle dismounted, made a short bow, tied his horse to a sapling. He handed Rust his sword, submitted to his search. Rustin pointed to me, saying something lost in distance.

Margenthar strode down the road. Rust sat himself on a rock, Mar's sword in his lap. He folded his arms.

So be it. Let him sulk. See if he could exercise his office as regent without speaking to me.

In a few moments Uncle Mar was near. "Ahh, Roddy." An exaggerated bow.

Abruptly I was aware I hadn't asked Soushire and Groenfil to absent themselves; they would hear every word. Could I cross the road and—no, it would be too obvious a snub. "Sir." I pressed my lips together.

"Well? What say you?"

"We thank you for your gracious offer, and—" By the demon's lake, I was in no mood to engage in polite charade. "The answer's no. I'd rather lose Caledon. Begone!"

Lady Soushire drew sharp breath.

Uncle Mar seemed unperturbed. "You may indeed lose Caledon. There are no terms on which . . . ?"

"None."

"I bid you farewell." He bowed to Groenfil and Soushire, as if in genuine respect. "Enjoy your exploits with the boy king." He strode off.

As soon as he was gone, Elryc ran to me. "Roddy, he's not worth it. Don't let him enrage—"

I retreated beyond the hearing of my lords. "In my cell, Mar came to me daily, to pleasure himself at my misery. It wasn't just . . ." My hand flew to my scar. "The things he made me say . . . better I'd cut out my tongue."

Striding down the trail, my uncle never looked back. As Mar neared, Rustin stood.

"We're well rid of him." Elryc's tone was soothing. "Larissa will understand. She thinks no better of him than you."

"Yes, she knows him." I ruffled his hair. My brother, near thirteen, stiffened at the indignity.

Margenthar untied his steed, bowed to Rustin.

"The formalities." I snorted. "We bow and simper, while—"

Rustin handed him the sword. Margenthar shifted his grip, leaned forward, rammed the steel through Rustin's throat. Rustin toppled, twitched once, and was still.

"Roddy!" Elryc's voice was a shriek.

I sprinted down the road. A scream, amidst the rasp of breath. Another. I cut it off.

Margenthar swung onto his saddle, cantered into the dusk.

My legs pumped. My heart pounded. The shrubbery crawled by at snail's pace.

I tore loose the clasp, let my cloak fall, galloped on.

At our camp, cries of alarm. Hoofbeats.

Margenthar disappeared over a rise. Behind me, trumpets sounded.

I skidded to a stop, threw myself into the grass. "Rust!"

The blow had near severed his head. Unseeing eyes stared. More blood than Lord of Nature should allow.

I cradled his face. *"Rustin!"*

Horsemen thundered past. They rode with swords drawn.

I staggered to my feet. "Kill him! Find Mar and kill him!"

Genard flew down the road, legs pumping. Elryc struggled behind.

"M'lor—"

"He's gone." I sank to my knees beside Rustin's still form.

"The Still, make him come alive—"

I shook Genard like a terrier, a rat. "He's *dead*!" With loathing, I cast him aside.

Elryc reached us at last. He stopped, hands on knees, chest heaving. He made to speak, but was too winded. His eyes said all he might.

I sat crosslegged, took Rustin's wrist, touched his fingers to my face.

He knew I loved him, did he not?

"Let the hateful greet the hateful."

I caught myself in a shuddering sob, quelled it.

I was king. It was not meet.

NINE

THREE LEAGUES FROM Fort.

I walked slowly down the road. My blood-soaked breeks chafed.

Behind me, Anavar, Elryc and Tursel carried Rustin, in my cloak.

Three leagues from Fort.

The whole camp had assembled alongside the road, jostling to take sight of the stricken king. A soldier, no older than I, thrust out my coronet, wiped clean on his shirt.

I placed it on my brow, three leagues from Fort.

Willows arched over the gloomy roadway, encumbered with spring's new shoots. Somewhere, a cricket called with relentless monotony.

It seemed an hour, the silent stroll along the wagon path in the dust. I mustn't get too far ahead of Rust.

Our camp occupied the road and the great meadow alongside. I turned from the trail.

Elryc, Anavar and Rustin followed.

Kadar and my bodyguard fell in beside me.

At a wagon, my footsteps faltered. Scores of soldiers stood aside. I found voice. "Lay him down. Six men as honor guard, all the night. We'll bury him in Cumber."

"What of Mar, sire?" Groenfil's tone was grave.

Our horsemen had returned from the chase, three fewer than set out. Margenthar had set ambush, and was gone.

I had to force my words through unwilling lips. "First, the Norland. After Hriskil, I'll pay Mar heed."

In an act of unparalleled kindness, someone had seen to it that my tent was ready. Slowly, as if dazed, I made my way to it. Troops stood aside. One or two held out their hands, as if pleading alms. A few wept.

I tore aside the flap.

Kadar motioned his squadron to their places, one to a side.

I beckoned my bodyguard close, seized his jerkin. "No one enters. All the night. See to it, on your life."

"What of your brother and—"

I thrust the flap shut and stood aching in my tent, three leagues from Fort.

My two clothes chests—Rustin's and mine, together—were in their usual place. I sat on one, in the flicker of the white hour-candle in its silver sconce that hung from the centerpole. The handle was a cunning lion's head.

Nigh on eighth hour, by the black line that crossed the candle at intervals.

Outside, the subdued sounds of a camp preparing for night.

My clothing chest was of oak, its grain lacquered and gleaming dark against gold. Black iron bands held the wood against the jostle of wagons, the unsteady grips of porters. Within, the chest was lined with cedar slabs that lent a refreshing scent to our garb.

I took out Rustin's favorite shirt, held it tight to my cheek.

The tent was golden yellow, its draperies royal maroon. Ropes hung loose from the centerpole, for the hanging of garments or other convenience. Our bed—feather-filled cushions on a canvas underlayment—was dressed, as always, with pale soft cloth, and an ermine blanket on top.

We'd need sleep, Rust and I. In the morn there'd be the ride to Cumber, and the ceremonial greetings.

Near the bed stood a three-legged stool, on which I perched when Rustin dried my hair after we bathed. A dark wood, walnut, perhaps. At the base of each leg the carver had skillfully fit an iron cover to keep it unfrayed. The seat itself was rounded, smoothed by infinite care of its maker.

A set of fitted rugs covered the canvas floor of the tent, notched to surround the centerpole. Assembled, they formed the royal seal of Caledon, in gold thread on black.

Hanging from the rope across the top of the rear wall was a tapestry, portraying Stryx harbor on a clear day. Whitecaps, frozen forever, sailed into the rock-strewn shore.

Come to bed, Rustin. It's grown dark.

The chest that held our bedcovering, when turned on its side, formed a table whose surface bore the royal seal, on which was set our ewer and basin. Near it, a silver to peruse my face. Its edges were an ornate filigree, intricate work that one such as Jestrel might render. The center, impeccably smooth, was polished to a perfect reflection. It had been Mother's favorite.

I rubbed my scar with the soft fabric of the shirting. Rust wore it on special occasions. He'd had it for my coronation, and our first banquet after we'd wrested Stryx from Uncle Mar's hands.

Uncle Mar.

Near our chest sat the inlaid wooden box of alternating cream and ebon slivers, in which we carted the delicacies that eased our travel. Dried fruits, hard sour confections, sweet-meats, each wrapped in a soft cloth. Tiny glass goblets, and a golden flask of sweet liqueur. Dried, salted beef and hard thin breads that satisfied night hunger. Roasted nuts in a silver jar. Wrapped carefully in cloth, peaches dipped in wax that they might not rot.

Soft night-shoes sewn of ermine lay at the foot of my bed. They were Rust's present, after I'd begged pardon for my tantrum at the market.

Rustin liked to see me wear them. I slipped them on my feet.

My eyes stung. I stared fixedly at the carpet.

Slowly, the camp stilled. Outside the tent, whispers. "Let me see him."

"It's forbidden."

Tenth hour, and part of another. I unlaced my jerkin. My breeks were stiff with dried blood; I paid them no heed.

I would wear them often.

In Cumber, we would order a rite of mourning. I would not attend, lest my grief be snatched from me.

Idly, my fingers played over the hilt of my dagger. I lifted it from its leathern sheath. Two small ruby eyes adorned a wrathful silver face. Nowhere as ornate as the dagger Anavar wore, my gift from Lady Soushire.

I closed my fingers over the eyes, grasped the hilt, wafted the razor point across my forearm. It barely scratched.

From the side, near upside down, the royal seal of Caledon under my feet seemed a woman's face. I smiled, ran the point across the flesh of my forearm a trifle more firmly. The effect was more satisfying: an angry red blotch; a drop of blood.

Setting aside the dagger, I shifted Rustin's shirt, so as not to stain it.

I rocked slowly, to and fro, clutching the shirt.

THIRD HOUR OF the morn, and the camp was silent as death.

In my soft furred night shoes I wove my way among flickering campfires until I reached the wagon. The soldiers of the guard, abashed, stood away.

The wagon was empty, save for my cloak, and the burden within.

I stood by the wheel, looking down at the stained cloak.

Below me, a stirring. Rubbing his eyes, Anavar crawled out from under the wagon.

"What do you here?" My voice was harsh.

"I knew you would come." Shivering, he hugged himself against the night cool.

"Go to your tent."

"No." But he retreated a handful of paces, to stand near the guards' fire.

My hand reached out to my cloak, pulled back as if burned.

Gritting my teeth, I forced my fingers to stroke the cloth, and the stiff flesh beneath.

After a time I opened the edge of the cloak, brushed the hair away from Rust's cold face.

Already he had transformed to what was left, after the essence departed. "Oh, Rustin." My voice was a whisper. "Who will love me now?"

I stood, silent, unmoving, for many breaths, until the ache of my legs forced me to shift.

I closed the cloak, made my way toward my tent.

Anavar fell in beside me.

"Get thee gone."

"Sir, say your grief."

Almost, I destroyed him on the spot. My hands closed on his shoulders to hurl him into the fire, but with fierce effort I quashed my inclination. We stood, eye to eye, a hand's breadth apart.

"I, too," he said, "know of death."

I gazed into his unblinking scrutiny until at last, despite my whole will, my head sagged, came to rest on his chest. His fingers, tentative at first, kneaded my shoulder blades.

At length, I pulled away. "Go to bed." I strode to the tent, knotted shut the flap.

I sat on the cushions, crossed my legs. Fourth hour, and half of fifth.

I started to doze, caught myself. I hammered my leg, above the knee, over and again, hard enough to cause a bruise that would keep me from sleep.

The tent swayed gently in a night breeze. The flicker of a hundred fires danced on the fabric.

In time, I would go out into day.

Across the tent, on my clothes chest, lay my dagger. I summoned the strength to retrieve it.

DAYLIGHT CAME, AND I put aside Rustin's shirt, laced my boots, opened the flap.

I had slept not a wink, nor tried to. My very bones ached.

I shook Bollert awake, in the back of a wagon. "Saddle Ebon." He jumped to his feet, ran off to do my bidding. To the guards surrounding my tent, "Sleep as long as you might. I need no guarding."

A grizzled trooper stretched, rubbed his back. "Kadar's orders—"

"Countermanded." I trudged to the cookwagons. Camp servants bustled about, raising the morning's meal. "Is there to eat?"

"Bread baked in the night." The cook gave me a loaf, still warm. "In an hour, porridge. And there's water for tea."

I grunted, my mouth full. Was it betrayal, to feel such hunger?

As the camp began to stir I leaned on the wagon wheel devouring my ration, my mind empty at last.

A timid hand sought mine.

I looked down at Elryc, devoid of expression. He squeezed my fingers. Then, a sharp breath. "What befell you?" His fingers brushed the angry red scratches that lined my arms, my legs, my torso.

"They don't hurt." Not nearly enough.

Elryc's eyes darted to my dagger. Abruptly he loosened the flap of its sheath. For a reason I couldn't fathom, he was weeping. As if dazed, I let him take my plaything. I'd find another.

In a while, he was gone.

Day lightened.

From afar, Elryc, Anavar and Genard regarded me gravely. It annoyed me. I returned to my tent, closed the flap, nursed the satisfying sting of my scrapes.

After a time, the flap opened. I winced at the unwelcome light.

Anavar peered round, spotted me crosslegged on the chest. "It's time the tent was struck."

Wearily, I uncurled myself. "Very well." I crossed to the entry.

He eyed me uncertainly. "Sir, your breeks . . ."

I glanced down at the bloodstained cloth. "What of them?"

A pause. His tone was chastened. "No matter, my lord."

Ebon, saddled and ready, nibbled at grass. Bollert was nowhere to be seen. I untied Ebon from the tent stake, hoisted myself into the saddle, waited patiently for our column to assemble.

The morn was warm and dewy, the sun bright, as befit days of sowing. Churls at their fields would be gladdened. Ebon's tail flicked at persistent pests.

"My lord King." A soft voice. Lady Soushire, on her palfrey.

"What do you wish?" I sounded harsh, and cared not.

"In the camp there's . . . consternation. None dare approach."

"If they doubt our cause, let them depart."

"It's not about the Norlanders, my lord. This morning you're an . . . apparition." Her wave took in my clothes, my manner, my mien.

"What would you?"

"Summon strength to show your men their king's still with them."

"I'm here. If they would more, they've but to ask."

"Rodrigo—"

The gossamer web binding my temper frayed. "I would be alone, my lady."

With a glance of reproach, she departed.

Presently we commenced our march. I rode alone, near the head of the column, encircled by my bodyguards. From time to time, despite myself, I dozed.

As we climbed the last of the hills and wound our way into

the green valley of Cumber, Tursel sent runners ahead.
Presently they brought Tresa's assurance we were welcome
and expected before dusk.

Our whole force seemed infected by a will to end our journey. Perhaps I was the cause; to me it mattered not. First
Anavar made to join me, then Elryc. I rebuffed them both.
Presently Tanner and Genard appeared, with a waterskin. I
drank deeply, handed it back, rode on.

The highest turrets of Cumber castle were visible a goodly
distance from the town. As always, bright banners flew. Even
in Uncle Raeth's absence, his holding reflected his inimitable
style.

We clattered over the cobbles of Cumber Town. Aproned
merchants came blinking out of drab stone shops to stare
silently at our procession.

The road turned sharply at the castle wall. From the ramparts, armed and helmeted soldiers watched our passage, grim
of face.

Today the gates were open. A year past, I'd been seized by
Margenthar of Stryx as I battled desperately to reach them.
My fingers drifted to my scar.

Our front guard turned, marched smartly through the narrow twisting entry, into the walled courtyard.

I guided Ebon past the turns.

On the steps to the keep, Lady Tresa waited.

Abruptly, Elryc spurred past me, cantered ahead to Tresa.
He swung off his mare, spoke urgently to her. Tresa's hands
flew to her mouth. After a moment her gaze found me, returned to my brother. She nodded.

Elryc stood aside.

I rode to the steps, tugged gently at the reins. Obedient as
ever, Ebon came to a halt.

Tresa made a deep curtsy. "Rodrigo, my lord King." She
held my bridle.

I bowed, a formal bow of respect. "My Lady Tresa of
Cumber."

"On Grandfather's behalf, we welcome thee. All that thou
seeeth is thine."

"We thank thee for thy grace, for thy kindness and thy welcome." I dismounted, the ceremony completed. Now we'd return to normal speech.

"My lord Earl Groenfil, my lady of Soushire, welcome." To me, "Roddy, Elryc told me. I'm so sorry."

I swallowed. "I would not speak of it. Is there a chamber to which I might withdraw?"

"Of course." She snapped her fingers, summoned servants.

"We'll need have swift burial," I said. "Near Pytor." Nurse Hester had brought my brother's body to Cumber, in a last act of service.

"It will be so. I'll call when all is ready."

"I thank thee." With what dignity I could muster, trying not to yawn, I followed the servant to the castle's high reaches, and solitude.

How long I sat amid the fine trappings of my chamber, I knew not. At length, a quiet knock. Tresa stood aside for servants with washbasin and ewer, and others bearing my clothes chest. With brisk efficiency she directed their labor, hurried them out the door.

Tresa remained. "My lord."

I made no answer.

Unbidden, she sat beside me. "Elryc's terrified. And Anavar."

"Yes, now that Rust—no one's left to restrain me."

"Don't be daft. It's that you're near unhinged with grief, and hold it within. You can't . . . my king, forgive me."

I regarded her warily.

Gently, she pulled my head to her breast. "He was everything to you, Roddy. Don't deny him."

"I have no need to show—" I couldn't say more.

"Oh, my king." She held me tighter.

Presently, I stirred, pulled my head from her dampened blouse. "I'm sorry."

"Whatever for?" She sat beside me. "Roddy, think you it's unmanly to mourn a companion?"

"Rust was more."

"A guide. A vassal. A bed-friend." Her calm acceptance nearly undid me. "I'm glad you had him so long."

"Long?" Our time was but a vanished instant.

"Time enough to evoke your wisdom, your grace."

"Hah." My tone was bitter. "Not a fortnight past, he beat me."

"No matter. He loved and respected you." A moment's hesitation. "I summoned a ritemaster for the mourning." A rite of mourning preceded burial. "We await you."

"Conduct the rite." I gestured a dismissal.

"Rodrigo, you mustn't—"

I gripped her wrist hard enough so she winced. "Know you the rite?"

"It's to grieve the loss—"

"No, my lady. To put end to grieving." I let go her arm, sorry for the red fingermarks in her flesh. "Rust knew my tears, my hopes, my failure as a man, and still he loved—" I swallowed. "Think you I'll set aside mourning? Not while I live!" This last I flung at her, as a sharpened spear.

"Were he among us, how would he bid you?"

"No doubt to carry on. I'll disappoint him in this, as so much else."

"As you wish, my lord." She rose. "You need dress for the burial."

"I am dressed."

She crossed to the clothes chest. "I'll help you select—"

"Madam, you are not my mother!"

She fingered my breeks, stiff with dried blood. "It's of respect you wear this. But consider, my lord, how your court will see it. A king so deranged—"

"I care not!"

"Or that you've such disdain, you'd see your friend to earth in stained garb that draws flies!" Red spots fired her cheeks.

I ran to the door, flung it open. "Out of my chamber, this instant!"

"My lord—"

"Out!"

The door slammed behind her with a satisfying crash.

I paced the chamber, savoring my wrath. My heart pounded.

Below, at the place of burial, there'd be erected a canopy, perhaps a tent. Rustin would be set out on a slab, garlanded with blooms. Three times would the ritemaster carry a taper round his still form, perhaps shielding it from wind; it was an ill omen if the candle guttered.

While the ritemaster muttered the sacred words, mourners would each lay a flower on the stony bier, or, if in dead of winter, a green twig, symbolizing the rebirth of spring. The ritemaster's taper consumed, as flames will, the collected grief.

Rustin would understand my absence.

My youngest brother, Pytor, was buried in the courtyard, under a bronze marker of Uncle Raeth's devising. Rust had liked him, more than I in my selfish youth. Now he'd enjoy Pytor's company through the ages. Perhaps he'd teach him to be a man, like he—like . . . I hammered my thigh with closed fist.

I flung open the window, peered down. Folk were gathering in the courtyard. I couldn't see Tresa among them. Foolish woman, who dared to upbraid a king. I was well rid of her. Willful, stubborn, blind to my needs. Stupid, like all her kind, and—

A soft knock.

"Begone! I've no need of—"

Not Tresa, but Anavar, peered through the half-opened door. He slipped inside.

"Must I set the bar, to have peace? Out."

"No, my lord. I beg pardon."

My hand flashed to my empty sheath. Maddened, I snatched the ewer, pitched it at Anavar's head. He ducked. A shattering crash.

My voice was hoarse. "Know you what you risk?"

Anavar took deep breath. "Full well." He came near, tremulous. "Sir, you—"

I slapped him. The sound was a thunderclap. His hand flew to his fiery cheek.

My voice dripped contempt. "You call yourself vassal, and obey not your king?"

"I protect you. From yourself." His eyes glistened. "Rustin's to be buried in an hour. It's time to dress, my lord."

"Tresa sent you."

"And Elryc. As would Rustin, if he had speech."

"How dare—" My mouth worked. Mute, I sank to my cushioned bed.

"Come, sir." His voice was soothing. He knelt by my feet, pulled loose a boot.

I jumped up, seized his hair, drew him upward.

Teeth bared from the pain, he rose.

"By what right do you defy me, Anavar of Eiber?" I stretched him to his toes, pulled harder.

"For your own sake!"

Abruptly, I released him. Rocking, eyes shut, he rubbed furiously at his scalp. He stamped a foot, rubbed harder.

My rage was doused. "I'm sorry."

He nodded, surreptitiously wiped an eye.

"I didn't mean to hurt—no, I'd have hurt you more, had I the means." Wearily, I slumped on the cushions. "Again, my cruelty."

Anavar opened the door, peered outside. "Tanner, warm water for the king. Be quick." Back to me. "Hold up your foot. There. Now the breeks."

I lay still, arm over my eyes.

The creak of my clothes chest. "Rustin must have liked these; he laid them out for you often. And this shirt. There's no time for a bath, sir, but we'll have water to wash. This scented soap was Rustin's. He won't mind your using it."

"I don't . . . I can't . . ."

"I'll help, sir. That's all right, let yourself cry. Lord of Nature knows you have cause."

Half an hour later, we descended the stair. As I'd clutched Nurse in my sorrows when a toddler, now I held tight to Anavar, afraid to catch an eye, to take a step beyond his.

In the windswept courtyard we laid Rustin into the earth, wrapped still in my cloak. Groenfil and Soushire, Tresa and Tursel had all gathered, along with the nobility of the place.

I watched in silence, my mind in flight. I was wondering how to make amends to Tresa, when unexpectedly, she slipped her hand in mine. Grateful beyond words, I stood dumbly between her and Anavar, and let them steady me when the first earth was thrown.

After, we walked to Raeth's sunlit dining hall, where viands had been laid.

I cleared my throat. "Lady Tresa . . . I know not what I do. I haven't slept in . . ."

"Two days." Anavar.

"I'm not fit to be king."

Tresa frowned. "Whyever not?"

"When Margenthar slaughtered Rust, I ought have turned in fury to Verein to oust him. Instead, I bid Tursel proceed to Cumber." My lip curled. "Duties of state."

"You need save your kingdom."

"To what end, if foul murder goes unpunished?" My voice was shrill.

"It's been barely a day." Her tone was soothing. "In good time you'll—"

"Rust cries for vengeance. Can you not hear him?"

Across the hall, Groenfil paused at his plate.

Tresa glanced at Anavar. "To his chamber, I think. I'll have food brought. Come, Roddy." Weeping, I let them guide me.

All afternoon I lay disconsolate. Anavar and Tresa spoke calming words. From time to time they fed me morsels. Dutifully, I ate.

I dozed, waking suddenly to nightmares and panic. Soft voices coaxed me back to my sleep.

I WOKE SNUGGLED in Rustin's embrace, an arm thrown casually over his flank. For a delicious moment I drowsed, basking in his warmth.

Anavar stirred. "Good morn, my lord."

Galvanized, I sat. Rage tore the cobwebs of sleep. "Out!" An ankle, at the small of his back. I propelled him to the floor. A thump.

"Ai!" He clutched his knee, rolled back and forth. "Why'd you do that?"

"How dare you take his—you've a bed of your own!"

His eyes were reproachful. "You begged me not to go. You clutched my wrist . . ."

I flushed at the unwelcome memory. "That's as may be. I was . . . agitated." He deserved more. "Forgive me, if you have it in you."

Cautiously, he perched on the edge of the bed, shivering in naught but a loincloth. "Tresa and I sat 'til past twelfth hour."

"I recall, now."

"Your sleep was fevered."

It would long be so.

"Twice in the night you called out—"

"Enough!" My tone had an edge. I rubbed my eyes. The welts from my scratches itched, and I had a great hunger. Still, I hesitated. "Anavar, shall I abdicate for Elryc?"

He snorted. "Don't play the fool."

"Think on it. He's . . . sedate. And wise."

"He's a child, and you're my liege." His voice was firm. "Sir, I'd speak of things beyond my station."

I nodded.

He wrapped a bedcover around his bare shoulders. "My father is a fair man, but strict. When I was young my mother Janna shielded me from his ire, and taught me a child's ways."

He took deep breath. "I was eleven when my mother passed from life. For months after—in truth, sir, years—I went about as if thrown from a horse, dazed and hurt. I wept without reason and shied from friends. Oft father was irked. But with time . . ." He blinked rapidly. "I learned to smile anew. You could not love Rustin more than I Janna. But Lord of Nature demands life go on."

"How long . . ." I swallowed. "Before it eased?"

His eyes glistened. "Every day I miss her, to this hour, as you miss Lord Rustin. But one grows accustomed." He turned away, and was silent. Then, "Be not alone in your grief, sir."

After a time I cleared my throat. "Did I hurt your knee?"

"It's a trifle."

"I'm sorry. I always am." Awkwardly, I patted his shoulder. "Come, let us dress." A new day was on us, and I must rise to play at king.

TEN

THRUSTING CAYIL ASIDE, I strode into the cave, my bedchamber fading to mist. "Why didn't you warn me?" My voice trembled. "Have you only shades of passion? Think you I'd not have given life itself to prevent it?"

Mother rose quickly. "What has passed?"

"Rustin's dead, madam, by your brother's hand." I whirled to Tryon. "May your Mar burn forever. May demons take his soul."

Instead of the rage I expected, Tryon cleared his throat uneasily. "Why berate me?"

"You spawned him. Better you were struck dead."

"Enough, Roddy." Mother sought to guide me to the fire.

"Bah!" I flung off her hand. "For this babble, this endless fire, I've given up manhood? I'll lie with Tresa and put an end to it. You gulled me, madam, to believe the Still had worth."

"Leave us then, if you won't listen." Mother crouched by the fire, rubbing her hands. "You were always willful."

Despite myself, I sank reluctantly at her side. "Speak on."

"What cause had Mar to slay Rustin?"

"They had no quarrel."

"Why, then?"

"To destroy me."

"Aye, he's half done that." Her appraisal was cool. "It's for you to hand him victory or defeat."

I flushed at her rebuke. "I have no calm in this, Mother."

"Devise one. The kingdom demands it."

"What care I now of Caledon?"

"Little enough, it seems."

Cayil loomed over us, touched my shoulder lightly with a withered claw. "Recall you not grief, Elena? Slacken his fetters."

"He's king, and must set sorrow aside." Nonetheless, Mother paused, reflective, exploring me with troubled eyes. "When you were three, and Rustin five, he taught you a game of ball and blocks. As seasons passed, I held my breath while the two of you rode to hunt." Her fingers brushed my arm. "You've reason to mourn him."

"Thank you."

"But not to berate us. If you want foreknowledge, seek the Ukra, though little good it does their Empur. Did ever I tell you the Still brought prescience? Chide us not for a gift beyond our giving!" Her eyes glinted.

"I ask pardon." The words came hard, but were merited.

Queen Elena seemed to weigh the boon. "Granted."

I held out my hands, in futile effort to take warmth from the cold flames. "What now, Mother? I'm without restraint."

Grandsir Tryon stirred. "You're weakened, and all know it." He scored the dust with a dry stick. "First, you lost a valued counsellor. Second, you're bereft, and act it. Third—" He jabbed at the dust. "—Mar tweaked you with impunity."

I started. "Tweaked?"

"Jabbed." Tryon waved it away, as if of no consequence. "Tantroth will know, and consider. And Hriskil will be emboldened."

"Grandsir . . ." I girded myself. "I'd have your advice about Margenthar. Surely you know the blood between us can never be expunged. But he's your son. How shall I know you speak to my benefit, not his?"

"I speak for Caledon." Tryon's tone was acid. "Neither you nor Mar signify. Only the realm."

"If you think him preferable . . ."

"You're crowned, and will join us after your day. We exist to guide you."

"How can I know that?"

"Because we say it. If you doubt, leave us!"

"Very well." I surged to my feet. "I shall."

MY ASSEMBLED NOBLES pored over a map drawn on sheepskin, while I sat lethargic and worn from my wield of the Still.

Elryc pressed my unsteady hand to his cheek. Until our meet of this sunlit morn, I hadn't realized how my derangement had alarmed him. Even Genard, usually my goad, refilled my watered wine and attended me as if I were his liege. I did my best to set my mind to our business.

"Grandfather blocks the Caled Pass at Pezar. Tantroth is

here, across Eiber." Tresa stabbed at lines drawn in dye.
"Hriskil is determined to hold them apart, though he needn't
take the trouble. Tantroth has no longing to join his allies."

Groenfil frowned, arms crossed. "Outnumbered as we are,
there's no great benefit in joining force."

I frowned. We'd left Stryx only to unite the armies of Caledon. Why question that goal now?

Tresa's tone was tart. "If we fear battle, why take the
field?"

"To seek the moment we might prevail," said Groenfil. "It
warrants patience."

Captain Tursel looked stubborn. "Cumber's the key to
Caledon. A strong base in the north prevents Hriskil from
lunging with his whole might through the kingdom. Duke
Tantroth must know our force here in Cumber prevents his annihilation. It's essential he join us."

I bestirred myself. "What say you, Anavar?"

My ward shot me a grateful glance. "Trust not in Duke
Tantroth." A pause. "But summon him, to augment your
strength and fight under your eye."

"Hriskil's overrun the west of Eiber," I said. "If Tantroth retreats east to join us at Pezar, we cede the Norlanders the rest
of his duchy."

Tursel scowled at the map. "Not if we advance westward
and give battle in Eiber."

"Abandon the pass?" Tresa was indignant. "Grandfather
fought all winter to keep—"

"Just so." Groenfil's tone was sharp. "If Hriskil maneuvers
behind us, not only are we cut off from return, but Cumber
and all Caledon are open to him."

I wondered, "If I summoned Tantroth, would he heed?"

At that, silence.

"We'll soon know." Wearily, I stood. "My lady, send couriers to Tantroth. He's to meet us at the Caled Pass and fall on
the Norlanders from the rear, 'til our forces join. We ourselves
leave for the hills at dawn. Tursel, make ready."

Murmurs of assent.

"Roddy . . ."

"Later, Elryc." I strode to the stone-decked veranda, but
Uncle's abandoned flowerbeds held no interest. I turned back
through the keep, to the massive wooden door and the stairs

to the courtyard. Reluctantly, I let my steps take me to the bronze monument. Soon Rustin's name would be placed alongside Pytor's. We'd need set another marker too, on a road three leagues from Fort.

I stared at the fresh-piled earth. Someone had placed a flag-stone near. I brushed it clean and knelt.

Ah, my prince . . .

I started. "You're here?"

So long as you remember me. His tone was sardonic.

"Oh, Rust, what will I do without you?"

Carry on.

"Do you really hear me?"

Silence.

"Rustin?"

A long while passed. A familiar lithe form settled at my side. "It's a nice grave, m'lor'. Plain, but where folk will see it. Who were you talking to?"

"Rustin."

Genard nodded wisely. "The Still serves you well."

"Not the Still, you toad! I imagine him!"

"Who's to say what—"

"I say. Think you I don't know the distinction?"

"I'm sorry, m'lor'." For once, the stableboy sounded abashed. "You've such great Power, I think you can do all."

"If it were so, Hriskil would be dead, and Mar flayed alive."

The venom of my words took Genard aback. "That's be-yond me, m'lor'." He picked at a clod of earth. "When we leave in the morn . . ."

"What now? You would ride at my side?"

"Not me. Lord Elryc." Genard's glance beseeched me. "He's lonely, and takes fright. I do my best to ease him by talking of small things—"

I snorted.

"It's all I know to do, m'lor'. I have no great mind."

"At least you know it." Then, after a moment, "Were Rustin alive, he'd beat me for that. I know no bounds." Tentatively, I laid a hand on his shou!der. "It's foolish speech, and cruel. I vowed you better."

"I don't hold you to it. You meant well."

"Demons dance on good intentions." I sounded cross, and was. "Before today, I was civil, was I not?"

"Yes, m'lor'. For a half fortnight."

"Then I'll resume."

He toyed with a fallen bloom. "It's that I know not what to say. When I would bring ease, I vex you. When I would vex, I enrage you. Old Griswold urged me to silence, but even he had to admit it wasn't my way." Reflectively, he rubbed his rump. "Only Elryc understands."

"I do, too," I said, surprising myself. "You mean no harm."

Genard settled himself closer. "Let's think of Rustin," he said presently.

FINGERING MY SCAR, I paced the soft-draped chamber, while Lady Tresa sat placidly. "I don't know how. Rust said I ought speak as to any man, and not take heed that you're a woman." That wasn't quite how Rustin had phrased it, but I was too flustered to do better.

"In your scrolls you do so, my lord." She studied the stone flagging.

"I ought have had them rewritten. Willem's clerk would make them more flowery."

"They'd have been ruined. I heard your voice, watched your quill fumble."

"Thank you." My tone was bitter.

"It made them precious." She colored. "The more so that you spoke your heart." She glanced to my face, and away.

"I had no one else." I realized what I'd said. "You see? I meant they were precious to me too, but it sounded . . ." Oh, Rust, tease me once more for my muddled speech. I swallowed.

"Come sit. You pace like you need a chamberpot."

I blushed. "Nerves." I sank at her side, on a cushioned bench, my best side turned toward her.

"I tended your wounds, my lord. There's no need for formal—"

"Roddy. You always called me that."

"There's no need for formality, Roddy."

Resolutely, I took her hand, raised it to my lips. "This is for your letters that sustained me." I lowered my hand, astounded I'd carried off the gesture without catastrophe. A year past, I'd near assaulted her in a fit of ardor; only her good sense stayed my loss of the Still.

Now, of course, ardor was beyond Tresa's considering, despite the protestation in her scroll. If I moved to embrace her, she'd run screaming from the room; my scar had made me ugly beyond belief. Only Rustin could delude himself enough to cherish my visage. Unconsciously I resettled myself, putting distance between us.

"What will you do now, Roddy?"

"Ride north."

"I mean, without Rustin. You made him your guardian, did you not?"

"More. I'll tell you a secret." I described how I'd set him as regent, and how he'd quietly guided my hand.

Her look was one of wonder. "How you trusted him!"

"Of course." I bit my lip, reluctant to reveal deepest flaws. "I had to, you see. The Still brings out . . ." I explained how the Power gave my cruelty full rein. "I'm on constant guard. Just this afternoon I savaged Genard, in harsh speech."

"I've not seen you cruel."

"Hah. When I think of last year's visit, I sweat through my jerkin."

"That was . . . inexperience." She smiled. "You're older now."

"But still vir—" I forced myself to finish. "Still virgin, Tresa, and a dolt with women."

To my astonishment she leaned close and kissed my cheek. "It matters so to boys, doesn't it?"

"More than you can imagine." It was as much as I dared say. No torture could make me disclose my fevered nights, my restless anguish.

"Pay no heed, Roddy. I judge you by more than rutting."

"Really?" My voice was a squeak.

"You freed yourself from Margenthar, rallied the kingdom, retook Stryx. Your troops respect you—"

"How know you that?"

"How many deserted on the road from Stryx?"

"A handful."

"Only a handful?"

"You really think . . ."

"You've been a good king."

"Ahh. Well." I shifted, finding sudden discomfort in the seat. "Hmm."

*   *   *

I EXAMINED THE delicate silver falcon. "It's exquisite. Thank you."

Jestrel the silversmith bowed his appreciation. "Your hospitality has been—"

"Lady Tresa's."

"Yours, until now. In your generosity, might I ask a boon?"

"It depends." My tone was cautious. If he expected me to pay for the keepsake after all . . .

"Cumber's sunk in war and taxation; my wares are wasted here. If I might ride with your troop, to the Ukra passes . . ."

"Granted." Thank heaven it was all he wanted. "Genard, don't break it." I held out my hand.

Reluctantly, the stableboy let go of my treasure. "It's beautiful, m'lor'."

"I have others," said Jestrel. "If you'd grace my chamber with a visit . . ."

"Yes, I'd love to. But not tonight." We would ride at dawn; I had soon to be abed. I stood. "Perhaps at Pezar."

"It would only take a moment . . . as you say, my lord." A deep bow, covering his disappointment.

I sought out Tursel, in his old quarters built onto the wall. We passed an hour reviewing the line of march, my relentless bodyguards pacing outside, while I struggled not to nod off. Really, I should study war, since I seemed destined to spend my life at it. At last I made my escape.

On the way back to the donjon I detoured to the flagstone, where Rust lay. "I'm off, sir. I'll be back, if I've breath in my body."

Fare thee well, my prince.

"I'm nothing without you!" It was a whisper.

Have I taught you so little?

"I had so much to say, and never found the words." My throat caught.

Ahh, Roddy. Don't weep. I can't abide it.

"I can't help it."

Perhaps when all's done we'll meet. Have ease, Roddy.

I stumbled to my room, blind from salt sting. I collapsed on my soft, luxurious bed, jumped up, ran to the adjoining chamber.

"Anavar? Do I trouble you?" I knocked again. "Anav—

could you sit by my bed 'til I sleep? I'd be grate . . ." I beat my thigh, 'til my voice was steady. "Anavar, I beg you."

THE ARMY OF Caledon toiled and creaked past the shadows of Cumber's bright towers.

Pezar was a day's ride, no more, for a man on a fast horse. But an army was not that. Heavily loaded wagons mired themselves in ruts and mud, and cavalry was constrained to the pace of trudging men. We'd be three days on the march.

Elryc rode to my left, and beside him, Genard. To my right, Lady Soushire and Anavar. Groenfil and Tursel rode up and down the line, a vigilant tandem of captains. From time to time Groenfil stopped to have word with Larissa, and Tursel to change horses.

We'd turned from the broadened road for a track that meandered into the hills, before I discovered Tresa was among us.

"What vexes you, Roddy? I have a tent of my own." She patted her spirited mare, soothing her.

"Uncle Raeth said you were to—"

"Let the king ride through Cumber unescorted? He'd be aghast."

"A lady has no place at war."

Larissa of Soushire chuckled. "Shall I depart? I'd take my retinue."

"Your pardon, Lady Soushire." I bowed at the thrust. "You're most welcome in our midst. And Groenfil would be most discomfited were you to leave."

She blushed. It gave me respite to turn back to Tresa. "Uncle Raeth sent you home to Cumber."

"A month ago. Circumstances have changed."

"He'll be furious. Worse, he'll think I arranged your return."

"Oh?" Tresa cocked an eyebrow. "I didn't know you feared him."

"Don't play that game." I rounded on Anavar. "What are you grinning at?"

"Nothing, sir."

"Bah." Scowling, I turned back to Tresa. "Well, don't ride in the brush. Here, to my right. Take Anavar's place. In fact, take his horse."

My Eiberian ward sniffed, nose in air. "I'll help Tursel. One of us ought to be useful." He galloped off.

"I see what you meant about cruelty." Tresa rode to Larissa's right, at the edge of our row. "Oh, Roddy, don't pout, I spoke in jest."

Larissa grunted. "You ought teach the king humor. His Rustin made him sputter and fume at will."

"Roddy hates being teased."

"Only when I don't know it." I cast about for a diversion. "Is Pezar tolerable?"

"It's small, dull, dusty. But Grandfather's built a stone kitchen. He sends weekly for spices."

"He would." I smiled at my memories of Cumber. Uncle Raeth made every meal a banquet. Even if he starved, he said, he would starve in style. Once, Rust and I were served a . . . my smile vanished. I rode with head bowed.

WE STOPPED TO water the horses at an icy stream. It was there a runner caught us. "Margenthar encamps outside Soushire Castle. He seeks the lady's hospitality."

Larissa bit viciously into a soft loaf, as if tearing off a foe's head. "He knows full well I'm with you."

I said, "Are you prepared for siege?"

"As well as can be. But his thousand outnumber my few."

Groenfil's gentle hand soothed her shoulder. "You stripped your defenses, my lady?"

"Not utterly. But was I to ride alone? I'm always accompanied by my troop. And the king ordered us into the field."

I hid a smile. No order could have bludgeoned her from Soushire, were it not her choice. She was plowing ground to seed my obligation, should Margenthar seize her holding.

I pondered. Should I send Larissa home to fend off Mar's thrust? Or better yet, send Groenfil on her behalf?

No, I ought not. Our soldiers who left the field wouldn't return; time, battle and other obligations would intercede. In fact, I should beware lest Larissa depart without leave.

Tresa's voice was soothing. "Surely Mar will be months at siege. When Roddy turns his army south, he'll flee."

Lady Soushire snorted. "What army, when the Norlanders are done with us?"

"If Hriskil bests us," I said stiffly, "there's no safety in Soushire."

"Nonetheless . . ."

I made a sour face. If Larissa held Soushire securely, and luck favored her, she might persuade Hriskil to accept tribute and homage, and keep her castle. The loyalty of my nobles was only as good as my strength. Such were realities.

Elryc whispered, "Be nice to her."

I frowned. Did I need a child sage to tell me the obvious? "No doubt it's vexing, my lady. But you have valiant men at arms."

"Old Quindar? He's an irresolute fool."

"And stout walls."

"But low, in the north quadrant. I was meaning to build them higher. I really ought to go set matters right."

"We're within a day of Uncle Raeth. Let's ask his counsel."

She motioned a groom to help her mount. "You must think me dense indeed."

"No, not at—"

"I'll stay because I gave promise and the peril's not dire." She hoisted her hefty form onto her patient palfrey. "No thanks to your honeyed words."

"Whatever the cause, I'm grateful." The day wasn't that warm. Why was I sweating?

"Hmpff. Groenfil, a word." A flick of her crop, and she moved out of earshot.

"Deftly done, Roddy." Tresa's eyes held a glint of amusement. "You have a gift with women."

"Did I claim to be silver-tongued? Am I a mummer, to cast a thrall?" I swatted an annoying fly. "I beg you stay home, and you ride. I beg her stay, and . . ."

"I'm jealous. Does her beauty blind you so?"

Larissa was fat, had yellowed teeth, and ate garlic cloves. I shuddered. Then, gamely, "No, my lady, yours does."

Spots of red in her cheeks; my point had found flesh. Advantage taken, best to retire from the field. "Ah, Tursel, hold a moment!" I wheeled after him. More quietly, when he and I were alone, "Keep us moving 'til we're at Pezar. Don't give Larissa time to withdraw."

"If she chooses to leave, rolling wagons won't stop her."

"I know, but . . ." I rolled my eyes. What more could I do, short of forging chains to bind my nobles?

PEZAR WAS ALL Tresa had promised: a dirty border town of no consequence, its rustic calm disrupted by Cumber's encampment. Two hopelessly overcrowded alehouses, a creaky mill, a blacksmith and a desultory market were all the town offered.

Anavar, Elryc and I rode with our bodyguards to the windswept hillside, where we found Uncle Raeth glumly watching laborers strengthen his defensive wall.

He'd placed our battlement directly across the road that ran the length of the pass; one end died in a steep, near-unclimbable hill, the other at a roaring stream that carried water from the mountain. Huge, thick wooden gates closed the road under the wall. All in all, a sturdy bulwark.

Uncle Raeth's wrinkled blue eyes lit. "Roddy! My lord king, that is." A bow, with a flourish. With the aid of a stout walking stick he dismounted the new-mortared berm he'd climbed. "Imbar's sending out a patrol; he'll be along shortly. You look ghastly."

My hand flew to my scar.

"Not that, my boy. Your eyes, your expression. It's Rustin, of course. I'm so, so sorry." He opened his arms. I nearly fell into them. "There, boy, it's all right."

"How did—did you—"

"Tresa sent word. Now, don't try to talk."

I didn't.

"Dry your eyes, Roddy. Folk are watching."

"Let them." But I did as he asked.

Perhaps to give me time to sort myself out, Raeth surveyed his defenses. "Hriskil threatens to go round the west Caleds, but this is the only sensible pass. I haven't budged, despite his allurements. And so we survived the winter."

"And Tantroth?"

Raeth's shrewd eyes met mine. "I do believe he'd cede his duchy if only he could keep Eiber Castle and the three leagues surrounding. He's obsessed with regaining it."

"Can you blame him? What if Hriskil took Cumber Town?"

"I'd husband my force, and govern from an alehouse." A contemptuous thumb toward the outskirts of Pezar. "I've not stooped quite so low. Ahh, there's Baron Imbar!" A welcome wave to a grizzled fleshy man I knew too well. "Make obeisance to your king. He's grown, has he not?"

I turned away from Imbar. "Remove him!" My final quarrel with Rust had been over Raeth's one-time valet, ennobled as a boon to Uncle Raeth.

The old baron's tone was pleading. "I wept when Rae told me." He sank to a knee. "Find it in your heart to forgive me."

"I do not." Nonetheless, I sighed. Imbar was Raeth's right-hand man, and defended my kingdom. I was too weary to be as angry as I ought. I waved vaguely.

"There, that's done. He has a king's grace, does he not, Imbar? Think you he's hungry after his long ride?"

"I'm here, Uncle. Ask me."

"Change my ways, at the last of life? Unlikely." But he bowed in my direction, rather formally. "I invite you to dinner, Rodrigo. We've a pavilion outside the hearth I insisted on building. The alehouse was unspeakable."

"I'd like that. Groenfil and Soushire, of course?"

"And your Baron Anavar."

I clapped Anavar's shoulder. "He'll escort Lady Tresa."

Raeth's head shot up. "You brought her?"

"She brought herself." I wouldn't take responsibility.

"You shouldn't have allowed it." He looked cross. Discreetly, I let it pass.

THOUGH RAETH MADE a fetish of gastronomy, I noticed he saw to it our troops were fed and sent to reinforce our defenses before we sat to dinner. I nodded silent approval.

Over ragout of venison with sage and tarragon, I studied him. Despite his animated conversation he seemed tired and careworn; winter in his wretched border camp must have been miserable indeed. Tresa eyed him with unconcealed concern.

"Word's been sent to Tantroth." Uncle Raeth looked glum. "He'll know he's summoned, if our runners get through. Last month four were caught. Try the spiced asparagus."

"Imprisoned?"

"Tortured. They're dead." With an effort, he wrenched the conversation elsewhere. "So, Anavar, has our king yet provided you lands?"

"Mar's estate shall be his." I spoke before Anavar could. "All of it."

Anavar's eyes widened. "Sir, I thank—"

"Don't spend your revenues. First we need secure them."

"Aye, sir." For the rest of the meal his attention was lost.

Afterward, in dusk, Raeth and I walked the camp. To my

surprise he agreed we need take battle to Hriskil, rather than wait on his pleasure.

"I'm too old for another winter of this, my boy." Gingerly, Raeth stepped over a steaming pile of horse dung. "And Lord of Nature knows what's befallen my garden."

"It's a bit bedraggled," I admitted. Scarce a year ago it had been a wonder.

"We've been lucky so far," he said. "Not to discount your prowess as a warrior."

I shot him a sharp glance, alert for mockery, but he seemed serious.

"Hriskil split his force to no purpose, Roddy. He sent your Danzik south of Stryx, led his own command in central Eiber and left more men here beyond the pass. Had Hriskil struck in one place with his full might . . ."

"He may still." A chill stabbed my spine. "What if he withdrew from Eiber and sailed down the coast to Stryx harbor?"

"He'd be King of Caledon." It was said simply, without menace, and was all the more frightful. "But he can't leave Tantroth behind to harry him."

"All the worse for us," I said.

"Yes. I'd be surprised if Tantroth hasn't already made overtures to the Norland."

I stopped short. "Uncle, tell me true. If Cumber were at stake, would you do the same?"

"And be vassal to Hriskil? No. His kitchens are an infamy."

"Be serious."

"I am," he said. "Do you think he serves mountain-iced sorbet to clear the palate, as I did tonight? Bah." A few finicky steps, through ruts and mud. "And there's the matter of an oath."

"It sits lightly enough on your peers."

"Oh, I don't know. Larissa's here, is she not?"

We hadn't spoken of Mar's threat to Soushire. I forbore to ask how he knew. This was, after all, Caledon.

"If it's the oath that binds you, I thank you."

"That was offensive."

I swallowed. "Uncle, I beg pardon. Your oath is as good as my own. It was callow to say otherwise."

"Ahh. Rustin taught you well."

Abruptly, the day was bleak. "Yes."

We returned to camp. Somewhere along the way, he took my arm, and held to it until we reached our tents. Before leaving me he tilted his head quizzically. "Was it wise, Roddy, to cart Danzik so close to rescue?"

"He's been teaching me." Rustin's murder had driven thought of learning from my mind. I sighed. "I'll resume my lessons."

"Guard him well." Raeth need not worry; Danzik was chained to a wagon, with three ever-present guards.

My tent spoke loudly of Rustin, but I was so weary I pretended not to notice. Tanner helped me ease off my boots. I thrust off my clothes. He stood by with towels while I lowered myself into the cramped wrought-copper tub. The water was tepid.

After, I shivered but felt better for the cleansing. I doused my candles and drifted into sleep.

Deep in the night I stirred, dreaming of the hunt. Horns blared, beaters shouted. Rust and I raced through the wood, spears poised. A sudden crashing in the brush . . .

The flap burst open. "Arm yourself, my lord!" Kadar, chief of my bodyguards. His garb was disheveled. "Horsemen in the night!" Trumpets bellowed a warning.

I leapt from my bed, grabbed sword and shield. "Who? Where?"

"South of camp. Stay among us." A half-dozen men enclosed me within a bristling spear-wall. The camp was a blaze of lights as sleepy men roused themselves.

I caught sight of a familiar figure. "Uncle Raeth, what's—"

"I don't know. They seldom raid at night, but . . ." He dived into the commotion.

Moments later Captain Tursel spotted us, flung himself from his horse. "My lord king, it's Tantroth. He slipped through the Norland lines."

"Alone?"

"Twenty horsemen. They rode up to our scouts as bold as . . ." Tursel shook his head.

"His army isn't poised to strike?"

"Twenty horse, that's all. His royal guard."

"Bid them welcome." I lowered my shield. "Tanner, my tunic, and be quick." I hesitated. "And my coronet, in the chest. It's wrapped in velvet."

In a few moments, the clatter of massed horse. Tantroth made a show of it, as he'd intended from the start. Racing into

camp in the earliest hours, his way lit by smoking torches, an
army routed out of bed for his welcome. Yes, that was my arrogant sometime vassal.

We waited for him, Raeth and I, with my nobles attending.

All the riders were dressed in Eiber black, even the duke. It
suited his style.

Tantroth reined in smartly, and his stallion reared. He
swung down. Carefully, he slipped his sword into a saddle-
scabbard, handed his dagger to a soldier. He strode toward
me, ignoring my bodyguards. They slunk out of the way.

His hair was grayer, his grizzled face more lined. And he
was thinner. A winter fleeing one's enemies will do that. "My
liege." Dramatically, he sank to one knee.

Uncle Raeth rolled his eyes.

"My Duke Tantroth." I held out a hand; perhaps his lips
brushed it. "We bid you welcome."

"Yes, and all that." He rose. "You summoned me?"

"With your army."

"You've only to command their presence."

I was tired, and not amused. "Very well. Depart, and return
with your company."

An instant's hesitation. His smile broadened. "You have
me, Roddy. I ask leave to confer."

"On how best to reclaim Eiber Castle?"

His eyes turned serious. "How best to repulse Hriskil and
bring peace to your domain."

"We'll speak in the morn." I glanced at Raeth. "Can you
find him a tent?"

Uncle's tone was acid. "No doubt there's room in the alehouse." He trudged off to make arrangements.

ELEVEN

"JESTREL ASKS A word with you," said Anavar, in my tent. "Tanner, have you no sense? Fold it, that it stay smooth."

For a moment I smiled; he sounded so much like Rustin. "The silversmith? Later, perhaps. After my lesson, Tantroth awaits." I laced my boots. Did war consist of stirring battles, or endless conferences? Every time we moved our men, the arrangements wanted hours of conclave and produced flared tempers, soothing words. I might grow old before our campaign was truly under way.

"Don't trust the duke, sir." Anavar looked apprehensive.

"At the moment we're allies." I clapped Anavar's shoulder. "As always, keep from his sight."

"Aye, sir." He settled on a stool. "I was at the alehouse . . ."

"My stipend put to good use, I see."

"The tavernkeeper had a horse. A guest died, leaving it. A stallion." His boot scuffed the floor.

"Of course it costs more than your stipend would allow."

"Considerably." His tone was subdued. "But I hoped . . ."

"You can't judge by a pretty mane, or whether he stamps his hoof. You have to examine the fetlocks, judge his wind, get a look at his teeth . . ."

"Perhaps you'd teach me how." His voice was eager. "This afternoon."

I snorted. "Are all Eiberians so cunning?" I could hardly imagine I'd been so obvious as a boy.

"Does that mean you'll go?"

"I suppose." I strode out, made my way to the wagons, where Danzik the Norlander sat under guard. I climbed in. "Avit, Danzik. Leste memor."

"Avit, Rez." He stretched prodigiously, settled himself. His eyes were somber. "Regre qa se modre Rustin."

"Don't speak of him! No insults or I'll have your tongue!"

Danzik spat. With contempt he said, " 'Regre' . . . 'sorry'."

"Oh." I put my head in my hands. Then, "Regre, Danzik. Rez Caledi regre . . . what I said."

"Qa diche."

"Qa diche. What I said."

Danzik grinned. "Regre qa Hriskil modra rez Caledi." *I'm sorry Hriskil will kill the king of Caledon.*

"Farang vos." I made a rude gesture.

Amenities out of the way, we got down to our lesson.

"TWENTY MEN, WITH me to lead them." Tantroth tried to look modest. "But to smuggle my whole force past the Norland army . . ."

Lady Soushire sliced a wedge of goat cheese.

I said sweetly, "You underrate yourself."

Groenfil rolled his eyes.

"Honeyed words, or truth?" Tantroth's voice was a growl. "Is all Eiber in Norland hands? No, though Hriskil threw ten times my number against me, and led them himself."

"Five," purred Raeth, "not to denigrate your—"

"Were it only three, you ought deem it a miracle, you old sybarite!"

Raeth smiled. "A pity King Freisart's gone. He'd have cherished your company, now you're without a duchy."

"Enough." I slammed my fist on the table; it shuddered. "The issue's how to join our forces."

"Which I spoke to," said Tantroth, "before that senile—"

"*Do you seek my displeasure?*"

After a moment his gaze dropped. "Why, no, Rodrigo."

"Then, don't try me."

"See, Imbar, how he puts upstarts in their place?"

"Nor you, Uncle!" I favored the whole company with a glare.

"My lords . . ." Captain Tursel sounded apologetic, as well he might in such august company. "To what purpose is this speech? Are we to dissolve in acrimony?"

"From the mouths of underlings, eh, Imbar?" But Uncle Raeth's eyes were steely. "If I may speak for the king, my lord Duke, will you join us or no?"

Tantroth ignored Raeth, answered to me instead. "We ought join forces, of course. But pray you, come to me. Combined, we've a chance to clear Eiber. That forces Hriskil to withdraw from Cumber. And he'd hardly attack Castle Stryx while—"

I growled, "If I order your presence?"

"I'd comply; you're my liege. But there are grave problems."

"I've no doubt you can work your way past Hriskil's forces."

"Perhaps. But my soldiers need be paid. Don't roll your eyes; it's an issue. I've lost the bulk of my revenues. And without pay—"

"They fight now, do they not?"

His tone was gentle. "They're in Eiber, my lord. They fight for their land."

Groenfil slammed his fist on the table, spilling wine. "Cowardice, that's what—"

Tantroth's hand flew to his empty scabbard.

"NO!" I shot to my feet. "I won't have it! Do imps dance in your minds? Can you not see this benefits only Hriskil?"

Into the silence Elryc spoke calmly. "What would it take, my lord Tantroth, for you to find a way to join us?"

I stared at my brother, marvelling that he put it so simply, so clearly, when all of us raged like barnyard hounds over a meaty bone.

From Tantroth, a bow of respect, interrupted by a long hacking cough. When at last he drew breath, his face was red. He groped for his wine, downed it in one swallow. "Perhaps if I might assure my men that once you broke the Norland force, you'd not leave Eiber until the duchy was fully restored to its people . . ."

I breathed a sigh of relief. An offer was on the table. Our work could begin.

"COLORFUL IS THE word you seek." Tresa perched comfortably on a rock.

I paced, brooding. "Never forget Tantroth is vicious and cruel. In Stryx he hanged children in the market square."

"You can't hold that against him if—"

"Can't I? He nearly seized my kingdom."

"—if you've made him ally. Did you not decide his sins were forgivable?"

She was right, of course. I couldn't remain united with

Tantroth while nursing grievances. I had put them aside with his renewed oath of fealty.

"Sorry," I muttered. "I didn't sleep well." After the commotion of Tantroth's arrival subsided, I'd lapsed into fitful dreams. And since morn I'd had my lesson, the conference of my nobles, a meet of my council . . .

Tantroth had exacted our commitment to restore him to Eiber Castle and make a strenuous effort to drive the Norlanders from all Eiber. He'd wanted an absolute vow that we'd stay until we succeeded, and I threatened to abdicate before giving it. He ceded the point.

Only then did he commit to maneuver his force past Hriskil's army, to our camp.

"You're sure you want his forces attached to yours?" Tresa looked doubtful.

"You think he'll do mischief?"

"I'm more worried about Hriskil."

"The decision's made, love—Lady Tresa!" I made a jerky reflexive bow of utter confusion, stumbling over my feet in my haste to put distance between us. "I'm sorry—I must speak with Tursel—good day!" I fled to my tent, barely managing not to stumble.

No wonder I was confused, drawn into discussing policy with a *woman*. Of all the presumption! She would overturn all our delicate agreements with her probing questions.

Even if I wished to alter our plans, time pressed. Tantroth was due to leave when darkness fell. Every rutpath of Eiber was his, he said, and he knew its ways in moonlight or dark.

A half hour's pacing my tent brought a semblance of calm. I stepped outside.

Kadar saluted. "My lord, Duke Tantroth asked your whereabouts."

I recoiled. Lord of Nature knew what new concessions he'd demand.

"My lord?" Jestrel was waiting, his tone diffident. "Might I tempt you with my creations?"

I tried to hide a grimace. The last thing I wanted was to examine silver gewgaws I couldn't afford. On the other hand, whatever would keep me from Tantroth's sight . . . "Very well. Bring them."

The silversmith looked crestfallen. "They're laid out in my

tent, my lord. It's not so elegant as yours, but I've refreshments set . . ."

Weekly acts of kindness, Rust had said. Obviously Jestrel yearned to entertain a king. For him it would be a stellar occasion, on which to reminisce over winter fires, and would cost me naught. "Very well."

My bodyguards trailing, Jestrel led me to a threadbare mauve tent near those of my nobles. It hinted of past grandeur; perhaps it was a gift from his patron Freisart.

An anxious servant kept watch outside and seemed much relieved when we appeared. I thrust in my head and understood why; costly silver sculptures were spread about on every surface.

Brusquely, Kadar brushed me aside, peered in, reassuring himself the tent was empty. Jestrel shot me a mute appeal. "Wait outside," I told the guard gruffly, and followed Jestrel within. With a flourish, the silversmith closed the flap.

He'd set two goblets on a tray. I frowned, hoping he knew the proper etiquette. The guest must choose his own glass, and the host drink first, to prove neither wine nor glass was poisoned.

I tried to hide a smile. Jestrel had also found—or hoarded—dried fruits for the occasion, and had piled them on a silver tray. It was to be a feast of sorts, as best as his circumstances would allow.

"Seat yourself, sire." Quickly he brought forth a stool. He filled two crystal goblets with dark red wine. "Would you refresh yourself?" Properly, he held them out for my choice.

My eye roved over his works, scattered about the tent. Animals, decorative objects, reflecting silvers for the bedchamber, all testified to the hand of a brilliant craftsman.

Jestrel saluted me with his glass. "Some think," he said, "objects of beauty need not have purpose. Like the hare, on that bench."

"I suppose one might use it to hold papers in a wind."

"Yes, but it does not itself have utility." He took a dried fruit, offered me from the plate. Dates, dried grapes, pitted cherries, a white fruit I didn't recognize. I took a date. It had been bathed in sugar and was quite good.

"Freisart was fond of these."

"His was a sad end," I said without thinking.

"Lonely and far from home," he agreed. "So, which of my works do you find most appealing?" He held out the tray of delicacies.

"Hmm. I'm not sure. Perhaps the fawn." I examined it, reaching for another fruit. "It has a look about it . . ."

The tent flap swept open. "*There* you are, Rodrigo." Tantroth. "I've been looking—"

Startled, the silversmith snatched up the tray, knocking the fruit from my fingers. "My lord duke—I was—the king was examining—"

"Do I make you nervous?" Tantroth's tone was dry. "I can't imagine why." Idly, he picked up the silver fawn, laid it down. "Might I have some wine while Roddy and I have speech?"

"Certain—I've only two glasses out. But . . ."

"I'll wait." Tantroth took a fruit. Jestrel twitched. A pity, that his long-planned meet with the king be so disrupted.

Chewing, Tantroth gazed at him, picked up the filigree tray. "Beautiful work. Your own design?"

"Yes, my lord."

Tantroth sifted through the delicacies. "Cherries, dates . . ." He came on the white fruit Jestrel had knocked from my fingers.

His manner finally drove me to speech. "My lord duke, I don't stand on ceremony, but, frankly, you interrupted a private—"

He sniffed the fruit, examined it closely. "Almost you make me regret my intrusion." He held out the fruit to Jestrel. "Eat it."

"I don't—thank you, they're for my guests, I've had my fill, and . . ."

I set down my wine. "*Guards!*" Kadar and his troops burst in. "Seize him." I stabbed a finger at Jestrel. "The fruit is poisoned."

"Not poisoned, sire." Tantroth was grave. He held out his palm. "That almond scent? Only one fruit has that aroma, and color. Though I've never seen it dried."

I snapped, "Speak plainly, or be gone!"

"The White Fruit of Chorr, my liege. Had you eaten it, you'd be his servant evermore."

I stared in horror. "But . . . he knocked it from my fingers. If it would make me his servant—"

"Know you not the Power of Chorr? The fruit binds one as servant to the first person his eyes fall on after eating it."

I blinked, still not comprehending.

Tantroth bent close, spoke softly. "Must I spell it out? I came in; had you eaten while looking at me, he'd have lost you."

"I'd have been your servant?" My tone dripped revulsion.

"You'd prefer the silversmith?" His tone was acid. "You, guard. Remove him!"

Kadar waited for my nod of assent, hauled the ashen Jestrel from the tent.

I stumbled out into welcome daylight, my mouth dry. "Why?"

"No doubt he wanted—"

"You, Tantroth. Why stop him? I'd have been yours to command." I started toward my own tent, and he perforce followed.

"Or possibly his. I couldn't risk—no, it's a moment for truth. You do me dishonor, sir."

I stopped, before my tent. "How so?"

"I swore oaths of fealty, did I not? Solemn vows of ancient ritual, binding me as your vassal. It was my duty to save you."

I snorted. "You made war on Caledon, routed me from my castle, killed—"

"Before giving my oath."

I strode through the flap. "You were vassal to my mother, Elena!"

"And I never attacked her. But she was dead; there was doubt you were king or ever would be. I felt free to pursue my interest."

"I'm no newborn. The moment it suits you . . ." I held open the flap for him to depart.

"Fool! Knave!" Tantroth strode my tent from wall to wall, a dangerous fire in his eyes. "Know you naught of Eiber, or of me?" He whirled. "I'm a vassal; you're my liege. I hate it! My hopes for Eiber are shattered. But it was submit or lose all to Hriskil. Look you!" He held up the vile white confection. "Only fruit blessed by the king of Chorr has the power to bind, and consecrated fruit never leaves Chorr. Know you its worth?" He came close. "Shall I eat it, that your fears be stilled?"

"Would you?"

For a time, silence. Then, a crooked smile. "Now that I've challenged you, I'd have to. My pride wouldn't allow less."

"Do it."

His eyes creased. Slowly, with great reluctance, he raised the fruit to his lips.

I stayed his hand. "We thank thee earnestly, lord Duke. Well has thou served Caledon."

"Ah, the high speech, to save an embarrassing moment. I'm not sure I could have done it, my lord. I might have preferred you kill me." He wrapped the fruit in a greasecloth. "We're fortunate I came in search of you. But, did Jestrel serve only himself? Let me have the silversmith for an hour. I'll have truth from him."

"Your ways are too . . . unsubtle for my taste."

"We've no time for subtlety."

I thought on it. Jestrel would have made of me a plaything, a devoted pet. He deserved Tantroth's attentions.

And yet, despite his new-shown loyalty, could I be sure Tantroth would tell me all his torture unveiled? And did I want to forgo the . . . yes, the pleasure of putting the question myself?

"No." It came out a bark, and I tried again. "No, my lord. I pray thee, sit." On my knees, I rummaged through a chest, pulled out a bowl, and a corked ewer of my precious stillsilver. For what I would attempt, water would not answer.

I poured the silver liquid, and immediately it was still.

I set down the ewer, let my palms droop across the bowl. My skin grew warm. Eyes closed, I murmured the familiar words.

The mists blew away, and I stood before the cave. In that far world I sat, composed myself.

My eyes sprang open. "Bring the silversmith."

Tantroth jerked to his feet. He hurried out. In a moment he was back, with my bodyguard and Jestrel.

I said to Kadar, "Leave him."

"But—"

One look was all it required. Hastily, he left.

Jestrel licked his lips. "My gracious lord . . ."

I muttered, and he was silent.

Again, I felt my way through a mist. I'd never wielded the Still so, and was surprised by the certainty that I could. Slowly I groped my way, and, outside the cave, Jestrel was before me.

Greed. Fear.

I slipped within.

A frightened boy in far off Orlot, prenticed to a choleric smith, whose specialty was fine filigree for royal tables.

The boy's first casting, made from collected scrap. A beating from his master. "Remelt it, that it be put to good use."

Stubbornly, other work, until his growing skill was noticed. Then the master smith wanted all.

Ai! Get out of my mind!

A runaway, attaching himself to a caravan. Sleeping with horses, clothes acrawl with vermin, until in a far Ukra town he saw the scarred and battered sign of a silversmith.

I opened an eye. Jestrel was sweating. I snapped, "Tantroth, a chair, under his legs." As if dazed, the silversmith sank into it.

Years of work. A growing reputation. A share in the smithy. Restlessness, a dismay that youth was passing.

A visit from King Freisart, and an invitation. The exiled king had not yet depleted all his coin, and to the earnest smith he seemed the opportunity of a lifetime.

Long years with the ever-more-penniless Freisart. Contempt, alloyed with reluctant affection; the old dethroned monarch had been kind, within his impoverished means. And he'd esteemed Jestrel's talent.

You've no right! Leave me!

I probed deeper, thrusting aside fibrous strands of memory.

Growing desperation. A man must make his mark. Where to settle? How to amass wealth beyond his young dreams?

A visit to Chorr. Introduction, of course, to the king.

Sleepless, sweating nights. Did he dare?

A casual word from the king, and a moment seized. Would you like to see my works, sire? Those pieces I've kept for myself?

Get out!

The king of Chorr himself, impressed by the awesome talent. And then the gamble, staking all on a cast of the bones. Half of what the king saw before him, if only he might . . .

An endless moment of appraisal. Yes, but not while he tarried in Chorr. Handed to him at the border, and he may never return.

Could the king be trusted?

What choice had he?

Half his worldly goods gone. An endless fretting journey

through the mountains, to the remote border. A guard waiting, with a sealed box.

Now, when to use it?

Not on Freisart; the old man owned naught worth the having. Hriskil of the Norlands—what a prize, but the barbarian fool had not the slightest interest in fine silver. He hadn't a chance of seeing the king alone, though he'd tried.

The Ukras tolerated Freisart, fed him, housed him, but even Freisart of Kant never had audience with the Empur himself.

In desperation Jestrel thought of feeding his foul gift to a king's treasure-keeper, and looting a royal house. But where then to flee? And who would protect him against limitless wrath?

Sheer anguish. *Let me die!*

To Caledon. After endless scheming, an audience with Elena. She loved his silver, but wouldn't touch the fruits. She didn't care for sweetmeats.

Despair.

Elena was drawn and pale. Rumors of ill health abounded. What of her son, the whelp—

Please, lord king! Please, gracious sire, humbly I beg you—

—the whelp Rodrigo. An ill-raised lout, to be sure, but—

I never meant you to know!

—he'll be king, unless his mother disowns him.

He's always off riding with his red-haired companion. Civil words in the corridor, to no avail. The boy stalks past with nose in the air.

My palms wavered. I hadn't known I'd met him. It must have been . . . I bent anew to my work.

A visit to Tantroth, but the duke was preoccupied with war and had no time for trinkets.

Years had passed since Chorr. He would have to lower his sights. But he wanted so to be eminent. To have splendid horses and servants. Perhaps a barony, or more; did not the finest hand at silver in all the world deserve recompense?

And so Freisart, old and wheezing, came again to Caledon. A sob. *Please . . .*

If Freisart hadn't died that season, Jestrel would have left him. It was past time.

Rodrigo wasn't much; from all signs he'd be no great loss.

And he barely held his castle. But he wore a crown, and if he thwarted Hriskil . . .

A man might have the prominence he deserved.

Slowly I peeled open my eyes. Tantroth sat deathly still.

"Call the guards. Escort the smith to his tent."

Jestrel wept silent tears.

When he was gone Tantroth asked, "What did you learn?"

"It was no plot of state."

"You read his being?"

A nod. My hands hovered over the viscous bowl.

"I'm impressed, my lord. As you intended." A bow. "With your leave . . ." He strode out.

I bent anew to the stillsilver.

The tent flap jerked open. Tantroth stumbled in, white of face, walking as a marionette. "Rodrigo, what—" It was all he could manage.

My eyes remained closed. "The fruit."

With a convulsive motion the duke reached into his shirt, dropped the greasecloth before me. Reluctantly I forced my fingers from the bowl. I opened the cloth to see the fruit, rewrapped it. "Thank you."

"Aye." A futile attempt at an airy wave. "Good-day, my lord." He abandoned the field.

OUTSIDE, THE YOUNG voices chattered.

"Anavar!"

"Sir?" He poked his head into the tent. "Lord of Nature!" He ran to me.

"A stool. Set it outside." Weak as a kitten, I clung to him, managed a few steps to sunshine.

"Are you hurt? Can you rise?"

"I wielded the Still."

He settled at my feet. "Tantroth looked like death. Did you have words?"

"I told you to keep from his sight."

"I doubt he saw me."

"He had a . . . demonstration." Perhaps henceforth Tantroth would feel less contempt when he thought of his king.

"Not like—when Genard . . ."

"I didn't torment him." Nor Jestrel, though I ought have. *Ill raised lout? No great loss?* He'd regret his words. His thoughts. Jestrel would know agony beyond the worst dreams of the night. When I was through he'd bless the death I allowed him.

"Roddy?" My brother, with his young shadow. "You're well enough to talk?"

I nodded.

"Genard, fetch him chill water from the stream." Without a murmur of protest, the stableboy ran off.

Elryc ducked into the tent, emerged with a second stool, plunked it next to mine. "I'm worried. This adventure with Tantroth . . ."

"It's the best compact we could get." First Tresa, now him. Would I have no peace?

"Our striving's become about Eiber, not Caledon."

I said, "Eiber is of Caledon."

"Oh, of course. But for Tantroth's three thousand men, you commit your whole force to his salvation. What of our own?"

I opened an eye. "Aren't you a trifle late?"

Elryc blushed. "He argued persuasively."

"Don't fret, brother. We do what we may."

"Roddy . . . ?" His voice was tremulous. "It's so hard for you without Rustin."

I lurched to my feet, stumbled into the tent, sank on the bed.

His voice followed. "I'm sorry. Truly!"

Suddenly I was encircled, by him and Anavar, and Genard. I covered my face.

"Give him privacy!"

"Get out of my—"

"Don't spill it!"

Despite myself, my lips twitched. "Listen to you. A worse gaggle of servants I've never . . ." I couldn't go on.

Anavar perched on the bed, cross-legged. "My lord, should we never mention him?"

"We won't," vowed Elryc.

"You must," Genard said.

We stared.

Elryc's vassal fidgeted, but his tone was stubborn. "You don't make him think of Rustin. He does that each day, if not every hour. My ma said sorrow festers if it don't see light."

Silence.

I sighed. "She's wrong. I'm king, and have no time for grief." I wiped my eyes. "It's just you caught me unaware."

"Father says—"

I groaned. I'd never met Anavar's father, and could easily loathe him.

"Death is like a blow to the eye. It's a goodly time before you see the world straight."

"Say you I don't see where I go?"

"It's a figure of speech. It means—"

"I know!" I cuffed him, but lightly. "Don't think me stupid."

He held my eye. "Did I deserve that, or was it cruelty?"

I chewed my lip, afraid of the answer. "Cruelty. I just wielded the Still, and it wells within me. Did I hurt you?"

He evaded my question. "May have a boon in lieu of pardon?"

"I suppose."

And so we went to the alehouse, to consider a stallion.

"I WANT HER returned to Cumber," said Uncle Raeth. He squinted against the setting sun. I shivered, still weak from my bout with the Still. The long walk to the tavern hadn't been wise.

"Speak to me, not the king." Tresa's eyes flashed.

Raeth snapped, "You order it?" I could have sworn his hackles raised.

"If you meant me to fear you, Grandfather, you ought have begun earlier." She planted a kiss on the tip of his nose.

He made a show of annoyance as he wiped it off, but failed to hide his smile. "You see, my liege? You failed to command her, when you could. I am aggrieved."

I rubbed my stomach, still full of Raeth's provender. "Think you she'd obey me, when love won't sway her?"

"She has love as well for—don't step on my foot, Tresa, my bones ache enough!" He sighed. "I'll face my death if I must. I won't face her death."

"Bosh," she said, cutting us off. "You'd rather I be Hriskil's whore?"

"Tresa!" The old man was scandalized.

"If the Norlanders tried to make me so, think I wouldn't die?" She looked from one to the other of us, crossly. "So I can't swing a mace with skill, or set a pike. Is that what you do?"

"I'm old, and command—"

"Just so. I'd be far more use here than at home."

I spluttered, "A noblewoman in camp? Outrageous!"

"Very well, I'll tell that to Lady Soushire. I believe she's in her tent." Tresa stalked off, her skirts billowing.

"Tresa, come back!"

She swept on.

I shrugged at Raeth and raised my voice. "My lady, I pray thee, return." She halted, placed hands on hips, regarded us quizzically. I put on my most courteous smile, and she retraced her steps.

Tresa would defy Raeth's authority if need be, and I wasn't about to test my own. It appeared she would remain.

I'D SELECTED A choice apple, and was on my way to visit Ebon.

"King?"

I pulled Bollert's fingers from my sleeve. "You're not to touch me."

"Aye, m'lord. Jestrel weepin' and says you'll kill him." The lights of a hundred campfires glinted from his eyes.

"He's under guard. How did you—" My eyes narrowed. "You spelled the sentries?"

An embarrassed shrug. "Didn' do harm. Left everythin' as it was." His words were quick. "No stealin'. Hadda know. Was it 'cause of Tanner an' me? His li'l squirrel an' all? We put him in noose?"

"For that you broke into—" I controlled myself. "No, it's not because of you." I collared him. "What must I do to banish your warped Power? Hood you? Put out your eyes?" I shook him. "You begged to be let free, and I—"

"King, didn't harm, didn't take nothin'." He was sweating. "Search me." He pawed at his clothes. "Didn' tell Jestrel nothin'!"

"It was that important you know?"

He started to speak, made a hopeless gesture. "All my life, never had more 'n copper coin. Hadda get boys t' steal. Wasn' much. Eggs, sometimes chickens. Never killed no one. Don' want Jestrel dead 'cause of me."

"Bah. You'd have seen Tanner dead."

"Steada what?" His tone was contemptuous. "Confess an' hang?"

"A thief with morals? Miracles abound."

"Don' understan'."

"Nor do I. What exactly did you do to the guards?"

Bollert scuffed his torn boots in the dirt. "Went up to 'em. Looked at 'em, asked proper. They let me in. After, thanked 'em, asked 'em not to tell king." He colored.

I waited.

"Lor' King, maybe wasn't right I made 'em, but I tol' you, didn' I?"

"Argh." I was at a loss. Rust, what would—"You like working with horses, don't you?"

"Aye. When they be fed, their minds calm . . . they have peace and like it."

"If you spell anyone—anyone, Bollert, do you hear?—without my permission, I'll take you away from horses. You'll wash clothes with the women and never touch a horse again!"

Had I threatened him with hooding, my words couldn't have had more effect. He cringed. "Won't do it, King! Never!"

"Remember when next you're tempted."

TORCHES SPUTTERED AND smoked. Quietly, Tantroth's company of horsemen gathered.

Tresa and I walked hand in hand among the pickets. Kadar and three guards trailed. Would I ever be free of them?

While a black-clad soldier held the reins of Tantroth's mount, the Duke strode among his men, tugging at cinches, checking bridles, tucking kitbags.

"What if he's taken?" Tresa's voice was no more than a whisper.

I said, "I cede Eiber, and go home." Without Tantroth, I'd have no choice.

"Really?"

"What else? I'd—" She squeezed my fingers, and I startled. "I'd be left . . . Hriskil would—aargh." I pulled free my hand. "I know not courtly ways," I blurted. "Don't mortify me."

She caught my hand, tickled my palm. I managed not to yelp.

"Roddy . . ." She giggled. "Are you afraid of me?"

"Of course I am." My voice was gruff. "How often must I tell you—"

"Here, let me show you." She took my head between her hands, brought it to her own. Our lips touched.

My heart did a somersault. I wrapped my arms around her, hoping my guards had enough sense to stand well away.

A cough. "I wouldn't dream of interrupting." Tantroth's tone was dry.

I thrust us apart. "We're not—it's just—what do you want?"

"To take leave."

"Again?" I couldn't help how it sounded. The duke and I had bid a formal adieu in my tent, an hour past.

"Since you ventured out . . ." A formal bow, which I had little choice but to return.

"Fare thee well, Tantroth."

He snapped his fingers to his groom, took his reins, swung into the saddle with a grunt. "Two days hence. Be set to march." His hand raised in a signal.

I expected a gallop, a swirl of dust, but they left at the walk, silent as ghosts. I groped again for Tresa's hand, held it in silence.

It wasn't 'til the horsemen were out of sight that I realized they'd set off in the wrong direction. I sputtered. "Eiber . . . the pass . . . Caledon—"

"They won't go directly, lest Norland scouts observe." Tresa's tone was matter-of-fact. "He'll circle the town, through the hills."

"He'll be all night." I felt a reluctant respect for his courage, and stamina.

"No doubt." She shivered. "I'm chilled, Roddy. Would you join me in my tent?"

"No! I mean, thank you, but . . . it wouldn't be meet."

"Poor Roddy. You'll have to get over it, if we're to campaign together." A quick kiss, full on my lips. "I enjoyed our walk." And she was gone.

The guards followed me to my tent, took up stations outside. Within, a sleepy Tanner roused himself to help me pull my boots, and set out my basin.

I sent Tanner to rest in a tarped wagon. In my night clothes, I fell on my soft bed.

Tresa's face floated before me.

Inflamed, I couldn't sleep. We'd held hands, embraced,

kissed. Was it possible she felt other than revulsion at my visage? I felt again the soft pressure of her bosom, tossed and turned in rising passion. At length I surrendered to boyhood, the only man in camp—in all Caledon—denied a woman.

TWELVE

I PASSED TWO days in lethargic fog, barely leaving my tent. I didn't demand solitude; on the contrary I welcomed Anavar, my brother Elryc, even Lady Soushire and Groenfil. But the persistent mist and damp were apt accompaniment to the haze of my mind.

I had no doubt that my probe of Jestrel was the cause. By cleaving the shield that cloaked him, I was assured, as I couldn't be otherwise, that only greed propelled him to his folly. Yet it left me listless, and I'd made myself worse by tramping about the camp, buying Anavar a splendid new mount, courting Tresa, banqueting with Raeth.

I tried, the second day, to speak to Mother and my grand-sires, but to no avail. It would be days before I could wield the Still anew.

Not that I had need.

Anavar galloped about, risking bones on wet ground, until I could stand no more. One of us must have sense for both. He was sullen about my rebuke, but I prided myself in paying no heed, and deemed that an act of kindness. Eiberians, all knew, opened their hearts for all to see; good or bad, I would know Anavar's moods. He wasn't circumspect, as I. Perhaps he could learn from my example.

Near dusk the third day, Tantroth came storming through the wood, dragging his carts along a hastily cleared trail. We'd had scant notice of his approach, and that thanks to the scouts he sent to forewarn us. I began to see how he'd evaded Hriskil these many months.

We spent a weary night organizing ourselves for the morn.

"What of Danzik?" asked Lord Groenfil. "Every man who guards him is one less to fight."

"Danzik rides with us." I'd grown accustomed to—no, I looked forward to—our daily lessons. I'd uncovered in myself a facility for the uncouth Norland speech. Today, for the first time, my thoughts had formed themselves in the foreign tongue.

"And the silversmith? Hang him, or send him to Cumber to await your pleasure." Groenfil brushed his cloak, set it carefully on his shoulders. "What's he done, by the way?"

"Offended me." I left it at that.

Deep into the night I plotted my revenge on Jestrel, while his silver falcon stared accusingly.

Flaying might suffice; I needn't stand near to hear his screams. Burning, if I could devise a fire slow enough.

I sat brooding.

Seldom had I felt so humiliated. Jestrel had had the power to bind me, and with me, Caledon. Yet he'd long scorned me as an unworthy prize, to be seized only in desperation.

After a time I sat on the chill floor of my tent, aware that his true crime, in my eyes, was his contempt, his reluctance to offer me the fruit of submission until all else failed. At length I roused myself. "Bring the silversmith."

I was shocked at the change three days had wrought. He stumbled in, haggard, his clothes hanging, deep orbs under his haunted eyes. Kadar's men watched him, hands never far from their blades.

"Leave us."

When they were gone I sliced through his ropes. He rubbed his reddened wrists.

"Gracious lord, if I may—"

"Don't speak." I took the better stool, gave him the other. "Know you I roamed your mind?"

He nodded. "It was as . . ." He colored. "When a woman is forced—"

"I know you, perhaps as well as you know yourself." In his mind I'd found fear, greed, vast yearning to be thought worthy. "For years you schemed, Jestrel, to raise yourself through the Fruit of Chorr. How old are you?"

"I was born two years after your mother, the gracious—"

"So much time wasted. You're past fifty, but you've still got your teeth. You've time yet, Jestrel, if imps don't sicken you."

He said cautiously, "Time to . . . ?"

"To make yourself the world's most renowned silversmith. To gain wealth, admirers, standing. Perhaps even a barony. Loan money to a king, that should do it."

"But I . . ." He dared not speak of it.

"Yes. I pardon you. Your penalty is that you must achieve prominence on your own, by your talent. Not by enslavement. Settle yourself, in any royal town. Visitors will hear of you. Word will spread. Send small, exquisite gifts to royalty who visit your monarch."

"But the cost, a proper shop . . ."

"Work in a barn at first, with a churl as bellows boy. They'll find you. Everyone goes to the Empur of the Ukras, soon or late. Or try the Warthen of the Sands."

He whispered, "Think you I'd succeed?"

I lifted the exquisite falcon he'd given me. "Its wings are poised to beat, its beak to stab. Make nothing common, Jestrel. There's witchery in your work."

He dropped his head. Presently a tear splashed to his lap.

"And don't sell yourself cheap." I said. "Make barons and earls pay what you're worth. The higher they pay, the more they'll value it."

He fell to his knees. "Rodrigo, if you toy with me . . . don't."

"You're free to go. Settle where you like. Anywhere but Stryx."

"PIR?" DANZIK ASKED in his uncouth tongue, as we sat together in the jouncing wagon. "*Why* do you chase Hriskil to your death? Why not stay and wait?"

I sought the Norlandic words. "Eiber is my land." Mine to defend, the cost of my vassals' fealty.

He grinned. "Tantroth says not."

I shrugged. *He set aside his aspirations,* I wanted to say, but such subtle speech was beyond me.

Perhaps Danzik understood. He said seriously, "Hriskil will kill you, Caled king."

"Regra vos?" *Will that sorrow you?*

"Quix iot." He leaned forward and shrugged, hands in air. "Quix." He did it again. Then he put thumb and forefinger together, an inch apart. "Iot."

I smiled. Quix iot. *Perhaps a little.* "Pir?"

"Because you learn quickly." It was a moment before I realized he'd spoken Norlandic. Perhaps he said truth.

"Tell me." I took a moment to form the strange words. "Why does Hriskil want Caledon?"

He spoke long and volubly, and his face gained color. He
slowed, and repeated himself several times.

When all was done I thought I had the gist of it. Stripped of
self-justification, his answer seemed to be: because it was
there.

ALONG THE TRAIL from Pezar into Eiber, we saw not a single
Norlander. By noon Tantroth assured us we crossed ground
Hriskil's scouts had roamed two days past.

I took stock. Eiber Castle was a day's fast ride, by horse.
Three days or more, for our army. From the castle to the sea,
another day by horse.

Hriskil would meet us on ground he favored, well beyond
the castle. And if he slipped behind us and broke through the
scant force we'd left at the pass, all Cumber was his.

Groenfil and Tantroth were as men possessed. Their scouts
and patrols roamed in constant search of the Norland foe,
while Tursel rode our line, keeping us together. I asked to
help, but my captain's look held such dismay that I subdued
my pride and rode instead with Anavar.

The Eiberian's young stallion was a match for Ebon himself, and my baron was beside himself with pride and joy.
Constantly he fiddled with cinches, patted the pommel, adjusted his stirrups until he drove me to distraction. Thrice
harsh words sprang to my lips; twice I swallowed them, con-
gratulating myself. The third time I was savage and reduced
him to tears.

"MY LORD, HE'S out there." Almost, Tantroth sniffed the late
afternoon's wind. "I know it."

We'd wound our way from the high pass. The terrain
smoothed and settled into a high plateau, and the pine forests
gave way to imperious oaks that fought a slow, tenacious battle with stubborn stands of beech.

We rode, walked and rolled in uneasy silence. Danzik sat
alert in his wagon, eyes roving from shrubs to hillside.

Quietly, Tursel issued extra arrows to the archers, set pikemen to walk alongside so that, were we ambushed, the archers
might be protected while they loosed their deadly volleys.

Our scouts ranged far and met no foe.

At last the majestic oaks gave way to meadows, and Tursel

chose our camp. The nobles' tents were all set in the center: Raeth and Imbar's, Lady Soushire's, Groenfil's, Tresa's, my own. Elryc asked leave to spend the night with me; no doubt it meant Genard also, but I acquiesced. I'd vented my cruelty enough for one day. I sent Anavar delicacies from my wooden box, but had no reply.

My brother watched from the corner. "What are you about, Roddy?"

I settled myself before the bowl. "A talk with Mother." I poured water, waited for it to still.

Nothing. I could see no cave, not even mist. I sighed. After I'd tormented the truth from Tanner, it had been five days before I'd seen my power return.

"Roddy, don't let me be taken." Abruptly, Elryc's voice was tremulous.

"I won't. Did I not promise Hester? And if you are, I won't rest 'til you're free. Our lives are as one. By the True, I so swear."

He calmed himself, and we settled to sleep. I was weary, and Elryc's thrashing about was a trial.

In the darkest hours, shouts and alarums.

I sat bolt upright, knocking Elryc's arm aside. "What—"

Snores, from my bed and the corner.

I thrust on boots and cloak, peered out. A tent blazed in the night; ineffectual men ran up with buckets. From the heavens, stars fell. I muttered words to dispel demons.

Kadar thrust me past a campfire. "Stay under cover, sire! Behind a wagon, or—"

"Who—"

"Fire arrows!" Even as he spoke, blazing barbs fell among us.

I dashed into the tent, roused Elryc and Genard. "Hurry!" We raced to a wagon, threw ourselves behind. I cannoned into a dark figure, fell heavily, head throbbing.

"Sorry, my lord."

"Anavar?" I rubbed my skull.

"Stay low." Ignoring his own advice, he peered over the sideboard.

I pulled him down, threw a protective arm over his shoulders. "I need you alive."

His look of gratitude caught my throat. I said gruffly,

"About today . . . I was tired and sore." I knew it wasn't enough. "At least this time it was only words."

"It's all right, sir. Think you they'll attack?"

"At night?" I shook my head. "They but harass us." A clever tactic; it kept us all awake, and caused us loss. Two wagons were ablaze.

"Groenfil's lost his tent." He gestured to the flames.

"No doubt Larissa will offer hospitality." Together we grinned at the ribald image. "Where's your bed?"

"With Tursel." He made a face.

I said carefully, "No one will take Rustin's place. Sometimes Elryc and Genard will join me, but if you care to share my tent—"

"Accepted." He wrung my hand. "I was worried you'd still be angry. I couldn't help myself. Edmund is so new to me—"

"Edmund?"

"My stallion."

A horse with a human name. Odd folk, Eiberians. I hoped the horse wouldn't expect to be seated at table.

THE MORNING SUN shone pale and cool.

"They passed our patrols?" My face was red.

Tursel looked abashed. Tantroth shifted uneasily. "We're a large camp. Had they come any closer we'd have seen—"

"Three wagons torched, all of us without sleep . . ." I waved in irritation. "How is it they find us, and we don't come on them?"

"I don't know." Tantroth looked cross. "You see what Eiber's been up against?"

I circled Ebon, checking his tack, trying to be thorough without seeming like Anavar. Last night, after the excitement died down my vassal had run to fetch his blanket and curled up in the corner of my tent near Genard.

I was certain I was making a mistake. A king ought live in regal solitude, not appear common. Yet Anavar was my ward, and how could I deny my brother Elryc? And where he went, followed Genard. I sighed. Perhaps I ought worry less about appearance, more about ruling well.

One by one Tursel's patrols reported. No enemy in sight. Fresh track, to the west. Day-old horse dung ahead, to the east.

Once more we lurched into motion.

Uncle Raeth rode up, slipped between me and Anavar. "Well, my boy, we'll see Norlanders this day."

"Think you so?"

"I'm sure of it. Any longer and we'd gain too much ground. Hriskil won't let us seize Eiber Castle and drive him from the duchy, else from Eiber Castle we'd hinder his campaign against Caledon. No, if Hriskil doesn't give battle today, he's already slipped past us and gone for Cumber, to put an end to it."

I reached across to pat his knee. "He wouldn't dare, Uncle. We're too large a force between him and Ghanz."

Raeth snorted. "He's troops aplenty to thwart us *and* besiege Cumber, with careful generalship." He drew his cloak tighter, despite the warming day.

"I'm glad, though," Raeth added, "that we fight each for his lord." We'd decided so in our conference back in Pezar. Lady Soushire's men would fight under her appointed commander, Groenfil would lead his own. And so for Cumber, and Eiber, and my men of Stryx under Tursel. It made for better discipline, despite my dreams of a united army.

"Fight each for his lord," I said to Raeth, "or run away each with his lord."

He raised an eyebrow. "You think that will—"

"After Llewelyn abandoned the Keep, I trust none but you." After a moment I added, "And Groenfil, I think. He'd tell me to my face, were he to withdraw."

"That leaves Tantroth and Larissa."

"Lady Soushire frets that Mar is at her doorstep. As for Tantroth . . ." I left it at that. Still, he'd made me a present of my freedom from the White Fruit. Perhaps he'd fight as a vassal ought.

"I worry for Imbar," said Uncle. "I'm older than I care to admit, and he's no youngsire. Yet he rides in all weather and makes no complaint."

I muttered something civil.

"I know you don't like him, Roddy." We rode on. "I'd have declared for you without Rustin's . . . sacrifice. It was mischief on Imbar's part. I was quite put out."

"That he strayed?"

"That he used meanly a soul as great as Lord Rustin."

I swallowed.

"There, my boy, I shouldn't have mentioned it. Think of the banquet we'll make when this is done. I'll start with tortoise soup, I think. Do you like shallots? And there's a trick with roast hare . . ." He prattled on, and despite my melancholy, my mouth watered.

SCOUTS CAME RACING along our line. They'd found the Norlanders moving west, as were we. Hriskil was fleeing before us.

"He is not." Tantroth was pale. He held a handcloth tightly wrapped, and coughed into it. "He draws us to the ground on which he'd fight." An aide thrust a cloak over his shoulders. "Thank you, Azar."

Larissa said, "Shall we turn tail? Let him pursue us."

Groenfil shook his head. "There's no suitable ground twixt here and Pineforest, unless you'd fight among the trees."

"Give chase," Imbar said, "at sober pace. Don't commit unless we approve the terrain."

I had to admit it made sense. And so we formed ourselves into companies, trod onward. Archers marched with full quivers. I rode with one hand on my scabbard, shield over my forearm. Kadar coaxed me into a helmet, but the air was dank and I sweated profusely. After a time I set it aside.

As the sun drifted westward I spurred to the head of our line, where Tursel sat quietly in the saddle. His horse nibbled the grass of a steep ridge overlooking a wide rolling meadow. Rocky hills protected our left. I said, "Here, Captain."

"We'd hold high ground, but would Hriskil meet us?" He peered round. "Our left's secure; Norlanders would break arms and legs rushing down that hill. Our right flank is the road, but see where it runs through that stand of trees? If we present our flank at the far edge of the field, Hriskil could come fast on our flank, but he couldn't spread himself wide."

We pondered.

"What's over that hill?" I pointed straight ahead, to a small rise at the far end of the meadow.

Tursel beckoned to the nearest scout, a small, wiry fellow, once of Cumber. "Reconnoiter the lay of the land." He pointed. "Take care."

The man saluted, galloped down the ridge, across the plain.

"My lord, you shouldn't tarry at a point of peril."

"Lord of Nature, Tursel, we can see near half a league in any direction." The scout shrank steadily as he rode off to the rise.

"Not over those hills to the left, or past the trees alongside the road. Norlanders could be upon us in . . ."

"Half an hour. I could crawl back to our troop faster."

The scout slowed his mount to a trot, worked his way up the rise. Abruptly he reined in, stared downward for a moment, hauled his mount about and raced across the plain. My spine tingled.

It was long moments before he was near enough. "Norlanders! About a thousand. They've made a rough camp. Below the rise, the land levels again. There are woods five hundred paces beyond. Their camp's near the rise. No defenses to speak of."

"Let's fall on them!" I leaned forward in the saddle, as if to charge.

"It might be a lure, sire." To the scout, "Did they see you?"

"I think not."

"I ought see." Tursel chewed his lip. "Come with me." For a breathless moment I thought he meant me, but he spoke to the scout. Together they rode across the plain, leaving me with Kadar.

At the foot of the far rise Tursel dismounted, handed his reins to the scout, trudged slowly up the hill. A good distance from the top he dropped to his knees, began to crawl.

Ever so cautiously he raised his head, gazed intently at the enemy camp.

Kadar said, "Stay back, my lord. If you're killed, Caledon falls."

"If I turn coward, who will follow me?"

"Will Hriskil himself lead the Norland charge? Did Danzik?"

"No, and look what happened—" I sighed. "I won't lead the charge, but I must be seen in battle."

"Amidst us." He gestured at his cohort of guards.

"Very well." I squinted. Tursel hurried down the hill. "Enough. He's coming. Wait here; they'll hear your horses!" Alone, I guided Ebon down the ridge, met Tursel in the plain. "What are—"

He rode past me, mouth set. I wheeled Ebon and followed. Tursel didn't slow 'til he reached the ridge. It was hard work steering our mounts up the steep incline, and it wasn't until we reached the top that I soothed Ebon with a pat, and spoke.

"How many? What were they doing?"

Tursel hurled his helmet into the dust. "You're king of Caledon, and ride alone into the field! Do I serve a simpleton?"

I gaped.

"I'm done, Rodrigo. I'll serve Raeth, or go home to Cumber. I won't serve a monarch who values himself as nothing!"

Kadar said nothing, but nodded firmly.

I gulped. "Captain . . ." A deep breath. "I ask thy pardon. Ah, humbly. Yes. Humbly ask." I tried to meet his eye. "I won't do it again. I'll ride where you advise."

"And in battle? At the first sound of horns you'll—"

I cried, "In battle too." My face was crimson. "It's only that I want—wanted—I'll let you protect me, sir."

"You swear so?" His glare didn't waver.

Now he saw my tears; he couldn't humiliate me more if he cut a switch. "Yes, Captain. By the Still."

"Very well, my liege."

I let them lead me back to our column.

WE CLUSTERED IN the rutted road. Tursel debated with himself. "Groenfil's horse will lead, from the left, by the hill. Tantroth's cavalry will file down the road past us, and charge from our right. They'll converge in the center."

I found it hard to concentrate. "Cavalry only?"

"For the speed of it. We'd be hours sending all our men down the ridge, marching them across the plain to the rise. We'd be noticed."

"Archers?" I'd snatched sleep the past night, despite the flame arrows. Why was I exhausted and befogged?

"I'll send a company ahead of the horse. They'll stop just short of the rise."

Were we taking too many precautions? "Surely this isn't Hriskil's main camp."

Tantroth bestirred himself. "Hardly. A thousand men at most."

And so confident they hadn't fortified their camp. We'd teach them better respect for Caledon.

"If you approve, sire . . ." The captain looked impatient. "We'd best get started." It would be near dusk, when we plunged over the rise to attack.

"Very well."

Tanner tugged at my sleeve, with a skin of watered wine. I drank greedily. The wine added welcome flavor to the chill water, and wasn't strong enough to fuddle me.

He stepped back, as Anavar sought me. "I'll ride with Groenfil's troop," said the Eiberian. It was half statement, half plea.

Should I give as I got, or as I'd hoped for?

I sighed. In Eiber, Anavar was fighting for his homeland. I couldn't deny him.

He waited, face fervent, body dancing.

I nodded.

With a bound, he was on Edmund, and gone.

As quietly as they were able, Groenfil's troop set off for their post on our left. Horses snorting, men trying not to jangle in their stirrups, they assembled across the brow of the ridge. Tantroth's horsemen filed past, filling the right of our line. Immediately Raeth's men on foot rushed down the road to guard our far flank.

So far we'd committed only our horse, but Soushire's troops and those of Stryx would assemble at the ridge when battle had commenced, as counter, if the Norlanders were reinforced. As it now stood, the engagement wouldn't be much more than a skirmish.

Tursel had bidden me stay within our main body of troops, on the road, and ride nowhere without my bodyguards. Specifically he barred me from the copse through which the road passed, that Cumber guarded as our flank. I pleaded with him to let me see the battle. He allowed me the edge of the ridge, but no further.

I chafed under his constraints, but obeyed them. It brought an odd comfort, as if Rust rode yet at my side.

As quietly as they might, our horsemen clambered down the ridge, reassembled at the foot of the plain.

At least I wasn't alone in my exclusion. Elryc sought me out, as did Tresa. The four of us—one must never forget Genard—huddled together at the top of the ridge, overlooking the field. I was in a fretful mood, and so was Elryc.

Uncle Raeth, on a sturdy brown gelding, trotted back and forth along the road. Our vantage point, at the center of the ridge, was as convenient a place as any for him to quarter himself, and so it was to us he returned from each jaunt.

A handful of scouts lay on their bellies at the top of the far rise. Occasionally one of them, ever so cautiously, raised his head to peer at the Norland camp.

A company of our archers trudged across the field.

Groenfil's horsemen rode at the walk, as quietly as they might, that the sound of their approach not carry over the rise to the Norland camp.

"When will they sound the charge, Roddy?" Elryc danced from foot to foot.

"How do I know?" I tried not to sound irritable. "When Tursel gives the signal." Increasingly weary, I tried to goad my thoughts.

Suddenly one of our scouts at the ridge crawled backward, leaped to his feet, ran windmilling toward our advancing horsemen. I tensed. "What—"

Captain Tursel spurred forward. They met; Tursel leaned over the pommel. Abruptly he reined about, raced to a captain of horse, conferred. The rider wheeled and raced toward our command post on the ridge.

Tursel raised his hand to signal the charge.

A flock of swift birds shot from the hills to our left.

Not birds.

Arrows, swarms of them. They fell among Lord Groenfil's horsemen. The stony hill was crawling with Norland archers, who'd climbed over the bristling rock. Horses screamed. Men and mounts toppled.

Tursel sounded the charge.

A well-trained archer could shoot an arrow every three breaths. If anything, the Norlanders were more swift; the skies were near black with their barbs.

Should I order a counterattack? Climbing the hill against the archers above would be suicidal.

Tursel's courier reached the rise. His mount struggled upward, fell heavily. The rider jumped off, scrambled the rest of the way. It was Azar, Tantroth's aide. "My lord, the Norland camp is reinforced. Troops are pouring out of the wood beyond. Tursel says to send down the foot soldiers!"

"By the time they cross the plain, the battle will be over."

Uncle Raeth ran to us. "What's this? Withdraw the cavalry, while we may!"

"Too late." Our charging horsemen plunged over the far rise, raced beyond our sight toward the Norland camp.

"Call them back!" His bony fingers gripped my arm.

"Tursel's in charge." My tone was bitter. "I'm only allowed to watch!" The unfairness of it rose in my gorge.

Dozens of our horsemen lay dead on the plain.

"Kadar, send word to the captain of foot soldiers. Form a line of advance at the foot of the ridge. Hurry. Shields high to the left, against the arrow swarm."

"Aye, my lord. Stay in this spot." He rushed off.

"Genard!" I was near beside myself. "Any kind of a bowl, and clear water. Hurry!"

He gaped. With sudden understanding, he ran.

I jumped off Ebon, tied him to a tree, used my boot to scrape a spot clean and level.

"Roddy, what are you about?"

"I'll ask Mother!" Our attack was a shambles. I needed her advice, her experience. I paced with increasing unease until Genard came racing back, out of breath.

"The bowl's plain and had soup. I rinsed it, but—"

I snatched it from his hand, set it on the level ground. Genard poured.

"Keep your voices low." I sat cross-legged, waited for the water to settle. I threw my hands atop the bowl.

Hoping, praying, I muttered the words of encant.

Nothing.

I bowed my head, screwed shut my eyes, tried harder. Time had passed; I was rested. Surely if I strained to my utmost . . .

"Roddy, they attack our flank! Call back the foot soldiers!"

I bent anew to my task.

"*Roddy!*" Uncle Raeth was frantic. "We've no time. Look. Thousands, pouring from the wood!"

"Why didn't our scouts . . ."

"They're incompetent, or worse. They were Tursel's choosing, not mine." His face was choleric.

From the battlefield below, screams.

"Tursel's your own man, Uncle."

"Before you corrupted him!"

I was speechless.

Larissa stalked across the road. "Enough, Roddy. We've lost; call it off. I depart for Soushire within the hour."

"Traitor!"

She slapped me.

Instantly Kadar's men seized her. I beckoned them let her go.

Elryc was in tears. "What's come over us? The foe is near; we can't afford to quarrel!"

"Oh!" I sank to the ground. "Uncle, it's the Rood of the Norlands! It sows confusion!" But that meant Hriskil himself was before us. And he wouldn't take the field without a strong force.

"Nonsense. If you knew what you were doing—" Grumbling, Raeth stalked off to his post further down the road, at what would now be our rear guard.

I placed hands over bowl. If ever in my life I must wield the Still, it was now. I said the words.

Again I spoke them.

And once more, with greatest fervor.

Nothing.

I rose to my feet. Oddly, a great peace descended over me. "Kadar, have the hornsmen blow retreat. Send word to Tursel, and Groenfil. Azar—" This to Tantroth's aide, who'd remained with us—"Bid my lord Tantroth withdraw on the instant. Hurry." I whirled. "Genard!"

The boy bounded forward.

"Tell Raeth: a rear guard action, 'til our men are over the ridge, and assembled on the road. Then we fall back toward Pezar."

Elryc said urgently, "Roddy, are you sure? We might—"

"Years ago Mother said the Still might counteract the Rood. Without it we grope in dark."

"We're confused and irritable, yes. But Tursel may prevail."

"No." I spoke with the relief of assurance. "Why didn't our scouts find the archers, or give warning of the Norlanders massing on our flank? Why, if not for the Rood, did we choose battle at so foolhardy a spot? Why are we at each other's throats?" I swung into my saddle. "Turn the wagons about! Elryc, Tresa, up the road with you. Quick, clear the ridge; our returning cavalry will be upon us!" I lashed Ebon, raced up our line. The road would be clogged beyond redemption unless someone took charge.

I slammed a frantic soldier aside with my shield, threaded my way to the wagons. "Get the carts turned or pull them off the road, lest they trap our men!"

Yeomen milled about. I stood high in my stirrups. "Captains, stand forward! You, gather your men, start them east at fast march. You, likewise. Lady Soushire's troops, assemble to the left. Cumber to the right!"

Behind me, down the road, cries and shouts. My spine prickled. I turned Ebon. Cumber's rear guard was giving way, far sooner than it ought.

A courier spurred up the ridge, his mount foaming. "Rodrigo! My lord!" He hauled on the reins. "What do you? Tursel needs the foot soldiers below!"

I snarled, "We retreat! Tell him to withdraw!"

"Groenfil's men are enmeshed. Tursel is desperate to clear them a path." The courier danced in his saddle. "Tursel says, 'Rodrigo, countermand your order!' "

"I will not!" I drew myself up. "Pull the archers back to the ridge; let them cover our horsemen's retreat from here. Tell Tursel he has a tenth of an hour's candle to free Groenfil."

"You abandon your men!"

I'd just said the contrary. Damn the man for—

It was the Rood. It drove us to crossed swords.

"Give my command, and be quick!" I beckoned a handful of soldiers. "Free that wagon! Move! You, in black! Your duke will be along presently; keep the road clear. Gather your men."

KADAR GRASPED MY arm. "Sir, you're flying about. You gave your word."

"Until Tursel's among us, who's to keep order?"

"You, but from the center of march."

Dusk was falling. The first of Groenfil's horsemen had appeared over the rise. The ridge, which once had seemed so safe, crawled with our soldiers casting anxious glances down the road, where Cumber's pikemen and archers fought desperately to hold the narrow path against Hriskil's thousands.

I'd already sent companies of Tantroth's Eiberian infantry to strengthen them, but dared not commit too many; if

Hriskil's main force charged the ridge, our rear guard risked being cut off. A demon's choice: if I didn't reinforce Raeth, our flank would be rolled. And if I did, I'd mire us in battle, and we couldn't pivot to make our flank our rear.

Obediently, I trotted Ebon to the center of our line. If I'd do no else this day, I'd keep my vows.

At the wagon that bore my tent, I slowed. "Tanner, where's Bollert?"

The scruffy urchin grinned. "Under the cart." It was as safe a place as any.

I gestured furiously; Bollert came at a run.

"Where do you march?"

"By the wagons. In 'em."

"Not today; they may be plundered. Both of you, run to the front of our line." I pointed toward what had been our rear.

"Aye, King."

"Elryc!" I craned my head.

"I've got 'im, m'lor'!" Genard cantered around a wagon, holding Elryc's reins.

"Stay in my sight! Alongside me, in fact. Larissa!"

She lashed at her palfrey with her crop. "You've befouled our nest, Rodrigo! Look at us! Imps are laughing. What have you done with Groenfil?"

"He'll be along." Pray Lord of Nature it was so. "Where's Tresa?"

"With her grandfather."

I reined so hard Ebon neighed in protest. "Is she crazed?"

"No more than Raeth. Or you!"

It was the Rood that made her speak so. Somehow, I must remember.

"I'll fetch her."

"You will not." Kadar barred my way. "Is your word worth nothing?"

In desperation I leaned across, grasped his jerkin. "As you value me, Kadar, go for Tresa. Raeth must be frantic for her safety. Bring her back, across your saddle if need be. I'll wait here with your guard."

"I can trust you in this?" His eyes searched mine.

"Please, Kadar!" Perhaps it was my tone. He nodded, cantered down the road.

I pounded my knee. I'd left the ridge, and with it, a view of the field. On the roadway, all I knew of the battle was what runners told me. It was no place for a leader of men.

In the prison of his wagon, Danzik tore at his chains. "Soa qi, Rez! Feran! Soa qi, Hriskil!" *I'm here, King! They flee! I'm here!*

"Strengthen his chains! Club him to silence!" Cursing, I spurred Ebon. "You, drover! Get that wagon about! Make way."

A gob of spittle, on my leggings. I paid no heed to Danzik's frenzy. "Haul him to safety, I won't have him freed! You there, with my tent, make way for his wagon!" Danzik held more value. Fuming, I watched them work the cart through the tangle of horsemen and foot soldiers.

A courier galloped east, from the last of the roadway we held. "Rodrigo!" The horseman reined in, his mare sweating. "My lord Raeth warns: the Norlanders assemble in force to attack our rear guard. Break off soon, that we may retreat."

"The moment Groenfil's extricated."

As I spoke, the furious clop of hooves along the road. A flurry of horsemen. Lord Groenfil himself, blood dripping from under his helmet. "Coward!" His eyes blazed. "Traitor to your cause!"

I said, "It was a Norland trap, well baited."

"You left us to die."

"Tursel's men fought their way to—"

"But for him, I'd be in Hriskil's hands!" A gesture that dripped contempt. "Faugh! I'm done with you this day."

It was the Rood.

I made my tone soothing. "We'll take counsel after. If you're determined to depart—"

"I'll ask not your leave." He wheeled off to regroup his horsemen.

Tursel's men, and Groenfil's, struggled up the rise to rejoin us on the rutted road.

Kadar threaded his way through the milling mass, leading Tresa. He had firm grip on her reins.

Her eyes flashed. "Was this your doing? Grandfather needed me!"

I shouted, "Would you become Hriskil's whore?"

It shocked her to silence.

Red of face, I cast decorum to the winds. "Have you no

sense? One lunge, and you're in their hands. How can Raeth do his work, or I, with your safety chief among our thoughts?"

"I—" She blushed. "Oh, Roddy."

"Stay with us, Tresa." It was a plea. I galloped toward the front of our line. Kadar and his troop raced after.

While Raeth maneuvered to withdraw our rear guard, we fell back eastward, toward Pezar. Groenfil threw his troops protectively around Larissa, and was of no other use. Captain Tursel, weary and distracted, toiled to keep our flight from becoming a rout. The road was too narrow for speed, but no one wanted to be rearmost, in range of Norland arrows or spears.

Atop Ebon, moving about the line, I issued a stream of orders, and helped reduce the chaos of frightened men on the march. But my roaming drove Kadar to distraction. At last I reined in, faced him. "I stay within our line, do I not?" I gave no pause to answer. "Look at Tursel's mount, bleeding from the kicks he gives it. He can't be everywhere."

"Sire, a Norland arrow, a spear—"

"I'm as safe in our center as ever I'll be." I lowered my voice. "Help me, Kadar. See the men's faces? They're near panic." As they would be, with the Norland host close behind. "Tursel's exhausted, and sore of soul. Unless we keep order . . ."

"My charge is to guard your life."

I cried, "What worth my life without all of you?" My wave took in our sweating yeomen, the wild-eyed horses, lumbering carts. The boys racing about, archers and spearmen, our wounded. "The army of Caledon *is* Rodrigo!" I tugged on the reins. Skittishly, Ebon turned about. "And who'll preserve order, if not I? Come, Kadar, let us save Caledon and ourselves."

With a look akin to awe, he followed.

Desperately I plunged past Tresa, past Anavar and Bollert, to the head of our line. The road had narrowed, and a cart was caught in mire. I halted a column of Soushire's troops, bade them push their wagon past the ruts, set Kadar as watchman to hurry us through the defile.

A twist of the reins, a gouge of unoffending flanks. "Go, boy." Dutifully, Ebon surged through the gap.

A branch leaned ever lower over the road.

Haul on it 'til it breaks, drag it free. Climb onto your patient mount.

"Tursel." I caught at his arm, in passing. "Where might we turn and face the Norlanders?"

"They're as many as in the meadow. More, now."

"We can't run before them long. Else the men . . ."

He nodded. Despite our forced cheer, they'd soon give way in their panic, and they'd cast aside arms, shields and life in desperate, bloody fear. "There's no good place, Roddy. But no widening where Hriskil might spread his men before us."

"The clearing where we camped?"

"Aye, there's that." Tursel's mouth tightened. "I'll send men ahead to throw up a defense. Raeth needs relief."

"Good. I'll hold us in order."

"Groenfil is . . ." He shook his head. "If he'd help . . ."

"Cajole him, promise, implore. Get him to the clearing. It's far enough away that perhaps the Rood would wane." I raised myself in my saddle, peered past archers clustered around an arms-wagon. A company in black, marching with their horsemen. "I'll have word with Tantroth."

"My lord, you do yourself proud this day."

"You too, Tursel?" We had woes enough without his sarcasm. "I ran from battle, but it was one we couldn't win."

"The meadow was a disaster. I speak of now. You ride among the men and rally them with your calm. Would that Lord Rustin could see you."

I searched his eyes, found only approval. I swallowed a lump. "Thank you." I wheeled off, toward our rear.

Frantic men in a shoving match over a cart, taut fingers drawing to hilts of swords. "Easy, lads." A smile, forced from calm I knew not I had. "We'll work together and be all right. Pezar's just ahead." Not so, we'd camped a night on our journey westward. But it wouldn't be all that far, once we were free of the Norlanders. And I doubted we'd find rest before the town.

After the road was cleared, I brooded in the saddle, while weary men tromped past. Kadar, dusty and damp, found me by the side of the trail. "Stay with the column, my lord."

"I have."

On the road behind us, a flurry of activity. "Look, Raeth withdraws. He'll take position by those trees, I warrant. It's

narrow enough to—come along, sire. We're near alone." The
body of our men had passed us by.

"I'll speak with Uncle Raeth." I stirred. "Fear not, if Hriskil
comes close—"

"A risk you need not take." Kadar's tone was reproving.

"He'll need relief soon. At the clearing Groenfil will cover
our retreat, but 'til then . . ." Cumber was old, and the tension
was exhausting. "Ah, there he is." I waved.

In moments Uncle Raeth and I had our heads together, in
the welcome shade of a grove of beeches. Cumber's men
brought arrow-filled sheaves for the archers who'd soon be
among us, while Kadar glanced about nervously.

"They press us sore, Roddy." Raeth wiped his brow.

"Can you hold?"

"As long as the road's narrow. But . . ." A grimace. "In truth,
if Hriskil's willing to pay the cost, he'll have us. A strong
enough charge, and . . ." A gesture, that scattered us to the
winds. He beckoned to an aide. "Have Imbar send the
archers." To me, "They provide cover while the rest withdraw.
Imbar will hold the line as long as he's able. The rear guard's
rear guard, as it were."

I looked about. "How if we add Soushire's men, or
Tantroth's?"

"And put them where?" Raeth's smile was wry. "But that's
Hriskil's problem as well. The road's too tight to mount a
proper charge, and the woods too thick to skirt it in force."

I peered down the road, at Cumber's men extricating themselves from the Norland menace, running to join us. "Is Imbar
skilled enough to hold the trail?"

"He was a soldier when we met. A boy, and handsome
as . . ." He sighed. "Not that you'd think it today. Bright as a
new-mint pence, to boot."

I flushed. "I'm sorry I dislike him."

"He gave you cause." Uncle's tone was curt, but his smile
was gentle. "Learn to forgive, my boy. Many's the affront
you'll bear in this long life. Think of your kingdom and its
gain, and don't hold—"

A whir.

Raeth pitched to the mossy earth. A feathered shaft quivered from his breast.

"No!" I threw myself down, to his side.

His hand fluttered to his chest. "You'd . . . best . . . call Imbar."

"Oh, Uncle!" I swallowed. "You there, fetch Imbar, at the run. Kadar, find Tresa!"

"I can't leave—"

"Do it!" I shoved him on his way.

From Uncle's lips, a pink froth. His mouth worked. "Sorry, my boy." But no sound came.

I squeezed his hand, drew it to my lips. "Don't leave us."

His hand twitched, and the pressure eased. "Cumber . . ." It was but the shape of words.

"To your bloodline forever, though it cost my crown to preserve it."

His eyes faded to something that might have been peace. "Thank—"

And he was gone.

I LED EBON down the dusty road. Beside me walked Kadar, shield raised. At my left, Anavar.

Visions of Rustin beset me.

My cheeks were wet, and I knew not why.

"Sir . . ." Anavar's voice was unsure.

I shook my head.

We trudged on.

Tresa rode alongside the wagon that bore her grandfather.

She'd come flying down the road, moments too late. Instead of him, she'd found me, brimming with inadequate words, useless solace. She'd thrust me aside without heed, knelt by Raeth's stili form.

Kadar had pulled me, protesting, to safety, but not before I'd summoned the duke of Eiber and put the guarding of our trail in his hands. In the cart, stout, grizzled Baron Imbar knelt by his master, desolate.

Perhaps Tantroth possessed some skill that Raeth had not, or perhaps the Norlanders merely tired. They fell back, leaving us the road.

Leading Ebon, I grappled with the enormity of my loss. When I fled Uncle Mar, it was Raeth who'd taken me in, succored me, given me the troops with which to reclaim Stryx. It was he, of all the lords, who'd first believed in me. He, who'd known and loved my father, Josip.

Where Larissa of Soushire was crude and irritable, Groenfil fierce with boorish rage, Cumber had passed his last winter in the lonely hills of Eiber, upholding my cause.

Azar found me, striding. "Sire, Lord Tantroth prepares the
next withdrawal."

"Be it so."

TANTROTH, GRAY AND gaunt, walked with his men, reins in his
hand. Absently, he patted his stallion's muzzle. "Raeth," he
said, "served you well."

I swung down, glad to stretch my legs. "About the field of
battle . . ."

"We'd have prevailed," he said firmly. Then, "But perhaps
not." His brow furrowed. "Orders flew and were revoked. No
one knew—"

"Just so. We'd have been annihilated."

"There's always confusion in war, Rodrigo."

"Hriskil himself is near, with the Rood. I felt it."

"Are you sure?"

I shrugged. "As can be."

He pounded his leg. "What an opportunity! If we can lure
him—"

"Think not of battle this day. We'll be lucky to reach the
pass unscathed."

"Hriskil will always have the Rood, my lord. Soon or late
we'll have to face him."

"But I have not the Still." I'd have bitten off my tongue, not
to have said it. Too late.

If he saw opportunity to betray me, he gave no sign of it.
"What befell you?"

"I squandered it, putting Jestrel to the question." I reddened.

"Brave men died, that you had no Power to succor them!"

"Who are you to—yes, my lord Duke." Raeth was among
those my folly had lost. I bowed my head. The shame would
be with me long.

Tantroth grunted. "I ought to seek advantage."

I shot him a curious glance.

"I don't have the heart for it, this day." His eyes were tormented. "Raeth's gone, we're in retreat, no place to regroup
short of Pezar. We came so close, Rodrigo."

"It's not over."

"Is it not?"

"No!" I stopped so abruptly Ebon bumped me with his muzzle. "Look to me, lord Duke!"

Startled, he did as I commanded.

"Doubt not, my lord." My eyes blazed as I swung into the saddle. "This is beginning, not end!" I spurred Ebon. "Eiber shall be ours, and with it, Caledon!"

PART TWO

THIRTEEN

WE THREADED THROUGH the passes, slowly enough to maintain good order. I sent Soushire's yeomen ahead to augment the feeble force we'd left behind at Pezar.

At the clearing in which we'd been beset by fire arrows, Groenfil set what barrier he might, to give us respite from the Norlanders. But we judged—Groenfil, Tursel and I—that we dared not camp there the night, lest Hriskil fall on us.

"Sol pur sol, Hriskil modre domu Caledi," Danzik told me with satisfaction, learning of Raeth's death. *One by one, Hriskil kills the Caled lords.*

"You're still prisoner." I rattled a chain that secured him to the cart. "Hriskil found you not worth saving."

Danzik grinned through gap teeth. Foul as his insults were, he never resented receiving one.

After my lesson I walked with Tresa of Cumber.

"Your men built us a casket, Roddy. With your leave, I would take Grandfather home."

"Of course." As if nonchalantly, I squeezed her hand. "I'd attend the mourning at Cumber, but the army awaits."

Reeling from exhaustion, we plodded on toward Pezar.

"I know." Tresa's glance shot to me, and away. My scar, no doubt. "I'm sorry I rebuffed you. It was—I felt—" She blinked. "He was kind to me. Always."

I suppressed a smile. "Except at dinner."

"Well, yes." The corners of her mouth turned up. Uncle Raeth's mealtime candor had been startling, until one got used to it. "What now, Roddy?"

"The pass at Pezar." We must hold it, or be destroyed.

"And then?"

"I can't think past that. I've lost my two most trusted counselors, and dearest friends." If I spoke of it more, I would be undone. "What of you?"

"I'll ready Cumber for Bouris." Her tone was placid. Bouris, her uncle and Raeth's son, would inherit. Perhaps he'd make place for Tresa. If not . . .

I asked, "Would you care to live at Stryx?"

"If you're there."

My heart thumped so hard I couldn't speak.

"I'll send word, if I may."

"Do more!"

She started, at my urgency.

"Tresa, when you write . . ." I sought refuge in the high speech. "Madam, speak thy entire heart to me, and I swear thee, I shall speak mine. It would be as if . . ." I took deep breath, forced reluctant words. "As if I were not denied thy presence." *As if I were not alone.*

Perhaps she understood. "I'm . . . in a daze." Abruptly, she halted. "Thank you for all, sire. I spoke with Tursel, made sure he'll serve you."

I waited.

"Imbar will also."

I could only gape.

"Nothing remains for him at Cumber, he says. Bouris loathes him."

"He's soft, and no warrior. A battlefield's no place for—"

"Roddy." She drew close. "If he wants a death such as Grandfather's, would you deny him?"

Learn to forgive, my boy. "No. Of course not." I would need schooling. Imbar would be my guide.

"Fare thee well."

PEZAR WITHOUT RAETH was a dismal, sorry town.

Earl Groenfil sat with head in hands, on the three-legged stool in my tent. "I stand by my words, Rodrigo. You abandoned us."

Defiant, as on the road. But why did he fail to meet my eye? "You're right." I surprised even myself. "No doubt it seemed cowardly. But it wasn't from fear."

He flushed. "I didn't truly mean . . . my temper was hot."

"My lord Earl." I made my tone gentle. "I reproach you not. But consider, if you will, what drove your rage."

"Your act. Don't evade the burden." A pause. "They pressed us. I felt befogged."

"Why?"

"Because I did!" He raised his eyes. "You're saying?"

"It was the Rood, my lord. I sensed it; perhaps the Still aided me. It drove us all mad. Our tactics were a muddle; we failed even to protect our flank. Even Uncle Raeth was snappish. And so I called off the attack; they'd baited a trap, they had the Rood, and we were driven to confusion and despair."

"Hriskil can do that?"

"When he wields it. Think you the Norlanders gain all their victories by force of arms?"

"That, and overwhelming numbers." For a time, Groenfil brooded, while I sat in patient silence. Then, "Rodrigo, how might we best him?"

My heart quickened. I said gravely, "We've no chance without your aid."

A grudging nod. "Deftly done, sire. Very well, I repent my hasty words. I won't leave you."

"Thank you." A short bow, to mask my relief. "We'll not do battle until I'm prepared. I'll ask my forebears—" I hesitated. How much of the Still's working did he know, and what damage could I cause myself by telling him more? A deep breath. "I'll take their counsel on how to counter him. With my Power, perhaps we'll prevail."

"Roddy . . ." Groenfil studied me. "If we must ride to our deaths, I want it to be in truth. If you can't forestall the Rood, you'll tell us, that I may save loyal men from annihilation?"

"Yes. By the True I swear it."

I had changed. Nary a chill swept me, as recklessly I committed my kingdom.

"GROENFIL MEANS IT, I think." In my secluded tent, Elryc toyed with my blanket. "I've the feeling he's less devious than most."

"But if not . . ."

"Roddy, if any of them abandon us, we're undone. Soushire, Tantroth, Groenfil . . ."

"I like it not." I scratched an itch. "I need silken words that don't suit me."

My brother suppressed a smile.

I said, "Well, they don't. Shall I pretend otherwise?"

"No. You're as you are."

I frowned, weighing if it was an insult. With a sigh, I put it

aside. If I took umbrage at all who called attention to my nature, I'd have no companions. Grudgingly, I let myself smile.
Laugh first at yourself, Rustin had once said. *Then others
won't.*

"You're lighthearted today."

"No. Tresa's gone, Raeth is dead, and we're thrown back to
Pezar." I grimaced.

"You've reconciled with Groenfil, Larissa's words were near
civil when we broke fast, and you're the talk of the campfires."

My ears perked up. "Oh?"

"Yesterday, on the trail. I'm proud of you, Roddy."

Any insults were forgotten. "Why?"

"You risked yourself among them. You worked to clear the
road, carried Raeth yourself to the wagon, held your temper
with Groenfil and Soushire. They'd never seen you so."

For a moment I let myself bask in his approval. Then,
"Tursel's scouts say Hriskil's troops dog our steps."

Elryc nodded. "It's sure they'll seek battle. Gathered together, we might be destroyed. Else Hriskil must chase us
from castle to keep."

I said hotly, "Would you rather we disbanded? What chance
have we then to—"

"Of course not. It's just . . . our opportunity is also his."

After a moment, I nodded. "Good counsel."

Elryc nodded, as if taking that for granted. "Roddy, when
you talk to Mother, ask if Bollert's power might be of use."

"Against Hriskil? Are you daft? He's a commoner."

Elryc rolled his eyes. "You're as you are, but sometimes I
wish you weren't."

This time, I knew it was insult.

TWO DAYS WE waited, while Hriskil assembled before us.

Danzik was gleeful. "Soon you'll be dust."

I grappled with his graceless tongue. "If you were dead,
you won't—wouldn't—see it."

"Oh, please, mighty king, don't slay me!" A contemptuous
laugh, that belied his words. "Think you I fear death at your
hands?"

"Why not?"

A moment's reflection. "My capture earned death. I'll be
lucky if Hriskil doesn't provide it."

"The Eiberians think as you." I wrinkled my nose. "Barbarians, the lot of you. You torture prisoners, fight without quarter, raze cities . . ."

"And we win." His eyes glowed. "Truly, Rez, I'll miss you. I'll light candle in your memory."

I smiled, patted his knee. "My friend, you amuse me. Perhaps, for your sake, I'll spare Hriskil's life."

His guffaw rang through the camp.

TRESA MADE SAFE journey home, and buried my uncle. She wrote that she chose a spot near Rustin and Pytor. I wept.

The next day I wrote her a long missive. As always my spelling was weak, my lines muddled. I cared not.

Rustin, what do I make of myself?

A king.

Why do I feel more . . . gentle?

You forgive yourself. And so you forgive others.

Are you real? Do you truly hear me?

Silence.

Rust?

Nothing.

"What is it, my lord?" Anavar looked wary.

"A mood." I shrugged it off.

In the night, fire arrows put our camp in uproar. Tursel combed the hills, and Tantroth, but found no foe. In the morn we were all weary, and sleepless.

LARISSA PACED FROM pole to pole, in her soft, sumptuous tent. "Margenthar probed my walls."

"How know you this?" With Soushire Castle under siege, no runner could set forth.

"I know." A spy, perhaps, or loyal observer outside the walls.

I mustn't let her leave. "Hriskil's within a league of our camp." Our patrols, prowling through woods and fields, reported the road clogged with wagons and supplies, and men amarch.

"Would you I lost my domain?" Her tone was testy.

"Of course not, my lady."

"We gird ourselves to throw back an attack." Her pacing stopped. "What if Hriskil does nothing, but waits?"

"We wait with him."

She lowered her voice. "That, I can't afford. I must be home, and soon."

"Uncle Mar hasn't the strength—"

"He's wily, and wouldn't besiege me without hope of victory."

I nodded reluctantly. "Unless his goal is to draw you home."

"Why, to aid the Norlanders? Even Mar wouldn't do that."

"Think you not?" My tone was savage.

She threw up her hands. "That's as may be. Five days, no more. Then I'm off."

Almost, I asked, "And Groenfil?" But I knew enough to keep the thought to myself.

Afterwards, I strode through the dusty town with Anavar. Kadar and a dozen men dogged our heels. "Can't she understand we need them all? If one lord leaves, another will follow. What if Tantroth decides he's better off roaming Eiber?"

Anavar snorted. "You'd profit of it. But first he'd need to pass Hriskil."

"Tantroth's an imp riding moonbeams. No one sees him in the night." In that, he'd earned my grudging respect.

"It's not so difficult, when you know the terrain." Anavar bent, tossed a pebble past a guard's nose. "What a meager town, Pezar. And my stipend isn't enough to—look, there's Tanner."

My bondservant raced down the road, arms windmilling. "M'lor! Lor' King!" The boy's face was red. "Tursel looks everywhere for you." He panted for breath. "Hriskil's coming!"

I looked about; not a horse in sight. "Let's go!" I dashed toward our camp, trailing guards.

I BENT, HANDS on knees, trying to regain my breath. Anavar cantered up on his stallion, Ebon's reins in hand. I'd been in too much haste to stop and saddle him; I'd raced through our camp like one demented, headed to our defensive wall. Kadar, who'd taken a moment to gather men and mounts, glared at me without cease. I did my best to ignore him.

When I could speak, I gasped, "I see nothing."

Tursel's thumb flicked past our battlement, to the Eiber trail. "Listen, sire." He cocked an ear.

All I could hear was the thudding of my heart. Then, the unmistakable creak of wagons, the soft clop of a thousand hooves, the trod of booted feet. "How far?"

"Past the next ridge."

I swallowed. Sweat sprang up. I could smell my fear. "Wouldn't he attempt . . ." I ought say naught, lest I reveal my ignorance before Anavar and my guards. But I threw caution to the winds. "Surely Hriskil knows we hear his approach."

"Aye, and that our scouts spotted him hours past. So why chafe his men with silent ride? They must organize themselves into order of battle. Besides . . ." Tursel pointed to the narrow pass, and beyond. "It's here he must cross, and he knows we know it."

"How long have we?" My mouth was dry.

"Lord Raeth chose well, to fortify Pezar. The road beyond constricts so. Hriskil will need time to bring up his archers, arrange his horse, send the pikemen—"

"How long?" Abruptly, my tone had a bite. Glancing at Anavar, I flushed, and sought to soften it. "Please, Captain. You know of war."

"Fifth hour, at the earliest. I rather think he'll wait 'til morn." Tursel paused. "I would."

Then Hriskil might not. I managed not to say it.

Somberly Tursel and I stared at the trail, and the hills beyond. Anavar swung down from his stallion and climbed the wall to my side. We gazed down at the unseen foe.

This very moment I should be astride Ebon, issuing orders, arranging the cavalry, the archers, the pikes, but my head was a jumble. "Tursel?" My voice was meek. "How would you dispose our force?"

"Archers there, on the hill, shieldmen and pikes before them. Cumber's men here behind our redoubt, where you see them."

"And?" I paced the stony battlement.

"What else? There's no room to deploy, my lord. That's why we chose this place. It makes our army the equal of his."

"But Hriskil's bringing up his horse and pikes, you said."

"Of course. Why would he not?"

"Why would *we* not?"

"Lord of Nature, Rodrigo, look at the terrain!" A pause, in which Tursel heard no answer. He gentled his tone. "Look, sire, past the walls. What do you see?"

"To our right, the Caled peaks."

"No, just out there." He pointed.

"Past the stream? A steep, rocky hill rising to a flat. It overlooks our fortifications."

"Precisely. If their archers took it . . ."

"We'd need retreat." From the earthworks, from the pass.

"So we hold it with archers and pikes. You of course note the rope ladders our bowmen climb to the plateau?"

I snapped, "I'm not blind!"

"They'll pull them up after. What's within our archers' range from the terrace?"

"The meadow, the road . . . everything. Almost to the wood."

"Yes, sire. Now, here." He pointed straight before us. "What do you see?"

I was a boy, at lessons of war. "Our walls curve across from hill to hill, like a dam across the valley. The land slopes down from where we stand; our footing is higher than the attacker's."

"Beyond our walls?"

"The meadow, then the woods beyond." I was calm now, and searching out features to describe. "The meadow widens with distance from the walls. That is, it's widest where it meets the woods. The peaks narrow the field as it nears our walls."

"Back there, where the wood is thickest, how much room to deploy?"

"I don't . . . I'm not sure." The admission shamed me.

Anavar stirred. "Look, sir, Hriskil will probably set his cavalry at that clearing to the left. A far reach for our bowmen." Though we had the heights, and a farther shot.

My eyes roved the field. "I suppose there, in the center, they could assemble cohorts of foot soldiers. Ten, easily. Three thousand men." Still only a fraction of his force.

"Good, my lord. And as they advance?"

Arrows darkening the sky. Screams. The thud of hooves. I grimaced; that wasn't what Tursel meant. "The field narrows. I already said that."

"Yes, my lord. How many men abreast, when they reach the walls?"

Would his questions have no end? "A hundred, at most."

"And their horse?"

"No room for them. Their track is uphill and crowded."
Uncle Raeth had done well. I saw it now, better than before.

"And on our side, my lord?"

"A few hundred on the wall, reinforcements below." I
turned. "Somewhere behind us, a reserve in case they break
through."

"They're positioned on the Mill Road."

"And our horse . . ." I studied. "Where?"

"Straight down Pezar Road, sire. At our campsite."

"You jest."

"It's, what, a moment's ride? They're out of arrow range,
guarding tents and supplies as well. Three men with sema-
phores, here, there at Mill Road, and in camp. Simple signals
already arranged."

I squinted, turned glumly to the wall. "You've no need of
me. I might as well be home in Stryx."

"Ah, Roddy." The hint of a smile. "Lord Raeth had months
to ponder the land. It's *his* deployment I set in train."

"One I should have studied." My tone was bitter. "All the
while we camped here, I was too busy. Babbling at Tresa.
Vanquishing a silversmith. Quarreling with my lords." My
fine words to Tantroth meant nothing, if I looked not to the
safety of my troops.

The canter of hooves. Tantroth, on his gray steed, his aides
and a dozen well-armed guards in tow. The duke of Eiber
sprang down, climbed our meager battlement with spry step.
"So, my lord, the moment approaches."

"You sound eager."

"Resigned, perhaps. A maiden can only flit from rock to
rock playing catch-my-sash for so long, before wearying of
the game." Tantroth glanced about. "And a sturdy playing
ground, this."

"Better than the last?" My tone was truculent.

"It wasn't the lay of the land that defeated us." His gaze
seemed curious. "Look you for quarrel?" At that, Captain
Tursel frowned, looked away.

Ashamed, I gave no answer. Then, to Tantroth, "If you were
Hriskil . . ."

"Yes, my lord?"

"What would you do?"

"On the morrow, or beyond?" He pursed his lips. "I'd test the wall, of course, to see if the child king has mettle. Were I rebuffed, I'd bring the whole weight of my force to bear. Who is that boy behind you, and why does he glare so?"

"You know full well—" No, perhaps he didn't. Before renouncing Eiber, Anavar had been squire to Lord Treak, a cousin of Tantroth, but that didn't mean the duke had met him. And until now, I'd carefully kept them apart. "That's Anavar, Baron of the Southern Reaches. My ward." A wave, as if it were of no import. "Baron, make your greeting, and ask Elryc if he would sup with me tonight." A feeble errand, but all I could conjure.

From Anavar, the shortest of bows, little more than a nod. He swept down from the wall, swung aboard Edmund, and was off.

"Now, where were we?" Tantroth's gaze flickered to mine. "Yes, I'd bring the weight of my force to bear. I'd build fortifications there, at the edge of the woods. You know, the boy lacks manners. Perhaps Lord Treak failed to teach him."

Gamely, I focused on our defense, ignoring the barb. "Why build fortifications?"

"When I split my force, you'd be tempted, would you not? To sally forth with Groenfil and old Tantroth, and push me from the pass? So, fortifications to hold you at Pezar."

"Why split your force?"

"This isn't the only pass, my lord, merely the best. Far more work to haul wagons laden with supplies through the Ukra, or down along the sea road. But it could be done. Soon or late, I'd be behind you."

I said, "He tried that, with Danzik."

"Ah, but you were down in Cumber, then at Stryx, not in Pezar. Here's the heart of it: if Hriskil withdraws from the pass, you follow, and Eiber's open to you. If he turns to press you, you retreat to the pass. Stalemate. But if he fortifies, Hriskil has more than enough men to hold you at Pezar. If you make for Cumber, his superior force will fall on you like wolves on a doe. So you're committed here. That gives him time. If he sends but half his men, even a third, by autumn he'll be in Stryx, or better yet, Cumber. If you turn to fight them, he'll take the pass behind you."

"We've lost?"

"Did I not say so, on the road to Pezar?"

My mouth worked, but I had no words.

Tursel took up my cause. "It's not so simple as that. A victory at the pass—"

"Would encourage Larissa, and if she stays, Groenfil must." Tantroth's tone was dry. "And Hriskil may take ill, or the Ukras stir." A wave. "Vagaries of war. But you asked what I'd do, were I he."

"Thank you." My voice was thick.

"As to that hill, again I offer you my archers. You can scarce have too many when—".

"Again?"

"Tursel refused them. I can't imagine why." His tone was sardonic.

"Because we have enough to—" Exasperated, Tursel broke off. To me, "My lord, arrows fly west as well as south."

I blinked, took in his meaning. "At us?" Our walls were well below the plateau; our defenders would be helpless against flights of arrows from the hill. I turned from his stubborn visage.

Neither Tursel nor Tantroth spoke. But Kadar had tensed, and the hands of the duke's riders were near their weapons.

Rustin, I need you. Take charge, regent, and end this madness.

Tantroth said tightly, "Naturally, a man of Cumber knows not the meaning of an oath, but that he voice his calumny in the presence of—"

Tursel reared. "Raeth knew you for a knave and traitor who—"

Kadar edged closer to me, hand on sword.

Tantroth rolled his eyes. "What keeps me in your camp, amid slurs and contempt?"

"Silence, the lot of you!" My shout echoed from peak to wall. "An end to this!"

"How, my lord?" Tantroth.

Yes, how? For a yawning moment, I hesitated.

Then I took deep breath. "Tantroth, your archers to the hill, and be quick, they're sore needed. Give their command to Tursel, who has charge of this place. Tursel, in private, you will ask pardon of the duke for doubting his oath. You object? Say not what is in your face. Do it, or leave us. Kadar!"

My bodyguard jumped. "Yes, my lord?"

"We thank thee for thy good service. When our realm is secure, we shall find thee reward. But thou hast no longer the care of our person. Protect Lord Elryc, who on our death is the last of our line."

"But—my Lord who'll—you can't! You must have guard!"

"Yes." I jumped off the wall, stepped into Ebon's stirrup, swung myself into the saddle. A twitch of my reins, and Ebon nosed his way among Tantroth's armed riders. "My lord duke!"

Tantroth raised an eyebrow.

"These men here, or such others as you choose. They'll guard my person and have the sole say of it."

"Roddy!" Kadar leapt off his mount, threw himself on his knees, clutching my stirrup. "Whatever I've done, I beg your forgive—Lord Rustin made me swear—please, sire!"

"Take ease, Kadar. You've done no ill. And I'm in good hands." Slowly, I turned. "Am I not?"

After a time, Tantroth's gaze fell from mine, and to the muddy earth. "Why," he said, "I suppose you are."

FOURTEEN

TANTROTH'S GUARD JANGLED alongside as we rode to camp.
The duke was silent a moment, then conferred with Azar,
Sandin and Pardos, his aides. Turning, he issued a few terse
commands to his men, giving charge of my bodyguard to Pardos. I cared not whom he named; I'd just put my life in the
hands of the man who'd once betrayed me to Uncle Mar. Insane, perhaps, but I could think of no other way. Were
Tantroth to ride off, or sit on his hands in the camp, Groenfil
and Soushire would likewise abandon my standard. His loyalty must be earned, and claimed.

"Hold, Rodrigo, if you will." Tantroth.

I reined.

"There, past the mill, something you ought see."

"Very well." I spurred, along the Mill Road. In moments
we'd passed the pitifully few yeomen we held in reserve
against Hriskil. Near the mill I reined in, alone with Tantroth
and his guard. "Are you satisfied?"

"With what, my lord?"

"That I consent. That my life is yours." Perhaps he
wouldn't kill me; perhaps he only wanted to learn, as would
I, the extent of my trust.

"Pardos, give us a few paces." Tantroth led me a short
distance, said quietly, "It wasn't necessary. I was irked,
but—"

"Enough to demonstrate Tursel's distrust to me."

"Well, yes. But I wouldn't have left. I'll give you back your
Kadar."

For a moment, I considered it, then smiled. "Our thanks,
Lord Tantroth, but no. We're safer in your charge."

"I'll fight for you, Rodrigo." He flushed. "It's in my self-
interest to hold the pass against—"

"Why, yes, but we prefer thy honor to self-interest." I
tugged at Ebon's reins. "Was there else, my lord?"

*   *   *

As the afternoon wore on, with no sign of attack, a hollow formed in the pit of my stomach. I could scarce swallow. The Norlanders were so many, our wall so low. I found myself sitting with Elryc, Genard and Anavar, in my brother's tent. Pardos, of course, had set guard, all about us.

"Take ease, sir, it's just that you want battle." Anavar.

Not just battle: decisive battle. Hriskil had halted our daring thrust into Eiber that might have forced his withdrawal from Caledon; now we were thrown back on the defensive at Uncle Raeth's border wall. A sturdy defense at Pezar would bring no glorious victory, but if we held, we'd at least keep Hriskil's forces from uniting into an irresistible river of men and horse.

I paced from tent pole to flap. "I want it over. Or deferred. How will we sleep this night, knowing the blood dawn will bring?" I sat for a moment, paced anew, as a thought struck me. "Anavar!"

The apple he was coring flew out of his hands and rolled across the tent. "Yes?" He leaped to his feet, blushing.

"Find my lord Groenfil, if you would. I wish an envoy sent."

"To Groenfil?" Anavar's brow furrowed.

"No, you twit, to Hriskil."

While we waited, I perched on Elryc's bed and retrieved the apple.

My brother's tone was cautious. "Roddy, a jest before battle wouldn't be meet."

I forbore to answer. In a few moments, hasty footsteps. "Let me pass, villain! I'm Lord Groenfil!"

"No one enters without—"

I poked out my head. "It's all right, Pardos. He, Lady Larissa, my brother . . . who else? Anavar. And your master Tantroth. They have access to my person."

A tug at my jerkin. "Tursel. And Genard."

I named them.

In Elryc's tent, Groenfil looked for a place to sit, found none. "What's this about an envoy?"

"To Hriskil. Will he honor a flag of truce?"

"He has in past. Why?"

"Send a message. For his ears, or none. 'To Hriskil, King of the Norlands, from Rodrigo, King of Caledon, greetings. Know why we have summoned thee to this pass: our vassal

Tantroth of Eiber laments that thy prolonged visit to his lands has sore afflicted his people.' "

"Roddy—"

" 'And beseeches us speed your leave. Accordingly, we extend you our hospitality until three days from this morning, then pray thee depart.' "

The tent flap fluttered in a sudden gust. Groenfil's eyes blazed. "You'd risk an envoy for a jape? I'll not send a man on this foolishness."

Behind us, a determined voice. "I'll go."

I gaped.

Genard held my gaze. "Really, m'lord, I'll do it."

"Why?"

He blushed. "Meet the Norland king? Speak for Caledon? When else would I—I'll go, I'm not afraid."

"You're just a—" But Elryc stirred, and I swallowed it. "Of course, Genard. My lord Earl, see he has the garments of a page, and a proper horse."

"What's the purpose, sire?"

"To hear Hriskil's response." It seemed lame as a mare with a stone in her shoe.

We walked him to the gate, Genard in elegant garments borrowed from Soushire's squire, sitting proudly on a great stallion that dwarfed him. I was regretting my impulse. But not only would I make a poor figure reversing myself; Genard would be heartbroken.

We opened the gate. He rode into the fading afternoon, a yellow flag of truce waving from a pole. His pace was cautious, barely more than a walk. If I could, I'd have held my breath the whole while.

He disappeared into the wood.

Waiting, pacing, my mood grew ever more vile. What had I done, sending a child to do man's work? Sending a stable-reared boor in place of a squire?

What was I doing, at the wall? In Pezar? On the throne?

At last, when I could no longer stand it, a cry from the wall; Genard's stallion, and our flag. From a distance, he seemed unharmed.

Inside the gate, Genard swung down, handed his reins to Baron Imbar, as if the older man were a stablehand. I frowned, but he paid no heed. "Hriskil himself! You should see him, a huge beard, big shoulders—"

Groenfil snorted and rolled his eyes.

Elryc said gently, "The message first. An envoy always gives his message."

"Oh, yes, sorry, Roddy. I mean, King. M'lor'. They translated for him, and for me. Uh, it was . . ." He wrinkled his brow. "From Hriskil, King of the Norlands, Eiber and Caledon—sorry, m'lord, it's how he said it—to the pretender Rodrigo, rumored son of the whore Elena . . ."

My teeth bared.

"Begone from our lands. If not, tomorrow you will die. To any true noble who hears these words, know that—I'm sorry, maybe I shouldn't say it—"

"Speak!"

"Whoever brings the head of Rodrigo, the child pretender, shall forever hold castle and lands as now he possesses, as my sworn vassal."

Silence, all round.

"Well, who would avail himself? Tursel? Groenfil?" My tone was harsh. No one spoke. "Genard, a message to Hriskil. Remount."

"No. He's done enough." Elryc. He had the right; Genard was his vassal, not mine.

"Who, then?" I looked about. "Very well, I'll go myself."

"I'll do it, sire." Imbar.

I gaped.

"What use am I? Let me go." He clutched the bridle, eyes searching mine.

"You, speak for Caledon? Fah!" I snatched the reins from Imbar, paid him no further heed. "Open the gate."

The gateman looked to Tursel, who shook his head.

"I command you!" My tone was imperious.

Anavar tried to seize my bridle. I kicked him aside. He fell.

Groenfil spat on the ground. "Let him. He'd destroy himself and us. He's not worth following."

"No!" Elryc. "Roddy gets—he's upset, don't you see, all he wants is—"

"Be silent, brother." I yanked the reins so hard my borrowed stallion whinnied in protest.

"I'll go, sir!" Anavar.

"Don't trouble yourself, I'm not worth following. Tursel, the gate!" I rode at it, would have ridden through the planks if need be. The gateman opened just in time.

"They'll kill you, Roddy!" I wasn't sure who spoke. Groenfil, perhaps.

I rode into the dusk.

Roddy, what in blazes are you up to?

I don't know, Rust.

Turn back to camp this instant!

No. I cannot. Not to Groenfil's contempt, Larissa's impatience, my own fear. Better Hriskil kill me.

That's likely. I think you a fool.

Do you, Rust? Do you really?

Nothing.

I risked a glance over my shoulder. A score of faces, peering atop the wall. I held high the yellow banner of truce.

"STAD, CALED!" *HOLD, Caledon.*

I tugged on the reins. Snorting, my stallion came to rest. "I am envoy to Hriskil, king of the Norlands."

"Esper." *Wait.*

I threw my hood over my head. The wait wasn't long. Just time enough for my bowels to dissolve to water, for sweat to dampen my jerkin. *Roddy, if you ever get out of this, use* sense.

They led me, on horseback, to a camp. A huge fire, a score of men around it. Behind the circle, a long, bedraggled tent. I tugged the reins, and my horse halted, in shadow.

"Enva Caledi, Rez." My guide bowed to a wild-bearded man whose matted hair had streaks of gray. I studied him. Was he king? He seemed a barbarian. He muttered something to a companion.

A stocky, graying man got to his feet, and indicated the seated barbarian. "You've found Hriskil." He spoke in the tongue of Caledon. "What say you?"

Yes, what say I? That on a whim I'd risked all, to see my foe's face before he struck me down?

I let my voice ring out, as had envoys I'd heard. "From Rodrigo, the child pretender, to Hriskil, King of the Norlands, greetings."

The translator gaped.

"Those are the king's words," I said.

He translated. Hriskil watched him closely. So did I. He seemed somehow familiar. He swung back to me, waiting.

I said, "Rodrigo is new to war, and wishes a pleasant night's sleep for your men and his. He proposes therefore that battle be joined at the morrow's twelfth hour, rather than dawn."

"Er rez graftig?" Hriskil's tone was sharp. *Is the king broken?* No, that wasn't right. I groped for unfamiliar words. Graftig. *Insane.*

I held tight to the yellow banner. "Rodrigo says, if you will grant him this courtesy, on the morrow he will kill you gently."

Hriskil's whole body convulsed with laughter. "Graftig, chazu graftig. Doz hur? Qay. Doz hur modrav dom Caledi." He climbed to his feet, still chuckling. "Dit ko, Llewelyn. Dit ko qa diche." He strode to the tent.

My mount's head shot up as I jerked on the reins. *Tell him, Llewelyn. Tell him what I said.*

Llewelyn of the Keep, in Hriskil's camp? Lord of Nature, why had I come? My finger flicked toward my scar, and away. I mustn't call attention to it. My hood was flung over my head; that would have to suffice.

"His majesty answers: yes, he will fight the child pretender at noon." Llewelyn, Rustin's father, betrayer of Stryx, had a courteous voice.

"I will convey his response. With permission?" I gestured to the trail.

"Go with grace, youngsire."

EVERY NOBLE IN our camp watched from the wall as I rode in.

They gathered at the gate. Elryc, Anavar, Tursel, Tantroth, Larissa, Groenfil. One held my horse, another helped me alight. In answer to a volley of questions, I related my tale.

Silence. Looks of reappraisal.

"It's true. I swear so by the Still."

"The king himself, Roddy?"

"Yes, brother."

Larissa of Soushire gave a grudging nod. "Bravely done, Rodrigo. But what now?"

"A good night's sleep. Tursel, send hot food to our archers on the high hill. And give rest to our reserves; they won't be needed 'til midday."

Groenfil spluttered. "Preposterous! You'd wager Caledon on Hriskil's word?"

"Oh, we'll man the walls. But no need to discomfit the rest of our army. Pass word: their king has secured them a night's rest. The camp's not to be roused until the sun's well up."

"Rodrigo!" Groenfil threw down his cap. "Have you no regard for the art of war?"

"What do we risk? Hriskil would be demented to mount a frontal assault in the confusion of night."

"At dawn . . ."

"Will we not see and hear their approach? Come, Anavar, you're yawning." In good cheer, I mounted Ebon and started toward camp. Immediately Pardos and his men formed alongside. As we rode, he growled, "Kadar warned me you were impulsive."

"Hmpff." But I let him guide me to camp.

Glad it would annoy him, I paid a visit to Danzik, still shackled to his wagon. The Norland chieftain seemed restless as I. "Pir vin?" he demanded. *Why do you come?*

"Liste memor." *I'm ready to learn.*

"Eb pir tal hur? Pir nota het vos morta?" *But why this hour? Why the night before your death?*

"You're so sure," I said in careful Norlandic, settling myself on the slats of the wagon bed, "your master will kill me?"

Absently Danzik corrected my verbs. Then, "Qay." *Yes.* "Norl haut Rood."

"But I have the Still." Not that I could use it. I'd squandered it, for the time.

His laugh might have held pity. If so, I could hardly blame him. We'd learned hard that the Rood of the Norlands was a fearsome weapon.

Yet if Danzik were right, no point in my struggling with his tongue. No point in anything, this night. Irritably, I snapped, "Rez Caledi verta rez Norl." *We're equals.*

He rolled his eyes.

"Your king may be strong . . ." I struggled for the words. "But he knows not all. Tonight, in secret, I visited his camp."

It was too much; I hadn't the words. I tried to pantomime "visit." At length, we settled on a word. And I learned a new one: mentrik. *Liar.*

In vain, I described the camp, Hriskil's appearance.

He dismissed it. "Kevhom vos diche." *The horseman told you.* My real envoy, he meant.

"Soa kevhom!" I jabbed at my chest.

"Han." He shook his head. Nothing I said could convince him. He launched into an impassioned speech, only part of which I understood. Hriskil was no fool, no savage. The king spoke four languages, ruled wisely and justly, wielded the Rood itself. No Caled boy could fool him. Soon he'd —something—sweep?—me from the pass.

Impasse.

Why waste my time with a dirty barbarian in a fly-specked wagon? I should be in bed, or if wakeful, walking the camp, soothing the fears of my men. Danzik was a superstitious savage, and his opinion mattered not.

"No. He isn't."

My guards started. I hadn't realized I'd spoken aloud.

"He's Hriskil's captain, and my teacher." Wearily, I stood. "Regra, Danzik. I've treated you ill."

He watched with suspicious eyes.

"Take him to the stream, let him bathe. Give him good food, decent clothes, see the wagon has real bedding, and a cover for rain. Move it so it's near my tent."

Pardos looked from one to the other of us. "Sire, he's the enemy!"

"Agreed. Do it." I jumped down, stalked to my tent.

Tanner was within, smoothing my bed, laying out my clothes under Anavar's watchful eye. I grimaced at my reflection in the silver. I was as unkempt as Danzik; no wonder Hriskil and Llewelyn didn't recognize me as king. Well, it had been a long, fearful day.

The ewer was full; I poured water into the bowl, set about washing. To Tanner and Anavar, "You may go."

Anavar waited until we were alone. "Here." Brusquely, he unsheathed the bejeweled dagger, once a gift from Lady Soushire. "Have Pardos impound it, before I'm let in."

I dried my face. "Why?"

"You kicked me! Before Genard, Tursel, the common soldiers! I'm of noble birth, a peer of your land and mine! Would you treat Groenfil so?"

I bowed my head.

"Harsh words I can abide; I'm boy to your man. But how dare you treat me thus, and rely on my honor not to bury my blade in your back! You ask too much!"

I swallowed.

"Sire, I *would* follow you." He brushed at his eyes. "Tonight you were a marvel. And on the retreat . . . you're noble indeed. And then you ki—ki—kick . . ."

I was exasperated beyond bearing. "Leave me."

He stalked out.

I finished my ablutions. Who was Anavar to rebuke—he was my baron, a noble, my friend. Never mind that. On the morrow we had to defend a puny wall against a force far our superior, and all Caledon hung in the balance. Couldn't he see I was tired, highly strung, fearful that . . . couldn't I see he was likewise?

Sighing, I sat, drew the bowl near. Why, of all my aspects, need the Still augment my cruelty? I set my palms across the still water. Perhaps I was rested enough to ask my ancestors. With Mother's help, I'd bind the impulses that drove me. I closed my eyes, summoning the words of encant. I'd go to battle tomorrow a better man, one who—

Aghast, I pulled away my hands. What fool was I, to squander the Still on personal affairs? Who knew what need battle would bring? "Demons take it!" I stumbled to my feet, paced the tent. I would live with cruelty, and Anavar must do the same. No time for weakness, maudlin self-pity.

I must be strong.

THE CREAK OF wood, low irascible words. I poked my head through the tent flap. A squad of Tursel's yeomen dragged Danzik's splintered wagon across the turf, amid muttered curses. I threw on a fresh jerkin, stepped into the cool night air. "Yes, good, over there will do."

They complied, in sullen silence.

Very well, imps take them if—no, Roddy, that's not the way. "Thank you, I'm much pleased. You, there—Coster, isn't it? What troubles you? The battle?"

Thus encouraged, the stubby fellow stuck out a disdainful

thumb. "Better 'n us, Danzik gets? Wagon, fresh bedding . . . what say you, King, shall we send him a girl from the tavern?"

No more than I deserved, seeking the opinion of a churl.

Not so, my prince. A faint whisper, as of a breeze.

Oh, Rustin, don't steal unseen into my mind. Give me warning, that I not blink tears before my men. I stood, mouth working. Then I managed, "You're irked. I'm sorry. Come sit with me by the fire." Murmurs of amazement as I led them to the nearest campfire. "Peace to all, no, don't get up."

I found a place. The wagon detail crowded around.

"You also served my mother, Elena, did you not? When I was a tyke, I'd watch you walk the battlements."

"Yes, sire." Coster's tone was wary.

"And here we are, far from home, in this imp-plagued mountain town." Is this the way, Rust? I haven't the knack of kindness. "You hate Danzik? Speak up, the lot of you."

Someone said, "He's one of *them*."

"He spat on you."

"A long time past." My tone was mild.

"*I'd* never forget."

"Best they drown him in that stream he washes in." A gaunt face, across the fire.

"Tomorrow . . ." Coster was hesitant. "If they—if he's freed, what mercy think you he'd show us?"

I admitted, "None, I warrant. But . . ." I swallowed, cast aside the caution I ought to safeguard. "Have you never wanted to be a better man than you are? As do I?" Abruptly I got to my feet. It was all I could do not to flee to my tent. "Kindness is foreign to me, Coster. I pray thee, don't berate my use of it."

Stunned silence.

"Well, isn't it so? I ride roughshod over goodwill, tramp friendship into dust. Does not the whole camp speak of it?" *Rust, bind my mouth before I destroy myself. I know not what I do.*

"Well, my lord . . ." From a few, nervous laughter.

Someone handed me a clay-made cup. Hot steaming tea. I took a grateful sip, glad not to look into the faces that surrounded me.

"Sire . . ." A soft voice. "Can we hold the Norlanders?"

"Tomorrow? I trust so. They're men, not demons." I risked

a glance. If I'd meant to reassure, I'd failed. "How clever can they be, letting the king of Caledon ride through their camp?"

"Is it true? We heard rumors—"

" 'Go with grace,' they told me in parting. Would *we* wave cheerful good-bye if Hriskil presented himself among us?" From the men, guffaws and ribald suggestions. I was encouraged. "And funniest of all, they haven't the faintest idea of their folly."

Coster chuckled. "Imagine Hriskil's face, if he knew he'd—Rodrigo? Is all well?"

I sat rigid, my mind awhirl.

After a time, I raised my head. "Who among you would take a stroll with his king?"

FIFTEEN

IT WASN'T SO easy as I'd wished, but at last we slipped over the wall and worked our silent way across the field.

Twenty men, armed to the teeth. Bowmen, near useless in the dark. More swords and pikes than we could comfortably carry. Shields. No horses, though, lest one neigh or snort.

We'd had more than enough volunteers. Lord Groenfil himself led them. When his best efforts failed to dissuade me, he'd insisted on taking part, in unspoken apology for his calumny that I wasn't worth following. Lady Soushire had embraced him at the gate, and a lively wind had snapped at my leggings.

Coster and three of his troop hauled along a precious burden.

Nothing could be heard but the sound of our breathing as we crept toward the wood. Though my men all wore black and I sweated under a black cape, a quarter moon gleamed; enough to betray us if luck favored the foe.

I glanced at Groenfil; his eyes shone through the black soot that covered his face. I grinned; his head bobbed in acknowledgment.

A muffled protest. I whirled, motioning Coster to go easy with the point of his dagger.

How much further? We were nearly out of arrow shot of the wall, definitely within range of their outguard.

"Roddy . . ." Groenfil's voice was barely a whisper.

"A few more paces." If we weren't close enough, all would be for naught. I stumbled over a root; with a sharp intake of breath someone caught me.

Finally, I murmured, "All right." Four shieldmen came forward, each man dropping on one knee behind his tall bronze shield. Groenfil took my shoulders, propelled me firmly behind the shields. He'd promised as much to Tantroth before the duke of Eiber would countenance our mission.

I took deep breath, began to shout. "Small men of Norland!" The problem was, I lacked proper insults. My vocabulary wasn't all that extensive, and Danzik couldn't be consulted. "Little men! Hriskil!"

Within the distant copse, a cry of alarm.

I shouted, "Voe graftig rez qa fartha Caled?" *Where is the crazy king who invades Caledon?* "Wake your drunkard King Hriskil!"

"Enough," snarled Groenfil, and pulled me to the ground. "Give them time to rouse themselves."

Within the wood, a flicker. A fire arrow arced into the sky, and another. They fell nowhere near us. We all lay on our bellies, absolutely still.

Except one, of course.

The Norland camp swarmed like an aroused beehive. After a time I got cautiously to my knees. Our shield bearers promptly did the same. I roared to the Norlanders, "Why do you let a drunk lead you?" Or, I hoped that was what I said. It might have been, "Why do you drink your leader?" In Norlandic, words don't fall in their rightful place.

"Soa embas Caledi!" *I am the envoy of Caledon.* "Do you not remember me at your camp?"

A volley of arrows whistled past. No fire, just deadly iron tips.

"Llewelyn! Tell your master you cannot conquer us! I walk with impunity through your camp! Soa Rodrigo, embas Caledi!" As signal, I turned, shouted it again toward our walls.

"Now!" Groenfil shoved Coster, who yanked the gag off our captive's mouth.

Danzik struggled desperately to free his bound wrists. "SA REZ CALEDI! MODRE KO!" He was beside himself. "ER CAMPA SA! AXT HOMU!" *It's the Caled king! Kill him! He's in the field, twenty men!*

From our walls, a dozen fire arrows launched. The nearest landed about a dozen paces behind us. Our closest shieldman dashed toward it, snatched it from the ground, raced back to us.

"HRISKIL, IV OT, DANZIK! MODRE RODRIGO!"

I rasped, "It's time!"

Our runner dived to the ground, fire arrow sputtering. Instantly, three torches were thrust at it. In a moment they caught.

Without ceremony, Coster and three men lifted the bound Norlander off his feet, ran with him toward our walls. "HRISKIL!" Danzik's voice receded. "MODRE REZ!"

Three shieldmen were on their knees, palms braced on the earth. Groenfil's iron grip on my arm helped me to climb on their waiting backs.

I threw off the black cloak. Under it was the garb I'd worn as envoy. Our yeomen thrust the torches at my face, blinding me before the enemy. Well and good; I wouldn't see the Norland arrow that snuffed out my life.

I bellowed, "Iv ot, Hriskil! Rez Caledi qa vit embas!" The soft hum of arrows. Something flicked past my ear. "Mor Rodrigo, qa han vos modrit!" *Look on Rodrigo, whom you cannot kill!*

"Aiye!" Behind me, a squeal. An arrow had gone home.

Groenfil hauled at my forearm, but I twisted free, thrust my face at the nearest torch. "Soa Rodrigo Caledi, embas ur rez!" From the wood, the thud of feet, the clank of iron.

"Retreat, you lunatic!" Groenfil hauled me off my perch. "Go!" To the lot of us, *"Go!"*

Our men flung aside their torches. We sprinted madly toward Pezar.

"RODRIGO? IT'S NINTH hour!" Tantroth sounded annoyed. "Awaken and dress yourself. You're a disgrace."

"Ohhh." My head pounded. How late had we caroused into the night? "What of Hriskil?"

"No sign."

"I told you." I suspected I hadn't seen my bed 'til near dawn. I'd had drink, and my recall was fuzzy. I poked out my head, blinked in the sharp lance of sunlight. "What of the men?"

"Long roused."

Last night, reaching the wall, we'd scampered up the rope ladders and onto the rampart, bearing our wounded companion, an arrow through his shoulder. He would recover, unless the wound turned putrid. I was immediately surrounded by wildly excited guardsmen, some of Stryx, some of Eiber.

An odd madness had come over me; I capered gleefully about the wall, and whirled Genard into a spin when he tried to grab me. Suddenly others joined my dance and frolic, and I led a line of shouting, laughing, careening soldiers all the way to camp. We dug out bread, threw chickens into pots, uncorked kegs of beer. In an hour the whole camp had joined our revels; Hriskil must have heard us in the far corner of his encampment. Tantroth and Groenfil had done their best to put a stop to it, but I said nay; we had until noon, and would make the most of it.

Now, in morning's light, I tried manfully to put myself together.

"Is he up?" Groenfil, outside my tent, his voice curt.

"Barely." Tantroth.

I stumbled into my breeches, grabbed a jerkin. "Good morning, my lords. Would you break fast with me?"

Groenfil glowered. "Is our play done, sire?"

"Please, sir." I waved at the camp. "See you no difference?"

"They're tired, befuddled, logy with drink—"

"What of their fear? Look at them!" It was true; our men, though preparing for battle, had lost their sullen dejection, the anxiety that ate at their souls. If our camp wasn't exactly festive, it certainly didn't lack for good cheer.

And we'd done more. Among the Norlanders, seeds of doubt had been sown. By what arcane power did Rodrigo walk among them unharmed? They wouldn't, I hoped, conclude it was by sheer good luck. And if our frolics kept us carousing the night, what, the Norlanders might wonder, did their Caled foe know about the morrow?

None of it could do us harm.

Tantroth grunted. "If Hriskil had attacked at dawn—"

"Half of us would still have been up." I waved it away. "Raeth's gone, and a meal won't be the same, but let us sit at table." I laced my boots.

HRISKIL FILLED THE field with shields, more men than a just Lord of Nature would allow under one standard. To my surprise, no horse. They began a slow march to the wall as the sun reached midpoint in its arc.

My whole soul reached out to sense the Rood. But no muddle obscured our thought, no cloud befuddled my wits. Perhaps Hriskil must recover from the Rood, as I the Still; when opportunity arose I would ask Danzik.

Much of the battle was fought by bowmen; ours loosed shafts into the advancing yeomen; theirs aimed primarily at our archers on the hill.

If Uncle Raeth's defense had a fault, it was that the battle-ments were too narrow to allow easy movement of men on the ramparts. But as needed, we crowded reinforcements onto the ledges, and for five hours, it was bloody work. We lost seventy men; they lost hundreds.

Abruptly, a blare of horns, and the Norlanders fell back.

We had won the day.

Bloodlust ebbing, I paced the wall, shield arm aching from the weight of the bronze. "Lord Tantroth, what think you?"

"That we ought attack Hriskil's camp within the hour."

I blinked. "We're tired, our wounded need care, the Nor-landers far outnumber—"

"Precisely. Could they imagine you so foolish as to attack?"

"I hope not." I waved away the absurdity. "So, what will he try next?"

"A real attack."

"But, the terrain is against . . ."

"Fah. Saw you ladders, or towers? Catapults?" He shook his head. "No, today was but a probe."

"Hundreds dead, in a probe?"

"To him, the cost is but a trifle."

Despondent, I rode back to camp.

I TRUDGED TO my tent.

"Imps eat you, evil king!"

I whirled? "Qa diche?" It took me a moment to realize we were speaking Norlandic.

Danzik bestrode his wagon. I took a hasty step back; he might at any moment leap for my throat. His guards were tak-ing no chances; spears were pointed, daggers out. From Danzik, a volley of oaths, only some of which I grasped. But they made clear his rage. I threw up my hands, left him to his choler.

At a campfire nearby, I came upon my bondsman Bollert playing idly with a sharpened stick, and stopped so abruptly Pardos collided with me. "Boy, have you naught to do?" My tone was sharp.

Bollert scrambled to his feet. "Can't fin' Tanner." He scratched his flank.

"That's not my concern. Have you a place to sleep?"

"Last night, unner cart."

"Find Tursel. Tell him I said to find you shelter. And bedding."

"Aye, King." He shambled off.

I opened my tent flap, peered in. My night clothes were set out neatly, and my soft bed of duck feathers invited my recline, but I hesitated. I wasn't yet ready for sleep.

Unthinking, I looked about for Rustin, and caught myself with a sharp exhalation of breath. The tent seemed so . . . empty. But Anavar had his own, and Elryc too, though he shared with Genard. I was beyond seeking solace—I must be king, and strong. Yet . . .

I turned about. "Pardos, *must* you step on my shadow? Look, there's a good man, stand back by the fire. I won't leave the clearing: Elryc and Anavar and Groenfil's tents mark my boundary. Please, else I'll go mad."

"A knife in the night—"

"Would you disarm my very brother? No, don't answer; I wouldn't know of it. Please, cannot my kingdom be a few paces breadth?" At last, I cajoled him, and with relief headed for Elryc's tent.

". . . say as you wish, Lord Prince, but I know what I see." Anavar.

I stopped dead, outside the closed flap.

Elryc said, "Roddy's impulsive."

"That may be his end." Anavar's tone was somber.

Rooted to the spot, I shooed away a fly.

"Why tell Elryc?" Genard. "Roddy barely listens—"

Anavar's voice was hot. "Last night, we beseeched him not to risk himself as his own envoy; did he answer? He kicked me into the dirt, rode off on a madman's errand."

"At the wall today," Genard said excitedly, "Tantroth wanted to attack their camp. Roddy just waved—you know how he does it, m'lor, the dismissal that makes you feel so small. Rode off without a word."

"A pity." Elryc. "Tantroth was softening. I could feel it."

Genard sniffed. "Think of Tursel, m'lord. Or Lady Soushire. She's near leaving camp."

"He knows."

"Imbar won't leave his tent. I ought tell Roddy, but he'd laugh, and I'd answer with spite, and he'd break his vow not to speak ill to me."

Elryc said gently, "It's not your place to tell him, Genard."

Anavar cried, "So many wished him well. If but he'd listen!"

Elryc sighed. "Rustin could guide him. He'll heed no other."

Yes, brother, betray me. I knew you had it in you. My fist knotted.

"But he tries so to be a good king."

Abruptly, my eyes stung.

Elryc added, "Recall that, Anavar, when he chafes you."

"I'll stay," said Anavar glumly. "I gave my oath." But then, "Would that I had not."

I stumbled toward the clearing. Pardos started in alarm; fiercely I waved him away. I was all right.

No, I wasn't. I was struck to the heart with a blade I'd my-self honed.

Whom else could I blame? My brother? Anavar, whom I'd shamed? Genard, who loved only his master Elryc?

Yet, it wasn't fair. I *did* try to be a good king. They spoke nonsense, they were mere children. I need not listen to—

I need not listen.

Appalled, I wandered to the fire, sank onto the damp grass, twirled the stick Bollert had dropped.

Rodrigo, who art thou?

Son of Elena Queen, of Josip her lord prince, grandson of Tryon, conqueror of—

Rodrigo, what art thou?

Seventeen, and crowned king of Caledon, liege to the Lords Groenfil, Soushire, Tantroth—

What art thou, truly?

I dare not say it!

"Sire, are you—"

"Get thee gone!" My voice was raw.

I'm an arrogant youngsire. Vain and foolish.

No more?

Frightened. Is that so—yes, frightened. And so lonely. When I wake in the night, I bite the pillow that my grief not be heard. *I miss him so.*

What resources hast thou?

Stryx, and the castle. The army about us. The Still, though I can't value its worth. Cumber, though without Uncle Raeth—

Within.

I'm stubborn; sometimes that's good. I'm terribly afraid of capture, of a gory death. But I quell my fear and summon the pretense of courage. It's almost as if I had it in truth. And at times . . . I speak well, and call forth loyalty beyond . . . my cause is parlous, yet so many have—have—many—

Why dost thou weep?

I'm ashamed.

Of?

What I am. What I do. Must I say it?

Silence.

I hurled the splintered stick into the fire.

I appoint advisors and won't hear their counsel, guards whom I won't let guard. Vassals I swear to uphold, and kick into the dust. And there's my cruelty, that has no restraint except what I myself provide. And I can't curb myself. Oh, I've tried. Did I not appoint Rustin regent and guardian of my person? Did I not abdicate my manhood to put an end to cruelty?

And now?

Now I'm lost.

Oh, my prince . . . are you?

Yes, Rust. Look at me, head drawn to knees, rocking before the fire. I'm so ashamed. Why cannot I master myself? Would you help me, Rust?

The crackle of flames.

Rustin, I can't abide your soft voice that flits unexpected in the shadows of my soul. If you're real, speak!

Silence, of a grave.

Rustin, I command thee, speak!

The distant sounds of camp.

Sir, my heart breaketh; I beseech thee!

Nothing.

Now must I acknowledge it: I was truly alone.

I drew myself closer to my knees, rocking in my calamity.

Sixteen

IN THE DAWN'S pale light I shivered, raised my head. A flutter of wind stirred the ashes of the fire.

Across the firepit, two vigilant bodyguards brandished spear and sword. To either side, some paces removed, others.

Ignoring the ache of my bones, I turned my head. Behind me, three guards, at a respectful distance.

Before them, on the damp grass, cross-legged, Anavar sat wearily.

Near my tent, on a campstool, Elryc, his eyes hollow, huddling under a blanket. At his side, solemnly, Genard.

Near my tent, standing, Tantroth, his arms folded, speaking quietly to Groenfil. Across the way, Tursel. Even Danzik's smoldering gaze bored through me, under the canopy of his wagon.

All eyes were on me.

Not often does one attend the dissolution of a king.

I tried to get up. My bones were stone; every muscle throbbed. I grasped a guard's offered arm and staggered to my feet.

"Sir . . ."

"Not now, Anavar." My voice was a frog's croak. "How long have . . . ?"

"As long as you."

Gently, I took his face between my palms. "Go, refresh yourself. Warmth, fresh clothes, hot drink." A pat of his cheek that might have signified fondness. I cloaked my embarrassment in high speech. "We thank thee, Baron, for thy attendance."

Still, he persisted. "What do you now?"

I shook my head. No more words of resolve, honeyed promises beyond my keeping. And, Lord of Nature help me, I would not be judged the man I've been.

Rustin, if you will not aid me, I must correct myself. It's a task I dread, but . . . I cannot abide what I am.

"Drink, sire." A steaming cup of mulled cider.

My mouth watered. "Later, Pardos." *When I've earned it.*

My calf was knotted. I limped from the campfire. Where to start?

"Farang vos, Rez!" Danzik.

As good a place as any.

I made for the Norlander's wagon, tried to hoist myself over the rail. Every muscle shrieked in protest. If you don't want aches, Roddy, don't squat the night at a campfire's fading embers.

Halfway over the rail, I hesitated. "Fea, Guiat?" *Please, Teacher?* Though in Norlandic, fea could mean "permission," or "may I," or . . . at any rate, it would serve.

Danzik snorted. I took it for assent and slipped over the rail; one could carry humility too far.

He rattled the chain that tethered him to his bed.

"I'm sorry about that. Guard, take it off; he's only to be secured at night."

"Or when you're with him, sire."

"Kadar? You're not . . . what do you here?"

"I'm bodyguard to the king. Pardos gave me leave," he added hurriedly when my scowl failed to abate. "I swore to obey his—sir, I *must* guard you. I gave oath to—please!"

"Release my teacher."

"Han guiat!"

"Yes, you are. Kadar, don't pout, sit beside me with dagger drawn, he won't hurt us. Will you, Danzik?"

A grunt that wasn't very reassuring.

We got ourselves settled. A small form detached itself from the knot of watchers, swarmed over the rail to crouch beside me. Genard, the shadow of my lessons.

I nodded assent. "I was about to ask about his fury of last night. What he shouted—qa dicha . . . diche?—Genard, how do you say 'dicha' when you mean yesterday?"

"Diche, m'lor'."

"Yes. Vos diche—that I couldn't buy . . ." Somehow, I wrenched it into the Norland tongue.

Danzik bared his teeth. "Why I teach?"

"Because I ask it." I made my tone meek. "What can I not buy?"

"Ot!" He pounded his chest. He launched into a long discourse, which I struggled to follow. I . . . owned? . . . held? . . .

his body; that was fortune of war. I could kill him. But he was
no traitor. I had no *vade*. To make him play my games with
Hriskil was *han kevhom*. I couldn't buy *vade* of a man. Not
'buy.' *Torsa*. Heavily, Danzik got to his feet, alarming Kadar,
and pantomimed snatching something, hiding it under a
cloak. "Torsa!" he growled.

"Steal?"

"*Torsa ot vade!*"

I threw up my hands. "What did I steal?"

"His soul," said Genard suddenly.

Crossly, I waved it away. "Only imps can steal a soul." One
took great care not to summon them in the night by careless
words. "Besides, I needed him to show it was me." Danzik's
shouted rage had confirmed that it was I, the king, who'd
taunted them in the night, and that I was the envoy who'd
boldly ridden into their camp.

"*Regra, Guiat.*" *I'm sorry.* Wearily, I stood. "I won't do it
again."

It wasn't a good time to ask Danzik about the Rood; instead, I left him to his recriminations. When I'd clambered
down, Kadar breathed a sigh of relief. "Now where, sire?"

"I don't know." If Hriskil wielded his Power, our every decision on the field of battle would be fraught with confusion
and raw seething anger that undid us. Above all, I must devise
a plan. Recover use of the Still, or . . . or what?

I knew not. With a sigh, I set it aside and led Kadar across
the clearing, to a tent I'd set as far from mine as I might. I
beckoned to Genard, who still trailed. "My respects—" I tried
not to choke on the word. "—to Lord Imbar, and would he
kindly receive his king?"

"Aye, m'lor'." Genard trotted ahead.

The frayed tent was sturdily made, without frills, but was
becoming shabby. No one had cleaned the accumulated mud
from its flaps. Nonetheless, it bore traces of the dignity with
which Raeth cloaked himself.

Imbar, smoothing his jerkin, stood aside. "Welcome to the
king." His voice was stiff. I eased past his protruding belly.

Inside, a trunk, a stool, a rope bed. Little more. Clothes
were strewn on whatever surface was handy.

"Have you no manservant?" I spoke without thinking.
Someone ought to tidy the place, if Imbar wouldn't bother.

"None." He scratched his grizzled cheeks.

"Did Raeth make no provision?" The earl of Cumber wanted his valet ennobled; it was *his* responsibility to look after the man. Did he think *I* would do it?

"A farm I might sell." Not now, of course, with Cumber impoverished, and all Caledon at war. A shrug. "Why come you, sire?"

"Why won't you leave your tent?"

"I haven't the courage." Defiant eyes met mine.

"No one expects a man your age to fight—"

"To kill myself." Imbar threw up a hand. "Give me time; I'll manage. A rope, I think. I've always dreaded the ooze of blood."

"I—but . . . why?"

"Why not?" He turned to the flap, peered outside to make sure we were unheard. He tugged at his sagging breeches. "They no longer fit. Rae would have approved." A fleeting smile.

"Don't you eat?"

"Now and again. Please don't make small talk; we both know you care not."

Astonished, he watched his king clear a space on his trunk, as might a page.

"Sit, Baron." It was between command and plea. "Tell me your trouble."

He eased himself down. "Raeth is gone. Look at me!" Imbar's wave took in his corpulent form, his unshaven face, the disorder of his tent. "Raeth saw in me what I once was."

I waited.

"In my youth I turned heads. I was slim, fair of feature. Can you imagine it? No, I see by your eyes you do not. How can I blame you?" He hesitated, found a hidden resolve. "Was a time when I'd inveigle some well-born boy to my bed, he'd go away laughing, shaking his head at the frolic or device which landed him, but not put out, Lord King, not revolted as your Rustin, ready to spit me on his blade but for your cause!"

For my very life, I could find no words. I concentrated on barring my fingers from the sheath of my dagger.

"Think you, Lord King, I am not punished for my folly? His disgust, his offense . . . I see them yet! And I see myself, fat and vain, a figure of contempt."

"Don't ask my compassion for—"

"Oh, Rodrigo," he cried, "who will love me now?"

A stab in my breast. His despair swirled a distant memory. I closed my eyes.

Learn to forgive, my boy.

Oh, Uncle Raeth, you ask much.

THE ADVANCING SUN bore mute witness to my halting efforts at reform. I was civil, and more, to Tantroth, Larissa, Anavar. I listened when they spoke, and considered what they said.

I told Groenfil, as I promised I would, that I hadn't yet recovered the Still.

He looked grim. "Hriskil's attack will be in force."

"I have no doubt."

"At the ridge, the Rood unmanned us. We were lucky to escape."

"That is so."

His sarcasm bit. "Trust you in luck?"

"No. I have a plan." It wasn't so, but I would make it true.

For dinner, a bowl of savory stew. Afterward, I took a moment to see that Tanner was properly housed. Feeling virtuous, I retreated to my tent, but though I'd not seen my bed for two days, it held no appeal. I paced, toying with a tooled scabbard, an inlaid cachet box, the chest with my royal seal that Rustin and I had shared.

I'd promised Groenfil a plan, and had none. Would the lie cost me my Power, or was it a ruse of war? Could I salvage my Power, or had I thrown away all on a moment without thought?

"Rustin, am I undone?"

Silence.

Suddenly, I couldn't bear to be alone. I crossed to the flap. The bodyguard stiffened. "Summon Anavar." My tone was brusque. "No, hold." I caught his arm. "I'm sorry. Say rather: if I don't disturb his rest, would the baron join me in my tent? Kindly join. Kindly." Cheeks crimson, I thrust closed the flap. The guard must think me demented.

"Ah, Rustin, will it always be so hard?"

A knock, at the pole by the flap. Anavar poked in his head, glanced about. "Who were you talking to?"

"No one, I—" I sighed. "I hear Rustin, sometimes. In my

heart. Sometimes I answer." I waved it aside, before he could ask me more. I'd made fool of myself enough for one night. "Anavar, what shall we do about Hriskil and the Rood?" I sank on the bed, put my arms behind my head.

"Tell me of it." He settled himself.

I said crossly, "You know the effect as well as—"

"The Rood itself. What is it?"

"A device, two sticks crossed. Bejeweled, some say made of gold. To wield it he holds it high."

"Is it . . ." Anavar pondered. "Like your Still, in that the vessels aid you, but any water in a bowl will do?"

I shrugged. "I don't know if the ceremonial Rood need be the one he holds."

"Because if it is . . ."

"We might capture it." Or bribe his troops, or destroy it, or . . . My mind reeled with possibilities. I brought myself back to reality. "But not by the morrow."

"No. That day at the ridge . . ." Anavar shook his head. "We were caught unawares, and the Rood made it so much worse. Orders flying, tempers ignited . . . thinking was like swimming through mud."

I grimaced. I hardly needed reminding.

He mused, "If only we'd known ahead of time what to do."

"Never mind that. The question is—" I jerked upright. "What did you say?"

"If only we'd known—"

"That's it!" I leaped to my feet. "Anavar, call them here!"

"Who?"

"Start with Tantroth. Don't scowl, he knows who you are." I thrust open the flap. "Pardos, my respects to Lady Larissa and Groenfil; might they join us at once? Genard, what are you doing by the fire? Who's with Elryc? I pray you, summon Baron Imbar from his tent. Then find Captain Tursel!"

"But—"

I held my temper; it grew easier each time. "It's below your rank, but would you, for me? You see, I've found a way!"

"Aye, sire." Perhaps my mood was infectious. Anavar and Genard bounded into the night.

Moments later, Groenfil found me, head on hands. I pulled myself together. "Welcome, my lord."

Soon we were gathered. Anavar watched wistfully, from the

tent flap. I beckoned him near, threw an arm across his shoulder, swept him into our conclave. "My lords, in a while—perhaps at dawn—they'll be upon us. Hriskil will lead the battle."

Tantroth raised an eyebrow. "You've spoken to him?"

"No need. They've wasted time and men. Now they'll mount their true assault. Towers and horse, ladders, catapults, all their implements of war. He'll be among them, to wield the Rood." I took deep breath. "I can't counter it; I haven't yet the use of the Still."

Groenfil frowned. "If there's naught we can do—"

"But there is." I spoke as if with confidence. "Tursel, the wall is yours to defend. It must not fall. Bring our reserves up from the Mill Road; we'll want them near."

"They'll only be in the way when—"

"The Rood is confusion; every summons is fraught with peril. Station our reserves in sight. Lord Groenfil, cede your horsemen to Tantroth."

"What?" His eyes blazed; a wayward wind whipped the canvas.

"For the day. You'll lead our reserve, all our footmen and archers. Ah, Baron Imbar, welcome." I made him a place at my side. "You're to keep the wall fit for battle. Lady Soushire, Imbar will need men, perhaps a hundred, if you allow? Baron, bring down our wounded and dead, send Tursel replacements as needed. See the archers are supplied, and fresh pikes for those broken."

Imbar's lined face stiffened with resolve.

I swung about. "Tantroth, you'll have our horse."

"To what purpose?"

"Tursel will hold the battlement until the Norlanders turn back. When they're halfway across the field—exactly halfway, we'll decide that now and vary not from our course—Groenfil's pikemen and Soushire's will rush out the gate, half to the left, half to the right. Attack, Lord Groenfil. A full run toward the retreating Norlanders. That leaves the center open for Tantroth's horse." Break their center, sweep up the flanks. Plunder their camp, if we get that far. Then back to the wall."

Tursel cleared his throat. "Sire, we can't set our order of attack until we see—"

"That's my point. We must!" I looked about. "The Rood." I

could see none of them understood. "We fight it by setting our dispositions in stone. Nothing is to be changed. No last-moment orders, counterorders, fury or misunderstanding. This won't be another battle of the ridge."

"But, sir!" Anavar seemed abashed to speak in this august company. "No changes, to meet a changed situation? If anything goes wrong and you've locked us into a plan of battle, we risk annihilation."

Groenfil nodded agreement, as did Tursel.

"Not if we carry out our assigned tasks. Tursel, the wall *must* hold. With it falls Caledon."

"Aye, sire."

"If Tursel holds, soon or late, Hriskil will retreat; our archers on the hill make encampment on the field too costly. When he retreats, Tantroth and Groenfil must have their chance. We need but take it."

They looked unconvinced.

"And you, sire?" Tursel.

"I'll remain by the wall, to hearten the men." To Tantroth, "It's what you yourself proposed two days past."

Larissa and Groenfil exchanged a dubious glance.

"I tell you, we'll defeat the Rood! It's the only way. And it will only work once."

"Why?" Tursel.

"Hriskil's no fool; he'll figure out what we've done, and come prepared."

"Then, next battle—"

"I'll have the Still." I looked about. "Trust me in this, my lords. I beseech you, swear that we will stay the course we set this night."

"Aye, sire." Anavar, dutifully. Gratefully, I squeezed his shoulder.

"Yes, sire." Baron Imbar. With dignity, a short bow.

"Very well." Tantroth, duke of Eiber.

One by one they acquiesced.

SEVENTEEN

"*To RODRIGO, KING of Caledon and my liege lord, fond greetings from his cousin Tresa. I pray you are in good health. Your firm defense of Pezar gladdens our spirits. But, Rodrigo, do take care. Your exploits in the night, however infuriating to Hriskil, risk all. One stray arrow . . .*

"*Shall I assure you all is well in Cumber? No, you bade me speak my heart. Here, the days are long, the air sultry and our people fearful of changes that a new lord's dominion brings.*

"*With great fanfare, my uncle Bouris arrived to take up residence at Cumber. Have you met him? He's muscular, impatient, quick to decide. Nothing like Grandfather. Almost his first act was to order the gardens Grandfather cherished torn out and replaced with kennels. He is decidedly fond of his hounds.*

"*In fact—*"

"Sire—"

I scowled at Pardos, who peered through the flap. "Now what?" It was barely dawn.

"The Norlanders."

My throat tightened. I dropped Tresa's letter on the wooden chest, laid a candlestick over it against a stray breeze. "Help me, please." I raised my arms to aid in buckling my scabbard. A last look around the tent I might never see again. "As we agreed, yes? I'll climb the battlement, but I won't seek the front rank."

My bodyguard pursed his lips. "As you say, sire."

"How soon before . . ."

"They form ranks across the field. An hour, perhaps."

Enough.

Outside the tent, Bollert held Ebon's reins. I'd been so engrossed in Tresa's letter, I hadn't heard them.

We cantered down the road to the fortified pass. Groenfil and Larissa were to one side, with their troops. Tantroth paced the wall, breastplate gleaming. Imbar waited the day with his squad amid empty litters, barrels, sheaves of arrows. I glanced about, as if to see Uncle Raeth's gaunt, weary form. I knew better, but . . .

I sighed. I might as well search for Rustin. No, I was alone, and on my shoulders the weight of our campaign. I climbed the wall, peered over the battlement. Foot soldiers poured out of the wood, clearing the way for towers on wheels.

I climbed the wall. "My Lord Tantroth, I wish thee fortune." I gave him a short bow, of familial respect.

He grunted, as if oblivious to the honor. "Look at them. The wood is thick."

I peered. Men poured from wood to meadow. The day would be grim indeed. Our archers wouldn't miss; they had merely to loose their arrows to find a target.

Across the field, a high platform lurched, almost overturned, righted itself. I frowned. The field was too level; we ought to have dug trenches and mounted barricades to disrupt the wheels of the siege towers. Were I not a boy at war, I'd have known to do so.

A clatter of footsteps; Anavar ran up the stair, sleep still in his mien. He bore shield, sword, helmet. I eyed him sourly. "Think you your place is in the front rank?"

"Eiber's my homeland!"

He was but a boy, and my ward. I'd soon cut him down to size. I drew breath.

Rodrigo!

Yes, Rust. I'm sorry, I didn't think. I cleared my throat. "About last night . . ."

Anavar waited, apprehensive.

"Speaking with the nobles, I gave you not your due. The idea to set in advance what each would do, was yours. Will you forgive me for claiming it?"

He searched my face. "Sir, do you toy with me?"

What was I, that my household was skeptical of my praise? "It's just that . . . coming from a boy, they might not have— still, I should have mentioned you. I'm sorry." To my surprise, I truly was.

His face softened. "I'm glad to help."

"Then you'll help me this morn? We'll go about and encourage the men."

His face fell. "But I want to fight."

"Please?" I made my tone meek.

"As you say." His look was dubious. "Are you well?"

No, I'm being kind; obviously I've lost my wits. "Yes, of course."

A NORLAND WAVE rolled across the sea of grass, in frightening silence. No signal rent the air. No hoarse cry, no shrill clarion spurred Hriskil's hordes to the charge. The enemy host flowed out of the wood, a grim-faced tide advancing inexorably toward our shore. Shoulder to shoulder, in lockstep they advanced, more men than I'd dreamed any foe might comprise, their boots scything the remains of the meadow's dry and scraggled brush. Most of Hriskil's men carried light, practical leather arm-shields, but the front line bore sturdy full-length iron-studded shields that covered their bearers from shin to helm.

On the hillside, our archers nocked arrows.

Across the field I searched a crop of bearded faces. If Hriskil was among them, he was but a kernel of corn in a wagonful.

On our battlements, all was silent.

"Steady, lads." My voice rang too loud. "Let them near. We'll give them something to remember." Inept, or worse, but all I had in me.

Pardos swore under his breath and tugged me from the arrowguard, though no man alive could aim an arrow across the breadth of the field.

With each step, the distance between us narrowed. Still, the Norlanders were but a third of the way across.

Tursel called urgently, "Look to your shields!"

Reflexively, my arm shot up. "Why?"

"Behind the spearmen, behind the ladders!"

Archers. Masses of them, trudging forward in tight formation, bows in hand, sheaves of arrows bristling from quivers.

As one, we looked to our hillside. On the plateau, Tantroth's Eiberians intermingled with my bowmen from Cumber and Stryx. An arm flashed down.

Our first volley loosed. By their hundreds, barbed birds of prey whirred from the sky and found their marks. On the field, shields raised. Most of our volley was deflected. Still, men staggered, fell. The majority marched on, as if oblivious.

Another volley. A shrill cry, cut short.

Why weren't they returning our salvo?

Our bowmen were on the hill and had greater range. But surely, by now . . .

As if they heard my thought, the Norland archers raised their bows.

"Down, Rodrigo!"

But the volley found no targets on the battlements. Instead, every arrow soared to the plateau.

The Norland bowmen, shooting upward, were at the furthest extent of their range. Most of the barbs fell short. A few did not.

"Now!" Tursel gave the order to our archers on the wall, but it was too soon; most of the arrows thudded harmlessly into the turf.

"Can't you see it's a waste of . . ." I broke it off. Tursel would do as he pleased, and demons take my orders. He was always stubborn and willful.

As if in a dream I watched the Norlanders lumber forward. Their front ranks made way for lurching wagons that bore tall ungainly towers. We ought do something to prepare, but the cries of wounded men burst my fragile thoughts. Now the Norland bowmen found the hillside, and our men were falling.

Men of Cumber, with pikes and shields, awaited the Norland assault of the hill.

Behind us, a tremendous crash. Anavar whirled. "What's that?"

As if in answer, a half dozen stones smashed into the parapet. A yeoman shrieked and flailed as a ricocheting shard pierced his eye.

"Catapults. Stay down." Foolish advice, I knew as I gave it. Nowhere was safe.

The Norlanders' pace increased to a run. Most swept toward our archers' hill, traversing the field. Our bowmen on the battlement loosed arrow after arrow, picking them off.

Leather-garbed Norlanders lay kicking, crawling, screaming, twisting, clawing at barbs.

"Reinforce the hill!" Duke Tantroth.

I said, "How? It's outside our wall."

"Send our horse against the Norland flank!"

"They'll be slaughtered."

"We've a thousand bow and pikemen on the plateau. Ten thousand attack!"

"Their siege wagons make for the wall."

"They won't need their towers, if they take the hill! They'll shoot down on us!"

Tursel overheard. "I'll pull the archers from the front battlement, send them to the right." He gestured. "Concentrate their volleys on the troops attacking the hill."

Tantroth's cheeks grew red. "Then we've no defense of the wall! Once they close . . ."

Tursel snarled, "What would you, my *lord*?"

"Down!" Anavar leaped upon us. We sprawled as stone flew close overhead.

"Get off me, you—" I clamped my mouth shut. Time for his insolence later.

Groenfil stalked onto the battlement. "Our reserves are too near! The catapults will find them!"

"By blind luck. The Norlanders can't see over—"

"Roddy, you fool, you'll get us killed!"

What came upon Groenfil, that he would speak so? I was his king!

I drew sudden breath. "The Rood!"

"What?"

"Hriskil's at work, can't you feel it? We're at each other's throats."

Groenfil paid no heed. "Move the reserves, you simpleton, or I will!"

Anavar snarled. His dagger glinted.

"*NO!*" I caught his arm. Had we all gone mad? What was I to—how could I think with—I gritted my teeth. I couldn't think. That was the problem. "My lord, last night we set our dispositions. We pledged agreement. I hold you to your oath." I swung to Tursel. "Don't move the archers. The hill must save itself."

Spitting curses, Tursel stalked off.

"Imbar!" My voice was a snarl. "We've a bloody mess up here!" It was little enough I asked of him. Why couldn't he—

The Rood. I swallowed.

With a mad rush, men and ladders attacked the steep hill.

"Sire, off the battlement, I pray you." Pardos.

I shook him off. "I must see."

Frantic men pulled the wheeled towers toward the wall. The first of them was but a moment away.

"You, and Kadar, take his arm!" Without ceremony, they hustled me to the stair.

I swore and raged, to no avail. They set me down in the roadway, surrounded me with shields.

A crash, as a tower leaned into the wall. Men swarmed up its supports, leaped over the parapets. A surge of defenders rushed to the spot.

A hail of arrows. Kadar yelped, clawed at his shoulder. I saw my chance, bolted to the parapet. Anavar thudded behind. "Stay back, sir!"

I whirled, teeth bared. "Get away from me!" Could they not understand? I must *see*.

Tower after tower lumbered to the battlement. Arrows thudded everywhere. Our bowmen aimed for the wagons, with flaming arrows dipped in pitch. Rocks flew. Arrows. A pike thrust. I cowered behind my shield.

The swarthy soldier in front of me grinned. "Hot work. They're—" An arrow thunked into his temple.

A dozen Norlanders were over the top, then twenty.

"Caledon, follow me!" My voice was shrill. Brandishing my sword, I charged into the fray. Anavar raced after. A few paces behind, Pardos and his squad charged to my rescue.

I slashed, threw up my shield, ducked away, slashed anew. Blood spattered, not mine. A howl. I sidestepped a blow, parried with my shield, ran to an upthrust ladder, hacked off an arm.

Someone kicked me in the stomach; I gasped, doubled over, lunged.

The day was an endless dream of combat.

I struggled to wake.

"Use our reserves on the wall!" Tursel.

I rasped, "No changes."

"We can't hold!"

Time drifted past.

Tantroth himself overturned an upthrust ladder with an outstretched pike. A Norland tower burned, sap steaming and hissing, as foemen jumped to safety, fire arrows still raining upon it.

A scream of agony from the parapet.

A barrel of arrows burst asunder from a catapult shot, scattered arrows splintering underfoot. Imbar sweated under his breastplate, leading his men with grunts and curses to salvage what they could.

Kadar nursed a bloody arm, refusing to leave me untended. Towers leaned crazily as sweating Norlanders rocked them toward the wall. Arrows. Arrows. The hill swarmed with bearded ants, struggling desperately up ladders toward the rise. Arrows.

"The gate! The gate!" A desperate voice, below.

Old, fat Imbar snatched up a pike, stumbling to the splintered barrier under furious Norland assault. Anavar leapt off the wall, arms windmilling, sprawled at Imbar's side, bounded to his feet. Fifty of our men raced to help.

On the hill, our bowmen fired steadily, through ever-increasing gaps in their ranks.

"Caledon!" My voice rang out. "Fight for Caledon and Eiber!"

"Rez!" An attacker pointed. "Rez Caledi!"

"Soa rez," I taunted. "Rez qa han modrit!" *The king you can't kill.*

Someone on a tower launched a spear. I skittered aside. It thunked into stone. I snatched it up. "Doa Rez Caledi!" *From the king.* I hurled it with all my might. *Kachunk.* It pinned a blond youth to the beam. His mouth fell open. His eyes faded.

A dozen of our bowmen thudded along the wall, took up station beside me, loosed mercilessly into the nearest towers. Gasps, shrieks, moans. For a moment a Norland soldier staggered, pierced through with arrows, then he fell, bowling over two comrades beneath.

Anavar, blood-spattered, appeared at my side.

"The gate?"

"Reinforced."

I licked dry lips. Would the day never end? The sun was barely at midpoint. The field swarmed with Norlanders. For an instant a jagged cross gleamed, across the field, near the wood.

Parry. Thrust. A lithe young boy, the image of Genard, swarmed up a ladder. I rammed my sword through his ribs. Dead, he fell like a sack of wheat.

Anavar and I stood back-to-back, sword and shield poised.

"Let me send our horse against the towers." Tantroth.

"No changes."

"No changes, no changes," he mimicked. "Must we die for your stubbornness?"

The Rood.

My sword arm ached. I risked a glance at the plateau.

The foothill below was covered with unmoving bodies. Obstinate Norlanders climbed over them. Behind our pikemen's shields, fewer and fewer bowmen still stood.

Imbar thrust me aside, prodded a body. "Dead. Check this one." Two litter-bearers knelt by a bloody swordsman.

When will it end?

"To the south! The south!" A frantic defender beckoned as Norlanders swarmed the wall.

"Charge!" I raised my sword.

Pardos caught my wrist. "Stay, lord."

"They need aid!"

He held tight. "It's our work to save you."

Somehow, I broke loose. "Save me by saving Caledon!" I thrust him toward the breach. "All of you!" I jumped atop a bulwark. My shout pierced the din. *"CALEDON! THE WALL MUST HOLD. To the south!"* I jumped down not an instant too soon; a dozen arrows whistled past. One caught at my tunic. I yelped, but it was a mere scratch. *"Save the wall!"*

Imbar and his litter-bearers joined the frantic surge. Twenty Norlanders were already over the top; they jumped down into the road behind the wall. With a roar, Soushire's reserves charged them, unbidden, undirected. Four hundred swords and pikes fell on the hapless foe.

On the wall, all hung in the balance. Our men and Hriskil's grappled for the southernmost battlement. I seized Anavar's forearm. "Together!"

His grin was feral. We raced along the parapet to the melee.

Our blades flew. Heaving for air, my every nerve straining, sword arm swinging, I caught glimpses of madness.

On the deck, a severed arm still gripped a sword.

Someone fell. A bloody hand clutched my ankle. Coster, with whom I'd sat at a campfire two days past. He tried to speak, failed. I kicked free.

In the field below, swarms of men. Bodies. A fire arrow missed a tower, embedded itself in a Norlander's chest. As he slid to the turf smoke curled from his jerkin.

A soldier staggered along the parapet, arms stretched before him. One ear was gone, and an eye. The other was spewing blood.

Calls, screams, death.

At long last, the Norlanders on the wall fell back.

We'd saved the battlement.

I looked about for men to kill, found none. I shook my head to clear it. "Now where?" I was so winded I could barely speak.

"Two more towers." Anavar.

"Where?"

"Closest to the hill."

"Pardos, round up your men, we're—"

"Look, sire!" My bodyguard pointed below.

In the meadow, the Norland host was milling about in disarray. Officers rode among them, shouting orders.

Panting for breath, I leaned on my sword.

Hriskil's men were in retreat. From our hilltop, a ragged stream of arrows sped them on their way. With them careened their surviving towers. A few men carried ladders that had failed to secure the plateau.

There was something I ought do. What was it?

Slowly, Hriskil's minions fell back. We were done. I had but to lie down . . .

I spun to Anavar. "Quick, the gate! Clear the barricade!"

He bounded down the stairs.

Tantroth heard and stormed across the battlement. "We can't, Rodrigo, we've taken too many losses. Now's not the time—"

"NO CHANGES!" My scream made my throat raw. "Why aren't you with your cavalry? Go!" I fought to think through fog. "Kadar, get word to Groenfil! We attack in—" I peered at the torn and ragged field. "In moments, the Norlanders would be halfway across. "On my signal. Tell him they withdraw!"

For a moment Kadar looked ready to object. Then, "Aye, my lord." He strode off, clutching his blood-soaked shoulder.

"Rodrigo!" Anavar shouldered past a guard. "Tursel won't clear the gate! He says—"

Unutterably tired, I marshalled my scattered thoughts.

"—the Norland retreat's a feint; Hriskil will turn at any moment. The gate's smashed, and only the piles of debris protect—"

I managed to sheathe my sword without unmanning myself. "Pardos, Anavar, all of you!" I charged down the stairs.

Tursel was before the splintered gate. So, to my surprise, was Larissa of Soushire, guarded by half her regiment. "It's madness, Rodrigo! My men won't take part!"

"Out of the way!" I took her by the arms, spun her from our path, threw myself against a rough-hewn beam. "Anavar, get that barrel of sand out of—it's what we agreed, madam."

"Before Hriskil butchered half our force!" Larissa's face was red.

"Pardos, must I heave this myself?" My eyes bulged from the strain, and the beam barely moved.

Tursel barred the path. "Roddy, you've lost your senses! We can't attack a force five times—"

"Ten. But it's the course we set."

"That was before—"

"No changes! The Rood drives us mad! Pardos?"

My bodyguard said wearily, "Help the king." A dozen hands took hold.

Soushire stamped her foot. "They're in retreat, what more do you want? *You* die, if you insist on it. My men go to camp!"

"Very well, madam, let Earl Groenfil fight alone. With luck, he'll survive." Brutal, but she left little choice.

"He's not so foolish as—"

"Who's at the road's bend?" I looked past her shoulder.

Earl Groenfil, mounted, led a long column of six hundred men toward the gate, at the trot.

"Imps take you," she snarled. A mastiff began to howl.

My spine prickled. "Control thy ire, madam. Tursel, help, or stand aside."

"You'll rue this day!" Still snarling, he helped throw aside our makeshift barrier.

Now what? "Anavar, what should I . . ." Why ask *him*? He was a child. "My lord Earl." I bowed. "On my signal."

His face was hard. "If I hadn't sworn to this . . ."

"Where's Tantroth?"

"They mass by the mill. Make sure he follows. I've seen treason enough!"

It was the Rood.

I made for the stair.

When the Norlanders were halfway across the meadow I rushed to the inner parapet. "Now!"

The splintered gate crashed aside. Groenfil's men raced across the field, dividing to left and right.

Shouts from the Norland officers. Their men paused in their stolid retreat. With admirable order, they set about making a stand. A Norland chieftain gestured frantically. Even from the battlement I knew he was pointing out our weak, almost non-existent center, trying to ready a charge.

And then the duke of Eiber cantered through the gate on his black stallion, three officers at his side. Behind them, four abreast—the most that could pass the narrow opening—thundered the mass of Caledon's cavalry, armed with sword and lance.

Tantroth raised his sword. The horsemen spurred their mounts. They charged the Norland center.

The thud of a thousand hooves, a mass of drumbeats, a sound like no other.

A few brave Norlanders held their line. The rest broke and ran.

The timing was exquisite. As Tantroth smashed their center, our racing foot soldiers rolled up Hriskil's flank.

Our horse caught up with the wobbling towers. Barely a moment's pause, and down they went. I danced from foot to foot, beside myself. If only I could have ridden with Tantroth. But I'd have had to slay Pardos first.

The charge became a battle, the battle a melee. Grunts, cries, shrieks of agony wafted across the bloody field. One couldn't tell who was winning, except that the fighting moved inexorably closer to the wood, and the Norland camp.

Then the Norlanders were breaking free, running, and Caledon was giving chase. I pounded Anavar's back. "We have them! Oh, we have them!"

He said thickly, "Take your hands off—"

A snap, within my mind.

Our startled eyes met.

I blinked, awakened from a dreadful dream. I could think again. I frowned. What had just passed?

"Sir, I meant no offense; I don't know why I . . ."

The Rood!

"Hriskil's in flight!" My tone was joyous. "He's set down the Rood!"

On the steep hill our surviving archers, their day's work done, lay down their bows and massaged aching shoulders. Imbar's troops continued their grim work of removing the dead and succoring the wounded.

The cries of battle receded. I watched anxiously. Soon, the only men moving about the battleground were ours. The Eiberians among them began walking the field, methodically slitting the throats of the Norland wounded, until, aghast, I sent frantic runners to put a stop to it.

From the wood beyond rose a plume of smoke.

Hriskil's camp burned. His tents, foodstuffs, wagons of costly supplies. That would give him pause. I wheeled, ran to the stair. "Tursel!"

"Aye, my lord." He came out from the gateway, discomfited.

"Send riders to Tantroth and Groenfil. Remind them not to chase Hriskil beyond the camp."

"Of course. We agreed so." He blinked, looked up at me with a moment's unease, before turning once more. "Lady Soushire, two horsemen, if you will!"

She gestured assent. In moments they cantered across the carnage.

There was no need. Tantroth and Groenfil were already marshalling their withdrawal.

"Sire, if I may . . ." Tursel again. "We ought strip their dead."

I grimaced. "We don't need gold so badly that—"

"Swords, shields, sheaves of arrows. What's left on the field is ours for the taking."

And Hriskil wouldn't have the use of it. "Quickly, then." In moments, our wagons jounced to midfield.

Gratefully, I unslung my arm from my battered shield. My forearm was cramped and sore, but nothing could dull my exultation. We'd won, soundly and utterly. Of course, the war wasn't over; Hriskil had been bloodied, not crippled. His force still vastly outnumbered ours.

I rushed from the wall to greet Groenfil and Tantroth. I called happily, "A glorious victory!"

They paused together, by a handful of wagons, as their troops filed past. Groenfil's face was bleak. Tantroth said nothing.

"Is it not so, my lords? We fought today for the glory of Caledon. Long will men remember!"

"Rodrigo . . ." Anavar, in a whisper.

I brushed away his insistent fingers.

"Pardon, my lord." Groenfil turned back to the wagons.

Why should Groenfil care about captured pikes and swords, at this wonderful hour? I followed him past our tired soldiers. "Rejoice with me, my lord! After this, Hriskil won't dare—"

Not weapons, but men were piled on the flatbed carts. "It was a glorious victory," I insisted, wishing he could understand. "Across Caledon men will be heartened. It will give us—"

I slipped on a damp rock, and fell on my rump. Instantly my leggings were smeared with foul effluvia.

Disgusted, I jumped to my feet, wiping my flanks, but stinking ooze soiled my hands. "Get this muck off me!" I swept at the revolting mess. "Anavar, a cloth!"

As I wiped my stained leggings I became aware that all had fallen silent. Men stared at me, with expressions that I could barely fathom . . . once, when I'd truly offended Rustin, he'd looked at me so.

But only once.

I swallowed.

What had I done?

I glanced at Anavar, but he retreated as if I had the plague.

I looked down at my rust-stained, bloodied hands.

At the ooze of blood that dripped constantly from the bed of the wagons.

Muck, I'd called it. In the presence of my dead, wounded, mutilated men. They and their comrades fixed me now with insolent, unforgiving stares.

Please, Mother Earth, swallow me. Imps and demons, take me now. I'll go gladly.

I put reddened hands to my face, sank to my knees.

After a time I whispered, "Anavar . . . take me to my tent."

Eighteen

I WEPT, I think, along the road, but I wasn't sure. I was in a daze, as if Hriskil again wielded the Rood.

I tethered Ebon, stumbled into my tent, yanked shut the flap. I should peel off my filthy clothes. No, I didn't dare; it would show disrespect.

Why hadn't I apologized? I ought have, but I'd felt it would make things worse. Now I was skulking in my tent, afraid to be seen.

I wiped my eyes, got to my feet.

Near Pardos, Anavar waited in the clearing, holding Edmund. His very presence was a kindness. Absently, I patted his shoulder. "Tend to the horses, would you?"

"Where will you be?"

"There." I strode to the surgeons' tent.

Wafting from inside, a foul stench. I took sharp breath, fighting an urge to bolt.

Blood, swarms of flies, and outside the canopy, a horrid pile of sawn-off limbs. Wails and cries. Half a dozen physickers, all our army had, tried to tend far too many stretchers of men awaiting dismemberment or sewing. Aides milled about, moving men, helping hold down those treated. Pardos a step behind, I sought out the surgeon Darios, whom I knew.

He snapped, "No time for talk, sire. Men are dying."

"I came to help."

"You've no place here." He turned away.

"Where else is my place?" I stood dumbly, hoping Darios would answer, but he was far too occupied. A surgeon straightened, beckoned the men to take away a stretcher.

I was ready, and had one end of the next litter. With a grunt, I helped raise it to the table. The wounded youth twisted and cried, thrashing his lacerated arm.

"Hold him steady." With callous unconcern an aide seized the boy's wrist, pinned it to the table. Gingerly, I applied my weight to his shoulder. He wailed and begged all the time he was sewn. After, I helped carry him outside. The aide dumped him unceremoniously in the grass.

I was incredulous. "You can't just leave him here!"

"Where else?" He gestured; the environs of the tent were crowded with writhing wounded.

"Have they water? Anyone to tend them?"

"Not my task." He dragged the litter to an overburdened wagon creaking to a stop.

"Then it's mine! ANAVAR!" The boy was nowhere in sight. "Pardos! A bucket of water, and be quick."

"I can't leave you."

I gripped his arm. "This instant!"

He hesitated. "I see no bucket."

"My ewer, in my tent. The silver one. Hurry."

Moments later, he was back. In a twinkling, thirsty soldiers had emptied the ewer.

I snapped, "A barrel of water!"

"Sir, there's no barrel; let the surgeons handle their own—"

"I'll get it." Elryc, softly, behind me.

"Be quick, brother. And my wine, all you can carry. Find Tanner to help."

His head touched my shoulder. "Take comfort, Roddy."

"Would that I could."

When Elryc returned, I helped him serve water and set him to dispensing wine to those in most pain. Wiping my scarred cheek with a bloody hand, I hurried back to the tent.

"You, boy, hold his legs!"

I did. The perspiring veteran kicked and bucked. I glanced upward, saw furrowed brow, sweaty forehead, terrified eyes, the relentless saw that ground through flesh, muscle, tendon, the white bone of his mutilated arm. I gagged. My blood pounded. The surgeons' tent receded into some distant mist. I hung on, resting my sweaty forehead on the patient's bony knee.

A long while passed.

"Move, boy!" Roughly, the surgeon shook me. I blinked. The soldier's eyes were shut. He was dead, or unconscious.

As I'd like to be. Wearily, I got him on a litter.

Outside, the day was darkening. I searched for somewhere to put down my burden. We had to trudge a long way from the tent. I spied Pardos. "These men need shelter."

His tone was belligerent. "And where shall we find that?"

I cast about. Someone should have organized . . .

Yes, someone. Someone in charge.

"My tent. It's huge; you can put twenty—"

"A drop in the—"

"And Elryc's. Anavar's."

"Where will *you* sleep?"

"Under a wagon! It matters not!"

In my absence Anavar and Bollert had commandeered a donkey cart. They drove up with a fresh barrel of water. Eagerly I took a ladle. "Thank you." I turned back to the carnage.

"Sir," asked Anavar, "are you well?"

"Yes. I gave away your tent. You may have my blanket."

I felt his stare as I retreated.

Hours passed. I learned to sew. I got the knack of thrusting a leather thong between a frightened man's teeth, urging him to clamp down. I fetched water, tore rags as bandages, held terrified men while they shuddered and died.

After an eon, a soft hand on my shoulder. "Come." Anavar's voice was gentle.

"They need—I have to—"

"They're caught up. There's no more wagons."

I looked about. No more than a dozen men still writhed and moaned, waiting for the surgeons' mercies.

Outside, I recoiled at the wounded scattered about the field. "I ordered . . . in my tent . . ."

"Full. And mine, and Elryc's. Groenfil's staking canopies. There's no rain tonight."

"I can't leave."

"Look, sir, Genard's bringing a stewpot. Groenfil said hot broth would—I've organized the boys. Tanner, Genard, Elryc and I . . . we're doing what can be done."

My eyes brimmed. "How can I repay you?"

"We'll not speak of that."

I walked awkwardly, my clothes stiff with dried blood.

Pardos and his squad fell in behind us.

As we passed campfires, men stared. Some turned away. One man spat in the dirt.

We neared my tent. I stopped abruptly. By my own command, I'd been dispossessed. "I don't want to . . ." Face them. "Water, and a cloth, I beg you. And whatever clothes are in the trunk. And my coronet, wrapped in that soft cloth."

After a moment Anavar emerged with loincloth, breeches and a tunic. Surrounded by tents and campfires I stripped to the skin, washed myself as best I could, gratefully donned fresh clothes. A cloth-wrapped bundle under my arm, I crossed to a campfire, rubbed my chilled fingers.

All talk stopped. Hostile eyes fixed on mine. "Muck," someone muttered.

I'd not been forgiven.

Hadn't I wallowed in gore for their sake? I endured the horrible stinking tent, carried them, gave them drink, lent them my very bed, all to show my contrition; could they not see?

Yes. They saw the sham of my remorse.

By this time I ought have use of the Still. Mother would know what to do. If ever an emergency demanded I seek the cave, it was now.

No. I needed the Still to fight the Rood. At all costs, I must preserve it. I stepped back from the light, out of the pitiless gaze of my troops. "Find Tursel," I told a bodyguard. "Call an assembly."

"A what?"

"Assembly. Of the troops."

He looked doubtful. "First you issue orders to your captains, then *they—*"

I sighed. "Bring me Tursel."

But it was Groenfil who appeared, the guard tagging at his heels. "Roddy, leave the men alone."

"I would speak to them."

"All, at once? It's not done." He dropped his voice. "They're sore and exhausted. You can't make them stand at summons half the night."

"I don't intend—"

He spoke even more quietly. "You can't call armed men before you except under discipline, and only when their captains are alert. A stray word, a flurry of anger: weapons are drawn. Royal houses fall over such clumsiness. Think of Halkir of the Ukra."

"I only—"

"You've goaded them enough for one day. Sheer stupidity it was, liege or no."

I reddened. "Agreed. But, my lord Earl, in this I will be obeyed."

He glowered, until he realized I would hold his eye. "Set your bodyguards before you; stand at least twenty paces—"

"To preserve my crown? The cost's too high. Call the men. Everyone. Strip the wall."

"You're mad."

"This is the one night I'm certain Hriskil won't attack."

Groenfil went about gathering our troops.

Anavar and Elryc stood vigil with me. Once, when I sighed, my brother said, "You meant no offense. They don't understand."

"I never mean offense, Elryc."

"What will you do?"

"What I must." With a gesture, I stayed his speech.

As the hour passed, knots of soldiers appeared among the royal tents, their numbers growing until they filled the meadow. They muttered among themselves, a low, uneasy murmur. I'd dispensed my bodyguards to fetch a sturdy wagon; the best they found was Danzik's; I stood on the flatbed, in the light of pitch torches lashed to the sideboards. "To your regiments," I told Kadar and Pardos.

"It's our duty to—"

"Not this night." I added, before Pardos could object, "Seek Tantroth's approval if you must. But tell him if he consents not, I'll abdicate."

As if by unspoken agreement, the gathering men stood back ten or twelve paces from the wagon.

As the assembly grew ever more packed I leaned over the sideboard. My voice was low. "Anavar, escort Elryc to the edge of camp. I charge you, see he survives the night."

"Sir!" He paled.

"Be quick."

"My place is with—"

I clutched his hand, in embrace or farewell. "Do as I bid you." Hurriedly, I turned away. When I risked a glance, he had a grip on Elryc's arm and was edging through the mass of troops. Unobtrusively, Genard followed, tucking a blanket across Elryc's frail shoulders.

Alone, I took a step or two, to unknot my calves.

"Get on with it, King!" A voice from the dark.

"Tell us of your glorious victory!"

Groenfil's mount thrust through the milling mass. The earl roared, "BE SILENT!"

I shot back, "No, let them speak!"

Groenfil glared.

Someone shouted, "Washed off the muck, did you?"

Mother, have you inspiration? Now is when I could use it. I should have sought the Still, regardless of the cost.

I held up a hand for silence, but the throng grew ever more restive. A burly fellow stooped, tore out a clod of turf. He hefted it, taking aim.

Desperately I shouted, "Come closer, all of you!" Urgently I beckoned them in. "I want you to hear!"

Groenfil slammed his fist into his pommel, startling his horse.

Taken by surprise, the men surged close. I could smell their sweat, their sullen fury.

I raised my voice, hoping even those most distant might hear. "I called assembly of the army of Caledon, because you've a problem, and must decide our course." Still, mutters of discontent. I pressed on. "What say you? Shall we go home?"

That brought silence.

"You fought bravely and well, but the Norlanders remain in Eiber. You learned today two things. That you can defeat Hriskil, despite the Rood. And that your king is a fool."

A sudden buzz, that quieted instantly. I had every eye, every ear. I paced my wagon. "You've all heard how I prattled about a glorious victory while our wagons of dead and dying creaked past. How I slipped in the blood of my vassals and called it muck. Hriskil wielded the Rood today, but it wasn't his Power that befuddled me. I'm thoughtless and callow. It's my nature."

"Enough, Rodrigo." Groenfil's voice was low, but it carried.

"Oh, not nearly enough. I'll tell you more. I passed my evening in the surgeon's tent. I gave drink to our wounded, helped hold men in agony, carried litters. And I'll tell you the truth of it: I loathed every instant of it, and only remained as a show of virtue, to earn your forgiveness. But you're wiser than that. Thank Lord of Nature some of us are."

"You're not fit to be king!" A thickset soldier, red hair turning gray, who'd brought along short sword and shield.

"I wish I were." I swallowed. "You don't know how I wish I were!"

It earned me a moment.

"I knew an old soldier once, of Stryx and Verein. Fostrow. Anyone remember him?" I searched for a nod of recognition, found one at last. "First he was my guard, then my pledged man. I drove him to distraction. I was rude, disrespectful of his years, heedless of his comfort. And still he served me, to death."

Their gaze fixed me, a butterfly on a pin.

"The last thing he said, as I held him while he died . . ." My voice dropped. " 'It's wars kill us, Roddy. Fight *just* wars.' "

"I can't say I'm worth your lives, but I do believe we fight a just war. Hriskil came unbidden to our land. Has he respect for our laws, our ways, our lives? Under his rule, we'd be less than naught. Ask Danzik; to a Norlander we're savages! You know their cruelty; it far surpasses mine.

"And so." A deep breath. I unwrapped my bundle, held up the coronet for their inspection. "I was crowned by the nobility of Caledon. By our laws their assent sufficed; as proof of it, I wield the Still, and next battle I'll use it to ward against the Rood.

"But in truth, the nobles' assent is *not* enough. I cannot be king without your approval. What I said today was callous and stupid. Were Lord Rustin alive he would beat me. Yet I meant you no ill." I paused, seeking some words of conclusion. I found none.

"Here." I tossed the coronet into the crowd; eager hands caught it. "I'll be in my tent. Bring me my crown, or your justice. I only ask that . . ." I swallowed. "If you'd have another king, give me a fast end. I'm not brave enough to . . ."

I gestured vaguely, gathering my composure. "And if you'd have me as king, be warned: I'll do it again. Even Rust couldn't control my thoughtless speech. But I give you leave to chide me when I earn it. That much, you deserve." I swung over the sideboard, hesitated. I raised my voice as high as I could. "Lord of Nature, bless these men, lead them to victory. Free our beloved Caledon!" I made a sign, as might a ritemaster.

It took all my effort to direct my steps to the tent. My legs were trembling so I thought I might fall.

With each stride, they opened a path before me. Here and there, as I passed, a man reached out, touched my arm, my tunic, my hair.

"Rodrigo." A low murmur.

A dozen more steps, no further. That much I had in me.

"RODRIGO!"

Only a few more paces.

"Rodrigo!" A chant, taken up by a hundred voices. A thousand. *"Rodrigo!"*

Rough, grizzled men barred my way to the tent.

I halted, bracing for the stab that would end my misery. "I'm sorry." No one heard me. "I'm sorry for who I've been."

One by one, they began to fall to their knees.

"RODRIGO!"

Fingers reached up, clutched mine. Dark eyes glistened, searching my gaze. The coronet glinted, passed from hand to hand.

A kneeling guardsman held it up to me.

"RODRIGO!"

I bowed my head. He slipped it on.

The breeze whispered softly, *Ah, my prince.*

It was more than I could bear.

THE MEN HAD offered me my tent; I'd forbidden that a single patient be moved. Another tent, then; their rage had turned to fierce adulation.

Cynically aware of the theater of it, I'd chosen the underside of a wagon. Anavar and Elryc had joined me of their own volition. My bodyguards made a campfire and sat nearby, guarding me in shifts; nothing I said could induce them to go.

I tried not to wake my companions, burying my sobs in a blanket. Perhaps Elryc heard; it was his hand that stole across my cover, lay protectively over me in the night.

By morn, I was wept out. I sat up slowly, so as not to slam my head on the underside of Danzik's cart. Behind me, Elryc stirred; to my front, Anavar was rubbing his eyes.

I sniffed. What was it? Hot porridge, with honey! I salivated. In a moment the bowl appeared, and then the rest of Genard. He handed it to me. "Gotta get the others, m'lor'." He disappeared.

I took a taste. "Now there," I said approvingly, "is a vassal."

Elryc giggled. "You can't have him. Ow!" He'd thumped his head. A moment's thought. "Roddy, would they have killed you?"

"I don't know."

"You were wonderful. Mother would be proud."

"How did you hear?"

"I didn't let Anavar take me far. Your voice carried."

Outside, a pair of boots. Leggings. I set down my bowl.

Earl Groenfil crouched, peered under. "Well, now."

Like a castle hound, I crawled out from my shelter. "My lord." I ran fingers through my tousled hair.

Groenfil crossed his arms, stood scowling. "What are we to do with you?"

I blurted, "What are the choices?"

"I wish I knew. At times I'd cheerfully strangle you."

"Is this one of—"

Anavar crawled out from under his blanket, stood listening.

Earl Groenfil held up a palm. "Then you redeem yourself with such grace, I . . ." Abruptly, he turned away.

"What?"

"I could wish you were my son."

I swallowed a lump. "Thank you, my lord." I bowed, a short familiar bow as a son to father, and managed not to spoil it by saying more.

"I wish," the earl said presently, "you'd maintain the arrogant disposition we've all come to know."

"Why?"

"By your virtue you shame me." He squared his shoulders. "Twice, now, in heat of battle, I've spoken to you with such foul—"

I said quickly, "It was the Rood."

"Nonetheless, I ask thy pardon."

"Gladly granted," I said.

"So. The wounded are under shelter. We've distributed food and drink; the men rest. We've scavenged weapons aplenty. When will Hriskil attack?"

I blinked. "You assume I know?"

"Yes." After a moment, "I trust your instinct. Ah, my lord Duke." Groenfil made way for Tantroth.

"He's rejoined us? A most impressive performance, Rodrigo." Tantroth gave a nod, almost a bow.

Was it compliment or accusation? Cautiously, I kept silent. Beside me, Anavar glared at the duke.

"The camp sings your praises."

Abruptly I tired of sparring. "I'm weary, and every muscle aches. Might we postpone our duel?"

"You misunderstand. I honor you." Tantroth wheeled to Anavar. "Youngsire, you lack manners. Were you not the king's favorite, I would offer correction."

Anavar hissed. "You're a foul—"

"Stop, both of you!" I spoke before I thought. "My Duke, with respect: he's my ward to chastise. He's renounced Eiber—"

"Without my leave!"

Groenfil raised an eyebrow.

"—and is my Baron of the Southern Reaches. As such he's beyond your correction." I raised a warning finger to Anavar. "And you, sir, are insolent to my ally the duke. I won't have it. If I strive to regulate my conduct, *you regulate yours!*"

Anavar gulped. After a moment, "I offer apology."

"And to the duke!"

He reddened, ear to ear. "And to you, my lord Duke." A reluctant bow, of lesser to better.

Tantroth grunted.

My tone was cool. "You have our leave, Anavar." That wasn't fair; without a tent, he had nowhere to go. The boy withdrew with what dignity he could salvage. I frowned. "Surely you didn't seek me out to bicker over my liegesmen."

"Why, not at all, sire." Tantroth's voice was smooth. "I came to extol your skill last evening. In fact, Groenfil, wasn't I just saying—"

I said, "Do you never tire of games, my lord?"

"Seldom." But after a moment Tantroth shrugged. "You are, in fact, the wonder of the camp. At the moment they'd follow you anywhere. So, where do you lead?"

The question gave me pause. I gestured for him to go on.

"Do we merely block the pass, sire, and leave the next cast of the bones to Hriskil?"

"Or?"

For a moment Tantroth looked older. "I was hoping you'd tell us."

"I have no miracles, my lord Duke."

"A pity. I could, perhaps, pick my way past the Norland camp."

"To what purpose?" Groenfil.

"Harry them from the rear. Make them think twice before throwing themselves at the wall."

I said, "With all our force, we barely held the pass."

"Oh, nonsense," said Tantroth briskly. "We can't squeeze even a third of our men onto the wall."

"Afterward, in the field . . ."

"Think you Hriskil will give us such chance again?"

"I don't know!" I shifted from foot to foot. "I'm but half awake and need to piss. A poor moment to debate policy."

"Then I'll leave you to your needs. We'll speak later." A bow, deeper than the last. He said to Groenfil, "Shall we oversee Tursel's repair of the gate?" They departed.

As I vigorously scratched myself, Elryc joined me, setting aside his empty porridge bowl. I asked, "What was *that* about?"

"Your nobility. They wanted to view it anew."

I scrutinized him, to see if he mocked. Apparently not. "Did they?"

"Enough. You set Tantroth back over Anavar; he tested to see if you would. And you honored Groenfil's admission."

"Hmpff. Why can't they just say what they mean?"

Elryc smiled. "Roddy, we are *Caledon*."

NINETEEN

" . . . MARVELOUS VICTORY, RODRIGO; Grandfather would be so pleased. And I'm sure you didn't mean it the way it sounded; it's an outrage so many took it amiss. You've every right to be proud of how you redeemed yourself. How I wish I'd heard your speech to the men. A clumsy fool? Certainly not. I knew that the moment I laid eyes on you.

"I must hurry; I bade the courier await my reply, and rushed to my rooms to dash off these lines. Now it's I who need apologize for blots and scribbles.

"So, has Anavar accepted his rebuke? Is Tantroth more deferential? What does Danzik think of his lord's defeat? Eagerly I await your response.

"As to your 'campaign of kindness,' I commend your perseverance. Act with all folk as you confide to me that you've resolved; it but brings to men's notice your true nature.

"My dearest Roddy—if I may so address my liege lord, the king of my realm—do write again, and soon. Life in Cumber is drear. The prosperity of our land is shaken, and the Norland threat looms. And if I may suggest it, do send greetings to Bouris as well, when next you write to me. He takes it amiss that his earldom is not in your regard, and the arrival of your courier rubs salt in the wound. He's given to biting remarks and petty retaliations. They trouble me not, but I worry lest he transfer his displeasure to you, my lord. You cannot afford the alienation of Cumber.

"In the hope this missive finds you well, and with the assurance you are always in my heart, I remain Tresa, of Cumber."

"OVE, GUIAT." *HELLO, teacher.*

Danzik grunted. "You live."

"Does that surprise you?"

"*Quix iot.*" *Perhaps a little.* A shrug. "My lord Hriskil is generous."

"No, it's I who was generous. After we burned his camp I let him go."

Danzik chuckled. "A Caled boy, defeat the Norland king?" He shook his head at the notion.

I hunched over, elbows on knees. "Why do you hold me in such . . . Genard, what's the word for contempt?"

"Redic."

"Thank you. Pir redic, Danzik? Pir?"

"*Ca vos sa redicas.*" *Because you're contemptible.*

I said nothing.

He snarled, "You're a Caled savage!"

My eyes held his.

The Norlander looked uncomfortable. "Ca . . . Hriskil is a man, a famed warrior. You're a boy with a mouth full of lies."

"You don't believe we burned his camp?"

"Impossible."

My eyes burned through him. He began to fidget.

I'd endured withering scorn from my own men; imps take me if I'd let an unlettered Norland oaf mock me.

Genard murmured, "Easy, m'lor'. Don't give him the satisfac—"

Abruptly, I stood. Madness, keeping a Norlander in my very camp. "Danzik, have you honor?"

A growl.

"Have you? Does a Norlander keep his word?" Of course not, but I'd play the game.

"Qay." *Yes.*

"Even to a . . . Caled han-kevhom?" *A Caled savage?*

He looked about for something, or someone, to smash. "Qay!"

"We'll see. Genard, help me explain this. How if I release you . . . Genard—?"

"I don't know. *Han pris?* Not capture?"

"*Han pris.* If I release you to ride your *kev* and see if the camp was burned? If I lied, you're freed. But you give *vade*, oath: if I told truth, return and be *pris* once more." As if he would.

His look was wary. "No other oath? Only return if you burned camp?"

"Qay."

A smile that grew to a toothy grin. "Danzik is free!"

*   *   *

GROENFIL, IN HIS tent, was beside himself. "Did imps seize your wits? To let him ride off thumbing his nose—"

"I doubt he'll do that."

"The moment he's out of bowshot!" The tent flaps swirled. With an effort he calmed himself. "More wine, Larissa? Roddy?"

"I'd like mine watered. And if he does?"

"Think of morale, sire! To say nothing of what he'll tell Hriskil. He's seen our camp, counted our—"

I took a sip. "Think you Hriskil hasn't his spies? There's little about our camp he doesn't know."

A reluctant nod. "That may be so, but men died to give you Danzik."

"They died to free the coast road and smash Danzik's camp. Sending him home doesn't negate their sacrifice. And his tutelage is no great loss. As Norlanders don't practice ransom, we'd have to hold him 'til war's end. This way we'll be rid of him. It feels right."

"Tell him that's no way to lead Caledon," said Lady Soushire.

"My lady," I said, "what good does the barbarian do us?"

"He's a symbol. Our men look on his chains and know the Norlanders aren't invincible."

"If you're bored with his company," said Groenfil, "put him to death. You saw the surgeon's tents. Why let a seasoned warrior loose to wreak more havoc?"

I went off to ponder.

TURSEL, TANTROTH, EVEN Imbar objected to Danzik's release. As peaceably as I could, I overrode them all, but their feelings were so strong I resolved to keep an eye on our bowmen while Danzik rode off.

"Ove, Danzik. Good-bye." I handed him his reins.

A nod that might convey grudging respect. "When we meet again . . ." Something I couldn't catch. He saw my confusion, leaned over the pommel, said slowly and clearly in his own tongue, "All before forgotten, when me guiat, you memora. War is kill."

"So must it be. Tursel, the gate."

The bar was lifted; the thick, battle-scarred door swung

open. The Norland chief kicked his heels. His mount
bolted.

"Danzik!"

He reined.

I held out a sword, one we'd carried from the field.

He raised an eyebrow. "Pir?" *Why?*

"That you go home with . . . vade." *Honor.* I handed it up,
stepped quickly out of range. I didn't trust his honor *that* far.

He grinned. "Salut, Rez." A vague wave, and the dwindling
clatter of hooves.

Tantroth joined me on the walk back to camp. "The most
imprudent act of your reign," he said.

My tone was sharp. "Why didn't you poison him in his
wagon? You had ample opportunity."

"He might have had some use. And I couldn't conceive, my
liege, that you'd be so foolish as to let him go."

We walked the rest of the way in silence.

In the clearing, I found my tent vacated, the flaps rolled
high to air out the bedding. I looked about, saw only Tanner
squatting to sun himself. I snapped my fingers. "The
wounded. Where?"

He pointed. "With others, m'lord."

"Why?"

He shrugged. "Dunno." Not a question to ask a servant boy.

My tone sharpened. "Get to your feet when you speak to
me. I'm king." Was it cruelty? No, by Lord of Nature. Simple
manners.

Listlessly, he did as I asked.

I peered into the tent. Bloody rags pitched in a corner. My
silver ewer, overturned. Carpets stained and disheveled, the
bedding awry. I swung open the trunk. Most of my clothing
seemed undisturbed, but if any was missing I wouldn't be-
grudge it. "Tanner." My voice was mild. "Come straighten
this out." It would keep him busy.

I perched on a trunk while he shook out carpets.

Tursel hurried up, saw the boy working. "Good, lad,
straighten the tent. Roddy will have a fit if he sees—oh,
sire!" He fell back, disconcerted. "The men . . . a delegation.
They demanded we return you your quarters. After last
night . . ."

"Yes. Well." I tugged at the comforter, straightening wrinkles. "What kind of fit?"

"You'd be annoyed. Have words with—sire, forgive me." His face was red.

"Easily done." I waved it away. "Where's Anavar, these days?"

Tursel studied his fingernails. "He took a bed at the alehouse."

"Was I too rough on him?"

"I wasn't present."

"But no doubt you heard." A king's life in camp did not lend itself to privacy.

Tursel glanced at the servant boy, moved closer and lowered his voice. "Anavar showed his ire to Tantroth. That's dangerous, as well as impertinent."

"Think you Tantroth would—"

"He'll never accept Anavar's desertion."

I bit my lip. "Well, from his view, it was treason."

"There's that, and pride."

"Is the boy's life at risk?"

Tursel said, "Tantroth's no fool, and doesn't think you one. Still, it were better they be kept apart."

OUTSIDE THE TENT the courier stood insolently, hand on hip. Perched on my bed, I read through his missive.

"From Bouris earl of Cumber, greetings to Rodrigo king.

"Sadly, I regret that the defense of my holdings makes it impossible to send the men or supplies Tursel requests. In fact, our walls are alarmingly undermanned, and I see no choice but to order the return of a portion of the troops who fight under your glorious standard. I relinquish to you the services of your Baron Imbar—"

"My baron!" I gritted my teeth.

"—and a hundred men-at-arms. I shall expect the return of Captain Tursel and the remaining troops in one week's time."

"What's it say, Roddy?" Elryc peered over my shoulder.

"That Hriskil's found an ally." I crumpled the dispatch. "What's Bouris to gain?"

With a sigh, Elryc smoothed the parchment, scanned the

letter. "He gives you a week to negotiate. What does he want?"

"Ah." I hadn't thought of it in that light. "Ask that lout kicking the sod in my walkway." He'd ridden into camp, bold as brass, and thrust his letter at Pardos without a word of greeting.

I asked, "Would Hriskil guarantee Bouris's lands and holdings?"

"He must offer something of worth. Llewelyn's in his camp."

I growled. Why Rustin's father had betrayed us still remained a mystery.

"Never mind Llewelyn." I said. "Bouris is a hard enough nut to crack. What do we tell him?" To jump in a lake of fire, if I had my way of it. His lands and castles would make a fine gift, if I wrested them from him. To Anavar, for instance.

As if reading my mind, Elryc said, "Remember your promise to Raeth."

I grimaced. *To your bloodline forever, though it cost my crown to preserve it.* A rash vow, with Bouris his heir. But now I couldn't dispossess the new earl without losing the Still. And, of course, my honor. What ought I to do? Ask Tursel? Did he serve Cumber or Caledon? At this point, did he himself know?

"Meanwhile," I muttered, "the courier waits. You, there!" I strode to the flap. "Thank the good earl for his message. Tell him he's invited here to a banquet, third-day hence, to celebrate our great victory and to consult with my lords on our future course. Can you remember that? Need I write it?"

"I'll tell him."

No "sire," no "my lord." I said brightly, "Are you sure? If it will tax your memory—" His cheeks reddened.

When he'd ridden off, Elryc asked, "Was that wise? Why pique him?"

"Because he's a clod, as is his master. Because I'm full to my throat with dispensing kindness and soft words, and if I don't pique *someone* I'll—I'll bite!" Congeniality wasn't in my nature.

"Thank you, sire," murmured Elryc slyly, "for making me feel at home." He put the letter aside. "And the banquet?"

"Pheasant, I think. A sauce of oranges, braised—"

He jabbed me in the ribs.

"The obvious reason. To see if he'd come." And by so doing, place himself for the moment in my power.

"Of course, Roddy, but why make Bouris commit himself?" As in better times, Elryc settled cross-legged on my bed. "What harm letting him stretch his leash?"

I said, "Who knows what mischief he'd commit? By speeding his hand, at least we deny him subtlety."

"It doesn't seem his strong point."

Glum, I sat with head in hands. "I miss Uncle Raeth."

After a moment, my brother said, "So does Imbar."

"What more would you? I included him in my councils, gave him employment in battle. He's had time to digest his loss."

"I know, but . . ." His eyes darted to mine, as if in measure. "If it were your loss we spoke of . . ."

"Uncle Raeth? Oh!" I drew sharp breath. Rustin. As long as I lived, his torn throat would be before my eyes. I swallowed a lump. "Is that what manhood consists of, Elryc? The tally of absent friends?"

"SIRE, TO THE wall! Make haste!" The runner gasped for breath.

I bolted from my tent. "Hriskil attacks?"

"No, not—please, my lord, hurry! Tursel . . . words cannot—"

I raced to the picket. "BOLLERT! WHERE'S EBON?" I fumbled to free my cloak, entangled on my scabbard.

Long anxious moments while the saddle was tightened; I could almost have run faster. Well, perhaps not. The moment Bollert thrust me the reins I scrambled into the saddle, wheeled Ebon, took off at a gallop through the dust. My bodyguard raced behind.

In moments I was at the battlement. Men paced back and forth, cursing. A few had swords drawn. At the far battlement, Tantroth stood with his aides. Abruptly, he gestured and Sandin left the wall, mounted and cantered off toward camp.

Captain Tursel beckoned me up the stair. "Here, sire."

I peered. In the meadow between Hriskil's camp and the

wall, just beyond arrow range, were a few Norlanders and a ramshackle wagon. Outside the wagon, what appeared to be a pile of clothing. "For *that* I raced through camp as if an imp bit my tail? Have you no sense? Only call me when—"

"Watch."

They helped a youth climb into the wagon.

"That's the twelfth so far."

A distant shout. *"Eyurf, of Brooksend village."*

Head down, he stood in the bed. He seemed curiously still. After a time I became aware his hands were bound.

The flash of a sword. He toppled to the pile of clothes . . . no, bodies. For a moment his feet scrabbled and kicked. Then he was still.

I frowned. "They're executing their shirkers?" Hriskil was savage enough, but why he would advertise his troubles to us . . .

Tursel's fingers locked over my wrist. Pardos looked askance but didn't interfere. "Eiberians," Tursel said softly. "Captives."

"Lord of Nature!"

A woman was next. She kicked and struggled. It took two Norlanders to hoist her up.

"Alla, wife of Sril!"

A Norland savage seized her hair, pulled back her chin.

A long, gloating moment.

"No!" A cry, from our wall.

"Silence!" Tursel.

A sudden wrench. They slit her throat. She fell lifeless.

I pried loose my wrist, rubbed the white finger-marks. "WHY?"

"Look at our men." Seasoned troopers, most of them. One full-bearded fellow wandered about, looking lost. Another soldier stood silently, tears coursing down his cheeks.

"Gena, wife of Sutlin!"

Sickened, I turned away. Tursel snarled, "If you value your throne, you'll watch."

"Is that a threat?"

"Advice."

I stole a glance aside. Bewitched as if by foul encant, every man's eyes were fastened on the gruesome spectacle. I gulped, did the same; the deaths deserved no less. "Send out Groenfil's regiment!"

Tursel's voice was barely audible. "Beyond the brush, at the edge of the wood."

I squinted. Norland pikemen, spearmen, Lord of Nature knew who else. Hriskil was daring us to intervene. "That son of snakes and demons. Spawn of—"

The stride of boots. Tantroth, duke of Eiber, loomed. His face was gray. "Rodrigo . . ."

"My lord."

"For every wrong I've ever done you . . ." His voice was thick. "I ask pardon."

"Granted." I offered my hand, but he drew back.

"Forrel of Keth!"

Below the battlement, the thud of hooves. Tantroth's cavalry trotted down the road, toward the gate and the field beyond. They came to a stop below us, and Sandin hurried up the stairs.

"Sire," said Tantroth, "I must . . . take my leave."

I said gently, "I can't allow that."

His eyes glistened. "We must put cease to it! A charge would scatter them."

"They wait at the wood for just that. You can't thwart them, my lord."

"Yet I'll try. My men go mad."

"And after your death?" Brutal, but necessary.

Tantroth said simply, "I won't see it."

I said, "I forbid—"

"I will not obey you in this."

"Pardos." My voice was low.

"Sire?"

"My lord Tantroth does not leave the wall. See to it."

Pardos took a step back, as if struck. "Rodrigo, he's my liege lord!"

"Stand away!" Tantroth, trembling.

I said quickly, "My lord, don't play Hriskil's game. He rubs his hands, hoping we'll—"

"Don't presume to instruct me, you callow child! Pardos, remove your hand or I'll slice it off!"

Drawing swords, two of the duke's captains sprinted across the battlement. Tursel's hand went to his scabbard.

In a moment, all would be lost.

"Jath and Kanna, sons of Lord Sleak!"

I took two steps toward Tantroth's officers, drew my sword,

threw it at their feet. It clanged on the flagstones. I tore open my tunic, bared my breast. "Come, regicides, honor your duke!"

They skidded to a halt.

"Sandin, Azar, no!" Even as he spoke, Tantroth struggled to free himself. "I forbid it!"

I turned, my voice ice. "Who are you, sir, to forbid a vassal?"

"I'm their . . ." Slowly, he crumpled. Somehow, he shook off Pardos and peered over the wall. "You know . . ." His tone was too bright. "Jath and Kanna are my nephews. A hundred times, in my lap . . ." To his credit, he'd been intent on his suicidal charge long before their names were called.

We watched two hapless youngsters dragged toward the wagon.

Uncertainly, Azar slid his sword into his scabbard. He appealed to his duke. "What do we do?"

"We wait." My voice was harsh.

"They slaughter Eiber!"

"Look upon evil, Azar." My voice rang out, to him and the horsemen below. "And you, Tantroth. All of you!"

"Brewer Jon, of Keth."

Tantroth gritted his teeth.

"When comes our time, remember this day!" I looked about. "I'm cruel of speech and callow, but compared to them, I'm sweet light itself! Know you why we fight! Know you why Caledon must triumph!"

THE GRISLY DAY wore on.

Unbidden, by twos and threes, then by tens and hundreds, our army began to assemble under the wall. Tantroth huddled with his men of Eiber, just off the road.

Men jostled each other for places on the battlement. Five deep, soldiers peered over each other's shoulders for a view of the atrocity.

On the hillside, our strongest bowmen loosed useless shots that fell thirty paces short. I had Tursel signal them, to put a stop to it.

I dared not step away, or avert my eyes. Surreptitiously, I massaged aching calves.

Afternoon passed toward eve, and still the Norland host

dragged captives to the wagon. Thrice they had to move the cart, to make way for bodies.

As dusk approached, they brought out torches, to light their work.

Like Tantroth, I yearned to give battle, but the narrow pass blocked by the wall was our only advantage. Without it, the foe outmanned us by such proportions as to make a fight hopeless. I dared not say so to my men, whose tempers had begun to unravel. First harsh words, then jostling. Quarrels, with an edge.

Eyeing the troops, Tursel made his way to me. "We need do *something*," he said. "When one man breaks, they'll . . ."

I nodded, knowing what must come next. "Clear the battlement."

He looked aghast. "They may not . . . sire, don't give an order they may not obey."

"Tell them the king will speak. Assemble them below the wall."

Tursel took deep breath, as if to gird himself. "You men, off the battlement. You there, make way . . ."

Much grumbling, but they did as they were told.

From the parapet I looked down on the upturned faces. "What the Norlanders do is an abomination that sears the spirit. There is vile magic in it that robs the mind of reason." I drew my cloak against the evening chill. "You may see no more."

An angry mutter, that swelled to a growl. "You'd let them die unseen? Throats slit by those savage—"

"No," I said. "I will watch, for Caledon."

Utter silence.

"You crowned me; the burden is mine. Find a ritemaster; let him break a jar to ward off imps, that my soul not be stolen this night."

Uneasy looks.

Someone blurted, "We have to *know*. Our friends, our kin—"

"I will say their names." My tone was sober, but firm. "Those of you who would, stay below on the road, that I may have the solace of your company. The rest, go to camp. I'll send herald when the nightmare ends." I faced the field, knotted my cloak.

"Sleak, lord of Rivendon!"

I turned to my men. "Sleak, lord of Rivendon." Anavar had fought for him in Tantroth's assault on my lands, and been captured.

Tantroth put his head in his hands.

I turned back to the battlement.

RUSTIN, I KNOW you're gone, your voice isn't real. I speak to what's left of you within me. Be silent other days; tonight I need reply.

"Lara, daughter of Sith!"

"Lara, daughter of Sith." My voice grates.

They are names, no more. Remote vassals I've never met. I know not these folk. So why do I weep?

Please, Rust! Murmur, "Ah, my prince." Tell me I'm a fool, that it's my blunders that brought us to such straits. Say anything; I only pray you: speak!

Our whole camp has gathered below. They sit, craning their necks for a glimpse of me. Some cry quietly, some slam their knee with knotted fist. One whittles a stick with such savage strokes the wood is reduced to splinters. A man who made a quip nurses a bloody mouth.

I don't want the throne, Rust, not if I must stand sentry to the slaughter of my churls. My legs scream with ache; if not for that penance, I couldn't stand it. Only the calm of my voice as I declare death upon death prevents the army's dissolution; if the king can abide it, it must be bearable. They credit me with the breadth of soul to absorb utter evil.

"Garst, plowman!"

My voice rasped. "Garst, plowman."

I'd known a Garst once. Captured with Anavar, he'd later betrayed me to Tantroth when I sneaked into Stryx. But now it's well into night; the doomed Eiberian Garst is but a silhouette amid flickering torches.

Even if we win, Rust, what worth a crown bathed in blood? If I were certain it would stop the slaughter, I'd strike my standard and submit to a Norland axe.

You know my ways, Rust. When I said I'd watch the butchery on behalf of Caledon, it was as a mummer on stage: fine empty words to impress the lords and ladies seated in the hall. How could I know that my speech would make itself true: that my tongue tastes of ashes, that my knuckles are raw where I've pounded them on the obdurate stones of the parapet, that sharp stabs clutch my stomach as if I were pierced by a dagger.

My countrymen die!

TWENTY

THE NORLAND WAGON remained in the moonlit field, bodies piled about it.

The ghastly slaughter had halted, but still I remained on the wall, lest it resume. I was not sure I could leave, even if I cared to. My knees were weak, my stomach roiled.

What's this? A horseman, bearing a torch. He rode toward the wagon. Was he the harbinger of a new squad, coming to resume their labors in the dark of night?

They'd made their point; we were sickened, to a man.

But he cantered past the wagon.

Toward our gate.

I licked my lips.

Hriskil must want parley. My life for the Eiberians? I should surrender, but tomorrow Hriskil might wreak on Caledon what he inflicts on Eiber.

"Guardsmen at the gate!" My voice was a croak. "A rider!"

The clop of hooves, as the horseman's brown gelding cantered near. Fire jogged in the night, as his torch jounced with the rest of him.

He reined in, a moment's trot from the wall.

"Rez Caledi!"

"What want you?" My tone couldn't be described as civil.

He called, "Iv ot, Danzik!"

From our hilltop, a whir. A dozen arrows flashed in the night. Four found his horse, who whinnied once and went down. The torch went flying. Another volley. Instantly Danzik scrambled to wedge himself behind his expiring mount. Four more arrows went home; the gelding kicked once and was still.

"Hold! *Hold your shafts!*" My voice rose to a scream.

Below, on the road, voices swelled. "It's Danzik!" "The whoreson's back!" "Get him!" The gate crashed open as a new flock of arrows whirred from the hill.

"No!"

A clamor of men surged through the gate.

Oh, Rust. Look what it comes to.

I leaped atop the parapet, threw myself from the battlement. It was a goodly fall, over two men's height. I crashed on hard ground as our men rushed the Norland chief. Had I smashed my ankles? No, I could move, if I hobbled. I stumbled to the dead horse, threw my cloak across Danzik. "He's mine! Don't—AIYEE!" I pitched backward, gazing stupidly at the shaft protruding from my left breast.

A charging Eiberian skidded to a stop. "YOU SHOT THE KING!" The voice held horror.

A burly soldier knelt before me, his battered shield raised to guard us both. He screamed to the hill, "Hold! No more arrows!"

A horde of men poured through the gate, Pardos among them, driving aside any who stood in his way.

I scrabbled at the feathered dart. I ought say something, knew not what.

"Sire, don't touch—a litter for the king!"

"I don't need . . ." Perhaps I did need. My fingers were strangely weak.

"Hurry, before Hriskil mounts a charge—"

Kadar's squad formed, blocking my view of the distant Norland wagon. They bristled with pikes, bows and swords.

"Snuff the torch!"

Danzik growled, "Qer vos mord, rez." *I wish you dead, king.* Then he added in his wretched tongue, "But by *my* hand."

"Watch it, that savage is alive behind the horse!"

"Kill him!"

"No!" I searched for a face I knew. Not Pardos; he'd never leave me now. "Azar. I charge thee with Danzik's care . . ." I coughed; fire blossomed. My voice was ragged. ". . . not harmed."

Men ran up with a litter; canvas wrapped across poles. A sea of hands lifted me into it. I cried out.

"Gently!"

"Get him through the gate!"

"Did you call Darios the surgeon?"

Rust, they'll cut me! I shuddered. I'd always been terrified of wounds, sewing, saws. My recent work only augmented my fright. My bearers stumbled over a rut, and I cried out.

The gate crashed shut behind us.

*   *   *

DARIOS STRAIGHTENED FROM my bloody bed. "It's not reached the lung."

Around the tent, a collective sigh of relief. Earl Groenfil leaned against the centerpole, his eyes for a moment shut.

"Time to get it out. Who'll hold him?"

I made a sound through gritted teeth.

Outside, a commotion. "—me pass, or I'll—NOW!" Elryc's voice was shrill. *"NOW!"* He burst through the flap. "Roddy—Lord of Nature!" His hand flew to his mouth.

"It's all ri—"

He threw himself to my side, careful not to sway the bed. "Don't die!" His voice wavered. "I need you."

My hand stole to his. ". . . going to cut me. Hold me tight."

"—with Lor' Elryc! Lemme in!"

"So much blood. Will he—"

"Not if I get him bound. First the shaft must out." Darios raised his voice, as one used to command. "You, Pardos, hold his feet." He set out his instruments.

"I'm here, Roddy." Elryc gave my fingers a firm squeeze. "It'll hurt."

"I know."

"—Elryc's man! Han' off me!"

Elryc said over his shoulder, "Let Genard pass." His voice was low, his tone not much more than a child's, but Kadar leaned out the tent and snapped a command. In a moment Genard's lithe form crouched near Elryc's.

I raised my head, managed only an inch. "Tantroth."

"Sire." Gaunt and gray, he stifled a cough.

"If I should . . ." No. Don't think of it. "While I heal, Groenfil speaks for Caledon." Lord Groenfil turned, stared at me fixedly.

Tantroth's eyes burned through mine.

Desperately, I gathered myself. "My lord . . . Duke, I have utmost faith in . . . your honor and skill. But what Hriskil has wrought—" I tried to nod to the battlement and the carnage beyond. "—you are but human. Forgive me."

"You, there, his left arm. Boy, move aside. Kadar, take his right, don't stretch it. My lord King, bite on this."

Darios leaned to his work.

A razor, red with blood. Anguished cries. Iron hands forcing me down. Entreaties. "Stop, I command—"

A howl.

"There it comes!"

Pressure eased. The room whirled. A bloody cloth, pressed to my wound. "Bind it tight!"

My cheeks, drenched with sweat and tears.

Elryc's white fingers, flexing. Eyes that glistened.

"It's all righ', m'lor', he's come through it. Don't fret. Now he needs rest—"

"Not another word, Genard!" Elryc shook his head as if to clear it. "Not now. Please."

IN THE MORN they let me sun myself. Nursing my bound arm, I sat weak as a newborn calf. Tantroth was the first to attend me. "Sixty-seven more during the night."

"Who watched?"

"Groenfil, 'til dawn. Then I." Hollows darkened his eyes.

I squinted at the cloudless sky. "Today they'll attack."

"Oh?"

I said vaguely, "I feel it."

"Then someone ought ask Hriskil why he wastes half the day. Battles begin at dawn."

"Where is it written?"

He said, "It gives an army time—"

The distant blare of a horn.

Throughout the camp, men paused, listening. They began snatching up clothing and arms.

Tantroth said, "It's eerie how you do that." A short bow. "I'm off to—"

Jaw clenched, I struggled to my feet. Painful, but I managed. "Elryc, bring the Vessels."

The duke studied me. "What have you in mind?"

"To wield my Power." Not to visit my forebears, but as when I'd made Tanner and Bollert speak, or Genard dance. Perhaps I might read Hriskil's thoughts. I knew it was possible; I'd perused the silversmith's soul, in his interrogation. With luck, the Still might counter Hriskil's Rood. Reluctantly, I told Tantroth my design. He nodded assent to my plan.

I settled in the back of a cart, my feet jangling, to ride to the battlements. On Ebon I'd have made a more noble figure, but doubted I had the strength to mount.

Elryc and Genard trudged alongside the cart. The dusty road seethed with men. Ahead, the battlement was crowded with defenders. Pardos spurred ahead to find me safe vantage. I didn't tell him it would be no use; if I were to help at all I must see. To pass the time I said, "Where's Danzik?"

Elryc said mildly, "Chained to his wagon."

"I gave orders he was to be treated—"

"By your order he's alive. The men don't like it."

"He's not responsible for Hriskil's savagery."

Elryc's look was quizzical. "How do you know?"

Our driver tugged at his reins; we were beneath the wall. I eased myself from the cart. "Pardos, a hand up the stair."

"But—" My bodyguard looked about helplessly.

"Now there, it's all right. See your Lord Tantroth? He has a special task, and I must help, or he'll . . . give me a shoulder, I seem to be . . . winded." It was more than that. I was sweating, and the bright clear day pulsed red.

On the hill our bowmen awaited their grim work. The Norland army had begun its plodding march across the field. Pikemen streamed around the vile wagon, half buried in a pile of corpses. I was appalled; even now, in midst of battle, guards hauled a bound and kicking figure onto the wagon's bed.

Tursel stalked across the deck. "It won't work, Roddy. Groenfil agrees. Call it off."

I smiled tightly. "It's the Rood."

"It's not the imp-cursed Rood! Had you a modicum of sense you'd—"

"Genard, the ewer." I reached for it, hissed as a lance seemed to pierce my shoulder. "Set the bowl on that flat stone, pour the stillsilver for me, there's a good lad." I peered through an arrow slit.

Wheeled towers lurched across the field. Sweating men hauled catapults into place, midway on the field. A long shot for our bowmen, even from the hill. But a long shot for the catapults too.

"Tursel, is Tantroth ready?"

"I suppose, but—"

"Don't suppose. Look, and tell me." My legs quivered. "Genard, a barrel for me to sit. Be quick."

"Aye, m'lor'. Then I'll take Elryc to the mill."

I nodded. It ought be safe there.

With a sigh of relief I eased myself onto Genard's barrel. "Now . . ." I flexed my fingers, extended my palms, closed my eyes.

Tursel growled, "Tantroth's ready, but Azar wants him behind the line. They quarrel."

"And the gate?" I tried to think through fog. The captain's tone irritated me beyond bearing.

"The barricade is cleared as you ordered. The gate hangs shut of itself, without a bar. A breath of wind will swing it open, and if so, Norlanders will pour through and we'll be lost. Are you satisfied?"

It was the Rood. I bent to my task.

"Hold that shield so. Cover the arrow slit." Pardos, to his men.

I opened my eyes. "Be quiet. And let me see."

"A stray arrow and you'll never see aga—"

"Be silent! I wield the Still of Caledon!"

Mercifully Pardos complied.

Again I extended my palms over the bowl. Even bent forward at the waist, it strained my shoulder beyond abiding. Muttering ugly words, I slipped off the barrel. "Pardos, move it close. Like so."

Once more I settled myself. My hands closer to my stomach, my shoulder didn't throb as much. Of their own volition my palms shielded the bowl. I squeezed shut my eyes. My lips moved.

The cave was empty. Perplexed, I looked about for a sign. I wasn't sure what to do next.

On the wall beside me, a tremendous crash. Debris scraped my cheek. A catapult had found home. Through closed eyelids I watched stolid Norland hordes striding ever closer. At the same time, I saw the gray dusty walls of the cave.

A hooded cobra slithered across the floor with surprising speed. Spellbound, I watched it until an instant before my life was forfeit. I leaped aside just as it struck.

Hissss! It raised its head, stared through me with black unblinking eyes.

I licked dry lips as the viper whipped across the rock. I backed away. My spine crashed into the wall behind. The snake coiled. Summoning my strength, I dropped, rolled across the floor, fetched up in a pile of sticks. The snake lashed itself after me.

The Norland host wheeled, archers and pikemen making for the hill, wagons rolling to our battlement.

"Get thee gone!"

The cobra paid no heed. I snatched up a stick, threw it at the snake's eyes. Its flattened head weaved, avoiding my missile.

A heavy hardwood log awaited the fire. With effort I raised it high, hurled it.

The cobra slithered aside. As the threat passed, it came for me, tongue flicking. I snatched up another stick, this one forked. We circled the firepit, seeking advantage.

Arrows flicked from the parapet's arrow slit.

The snake struck. With my stick I fended it off. It coiled and struck again. I rammed the stick down, caught its head between the forks. The viper thrashed free.

The Norland towers rumbled near.

My eyes were glued shut. *"Say to Tantroth, the time is now. I contend with Hriskil."* Again we circled, wary. I jabbed the forked stick. *"Do you hear? Tursel! Pardos!"*

"The signal is given, my lord."

With two minds, I watched the snake and the field. Tantroth, a goodly number of paces behind the wall, set his lance. He raised his hand. A moment, and it shot down.

Four abreast, lances set, the cavalry of Eiber galloped past the Mill Road toward our closed gate.

The snake struck. Its fangs caught the shin of my boot. The leather tore.

Tantroth, Azar, Sandin lashed their mounts.

I caught the snake, but too far from the head. It twisted, lunged, broke free.

At the last possible moment our guards threw open the gates.

Tantroth's horsemen charged onto the field. Lances set, they thundered toward the Norland line.

The cobra threw itself across the firepit. Its tail lashed my calf. I staggered, threw up my staff just in time to deflect the snake's aim. I smashed the snake in mid-body. It rolled aside.

Wield the Rood, Hriskil. Take your attention from me. Just for a moment.

The Norland pikemen wheeled, to present their front to Tantroth's charge. His massed horse tore through their line. He waved a signal; his men regathered and charged across the field.

As if desperate, the cobra flipped about, coiled itself, lunged.

"Aiye!" Fangs brushed my cheek. I backed toward the wall. The snake sought advantage.

Hriskil's men rushed our wall.

Tantroth reached the first of the siege towers. He dug at foemen with his lance, while Azar and his men slung ropes. They spurred. The tower crashed. On to another, while squads of horsemen elsewhere did the same. One by one the towers toppled.

A few of our riders carried torches. They worked their way to the fallen towers.

On the wall, shouts, cries of pain. Clanking steel. The thunk of arrows.

The cobra coiled itself, weaving. Panting, sweating, I followed its head. Its motion never ceased.

Tantroth, back to the gate. I couldn't hold much longer.

Lances extended, our Eiber cavalry charged the Norland catapults. Hriskil's soldiers broke and ran. Tantroth threw aside his lance, drew his sword. His men followed suit. A slash; a foeman rolled headless across the field.

The duke shouted something I couldn't hear. A dozen of his horsemen gathered, charged across the field, farther and farther from the safety of our wall. Others raced after.

The viper struck. In the very nick of time I wrenched the staff in front of my eyes. The hooded head smashed it into my face. Blinded, dazed, I fell back.

Tantroth reached the wagon of corpses. His cavalry surrounded it. They pulled it onto its side. Two torches flew through the air, three, four. The hated cart began to blaze.

My fingers twitched over the bowl. *Tantroth of Eiber, I summon thee!*

He jerked, stared at the battlement.

Get thee to the gate!

The snake lunged. I stumbled, rolled slowly to the wall.

Tantroth shook himself, as if to wake. He shouted, and his

men began to gather. Once more they raced across the field, this time toward our battlement.

I tore my thoughts back to the cave.

For eons the cobra and I feinted and parried. Twice I caught him with the fork. At last he, too, seemed to be tiring.

The fork of my stick splintered. I wielded it as a club to smash the cobra's spine. It evaded my hammer blows.

"Rodrigo."

Not now. The viper coiled. It lunged, but without the blinding speed of before.

"King!" Fingers grasped my forearm.

Get thee gone! Without hands, I thrust away the intrusion, protected my bowl.

A yelp. "Roddy, please!" Elryc. "Open your eyes. It's done."

Stalking, I bared my teeth at the snake. It hissed. It launched itself into its rolling gait, but toward the mouth of the cave. I darted to intercept it.

"My lord!"

The voice distracted me a crucial instant. The snake slithered outside, into dark.

Fingers pried at mine. Wearily, I unlocked my grip on the bowl and opened my eyes. Deep red marks scored my palms where they'd pressed into the rounded edge. Bright lances of pain gouged my shoulder.

"What . . ." I cleared my throat, tried anew. "Why'd you summon me?"

"My lord King." Groenfil. His tone was . . . odd. "Sire, look upon the field. If it please you."

I raised my head, peered through the arrowguard.

Wooden towers blazed in the dry grass. Smashed catapults burned. In the distance, Hriskil's men were melting into the wood.

"It's done, sire. We won."

"Did we?" I tried to lift myself, failed. It brought a stab of pain. I looked down at my crimson bandage. "I'm . . . torn." With each moment, the hurt grew. "Water."

Someone brought a skin. I couldn't hold it to my mouth; my chest and shoulder blazed. They squeezed it while I gulped cool liquid. "Elryc?"

"I'm here." He pressed through the throng.

"Best get me to my bed."

"Yes, Roddy."

Solicitous and awed, they helped me down the stair. I teetered at the edge of a deep black well. "Lie me down." They did, in the cart.

Eons later, we were at my tent.

"Let me." Groenfil's voice was gruff. He and Tantroth carried me within, laid me gently on my bed. "You need be resewn."

Salt tears leaked from the edge of my eyes. "Don't tell them, I beg you."

"What?"

"That I'm a coward."

Groenfil closed my hand, lifted it gently, pressed his lips to it. "My liege."

THE SURGEON DID his grisly work, and left me clutching a soft cushion to allay my misery. Sleep was beyond me; I drank icy spring water—my thirst was insatiable—and called for Danzik.

They brought him in chains. Scratching his beard, he studied me from beneath bushy eyebrows. "You die soon." Satisfaction in his tone. My bodyguards knew none of the Norland tongue, else they'd garotte him on the spot.

I forced my thoughts into Norlandic. "That pleases you?"

A grin. "Quix iot." *Perhaps a little.* Always, we came back to the phrase. He rattled his chains. "Pir?" *Why?*

"They blame you." I sought words I didn't have. "The wagon. The Eiberians."

He shrugged his indifference. "War."

"Was it," I asked casually, "your idea?"

"Hriskil. Done it before. Always drives from city."

I stirred and immediately regretted it. My forehead grew clammy. "Why do you return?" That wasn't quite right, but . . .

He scowled. "Vade." Oath, or soul. To them, it was the same word. "Not right Hriskil be angry. Said not right I give oath. No ransom ever. I die in Caled camp, he not weep."

I coughed, and the world went red. "You'd better go." After they led him out, I recalled I ought do something about his chains, but it seemed too much trouble.

*　　*　　*

A LOUD VOICE. "How is he?" Anavar.

"Sleeping." My brother's voice dripped scorn. "You're drunk."

They regarded each other warily. Ignored, I watched through half-closed eyes.

"Yes, what of it?" Anavar sat, or fell, on the trunk.

"Hear you!" Elryc grasped the Eiberian's crumpled tunic, held it tight. "You owe Roddy your very life! Was Tursel not about to slit your throat when he intervened?"

"Yes, but—"

"And Roddy raised you from servant to baron?"

No reply.

"He gave you honorable refuge from his enemy Tantroth. Yet now not once, twice, you vexed the duke. He needs not much provocation to be gone, and then where's Roddy's cause?"

"I—I didn't mean . . ."

"You snarl at a lord, an elder, ally of your guardian and liege? And when rebuked, you guzzle wine while he saves Caledon!"

A long silence. Then, "Urk." Anavar bolted to the flap. Outside, the sound of retching. In a while he returned, wiping his mouth. Shakily, he sat on the trunk. "You're unjust. I set aside my grievances, come to inquire—"

"What grievances?"

"Before the whole camp, he kicked me into the dirt. And in view of Tantroth of Eiber he humiliated—"

"You can't hope to replace Rustin in his heart, unless—"

"I don't! I won't be his bed-friend!"

"I never supposed that. Besides, he's grown beyond that."

A long silence. At last Anavar said, "Unless what?"

Elryc glanced at the bed, lowered his voice. "Think you he didn't wound Rustin to the heart? Rustin had the grace to forgive, over and again. Have you that?"

Anavar's gaze fell. "I would."

"As he forgives you?"

"How has he—"

"Your days in the alehouse . . . did he summon you?"

"No."

"Send a squad of guards to haul you home? Reduce the stipend you toss to the winesellers?"

"No!" Anavar's voice was subdued. "I beg you, enough!" He slipped from the tent.

Elryc sat on the trunk, staring at the carpet. After a moment, he said to no one in particular, "You weren't supposed to hear that."

I opened my eyes fully. "How could I not?"

"It's all true."

I said carefully, "The part about Rustin . . ."

"Anavar so envies your love. Did you not know?"

I turned my head to the tent. The answer shamed me.

TWENTY-ONE

"GENARD, I WOULD go outdoors."

"Aye, m'lor'." He helped me to my feet, wrinkling his nose; I realized I smelled foul. Rustin would be most annoyed. "Afterwards, a basin of water."

In the distance, a commotion. If it was Hriskil, he was welcome to the camp. To Caledon.

I sat sweating.

"Is he up?" Tursel. "Ahh. Sire, you ought to come see . . ." His glance appraised me, a horse at market. "Stay, I'll bring them. Boy! This way!"

My guards surrounded a ragged peasant lad, Bollert's age, or my own. He wore a soiled gray blouse, as churls might don for market. He led a brown stallion, too fine to be his. The horse had a rider, slumped over the pommel, an arrow protruding from his ribs. Blood had soaked through his jerkin, his leggings, the stallion's flank.

"Well?" I couldn't keep impatience from my tone.

"He killed—"

"Did not!" The boy's voice was shrill. To me, "Fulmon tol' me to find king, in Pezar. Would give me coin." He shot a look of indignation at his captors. "I wanted take him to ritemaster. He said he'd seek healer in Pezar."

Too late. No healer could follow where Fulmon had gone.

I said wearily, "What was his hurry?"

"This, m'lor'." The boy reached into the saddlebag. My guards tensed, but he only brought out a cloth, wrapped around a parchment. "Fulmon rides for Cumber. Letters an' orders an' such. Been passin' our cottage now an' again since I was a boy. When he stopped, thought he wanted water. Never thought he'd ask help. Didn't see arrow."

Tursel growled, "More likely this churl killed the courier."

"Why I come here then? For coin? When I had his stallion an' saddle an' good boots? Coin in pocket too, prolly." His look added, *more than I'm likely to get here.*

I asked, "What's in the letter?"

"Dunno." Which meant he couldn't read.

"Give it here. Who shot Fulmon?"

"Dunno. Was leaning over saddle when he came to cottage. Wasn't bleeding much, said he could make Pezar if I led horse."

The seal looked intact. I broke it. My heart gave a thump.

"To my dearest Rodrigo, king, from Tresa of Cumber, greetings. I've no time to dally. I leave within the hour for Certha."

I looked up. "Where's Certha?"

Tursel said, "Three hours ride from Cumber. A village in the hills."

"Why would she—" I compressed my lips.

"I've decided to visit my old nurse who lives there; it's been years since I've seen her. A pity I'll miss the festivities; I just learned Duke Margenthar arrives this afternoon, to confer with my uncle Bouris. He'll arrive before dark. Bouris is quite busy readying a feast, so I won't bother him with news of my journey, but I wanted you to know.

"I've no time for more. I pray this finds you in good health. Fulmon, who brings this, is an old friend. Don't hesitate to ask what you would know. I am, as always, your ally and servant Tresa of Cumber."

"Feed the churl, give him coin and our thanks. Genard, help me stand."

Somehow, we made it to my bed.

Had Fulmon been shot for what he knew, for what Tresa had said, or for what they were afraid she'd say? How had he escaped his pursuers with his wound? Perhaps they'd shot from long range. If he'd spurred hard, lost them in the winding hills . . .

Tresa, are you safe? Should I send troops?

My hand caressed my scar.

THE SKY WAS brown and blotched, and wrinkled where it crossed over my bed. Flies mated on its surface. The sun was but a haze. Elryc's face loomed, wan and gaunt. "Drink, Roddy."

"Umh." I rode a wave of fire.

He pressed a cup to my lips. I tried to turn away, but he held me until I sipped. Exhausted, I laid down my head.

Night.

The tent was hot. I tossed off the cover.

"I'll watch, m'lor. You rest—"

"Genard . . ." Elryc's tone held warning.

I slept.

Rustin and I were tykes, playing in the Keep. The day was dreadfully hot.

"How is he?" Groenfil.

"Delirious."

Later, Darios sniffed my wound. "It putrefies. Summon a ritemaster from Pezar."

I swam to the surface. "No!" If they tried to expel Varon, I'd die.

"The rite of healing—"

"No rites!"

Morn.

Outside my tent, Tantroth's grim voice. "They've set out another wagon. A hundred twelve souls today. One by one. Will Hriskil never stop?"

I tossed in my bed.

"Not if there's a chance he can lure you—" Larissa of Soushire.

"Chance? A near certainty. I'm pledged to the boy, not your paramour Groenfil. If Roddy's no better of the morrow, I'll sally against—"

"My lord Duke!"

"What would you? How can I claim Eiber's loyalty and cower behind stone walls while my people—"

"Have patience."

"Patience, Larissa? Is that why you ready yourself to leave camp?"

"Margenthar left men at my walls; his ranks have swelled to two thousand. Would you I lost my domain? I gave Roddy five days."

Their voices faded.

A sharp instrument at my swollen shoulder. A plunge.

I convulsed, and fainted.

"How is he today?" Groenfil.

"Feverish, m'lor'."

"Is there some draught . . . I'll ask Darios. The king must

rise. Hriskil will attack again, and if not, I can hold Tantroth no longer. Pah; why do I tell you this?"

"You're worried, m'lor.' Old Griswold used to say, even a horse is good company when—"

"Good-day." Receding steps.

"Genard, where's Elryc?"

The stableboy peered over me. "Sleepin'. He broods over you day and night. Yester eve he claimed he saw imps about the campfire. I gave him unwatered wine, an' at last he rests."

"How long have I . . ."

"Thir' day. Drink some broth. Lanced you last night. Smelly pus."

I drifted on a gray sea to forever.

"PUT HIS HANDS SO." Someone placed my palms flat over a bowl, balanced on my stomach.

I shifted, spilled thick liquid.

"Let it be still, Roddy." Elryc. "Talk to Mother. Ask her—" His voice quavered. "—how to heal." A cool compress bathed my fiery forehead until I dozed.

I dreamed. A snake, distant, prowling, eyes glowing. The cave. Mother, radiant, with ethereal beauty, such as I'd never seen her. My head was in her lap. She soothed me with cool hand. "Shhh, Roddy. All will be well."

Mother, I think . . . I'm dying.

"My son. My Caledon." She patted the floor. "Time comes, you'll sit here, twixt me and Tryon."

How will we pass our days?

"Waiting for the king. Drink, the water's cool." With tender care, she brought the warm cup to my lips. The heat chilled me. "Ah, Roddy, I always loved you."

Did you, Mother? Really?

"How could you not know? Later, we'll speak of it. We'll have ample time."

But not now?

"No, son. You've a life to live."

Mist, cold, swirling, gray. The cave faded. The jangle of spurs, the chatter of men at campfires worked their way through my mind.

A face, grizzled, old, lined. Tantroth. "The fever's broken." To me, "I think I'd have missed you."

"You may yet." My voice was a wraith.

"By your leave." He pressed his gnarled knuckles to my forehead. "Ahh, much better. Yesterday, you threw off as much heat as the alehouse hearth."

I said presently, "Why am I spared, Tantroth?"

He blinked. "Shouldn't you be?"

"I'm not much of a king."

"Oh, I don't know. Against all odds, we still hold Pezar. Hriskil is thrice repulsed. Groenfil's face softens when he speaks of you. Lady Soushire remains encamped, despite her threats."

"And yourself?"

His eyes met mine. "I risked more than I knew when I moved against Stryx."

The flap thrust open. "Is he better? Oh!" Anavar reddened. "Pardon, my lord."

Tantroth's tone was dry. "To whom do you speak, youngsire?"

"You, sir." With obvious effort, Anavar made his tone meek. "I meant not to intrude."

"Then," said Tantroth, "don't." When Anavar was gone he added, "The lad makes himself ever harder to overlook."

"Yet you struggle at the task." My tone was dry.

"Out of respect for you." He frowned. "Else the boy would lie below grass. Don't glare, Roddy. It wasn't a threat. What will you do about Cumber?"

I sought elusive memory. "What's Bouris done?"

"Accepted Mar's assurance that he races to your aid, and granted Verein's troops passage across his lands."

I bolted upright, or tried to; I fell back groaning. My heart pounded, and with it, my wound. "Why didn't someone tell me?"

"I just did."

I waited for the throbbing to ease. "How did you learn of it?"

"A question a noble spirit doesn't ask. We all have our private means, have we not?"

I let it go. "When will Mar get here?"

"Yesterday at this hour, near a hundred wagons passed through Cumber Town. Bouris sends generous escort; it's said loudly they'll turn back by nightfall." Which meant, of course, that they wouldn't.

Slowly, the tent began to drift. "We ought prepare . . ."

"For what, sire?"

The canvas spun faster. "For Margenthar."
Black.

I SPENT THE afternoon sitting on a cushioned trunk, receiving
a procession of supplicants: tanners, wagoners, leatherers and
the like. All had problems only the king could solve, and that
with coin. And we had near none. As for Cumber . . . while
Raeth lived, I could count on his support. Now, Bouris was
quite another matter.

Well, I'd forced the new earl to commit, hadn't I? Unfortu-
nately he'd committed to Margenthar, not to me. On the other
hand, better Mar than Hriskil. Unless they were one.

When my last petitioner was gone, I stood, tossed the cushion to my bed. The flap moved; I sighed. "Now what?"

It was Anavar. We exchanged wary glances.

"What do *you* want?" I was weary; it had been a long day.

"To see how you bided. I shouldn't have bothered." His
tone was belligerent. "I'll return when I'm wanted."

"You've no leave to depart. Sit."

Obeying with literal effrontery, he sat cross-legged on the
rug, in mid-tent where it would be the most trouble to go
around him. "Now what?"

"Now, youngsire, you'll be silent." He'd loitered in an alehouse while his countrymen were slaughtered. I'd fought
Hriskil, sustained a grievous wound, and where was my
baron? On the other hand, he'd come to see me a day past, and
met Elryc. And he was here now, inquiring after my health.
He wasn't utterly without concern. "You are rebuked," I said.
"Your behavior does you no credit."

"And yours?"

I took sharp breath. It was impudent, from guardian to
ward. From youth to elder. From baron to king. I said, "You
provoke me with purpose."

His tone was sullen. "Which is?"

"To rid yourself of shame."

"You know not my soul!"

I raised my hand. "Go to the willow at the edge of camp,
cut a switch no thicker than your finger, and bring it here."

When he returned, switch in hand, I flicked a thumb at my
bandaged chest, said, "I'll not injure myself for you. I'll need
a proxy." I considered. "A highborn; it's unjust that a com-

moner beat a noble." I crossed to the flap. "Kadar, call Lord Tantroth."

"No!" Anavar fell to his knees. "Anyone else! I beg you earnestly, sir. Not the duke!"

The humiliation would do Anavar good, and it might mollify Tantroth. Almost I ignored his protest, but might my incentive be the cruelty within? "Hold, Kadar. Groenfil instead."

And so it was that Anavar of Eiber stripped off his tunic and leggings and bent before the earl of Groenfil. I took great care that he not be beaten hard enough to break skin, but a willow, properly stripped, conveys a fearsome sting. When Groenfil was done, Anavar stood hugging himself, his eyes watery.

The earl left us.

"Now then, youngsi—"

"I apologize, my lord. I'll speak with respect and mind your commands." His words came so fast I knew they'd been practiced. Poor Anavar. I wondered if he knew how determinedly he'd had himself punished.

I said sternly, "I think you've had enough of the alehouse."

"Aye, sir."

"Clearly you need more governance. While I recover, you'll stay near and do me service. Sleep in my tent."

"Yes, my lord." A deep breath. Visibly, the tension left his form.

Now, perhaps, I could rest.

I WOKE IN pitch black, instantly alert. My whole body tingled. Something was amiss. I wrenched my dagger from its scabbard. In the corner, steady breathing; Anavar slept on a pile of blankets.

I poked my head out the flap. It rustled; a pacing guard whirled, clutching his sword. He gulped. "Sire, you startled me."

I looked about. "Is there an alarm?"

"No, my lord."

In the tent, I worked a blanket over my shoulders and settled wearily on my trunk, watching the slow rise and fall of Anavar's ribs. I grimaced at his welts, thought of Eiber and the Norlands.

Savage or no, Hriskil must know his murders were evil. But

they hadn't weakened our resolve; would Hriskil perforce call them off, or redouble them?

Despite our victories we weren't strong enough to leave our stronghold. And Uncle Mar's arrival would complicate—

I sat bolt upright. Uncle Mar was nearing; almost I'd let myself forget. I'd been groggy when Tantroth told me, as if that were excuse.

What did Mar mean to accomplish? Surely he knew I couldn't forgive him Rustin's death on that road to Fort.

Of course he knew.

Which meant he wasn't riding to strengthen us.

When he reached Pezar we'd be trapped, Hriskil before us, Verein's forces behind. It hardly mattered which of them mounted the first attack. The other would fall on our defenseless rear.

What was Mar's reward? And what advantage to Bouris?

Forgetting my shoulder, I shrugged.

It mattered not. *Mar was riding to Pezar.*

I'd frittered away an entire day. Cursing my stupidity, I stumbled to the flap. "You, guard! Wake Tursel. Summon him in the quarter hour."

I began pulling on my clothes.

TWENTY-TWO

A PALE MOON sailed overhead. I clutched Ebon's pommel, my throbbing left arm bound tightly to my chest. Disheveled, his hair wild, Bollert stood dozing against the stallion's flank, holding my reins.

While sleep-eyed soldiers struck my tent and slung it onto a wagon with the rest of my equipage, I stifled a yawn, gazing blearily at the beehive of our camp.

Captain Tursel, despite his reservations, had risen magnificently to the occasion. With but a few moments' warning, he'd sent runners about the camp to each flickering campfire, urging the men to rise in silence. Their packs filled, they quietly hitched muffled-hooved dray horses to wagons, stowed gear, made ready the march. No new fires were lit or old ones doused; no light or sound must escape to alert the Norlanders. At the edge of camp a blacksmith and his muscled boys dragged their anvil to a sturdy cart. At the baker's hearth, men piled bags of flour high atop flatbed barrows, covered them with tarpaulins in case of rain.

We march at dawn, I'd told Tursel. Earlier, could we manage it.

Lord Tantroth, when informed, was aghast. How could we forsake his countrymen to slaughter?

Hriskil had no reason to kill them, I said, were we not present to watch.

But what of Eiber? Had I not pledged to succor his campaign?

Did he want us crushed between Mar and Hriskil? Would that serve Eiber's cause? Hriskil's force was overwhelming, Margenthar's was not. We'd lunge at Mar, scatter his force, wheel to make a stand against the pursuing Norlanders.

Why now, Tantroth had asked. We'd had a night and a day to break camp.

Had I not told him I wasn't much of a king?

Yes, but you didn't have to prove it.

I sighed. Tantroth would be Tantroth. I was becoming accustomed, as to a nagging tooth.

As gently as they might, men lifted the wounded to straw-
strewn carts. We'd not leave them to Hriskil. Across the field
stablemen rolled precious round bales of hay up ramps to
flatbed wagons; horses, too, must eat.

Anavar led his Edmund alongside Ebon, took to his saddle
with a grimace. Almost, I regretted his stripes.

He looped his shield around the pommel. "May I have
place alongside you, sir?" His tone was carefully polite. I gestured assent.

Our scouts had long since fanned out in the hills along the
Cumber road, to probe for Verein. They need hardly look; I
imagined one could sense my uncle's brooding malice for
leagues.

The assembled column began to move. As the motion rip-
pled its way toward us, I urged Ebon forward with my heels.
Riding one-handed was no joy; my bound arm interfered
mightily with my balance.

Slowly, as the eastern sky began to lighten, we snaked
through the dust of Pezar.

Tursel had set Groenfil's men before us, an advance guard
who would be our front line, were we drawn unexpectedly
into battle. Tantroth would set our rear guard; he'd shown
great skill on our retreat from the ridge.

Once on the road, the column moved with speed. We
pushed the men at double-march; the more distance we put
between us and Hriskil the safer. And the further from
Pezar we met Uncle Mar, the more chance we'd catch him
by surprise.

Elryc, Anavar and I rode just behind Groenfil's troops.
Tursel rode up and down the column, hurrying wagonmasters,
urging scattered contingents to keep order. He'd wear out his
mount before the sun was high; a string of spares plodded behind his wagon.

On the battlement we'd abandoned, a dozen men tended the
usual watchfires. They'd maintain an illusion of vigilance as
long as they might. But soon or late, a sharp-eyed Norlander
would notice our bowmen had disappeared from the hillside
above. Immediately, they'd swarm the parapet. Mounts were

tied below the wall, on which our last men might escape to rejoin us.

Elryc shivered. He'd taken an ague, and shouldn't be riding, though Genard had him bundled well. Almost, I ordered him to a wagon, but forbore, for his pride's sake. If it came to it, I'd dismount and ride with him in the cart. No doubt poor Anavar would be glad to do the same. I smiled; a fine sight the three of us would make. No need for Hriskil to attack; one by one we would afflict ourselves.

Groenfil waited by the side of the road until we drew alongside, then jogged his chestnut mount. "What when we meet Margenthar? Parley?"

I snorted. "If he presents himself in chains, neck shaven for the axe."

"What, then?"

"Treat him as you would Hriskil."

Groenfil rode a few moments, in silence. "You recall, of course, that the duke and I are bound in blood." Groenfil's sister Varess was Margenthar's wife.

I said grimly, "The duke and I are likewise bound in blood." Rustin's.

He gave a short bow, acknowledging a point scored. "I won't don his colors, as I assume you know. But to attack him without warning . . ."

I said somberly, "That's the worst of war, is it not? We must choose our loyalties."

"Indeed. And mine is to you, sire, as I trust I've made clear." A wave, as if to ask leave, and he cantered off.

MIDDAY, AND THE runners said Hriskil had not probed our battlements. Tantroth rode close to the rear of our line, selecting sites where he might make a stand, building each new rear guards's strongpoint before abandoning the last. With feverish energy his men threw logs across the road, dug out fords, made the road behind him as impassable as they might. But Hriskil had swarms of minions to haul logs to the side, and artisans aplenty to repair fords. And, if necessary, his yeomen and cavalry could outstrip his wagons. Short of throwing up a new battlement, there was little we could do to stop their determined pursuit.

At the dinner hour, the first of our remnant at the Pezar battlements caught up with us. Hriskil had discovered our ruse, and the wall was his. The last of our men saw the gate behind them thrown open in triumph.

We hurried on.

Not satisfied, I demanded Tursel increase our pace.

"We're pushing them fast as we might, sire. Would you have an army, or rabble? Forget not that we rush toward Margenthar, where battle awaits."

Burying my misgivings, I grunted assent.

Near eve, a scout came racing to camp on a lathered mount. "Margenthar's army is encamped a league hence!"

Tursel struck his pommel, startling his obedient gelding. "Where?"

The courier wiped his brow, unknotted his waterskin. "Lord Groenfil says, between Oak Dell and the abandoned mill. They've set tents in the field, rounded the wagons, thrown barriers across the road."

So. Were it not for Margenthar's malice, we'd be safe—as could be—behind Pezar's sturdy wall, blocking Hriskil's main force from Caledon. Mar would sacrifice all for his hatred of me. Yes, I was right to meet him as far from Hriskil as possible.

I asked grimly, "How strong is he?"

"Wagons, a hundred and a score. Horse, three hundred at least. Men of Verein, but Cumber as well."

Tursel and I exchanged glances in the dusk. Bouris of Cumber had made his choice. What, I wondered, had Mar offered?

"Return to Groenfil," Tursel told the courier. "He's to withdraw his scouts before he's seen. We'll make camp here; at dawn we strike. Have him set pickets—"

"No," I said. All looked to me. "Tell the earl to make ready for battle. A league? We'll be upon Mar in an hour; another half hour to set our line. Groenfil's to lead the attack."

"Roddy, not in night."

"It's full moon; remember this morn, when it lit our withdrawal?"

"Archers can't aim in—"

"Then neither may theirs." I rose in the saddle. "Hurry the troops! At the full trot!"

"*You don't make war at night!* No battle is fought—"

I demanded, "Margenthar knows this?"

"Of course."

"And Hriskil?"

"Anyone with sense knows—"

"Then we attack. Go!" The rider lashed his gray, galloped down the road.

Tursel threw up his hands, but said no more.

"Speed the wagons!" I pranced Ebon about and nearly toppled from the saddle. Barely I righted myself. "Why isn't that cohort at the trot? Hurry! Hriskil isn't far behind us—"

"Nearly a day's march."

"Don't count on—"

"My lords! My lords!" A black-clad Eiberian raced from the rear.

I glared. "Now what?"

"Hriskil's cavalry gathers at the oxbow ford."

"A full day's march?" I snorted. "An hour, two at most."

Tursel demanded, "What of the Norland footmen?"

"Horse only, so far. They gathered their strength before crossing, lest we lay in ambush over the hill."

I demanded, "Why didn't we?"

He had no answer.

My tone was ironic. "Doesn't Hriskil know he's not to battle at night? Tell Duke Tantroth our rear guard must hold them for two hours."

"What then?"

"We'll be victorious, or our cause is no more. Tursel?"

"We give battle to Margenthar." An admission of defeat. "Lady Soushire, your troops block the road. Send them to the front."

"I won't ride unguarded!"

"Put them in that meadow, then. Tarry where you may." He galloped off.

"Genard, find my brother a comfortable place in my tent wagon. Pardos, see he's well guarded."

"And you, sire?"

With disgust I peered down at my bandaged chest. "I'm useless as teats on a boar. I'll watch."

"From the center, well back—"

"Don't be daft." I spurred toward Groenfil and the front. Cursing, Pardos and his troop chased after.

We cantered past row after row of weary men trotting with

dogged perseverance toward Oak Dell. On horse, in moments we were beyond the foremost of them. The darkening road was silent; not even the chirp of birds lightened the gloom. I was glad for my bodyguards' presence, though not even they might save me from an imp's malice. "Come, Ebon, it's all right." I patted his neck.

"Hold, sire!" Two pikemen waved me down from the shadows. "It's not safe, Verein's outriders may . . ."

"Where's Groenfil?"

"Over that rise."

"I'll go no farther." Before they could object, I cantered on. In moments I found the earl conferring with his officers. He raised an eyebrow, looked over my paltry guard. "Thank you for the reinforcements."

"They're not here to—oh, don't joke. I'm not subtle."

"One would never know. What do you here, sire?"

"Do you think I'm benighted too?"

Groenfil blinked.

"My not wanting to wait 'til dawn."

"Oh, that. Hmm. Would my blessing sway you?"

I blurted, "It's as close to a father's as ever I'll have." *Lord of Nature! What possessed me to say that?* I blushed furiously.

To his aides, "Leave us, a moment." Then, "Rodrigo, are you king, or boy in need of guardian?"

"I'm—" How could I know?

He held up a palm. "If you're king, you need not my sanction. And if a youngsire, it's madness to order us about as if you knew what you do."

"Is it madness, my lord?"

"To fight at night? Outlandish. We'll blunder about, likely to spike each other as the enemy. Couriers will get lost, orders go awry."

"Then—"

"On both sides. And by dawn, we'd have lost surprise. Your cause wants daring, my liege, and you supply it."

I swallowed. "Was that a blessing?"

"Imps take you!" For a moment, Groenfil turned away. When again he met my gaze, his eyes glistened. "*Must* you turn respect into more? I *have* sons, Rodrigo. I sought not another."

"I'm sor—"

"I bless your daring, your grace, your nobility. Now, would you linger in converse, or smash Verein?"

The night was chill, but a fine warmth sustained me.

"SIRE, ARE YOU well?"

The clarion call of trumpets exhorting our charge.

The whir of a thousand arrows across the bloody meadow.

Margenthar's flimsy barriers, cast into the ditch.

Cries of the chase, in the wood. Ebon snorting, pawing, eager to answer the call.

A dozen pikemen gutted like fish, flopping in the dust, struggling, breathing their last. Groenfil's men, Cumber's, mine.

"My lord King?"

Margenthar's wagons thrown over, a few burned before Tursel could put a stop to it. Grimy, ragged, exhausted men of Caledon staggering up the road, to be thrown piecemeal into the fight.

The throb of my jostled shoulder. My throat, raw from shouting.

Tents aflame.

Blood in the air, a scent that drives men mad.

"Rodrigo!"

Imps riding the moon, chortling at death.

Anavar, exultant, his sword sticky with blood. The scream of a wounded horse. A pikeman, demented, running about the meadow, stabbing at anything on the trampled grass that twitched. The embers of a score of campfires.

"Take his arm, Kadar. Gently."

The distant peal of retreat. Jubilant men of Caledon milling about the field, Groenfil and Tursel struggling to impose order. Broken cartwheels. Ragged canvas. Splintered slats. A headless man at rest under a drooping elm.

"To his wagon. Kadar, find him hot mulled wine."

The throb of my wound.

"Lord Elryc?"

"What's beset him?"

"He's dazed. Make room."

"Come up, Roddy."

"Sit. No, sire, let him cover you."

Fading cries.

Blood.

"RODRIGO?" A TENDER hand, on my knee. "Are you fit?"

"My lord Groenfil." My voice was a rasp. I sipped my wine.

"The men are spent. Hriskil's cavalry are probing Tantroth's rear guard. Give battle to the Norlanders here, or cede them the field?"

I set down my cup, rubbed my eyes.

"It's a good place to camp, but as Margenthar discovered, not so defensible. Past Oak Dell there's a better."

I cleared my throat. "Is the duke ours?"

Groenfil said, "Not yet."

"I was no help."

"You were splendid. You stood in the saddle, bathed in moonlight, urging us on, your clenched fist held high. All that one could ask."

"Margenthar's supplies . . ."

"We've most of his wagons, and half his provender."

"Can Mar regroup?"

"In time."

I asked, "Our men?"

"Utterly spent. We need take care that our retreat not become a rout."

"Then we're too exhausted to fight. And if Tantroth's done his work, Hriskil's cavalry have well outrun their wagons and foot soldiers. Soon or late, they too must rest."

"So?"

"Move on. Let the whole threat be behind us."

"Aye, my lord."

"You have no quibble, no unease?"

"Why no," Groenfil said. "I think you know your mind." He wheeled his mount and left me, already snapping out orders.

From the next wagon, a gleeful chuckle. "Homu Caledi en sa lucha." *The men of Caledon fight among themselves.* "Less work for Hriskil."

I ignored the Norlander's pleasantries. "Danzik, do you understand parole? I let you walk free, you give, um, your *vade* not to escape."

"Pir rez iv dese?" *Why does the king want it?*

Why, indeed? "I'm lonely."

"I walk free, your guards kill me." He made a slicing gesture across his throat.

"That's a problem." I drained the last of my wine. "Shall we risk it?"

WE CAREENED DOWN the road, our teamster keeping his drays a nose behind the tailboard ahead. We asked much of our men: roused at night from sleep, run down the road toward Cumber, thrown into battle, set again on the fast march. But we were near escape.

Tantroth had set cunning ambush for Hriskil's reckless cavalry. Two hundred of our archers, hidden in the brush alongside the rutted road, rose on Azar's signal. Their relentless shafts decimated horses and men. Now, Tantroth struggled to return our straggling wagons and carts to our fold, his task made no easier by our headlong plunge toward Cumber.

Elryc's head lolled on my good shoulder, to Genard's resentment. Across the wagon bed, Danzik rubbed his chafed wrists. "Qa capto soa?" *What kind of prisoner am I?*

"One with honor, I hope. My life is in your hands."

"And when I have chance to kill you?"

"You cannot, with honor."

"Bah. My king has simpler solutions." A stabbing motion. "No *capto*. No worry about loyalty."

"And then where would you be?"

Danzik had no response. After a time he said, "This *kevhom* of Caled—Mar—was once in your hands?"

I gritted my teeth. "Yes." And I'd had Rustin escort him from camp.

"You let him loose?" He shook his head. "And they allow you to remain king?"

I stiffened so that Elryc murmured, "What is it, Roddy?"

"Nothing, brother. Sleep."

"Tell me, Caled King. Why does this man beset you?"

"He's in league with your master." Actually, I said something like, "He rides with your master," but Danzik gathered my import. I added, "Why?"

Danzik shrugged. "Mar first rode with Tantroth of Eiber. Why?"

"Ambition." But I knew not the Norland word. In any language, it had a sour taste.

TWENTY-THREE

WE MADE BIVOUAC near midday. Men staggered into camp, threw down their sacks, laid themselves on the turf without fires. Exhausted groomsmen tended worn horses before curling up in hayracks.

Grimly, surgeons' aides laid out for burial the wounded who'd died during our exodus.

So, Roddy. You've opened Cumber to the Norlanders. Now what? Strike again at Pezar, hope to catch Hriskil unready? Fall back on Cumber Town? Would Cumber Castle open to us? Where was Bouris?

Where was Mar? What welcome, when Hriskil's outriders came upon him? For now, I could only rest. Those with whom I'd counsel were dead to the world. Tantroth withdrew his rear guard among us and rode into camp last of all, his face more gaunt than ever, his eyes sunken in dark caves.

Anavar and Tanner raised my tent. The five of us—add Elryc and Genard—sprawled within, a litter of puppies seeking warmth. Bollert had led Ebon away for care. I was grateful and offered him shelter, but he shrugged, said he'd found a wagon.

Danzik stalked to our campsite. "*Han capto* means I can't sneak out of camp?"

"Not exactly." I fought a smile. "It's *vade* that prevents you."

With a growl, he stomped off. The Norlander slept in a small tent, unchained. Kadar insisted on posting guard, and I was too weary to dispute the point.

I dreamt of Mother, and Rustin, and Stryx.

BY NIGHTFALL A few of us were awake, enough to post adequate guard.

I tended to my ablutions, glad to peel off my grimy tunic. Darios the surgeon stopped by to examine my wound. This time the dressing barely stuck. He probed and sniffed my scab, and nodded approvingly. "You mend, sire. In a few days time . . ."

Anavar helped me dress. His gaze fastened on a corner of the tent. "I'm glad you heal."

"I'm glad you share my tent."

Reluctant eyes met mine. "Sir, I want so to be friends again."

"We've always been." We clasped hands, and put behind us the quarrel we both regretted.

It was morn before the camp was fully roused. Tursel brought Tantroth to my tent. The captain said, "We've a few captives from Margenthar's encampment."

"Oh?" It wasn't the Cumber way, or the Eiberian.

"But Mar escaped. He was seen riding east." Into the hills. "More important—"

"Bouris." Tantroth.

I asked, "What of him?"

"He wasn't there."

"You said . . ."

"His men were. The escort that failed to return home. But Bouris stayed safe in Cumber."

"That means . . ." My eyes met his and lightened. Bouris had tried a gambit, but hadn't fully committed himself. Now he could deny all participation in his escort's betrayal.

Tursel said, "Now, he's weakened."

I nodded approvingly. "After this he's at a disadvantage, politically. No more talk of—"

"In *men*, my liege. Bouris hadn't yet recalled our company from Pezar, where Raeth had sent every man he could spare. By augmenting Mar with an escort, Bouris further stripped his walls. He's dangerously weakened." Tursel's face said he disapproved.

I smiled. "So, then. Shall we pay him a visit?"

"What of Pezar?"

I hesitated. "What of you, Captain? Bouris demanded your return to his service."

He didn't hesitate. "May I serve you directly, sire? I'd not be his vassal."

"Very we—"

"Raeth loathed him. Told me he wished he weren't heir." Tursel looked abashed. "I probably oughtn't mention that."

"Under the circumstances, Raeth wouldn't mind." I pondered. "My lord Duke, should we go to Pezar or Cumber?"

"Pezar." Tantroth's reply was instant. Naturally; Pezar was the border to Eiber.

"Can we retake it?"

"Our wall guards against the north, not south."

I said dubiously, "We'll need meet Hriskil in open field."

"And they outnumber us. But . . . Roddy, think how often we've mauled him. That counts for a regiment." Seeing my puzzlement, Tantroth added, "In their minds. The Rood is countered; their towers burned, their men thrown back over and again. Now they've no assurance."

Still, I hesitated. "Full council, in an hour. I would be advised by you all."

The lords of Caledon gathered.

Imbar, Elryc, Anavar. Lady Soushire, gnawing a candied apple. Groenfil. Tantroth. Tursel, of course. And myself, pacing with worry. "If we go south, we'll prevail on Bouris to open his gates. Cumber would make a sturdy refuge."

Tantroth held his peace.

Lady Soushire said, "Cumber. It's closer to all our domains."

Groenfil said, "We'd have time to regroup. Rest. But we were besieged there once, by a force not nearly as large as Hriskil's. We couldn't break the siege." He took care not to look at Tantroth, who'd conducted the siege at issue.

"The Norlanders aren't nearly so well led," murmured the duke. "And, my lady, Margenthar's no longer a menace. You need not concern yourself for your walls, unless—"

"I'll be judge of that!"

"—unless Hriskil reaches them. And the best place to stop him is Pezar."

I said, "Elryc?" It was his future too.

My brother looked peaked, but better after a day and night's rest. "If we turn and fight, we meet a greater force in open field. But if we retreat, all Caledon is open to them. Roddy, Hriskil's army need not take Cumber; they need only hold us at bay while they bypass it. Then, Groenfil, Soushire, Stryx . . . even the Sands. We'd have no way to stop him."

I paced. "And if Hriskil destroys my army, where do I gather another?"

Tursel said, "If we give battle here, the Norlanders will annihilate us. Cumber is at least a refuge."

Imbar said, "Pardon, my lords, but do any of you *know* Bouris?" He looked about. "He has Raeth's capacity for intrigue, without his subtlety. And little honor. My point, Rodrigo, is that at Cumber we're none of us safe. Whether he'd open the gate or poison you . . ."

The duke frowned. "Bouris has little respect for you, Roddy. He gibes openly about—pardon, but you insisted— your lack of manhood." He hesitated, added gently, "It's a reflection on him, not yourself, my liege."

"Thank you." I gathered what dignity I could. Manhood? Rodrigo, the virgin king? At times I thoroughly hated the Still.

A pause. Then Groenfil cleared his throat. "So, my lord?"

I said, "Not yet. There are others I would consult." I opened my trunk, reached for the Vessels.

"MOTHER?" I RUSHED into the cave, fearful I'd find it abandoned as before.

"She'll be anon." Old Tryon broke dry sticks over his knee, tossed them one by one into the flames.

"Grandsir." I bowed with respect. "May I?" I crouched at his side before the chill fire.

"Almost, you joined us."

"My wound? It's better now. I had a dream . . . Mother . . . did she . . . ?"

He made no answer.

"Sir, know you I routed Mar?" He'd best hear it from me; Uncle Mar was, after all, his son.

"Tell me of it."

I did.

Tryon grunted. "Steady in his resolve."

"You approve?"

"His malice is wearing. Ah, Elena."

"Madam." I stood. "Elryc sends his love."

"And you?" A brief smile.

"As always. And for your succor . . ." For a moment I couldn't speak. "I thank thee."

"You sensed us? I wasn't sure. You were half before us, an apparition in a mist." She settled herself at the fire.

"Yes. Well. The army of Caledon awaits my decision.

That's why I'm here." Quickly I apprised them of the facts. "Onward to Cumber, or back to face Hriskil?"

Tryon frowned. "What does Rustin say?"

"He's dead, grandsir."

"Ah, I forgot. What counsel gave your lords?"

"On the whole, to barricade ourselves at Cumber. Tantroth, of course, wants to fight." And Anavar, perhaps. Imbar, too. But their words carried less weight than Groenfil, Soushire, Tursel.

"You've no clear course." Tryon toyed with a stick. "Obviously so, or you'd decide without us. But allow Hriskil to hunt you from castle to fort, and you'll lose more than land; adherents will fall away."

"But if we attack, will I face the Rood? That is, need Hriskil rest between uses, as I must with the Still?"

Mother said, "All personal power is wearing. The Warthen, after a Return, must rest for weeks. The King of the Chorr . . . they say he sleeps the sleep of the dead for days after."

"After what? I thought he used a fruit that grows only—"

"After consecrating it. Surely you didn't think any white fruit that falls from a tree . . ."

"So Hriskil . . ." Cautiously, I returned to the topic, "must rest as do I? He won't have use of the Rood before I have the Still?"

"Tryon?"

"I think not. What say you, Varon?"

A deep voice from the dark recesses. *"I say, 'disturb me not.' "*

A small man, thin, flighty, came out of darkness to crouch opposite. "Ask Cayil, proud and foolish ones. I, at least, encountered the Rood."

Tryon spat. "Proud, yes. Foolish? This from a—"

"Grandsir, please!" I held my breath, but instead of an explosion, I provoked only grumbles. "Cayil, I ask. Humbly."

"At least the boy knows his manners. Unlike some in this cave, who strut about as if—"

"CAYIL, GIVE IT REST!" Varon's roar nearly hurled me to the wall.

"—as if they're lords of all creation, though they took Caledon by stealth and treachery. Four days, five perhaps, the Rood will be of no service to him. Best you strike immedi-

ately after he's used it; it's what I did, and threw him back to
Ghanz. Not Hriskil, of course. His grandsire, or before. Old
Vintal, it was, a brute of a man, a savage. He slew envoys and
sewed their heads in sacks—"

"Cayil, you're sure of this?"

"I opened the sack myself; think you I'd forget—oh, the
other? Yes, four days I know of. Six, once."

"Yet I'm here, and wielded the Still when he did the Rood."

"You're among us, but you'd wield no threat to the cobra."

"His Power seemed a viper to you, too?"

"That's its usual form." Cayil rubbed his hands.

"Thank you, my lord. Mother, I have a day, perhaps two before Hriskil wields the Rood. What ought I do?"

She bit her lip. "What is your heart?"

"To find safety. Yet I grow weary of war and waste. I would
make an end to it."

Her eyes met mine. "Would you?"

I PACED ON the bed of the wagon, waiting for men to gather.
Engulfing Pardos and Kadar by sheer numbers, they crowded
close.

I raised my voice and spoke through cupped hands to the
envoys from each campfire. "I've consulted your lords and
taken the wisdom of Caledon. Now, as I am king by your ap-
pointment, I seek your counsel." I explained our choice.
"You've been sore pressed. Yesternight's march was great
trial. To evade the Norland host we'll need exhaust ourselves
darting about Caledon awaiting the ideal moment to give battle. To lunge for Pezar and the protection of the wall hazards
nearly all on a cast of the bones. What say you?"

I waited, while the yeomen debated among themselves.
Murmurs grew more agitated. Finally, I held up a hand. "Di-
vide yourselves; those who would do battle, to my left; those
who would continue to retrea—to withdraw, stand there."

Men began to drift about, uncertain.

Disapprovingly, Tantroth caught my eye. When I'd told him
my intent he'd snapped, "While you're at it, ask them whom
they'd appoint duke. Or whom to set as sentinels."

Perhaps he was right, in that I overturned the world's natural order. On the other hand, the men ought have voice. It was
their limbs, their existence we risked along with ours.

"Make end to it." One voice rose over the others.

"Get it over with!"

"End it now!"

"Finish, so we can go home!" One voice after another took up the refrain. "End it now."

Men strode to my left. A surge. Near a stampede. "Get it done! Knock Hriskil's head!"

Nearly all our men had cleaved to the left. Sheepishly, the few who'd held out for retreat joined them. Only a handful of soldiers stubbornly held the opposing stance.

I raised my arm for quiet. "Prepare to break camp. Await Captain Tursel's commands." Exultantly, I jumped down, strode to my tent. Groenfil, Tantroth and the others joined me. "Satisfied?" I couldn't stop pacing. "It's nearly unanimous."

"Terrible precedent." Groenfil folded his arms.

"Undoubtedly." Larissa of Soushire. "Now they'll always expect to be heard. You've surrendered right of command."

"But they'll fight the harder, for my asking. Tursel?"

The captain smoothed out a parchment and quill, sketched the road to Pezar. "We ambushed their cavalry here. Hriskil's main force must be about . . . here." He stabbed at his map. If we meet them here . . . remember that rise, my lords? We'll hold high ground. And they won't expect us to wheel in our tracks."

I peered. "A half day's march."

"At least. We'd best start. We'll make final dispositions along the route."

I took deep breath. "Are we resolved, my lords?"

No one said nay.

STUMBLING, I LED Ebon along the muddy road; he was too spent for more.

"Sir . . ." Anavar, his voice gentle.

"Don't speak!"

How could I have been so sure, and so wrong?

We'd wheeled to meet Hriskil on ground of our choosing.

At first, it seemed we'd succeed. We threw back the first Norland charge. The second came soon after, and when we were fully engaged fresh savage hordes swung out to roll our flanks. In mere moments our line collapsed as our men clawed desperately to safety. They clogged the road, making with-

drawal near impossible. Groenfil rallied his infantry, charged
the enemy left, bought us precious time. His valiant chestnut
was shot out from under him; barely he escaped by leaping
onto an abandoned mount. Tantroth seized the opportunity
Groenfil gave us and cleaved order from chaos, turning our
rearmost wagons, racing them ahead, clearing the road for our
retreat.

Only the valiant efforts of Groenfil and Tantroth warded off
utter collapse. Nonetheless, we'd lost valuable carts, precious
cargoes. Worse, hideously worse, Hriskil had overrun our wagons of wounded. I was thrown from Ebon in our desperate
charge to reclaim them and dragged cursing to safety by Pardos and Kadar. Over the rise wafted screams, tapering to none.

We'd fared worse than in the battle of the ridge. Hriskil had
recovered the Rood, I was sure; Cayil knew no more its use
than I. And I had not the Still, no more than a shadow of its
wielding. The cobra seemed weakened as well, but never was
I able to trap its head in the cleft of a stick. Thrice the viper
chased me from the cave; ever more reluctant was I to return.

Tantroth's aide Sandin was killed. And Imbar, trampled
with his litter-bearers under the thundering hooves of venge-
ful Norland horse. No doubt I'd mourn him, were I not numb.

Now, our army shattered, we fell back on Cumber as best
we could. Norland cavalry harassed our every step. I doubted
their infantry was far behind. Like us, they'd had a day's rest.

"Sire!" Azar, Tantroth's lieutenant, galloped past the column; reaching me, he reined in hard. "Your tent wagon . . ."

"What of it?" Calves aching, I plodded along as fast as I
could.

"It lost a wheel at the ford. They were resetting it when . . ."
His mouth tightened. "The Norlanders took it."

"So be it."

"Your tent, your clothes—"

"I know."

He looked about, jumped down, put his head close to mine.
"The Vessels."

"I don't need them." They eased wielding my Power, but I
had others. Anyway, Uncle Mar had the true Vessels hidden in
Verein.

Azar's voice dropped lower. "Your treasury."

I gasped. The treasury wagon should have been the most

heavily guarded in our train. An army marched not on loyalty and courage, but on gold. Gold coin to pay the men—a stone's weight per year for each eight soldiers, near a thousand weights in total—and as much again for horses, gear, provender . . . our laden chests were not nearly enough, and now even they were gone. In the instant I'd become a near pauper. I'd be lucky not to suffer mass desertions when my plight became known.

"Lord Tantroth said you must be advised."

Now would the duke consider well his loyalties. I suspected soon he'd be gone.

Sudden doubt assailed me. "Who, beyond yourselves, saw the wagon overrun?" For all I knew, Tantroth himself had seized my treasury.

Azar drew back as if struck. "Sire!"

"Don't 'sire' me, you—"

Roddy, what are you doing?

Is that you, Rust? I know not what I do. "Sorry. I was only asking." It sounded worse than inane. I forced my eyes to his. "I've no reason to suspect—I'm vexed beyond words and lash at shadows. Forgive me."

After a moment, a grudging nod. "Understood." Azar swung onto his steed. "Tantroth needs all the help . . . your leave, sire."

"Granted." I trudged on.

A sorry spectacle we'd make at Cumber. With Hriskil hot on our heels, Bouris could again afford to bar his gates; we'd not tarry long. Of course, Bouris might expect the Norlanders to prove more unfriendly than ourselves. I could do nothing but wait and see.

No, that wasn't quite the case. I bestirred myself. "Anavar."

"Yes, my lord?" His tone was eager.

"Has Edmund much wind?"

"More than Ebon. Would you ride him?"

"No. I charge you as envoy; ride to Cumber. Set flag of truce, I don't know you'll need it, but I wouldn't have you harmed. Remember my words and say them exactly. To Bouris our vassal and earl of Cumber, greetings from Rodrigo, king."

His lips moved with the effort to record my speech.

"We bid thee open thy gates to receive us a dozen hours hence. We bid thee prepare five thousand loaves and meat and

drink for all our force, that we may refresh ourselves. Also,
hay and water for our mounts. We bid thee ride from Cumber
and meet us on the Eiber Road, accompanied by a guard of no
more than twenty, to escort us home to Cumber. Say you yea
or nay to this our envoy, Anavar, Baron of the Southern
Reaches." I nodded. "Repeat it back."

With only a few stumbles, he did so.

I fished for my purse, unknotted it as best I could with one
hand. "These silvers for food and drink, but be chary, there
may be no more." After giving it, I hardly needed bother re-
knotting the purse.

"Aye, sir!"

"Be off, then. Take care, youngsire."

"I will, Roddy!" He blushed. "Sire, I meant. My lord King."
He swung a leg up, sat himself. "Fare thee well." He cantered
down the road. At the wagons ahead, he slowed, searching. In
a few moments he galloped off, yellow flag of truce stuffed in
his bag.

A tired mare trotted up, with a huge pair of legs, longer
than the stirrups. Danzik swung down, patted his mount on
the forenose, took up pace alongside me, reins in hand.

I raised an eyebrow. "Who gave you horse?"

"Found. Owner need it no more." We spoke in the Norland
tongue.

All too likely true. I sighed.

He asked, "*Vade,* still, after battle?"

"Until you're freed, or Hriskil recaptures you."

"All right to walk slow?" I stole a glance; he was smiling
under bushy beard.

"No slower than I." I increased my pace. Easily, he did the
same. "What do you here, Danzik?"

"Danzik, now? Not 'Guiat'?"

"I'm in no mood for a lesson."

He nodded. "Hriskil gave one, this day."

We walked in silence. At length I said, "Too many dead.
Too much hurt. I cannot joke of it."

"Qay." Then, to my amazement, "You try be . . . ben rez."
Good king.

I finally managed, "How would *you* know?"

"Hear talk to men. You gentle to boy you send riding. Rodrigo . . ." His tone was cautious. "Truce, I talk to Hriskil. Cetar han vos modra." *Arrange he not kill you.*

"In return for Caledon? Danzik—" I groped for words in his language. "Rustin, the friend of my life, is dead. And Raeth. Hundreds more. Caledon is—Lord of Heaven, how do you say 'bespoiled?' *Graftig.* Broken. I cannot walk away with my life. I owe it to—owe it—I—"

I trudged down the road, cheeks damp.

"Ben rez." He said it quietly, as if to himself.

TWENTY-FOUR

BOURIS ESCORTED US to Cumber. After the formalities we barely spoke.

Milling about his castle courtyard, my troops fell on the rations he provided. Vigilant against treachery, my bodyguards surrounded me. I wandered away from the throng, settled on my brother Pytor's stone, next to Rustin's unseasoned grave. It was well tended; I nodded, acknowledging a debt.

So, Rust, I've made a hash of it.

Silence.

I gambled all and lost. Rebuke me. Tell me the fool I've been.

Nothing.

Please, Rust!

What would you I say, were I more than your chiding conscience?

Have you never been more? If ever I needed you, it is now.

Ah, my prince. The barest whisper.

Once, I swore I wouldn't put end to myself, but what's left? A few hours rest, then we must push on, lest we encage ourselves for Hriskil. Cumber can't withstand a determined assault; its walls are too long. One by one my lords will default. Where shall I go, Rust, becoming ever less a king? I should end it.

And then, what of Caledon?

"What of Caledon now?"

"To whom do you speak, sire?" Pardos.

"Nobody. Pay no heed."

"Ah, there you are." Lady Soushire strode up, rubbing her hands. "Now where, Roddy? Or shall we make terms?"

"Is that your wish?"

"The sooner, the more chance to salvage our domains. Perhaps he'd even grant you Stryx, as his satrap."

"Does Groenfil concur?"

Larissa colored. "I know better than to propose it. Beneath his skeptical hide, he's a true romantic."

"You'd make peace without him? Leave him to fight?"

"One would hope not." She patted her pouch, emerged with sweet bread wrapped in a cloth. "I hope—" A determined bite. "—he'd soon see reason."

I said stubbornly, "And if not?"

She waved it away. "Conjecture. Will you treat with Hriskil?"

"No."

"If your army beseeches you?"

I said promptly, "I'll hang who suggests they do so." Else, she'd be at them within the hour.

Lady Soushire wasn't fazed. "What would your Rustin say? How long would he countenance a hopeless quest?"

"Odd." My voice was musing. "He always told me to trust you."

She had the grace to blush.

"I'll think on it, my lady." A bow, and I headed toward the donjon.

Bouris crossed my path, managed to bar my way. "How long will you, ah, grace us with your presence?"

My gaze was cold.

"Er, *sire,* that is. How long?"

"You set a limit?"

He scuffed the earth. "Hriskil won't be far behind. Will you do battle in the city? Here?"

"You'll know shortly." When I do. I moved past him.

"And also . . ." He made his tone resolute. "My niece Tresa. Kindly return her to my custody. It's not meet she ride with you unchaperoned."

Ahh. Interesting. "Then, why'd you grant her leave?" What will he tell me? See, Rust, how I remember our lessons?

Bouris reddened. "My mind was on . . . I mistook her intent." A bald lie, that. She wrote she meant to slip out when he was unaware. "I didn't see her today, in your host, but hidden or no, return her. I'm lawful guardian."

"Of course. I'll see she's spoken to."

And, by Lord of Nature, that I would.

KADAR SAID, "SIRE, this is madness."

"Do be quiet, and ride." I urged my unfamiliar mount onward. I'd given Ebon much deserved rest and took particu-

lar satisfaction that Bouris had lent us mounts, unknowing
of our errand. I'd wandered about his castle gate, strolled
through when few seemed to be about. My bodyguards,
forewarned, had gone ahead and were waiting with the
horses, or trailed me as nonchalantly as they might. Now,
we rode for the hills and the village of Certha. I made my
tone as placating as I could manage. "It's only three
hours."

"And three back. If Hriskil—"

"He's mighty, but he doesn't work miracles. You know as
well as I he can't invest Cumber's walls by sunset."

"We'll be riding well past sunset."

"Midnight, then." The road twisted around an escarpment
festooned with brush and stumps. I patted my gelding en-
couragingly.

"Groenfil will be frantic."

"Elryc will tell him, as agreed." Until nightfall, I was to be
indisposed, resting in my chamber.

Dour of mien, Kadar shook his head. "How did you talk me
into this?"

"Because else I'd go without you. Because you enjoy the
guarding of me." Poor Pardos; he and five men unknowingly
stood guard over my vacant chamber. But if I'd asked his consent, he'd have rounded up the army and galloped us all into
the hills. I sighed. Between Kadar and Pardos, a king had no
freedom. They were worse than Rustin, when he . . . I pursed
my lips.

Yes, it was madness.

But our army was soon to quit Cumber, our future uncertain. If I didn't seek Tresa now, Lord of Nature knew when our
paths would cross. And any fool could read between the lines
of her hurried but cautious missive. She'd fled the castle,
scarce ahead of Mar. What fate did she dread? I knew not
Bouris, but what villainy was beyond Margenthar of Stryx?
What refuge had she?

It was past dusk when I found out.

"None, Roddy." Tresa and I sat before a sputtering fire in a
miserable hut I feared might fall on us at any moment. Must
all retired nurses live in hovels? The old woman had gone outside to sit on a rock, that we might speak.

"I thought . . ." Tresa gazed into the fire. "I have no domain, no lands. So one would think I'm of no value in games of state. But . . ." She shot me a glance, looked away.

"Yes, what is it?" My tone was cross; it had been a long ride, and my thighs chafed. Why was she blushing? Why couldn't she simply say what she meant?

"Margenthar might imagine my well-being has some importance to the king. And if so, t'were best I not be in his grip." She added quickly, "So as not to trouble you."

My heart swelled. "Why not flee to Pezar? I'd have shielded you."

"And give Bouris pretext to condemn you?"

I frowned. "He needs no pretext."

The corners of her mouth turned up. "Besides, the Eiber Road was well watched."

"And my protection useless. Tresa, I've lost all."

"Not yet." She watched my face, in the flickering light. Casually, I leaned my scarred cheek on my palm.

"I've lost enough," I said. "There's no safety in Cumber. Where might I flee?"

"All through Caledon, men will rally—"

"That's so only in heralds' tales. In life, churls melt into fields and haylofts when the king's man comes. And I've no gold for provender, we're exhausted from—"

"Sire, pardon." Kadar stuck his head in the sagging doorway. "We must be off."

"Soon. Wait outside."

Tresa asked, "Is there gold in Stryx?"

"No doubt Willem's kept *something* aside; he's a chary fellow. But the journey to Stryx bares Cumber, Soushire, Groenfil's earldom . . . think you my nobles would ride past their own lands?"

For a while, she was silent. "Rodrigo, can you abide the loss of Caledon?"

"It seems I must."

"You won't . . . be desperate? Harm yourself?"

I thought of it. "To save Caledon, yes. Not to mourn its loss." Was I so sure? Could I stand to become another Freisart of Kant, a king without lands? I shivered. "Not," I said gamely, "if I had—" I swallowed. "—you."

"Roddy, why do you cover your cheek?"

"I can't abide that you see it!" I pressed my hand tighter. "I'm so ugly, a demon couldn't love me."

"Not so."

"Tresa, if somehow I managed a visit to the Warthen of the Sands and arranged a Return . . . were I free of this frightful scar, could you see a marr—marri—demons take it!" Cheeks red, I stumbled to my feet, said harshly, "I must go." I looked about. As was the hut, so the village. "If Hriskil invests Cumber, you're not safe here."

"Safer than within Cumber's walls."

"I've no place to take you. No refuge."

She said low words.

"What?"

Louder, "My lord, you are my refuge."

"Oh, Tresa . . ." Almost, my heart broke. "Would I were clean-visaged, a man, a king."

"Sire, *we must leave!*" Kadar was adamant.

"Stryx," I said. "It's all I have to offer. And it may not be safe long. Ride with us until the trail diverges."

She smiled. "And sleep in your tent?"

"I have no tent. They'll find place—"

"But, someday, when you put down the Still."

"What? Yes, I supp—I mean, if your ladyship—it's . . . please don't laugh!"

She came close, whispered in my ear. "And I'll teach you to . . ."

"WHAT?"

She repeated it.

"Lord of Nature!" How could a gentlewoman speak so? Somehow, I managed not to bolt from the hut. I flung open the door. "Shall we, my lady? Kadar waits." Casting a nervous glance over my shoulder, I scrambled onto my grazing mount.

Presently, Tresa emerged from the hut, tied her gear behind her saddle, bussed her nurse on both cheeks. "Steady, boy." I *think* she spoke to the horse. Demurely, she climbed into the saddle.

THE RIDE TO Cumber was nerve-racking. The moon was obscured by clouds; the night was near pitch black. The land sloped downward, which made it all the easier for a horse to slip or slide, or worse, catch a foot in a chuckhole. I peered into the dusk toward Cumber, lest the castle be engulfed in flames. Not that Hriskil would have cause to burn it; the moment we left, Bouris was likely to hand Cumber to him without a fight. What was it Imbar had said of him? *He has Raeth's sense of intrigue, without his subtlety.* Poor old Imbar.

What? I blinked, clung to the saddle, my mind awhirl. Rust, forgive me; I didn't mean to mourn him. He dishonored you. That, I'll never forget. Imbar is offal, to be dumped into a foul alley. And yet . . . Rust, he faced his demons and served me with courage. If I salute him, will you forgive?

I gathered my cloak; the wind was chill.

We came over a rise, and the castle loomed in the valley. It was an anthill; men swarmed in the courtyard, up and down stairs to the great hall. Here and there drizzle dampened the night. Torches on the battlements whipped to and fro in the gust.

Tresa said, "Rodrigo, Bouris will . . . be displeased."

"He need not know I brought you home. Kadar, there is a decent inn on the street of the potsellers."

"Yes, my lord?"

"Secure Tresa a room and bring her to it well-cloaked. Tomorrow, before we go, you'll escort her to our wagons."

"Aye, my lord. I'll send two of our lot."

"Hurry. I'd know she's safe before we meet Bouris."

WIND WHIPPED DUST about the courtyard as we rode through the gate. I kept myself hooded and my head low. On an unfamiliar horse, perhaps none would know it was I. A groomsman ran to seize my reins: Bollert. He muttered, "Trouble inside. Lord be angry."

"Bouris? I care not." I strode to the steps.

"No. The other."

Rain splashed my cloak as I reached for the door. I forced it open against a contrary gust of wind; the handle nearly flew from my grasp.

A footman bowed; I handed him my cloak. A slim figure rose from the tower stair. Elryc.

I wiped my face, sipped from the watered wine someone handed me.

"Hurry, before we meet Bouris." Elryc urged me up the steps.

"It's his castle, we can't avoid—"

"Be quick." Elryc prodded me to a chamber on the second floor. A knock. "Do your best, Roddy. He's really—"

The door flew open. "I said no . . . oh. You!" Lord Groenfil paced the chamber. Behind him, mauve drapery swirled. He snapped, "We've nothing to discuss!"

I motioned Elryc to retire. "Why not?"

"You're my liege; I cannot speak freely."

I shut the oaken door behind me. "You have leave."

"Have I?" Groenfil regarded me coldly. *"Have I?"* He picked up a bronze wineglass, studied it, hurled it at the wall. It clattered across the flagstones. "Imbecile!"

I gaped. Even though I'd given him leave, that was unseemly.

"Leaving the castle, deserting your army, riding into the hills on a lark! Our domains, our very lives are in your hands! I grieve the day I swore your service!"

"My lord—"

The shutters banged shut, as if in a gale. "Know you the damage you've done? Where's Hriskil?"

"I don't know."

Groenfil stalked closer, halting only when we stood nose to nose. "That's right, *you don't know!* What if we were besieged, and you cut off from—"

"I judged they wouldn't reach—"

"A forced march, and they'd be on us before dawn. Did you ask Tantroth his whereabouts?"

I shook my head. He knew I had not.

"Did you command our withdrawal?"

"No, but—"

"Is Cumber Castle fit for a siege?"

"I don't know." The admission shamed me.

"It's your obligation to know! You're our king! But you sneak off, as if dodging a tutor's lessons! You—you child!"

I gulped.

"All without our counsel. And if the injury were not enough, you charge your baby brother with telling me. Why? *BECAUSE YOU'RE A LOVESICK CALF!"* His bellow echoed off the walls.

I made a shushing gesture. "Bouris will hear!"

"Imps take Bouris of Cumber! He's a knave, a traitor, a dishonest fool!"

That tore it. Now we'd have blood feud. "I had an—an errand that couldn't wait."

"Oh, I know of your errand. Are you sated, youngsire? Are you yet fit to wield the Still?"

My face burned bright. "Yes!"

"How can I know you didn't rut with her?"

"I swear it!"

"I repeat, how can I know?"

"Sir . . ." My jerkin was damp with sweat. "I may be foolish, but never have I given cause to doubt my word."

"Never?" Hands on hips, he glared. "Well, perhaps not." He stalked across the room, stooped for the dented cup, set it roughly onto a plank table. "You're a callow dimwit, a dunce, but an honest dunce. Gahrr!" His fingers made a twisting motion, as if grasping my throat. "Your very cause hangs in the balance this night; we *must* hold counsel and set our path. But no, you gallop off to your lover. If you were my son . . ."

I braced myself. "For the night, I obey you as a son."

He seized my chin, forced my eyes to his. "You mean that?"

"Yes, my lord." To my shame, my voice quavered.

Slowly, the howling wind calmed. "Ah, Roddy." He released me, paced from wall to window. "You vex us."

"Us?"

"Me. Tantroth, Larissa. No doubt Bouris too."

"I'm sorry, my lord. Tresa fled when Uncle Mar—"

"Yes, to Certha. Clever of her. It denied Mar a hostage he'd certainly have sought. But it irked Bouris."

"As you said, a knave."

"What matter, if his men shouldered arms with us?"

"May I sit?" My knees were weak. I sank into the chair by the fire. "Sir, you know Caledon. If I told the lords my errand, Bouris would know, and she'd be in peril. Did you know he had her courier killed? I feared . . ."

"Rodrigo, do you fight for Tresa, or Caledon?"

"Must I choose?"

"Do we risk death for you, or her?" He ceased his pacing. "Well?"

"For me, sir." That I deserved his rebuke made the humiliation no less.

"Then you must preserve yourself for our cause. Even if it costs your Tresa."

"I cannot!"

"Youngsire, you cannot be king and do other. You owe it not to yourself, but us." He held my gaze until I was forced to look away.

"You likewise owe us candor. Henceforth, Roddy, your nobles' disapproval must be met, not ignored or evaded. Will you agree to this?"

"I swear by—"

"No grandiose oaths! A simple promise, boy to man." He hesitated, then muttered, "Son to father."

"I promise, sir!" My eyes stung.

"Where is she?"

"I'll . . . please don't ask that."

Groenfil bent to my ear. He breathed, "The inn?"

Almost imperceptibly, I nodded.

"Probably wise. Have you had refreshment?"

"Not since . . ."

"Don't, unless Anavar brings it to you, from me."

I looked up, startled, "Is our host that foolish?"

"Perhaps not."

I drew myself together. "What now, my lord?"

"Council, sire. All of us."

"How do we . . ." I lowered my voice. "Hide it from Bouris?"

His smile was grim. "We don't. He's invited."

On the way to the great hall, I mulled it over. I suspected his including Bouris made sense. Ears would be pressed to spyholes; Bouris would inevitably learn of our deliberations. So, let him take part. Force him to commit before us all.

As we strode in, Anavar slipped alongside me. "My lord earl didn't run you through?"

I glanced back, to Groenfil. "He was . . . irked."

"I had no chance to warn you. Sir, there'll be refreshments . . . the flagon with the flowered intaglio is safe. Genard's eye is on it. The others know."

I nodded thanks.

"I can't vouch for the meats. The bread's ours."

*   *   *

DEEP IN THE night, we met in council.

Bouris ceded head of table; after all, I was king. He took the foot, as if in opposition. Foolish man, to declare himself so.

"If I may . . ." Bouris seized the lead. "Now Tursel's finally home—with our men—we might withstand siege. I offer you refuge."

"Why, thank you." My tone was exquisitely courteous. On which dark night would the gates be thrown open while I slept? "I rejoice in your loyalty. What supplies have you?"

Wells flowed inside the courtyard; I knew that from Tantroth's siege, a year past. At the moment, Cumber's granaries were half full, but there was no more than two fortnights' fodder for the animals. As to weaponry . . . I half listened. It mattered not; I had no intent to barricade myself at Cumber. We were opposed by too many Norlanders, too well armed. The castle would fall.

I asked, "My lord Tantroth, when may we expect Hriskil?"

A tight grin. "His advance guard? By morn. But to arrive in strength . . . he must first rebuild the bridge we burned at Miller's Ford."

Bouris bristled. "My bridge? At my village?"

"Why yes, my lord, it was a merry blaze. They won't want to wade the stream; my men busied themselves with axes the whole day, and the riverbed's a jumble of jagged logs, stumps, branches. It will be a time before the Norlanders cross." He considered. "Dusk on the morrow, I'd say."

The lord of Cumber spat on his polished flagstone floor. "Tell him, Rodrigo, that bridges run both ways. That we'll have no more ease crossing north than Hriskil crossing south. That—"

Tantroth rasped, "I was fending off raiders when you were damp sperm in your father's—"

"Yes, my lord. Point taken. And yours, Bouris." I might sound placating, but not to both at the instant. I took deep breath. "A necessity of war. You'll be compensated."

"By the crown?" Cumber's sarcasm was labored. "Oh, I am reassured. Your treasury is so vast."

"But I'll esteem the subsidy you'll grant this day." I might be—what had Groenfil called me?—imbecile, dunce, dimwit, but imps would dance on my nightshirt before I'd allow such insolence in the presence of my lords assembled.

Bouris was wise enough to swallow his rejoinder. Perhaps he realized that at the moment I had more men in Cumber than he.

We went round the table. Lady Soushire pointed out the advantages of accepting siege: sturdy defense walls at hand, union of our force with Cumber's, a civilized base and so on.

Groenfil was restrained in his reply, though I deduced he preferred to fight where he might defend his own domain, and Larissa's. I, a lovesick calf? He exceeded twice my age and fawned upon the lady like . . . I sighed. Perhaps, when I set down the Still, such mysteries would be revealed.

Tantroth spoke of the marvelous opportunities we were offered: we could melt into the hills and harass the Norlanders without mercy. He, for one, was experienced in the conduct of such a campaign.

Elryc, sitting at my right, said simply that we should go on, that Caledon wanted rallying, and we couldn't do it from here.

Anavar advised . . . well, I wasn't sure what Anavar intended to say. Tantroth fixed him in an implacable glare, and my ward was reduced to mumbles and shrugs that signified naught. Pink-cheeked, he subsided with a muttered apology.

I turned to Tursel, but before he could utter a word, Bouris slammed the table with a gloved fist. "I alone speak for Cumber."

"Would you mind?" Larissa's tone was ice. She dabbed at spilled wine with a serving cloth.

I said mildly, "I'd care to hear his views."

"But I would not, and I'm his liege." To Tursel, contemptuously, "And no royal upstart shall say otherwise."

For a moment, I was speechless. What was Bouris's aim? Was giving offense an end in itself? It mattered not. "I, Rodrigo, king, do arrest your person. My lord Groenfil, take hold of—"

Bouris shouted, "On what charge?"

"Slander of the royal court. Public disparagement of the sovereign." It didn't matter; I suspected he knew even less law than I.

"Rodrigo . . ." Lady Soushire's pudgy hands fluttered. "Surely it's not neces—"

"Cumber is my domain! You may not depose me!"

"No, I must keep a foolish promise to your father. Cumber must be yours forever, though it cost my crown. An earl you remain, but I seize you until my pleasure."

"No charge may be brought until the justiciar—"

I said smoothly, "Unless the offense is committed in the king's own presence. Groenfil, *will* you take him or no?" Quickly, please, before my bluff wears thin.

With surprising calm, Bouris unsheathed his blade.

"I'm sorry, Rodrigo." Groenfil dropped his voice as if to confer with Bouris. "My lord . . ." He leaned close, suddenly clubbed the earl across the temple with his mailed fist. Bouris reeled. Groenfil pried loose his dagger, held it to Cumber's throat. "Tursel, your three best men, and be quick."

Tursel ran from the room.

"Rodrigo, have you lost your—"

"Not now, Larissa." Groenfil.

"But he . . ." The lady shook her head. "And you . . ."

"May I have him, Roddy?" Tantroth's voice was a purr. "We have unfinished business. Last year, on the border—"

"I COMMAND ALL HERE BE SILENT!"

Though once or twice Bouris groaned, I didn't fault him for it.

After a time Tursel threw open the door, ushered in three nervous aides. They seized Bouris of Cumber. Groenfil distanced his blade from the earl's throat.

I asked Tursel, "Can they be trusted?"

"As myself."

It would do. "To the captain's chamber, in the guardhouse under the wall. Guard him well. Not you, Tursel."

In uneasy silence, we all took our seats. Tursel said, "I will not serve him. If that be treason, call me traitor."

"I call you friend. And release you from his service. As king I have that authority, do I not, Tantroth? My lady?"

He grunted assent; she merely shrugged.

IN MY CHAMBER with Anavar and my brother, I unbound my arm and carefully flexed my shoulder; my wound knitted well. On the morrow, I'd need at most a sling.

Moodily, Elryc rested his chin in his hands. "What about Bouris?"

"I can't leave him; confederates will free him the very day."

"I meant, Roddy, what was his design?"

"I'm not sure." Whatever obscure path Bouris trod, I could rely on him for nothing, and would be well quit of his domain.

"At first I thought he meant to separate you from your lords, mocking your empty coffers. But he promptly piqued the lot of them."

I shrugged. "Perhaps with his scorn Bouris sought to ally Tantroth."

Anavar giggled. "Pardon, my lord, but all men of Caledon insist on seeing wheels within wheels. What if there are none? What if Bouris says what his mind holds and simply lacks guile?"

Elryc and I exchanged glances.

"No."

"Impossible." I elaborated, "It's not our way. Surely he learned *something*, if not from his father, Raeth, then visiting his cousins. Among nobles, everything said has motive beyond."

"Everything?"

I waved it away. "Unless he's an utter simpleton."

I WANDERED THROUGH the mud to the grave marker in the courtyard.

So, Rust . . . I botched our campaign, and now we flee. Is this our last farewell?

As ever, silence.

Do you recall the day our fresh-set standard snapped in the stiff breeze, as hopeful churls and yeomen gathered to our cause? "Travail and blood lie ahead," you admonished. But not yours, Rust; gladly I'd have spurned Caledon to save that!

You see how I've tried to act the man? I even practice kindness, now and again. Genard no longer flees my company; Tantroth addresses me with as much respect as he's able. And Groenfil . . . he's not father, nor elder brother. Yet he takes on the role because I need it. And my heart breaks. I need *you*.

A clatter of horses, as Kadar's squadron returned from the inn, Tresa riding openly among them. Wearily, I rose.

Fare thee well, Rustin of the Keep.

I strode back to Ebon.

I had time for but a brief nod to Tresa—"Good-day, my lady,"—before I was caught up in the chaos of departure.

At last, I ordered Bouris released from the stronghold and set on a mount, then took my place in our bedraggled column. Danzik spurred his undersized gelding to ride nearby. *"Vade,"* he growled, his disgust evident.

"Hold, Guiat." As we set off, I beckoned him closer. "Pardos, take ease, we practice our honor. Danzik—" I switched to his tongue. "I would give you a task."

He studied my expression. "I cannot aid you against Hriskil. Surely even a Caled knows that *vade.*"

"It won't hurt Hriskil. Not even *iot.*" My fingers made the sign for a merest trifle.

"What, then?"

I jerked my finger at Bouris, who rode sullenly two rows behind. "Look: three men, watching lest he . . . *desera.*" *Escape.*

Danzik craned, swiveled back to me. His eyes widened. "You want me guard a Caled lord?"

"It would amuse you. He has nothing to do with Hriskil," I added, hoping it was true.

"If he . . ." Danzik pantomimed running away and taught me new words.

"Stop him. Don't kill him."

"Hurt?" Danzik looked hopeful.

"If there's no other way."

After a moment, "Qay."

I dismissed the guards, translated my orders that Bouris understand. Cumber stiffened in outrage, but said nothing. Danzik dropped back to ride at his side. Legs dangling under his steed, the Norlander dwarfed the sullen earl.

TRESA SHOT ME a disbelieving glance. "You what?"

"Arrested his person. He rides back there, with Danzik."

A long silence. "I wish you had not."

I asked, "Why?"

"Who'd defend Cumber better than he who holds it?"

"Tursel appointed—"

"Yes, my lord. But Bouris had a powerful self-interest."

I grunted. Perhaps, but he might have protected his self-interest by a covenant with Hriskil.

"Roddy, where do we ride?"

"To Groenfil, and thence to Stryx." We hoped to draw Hriskil's force past Cumber and play catch-my-lady in the hills, until the moment was right for battle. I smiled, glad Tresa's palfrey was to my right, where she had no view of my scar. "Without knowing our destination, you cast your lot with ours?"

"Yes." Her tone was placid. Then, "I'd not endure siege by Hriskil."

"You may see worse."

"I'll see you." Her tone was light.

What a site for the words my lips formed. In a column slogging through drying mud, Danzik the Norlander and Bouris the imprisoned earl behind me, Anavar and Tursel in the row ahead. A mild wind blowing my hair awry, sweat drenching my flanks at the audacity I measured. But I'd stumbled once before and meant now to have it out.

"Tresa?" I licked my lips. "Would you consider—I mean, I've nothing to offer—you've more estate than I at the moment . . . but after things are settled . . ." Desperately, I tried to pull myself together. "Consider bec—coming my—" Violently, I cleared my throat. "I—I want—I mean, love . . . oh, Tresa, help me, I can't do this alone!"

"Do what, Roddy? Rule?"

"Put two words together! Surely you know what words I seek!"

Quizzically, she rubbed a finger against her lips. " 'Marry me'?"

"Yes! Will you?"

"I might, if you ask."

My cheeks were crimson. "I just did!"

"Hardly, sire." Her gaze was straight before her, as if not daring to ascertain the effect of her obstinacy.

Well, marriage would hold worse. I gritted my teeth. "Tresa of Cumber, I ask—ask—" I bowed my head, concentrated on the pommel. "Not now. I must hold myself for the Still. After, though, I ask thy hand in marriage." My palm shot up. "Wait, not yet. I'll do my best to love you, through what life will bring. You'll teach me, along with . . . the other." Earth, swallow me up. I thought I'd known humiliation before, but I had not, until this moment. "And I swear, I'll have done with this awful scar that disgusts you. You won't have to look upon it."

Her voice was gentle. "How might you do that, Roddy?"

"A Return. Somehow I'll gather the funds. The Warthen of the Sands, his Power . . . I'll have Return to the cell in Verein, I'll avoid Uncle Mar's dagger . . ." In this moment, a man ought not to sound desperate. "I promise you, it will be gone, or we won't marry. If you say aye."

Ebon plodded along, a step, perhaps as many as two. I could stand it no longer. *"Well?"*

"Aye."

Ahead, Anavar dug his heels into Edmund's flanks. "Elryc! *Lord Elryc!*" Whipping Edmund's flank he raced down the road, his voice fading. "He did it!"

When I got my hands on him, I'd thrash him within an inch of his life. He'd rue the day he met me, the day he spied on—

Tresa's fingers hid a smile that her eyes betrayed.

Hmpff. Anavar would never know the agent of his pardon.

Tresa looked reflective. "And we'll need consent, of course."

Lord of Nature. Bouris would never . . .

"From the king."

"I'll ask, the moment—arggh! See, my lady, what you do to me?"

WEARY DAYS, UPON the road. The Norlanders surrounded Cumber, but did not take it. On the battlements, Cumber's loyal guard braced for assault that was mysteriously delayed.

Nor did Hriskil race after us, which troubled me night after night in my frayed and borrowed tent; I knew Caledon was not his while my army survived. Why, then, did he tarry? Even now, we rallied yeomen from the villages and fields, and melded them into our impoverished ranks. I did my part, donning royal cloak and coronet, planting standard in earth while Groenfil, Tantroth, even Anavar gave the call.

Lady Soushire looked to her comfort but otherwise said little. With ease, she turned aside my probes. Groenfil conferred with her by night, but I knew better than to ask the subject of their discourse.

The further from Eiber, the moodier grew Tantroth, and the more perfunctory his courtesy. I assured him we'd strike north as soon as our strength allowed, but my assurances fell on deaf ears.

At last we reached Groenfil's lands, and the refuge of his keep. He introduced me to his sons Franca and Horst, who held the castle in his absence. Each was the image of his father, down to the dour expression he habitually wore. I was glad of his warm smile on greeting them, that melted the chill from their gaze.

After a day and a night a full thousand adherents augmented our force.

We rejoiced with a banquet of roast boar. We were still at table when word came that Cumber had fallen. Perhaps Hriskil had set the Rood on the defenders, and they'd quarreled.

Tursel woke me while the moon rode high to tell me Hriskil's army was again on the march. They pursued us to Groenfil's domain. I considered battle, but why risk dashing my resupplied force against a Norland rock? Stryx awaited us, and reinforcements.

Before dawn, I paced Groenfil's courtyard while we made ready for a dash to Stryx. At first light we were off. In our march, untrained recruits replaced many of the grizzled veterans, who deserved rest, and were assigned to Groenfil's battlements. Groenfil himself looked tired; he'd conferred most of the night with his sons.

Through hills and vales we would pick our way to the seacoast. We'd long since smashed the Norland forces around Stryx, but Tursel's wary scouts ranged far ahead, probing for foes.

Behind us, a commotion. A clatter of hooves. Anavar whirled, drawing sword, but it was only Danzik, galloping away along an overgrown trail. I muttered silent curses. Let him go; honor had held him longer than I'd expected. But a quarter hour later, he was back, leading an empty-saddled horse, a bundle across his pommel. He maneuvered his overworked mount into line, threw the bundle at my feet with a thud.

It was Bouris, his face bloody. I raised an eyebrow.

"Ran. To piss, he said. No *vade*, your Caleds."

"Get him mounted."

"Wake him first." Danzik unknotted his waterskin. "An' need bigger horse. Can't *perse* lordling on . . . on pony." He regarded his undersized mount with disgust.

"Pardos, arrange it at next rest."

My bodyguard grunted. "What faithful stalwart shall I un-horse for your . . . Norland friend?"

"Come now, Pardos. We find our friends where we may." Though I sounded lighthearted, I fretted. When Danzik's true allegiance burst forth, what harm would it occasion?

That night we camped in an overgrown field. Tresa dined with Lady Soushire. Weary of Anavar, disconsolate at the thought of my cramped quarters, I sought out Danzik at a campfire. "How does Hriskil sleep, Guiat? Tell me of his tent."

He studied me, apparently deciding the information had no military value. "Grand." Widespread arms emphasized the term. "Rope bed, silver-top table. Much . . . *preci* than yours."

Fancier? I filed the word with so many others.

"You only . . . *youngsire*." Danzik used the Caled word. "He king of all Norland. Need *preci* tent." Then, slyly. "King of Norland, Eiber, Caledon."

"Not Caledon. Quix pron," I added wearily. *Perhaps soon.*

"Pron," he agreed. "Come." He patted a log across from where he sat. "I teach you Norland words to ask Hriskil for your life."

"Don't be hateful."

His eyes searched mine. "Rez, soon this—" His wave en-compassed the fire, the camp, the army. "—must end. You *valous*, brave. It not enough." Oddly, his voice held a note of . . . solace? Regret?

"I'll not beg Hriskil for life."

"No, kings are proud." A sigh. "We'll talk of happy things. *Farang.* Means . . ." He made an obscene gesture.

"I know farang. *Farang vos mata.*"

"Ru vos." *And yours.* "*Corti.* That means, when you make a girl put . . ."

An hour later I freed myself, to toss restlessly the night.

TWENTY-FIVE

PAST HAMLETS AND fields I knew of old, we made our way toward the coast road. A summer past, my fledgling force had charged through the crossroads Danzik guarded, to seize Stryx. Danzik too must have recognized our environs, but no flicker of expression betrayed his emotions.

When I granted audience, Bouris hotly protested his mistreatment and demanded I release him.

"Where would you go, my lord Earl, now Cumber is fallen?"

"Is that the king's affair?"

Perhaps not. I shrugged. "Be patient; at Stryx you'll answer to charges."

"That I was rude? Fah! You know you can't hold me for—"

"I fought Margenthar to escape Pezar. Why were your troops with his?"

Bouris raised his hands, as if in amazement. "Troops? A mere escort, to see he departed Cumber as he warranted."

"They aided an enemy of—"

"I assert Margenthar rode to aid you."

"Nonsense. I had to batter my way through—"

His jaw jutted. "Did you parley? Did you ask Mar's intent?"

"Oh, please." I waved him silent.

I'd have said more, but at that a rider stormed up the road. His mount foamed. He burst through our advance guard, slowed only when he was in the midst of our column. "Where's the captain? Who speaks for the king?"

Tursel held up a hand.

The rider cantered over, pulled up short. "Are you Tursel? Good. Is the king at hand?" His eyes fell on my scar, looked away. "Sire. Tidings . . ." Abruptly, for all his hurry, he seemed reluctant. "Stryx . . . the harbor . . . Norlanders . . ."

"Say your piece." Under the circumstances, my tone was remarkably cool.

"Stryx is fallen! The harbor's black with Norland ships. Already they land men, horses, supplies. At noon Willem sent word down to the Keep that I should ride; I had to detour through the fields, they swarm the coast road, I can't return . . ." His mouth worked. "The castle holds. Willem says: 'tell Rodrigo I'll do my best.' But, sire, he hasn't the men. The Keep is bare guarded, and—"

"I know." Were Caledon united, still we'd be hard pressed. As it was, we lacked men, provender, time. Willem was a sturdy soul, but no warrior.

"So many ships, sire! We're undone."

A calamity, but surely magnified; the fellow's report was so disjointed, Lord of Nature knew the actual circumstance. "Tursel, we're, what, an hour from the hill that views the harbor? Gather a squad; we'll assess what we may."

"I'll send scouts, but it's too dangerous for you. They may already be—"

I said, "Leading their protesting horses down gangways, assembling their squads, preparing to dig in. We won't meet them in the hills, not yet. You know this, Tursel."

He sighed. "The high hill, no further. Pardos, you'll ride with us?"

My bodyguard turned in the saddle. "Kadar, guard Prince Elryc. Keep special eye on that Norlander whom Rodrigo calls friend."

Danzik, friend? Ridiculous; I'd never called him such. Gingerly, I tasted the thought. Perhaps it had become nearly so.

OUR SCOUTING SQUADRON had grown; now it might almost be called a war party. Groenfil and Tantroth had joined, with officers and cavalry escort. My guard, and Tursel. And Anavar. He'd shown such dismay when I bade him stay with the column that I relented, and Edmund galloped at Ebon's side. He—Anavar, not Edmund—had thanked me over and again for my consent, with the deference due from youngsire to elder.

"A Norland raiding party," I told him, hoping to convince myself, as we left the road to lead our horses up the steep hill. "They'll torch the town and be gone."

"Hriskil's main force is in the hills," Anavar agreed. "He can't twin himself."

But from the hilltop, we stared aghast.

Stryx harbor swarmed with sails. From our vantage the coast road was obscured, but laden ships sat in the harbor not far from shore; obviously they awaited their turn to disgorge cargoes of men and material.

In the distant haze rose the battlements of Castle Stryx. Below it, woodlands blocked our view of the Keep, but no curl of smoke rose from castle or town. The Norlanders had come to occupy, not destroy.

I said hopefully, "Could we beat them back?"

Tantroth shook his head. "A full ten thousand troops, I warrant. At least half are ashore by now, more by the time we threw ourselves on them. And they'll be ready for us. If they've any communication with their king, they know we're wandering the hinterlands."

"What, then?"

"It depends on the orders of their commander. And his mettle."

"How can we know that?" No one answered. I jerked, as if struck by a shaft. "I have it. We'll need envoy."

"Why?" Groenfil.

"Ride to the city under truce. Say Rodrigo's army would discuss terms. Ask—"

"Roddy!"

"Ask with whom we treat."

"And what good that? We know not the Norland chieftains!"

I smiled. "Is that so?"

IN TWO HOURS, our column turned about in good order, to make for Soushire. We judged we'd have one good night's rest before Hriskil might near us, and forced marches thereafter.

At dusk our envoy from Stryx found us camped. His horse was spent, and his forehead and clothes bore the dust of the road. He crouched by the log on which I perched with my dinner. "Sarazon, sire. Related to the king. He's authorized to take your surrender and give you passage to any realm that will have you, once he has suitable hostages."

"Hostages?"

"Your brother, and certain nobles."

"Bah. Take a bowl of stew. Bollert, see his horse is well tended." I set down my plate. "Genard? Elryc, might you spare your man? It's time for our lesson."

Danzik sat in front of his tent. I gave it a baleful glance; it was near as good as the canvas I now shared with Anavar and sometimes Elryc. I missed my opulent royal shelter—the carpets, the clever devices, most especially the chest full of my clothes and Rustin's.

"Guiat." I bent stiffly, a short bow, as one might confer on a tutor. "Liste memor." *I'm ready to learn.*

"Rez Caledi." He nodded. Nothing today about our mothers. Perhaps we'd grown beyond that.

"Your king sends—Genard, how do you make *enva* into 'sent'?—*enve* many ships. They occupy Stryx."

Danzik's eyes lit in satisfaction.

"I might—" I spoke carefully, so not to violate the True. "—might take up your offer to speak to Hriskil."

"I save your life. But not your army."

"Sarazon too offered me safety, but I don't know that I can trust a fat old man. Genard, help me say it right." Together, we pieced it out. "One who commands only because he has the king's blood."

Danzik scowled. "Sarazon more than uncle to king. Fought Ukras for years."

"Guiat, would I be safe with him? Does he keep his word?"

The Norlander twisted his beard. "*Vade* is different for you Caleds. Our people think . . . much honor in clever trick."

"He thinks so?"

"Once, when the Ukras sent envoy . . ." He launched into an involved tale wherein a Norland force savaged a Ukra column that thought it had negotiated safe-conduct. In the telling, we had to act out a host of unfamiliar words.

At length I said, "But you could trick us and *desera*, escape, and didn't. Why? Isn't there *vade* in it?"

"Qay, er campa Hriskili." *Yes, in Hriskil's field.*

I shivered. "To board a Norland ship, be in Sarazon's power . . ." Genard shot me a glance but said nothing. I said impulsively, "Tell me of this man."

"He not command ships self. He wars land, not sea." Danzik broke a branch across his knee, tossed it into the fire. "Land, good soldier, keeps army fed, enough wagons." He grinned. "On sea . . ." He made a retching motion, hand to mouth. "Don't like waves."

"How old is he? Has he children?"

"Sixty summers? More. Two girls. Put aside three wives for boy. None."

I blurted, "Have you children, Guiat?"

His face grew somber. "One. Had. Dead."

"War?"

"Not battle. Ukra raid. My family *desera*. Ukra *perse*, to hills. Son die, cold." He smiled. "Have you children, rez?"

For what I'd asked, I owed him answer. "No. Do you know what is required of me?"

A mischievous glint. "Han farang."

"Yes," I said quietly. "Han farang."

Danzik stared into the flames. At length he said, "Sarazon good at lead many men. They eat, shelter, horses fed. Not clever at fight. Don't like . . ." He scratched his head, acted out a new word: fova. Small battle? No, few men. Aha: *skirmish*.

"Nor do I. Danzik, have you ever seen Ghanz?"

His look wondered if I'd taken leave of my senses. "Of course."

"You saw Stryx, from a distance. Which is bigger?"

We passed an hour while Genard yawned. I learned of Ghanz's thriving markets, of Winesellers' Way, where each stall's wares were unique, not to be found at the neighbors'. I fished out a few Norland coins; Danzik taught me their money and what it would buy. When we were done, I called for cold wine, tilted it over my head, had a mouthful, left Danzik the rest of the skin.

I wandered about until I found Groenfil, took him to Tantroth's tent. "Sarazon's about sixty, has been through three wives, has two daughters. Has no honor as we know it, but loves a good trick."

Tantroth's jaw fell.

"He's no admiral, seasick whenever he leaves port. He's Hriskil's uncle, primarily an administrator. He'll tend his supply lines, but he's no tactician. Prefers a decisive set battle to skirmishing."

"Roddy?"

"Yes, my lord Duke?"

"How do you do that? Is it the Still?"

I swelled. "I listen. I've learned how, of late."

FOR THE MOMENT, we judged, Sarazon would be content to deny us Stryx while he formed his troops for battle. Only when all was ready would he set forth to smash us on the anvil that was Hriskil. Some relief that; it afforded us days, perhaps weeks, to maneuver.

Meanwhile, Hriskil's massive army approached Groenfil's domain. The castle walls were thick and cunning, the granaries and barns well stocked. If the Norlander was utterly determined, the castle would fall, but not this season.

The southern hills were full of brush-filled ravines and steep canyons. An army, ours or his, could hide itself for days. Tursel's scouts would be busy, seeking our safe passage. If Hriskil paused to subdue Groenfil, our way was clear east to Soushire and beyond. Or, should we choose, we could tarry in the hills and strike from time to time at his besieging forces.

But if Hriskil bypassed Groenfil Castle and spread himself across the hills, he'd block our path to Soushire and force a battle for which we were ill prepared.

Tresa came to visit, while I fretted in my tent. "What news of Castle Stryx?"

My tone was bleak. "None."

"Your affairs go not well."

Did she chide me? I studied her gaze, but found no accusation, no pity. "No, my lady." I grimaced. "I meant to give you sanctuary, in Stryx. Now I cannot."

"There's rumor—" Though we were in my tent she looked about, dropped her voice. "—that you weigh throwing yourself on Hriskil's mercy."

I shot to my feet. "Who spreads such calumny?"

"You, I think." The ghost of a smile. "I heard it from Genard."

"Where would he get the notion—oh!" Our talk with Danzik. Naturally, I hadn't taken the stableboy into my confidence. "Is he fool enough to tell the camp? We'll have desertions by the score!" I flung open the flap.

"I admonished him. He'll be silent." Her voice coaxed me back to the stool. "I told Genard it was a ruse."

"How did you know?"

"By knowing you."

I sat on my rude stool, covered my face with my palms. "Tresa, when we're vanquished, what will become of you?"

"Would you I shared your exile?"

I nodded, not trusting myself to reply. I would have no exile. Any Norland ship that carried me would mysteriously disappear, after my bloodied corpse sank into the deep. I sought to divert my thoughts. "How might we restore our fortunes?"

She pondered. "When did Caledon last send envoy to the Ukras?"

"In Mother's reign, many years past. Josip, my father, lived. Why?"

"Tantroth was your foe . . . until Hriskil fell on Eiber."

"Yes, he couldn't guard his back and—you'd have me entice the Ukras to attack?" I gaped. "Do imps dance on your shoulder? Their realm dwarfs the Norlands, which overwhelms ours. Once roused . . ." The Ukras would certainly command Hriskil's attention. What might incite them against Hriskil? Then my senses returned. "Would you have war engulf our world? Where our refuge then?"

"Where our refuge now?"

HRISKIL MADE BUT a languid siege at Groenfil. No miners, no sappers, no towers abuilding to threaten the battlements. Almost with indifference, he waylaid the castle environs.

On the third day, a wagon appeared in the field before the gate. The slaughter began.

Groenfil's son Franca led a sortie and was repulsed. The wagon was wrecked, but what matter that? Another creaked into place.

In Groenfil's tent we held council of war. Before he could speak I said, "We must draw Hriskil away." And put end to the wagons of corpses.

Lady Soushire stirred, her eye on a tray of sweets that had not yet been passed. "Where would you fight? The terrain offers no advantage."

"In open field, then." I paced the confines of the tent, far more comfortable than my own. "If fortune smiles, we'll maneuver to our profit."

Elryc said mildly, "You can't wish them from outnumbering us."

"What, then?" My glare withered each in turn: Tursel, Groenfil, Tantroth, Anavar, Soushire.

Tantroth said wearily, "Eiber is Hriskil's. Better I'd remained in our hills to harass him. Cumber is his, and now Stryx. Of strong points, we're left but Groenfil and Soushire."

"And Verein." Lady Larissa. She stretched for the tray, chose a sweet, reluctantly offered the assortment to Elryc, who sat near.

My tone was dour. "Verein's more Hriskil's than ours." I knew Uncle Mar would cede Verein to the Norlanders rather than see it mine.

Since Margenthar had fled into the wood after our attack on his camp, little had been heard from him. Perhaps he'd slipped home, with a remnant of his force. Perhaps he was this very moment comfortably ensconced in the Norland fold. And if so—

"Roddy, do you agree?"

I blinked. Groenfil waited expectantly.

"I'm sorry, my lord. I wasn't . . ." I steeled myself. "I wasn't listening."

To my surprise, the corners of Groenfil's mouth turned up. "Thank you for your candor. I asked if it would not serve us best to meet Hriskil before Groenfil Castle, whose defenders may sally forth in concert. And if we break through to reinforce my sons, we'll make his siege a great travail."

"If that were our aim, better we'd remained there." I sat, scratched my head. "I confess, I know not what would best serve us. A solution is beyond me."

Groenfil's tone was dry. "A touch less candor, my liege." To Larissa, "My lady?"

"What you'd add to your walls in strength, Sergo, you'd cost in food and fodder. How long would our army's presence diminish your ability to hold out? A year?" *Sergo?* Had he another name? For a year, I'd called him naught but Groenfil.

"We'd consume substantial provender. Your point?"

"Why not Soushire?" She spoke by turns to us all. "You've all seen my holding. My walls are high, my granaries bursting to overflowing, my barns exceeding well stocked with hay and corn."

Her voice sharpened. "No accident that it is thus. I've squandered no silver on fripperies, no gold on silks, puff mattresses, fine-carved chairs. For these four years, since Elena sickened, I've feared it must come to this, and I've prepared. Soushire has sturdy walls, swords, arrows, pikes and oil for a host of defenders, ample dwellings to house a garrison. All it lacks, sire, is men."

"Madam—"

"I'm ludicrously undermanned! Troops you've beguiled from me in hopeless quest of your crown!" Her eyes flashed fire. "Do I complain, Roddy, and saddle my mare to ride this very night? No, though you've squandered your patrimony and made no decent defense of your kingdom, I invite you, my liege, to share my bounty. I only ask, help me deny it to Hriskil!"

Well.

None, including Groenfil, cared to speak.

I cleared my throat. "There's the wagon of death."

"What purpose that Hriskil soak Groenfil's earth with blood, if you won't be drawn?"

"Soon or late," I said, "the wagon will appear at Soushire."

Larissa popped the last sweet between her teeth. "No doubt it will." She chewed. "Rodrigo, to accept war is to accept death. If you're so thin of skin as to abhor the loss of churls, why, then, abdicate."

All eyes were on her.

"Well, it's so! He'll set the wagon by the orchard, I warrant. A fine view from the wall, but out of archers' range. Will I tear my hair like our dear friend Tantroth? No. Will I demand we sally forth to put end to it? No, I won't call my compatriots to futile death." She swallowed, looked sadly at the empty tray.

"Madam, we can't let—"

"Sir, we can!" She stood, smoothing her skirts. "Further, we must! In your eagerness to cloak yourself with blame, you overlook the cause. Hriskil kills our folk! WE DO NOT!"

Groenfil cleared his throat. "Larissa . . ."

"No, Sergo, it must be said. Roddy beats his breast so, it must be constant black and blue. But ours is not the guilt! Let Hriskil wipe the villages of those yeomen too witless to flee, I'll hold fast! Because we do not this awful thing, Hriskil does! Can you men not comprehend?"

Anavar shot to his feet, knocking over his empty flagon. "I comprehend that you care not for—"

"Youngsire, do not—"

"I pray thee, Rodrigo, let me speak! *Please!*" His eyes glistened. "My lady, I feel yet the knife Tursel's minion held to my throat, the day of my capture. He'd have put an end to me, and why not? We did the same, our men of Eiber, in the borderlands with Cumber. My lord Tantroth—" Anavar swiveled. "—with respect, sir, you were wrong in this. And you, Captain Tursel. The king taught me mercy. And as he's learned compassion, so have I!"

"It's *Hriskil* who kills, not—"

"Aye, my lady, but it's we who must halt him. We cannot bolt ourselves into castles and watch our vassals butchered. By their oaths to us we owe them their lives!"

Tantroth of Eiber stirred. "Our liege *has* taught you, youngsire."

Anavar said, "I beg thee don't mock, my lord. I spoke my heart."

"And mine." For a moment, their eyes met. Some understanding passed between them. "My lady," said Tantroth heavily, "I cannot accept your gracious offer. I shall seek Hriskil. I'm sorry, Roddy, if I must disobey you in this."

I took deep breath. "You do not."

TWENTY-SIX

BEFORE GROENFIL CASTLE, the army of Caledon formed in line of battle, Tantroth's horse to the left, Groenfil's to the right, Tursel commanding the center.

Beside him, I sat astride Ebon, for our soldiers to see. Not an hour past, I'd exhorted our men until my voice was hoarse. We could not flee evil, I'd said. We must best it, lest the wickedness snuff our souls like a damp blanket a fire. One more victory, and Hriskil might tire. One more stand, and the Norlanders lose heart.

Almost, I believed it. But the battle, I knew had purpose. A week past, when we'd marched bravely out of Groenfil, Stryx was open to us. Now, with Stryx Castle under siege, Groenfil was one of our last bulwarks. We must deny it to Hriskil.

Our supply wagons were half a day's march to the rear, at our camp twixt Groenfil and Soushire. Elryc, despite his pleas, languished among them. Bouris too, under Danzik's guard. And, of course, Tresa.

Behind our line, Lady Soushire's troops awaited orders, our meager reserve. The lady herself sat stolidly on her palfrey, perhaps unwilling to be separated, even for hours, from her guards.

Anavar waited alongside me, entrusted with my Vessels. The moment I felt the Rood at work, I would dismount and set my palms over the bowl.

Tantroth turned his horse, trotted the distance of our line. "Sire."

"My lord."

"Fare thee well."

"And thee." I added abruptly, "You shall not die this day."

Tantroth looked startled. Then, "If you err, I shan't forgive it." He wheeled, cantered back to his troops.

Anavar murmured, "Was it the Still told you?"

No, but what harm the gift of hope? I had little else to bestow.

"Will I die, sire?"

I growled. "Not until you repay the last advance of stipend."

"Then, pardon, sire, I shall keep your silvers." Anavar's nerves were as taut as mine.

I said to Tursel, "Franca and Horst will know when to break out?"

"Their father, Groenfil, assures us. Sire, it's time."

I hesitated, thrust down dread. "Advance the center."

At the signal our men trudged forward, pikemen before all. The archers strode behind, weighed down with sheaves of shafts. As always, pikemen would protect them while they loosed through and over the Norland lines.

Anavar asked, "Groenfil knows when to charge?"

"Of course." I frowned. A foolish query.

Tursel paced his mount, standing in his stirrups to watch the field. "If Tantroth delays again, men die without need. What's Azar doing? Can't he hold his place?"

"I don't need your chatter, you—" Astonished I bit it off.

Anavar's eyes met mine. "The Rood."

"Yes." I swung out of the saddle. "Quickly now." I sat cross-legged on the crushed grass. The boy jumped down, unwrapped the bowl, set it in my lap. Quickly he unstoppered the ewer.

A runner dashed across the field. "My lord Groenfil warns you'd best look sharp when the lines clash. Wait too long, and—"

Tongue between his lips, Anavar poured the thick stillsilver. In an instant it was still.

"—he won't see his men dead by Tantroth's stupidity or Rodrigo's!"

I set my palms across the bowl, squeezed shut my eyes. The words of encant. My lips moved silently.

Our pikemen strode toward the Norland host.

Mother, will I meet you or the viper?

The mist grew.

I felt my way forward.

The cave mouth loomed.

I peered within. The cobra struck. Fangs gashed my forehead. Venom burned. I reeled.

"Imps and demons, Groenfil won't watch for my signal! He's a fool, a knave!" Tursel's voice faded.

The snake coiled. Blood trickled to my eyes. I wiped stinging skin with my forearm. The hooded head flew upward,
buried itself in my jerkin. I tore free, staggered backward,
slammed into unyielding rock.

I can't see! It wasn't the blood alone; venom coursed
through my veins. The cobra slithered, black eyes seeking
mine. My hand fell on a pile of firewood. I hurled a log; it fell
nowhere near him. I snatched up another, slammed it down
where the snake had been an instant before.

No logs left, only sticks. Dizzy, I searched among them.
One had a fork. I hauled myself to my feet. The viper tracked
me, coiling, slithering, weaving. I blinked away blood.

"Demons take him! Tantroth! No!"

I stabbed at the cobra. Bobbing, he avoided my cleft. I
lunged. He struck. Fangs embedded in my boot. I smashed
down with all my might. The stick cracked in half. Cursing, I
snatched up the forked end.

Mother, you're here, though I can't see you. Aid me. Aid
Caledon.

"What, sir?" Anavar. "You're mumbling, I can't—"

Slit the skin.

"The cobra's? I can't catch—"

Yours.

I felt for my dagger, drew it, slashed at my forehead. Blinding pain. I squeezed; blood and venom coursed.

The snake drew back, weaved its flattened head, eyes
locked on mine.

I held out my dagger, point first, staggered to my feet,
reeled across the cold firepit.

The cobra followed.

Retreating, I slashed at my tunic with the blade, tore off a
fragment of cloth, held it tight to my brow. With my free
hand I wielded the stick.

We circled.

The snake struck. I avoided it. It coiled again; I knocked it
from its spiral, caught the head in the cleft of my stick. The
cobra struggled and thrashed. Grimly, I held on.

As long as I pressed my cloth tight, the blood was contained.
I could see.

"Good, they have our signal! Go!" Tursel, far distant, his
voice eager. "Oh, you have them, my lord Groenfil!"

With a mighty heave, the viper broke free. It threw itself across the firepit, coiled to strike. My gash pulsing, I flung myself back, fetched up against the unyielding rock wall. A protuberance ground into my spine.

The snake wriggled after me, but slowly. I breathed hard. We regarded each other with hatred.

"The gates open! Franca and Horst lead the charge."

I jabbed at the cobra.

"Captain, our center."

"Not now, we're—Lord of Nature! So many of them!"

The cobra hissed.

For eons, while babes aged and saplings grew old and stooped, I vied with the black-eyed viper for the dusty cave. Though I couldn't catch its head with the cleft of my stick, neither could it sink fangs into my flesh.

I ached. My forehead throbbed. My arm cramped, holding the cloth. My mouth was dry as desert sand.

"Rodrigo." A shake. "Sir, wake yourself."

Slowly, as if mesmerized, the snake coiled.

"Hurry him, youngsire."

"I do, Pardos. Roddy, let go the bowl!"

I blinked. Sunlight stabbed. I stretched aching palms, stared stupidly at my fingers. "Oh." I pressed fingers to forehead, sat rocking.

"What, sir?" Carefully, Anavar poured the stillsilver to the ewer.

"It hurts so. Wipe the blood."

"There's none, my lord. Can you rise? We must get you away." He wrapped the bowl, thrust it into his saddlebag.

"He bit me—get me away?" I tried to look about, winced from blinding shafts of light. "What has befallen us?"

"We withdraw. On your feet . . . hoist yourself by my arm, that's right, sir. Pardos, help him with the stirrup."

"The field's theirs?" My heart plummeted. "I failed. The Rood's too strong to—"

Anavar said, "Not the Rood, I think. Just numbers."

"How great our calamity?" Carefully, I dabbed at my brow. No blood. I marveled.

"We're in good order, as yet."

Clinging to Ebon's mane, I peered across the plain. The last of Horst's castle yeomen battled their way to the safety of their gate, while Tursel rode about behind our men, shouting orders, orchestrating our retreat, oblivious to the arrows that sought him.

The remains of Groenfil's cavalry thudded up the rise, leaving Norland footmen behind.

"What of Eiber?"

Anavar tugged on my reins, turning Ebon toward the road. "Azar's taken alive. A good number of horsemen are lost. Tantroth lives. Sir, that Norland cohort sees us. They make haste."

"They're on foot."

"Sir, rouse yourself, or I'll lead you."

Wearily, I tugged at the reins, guiding Ebon alongside my escort.

We made our way into the hills, toward our waiting camp. As day stretched toward dusk we filled the road. All of Groenfil's troop had become my guard. Tantroth and Tursel labored behind, to speed our troops and hinder Hriskil's.

From time to time Tursel sent a dispatch: trees were felled across a narrow way, a ford blocked the path. And then: "Quickly, my lord. They pursue us in strength. Find high ground where we may turn and hold."

We spurred our tired mounts, but had gone scarce half a league when two score horsemen galloped down the road toward us.

"Hold! We're Caledon!" The foremost, a swarthy fellow, bore a Caled standard. "We're of your camp!"

"What do you here?" My voice was hot.

He reined in. His steaming stallion heaved and snorted. "Rodrigo . . . sire, the wagons."

I flinched. "What now?"

"Norlanders . . . nigh on a thousand . . . from Stryx."

I reared in my stirrups. *"What of my brother?"*

"Here, Roddy." A weak wave.

I stared, speechless. Elryc sat on a fine stallion, cradled in the arms of . . . Danzik. *Danzik!* My mouth worked. "What do . . . what do you . . . how . . . ?" I gave it up.

"Danzik brought me." A giggle. "It annoyed Genard." Elryc slipped down, ran to Ebon, embraced my leg in the stirrup. I reached down, squeezed his shoulder.

Groenfil's hard voice brought us to our senses. "What of the camp?"

"Overrun," said a familiar voice. Tresa. My heart skipped a beat.

She added, "The wagons were alight when we fled."

"How many dead?" My voice was harsh.

"I don't know, Roddy. They came on us so fast . . . many ran to escape."

I stared at scraggly clumps of bracken marking the road-side.

From behind, a rider. "Tursel asks, have you found where we might . . ." He saw our faces. "What is it, my lords?"

Groenfil said, "Sarazon is before us, Hriskil behind."

I goaded my flagging mind. "Hriskil planned this, and or-dered it. It's not in Sarazon's nature. A thousand men from Stryx, so soon? You know what that means?"

"We're trapped," said Groenfil.

I waved it away. "Sarazon's set out without wagons, with-out supplies. Else he'd still be laboring up the slopes. A day's skirmish and he must turn back."

"So?"

Couldn't he see? I said, "Sarazon won't pursue us far. And he won't add to Hriskil's strength when they join."

"Pursue us? It's we who must smash ourselves on him; he has the road."

"But not the hills." I looked for comprehension. "Come, my lord, we're in your domain. Have you no vassal to guide us?"

"Where, Roddy? And how?"

"Why, anywhere, now we've no wagons to hinder us. We'll gather Tursel and Tantroth and sneak past Sarazon. If he meets us it can only be with a fragment of his thousand. Once past him, we're free. We go to Soushire, or the Southron hills. They abound with canyons and dells."

"If Sarazon must turn back because he has no supplies, what of us?"

"We live lean, or go hungry. We're better able than he."

"Why, sire?"

"We won't surrender Caledon!" I raised myself so all could hear. "We'll lead Hriskil a merry chase. We'll tweak his beard, outfox his every patrol. We're game gone to ground, in a meadow that's home!"

Anavar tried to smile, but his eyes were bleak.

* * *

ALL MY BRAVE words couldn't conceal the scope of our disaster. Not only had we met defeat, but to meld Tantroth's rear guard with our meager numbers, we must tarry, while each hour Hriskil raced ever closer to the main body of our force. Groenfil's scouts had long since fanned out to seek tracks and trails that might deliver us.

It was dusk when we veered off the main road, on a footpath that climbed sharply through birch groves and tall grass.

Tursel wrinkled his nose at the trampled brush, the snapped boughs. "A blind washerwoman could track us."

My tone was soothing. "Once we're past Sarazon, it matters not."

"Rodrigo, despite your declamation, we must have provisions."

"I know. We'll make for Soushire."

As we guided Ebon through the brush, I found myself with Danzik by my side. I said, "Sarazon didn't get close enough to free you?"

The Norlander scowled. "I had only to run across the field."

"Why did you not?"

"That . . . that iot hom." *Trifling man.* An odd phrase, though Elryc, with his serious ways, was more a little man than a boy. "El-e-rek told me rez gave me no leave to escape. That I owed you my . . . self. *Vade.* Until."

I asked, "And Bouris?"

"Looked around, saw Caled lord running into woods. I thought *perse.* But short boy scrambling to catch horses, El-e-rek standing waiting, Norl arrows falling near. Thought, rez want *iot hom* more than Cumber lord Bouris?"

"Yes!"

"I too think. So where is vade? I —" A motion, of snatching up a bundle. "—took. El-e-rek try to bite. Not understand I say no hurt." A wolfish grin. "Only stop biting when I catch up Caleds."

"Danzik . . . I thank you." It warranted more, much more. I was surprised by the sadness in my tone, "The king gives you leave, Norlander. You are mine no more."

Danzik rode a few paces, silent. "Free? Go home Norland?"

"Yes."

"With Hriskil? Fight?"

"Aye." For Elryc, I owed him no less.

"Qon?" *When?*

"Now," I said. "You may take your horse."

A pause. "Tem asta?" *Later too?*

I gaped.

It took me a moment to work through what he said then. "Vestrez coa tern, Rez." *I would see how it ends.*

PART THREE

TWENTY-SEVEN

"I EXPECTED TO host an army, not a rabble." Larissa's tone was aggrieved.

"The men are blooded, but fought well. They'll fight the stronger, behind your walls." We stood under a willow that offered scant shade from the cold drizzle. Ebon grazed through his bit.

"Aye, but now I must feed them, shoe their mounts, open my armories. You've lost wagonloads of arrows, blankets, food, tents, the means of war." She pursed her lips.

Enough. Was she liege, and I the supplicant? "I understand, my lady. We'll move on."

"Where?" She was skeptical.

"The hills. Verein." It mattered not; Hriskil would hound us through Caledon. "With fortune and surprise, we'll reach Groenfil's gates."

"A waste of your remainder." She sighed. "Very well, join us."

"You're most gracious." My tone was bland.

As she left for her tent—the closed-fisted lady had managed to protect it despite our rout—I drew my cloak tight. After three days camping without gear I was tired, dirty, despondent. Tresa beckoned, from a campfire. She'd propped a precious tarpaulin from a bough, and perhaps it shielded her from a share of the drizzle. "Tea, sire?" She wrapped her skirt around the handle, and pulled the pot from the coals.

"Sire?" I snorted. "That, between us?" Gladly, I took the cup she offered, and warmed my free hand. I asked, "Did you overhear our speech?"

"Yes. Regardless, she wants you at Soushire."

"Of course. We've bodies to sacrifice on her wall." Perhaps that wasn't quite fair. "Tresa, my—" I blushed. "My love, we've no choice but Soushire, at least for now."

"I understand."

"The army needs respite, but if I'm penned in Soushire, there's none to rally Caledon."

"Oh, Roddy, is there Caledon to rally?" Her cry uncloaked despair.

"Of course." I made my tone hearty. "But I know not what to do with Elryc."

"Soushire."

"You have a good heart, my lady of Cumber."

It took her a moment. "She wouldn't!"

"Perhaps not. But in all Caledon, whose head, save mine, could buy her such fortune?"

We sat by the fire, mingling converse with the sizzle of sap-filled firewood. We spoke of our comrades, and the hardy band who held Stryx under Willem of Alcazar.

It was I who brought up Bouris. "There's one I'm well rid of. Though I'll grant his loyal support would have been most welcome. I'd grown to count on Cumber."

After a long quiet she said, "He's not Grandfather."

"In no aspect. Even his banquets . . ." My smile was grim. "I wonder where he's gone." To Hriskil, I supposed. But Cumber would remain his, despite abandonment, treason, even regicide, should he attempt it. My farewell gift to Uncle Raeth. *To your bloodline forever, though it cost my crown to preserve it.* "A pity I had to pledge—" My eyes widened. "He's your grandfather!"

Her brow knotted. "Uncle Bouris?"

"No, you silly—Raeth! By Lord of Nature, I'll do it!" And savoring my delight, I said no more, until my nobles and I met by morning's light.

Before my nobles, and Tursel, as our captain, and Tresa, I declared Bouris's lands and title forfeit, and proclaimed Tresa lady of Cumber, holder of the lands and titles that had hitherto pertained to Bouris. I could see it made Larissa uneasy, and perhaps Groenfil, though his face was less expressive.

If so, the better for it. Let them know that no noble abandoned the House of Caledon with impunity. In any event, I'd kept my vow. Tresa was of Uncle Raeth's bloodline as surely as was Bouris.

I hurried on to my more significant announcement, while Tantroth, gray of face, coughed uncontrollably, cupping his tea to inhale the mist. Tursel swayed, near asleep on his feet. Even Anavar looked peaked. Only Groenfil, who'd shared Larissa's tent, seemed near rested.

Larissa protested, "Not join us? Rodrigo, what mean you?"

I repeated my argument: that I must rally Caledon. I would ride with six hundred men, leaving the rest to strengthen Soushire's walls.

"Six hundred men are no army. You'll be unable to meet Hriskil in the field."

"But we'll move quickly and harry his lines. At the moment, that's the best we can do."

"Let Caledon come to you," she said. "Take refuge in Soushire. All will know you're among us," she said.

"Especially Hriskil. If I'm bottled behind your battlements there's none to deny him the realm."

"There's already none—" She bit it off, as Groenfil shifted uncomfortably from foot to foot. "Your folk—Anavar and Elryc, Lady Tresa—they must have haven. You recall the quarters I gave you last year? Ample fires, soft beds . . ."

I smiled. "Don't tempt me, my lady."

"I insist on their rescue. Don't deny them life. Your beloved will abide at Soushire."

Anavar, whom I'd carefully coached, said, "I, madam, go with my guardian. And as for the others . . ."

"Yes, youngsire?" She sounded impatient.

"Who might ride with Rodrigo as your pledge? You know the forms."

Larissa summoned an outrage that perhaps she actually felt. "Hostages? You dare—after I risked—if *I'm* not loyal, then who—"

"It's custom, my lady. Not for a moment do I think you'd . . ." Anavar tried an ingratiating smile that to my eye appeared more a leer.

Her tone was ice. "I've no hostage to offer. No son you may slaughter for my betrayal."

"I'll stand surety."

All looked to Groenfil.

"Rodrigo, my lord king . . ." The earl bowed, a sharp nod signifying submission and assent. "Now do I offer my body as pledge of my lady Soushire's fidelity, that should she cause or allow harm to your betrothed or your brother whom you bestow to her custody, I be extinguished as reprisal."

"But Sergo, you're to stay with us!"

He offered her a sad smile. "My lady, I cannot. I'm pledged

to Rodrigo. Where he rides . . . don't look at me so, I beg you. He's right in that Hriskil need mount no assault; by surrounding us he takes Caledon. My domain will fall, and thereafter yours. With Roddy, I may save us both."

"I . . . see." She swallowed. "My lord Groenfil, I hold your trust to my heart."

WE SAW OUR force to Soushire, where I bathed in a cramped copper-clad tub that I found the lap of luxury. I wallowed in warm water. *If only Rustin could see me now.* "I've changed," I said to no one in particular, and nobody gave response.

Tresa seemed subdued, and the second evening, sought me out. "I can't stay behind, my lord, while you fight for Caledon."

"You must. I order it." Couldn't she understand? If I weren't sure of her safety, how could I carry on?

"I refuse." Her tone was soft steel. "I'll be of more service in Stryx. Even in Cumber."

I threw up my hands. "Raeth would tell you it's not right you leave Soushire without so much as a—"

"Why?"

"BECAUSE YOU'RE ONLY A WOMAN!"

Her voice matched mine. "YOU'RE ONLY A BOY!" Her tone subsided a trifle. "And a rude one." She rose. "Cumber must be rallied. I'll leave within the week. Arrest me if you will." She swept out.

Meanwhile, the news grew daily grimmer. Hriskil's men roamed the countryside unhindered. Homing birds with banded legs brought word to Soushire that Castle Stryx still held for Caledon. Sarazon hadn't attacked it, though he had seized the Keep below, and Willem dared not sally forth.

Groenfil Castle was besieged.

Each day we tarried amid Soushire's plenty was a misery, though men and horses grew stronger. As we gathered our provisions and made ready for war, I was not alone in my unease. One misty day, walking the damp courtyard, Tantroth accosted me. "My lord, this won't do, and you know it!"

I sighed. "Of course. I'm no fool." I closed the distance between us. "What would you?"

He coughed, wiped his mouth. "It's time I went home."

"Hriskil has your home."

"Norlanders, but not Hriskil. Their king sits outside Groenfil Castle. I need but slip past—"

I said, "Norland troops hold Pezar and the pass."

"It's not the only pass. Without wagons, I may—"

"If you go, what of Caledon?"

The duke of Eiber regarded me gravely. "My liege, if I stay . . . what of Caledon?" I had no answer. He added, "It's time, Roddy. I'd like your blessing."

I said bitterly, "Six hundred become four hundred, and four hundred become two, then a handful."

He leaned close, spoke softly. "Your cause is lost."

"And so you desert me!" It wasn't my most regal moment.

His gaze was steely. "I do not. If you insist, I'll fight Norlanders in your hills instead of mine."

"I insist!"

"Very well, my liege." A stiff bow. He stalked off.

"Tantroth!" I swallowed bile. "One battle, at least, that we have the advantage of your strength. Then, if you . . . go home with my blessing."

His voice was quiet. "Thank you, Rodrigo."

"But should I . . . *when* I call . . ."

"I'll answer."

He strode into the mist.

BOWS, OATHS OF fealty from Larissa, embraces twixt her and Groenfil, between Elryc and me. Stiff good-byes between Tresa and myself. She'd not yet left Soushire, and I'd given no orders for her arrest. Perhaps she would come to her senses.

And then we were off.

Now we were little more than bands of marauding cavalry. Four hundred of Groenfil's, half that number of Tantroth's loyal vassals. I'd even bidden Tursel stay behind, to lend his experience to Larissa's defense. It was of great importance we not lose Soushire, but of as much urgency that we carry the battle to Hriskil. So, we split our force.

Danzik, Anavar and I were all that remained of my personal party, saving my servant Tanner. Bollert came along to look after horses, and I had my ever-present guards. Tanner served without pay, of course, and I'd told Anavar I no longer had coin for his stipend. He'd looked unhappy, but merely nodded.

For the moment, we rode with Tantroth, to harry the Norlanders in Groenfil's domain. Soon or late, he'd turn north, work his way through obscure passes home to Eiber. When fortunes turned I'd join him. In the meantime he'd strike from the hills at Hriskil's caravans, and I'd harass Sarazon at Stryx.

Cavalry travels light, on four feet. Tiny tents shared by two or even more, cold meals more often than not, tea or broth made in a few precious pots. Spare horses burdened with gear, led by reins tied to the pommel of the mount ahead.

WE RODE ALL the day, avoiding roads, threading our way to Groenfil. I was in foul temper. Anavar tried, once or twice, to lighten my mood, but my growl was so ominous he withdrew. Late in the afternoon we fell on a small Norland outpost, and left blood and fire in our wake. We took no prisoners except a brace of hens ready for the pots, and dined well that eve.

Next day we stumbled on a strong column of Norland horsemen, who took after us in a wild scramble. We outran them at last and lost ourselves in wooded hills. Our predations had made Hriskil's troops more watchful, and for two days we roamed, probing, finding no weakness we might exploit. We were grimy, weary and unkempt.

At last, we came upon an overgrown goat-trail that meandered toward the outskirts of Groenfil town. We rode it single file, all that the narrow way would allow.

As luck would have it, a Norland patrol was trudging along the road where the trail crossed it. Forewarned by our scouts, we divided into squads, drew swords, and at the flash of a silk, thundered down the rise to fall on the stunned yeomen. We'd hoped to destroy them all, but three wiry runners got away to alert their fellows. Still, twenty-seven dead was something, and only one of ours.

Tantroth seemed not pleased.

I said, "Why, my lord?"

"Six hundred of us, and surprise lost, to blood a puny patrol. Now what? Another week skulking the woods, to unearth another vantage?"

"Of small stones are great battlements bui—"

"Bah! We need victories, not homilies."

"Is this not victory?" I squatted to pick up a Norland sword, better than my own, and made stabbing motions at an imaginary foe.

"If it is, my lord, then my pledge if fulfilled. Three battles I've given you, not one. I must see to Eiber."

I knew not how to refuse him.

WE RODE OUR horses ragged, seeking a chink in the Norland armor. With Tantroth gone we were fewer, but movements were quick. And Groenfil's scouts knew the terrain.

The second night, we'd barely settled into a miserable camp when an outrider raced through our guard. "Norland cavalry, about a thousand!"

Groenfil rubbed his forehead. "How far?"

"The end of the valley. An hour at best."

"Riding where?"

"At us!"

In desperate haste we threw saddles on weary steeds and made fast bridles and bits. Bollert loped across the field, Ebon's reins in one hand, Edmund's the other. I swung the groomsman up behind me, galloped to the stakes where the spare mounts were tethered. He grabbed a handful of reins, swarmed aboard a neighing stallion. Groenfil gave a harsh cry, waving to the trail. We were off, none too soon. Danzik looked back, somewhat forlorn. But he was free to rejoin his countrymen; it was at his choosing that he shared our fatigue.

The Norlanders chased us half the night. We dared not run our mounts to death, but Hriskil's troops too had to dismount and walk now and again. At last, near dawn, our band gathered in a ravine and fell on the ground, not bothering with tents.

Three hours later dogged Norland scouts searched us out, and we took to our heels. Half the day we sought to flee, oft leading our worn and weary mounts, stopping at brooks when we could to give them water. At one point we blundered on a column of Norland foot soldiers, as startled as we, and hacked our way through.

Seven dead.

That night, further from Groenfil Castle than we'd begun, the earl came to my frayed, tiny tent. "Roddy, we can't go on like this."

I nodded, in defeat. As if it mattered not, I inquired, "You'll go home?"

A swift breeze billowed the canvas. "Sire, to whom do you imagine you speak?"

I climbed to my feet. "My lord?"

"You do me dishonor." His voice was reproving, but not cold. "I'm pledged to your service, am I not? I came to say: we cannot go on like this. So, where next?"

"My lord . . ." My voice was unsteady. "I don't deserve you."

"Perhaps not. But you have me."

I rubbed my face, trying to gather my thoughts. Pitched battle was out; our numbers were too small. Moreover, the Rood had proved stronger than the Still; by the time I sensed Hriskil's power in use, our men were at each other's throats, our strategies in disarray. All my contest with the cobra accomplished was to stave off utter defeat.

We couldn't break through to Groenfil, we were resolved to avoid being penned in Soushire. Stryx was out; Sarazon held the roads to the castle. Castle Verein was Margenthar's. That left . . . I looked up. "The Sands."

He raised an eyebrow. "A year ago, the Warthen wouldn't let you in." He guarded well the high pass, and on my quest for the crown, had barred my way.

"Last time, I wasn't king."

The Sands was far to the east. Retreating from Groenfil, we gave Soushire wide berth. I wanted none of Larissa's importuning, and cared not to lead Hriskil to her domain.

Saddle-sore, grim, we rode for endless dreary days. At least we seemed to have shaken our pursuers. We passed through a few sparse villages, where we made no attempt to hide our identity. I even had our standard unfurled and tried to make a brave show. We'd have been better sneaking past the inns and barns, or pretending to be Norlanders. Better they not see the straits to which their king was reduced.

OUR WEARY BAND made its way into the Desert Range. Unlike the environs of Pezar, these hills were *cold*. Horses' breaths steamed in the morning breeze, and we all wore cloaks and covers. By oversight or loss, Bollert and Tanner had little to wear beyond the light clothing on their backs. Reluctantly, I parted with a few coppers, that they not freeze. Tanner accepted it as a matter of course—after all, a master provided for his man—but Bollert was pleasingly grateful. "Coulda got in Elm, but better you give."

I was outraged. "You had coin?"

"Nah." A finger, to his eye. "Coulda got."

"No witchery, you. You've been warned."

"Didn'!" He sounded aggrieved. "You know I didn'!" True, else he'd have been well clad.

Day by day, swaying in the saddle, my thighs chafing, sun beating down on my tangled hair, I came to a reluctant conclusion. One that was no less valid for my lack of enthusiasm.

At last, our winding road led us upward toward the High Pass, long fortified into the Warthen's Gate. Before my birth, Mother had, wielding the Still, secured the Warthen's renewed oath. On her death, he withdrew beyond his borders, adopting a waiting stance.

Before sleep, huddled under our blankets, I described for Anavar what I remembered of my one visit to the Sands, as a youngster. "High, colored cliffs of sandstone. A long way between wells. At Sandhelm, a rocky keep. And his eyes . . ."

"What about them?"

"I can't describe it." A distant awareness of some secret pain. A mere glance had left me uneasy, and I was loath to endure another.

"Sir, what do we seek there?"

"The Warthen's aid."

"Will you get it?"

"There's always a chance." Then, after a pause, "No, Anavar, I will not."

He raised himself on an elbow. "Why then do we go?"

I hesitated, knowing trust was folly. But without Rustin, I must have *someone*. "You mustn't tell Groenfil."

"I swear not."

I lowered my voice to a bare whisper. "I've lost Caledon. I can't best Hriskil. I'll take what I may."

"The Sands?"

"No, you twit. Tresa."

"You said she—"

"This scar makes her flee." I rubbed the uneven skin. Maybe when I was older, and had a beard . . . I sighed. Perhaps the skin of my cheek was so destroyed, hair wouldn't grow. If Mar meant to ruin me, he'd had done well.

"What, then?"

"A Return."

"Elryc spoke of it. You may go back . . ."

"To any one event, and relive it until it comes out right. Somehow, I'll not be caught, or evade Mar's knife. I *did* free myself from his cell. I'll just have to escape sooner."

"Sir? Roddy?"

"Yes?"

"Elryc said . . . the Warthen . . . one has to pay him vast sums."

"For his pain. The Sands has little resources, save what he acquires by lending his Power."

"You can't even pay my stipend."

"I know." I reached out, put finger to his lips. "Still, I have hope."

He watched me, silent, wondering, until I fell asleep.

TWENTY-EIGHT

WE ASSEMBLED BEFORE the rocky wall that seemed to spring from the stone cliffs to either side. A small gate at its base, firmly shut.

Anavar volunteered as envoy. He returned fuming. "From Badir, keeper of the Pass, to Rodrigo of Caledon, greetings. My master the Warthen has closed the Sands to all combatants. He bids thee, go hence from this place. Roddy, I told him—"

"Just the message!"

"Go hence from this place. Forthwith. He said 'forthwith' to the king! Know that his master the Warthen receives no messengers from the High Pass, and turns his gaze west."

"To the Ukras?" I turned to Groenfil. "He trades with the Ukras?"

"They're his neighbors."

"Um." I glowered. "No messages, either. How can I demand he open?"

"You can't."

"Bah. I'll speak with Badir myself." I urged Ebon forward.

"No you won't!" Pardos grabbed my reins. "See the bowmen on those walls? I didn't come this far to see you killed. You will *not* ride into a salvo of barbs."

"You're right, I'd best walk. Anavar, who has my coronet?"

"You do, sir. Your left saddlebag."

I fished it out.

"My lord—"

I spun. "Pardos, this must be done. Else, we disband, and I seek work as a blacksmith's boy. Groenfil, tell him."

Groenfil shrugged. "I doubt they'll shoot at him. And I suppose I agree. He must take the risk."

Pardos said plaintively, "I swore to my lord Tantroth . . ." But he made no move to stop me.

I trudged toward the looming wall, smoothing my cloak, nudging my coronet to the center of my scalp. From the battlement, a hundred faces peered down.

I took deep breath. "I am Rodrigo, your king. I bid you, open the gate."

One helmet bobbed. "I am Badir. I keep the pass. My master is Vasur, Warthen of the Sands. He bids me nay."

My neck ached; it was a high battlement. Perhaps I'd have looked more dignified at greater distance. "At least come forth and speak with me."

"I cannot."

"Your master requires discourtesy to the king?"

He considered it. "Very well. But my answer cannot be changed."

In a moment the gate opened. Quickly it shut again.

The villein wore sword and shield to greet his liege! The impertinence pricked my pride, but I appeared to take no notice. My tone was patient. "The Sands is my domain. Your master holds it at my behest." Not quite so; he'd received it from Mother, before my birth.

"I do but what I'm told."

"Let us send envoy to the Warthen."

"I cannot."

"One man can cause no harm. We'll wait while—" Now I was begging. I bottled my fury.

"I'm sorry, my lord. Vasur forbids it."

No point in further belittling myself. I turned.

"I'll bring Ebon!" A cry from below. Bollert ran among the rocks, Ebon trotting behind. "Here, sire. Your horse!"

My rage shifted. The peasant fool made me look a petty country lordling, served by an untrained churl. *Oh, Rustin, look what I've come to.* The moment we were turned about, I'd have the skin from Bollert's back.

Sweating, he clambered up the slope. "Here's Ebon, sire! Take the reins!" His eyes were wide.

Badir said, "I'm sorry, Rodrigo. Our conclave is done."

"Take Ebon, my lord!" Bollert thrust me the reins. His maniacal stare was fixed not on me, but over my shoulder. "May we go through the gate now? Please?"

I snatched up the reins, threw myself on Ebon. Another word and I'd drag Bollert down to the trees where Groenfil waited; demons take my dignity. "No!"

"Oh, we come so far, couldn' we please all ride to the Sands?"

"No, we're going—"

"I suppose you have," said Badir. "Yes, take your men through." He cupped his hands, called up to the battlement. "Open the gate! They have leave to pass!"

I gaped. Bollert ducked under my arm, danced in front of Badir, eyes wide. "All of us, an' no harm?"

The guard called to the wall, "Set aside your weapons! No one is to draw sword!"

I beckoned furiously to the trees, and Anavar. He lashed Edmund. Galvanized, his horse leaped up the rise.

I snapped, "Everyone, and quickly. We're allowed through."

Anavar's eyes widened. He wheeled and galloped recklessly across the rocky field.

Bollert capered. "Oh, look, m'lor', see how happy I am?" Sweat poured from his forehead. "Look, I'm dancin'!"

Badir's gazed fixed on Bollert, who crooned, "All of us, ride through, 'cause you wan' king safe behin' wall, hurry, sire, can't for long, oh, m'lor', we're so happy . . ."

Five abreast, our cavalry trotted toward the gaping gate.

"Happy, happy! Look, m'lor! We're glad we go through, aren' you glad too? Tell 'em again, glad king goes to see Warthen." The boy danced and gibbered.

Badir's eyes never left his. "All is well." His voice rang out to his troops on the battlement. "Our king visits Vasur at Sandhelm." I left him in the rocky field, whispered commands to Groenfil as we cantered through the Warthen's Gate.

There was no town at the High Pass, but as a regiment of guards was always on hand, a hamlet of sorts had grown up near the stone barracks. A blacksmith, a hovel and barn that might have been an inn.

We took no notice; our band clattered across the rock-strewn common, through the meadow beyond and onto the road that began the slow, circuitous descent to the dry land below.

As I'd hurriedly arranged, at the gate our last rider slowed, scooped Bollert into the saddle behind. Their obedient gelding trotted past the battlement. The boy clung to the rider's waist. They spurred, to close the distance between us. My back itched; each moment I awaited the shaft that would pitch me from the saddle.

None came.

When we were clear of the fortress town, I fixed Bollert with a glare, then turned to Groenfil. "He's a sport of nature, a freak. *Peasants don't wield powers.*"

Anavar tugged at my sleeve. "He's done us no harm, sir." As ever, since our reconciliation, his tone was determinedly polite.

"Not yet. But some night . . ." I shivered. "Don't expect me to thank him. He makes my skin crawl."

Bollert looked to the earth. Anavar pursed his lips.

I remounted. "Arghh!" I gritted my teeth. "Thank you. Thank you, Bollert, for opening our way." I glared at Anavar. "Satisfied?" I spurred down the dusty road.

EAST OF THE Desert Range, the plain grew ever more dry. Whenever we found water, we gave the horses their fill and soaked our wineskins full. A day from the pass, the ground was dry, the sparse vegetation withered and sere. We pressed on.

Sandhelm was in desert, but, I recalled, the greater wasteland lay beyond it. We had but a half day's ride to Vasur's stronghold. That near accomplished, I set my coronet on my scalp, changed to the better of my two sets of breeches. "Pardos, set your men, so, as if an honor guard." We'd make what show we could.

It was hardly worth the effort. Though four hundred strong, we were a sad proposition: ragged, dust-covered, ill-clothed and weary. Not exactly a royal procession.

Our lancemen rode with points set. In the flatlands the road widened, and we rode six abreast. Two villages were planted along our way, and I negated Groenfil's thought to skirt them. At the walk, we rode through them, eyes straight ahead. Robed and turbaned tribesmen came out of stone huts to mark our passing.

I doubted not that the Warthen had word of our admittance; homing birds made admirable couriers between two fixed points. I wondered how Badir explained his misadventure and whether his head sat firmly on his shoulders.

No guard, no envoy came to greet us. On the other hand, no warriors barred our way.

The stronghold was the tallest edifice in Sandhelm, a wind-blasted, austere but imposing refuge. We rode directly to it.

The gate was ajar. We rode through, four hundred horsemen crowding the courtyard before the donjon.

A lone footman came trotting to hold Ebon's bridle. He made a respectful bow, of commoner to noble. "My master asks, 'What do you here?' "

"Tell the Warthen I will speak of it to no ears but his."

"He will not see you. The stable's there." He pointed.

For an outraged moment I thought he offered me shelter within, but he was only explaining where he would take Ebon. I said, "A nosebag of grain and a rubdown. Not much water at first."

"Aye, my lord."

I looked about. Not a soul had emerged from the donjon. And if this churl were the only stablehand, our horses would go a long time unfed. Even as the thought crossed my mind, a procession of like-garbed attendants emerged from the barns.

At the same moment, a rotund fellow of middle years descended the donjon steps. He made his way to me. "My name is Tajik. You are Rodrigo?"

"King Rodrigo."

"I am corrected." A bow. "Vasur welcomes you. If you'll bring those you'd have accompany you . . ." A gesture to the steps.

"And the rest?"

He nodded to the outbuildings. "We'll find them quarters presently. For now, refreshment awaits you within."

Groenfil made a warning sound. I nodded. "They'll follow the forms, I'm sure. They did with Mother." They would offer no food, no drink they didn't sample before us. We would keep our arms. It was expected, and no offense offered or taken.

Danzik looked about. He would accompany us, I decided immediately. He'd traveled far and deserved a seat before the mummers. I asked, "What do you think of it?"

"Dry."

That, it was. Even with the revenue his Return produced, I wondered how Vasur kept his domain stocked with foodstuffs and other necessaries. I imagined not much would grow in this climate, save dates, figs and other esoteric produce good for a novel gift, but not daily sustenance.

"Anavar, my lord Groenfil, Pardos . . ." I named two dozen

to join us in the donjon, not excluding Tanner, so I'd have a servant not the Warthen's man, and Bollert, whom I dared not leave unwatched.

Following Tajik up the worn sandstone steps, it occurred to me Bollert's sorcery could gain what I sought from the Warthen. Immediately I discarded the thought. If I used witchery, I became myself a witch. Demons would ride my shoulder, their steel-sharp toes hooked into my flesh.

Besides, it had no *vade*.

In the entry hall, Bollert's gaze swiveled from pillar to stair to statue, his jaw dropping. Though I didn't show it, I felt as he. Sandhelm Castle had no opulent beauty about it, but its austerity was . . . well, impressive. Stryx may have awed the visitor not used to better, but born there, I was too accustomed to it to take notice. Here, though, all was exotic. Outside, I'd seen foundations of granite blocks, but within the dark and cool keep, carved marble pillars supported mosaic arches, and marble statues abounded, their features painted in lifelike colors.

Tajik led us to an airy room giving onto an inner courtyard. Immediately, very young servants padded in, bearing silvered trays. Their eyes were fixed on the colorful rugs, or their own feet. Not once did one of them allow his gaze to meet ours.

The trays were filled with exquisite silver goblets. At random, I selected one, handed it to Tajik, picked another for myself. He drank, lifting his chin to quaff the dregs.

It wasn't foolproof; fanatics had been known to accept their own death to secure that of their foes. But what could one do? Cautiously, I sipped the liquid, finding it sweet and deliciously cool. "Thank you," I said.

Tajik's bow was short and perfunctory. "My honor is to serve you."

If Rustin were among us, he would have caught my eye to counsel patience, but I said, "It's been years since I've seen Vasur." For Caledon, appallingly blunt.

Seeing Groenfil down a mouthful, Danzik swished his drink doubtfully, took a gulp, grimaced at the taste. Anavar, I noticed, held goblet in hand but did not drink.

Tajik said, "You were a child. He remembers you well." A moment's hesitation. "How long, sire, will you honor us with your presence?"

"That depends, I think, on our parley. Will he dine with us?"

"I'm afraid not." Tajik even managed to sound apologetic. "My master is indisposed."

"Until?"

An expressive shrug. "What man can say? Please, refresh yourselves. Your horses will be attended to. Dinner will be served in the Great Hall." He left us with courteous bows.

In my chamber, I requested water for a bath. While I soaked away my aches, Anavar perched on the edge of the tub. "Is the Warthen truly indisposed?"

"Perhaps." I doubted it.

He handed me the soap. "Shall I scrub your back?"

I stiffened. "Do not touch my person!" I twisted, to meet his gaze. "I will not be coddled, or held. You are not Rustin!"

"*Sir!*" His voice was a squeak.

"Rust is gone forever. Though we share a chamber, youngsire, his place is not yours."

Anavar's face burned. "Sir, I'm not—I meant no—" He jumped to his feet. "Have I leave?"

"No." I controlled my breathing. With an effort I added, "You're rebuked, but you're still my friend."

Anavar sat hunched over, head in hands.

I owed him more. "It's just . . . we knew each other all our lives. He was the best friend ever I had."

"You were sun, moon and stars to him." Anavar's voice was muffled. "He'd give his life for you."

"He *gave* his life for me!" I hoisted myself out of the tub, wrapped a cloth around my waist. "If we speak more of him, I'll be cross."

Dressed and combed, I gathered Groenfil and Pardos and their aides in an anteroom.

"Tajik mentioned dinner," said the earl. "Downstairs, in the Great Hall."

"If the Warthen's present—"

Danzik burst through the doors. "Outside, Rez! See!"

Groenfil looked blank, until I translated. Then we rushed down the stairs after the Norlander. Shoving aside the guard, Danzik flung open the iron-studded door.

The courtyard was packed with mounted men, no less than a thousand, armed to the teeth. A few held their horses' reins, walking about to stretch their legs. The Warthen's army—had he stalled us with false hospitality, awaiting their arrival?

Groenfil hauled me back. "Upstairs! Bar the door! Pardos, seek a way to the stable. Danzik—"

"No," I said, freeing myself. "It's what Vasur wants. Wait here. Especially you, Pardos." I reached to the door.

The earl blocked my path. "You need explain."

"I order—"

"Your nobles' disapproval must be met, not ignored or evaded. Did you agree thus?"

I swallowed. "Yes. My lord, I must go to them; I pray thee don't oppose me. In statecraft, at times I have an instinct. If I'm wrong in this, I ought not be king. But now they've seen me, the sands of time run low."

Groenfil glowered. "You forgive me if you're killed?"

"With all my heart." No time for more, I thrust open the door.

The steps had lengthened, or my legs had grown weak. I made my way down, as all eyes followed my progress. The courtyard was deathly still. Of our men, there was no sign. I hoped they'd been dispersed to their shelters. Surely they couldn't have been dispatched in combat without our hearing a sound. Besides, I saw no blood.

Near the steps a bony fellow stood holding a brown star-faced stallion. He had no insignia of rank. I strode to him, nodded, said pleasantly, "I am Rodrigo, your king." I held out my hand, knuckles up.

Uncertainly, he took it. Gently, I guided it to his mouth. "Your name?"

His lips touched my ring, jerked away. "K—K—Korwen. Sire."

"Your captain is . . . ?"

"Yassat." His eyes flicked to a swarthy bearded man, sitting astride his mount. In his scabbard, a sword whose haft bore nicks and gouges of extensive use.

"I should like to meet him." The man did nothing. After a moment I prompted, "Acquaint us, Korwen."

He yanked hard at his reins. His horse whinnied but followed his shambling steps. We crossed the courtyard, detouring around twenty men.

Yassat stared down at us, his eyes expressionless.

"I am King Rodrigo. You've an impressive unit. From what province are you?"

For a moment I thought he wouldn't answer. Then, "Shallowells."

"You're tough men, and hard." I looked about approvingly. "Even the Ukras would give ground. Are you bound to the Warthen directly?"

"Vassals of Lanat, his sister's son."

"Oh, good. Is Lanat among you?"

"At the gate."

"Come, let's meet him." I started on my way. "You, of course, are his principal deputy?"

To answer, he had to follow. Ill-at-ease, he swung off his mount. "Regarding the cavalry, aye."

I gave him my hand and grinned. "You can tell your children you spoke with the king."

Awkwardly, he raised hand to lips. Then, when we were nearly to Lanat, "Once, I met the queen."

"On her visit. I was the ill-mannered boy always underfoot." His visage softened to what might have been a smile. "My lord Lanat, his majesty King Rodrigo."

Lanat looked down at me with cold eyes. I said, "Marvelous. How did you train them so? They'd frighten imps in the night. You must tell my Earl Groenfil how you do it."

He regarded me.

"I should like to meet those you deem most proficient."

A long silence. "They're all proficient."

"Then I'll meet them all; form them in a line. We'll have to hurry; we sit to dinner soon. I presume you're invited."

As I held out my hand to the first of them, I glanced to the keep. On a balcony outside the great hall, my men gaped. Airily, I waved.

I CLIMBED THE steps. My arm ached from extending my fingers, but Lanat was volubly describing his cavalry's response to the occasional Ukra raid, and my elbow was twined cosily with his.

Dinner was a strange affair. All the local highborn took part, saving the Warthen. Tajik offered me head of table, which I allowed. After a while, I ceased to watch who had sampled what; dishes were passed with abandon, and much was had to drink. I watered Anavar's wine, much to his annoyance, but no more than I watered my own.

Lanat's men ate from cooktents raised in the courtyard, and my four hundred mingled among them. Groenfil had promised death to any who gave or took offense.

Afterward, we retired. Despite my precautions, Anavar's face was flushed and his gait unsteady. I guided him to his couch, helped him remove his boots.

I lay on my cushions, and moonbeams came to transport me. I climbed them, and slept.

A soft tapping. I blinked awake. Reflexively, I unsheathed my dagger.

Another tap.

I tossed off the covers, padded to the door. Two stout bars. I dropped one, nearly on my toe. Cautiously, blade in hand, I opened the door.

My guard sprawled on a bench, mouth wide, snoring. So much for Pardos and his endless vigilance. But, who had knocked?

Again the tap, behind me.

I barred the door, stumbled across the dark room, blundered across Anavar's bed.

"Whazit?"

"Sleep." Once more I let my eyes accustom themselves to dark.

The tapping came from a high wardrobe on the far wall. No, from the tapestry beside it. I yanked it aside.

A door we'd not known. Thank Lord of Nature it was barred, else I could have been stabbed in my sleep. We really must inspect our quarters more thoroughly.

I knew I ought wake my bodyguard, but I'd taken so many risks of late. Besides, if Vasur wanted me dead, he'd let pass many a chance. I lifted the bar.

A dank, dirty corridor, the sort of place you'd expect to see a forgotten skeleton snoozing on a bench. It was lit only by two fresh-placed candles in a sconce. A girl, ten or eleven, swimming in an overlarge, threadbare robe. Dark eyes stared up at me.

I realized I wore nothing but a loincloth. I retreated to my bed, wrapped myself in a blanket. "Well?"

"Come." She beckoned.

"Where?"

"Warthen."

"Oh, please." My voice dripped scorn. "Spin a finer tale than that."

She put finger to lips, beckoned again.

Perverse, I let my voice rise. "In his own castle, what secret need he keep?" It seemed to distress her; she glanced about with unease. "Tell truth, who sent you?"

She fished in her robe. I tensed, lest her small fist dart out with a sharp blade. But her fingers uncurled to show a small gewgaw. A tiny crown, cunningly made, of a metal I thought might be silver, but if it were, a scullion or bedservant would be flogged half to death for stealing anything so valuable.

"Who?"

As if by answer, she dropped it in my hand, beckoned again.

I sighed, half tempted to follow. But this wasn't statecraft, for which I had a flair. It was a personal affair, in which over and again I'd proven notoriously foolish.

And yet . . . I eyed Anavar, his mouth half open, breath snuffling. *You're an idiot, Roddy.* I threw off the blanket, slipped into my jerkin, wriggled into my leggings. *A dunce.*

Hopping into my boots, I brandished my blade. "Betray me and I'll slit your throat."

"Come." Lifting the bronze candelabra from the sconce, she padded down the hall. I had little choice: either return to bed, or follow.

An utter fool. I strode down the damp, dingy hall.

The corridor narrowed, so I had to take care not to brush against the cobwebbed walls. Twists and turns left me disoriented. I clutched my dagger, wishing I'd had the presence of mind to buckle on my sword. At any moment, a bend might hide—

She threw open a door, scuttled through. A wave of warm air, and with it, a blaze of light. I ought be cautious, but if I lost sight of her . . . I lunged into the light, blade extended. Half a dozen multipronged candelabras held two score of tapers, whose flames flickered and danced.

The girl was just disappearing through a far door.

In an ornate armchair against the far wall, by a table bearing a silver falcon, sat a gaunt, sallow man. Deep-socketed, unblinking eyes, in the shadows cast by the hood of a cinnabar robe.

We were alone in the room. I sheathed my blade. "My lord Warthen, I am Rodrigo."

His lips twitched in what might have been a smile. "I know that." His voice was deep, guttural.

"I'm glad we meet."

"Some oppose it. But a favor was begged, by a servant I hardly wish to offend."

"Whomever he is, I thank him."

His eyes widened. "You know not? Ah. I thought you and he had colluded." Again, the wave. It took in the silver falcon.

I approached, first shutting behind me the door to the dank passage. "May I?" I lifted the bird. Folded wings, a stare of challenge, each claw delineated with exquisite detail. I knew but one who could do such work. I breathed, "Jestrel? He's here?"

"Three months. He's . . . silversmith to the court. The Ukra envoy was much impressed. We cast him a boar and a hart."

I said cautiously, "Whatever Jestrel said, I urge you hear with caution. He bears no love—"

"But less enmity than you suppose. He said he paid a debt. So, let us proceed. I refuse."

"Huh?" It wasn't my finest moment.

"The levy you covet. Men. Arms. Gold. But not a chair; sit, if you wish."

This wasn't going as I'd hoped. I pulled up a lesser seat. Like all in the chamber, it was lower than his. "I am, after all, your king."

"Hriskil disputes that. And Margenthar. And lately, Bouris of Cumber." His information was dismayingly accurate.

"Do *you*?"

Vasur said, "I never swore fealty to you, Rodrigo of Stryx."

"You swore to Elena, and she named me heir."

"So it's reputed."

"I have documents, the seal—"

He held out a hand. "I won't consider them." No smile in his eyes or mouth.

"Is that why you wouldn't see me?"

"It's why I tried not. Though fate, Badir, and my silver-smith, decreed otherwise."

I said, "It's not the first time you turned me away at the Warthen's Gate."

"A convenient barrier, is it not? Stakia, late keeper of the Pass, was shortened by a head for taking Jestrel's bribe. What, I wonder, shall I do with Badir?"

"It was hardly his fault."

"It was hardly not. What demoncraft did you employ? The Still doesn't confer such Power, else you'd not be in such a plight as you are."

"There's much you don't know about me," I said. A weak parry, but I had no better. Gamely, I lurched on. "It's unseemly to deny your liege, the worse in that you haven't heard him."

"Then I am unseemly. I refuse. Make your plea."

"Caledon may fall without your aid." The realm *would* fall, with or without his aid, but I could hardly say that while there remained an iota of hope.

"But," he said, "Hriskil will not seek the Sands."

My heart sunk. "What treaty have you—"

"I need none. His soldiers are hillmen; what know they of desert war? You saw the Pass. Think you his army could force it? Pezar is more to his liking. No, he'll not risk defeat for a gain so slight."

"I offer remission of taxes—"

"I pay none."

"But you ought. A covenant of mutual aid—"

"I need it not."

"My ear as counsellor—"

"I keep my own counsel."

"Have you no honor?" My voice was hot.

Vasur ignored it. "Is there else, Rodrigo?"

I thought a long while, defeat sour on my palate. I'd foreseen his refusal, but nonetheless, I'd hoped . . . my hand strayed to my cheek. Once they'd called me handsome. I'd wear no coronet, but Tresa seemed not to care.

"I refuse that too." His voice was a harsh rasp.

"What do you say?"

"A Return."

"Why?" It was a cry of dismay. Never mind that the Warthen seemed to read my thoughts.

"Know you the cost?" In his tone, despair.

"Gold, castles, there's no limit to your—"

He threw off his hood. Hair gone white. Deep, sunken eyes, a lined face racked with pain. "How old am I?"

"I'm no judge. Sixty-five, perhaps seventy—"

"Forty-seven summers. I endure it that my people may live."

I was silent.

He said, "I measure the use of my Power, that I not enfeeble myself. And it's but a month since last wielded."

"How often . . . ?"

"Thrice a year, 'twere best." Vasur's smile was grim. "Not that my supplicants oft time their distress to mine."

I studied him curiously. "Is it your pleasure to refuse all you're asked? Twice you turned me away at the High Pass. I prayed your company to dine, and was refused. You denied me aid, and now a Return. What defect warps your soul?"

"I refused you at the Pass to protect us from your entreaties. I dined not with you because I am near prisoner of Tajik, who would deter the overuse of my Power, to safeguard the realm's profit. He'll be irked tomorrow, when he learns of our conclave, but tonight we're secure; I drugged his wine."

I gaped.

"When you appeared at my gate, my servitors wished me to fall on you like a wolf on a doe; I declined. They are most vexed. I deny you aid because it's not in my interest. I refuse a Return partly to please them. But regardless, you have not the wherewithal."

"In Stryx I have—"

"Stryx is lost to you."

"My oath, on the True—"

"Will not suffice. I require payment."

For a moment, I studied my fingers. Then, "A pity we'll disappoint your servants."

"Your pardon, Rodrigo?"

"I have the means."

"The chest you keep holds a paltry seventy coins of Caled gold. It's not the hundredth of what my service would require."

How did he know my funds? "I'll not pay in gold."

"I won't accept—"

"We are king! Thou shalt be silent!" My voice had an edge that unnerved even me. Impressed or not, he complied. I

leaned forward, made my voice more affable. "Of all our Powers, my lord Warthen, is not yours the most arcane?"

A twitch, that might have been a shrug.

"It has a . . . strength," I said. "A utility beyond that of Groenfil's winds, or Raeth's flickering candles. Even my Still cannot compare, though I rule Caledon, and you a mere duchy."

"What of it?"

"Power attends the rule of land." True, as a general principle. I would not mention Bollert's aberration.

"Of course." He awaited my ploy.

"Imagine, then, the potency of Return, were you sovereign over the Sands."

"To all intents, I am."

"But not in form."

Vasur seemed astonished. "You propose I proclaim my autonomy? That to augment my Power, I declare myself free of Caledon?"

"What good that? Powers require authority, properly vested. Could any fool don my crown and wield the Still, or slay Hriskil and raise the Rood?" Still, he seemed not to follow. "I offer what you might procure from no other. That I— Caledon— relinquish dominion over the Sands. That you be vested sovereign of your land."

THE SUN WAS well up. Yawning, I roused myself, threw off the sheet, peered about.

Anavar slept like the dead.

I padded to the door, flung it open. The guard shot to his feet. "Ah, you're awake," we said at the same instant. He gaped; I hid a smile.

I asked, "You stood watch all night?"

"Aye, sire."

"Very well, summon that surly servant who—ahh, there you are. Bread and cheese. Warm drink. First, fresh water for my basin." To the guard, "I'll meet with Groenfil anon. And with Danzik, he's earned it." My tone was cheerful.

"Aye, my lord."

I swung shut the door. "Up, you Eiberian lout." I clapped hands.

Anavar jerked convulsively, covered his ears. "Don't shout, I pray you."

"Come, me must be about. It's . . ." I peered at the hour candle. "Tenth hour. The day's half gone."

The boy tried to rise, fell back, held his head. "Oh . . ."

I was in inordinately good spirits. Dressing, I clapped hands again. "Up, laggard, or I'll cut your stipend."

"You pay no stipend; even Tanner's purse is fuller than yours. Arghh." Anavar squinted. "Might you close the shutters?"

I perched on one of his cushions. "Have I sympathy? No. I watered your wine, but I see you guzzled another bottle. Don't deny it, you suffer the effects of—"

"*Please* stop shouting. I did not. I drank what you allowed me."

I considered. "Last night, you sat near Tajik? That explains it."

Anavar groaned. "How?"

"You poured your wine from his bottle. You'll be well. It wasn't your fault."

He belched, made an unhappy face. "What's your hurry to rise?"

"The Return. I must ready myself."

That roused him. He peered. "I think not. First you have to entreat the Warthen."

"Done. Last night."

Anavar sat, hugging himself. "Sometimes, sir, a dream seems so real, you think . . ."

"In that case, we still sleep. Who knocks?" I pulled open the door. "Put it there. Warm bread, Anavar. I don't advise else."

My ward was of the age when illness was light and recovery swift; by the time I'd finished my cheese, he'd perked up considerably and soon after accompanied me to Groenfil's chamber. When Danzik had joined us I related the night's events. Anavar still looked askance. I didn't fret; time would prove what I could not.

Danzik said in his own tongue, "How long do this thing?"

I frowned; admitting a Norlander to my councils meant I was perforce the translator. "Tonight we start. Vasur warned it may take several attempts. Anavar, you'll attend me. When I emerge, I may be weak." The rest, I chose not to mention. The Warthen bore much of the pain, but not all. Some Returns failed when the suitor lost heart. But I'd borne pain and come through to the far side, though I was clammy at the thought of it.

I hoped Tresa would appreciate what I'd endure for her.

Afterward, walking back to our chamber, Anavar was silent. The moment the door was shut he whispered, "How did you persuade the Warthen? What payment?"

"I'd rather Groenfil didn't know until it's done." Not quite fair, given my promise to the earl, but I couldn't risk his disapproval. My hope of marriage rode on my quest. "I gave the Warthen what another could not."

"Tell! I dance on coals waiting."

I explained.

His gaze was doubtful. "You dismember your realm, without advice of your council?"

"What sway had I over the Sands? I conceded only what I'd already lost."

"That so, why did he accept?"

"For my acquiescence. Only with it might his Power augment."

"Will it, sir?"

"I know not. We cross into the unknown." But I would have Tresa. I was sure of it.

TAJIK'S FACE WAS impassive. "Lie you here, my lord." He indicated a bed of cushions. Across the chamber, beneath doors to a sheltered balcony, lay another.

"And Anavar? I want him near."

"It were best he wait outside. The Return costs anguish, yours and my master's. Your vassal may be alarmed."

"He'll stay. Baron, I bid you not interfere."

"The boy must be silent. The slightest sound, even a touch, may summon you home. Then, next day, the travail must be endured anew."

"I'll be still." Anavar slid out a spare cushion, settled himself beside my bed.

I asked, "What must be done?"

"You lie, as if to rest," said Tajik. "In a while, the Warthen comes. Speak not to him, before or after. He takes the draught—"

"What draught?"

"A potion to settle his mind for sleep. You know of it." An

edge to Tajik's tone, though his face showed nothing. "Direct your thoughts to where you would be sent. When he sleeps, his Power manifests. You will hear a voice within: *Whither would you go?* And where you name, you are transported. For my master's sake, I beg you, be quick, do what you must and return to us."

"I shall."

"Now, my lord, settle yourself and contemplate what you do. Only one Return may be had in all your life, but as oft as required to complete the task. Seek only the place where it may be had. Use this gift for your heart's deepest desire; all else is waste. Youngsire, when your liege awakes, he may be confused, fearful. It is often so." A short bow, as he left us.

I lay back, unbuttoned my tunic. I muttered to Anavar, "I'm *already* confused and fearful."

"Sleep, sir. I'll guard you from harm." His tone seemed an echo of Rustin's. My eyes stung. *Oh, Rust, that you were here, to see this marvel.* In an hour, perhaps a day, I'll have again my face. And with it, I'll be content to trade Caledon for Tresa. It's time I were a man. And time I not loathe myself in the silver. Of all the world, only you could gaze upon me unblinking; only you accepted my ruin. I cherished that, but I cannot live out my life so disfigured.

Across the room, a quiet rustle. Breathing, that slowly calmed.

So now I must think of Verein. Of my wretched, stinking cell, of the louse-infested straw. Of Margenthar's heartless dominance, the dance of self-abnegation he forced me to perform. Of the biting slice of his blade. Of my desperate escape. Of creeping about on Verein's parapets, gathering rope for my climb over the wall. Of Lord Rustin of the Keep, scaling the wall, heedless of his life, to save me.

Verein. The cell. Uncle Mar's knife. My hateful scar.

WHITHER WOULD YOU GO?

My fingers flew to my cheek. A sob. "A country road, three leagues from Fort."

TWENTY-NINE

A FIERY BLADE sawed my innards. I took sharp breath.

Slowly, the torment eased. I looked about.

"Be silent!" Rustin's eyes flashed steel. "We won't speak of it."

"I only meant to—"

"—to tread where you're not wanted!"

I stopped short. "At times you're hateful."

"My lord King!" A soldier rushed up, flushed of face. "The duke of Stryx." He pointed down the road. "He comes alone."

"I'll escort him." Rust strode off. "Let the hateful greet the hateful."

NO, IT MUST NOT BE! I spun the guardsman about. "A dozen men! A score! Follow and keep him safe!"

He seemed puzzled. "There's only the duke."

"This instant, or I'll have your head!" I chewed my fingers, enduring an agony of anticipation.

He rushed about, gathered a squadron, loped down the dusty road after Rustin.

What was my task? Rustin would live; I must confront Mar. Hastily, I donned my coronet. A hundred paces distant, Rust stalked to Margenthar, surrounded by the guards I'd sent. My uncle dismounted, made a short bow, tied his horse. He handed Rust his sword, submitted to his search. Rustin pointed to me, saying something lost in distance.

Margenthar strode down the road. Rust sat himself on a rock, Mar's sword in his lap, chatting with our guards.

In a few moments Uncle Mar was near. "Ahh, Roddy." An exaggerated bow. Groenfil and Soushire watched.

I bared my teeth. "What do *you* want?" I ought kill him this instant.

"What say you to my offer?"

I was in no mood to engage in polite charade. "The answer's no. I'd rather lose Caledon. Begone!"

Uncle Mar seemed unperturbed. "You may indeed lose Caledon. There are no terms on which . . . ?"

"None!"

"I bid you farewell." Again, a bow. To Groenfil and Soushire, "Enjoy your exploits with the boy king." He strode off.

As soon as he was gone, Elryc ran to me. "Roddy, he's not worth—"

"Later!" Only paces behind Margenthar, I rushed to the road, watched my uncle stride the endless hundred steps. *Warthen, I did as told. It's changed now. Let Rustin live.*

Margenthar untied his steed, bowed to Rustin, who handed him his sword. The guards, alerted by my unease, kept between them. Margenthar lingered a moment, finally mounted. To Rustin and the guards, a salute. Then in one smooth motion, he pulled loose a dagger, hurled it at Rustin's throat. Rust toppled.

"NO!" I bolted down the road. *"Not again, I can't bear it!"*

Mar spurred and was away.

Pain gripped my innards and my soul.

Clutching myself, I thrashed about. It was horrid. Sweat popped from every pore. I howled.

"Sir! Sir!" Anavar shook me, danced back, darted forward, hand to mouth. "Oh, don't!"

I clutched at him, and choked. "I failed!" I sought the balcony's wood frame, banged my head over and again. "Rust, forgive me!"

Anavar seized me, buried my head to his chest. "I beg you, sir, take ease." He rocked me, like a mother her babe. "You'll try again, that's allowed, is it not? Don't weep." He released me, ran to the door, flung it open.

He and Danzik escorted, half-carried, me to my chamber. I lay for hours, berating my folly. It was eve before my grief subsided. My stomach griped like a wound half healed. Rustin was slain, and I'd lost Tresa for naught.

Tajik appeared at our door. "In the morn, at sixth hour."

"So soon?" I swallowed. "So be it."

Anavar brought a cold compress to bathe my brow.

He was highborn, not bodyservant. I said, "That's Tanner's task."

"I don't mind."

"How not?"

"I'm your friend."

Why must I hear Rustin in all he said? I turned my face to
the wall.

MORN CAME. I made myself dress.

Not daring to break fast lest a meal congeal in my gut, I
strode to the Warthen's chamber, making my feet belie my desire. I laid on the cushions, rode a whirlwind of pain to the day
of my dread.

Three leagues from Fort, I drew Rustin aside. "Tomorrow
we'll be in Cumber. If you meet Baron Imbar . . ."

"He's in Pezar, with Raeth." Rust turned back to the trail.

"So we assume. Soon or late, your paths will cross."

Rust was calm, betrayed only by his bunched fists. "Don't
concern yourself."

I made my voice soft. "As Mar grates on me, Imbar abrades
your—"

"Be silent!" His eyes flashed steel. "We won't speak of it."

I must turn it aside! "I only meant to—"

"—to tread where you're not wanted!"

"My lord King!" A soldier rushed up, flushed of face. "The
duke of Stryx."

I snarled, "Let him wait!"

Rustin made a gesture of disgust. "If you haven't the courtesy to greet him, I do." He strode off.

"No, Rust!"

"Be silent. I order it!" Helplessly, as in a dream, I watched.

Afterward, I woke gripping Anavar, sobbing.

In time Tajik appeared, and glanced at the hour candle.
"Tonight. Vasur will recover by dusk."

"I cannot." Nor could I meet his eye. "It is done."

"No, Rodrigo!" Anavar fell to a knee, shook me. "You
don't mean this!"

"Do I not?"

"Not, my lord, if you would live with yourself."

I put head in hands. A long time passed. "All right." My
voice was barely heard. "Dusk."

Groenfil begged audience, in my chamber. I sat on my bed.
He regarded me. A grim smile. "I hope what you seek is
worth the cost."

Had someone told him I'd ceded the Sands? Surely not, else he'd not look so benign. "Know you what I seek?"

"Anavar told me: Rustin." Awkwardly, he stooped, patted my knee. "You could ask for no better."

I braced myself. "Has he revealed the price?"

"He refused. I presume it's appalling."

I told him.

Groenfil opened the shutters, stared across the courtyard. For a moment, a breeze swirled sand. Then, "Clever. But Elena would be not pleased."

"And your displeasure, sir?"

"Relations among vassal and liege are for you to settle. I have not the say of it. Let us speak of things more pressing. Have you seen your face?"

My hand flew to my scar. "I know what I lose—"

"You look ghastly. Can you bear more?"

I said bravely, "What choice have I?" Inwardly, I shuddered.

As night fell, I lay on the hateful cushions. Anavar fretted on his seat, picking at his knuckles. The door opened slowly; two servants helped Vasur to the bed. He was half doubled over. His breath was ragged. They gave him a flagon; he threw back his head and swallowed. For an instant, haunted eyes met mine.

I DREW RUSTIN aside. "Tomorrow we'll be in Cumber. If you meet Baron Imbar . . ."

"He's in Pezar, with Raeth." Rust turned back to the trail.

"So we assume. Soon or late, your paths will cross."

Rustin was calm, betrayed only by his bunched fists. "Don't concern yourself."

"Yes, sir. I won't. I'm sorry."

He raised an eyebrow, nodded with grudging approval. "No doubt you mean well."

"Rust . . ." I had to hurry. "Would you do me a great favor?" I hesitated. "Elryc is peeved, and I know not why. You know my tongue; if I ask, I'll only make it worse. Would you be my envoy?"

He sighed. "How did you irk him?"

"Truly, I know not."

"If I must," he said. "Tonight."

"I'll need Elryc's counsel. Might it be now? Please?" My tone was meek.

Rust studied me. "What's come over you?" For an instant, his fingers flitted to my hair. Then, "As you wish, my prince."

No sooner had he disappeared from sight than a soldier rushed up, flushed of face. "My lord King! The duke of Stryx." He pointed down the road. "He comes alone."

"Require that he surrender sword and dagger, and bring him on foot. Then assemble a guard of ten to escort him afterward to his mount."

"Aye, sire." The guard wiped his brow, hurried off.

Uncle Mar was brought to us. Groenfil and Soushire watched one and the other of us, spectators at a joust. Elryc peered from behind a wagon. Imps and demons; what if Rustin came upon him? He'd be outraged I hadn't summoned him to the meet with Uncle Mar. Might he have harsh words and then—Lord of Nature forbid—stalk off down the road?

Beside myself, I played our scene, hearing not what I said. No, I would not have Mar's thousand men, were Caledon itself to fall. Yes, I was certain. My regent, Lord Rustin? Occupied. He conveys his regrets. Was there else, my lord Duke? If not, we must be off to Cumber.

Mar seemed disposed to linger. He made small talk, no doubt precisely because it maddened me. To be rid of him, I did the same, even offering to send for elderberry wine, which I knew he hated.

At last, the longed-for words. "I bid you farewell."

Seething with hatred, I bowed. One must observe the forms.

He bowed to Groenfil and Soushire. "My lady, my lord. Enjoy your exploits with the boy king. Roddy, tell Lord Rustin I missed his sage counsel." He strode off. The guards fell in alongside.

The moment they were out of sight I whirled, beckoned Elryc. "Where's Rust?"

"Whatever did you mean, we quarreled? Other than how you spoke to Genard—"

"WHERE IS HE?"

"He's irked. Roddy, he's regent, and you convened with Mar without so much as—don't shake me! He said he'd bid Uncle Mar adieu. He's down the road, with—where are you going?"

I tore off my cloak, pitched it with my coronet at Groenfil as I galloped past. "Rust!"

The guards were nearly at the sapling to which Mar's steed was tied.

Where Rustin waited, arms folded.

"RUSTIN!" My bellow tore still air.

He spun.

Mar's hand slipped into a saddlebag.

"It's Orwal! He's hurt!" For my life, I could think of no other that would draw him.

Mar's hand whipped out. Rustin bolted down the road, my uncle forgotten. Mar stood frozen. Rust's legs pumped. I raced toward him. He called, "Where is he? Who did—"

I threw myself into his arms, knocking us both into tall grass. I wrapped myself around him. "You live! Lord of Nature be praised! Warthen, thank—"

Down the road, Margenthar swung into his saddle. Without a hindward look, he cantered off.

"Unhand me, you dolt!" Rust's words were muffled in my embrace. "What of the horse?"

"I made it up, Orwal's fine, you live, you live!" My babble mixed with sobs. *"You live!"*

"ARE YOU UNHINGED?" His voice was hot.

"You don't understand, I—"

A dagger twisted in my guts. Mist obscured my sight. White hot agony cleft me in twain. I wailed.

Even this, Rust. For you.

IN THE WARTHEN'S stronghold, Rustin scowled from over my bed. "You're well served, for eating like a pig."

I groaned, clutching my stomach. Behind my eyes, a dreadful ache that swelled and fell. I swallowed, hoping not to spew bile.

"Moderation at a banquet, Roddy."

Another word and I'd scream. "Yes, sir. Let me rest, I pray you."

"Very well. Come, Anavar, we'll see Sandhelm."

"Let me stay, 'til he sleeps."

"You'll find me on the street past the wineseller's. They say that silversmith's set up shop in Sandhelm."

"I'll be along, my lord."

When the door shut, Anavar's eyes met mine.

I said, "He doesn't know. Do you?"

Anavar had a faraway look. "As in a dream. Rustin didn't save us in the Southron Hills, ride with us through the High Pass. Or am I . . . No. It must be so. You bought a Return?"

In my throat, a lump. "You don't recall? You sat with me while I—" A spasm made me yearn to die. I turned away my face. When I could speak I said, "If not for you, he'd be forever gone."

Anavar was pensive. "Did I . . . urge on you another attempt?"

I nodded.

"Ah!" He fair leaped from the bed. "The memory is moored to my mind. But, Rodrigo . . ." His features screwed in puzzlement. "The other is true as well. Rustin *didn't* die. He rode with us to Cumber. When you were so . . . pardon, sir—clumsy with Tresa, he set you straight, delivered your apology so you left friends. Is it not so?"

Dismayed, I nodded.

"In Pezar, he held Raeth while he died. And that night you had the wild notion of sending envoy to Hriskil—it was he who forbade it. After, when you yourself would go—*Oh*!" He rested head in hands. "But I recall your grace. Surely that can't be gone."

"Stand away!" I retched into a basin. Weakly, I wiped my mouth. "Is this the Return, or too much roast pig? If Rust's alive, I had no need of a Return."

"Both can't be true!"

"Both are." I gripped his arm. "Anavar, Rust's with me again! What else matters?"

"He shares your tent." The boy's voice was quiet. "As always."

"Anavar . . . in the other life, so much misery, such awful pain . . . it's gone now. I have him."

"Yes." Anavar's eyes were bleak.

"Does it trouble you? You and I never—well, in our dream we drew closer, did we not? But now . . ."

He said firmly, "Now, all is as before." He stood. "Have I leave, my lord? You should rest."

*   *   *

ILL AT EASE and self-conscious, I made ready for bed.

Rustin paced idly. "Groenfil's thoughts are troubled. He looks at me strangely." A pause. "For that matter, so do Danzik and Pardos." He shot me a sidewise look. "Have you brought them complaint?"

"No. No, sir." My speech was well in hand, as it had been for months. Rust was a hard taskmaster, but I'd grown used to it.

Later, the candles doused, he lounged on the pillows. "So, my prince. We came to Sandhelm, and are spurned. No aid, no soldiers, not even sight of the Warthen. What now?"

"We go back."

"To what? Hriskil wanders Caledon unopposed. We can't retake Stryx. How long will Groenfil and Soushire hold out?"

"Not long."

Rustin ruffled my hair as if I were a boy. "Ah, my love. I wanted so to see you restored." His voice was sad. "Ironic, is it not? Once we whispered of a Return to erase the blemish that troubles you so. But we've no gold for the purchase."

Carefully, I breathed, in and out. In. Out. "I need no Return, sir." How might a voice be so careless, when one's heart was cleft?

I lay awake into the night.

"IT IS EVER thus." Tajik leaned forward to adjust his sandal. "He alone will not know." Behind him, Danzik stood at the door, arms folded.

"But . . ." I scratched my head. "Which is real?"

"He lives; all that follows from it is real. But you are what made you. What you recall is part of that." A shrug. "The Powers are mystery."

I needed no platitudes. "Can the event be explained to him?"

"Always, their minds struggle to surround it. I say 'always'; my lord has brought many to life. It is perhaps the most desired Return."

"And what other?"

"Lost love." Tajik glanced past the balcony at the sun, past midday. "Is there else?"

"If *you* bought a Return, what would move you?"

He seemed startled. "A dead child, I think. I can imagine no else."

"So, then." My voice was casual. "What would you swear on, Tajik? What binds your soul?"

"My oath is—"

"Of course. But on what sworn?"

He stared a moment, as if puzzling me out. Then, "In the Sands, oaths given on a father's life are beyond sacred. Men go mad who break them." He rose. "I must—"

"Not yet." I leaned forward. "You know my payment?"

"Renunciation. In secret, it was given."

"I'm no longer Vasur's liege, yet would do him one favor."

"What is that, my lord?"

"Rid him of you."

Tajik backed to the door, nearly ran into Danzik. "If I shout—"

"Your neck would be wrenched in an instant. Danzik's strength is formidable."

Tajik's eyes darted between us. He licked his lips. "What would you of me?"

"Your oath that henceforth you serve Vasur, not the Sands."

"They're one and the—"

"They are not!" I stood. "What cajolements you use, with what silken threads you bind him, I care not. It will cease, if you would leave this room alive."

For an instant Tajik debated. He even drew sharp breath, to cry out. But he was a realist; in a moment, he slumped. "Why do you this?"

"For his pain."

Tajik's eyes sought mine. "Know you that I love him?"

"Yes. And so you'll serve him."

Living under the sword of the True, I knew of oaths. And so, I well and truly bound him. Afterward, Danzik threw open the door.

AN HONOR GUARD of Lanat's hundreds escorted us to the pass. At least, I hoped it was so; perhaps Vasur wanted to assure we took no excursions through his realm.

On the long ride from Sandhelm, Groenfil found us a moment alone. "When will you tell Rustin?"

"Ask not when, but if."

He looked about, kept his voice low. "Roddy, I recall well what was. Do you?"

I nodded. "In every detail."

"Now you're . . . altered." Groenfil's tone was uneasy. "Well-behaved, I'll grant; Rustin's done well in that. But so much you did is . . . lost."

It was so. Under Rust's guidance I hadn't ridden to tweak Hriskil in his camp, hadn't jumped from the wall to save Danzik; Rust himself had quelled the rush to harm him. I hadn't spoken the names of Eiber's dead churls. I hadn't . . . I said firmly, "I mourn none of it. Until he died, I knew not how I loved him. Now I know."

"But—"

"No 'but', my lord Earl. I am content."

And I was. Caledon was still lost to us; in that, even Rust could do no better than I. But he eased my soul. For months I'd not lacked companionship, or warm heartbeat in the night. Now and then, I expected him to seek comfort in my limbs, as of old. Yet, he did not. Perhaps some memory of my vanished solitude crept into my mien or speech. Occasional affection was all he allowed himself, and I was too relieved to inquire the cause. Now, as before his death, I bathed when he asked, donned clean clothes, spoke kindly to servants and men. So what if I'd taken all that on myself in our other life, and by and large succeeded? I knew I'd done so, even if he did not. Soon or late I would be a man. For now, I'd be the boy Rustin knew.

Groenfil asked, "How could you not tell him?"

"I am content," I said again. Then, "Did you try?"

"Aye. It was as if I spoke our own tongue to Danzik. Rustin stared uncomprehending, then left me."

At the Warthen's Gate, we were greeted with generosity. Badir opened his stables to our mounts, made sure men and beasts were fed and watered before sending us on our way. Anavar had charge of my servant Bollert, keeping him well among our own, and if possible out of Badir's sight.

We passed through the gate at the walk, in single file. For a show, I wore my coronet, though Rust didn't really approve. But I'd recalled the art of coaxing what I wished from his generous nature, and he seemed content.

During our expedition to the Sands, Hriskil's lieutenant Sara-

zon had taken to the hills in force, and now blocked our path to
Soushire. Making camp, we conferred, Rustin, Groenfil and I.
The Southron hills ranged far and wild; we might evade the
Norlanders for long. Rust seemed to favor it, though Groenfil
clearly yearned for his imperiled domain. Not as much, though,
as I yearned for Stryx. But every castle of the land was barred
to us. Sarazon was between us and Stryx; Groenfil Castle was
under Hriskil's siege. The Norlanders held Cumber, and
Verein . . . I snorted. I retrieved a stick from the edge of the fire,
waved the smoldering end to write in air with the glow.

"Supplies," said Groenfil, "are the key. If but one domain
were open to us . . ."

"If wishes were horses . . ." Rust glanced at me, frowned.
"You'll cause hurt, my prince." Gently, but firmly, he pried the
stick from my hands, broke it, tossed it in the flames. My
cheeks reddened at the nonchalance with which he made me
a babe. I sighed. Had it not always been so?

"Castle Stryx is not yet fallen," said Groenfil. "If we evaded
Sarazon and gained entry . . ."

"We're too few. We decided that long past. There's
nowhere."

"Verein." I cleared my throat, said it more loudly. "We
strike for Verein."

Rust blinked. "Why, Roddy?"

"Uncle Mar's left it; he's twixt Pezar and Cumber dodging
Hriskil."

"We don't know surely—"

I said, "He *was*, at any rate. And to oppose us, he stripped
Verein's walls." I looked up. "Well, he *must* have, Rust. What
other men had he?"

"What good Verein without Mar? You can't take vengeance
on stone."

Annoyed, I climbed to my feet. "Verein is refuge, not
vengeance. It offers supplies, a roof, lands Norlanders don't
yet roam. A defensible base." I looked from one to the other
of them. "Are we not better there, than—" I gestured at our
meager camp. "—here?"

Their eyes met. Groenfil nodded. "Agreed? I'll send out our
scouts." He strode off.

After a time Rustin sat alongside, folding his legs under
him. "Well spoken, Roddy." He patted my knee. "But were it

not best that you broached ideas first with me? Am I not still regent?"

"Yes, sir." Immediately I was contrite. "I beg pardon."

"Thank you." He toyed with a burning stick, until he saw my eyes on him. He flushed, threw it aside. "There's more I would speak of with thee."

"What did I do?" I sounded anxious, and was. Since Sandhelm, I'd tried so to please him.

"I charge you with no fault." A pause, while Rustin seemed to gather his courage. "If we're friends—are we?" His voice caught.

"Yes!"

"Then hide not matters of import. I pray—I beg thee." For a moment he turned away. Then, with resolve, "Since the day we rode from Sandhelm . . . I know not what it is. Anavar sulks. Pardos looks at me as if a demon rides my shoulder, and he would break and run. Your mood is changed, my prince, though manfully you conceal it. Groenfil mumbled once about a Return, words that made no sense. Is it . . ." He swallowed. "Have I failed you as regent? Would you overthrow me? Because if so, no need, gladly I'll give up . . ." His eyes glistened. "For your frien—friendship—I'll—"

I seized his shoulders. "No, Rustin, it's not that, I swear it! You're regent of Caledon. You're guardian of my soul. I wish it ever so!"

His fingers crept atop mine. "Speak of it, then."

"In Sandhelm . . ." Why did my throat lock away the words? "In Sandhelm, Rust, a Return was had." Groenfil ambled toward the campfire, urgently I waved him elsewhere. "I underwent the rite."

Rust bristled. "Without my consent? Am I regent or no?" After a moment, "To what end?"

"Do you recall that day, months back, when we rode through Fort and on toward Cumber . . . ?"

"One day of many sewn together. Dust, flies, griping men."

I prompted, "I told you Orwal was hurt."

Pondering, he tapped knuckles to teeth. "You met with Mar in secret and afterward came screaming down the road like a drunken child, before I could do him the courtesies."

"Aye, *that* day."

"Orwal was unharmed. You leaped on me prancing and gibbering like a loon. I slapped you."

"Yes." I could smile now, at the recall.

"What of it?"

"You di—d—died." The shadow of anguish engulfed me.

"Roddy, my love, what fancy is this? Look at me!" He pinched himself. "Is this not flesh?"

"Yes."

"Why spread such caprice? You muddle even Groenfil's thoughts."

My fingers clasped his forearm. "Rust, had you no . . . dream, perhaps? Of dying that day?"

"None I recall."

"That we had words?"

"No."

"That Uncle Mar lunged—"

For an instant his eyes narrowed. "Ahh, did I tell you of it? An imp in the night. Next morn, I thought no more of it."

"It's true. Mar struck you dead."

"You're daft."

"No, he's not." Behind us, a defiant voice. Anavar.

Rust said, without looking, "Get thee gone, youngsire. This solely concerns the king and me."

"Roddy, he'll never believe you. Let me—"

"Baron, you try my patience." Rust's even tone belied the menace in his eyes.

I said, "Sir, I pray you, let him sit. He would tell you what we both know."

"That I'm dead? How can it be?" Rust got to his feet. "I'll hear no more of it! Control your fears, the both of you, lest you unsettle the camp." His departing nod to Anavar was less than cordial.

"My lord . . . ?"

"Oh, sit, Anavar." I hugged my knees. "Sometimes we seem in a maze without exit."

"You *were* king without regent. He *was* buried in Cumber."

"Yes, but . . ." I brooded. "How oft have you seen me weep since that day?"

"Not once. Oh, about the Norland wagon outside Pezar, but other than then . . ."

I twisted my jerkin, bared my shoulder. "Look."

"There's nothing to see." Anavar knotted his brow. "Oh! No scar from the arrow!"

"I'm better off with Rust. And it's best we let the matter drop."

"If you say." He seemed doubtful.

"And put down that flaming stick, you'll cause hurt."

THIRTY

FOR SAFETY WE avoided the main roads, which slowed us. Nonetheless, at day's end we threaded our way through the heavy wood that marked the eastern border of Verein. As we walked our steeds, Rustin asked, "Do you propose we mount a siege?"

I smiled. "No." The very idea was preposterous: a band of cavalry dragging behind them catapults, towers, the accoutrements to storm a well-defended keep?

"What then?"

My tone was cool. "Why, I'll ride to the gate and demand entry."

He snorted. "That would be like you. I'll pull out the arrows, after." He guided his Orwal around a clump of nettles. "I doubt Mar's folk will be as amiable as Badir." Rustin had smooth-talked the Warthen's envoy into opening the High Pass, making possible our late unsuccessful mission to the Sands.

I said, "We'll see. I doubt they'll have men to oppose us."

"It won't take many. Horses don't climb walls."

"But you did." For a moment, behind closed eyes, I recalled our exploit, a year past. At Verein Rustin had swarmed up a rope to search for me, just as I searched for a way down. He'd taken me, wounded, home to Cumber.

Rust pursed his lips. "In the tent last night, we didn't speak of that nonsense by the campfire." He matched Orwal's pace to mine. "What means *modru*?"

" 'Killed.' You've been speaking to Danzik?"

"Margenthar vos modru." His lips moved, piecing it out. "Even your Norlander thinks it's so. You've bewitched them all."

"I'm sorry, Rust. I shouldn't have."

He stared a while at his pommel. Then, "You're an inept liar. It's what I like about you."

"Above all?"

"No." His tone was despondent. "Please don't tease just

now." He flicked away a fly. His voice was so soft I barely heard. "If I'm dead, what am I?"

"You're as alive as I."

"But was I always?"

"Who's to say what dreams—"

"Don't, Roddy."

I despaired of truth. How could I help him underst— I caught breath. "Tonight, if you'll give me your trust." Relief made me weak. "Besides, we need make camp. We must approach Verein's wall before first light."

"Why?"

"It will unsettle them more." I urged Ebon along, contemplating my intent.

A league from Verein, well before dusk, we camped in a wooded valley.

In our shabby, frayed tent, I sat cross-legged on the floor. Rustin watched, apprehensive, from the cushioned straw. I uncorked the ewer, brought forth the bowl.

He licked his lips. "How will you—"

"Shush. I know the way of it."

"You tortured Jestrel, 'til I forced an end." He chewed his lip. "Genard, that day you made him dance. Tanner too. The cruelty of your Power—"

I studied his face. Then, with a sigh, "Fear not." I thrust home the cork, rewrapped the ewer in its soft cloth.

He hauled me close, shook me hard. *"You call me coward?"*

"No, sir."

At length he let go my tunic, smoothed the fabric, gave me an absent pat. "You ought. Look at me." His eyes were troubled.

I settled myself at his feet, my back toward him, and placed his hands on my shoulders. "Regret nothing, my lord. As I do not."

For a long while Rustin kneaded my shoulders. Then, at last, "Get it done."

"You're sure?"

"As ever I will be."

I poured the stillsilver, leaned back against the centerpole, spread my palms over the bowl. My lips moved.

When Genard danced, I'd moved him by my will. When I'd sweated truth from Tanner, the same. And so with Jestrel. No doubt it was how Mother had bound Tantroth, and Vasur the Warthen. I'd forced Genard and my servant boys, but in this summoning, I must be tender. And I must not only read thoughts, but create them, that Rust see the past as I do. Had I Power to achieve so much?

Rustin sat before me, a calm block of fear. Gently, so gently, hands tight over the stillsilver, I stroked him. His eyes shot open in surprise. I paid no heed.

How to do this?

I must not invade him. Instead I would present him my sight, my hallowed memory. I dredged up my recall, smoothed it. That dank day, three leagues from Fort. Rustin's ire, and my own. "Let the hateful greet the hateful!" Rust drew sharp breath. *No matter, Rust. It's over and done.* Mar's sneering conclave. My refusal.

"Roddy, stop!" From great distance, a plea.

I cherish thee, guardian of my soul.

My uncle strode down the road. Idly, I watched. Rustin bestirred himself on his distant rock.

"I remember that, but—"

Mar neared.

"Where are the guards you surrounded him with?"

At the rock, Rust handed Mar his sword.

Poring over stillsilver, I whimpered.

On the bed, Rustin cried, "Whatever it is, don't show me!"

Mar plunged the sword through Rust's throat.

My world ended.

Blood-drenched, I reeled in torment.

From the bed, a howl. "Oh, stop! If you love me, I beg you, don't—"

I am thine, my lord, now and forever. I sent it to him and made it soothe. But I must persevere, that he know.

I sat dazed in my royal tent, toying with my blade upon my skin, drawing fine droplets of blood.

From the cushions, a cry.

I bent, rocking, to my stillsilver.

Anavar, Elryc, Tresa, all tried to coax me from my breeks stained with Rustin's blood.

In Cumber's courtyard, the mound of earth. Desolation, then and forever after.

"No, Roddy, be it not so!"

It is not so, my friend of life. I could not bear it.

"But to use your only Return! Your scar, Tresa, your marriage . . ."

I'll pay a whore, or wear a sack on my head. What value fucking, if it costs me you?

From the bed, such anguish as I'd never conceived. I stroked it, tried to draw it off, failed.

"I can't—no more—I beg you, King!"

That's the worst. There's only . . .

Cumber, Uncle Raeth. The wagon at Pezar. Danzik and vade. The dreadful victory, my penance in the surgeons' tent. My wound that festered. The loneliness I couldn't bear.

Rustin lay, eyes closed, knees drawn up. Inwardly I spoke, had no response. I bathed him in a loving light, sustained it as long as I might. Slowly, with my strength, it faded.

Presently, I became aware of the dingy tent, the feeble flickering tapers, the drawn still figure on the bed.

I unclenched my aching palms, rubbed the indent from the hard-edged bowl.

I dried my cheeks on my sleeve. Carefully I poured the stillsilver into its ewer, carefully replaced the cork. "Rustin . . ."

His voice was muffled. "I pray thee, leave me."

I struggled to my feet, weak as a cub. "I'll go walk—"

" 'Til morn. Let me see only myself. I beg it."

I stumbled into the night.

ALL WAS STILL. The campfires burned low, except for one. I drifted toward it. Danzik was seated on the trunk of a fallen tree, occasionally feeding the fire a bone-dry branch from a pile he'd assembled. Wordlessly, I slumped alongside.

"Rood is simpler," he said presently, in his own tongue. "Hriskil carry, enemy go this way and that. Confuse."

I glanced at the tent. "You heard?"

"Hear him cry out like silversmith at Pezar. You hurt?"

"More than I meant." I brooded.

"He blood-friend?"

"Beyond." Did all Power bring misery on the wielder? "Danzik, when Hriskil uses the Rood . . ." Haltingly, I translated my question.

"Not pain like Warthen, but . . ." He pantomimed great weariness. "Every time, even when only one."

"Only one what?"

"Person he use against." Seeing my incomprehension, he added, "Like Llewelyn."

I jerked up straight. "The Rood brought Llewelyn to his camp?" Rustin's shame was deepened, not knowing why his father, householder of Stryx, betrayed his Keep to Tantroth of Eiber. A moment afterward, I realized I must have mistranslated; Llewelyn had surrendered our Keep months before the Norlanders took Eiber.

"No," I said, "Hriskil must be near to wield the Rood. It was in Stryx that Llewelyn proved himself traitor."

A sly smile widened to a grin. It threatened to consume his face, beard and all. "You never knew."

I waited, but Danzik played at keeping his secret. In sudden fury, I lurched to my feet, stumbled off to find Anavar's tent.

"Hriskil went to Stryx."

It caught me, like a baited hook a pike.

Danzik reeled me in. "Seven men. In trade ship. *Coura*." Brave. "Why Caledi will never beat Norl."

I half-fell on the rotting log. "Hriskil sailed to Stryx? In secret? To suborn Llewelyn?"

"With Rood. No harm tell now; he win Caledon."

"But, why?" We hadn't been at war; it was near a year before the Norland invasion.

"By taking Keep," Danzik said in his own tongue, "Tantroth could attack Stryx."

"And?"

"Then Tantroth army was not in Eiber." How, with most ease, might Hriskil clear his way to Cumber? By luring Tantroth to Caledon, leaving Eiber scarce defended.

Danzik said more, but I staggered into the dark, my mind awhirl. Daylight would be time enough to weigh Hriskil's vile cunning.

I was king of Caledon, or what was left of it, and had not a place to rest my head. Muttering foul imprecations, I stalked past Danzik's campfire. I'd sleep under stars, near Ebon. In the morning I'd be stiff and sore. So be it. I paced the camp, to tire myself for sleep.

I passed my tent. Within, a sound I hoped never to hear again. I stopped dead.

It won't do, Roddy. He made you what you are. You can't leave him so. I stared into the night. Slowly, I eased myself to the ground.

A long while I thought, before I stirred.

A solution was at hand.

For a moment I hesitated, fearful. *Be not afraid,* I told myself. *It's no more than you want.*

"Rust?" I pushed open the flap. "For the pain I caused thee, I beg pardon."

His eyes were bloodshot. "Away, or I'll pitch you out."

"I'm sorry, but, no, sir." I squatted by his side. "Why is it one or the other of us must be miserable?"

He raised his head. "We're star-crossed. What do you want?"

"Why do you weep?"

"For what I cannot have."

"Me?"

A nod.

"I am yours."

"You are made for marriage, my prince, and a woman's sweet loins."

"But I—"

He raised a hand. "And if you can't have that, it's because you think yourself ugly, yet squandered your Return on me. I'd gain happiness from your misery. That, I cannot abide."

"I have a solution." My heart thudded as I pawed through my saddlebag. "Rouse yourself and help."

"How?"

"Knot the flaps. Tightly."

"Why?"

"Do as I ask." My false calm moved him; he strung the upper and lower cords, knotted them well. I pulled out the ragged cloth I sought, threw aside the saddlebag. Slowly I unwrapped the content. "Light another candle, Rust."

He did.

Staring fixedly at his eyes, I rolled the wizened white lump in my hand, opened my mouth.

Bewildered, he watched. Of a sudden, he cried out in horror, struck the dried fruit from my hands.

Doggedly, I scrambled to retrieve it.

"No, Roddy! Never like that! Do you think I'd have it so?"

I could bare speak, from deliverance or loss. "Sir, I am content." In a way, it was so. Without Tresa, Rustin was all I might love.

"Lunatic! Imbecile!" His tears dampened my cheeks. "Dimwit!"

I could scarce breathe. Wriggling, I eased the vise of his arms. "May I stay, sir?"

A nod, all he could manage. With great care, he rewrapped the White Fruit of Chorr.

I crawled under the covers.

Determinedly, I closed my eyes, wondering what choice I'd made.

WE ROSE BY moonlight. I glanced at Rust, blushing, but he wasn't the whole cause; after he'd slipped into a doze, I lay awake, contemplating the enormity of the gift he'd declined, and ashamed of my relief.

Throughout the camp, silent men stowed their gear, tightened cinches, set bridles and stirrups. Bollert brought Ebon and Orwal saddled and ready to mount, a blessing indeed.

"You're serious?" Groenfil's distaste was evident.

"Yes, my lord." I met his stern gaze.

"Rustin, stop him. You've sway over our wayward liege."

"Not when the moon is full." Rust hesitated. "Roddy, you're sure?"

"Yes, but I give you all leave. None but I need take part."

"Ah, now, that's why you made me regent. I countermand you. None have leave; all ride, by our order."

And so we made our way through darkened fields, across a winding road, to a gully I remembered well. Idly, I rubbed my thigh, where the shaft had sunk.

At the walk, we came out of the gully, four hundred ghosts of the night. Hooves muffled, we took our places before the battlement of Verein. Motionless, we waited in silence astride our mounts.

We'd timed it well; within half an hour the eastern sky kindled first light. Not long thereafter, a lethargic guard glanced over the parapet. His yell shattered the night. In moments, a dozen faces peered.

Shouts. A horn, blowing call to arms. Disarray. Someone

thought of fire arrows, but by then there was no need; nascent day brightened the field. Five rows deep, eighty wide, the remnant army of Caledon stood as mounted statues before the wall. I sat in the front row, coronet on my brow. To my left, Earl Groenfil, to my right, Rustin.

Baron Stire, Uncle Mar's chief lieutenant, shouted, "Would you be shot through?"

Rising in the saddle, I spoke not to him, but to all. "Hear the king! The time for civility is past. I will have Verein this day. Open the gate this moment, or I swear by the Still of Caledon I wield, that when my army—" I glanced over my shoulder, to the distant gully—"reaches this wall, all within shall be slaughtered without quarter! Every man, woman and child, every highborn, every servant. Every master, every man. Pikeman, cook, scullion, bawd, ritemaster, stableboy, cooper, leatherer, reeve. All, without exception!"

"What army? You bluff."

"I bring pikemen, archers, swordsmen. I swear by the True."

"Show us—"

"Tanner!"

The boy jumped off his mare, cast himself at my feet.

"The candle."

A tiny tallow, a quarter hour's measure, its base melted to a plate. He set it on the ground, struck flint to it over and again until the wick caught.

From the parapet, Stire watched, uneasy.

My voice rang. "You have until the candle gutters."

Stire's tone was a sneer. "Isn't that Groenfil beside you? Will his sister's death move him? She's Mar's wife, you know."

"You'll know not, nor any other on the wall. You will be first dead."

"Show us your army!" Stire made a show of peering past me.

"I shall." I paused. "In the quarter hour."

Perhaps, if they'd had the men to make a fight of it, the baron could have rallied them. But as I'd guessed, in a bold gamble Uncle Mar had stripped his walls. From within the battlements we could hear murmurs of protest that grew to outright challenge. Well before the candle was but a nub, Stire poked his head past an arrowguard. "If we open?"

"Verein is mine."

"And our lives?"

"None will die by our hand."

"Give us leave to ride to—"

"Look! The candle gutters!" It didn't, not quite yet.

"Just a mome—"

Below him, the gate flew open. A dozen men ran out, fell at my feet. "Mercy, lord King!"

My eyes met Groenfil's.

He gave me, from the saddle, a short bow of acknowledgment. In his gaze, respect, a hint of humor. "Shall I summon your army?"

"Take the castle. I'll send Bollert."

As the sun rose, I watched from the parapet the bustle of our occupation. We housed Stire in the cells where I'd fretted my days; his venom equaled Uncle Mar's, and he couldn't be left loose. For the moment, we'd disarmed Verein's few soldiers, though they were free to move about. Rust and Groenfil would sort them out. Our own men, dressed in Mar's colors, took the guardposts, letting none leave. The longer Hriskil had no word of my refuge, the better.

Summoned by Bollert, our "army" of two horsemen, two archers, and two sword-armed foot soldiers trudged across the field and into the gate; my oath had been True, if barely so.

On the Keep's front stair Danzik sat whittling a stick. As I passed, he inclined his head in a short bow, in the Caled manner. "Rez Caledi haut coura." *The king is brave.* He drew his hands apart mimicking a stretched bow.

I shrugged. "You, too, rode with us."

"Yes. Be not so brave next time." A grin. "Toda vestrez coa tern." *I would still see how it ends.*

A SMALL FORCE like ours might slip through the wood and fields. Hriskil's army, or Sarazon's, by its sheer mass would make itself known. Our scouts roamed as far as Seacross Road, sniffing for an approaching foe.

Two days passed, and another. We ought, I knew, be out harassing Norland patrols, making our pinpricks felt where we might. But, truth to tell, I, like all our band, reveled in the luxury of a defensible encampment with foodstuffs, dry roofs not of canvas, wells instead of brackish ponds. Quickly, men and horses lost their lean and hungry look, as Verein's larder emptied.

Lady Varess, sister to the earl of Groenfil, trod a narrow and difficult path. Married to my hated uncle Margenthar, her loyalty must be to him. If she knew the zeal with which Groenfil had curbed my wrath, making sure it extended no further than Uncle Mar himself, she gave no sign.

At least one travail I was spared: my cousin Bayard was out making mischief with his father. Eighteen and haughty, he'd been the bane of my childhood. To rub shoulders with him in Verein would have been insufferable. To my joy, we discovered a trunk of his outgrown clothing, which I loftily confiscated. Once again, I had suitable wardrobe. His father, though oft cold and a demanding parent, had denied him little.

"Why so pensive, my prince?" Rustin came up behind me. As Verein's abundance had relaxed tight muscles and unknotted sinews, his eyes seemed less haunted. I'd done my part, feeding him tidbits, deferring to him in matters of state, permitting him to command my person without cavil.

Clapping his hand on my shoulder, he followed my gaze out the donjon window to the listless grass of the sunbaked fields. He asked, "Where would you be in a month's time? Could we buy a wish, what would be yours?"

"Stryx." His puzzlement showed it wasn't enough. I added, "When we captured Danzik, we relieved the castle for a winter and thaw. If we could evict Sarazon too . . ."

Rust curled hands behind his neck. "Danzik lived off the land. Sarazon's force is larger, well supplied, and the harbor's full of his ships."

"I know."

"Well, I'll think on it. Tonight at dinner, assuage Groenfil as best you may. His thoughts turn ever more homeward. And wear that green velour. It shows your color to advantage."

I was no child; why did he treat—Firmly, I bit it off. Had I swallowed the fruit, my adoration would have no bounds, and gladly I'd endorse his every whim. Let him choose my garments, and I'd count myself fortunate for the trunk.

I'd spent too much time in Uncle Raeth's company to have the simple tastes of a soldier: meat, bread, cheese. Dinner was

to be roast ox, garnished with greens lightly breaded and fried
in oil. My mouth watered. Kitchen boys hauled in the meat on
a great wooden trencher built across carrying poles and set it
before us, where I could fill the first plate. Expectantly, the
table waited. Anavar, seated toward the foot, stared at the ox
in rapture.

Before I could spear a portion, a guard raced into the great
hall. "Riders cross the field, my lords!"

"How many?" Rust's shoulders tensed.

"Perhaps two score, no more."

Not Hriskil, then. I let myself exhale. "Mar's stragglers."
My heart thumped.

Lady Varess shot to her feet.

"No, stay, Madam." My voice was curt. I opened my mouth
to give order, remembered in time to turn to Rustin. "Have I
leave, sir?" My tone was courteous.

"Continue." He watched, a worried look on his face, ready
to veto my edict.

To the guardsman, "Make haste, assemble our men. Overwhelming strength, but concealed in the courtyard. Open
when the riders ask it, close the gate after. Disarm them all."
To Rustin, when the guard hurried out, "At least we'll find
where Mar's gone."

"If they're loyal, they won't speak."

I caressed my scar. "Oh, yes, they will." Learning where
Mar had gone to ground was the next thing to seizing him. I
had no compunctions about breaking his soldiers' silence.

The ox could wait. I scraped back my chair. "Let us go."

"My lord King." Rust's voice was quiet. "If they see you,
the game is flown."

"Within the courtyard, it matters not." I made a gesture of
appeal. I *had* to see.

"Be seated, my prince." Seething, I acquiesced. "Thank
you." Rust patted my hand.

I tried not to bare my teeth.

Outside, the clop of hooves.

Lady Varess was pale. Unseeing, she stared at our forgotten
plates.

"Do you love him?" Lord of Nature knew why I'd asked,
but too late. I'd already blurted it out. From the corner of my
eye, I saw Rustin roll his eyes.

Fluttering fingers pushed away her pewter plate. "Sire, he is my consort. The father of my son."

It was no answer. Grudgingly, I let it be; my quarrel wasn't with her.

Shouts. The clang of steel.

"When I was given in marriage, I found him kind." Her voice was strained. "To me, he's always been so."

Guardian or no, I yearned to tear past Rustin, throw open the shutters, take heed of the courtyard doings.

Varess's glance flickered between me and her empty plate. "Like Elena, in affairs of state he's hard. I know that to others . . . to *you*, sire, he's given offense."

"Given offense." I tasted the phrase, marveling at its bland savor. "One could say so."

"Roddy . . ." Rustin's tone held a warning note.

"Bayard oft ran to my skirts to weep grievances about his father. But it's a boy's chore to harden, that he become a man. And not my station to interpose myself. As should be, Mar raised him these last ten years."

Outside the shutters, silence.

I said civilly, "I am answered, Madam."

"Mar's stood by his son, and granted me dignity and respect. I love him for that."

The door burst open. "Sire, we have them!"

"By your leave, Rust!" I threw down my cloth without waiting for answer. My chair teetered; I caught it, set it straight. "Let's see what . . ."

"Ahh. It seems we have company." A familiar voice.

I stood frozen. It couldn't be. My hand shot to my dagger.

In the doorway Margenthar, duke of Stryx, my uncle, was surrounded by three of Groenfil's guards. His scabbard was empty, and his sheath. His garb was disheveled. "Do be seated." His tone was dry.

"Get him out!" My tongue stumbled in my haste.

"Roddy . . ."

"No, Rust, in this I defy you, at whatever cost. Groenfil, Anavar, I charge you: choose a cell that won't be breached. Secure him within."

Rustin said, "You thirst to revenge Pytor—"

"To revenge *you*!" My eyes blazed. "And I will not be denied!" I stalked from the room, took the stairs two at a time to my chamber, barred the door. I paced the room, dagger in hand. I would avenge Rust's murder.

As I worked off my fury, unwelcome thoughts intruded. Was it murder, though, if Rust lived? Yes. I knew what had been, and surely so did Mar. But should one be made to pay for an act undone?

A knock. I ignored it.

"Roddy, open, or I'll be a tad annoyed."

I stalked to the door, threw aside the bar. "He's not guest, not family, not a noble of Caledon! He's foul Margenthar, and I won't treat him as else."

"Lower your voice."

"What matter that they hear? Is there one in Caledon who doesn't know—"

"You haven't the calm to see: the realm is in such disarray, only a thread binds it. Your nobles watch; perhaps some sway to Hriskil. Mar is a noble, and—"

I stalked to the shutters, flung them open, stared down at the courtyard. "Which cell? Did they pick the one I rotted in? I want him—put down the pitcher; I need vengeance, not a faceful of water!"

He regarded me doubtfully. "You're beside yourself."

"Of course." I rushed to the silver, peered at my cheek. "This is what I gaze upon each morn. *Look at me!*"

"I always do." His tone was soft.

"Blindly! You're the only one won't see—won't—" My voice caught. "Because you lov—you—" It was hard to see him through the haze of my eyes. "I've dreamed of this day, it's sustained me when . . ." I threw up my hands.

"Hate him, Roddy. Despise him. Gloat too, if you would, but quietly. The king's every mood oughtn't be carved on his—"

"IT'S NOT A MOOD! THIS IS *MAR*! I MEAN TO TORTURE AND KILL HIM!"

He slapped me. The report echoed.

I rubbed my stinging cheek.

For the instant, Rust was every iota a man to my boy. "Stupid creature, you just told Hriskil, Lady Varess, Tantroth, Lord of Nature knows who else, your intent! You can't conduct statecraft so!"

I sank on the bed. "I have no state."

"Perhaps this is why. Mar is a noble, brother to Queen Elena. Killing him, torture of any kind, raises the specter of your cruelty, of which we best not remind your lords. But, more to earth, they're nobles too, Roddy. What you do to Mar, you might do to them."

"But I wouldn't!"

"Inwardly, they cannot know it. So if you'd keep Caledon, put aside vengeance."

I beat the pillow.

"Only for now, my prince. 'Til the war's won."

"When might that be? Hriskil chases us from town to field. Our raids do him no harm." I'd known since before the Sands that my cause was lost. "It must be now." I took deep breath. "I won't agree to other."

Rust's gaze was cold. "Am I not guardian of your person?"

"This is not personal!"

"Am I not regent?"

"Yes, but . . ." I gritted my teeth. "Yes, sir, you are."

He raised my chin. "As regent I decree: you will grant Mar life. You may not touch him, or cause him to be touched. No fire, no rope, no knife or other physical torture. You will swear this."

"Why?"

"Because I love you, and require it."

I protested, but in the end, as always, he had his way.

Afterward I sat cross-legged on the bed, musing. As Rust said, I ought not strew about my rage as a plowman his seed. But, by Lord of Nature, I was not done with Mar.

Thirty-one

RUSTIN HAD MAR moved to the best of the cells, a locked chamber that had nothing of the dungeon about it.

Anavar did his best to console me. "You'll have him, soon or late. My father says revenge is a sherbet, best enjoyed—"

"Cold. None of your Eiberian proverbs, youngsire."

Anavar looked about. The room was spare, hard, boasting few amenities. "Are you bound to your chamber, sir?"

"No, but for the nonce, I'm avoiding Rust."

"Until?"

"Until I make it up to him." Who but a dimwit knew not how I felt about Margenthar, or my resolve to settle his score? Nonetheless—a long sigh—Rustin was right. He usually was.

"It's he makes you act the boy." Anavar's eyes were fixed on the flagstones.

"Don't be daft. He'd give an arm—well, three fingers, anyway—to see me a man."

"Think you so?" Anavar got up, stretched. "I crave daylight. Would you visit the stables?"

I let him coax me from my room.

FROM THE RUGGED granite wall, Rustin and I looked out over the deceptively peaceful field. Refreshing wind swept our hair and made us into urchins. Behind us, in the courtyard, stableboys walked horses for exercise.

"Groenfil urges a probe," Rust said presently. "Toward Stryx."

"Sarazon is astride the road."

"And we need know his strength. The array of his force."

I said, "Good. When do we leave?"

"*We* don't. Tomorrow, he'll send a score of men, no more."

"Why so few?"

"They hope to go unnoticed. And we mustn't reduce our defense here, lest Hriskil strike." A pause, and Rustin added in an offhand manner, "I ride with them." Abruptly, he seemed fascinated by a juniper growing outside the wall.

I said nothing.

"Don't pout, Roddy, it doesn't become you."

"Ride to the Ukra Steppe, if it please you."

"Yes, I know. But I would see the coast road for myself."

"Tell truth. While you're gone, will you put Groenfil in charge?"

"No, it's you. But I'll set men to provide Mar's victuals. You're not to interfere."

"I promise."

"I need not remind you . . . ?"

"I won't touch him, I won't go into his cell, or send anyone. How many times must I swear?"

ONE NIGHT, PERHAPS two, Rustin said. I need not worry unless it stretched to more than three. Even then . . .

I swept him into a bear's hug, in front of all. "Fare thee well, sir." Behind me, on the steps, Bayard smirked. Inwardly, I smiled. There'd come a day Mar's son and I would have words.

As twenty men rode out with little ceremony, Lady Varess gave a small curtsy. "May I have the king's ear?"

Pardos didn't approve, but I led her to a chamber where the highborn were used to hang cloaks, outside the great hall. "My Lady?"

"I pray mercy for my husband the duke."

Immediately I shook my head. "For him I have none."

Let him be released, she begged. On his behalf she'd give parole—he would too, the moment it was proposed—that he'd attempt no escape, nor try to wrest control of—

No. I would not.

I'd paroled Danzik. If I let a Norlander roam—

Danzik, I trusted.

For her sake, then. She yearned for a husband, a father to her son. She had done no wrong.

I refuse. Is there else, madam?

Did not her brother Sergo serve me well? For him, might I alleviate her misery? At least let Mar be confined to their boudoir.

Sweating, I made my escape. When I could, I drew Pardos aside. "Keep her from me. She has the tenacity of a ferret."

I passed the first afternoon kicking a stuffed ball with Anavar. My young baron had fearsome energy and raced after every stray ball. Setting aside my dignity, I strove with him until I noticed Bayard scowling from a window above. Thereafter, the game lost its allure.

In the evening, I walked with Groenfil. "It's time we made new attack," he said. "If we're to cower behind battlements, I prefer my own."

"We can't get to yours. Hriskil surrounds them."

"Aye, and will, until we draw him off." He ambled past the stables.

I asked, "Is that why you sent our patrol to the Stryx road?"

"*I* sent? Wherever did you get that idea?"

"Rustin told—"

"It was he proposed it."

"Why?"

Groenfil smiled. "He said nothing was dearer to your heart than Stryx."

Was it true? I'd been a boy there, for good or ill.

We wandered along the wall of the keep, Pardos and three guards trailing behind.

"Perhaps," Groenfil said, "we ought to risk all on a cast at Stryx. I'm weary."

"A few days of rest, good food—"

"Weary of war. Of blood, and the loss of good men." His voice, too, betrayed his fatigue. "And I envy Larissa, defending her own earth."

"If we go anywhere, it ought be there. Elryc frets for me."

"How know you?"

I smiled. "I know my brother."

"He has his stableboy. If he's a chick, Genard's the hen." We detoured around a decrepit stone hut.

I made my voice placating. "As soon as the way's clear, we'll ride—*what is this place?*"

He sniffed. "A smokehouse, is it not?"

I recoiled. "Let us away!"

Odd, what one remembered at such a time. My torn, oozing thumb. My ragged, filthy clothes. The stench of me. The salt tang of blood, from the guard's throat I had torn out with my teeth, in a desperate frenzy to escape my fetid cell. My jagged half-healed scar, my acrid, all-consuming fear.

Pardos, sword drawn, shielded my right. "What is it, Rodrigo?"

A demon cackled on my shoulder. I made a sign; I couldn't speak. Behind us, Groenfil hurried to keep pace.

At the stable Pardos panted, "My lord, what vexes him?"

"It seems he has no love for a smokehouse." Groenfil's tone was dry.

I whirled. "For *that* smokehouse. It's where I emerged, when . . ." My eyes glistened. "The worst night of my life, until Rustin . . ." No, that hadn't happened. But they recalled, and nodded. "I was drenched in blood. If I were seen, my life was forfeit. I had no place to go, no one within twenty leagues who gave a brood mare's fart if I lived or . . ." I swallowed. *Easy, Roddy. It's long past. And you could have erased it, if you'd not been set on undoing worse.*

I took deep breath. "Your pardon. I was . . . unnerved." As quickly as I might, I took my leave, retreated to my chamber. I called for water, immersed myself in a warm bath. I soaked, knowing I'd made myself a fool in the eyes of vassals. For that, too, I could blame Mar. Always, he had a hand in my undoing.

I ought think of else. No, I didn't *want* to think of else. Truth was, I was consumed by my anger. And more: anger, fear and loathing.

But why now? For months after he killed Rust, and months again, I'd been able to go about my affairs, not obsessed with but one desire. Why was I now beside myself?

Because Mar was *here*. We shared a roof, dined from the same larder. Easily fixed, except that Rustin had barred the way. I couldn't kill him, couldn't put him to torment, couldn't exact revenge for an iota of the misery he'd inflicted. Well, actually I could, but the broken vow would cost me the Still.

Rust made me forswear knife, fire, rope . . . a lingering drowning would satisfy, but I couldn't share a room with him, nor send another to do my bidding, nor for that matter, touch him or cause him to be touched.

No, Rust knew me too well. He'd foreclosed every means by which I might exact what was due. I sat in the chilling water, ruing lost opportunities. Rust had fenced every pasture, sealed off every trail. I stared at nothing, and stiffened.

All save one.

PARDOS FELL IN alongside me, glanced at my still-damp hair. "Where to, my lord?"

"I go alone."

"In Verein you're not well loved. What's that you carry?"

I held out my palm, he stopped short, so as not to run into it. "Your lord Tantroth roams his hills. Rustin is on patrol. There's none to gainsay me. I command you: await me at my chamber." I left him in the anteroom.

One great room gave onto another. At last, in a far nook, the chamber I sought. Three well-armed guards, two lounging on a bench until they caught sight of me, the third standing before a heavily barred door to what had once served as scullery.

"Where's Mar?"

"Within, sire. No one's to enter, except the servant who brings—"

"Yes, of course. I won't enter. Begone!"

"We cannot—"

"Complain to Groenfil, then. *But I will be alone!*"

Protesting, they took their leave.

I sat myself on the floor, my back resting on the bench. I unwrapped my bundle, uncorked the ewer, poured into the bowl.

Today I sought no cave.

My brother Pytor had been eight when Mar knotted the cord around his slender neck.

I would not touch him, nor enter his cell, or send anyone to do my bidding. I would preserve my vow, and the True.

I settled myself quickly. Groenfil would soon be upon us, and of more import, I could not use the Still long. I must conserve myself. I closed my eyes, murmured familiar words.

Presently, from within the scullery, a strangled cry.

GROENFIL RACED TO the guardroom, Mar's warders at his heels. With but a part of my contemplation I held him off until I was done—only a few moments. Then I wrenched palms from bowl, looked about, bobbed my head in greeting. "Resume the guarding, my lord."

Groenfil's face was grave. "What roguery is this?"

I got to my feet, weary, but less exhausted than I feared.

He demanded, "Have you been at Margenthar?"

"I've kept my oath in every particular." I would say no more.

Afterward, Anavar dared to question me, and I beat him.

The day after, I gathered myself, again made my way to the guardroom outside Mar's cell.

Of all the castle, only Groenfil was unafraid. Afterward, he took me squarely by the shoulders. "Know that you do evil."

I was spent, and the cruelty high in me. "I revel in it. See whom you serve?" I shook myself free and went on my way.

Next morn, on the way to break fast, a figure darted out of shadow. Pardos had him in an instant, dagger at throat, but it was only Bayard, Mar's son, unarmed. "I seek word with thee, majesty!"

"Then speak."

"Alone?" His glance rebounded from my guards' stern faces.

"Don't, sire."

"Take ease, Pardos. I've no fear of *him*." My voice dripped contempt.

"He more than most has reason—"

"Don't speak of it." I reversed course, took Bayard to the chamber that had been his. To spite Pardos, I barred the door, locking out his rescue. "Well?"

From Bayard, a formal bow, one of deep courtesy. He took breath, as if gathering resolve. "Sire, I ask a boon."

"Denied. What is it?"

Abruptly, he seemed uncertain, and rubbed his short-shorn scalp. "It's true I've been no friend." Almost, he hugged himself, but calmed his restless hands. "I appeal to your grace—your gracious mercy, for which you're known through—"

"Lord of Nature, no rote speeches! Say what you want."

"My father . . . the duke is severe, and single-minded in pursuit of . . . to us he's decent, sometimes kind—*I don't know how to do this!*" Bayard swallowed. "Know you what I would plead? Leave him his mind, I beg you!"

I was silent.

"He found me wife, stewards my lands, refills my purse. When I was young, even when he beat me, he'd hug me after. He's not a usual father, even among nobles, but I have no other, and want none! I beg you!"

Slowly, I shook my head.

"I don't ask that you forgive . . . but, sire, have mercy. Last night, when his screams echoed . . . I was with Varess, my mother . . ." His eyes were liquid.

I opened the shutter, stared down at the sunswept courtyard. When I spoke, my voice was hard. "Pytor my brother was brought here. HERE, in his care, in this keep! Perhaps his shade remains!"

"I know not what—father sent me away that day, sire. Later it was whispered . . . in truth, I cannot say it was done."

"How kind of him to shield you." Perhaps my derision was lost on him.

"Yet what gain to Pytor if you—"

I whirled. "Pytor is not all! Mar cost us Pezar, and with it Cumber. Perfidy without end. Come hither!" I grasped his wrist, put fingers to my scarred cheek. "Feel that! Don't dare pull away!"

Bayard whispered. "Father hated that you were Elena's and your life barred me from the throne. I cared not, but he . . ."

My gaze was stony. "For Pytor, for my ruin, for the wound done Caledon, I exact recompense." *And I relish the quiet glee his pain brings.* I would not speak of that.

"Sire, merciful king . . ."

I yearned to cover my ears. For pride, I could not.

Bayard got down on one knee, then both. "I beg thee." He raised hands, palms pressed together.

"No, no, and over again, no! Have done with it!"

"Wouldst joust with me, for his life?"

I gaped. "That's not our law."

"Custom, not so long past." He gazed up hopefully.

"I will not joust for Mar. I have him, and will keep him."

A shuddering breath. Then, determinedly, "Sire, trade my life for his. If you've any mercy, do this thing."

I threw down the wooden bar, flung open the door. "Pardos, I would be alone!"

Fixing my gaze on a distant willow, I closed my ears to Bayard's fading entreaties.

Before dinner, I brought my Vessels to the guardroom.

AT DUSK ON the third day, Rustin led twenty worn, tired riders through the gate. Watching from my chamber window, I yearned to greet him but refrained, knowing the hypocrisy of it.

Bollert ran out to hold Orwal. Rust swung down. Groenfil took him aside. Rust listened, jerked his gaze to my window. After a time, I turned away.

I sat on my bed, filled with sullen unease, as if awaiting Mother's summons to Chamberlain Willem's strap.

I expected Rust to bound up the stair, but he did not. Pardos told me he'd sat to dinner. I found I wasn't hungry. I toyed with the sheath of my dagger. Once, in the dream in which Rustin died, I'd scraped welts into my skin, to ease my pain.

What will ease me now? I lay back on the cushions.

The Still is a cruel gift.

Where, I wondered, was Tresa now? She'd meant to leave Soushire; no doubt she'd done so. If I found her, would she take me to her bed? I ached for nothing so much as her embrace. Someday, when we were married . . . I could bare imagine our loveplay. Her solicitous fingers, exploring, arousing me, my eager thrusts . . . no, that wouldn't come to pass. I'd promised her a Return and a face that might withstand her gaze.

There could be no marriage.

She wouldn't lack for suitors, even in exile. She was comely, courageous, sharp of mind and gentle.

All that I was not.

Whatever did Rustin see in me?

Poor Rust. He yearned for my embrace as I did Tresa's. Neither of us would be fulfilled.

Soon he would confront my villainy. I swallowed.

No matter how he hurt me, I would not utter a sound.

"You sleep? You lie snoring?"

I jumped to my feet. "No, sir. I mean, yes, I was. I beg pardon." My foot tingled; I shook it awake. Outside the shutters, a pale moon sailed.

Rust leaned against the open door, arms folded. "You kept your vow," he said. "I concede you proved me stupid."

"No."

"I pray you, don't speak."

I nodded assent.

He crossed to the window, drew closed the shutter. "I saw him. Will he mend?"

I said, "I don't know." When I'd left him, Mar was all twitches and tics, his nails chewed ragged. Or so it seemed through the stillsilver, from the room beyond.

"Lady Varess begged you. Bayard pled for him. Even I entreated you." Not fair. Rust had ordered, not begged. "But King Rodrigo had his way. So be it." He unknotted his cloak.

"What will you—" —*do to me,* I'd meant to ask. But he'd bidden me not speak.

He washed at the basin, settled himself on the bed. For a long while he was silent. Then he said, "Know, my prince, that you break my heart."

MORN CAME, AND we'd not spoken. Nor had I slept.

As Rust dressed, I broke the chill silence. "Will I be forgiven?"

His eyes were bleak. For a moment he drew my head to his, rested his forehead on my breast. He buckled his sword, went down to the great hall.

Groenfil was there to break fast, and Anavar. Lady Varess, too, pale and hollow-eyed. Even Danzik. But of Bayard there was no sign.

I took Anavar aside. "When I beat you, it was my cruelty, brought out by the Still."

"I know."

"Why did you not protest?"

"Your rancor needed vent." He held my gaze, until mine turned aside.

"I'm sorry. I think."

He shrugged. "Beyond that, I was rude."

I sat elsewhere. I could not abide decency, this morn.

When Lady Varess left, Rustin beckoned to Groenfil. The two seated themselves at my table. Unbidden, Anavar wandered near. Rustin frowned at him. "Don't stretch your ears. If you'd sit with us, ask it." He did, and was given consent. "Roddy, tell Danzik we need to speak privately. Say something about *vade.*"

I did, and the Norlander bared his teeth. But he rose, lumbered out.

Rustin bent close, lowered his voice. "Sarazon's moved most of his men to the hills. The Seacross Road is his supply line from Stryx. We could evade it, and him. But, even so, there's so many Norland troops . . . I'm not sure what we could do in Stryx."

I blurted. "Draw him back." They looked at me. "That's what we'd do."

"To what purpose?"

Inwardly, I sighed my relief. Rust might well have ordered me silent, or treated me like the boy I'd shown myself. I said, "Sarazon's a cautious man. If we—"

Rust said sharply, "How know you that?"

"Danzik told me, in the time you were dead." I hurried on. "If we sting Sarazon at Stryx, his base, he'll withdraw from the hills to protect it. That clears the lands around Verein and prevents his linking with Hriskil near Soushire."

Groenfil chewed his lip. "Four hundred of us. Perhaps fifty added from Verein, if we entirely denude the walls."

"We can't all go." Anavar. All looked his way. "Not since Roddy . . . after Mar, they'll . . ." He glanced about, blushed. "Pardon, my lords."

Nobody's eyes would meet mine. I said with determination, "Our baron's right. My barbarity to Uncle Mar makes him a figure of sympathy. Now Mar can't—isn't capa—" I swallowed. "Today, Mar isn't capable of schemes, but Bayard . . . unless we imprison him, he'll avenge his father's torture." I looked about. "You mistake my meaning," I said quickly. "I don't propose it."

Rustin said only, "That's a comfort." My ears went red.

Groenfil knotted his fists. "We're stripped to a handful if we leave fifty at the castle to guard the fifty Mar brought home."

"No," I said, casting aside my caution. "We bring the men of Verein. Leave but a score of our own, to man the gate."

"And Bayard?"

"I'll see he gives parole."

"Fah. What could you offer—"

"I'll find way."

Groenfil said, "You'd trust his honor after—"

"Who's left for him to subvert, if Verein's soldiers ride with us?"

The earl shook his head. "Be practical, Roddy. A keep the size of Verein, with but twenty defenders? It will fall to the first patrol that wanders past."

"With Stryx, we'd have no need of Verein." I added, "In fact, we ought—"

"Enough, Rodrigo." Rustin's voice was quiet.

"But—"

"I'll think on it and give answer anon."

"Anon" came past midday, but by then I knew his mind. It took no great wit to observe the blacksmiths hard at work reshoeing the horses of Groenfil's troop, or to notice seamsters gathering every last scrap of canvas for sewing into tents. Three light, well-built wagons appeared in the courtyard and were slowly filled with dried meat, fruit, flour, implements of war.

The remnant army of Caledon girded itself.

Rustin sought me out in the stable, where I fed Ebon and Edmund from a stock of apples. "As to Bayard . . ."

"I'll speak with him."

"As you spoke to his father?"

"No, Rust. I promise."

"Bah, what good your vow? You keep its letter but shatter its spirit."

"Not this time. Leave me if I do."

Bayard was not to be found. At length, I went to Lady Varess and demanded she produce her son.

It took an hour.

Bayard regarded me sullenly. "I'd prefer a cell."

"I offer inducement. Your father."

A hiss of breath. "You'll release him?"

"Not quite yet; perhaps on our return. But for your parole not to overthrow our authority, I'll vow not to . . ." I hesitated; there was no word for it. "To molest him again. Ever." Lord of Nature, I felt shabby.

A whisper. "How can I trust you?"

"I don't know, Bayard; I'll grant I'm not terribly scrupulous. My oath on the True, and all that."

At length he agreed, and we exchanged vows. He departed. I watched, knowing what I hadn't told him: after my last assault, I doubted Uncle Mar would ever be near whole. I need not bother him more.

At dinner Rust said, "We've one decision left: whom we leave to defend Verein."

For a moment my resentment flared. "*You're* regent. What say you?"

"I say, let the boy king decide." His tone was sharp. "Good practice for when he's a man."

No more than I deserved. "My lord, I beg pardon." I thought a moment and had the answer.

After the meal, I took Anavar aside. His eyes grew wide. "You don't tease me, sir?"

"Not in this."

A whoop, and he threw himself on me in a fierce hug. "By myself? Truly in charge?"

Smiling, I disengaged myself. "It's not as if you'll command an army. Or even a regiment."

"No, but . . ." His brow furrowed. "Only twenty, you say? It means an old washerwoman could force the gate, if she'd had enough drink. Still, beyond the troops, there's servants and storemen and . . . truly, you leave Verein in my hands?"

"As rehearsal, youngsire. I always meant it to be yours." Little enough chance of that now. Better leaving Anavar behind than engaging him in a suicidal dash down the coast. Perhaps Verein's walls offered a pinch more safety, if he had the sense to surrender them.

THIRTY-TWO

WE JANGLED THROUGH the gate at dawn. I rode with Rustin, Groenfil and Danzik. Anavar saw us off.

I doubted the boy had slept a wink; he'd rushed about the castle checking arms, learning the names of his men, conferring with Lady Varess. She might hate me, but her brother served my cause, and as only my meager army stood between her and Hriskil, her welfare was bound to mine. In any event, she was civil enough to my young baron.

During the night Anavar woke me twice. He'd loaded extra stores in the second cart, for us to take; Verein wouldn't need them. By the way, could he have Bollert, to help tend horses? Go to bed? Of course, sir, as soon as all was in hand. Rustin merely groaned and stuck a pillow over his ears.

We rode from Verein with scarce a look back. Of all my domain, I liked it least, and its lord was the cause. Well, I'd settled that account. As I told Rustin after he made a rather tart remark: if I must assuage Mar to keep Caledon, I didn't want the kingdom. Then take heart, he'd replied; I'd probably accomplished that very thing. For an hour afterward we had little to say, until our hearts thawed and we exchanged unspoken apology.

By the road, it was a day west to Stryx, but we were perforce more circumspect. And even with six horses to each wagon, we were slowed somewhat. Wheels could not go where hooves might. Twice our scouts reported a Norland supply column wending its way toward Seacross. Easy takings, but surprise was a coin spent but once. We agreed to expend it nearer Stryx.

My spirits didn't flag, but with each step, Rustin grew morose. It took no ritemaster to discern the cause. "He's not in the Keep, Rust. He's with Hriskil."

Rustin's voice was flat. "Ever more treason." As always, his father, Llewelyn's, betrayal gnawed at his soul.

"He couldn't help it." I was surprised at the clemency I expressed, and felt. My guardian and I had long assumed, without saying, that Llewelyn's life must be forfeit.

"As Mar couldn't help strangling Pytor." Rust's tone was acid. "And so we forgive."

"It's not the same. Hriskil . . ." I stopped for thought. "I don't think I told you. The night I helped you see your death . . ." I explained what Danzik had disclosed: that Hriskil had brought his Rood to Stryx and there undermined Llewelyn's loyalty.

A flicker of interest. "The Rood's that potent? We must remember." Then his face fell. "Yet, what matter? If you excuse it, any traitor may throw himself on your mercy, claiming a Power forced him." He held up a hand. "Speak of else."

As midday passed into afternoon, my mood too grew somber. I missed Anavar, Tresa, Elryc. Even Genard. Our army gadded about, sparring, fleeing defeat, growing ever weaker. I was king of what, now: Verein? In that meager domain, I was liege only of a grieving boy—with more courage than I— whose father I had undone.

It must end. If our foray to Stryx produced no great benefit, I would abdicate.

Just before dusk, we gathered on the wooded hill that overlooked Stryx. Far below lay the harbor, and beyond it, the town. But it was the bay that took one's breath.

Sail upon sail, vessels of all sizes crowded tight, or so it seemed from our height. Lord of Nature, where did Hriskil gather such a fleet? How vast must the Norland be, to support it? How many more ships had arrived, since we'd gazed down from this hill at Sarazon's arrival? Only Danzik showed no dismay.

Groenfil said glumly, "We mean to worry at Sarazon's supply line? Look you: his supplies are without end."

Rust admitted, "It does seem burning a few wagons here or there hardly throws the balance."

I sniffed the air. "Comes a storm? Did a soothsayer predict foul weather?"

"Why, Roddy?"

"They're all in the bay. My eyes are good; yours are better. See you any sails beyond the breakwater?"

"Only a few. That's not the issue. Do we turn east and seize a handful of wagons, or sneak back to Verein?"

"We ride to Stryx."

"I beg pardon, my liege?" Rustin's tone held warning.

I gritted my teeth. "Yes, sir, our squadron's yours to command. I beg pardon. But before we mount an attack we need know what Sarazon's about."

"The garrison would overwhelm our four hundred—"

"But not a handful, riding without notice. Yes, glare if you will, but pay heed. We need go to Stryx." I spoke as to a simpleton. "Why? The enemy's there. We need learn his numbers, where he stables his horses, who mills his wheat. Why? We can't defeat him in dark. It's time, my lords. If Sarazon is free to roam, Verein's soon taken from us, and Soushire as well. Here I make my stand."

"How noble, Roddy." Under Rust's calm, he seethed. "This is, what, your fifth last stand? Each time we're decimated, we fall back and—"

"In this I am right. I know it. Do not you?"

Rust rubbed his face, as if weary. "Go down to Stryx? I suppose I could send a few—"

"Us." My wave took in Rustin, Groenfil, a few others.

"Of course. Your scar would go completely unnoticed."

"The bandage I'll wear? Perhaps I won't scar, when it's off." Resolutely, I met his eye.

"The inns are full of Norland soldiers. We speak no—"

"I do. Enough to get by." I had few enough barbarian words, but spoke them well.

"If you're taken . . ."

"We'd be done at last. But, kill me first, I pray you." I tried not to think of my life in Hriskil's hands.

"Why wait? I could kill you now." Rust tugged at his reins, guided Orwal into the wood.

A GRIMY BANDAGE ran up my cheek over my ear and hair and down the other side. It was stained with a touch of blood from a chicken soon to go in the pot. Though I had no silver in which to peer, from our troops' expressions, I must be a sight, but I knew the dressing served its purpose and hid my scar. I tied the bandage under my chin.

Unlike Tantroth's Eiberians, Hriskil's army wore no set garb, though they were inclined to homespun woolen tunics and leather leggings. Making the rounds of our four hundred, we

borrowed or appropriated enough gear to clothe a motley, if unlikely, Norland squad. In any event, we need seem Norlandic
only for the canter down from the hills. Once in Stryx, some of
us could be Caled. Unless, of course, the taverns were closed to
native folk.

Rustin fussed interminably, until I feared we'd lose the
night. I ventured, "Take ease, sir. I've done it before." When
Tantroth invaded, before our peace, I'd ridden boldly into
Stryx to seek Vessa, speaker of the city.

"You were taken. It was Anavar freed you."

"Ill fortune." I shrugged it away. "Come, Rust; a horse is a
horse."

"Now he looks a Norland horse." He patted Orwal, swung
into the saddle.

I'd switched Ebon for another, not caring to risk losing him
in case we had to retreat on foot. I repeated my promise to
Groenfil, that we would send word or return by night's end.
An encouraging word to Danzik, who seemed disheartened
that his Norland comrades were so near yet so far. And we
were off.

EVADING PATROLS WAS easy; we stayed clear of the road. The
hard part was picking our way down the rocky hillside without breaking our necks. At last, near twelfth hour, as best I
could tell, Rust and I led our disheveled seven down the center of the muddy Potsellers' Way as if we owned it. For the
benefit of any who strolled in the night, I chattered in Norlandic, though too nervous to make an iota of sense. From
time to time Rust grunted in reply.

Our precautions were for naught. We ran across no patrol.

"Now what?" Rust's lips barely moved.

"The Keep."

"Lord of Nature. Why?"

"Is the gate kept open? How many men? How many
horses? Is the wall manned? Do they store fodder—"

"Please!" In his tone, real anguish. "Don't prattle."

"This way." I led them to the harbor road. Bold as magpies
we trotted along the cobbles, past the inn, past the swordsmith
at whose door I'd first heard of Mother's death. At this hour,
all was dark within.

The main gate of the Keep was closed, though torches

aplenty burned on the wall, and the postern was ajar. For a moment I debated dismounting, peering within, but it might earn me Rustin's knife in the ribs.

Rustin muttered, "Do we have names?"

"Not our own." I hesitated. "We're Mar's men, kicked out by Rodrigo. You're Garst. Jatho is himself, no harm in that. Pardos, you sound Eiberian. What say—"

"I *am* Eiberian. Sire, in days of war men of all nations are found—"

"Don't call me 'sire'; it's warrant of death."

"Call him Genard." Rust sounded disgusted. "And you, youngsire, answer to it! Now, turn about; if you glance at that gate one more time, I'll skin you."

"Aye, m'lor'." For some reason I found it funny. "Oh, look, a beerhouse. Ol' Griswold tol' me 'bout it. What say we—"

"Roddy, for the love—GENARD!" A lash with his crop, that caught my calf. I stifled a yelp. Rubbing my smarting leg, I unhooked my saddlebag and followed him to the alehouse. We dismounted.

Bare two or three mounts were tied to the post, but in the haze of smoke, most of the tables were full of raucous drinkers. We crowded at a splintered table in the corner. I listened, said quietly, "Caled speech, mostly. Except along that wall."

A plump barmaid set down pitchers at a nearby table, looked us over. "Qa dese?" *What do you want?*

My eyebrows went up. "Er Norl?"

A harsh laugh. "Han." *No.* "Wonde, of Fort town."

How many were we? Seven. "Doa urne." *Two pitchers.*

When she was at the barrel, Jatho said softly, "I thought we were Caled."

"She wants us to be Norl. You and Koz wander to the table with the dice players. Remember, you're from Verein. Wonder about local matters. Learn what you can."

"Aye, si—Genard. But I'm a fish out of water. I've no talent as a spy."

"Learn in haste."

"Genard . . ." Rust's fingers gripped my knee. "For a stableboy, you give orders like a noble."

"Aye, m'lor', I hear 'em when they come for horses. Keep me talkin' so, and see what the serving girl makes of it." I glared.

"Exactly. We shouldn't be here. We speak only Caled; she thinks we're—Ahh."

The barmaid set down two pitchers, foam slopping over the sides. "One silver." She corrected herself. "Sol argen." I fished out my purse, threw down a coin.

Clutching his mug, Jatho sidled along the flyspecked wall toward the dice players. Glumly, Koz followed.

Rust had poured me scarce a quarter glass. I sipped, licked foam off my lip. "I ain' a sot, m'lor'. Coulda give me more. I wouldn'—" A shadow loomed. I glanced over my shoulder, finished, "—drink more'n I should." To the newcomer. "Leng Caledi sper memor." *Caled is a hard tongue to learn.*

A big black beard, more wild even than Danzik's. Small, beady eyes. "Norl?"

"I am," I said in the same language. "But not my friends."

"How hurt your face?"

Rust watched each in turn, as at a joust. Coolly he drained his mug.

I made a gesture of disgust. "Faranga Caled patrol. Spear." Heart pounding, I stood, to meet him eye to eye. I failed, by a good hand's breadth. "Genard, of household regiment." I dared not say more; my accent was slipping. One by one, our companions drifted away to mingle in the crowded inn.

"Coth."

What word was that? My panic soared.

"Pike captain."

Oh. Perspiration beaded my lip. *Coth* was a name. Gamely I stuck out a fist, rapped his knuckles in the Norland soldierly salute. Thank Lord of Nature for Danzik's teaching. "I'm nothing. My brother's an earl." I smiled, as depreciatingly as I might. I wanted *some* rank, but not too high to justify a grimy alehouse.

"What do you here?"

Yes, Roddy. What do you here?

I'm blundering about, waiting to be unmasked. "I bring dispatches for Sarazon." At the name, Rustin blinked, but I paid no heed. "Rezia." *From the king.* "But . . ." But I've run out of nursery tales. Is it my bedtime?

"But he's not here," Coth finished for me. "He's in the hills."

"Qay." *Yes.*

"Tomorrow, he takes Verein. Even now he marches." The giant Norlander glanced at his empty glass, at our pitcher. Obligingly, I snapped my fingers at Rust. "*Sihr.*" *Pour.* With an apologetic shrug to the Norl, "Pour 'im beer, Garst. Coth drink wi' us."

"When you get here?" Coth's query might be idle conversation, or the start of an interrogation.

"Tonight." Frantically I summoned words, any words. "On Nightwinds. From Ghanz, to coast, then ship." *Still your tongue, Roddy, while you have one.* "Harbor full."

"Mmn." A sharp glance at Rust, who cheerfully raised his mug in salute. "Just landed? And you have Caled friends?"

"Oh, I've been here before." I drew myself up. "Fourth time with dispatches."

"Where you stayed?"

"His house." I flicked a finger at Rustin. "Near Keep."

Beer went down the wrong way; Rust choked. Obligingly, Coth pounded his back, nearly driving him through the rickety table.

"Just landed," I said, in a mad effort to divert Coth. "Harbor . . . so many ships. No . . ." I had no word for wharf. Pier. Dock. *Try "idiot."*

Coth grinned. "Aye, their fishermen are beside themselves. No *fote* to repair boats, no fote to land their catch. Bring fish by mule carts from south. But Sarazon won't risk enemy attack outside the bay." Focusing my entire wit, I caught the gist of it.

"What enemy?" I made my tone scornful.

Across the room, shouts.

"Exactly. Child king has no ships. Sarazon afraid of his own shadow. When he lived in Keep, it was packed full of guards. In hills, even with army, took all his guards along. Afraid he'll end like Danzik." At that, it was my turn to choke. "Their Keep near empty. Vena ot!" *I'm coming.* He waved his mug at his compatriots. "Vena vos. Kara vos urne." *I'll buy you a pitcher.*

I grinned. "In a moment." I shot a mental arrow at our companions, somehow caught their attention. I flicked my eyes toward our table. They drifted back. My lips barely moved. "Outside, a pair at a time. Slowly."

On the street, I breathed clean air. Our horses pawed the

dust. Rustin turned to the rail, bent over it, vomited. Shamefaced, he hauled himself into the saddle.

Startled, I said, "You're sick?"

"I'm terrified."

"*You,* afraid?" An outrage; Rust was the bravest soul I
knew. He spurred off, declining further query. Determinedly, I caught him half a furlong down the coast road.
"Why, sir?"

"Half for you." With effort, he met my eye. "But for myself
as well. It seemed . . . a shabby place to die." A glance behind
him, at the torchlit Keep. "And too close to home."

I clasped his forearm, held tight until I had his gaze. "Sir,
know I esteem you."

A weak smile. "Thank you, Roddy."

"*Genard.* It's nothin', m'lor'." Our other riders slowed as
they reached us.

We'd come upon that part of the harbor where steps led to
the water. Two score or so of sailors lounged about, some with
bottles. It wasn't a good place to tarry. "Let's go."

Fingers snatched at Rust's reins. "Caled pigs don't need
horses!" Grinning friends jumped up to see the fun.

I reared in my saddle. "VAN ATRA!" *Stand back!* I
snatched out my dagger.

The drunken sailor dropped the thongs. "I didn't—I
thought you were Caled, I—"

"What ship?"

"Pardon, my lord, I meant no—"

"QUA VES?" *WHAT SHIP?*

"What goes here?" A Norland officer.

I made my voice ice. "Your man is drunk. Almost, he lost
his fingers."

The officer rounded on the unfortunate seaman. A string of
oaths. I spurred my mount; we trotted on. My band knotted
close, as if there was safety in our small numbers.

I took the first turnoff, reined in at a closed stall. "Let's pool
what we know."

Jatho shrugged. "All I heard was talk of the castle. When
Sarazon gets back, they think he'll mount an attack."

Koz nudged him. "Stables."

"Aye. The Norlanders crowd every stable in Stryx. They
even quarter their animals in homes, if the doors are wide.

Someone left huge stacks of fodder out on the quay, and it rained. Now there's a shortage."

Pardos had asked how many men were in the Keep and had gotten a scowl for an answer. From the lot of them, no more useful information.

I said, "That business with the drunken sailor tells us . . ."

"That we oughtn't be here." Rust.

"That the Norlanders aren't well liked. Our fishermen are crowded out of harbor, and resent it. Their sailors are arrogant, probably their soldiers too. It's unusual for Norls to consort with Caledi; it made Coth suspicious." *Careful, Roddy. You're sounding ever more Norl. Er, Norlandic.*

"Of what use is that?"

"I'm not done. You heard Coth . . . pardon, sir. I forget we spoke his tongue. Let's see, now: Sarazon has taken his command to the hills. He attacks Verein in the morn."

Rust stiffened. "WHAT?"

"He marches even now." Poor Anavar; another friend lost. Thrusting aside gloom, I focused on the job at hand. "And why is there no dockage for our fishermen? Because Sarazon's entire fleet is crowded into the bay. He fears attack, though we have no Caled ships. He's afraid of his shadow. I told you he was cautious. Norland soldiers frequent the tavern, enough so barmaids learn their tongue. Let's see, what else? Oh. They're cautious, but not expecting attack. And the Keep's half empty; Sarazon's so afraid we'll capture him as we did Danzik, he only moves with a massive headquarters guard."

Rustin's eyes fixed on mine. He chewed his lip.

I scratched, shifted from foot to foot, finally managed with great effort to still myself.

At last he said, "You learned all that?"

"Yes, my lord. We ought go now to that seedy tavern you never used to let me in, the one in that village at harbor's edge. Where the fisherfolk gather." Still, he stared. I added meekly, "If it please you, sir."

A defeated wave. "As you will, my prince." As we made our way, his perplexed gaze sought mine, as if in contemplation.

It was past second hour of the morn, by the tavern's hour candle. The place was small and squalid, as befit the village of Stoneshore, no match for the inn by the docks. Even at that hour—or perhaps, because it was that hour—a dozen men, two or three bleary-eyed women sat hunched over bottles of strong brew.

The keeper stood by his barrels, arms folded. "Norl?"

I grinned. "Aye, an' you be a horse's cock. Norl, my buttock." I slapped the part I'd named. "Hey, Garst, he says we look Norlandic." I dumped my saddlebag on the grimy table.

Rustin snorted. "Insult us, we take our trade elsewhere."

The innkeeper unbent a notch. "Asking, was all. Sometime, they come in."

I hauled out a chair. "Any Cumber ale?"

The keeper looked mournful. "Two barrels left. Half a silver a pitcher; dunno when I'll see more."

I peered into my purse, ordered two despite the price. The keeper brought them himself; no plump perspiring barmaid here. At least one of the frowsy women hunching over her bottle looked to be a whore; of the other, I wasn't sure. Perhaps she was a fisher's wife, sharing her mate's sullen leisure.

Her man looked us over. "You're no sailors."

"Aye." I looked about. "Is the inn reserved for seamen?"

"Depends." His tone was short.

Rust and the others seemed lost. They could hardly join a conversation, as there was none, just a sputtering fire, smoky acrid air and slumped shoulders. I lowered my voice, said to the inn in general, "Hriskil's sailors laugh about your plight."

The drinker spat; his blob of spittle glistened in the grime of the planks. "No piers open. Norland ships tied to every post."

"We saw." I made my tone sympathetic.

Another fellow took up the tale. "Like Jahl says, they unload and won't move. Bay's so full there's no fishing it, so what's the point dropping nets outside? We've no carts to haul fish across town. Herring spoil 'fore we get 'em sold. And Fiegel, what they did was crying shame."

I looked blank.

The barkeeper grunted. "Fiegel unloaded from a breakwater a league south. Borrowed three mules, loaded a cart high. Imp-cursed Norlanders overturned the cart before he got to market. A thousand fish rotted in the sun, and laughing Norland pigs kicked him and his sons as they tried to gather their catch." Gloomily, the keeper sampled his own wares. "No wonder my place is empty. Who has coin for ale?"

Jahl said, "Half the fisherfolk of Stryx be gone to—"

"Jahl!"

"—gone," the man finished lately. Nothin' for 'em here."

I glanced at Rust. His eyes took in all, but he gave me only an imperceptible nod. Encouragement? I hoped so. I took deep breath. "If it hangs me, I'll say it: I'm for Rodrigo, king of Caledon. May all Norlanders rot in the lake of fire!"

A pause. Men looked at each other, then away.

A moment passed. Then, one by one, eyes not on each other, they raised glasses and bottles and gave silent toast.

Jahl said cautiously, "Where be you from?"

"A month past, we fled Cumber. Now we come down from Verein." A salute to the True.

"Margenthar!" He spat again.

"We're not his." My tone was quiet, but intense.

"They say Sarazon took Verein."

"Not yet. I heard he marches tonight."

The barkeep asked, "How missed you his force?"

I grinned. "The fat old Norlander likes a road. Garst—" A wave to Rustin— "prefers goat trails."

Our "Garst" said abruptly, "Where your fisherfolk went . . . might we go? To fight Sarazon?"

The innkeeper said immediately, "No one said that."

"No need to." Rust scratched behind his ear. "If you'll not tell us, so be it, no hard thoughts. But once . . . I met the king." His tone was fervent. "And I would aid his cause."

With thy life, my great friend. My eyes stung.

"I know nothing of it," the barkeep said offhandedly. "There's those say the Lady of the Hill gathers them in. She who rides at night."

My heart fell. Peasant myths. Mother was long gone. Why did simple folk sustain themselves with legend, rather than *doing* what would improve their lot? Elena Queen could no more save them than . . . than Ebon.

"Mustn't forget Willem," said Jahl. "He yet holds Stryx."

"Aye, he's old but has valor," muttered a sailor. "Where's the boy king when you need him?"

"Didn't Rodrigo fight at Pezar?" My voice was hot. "At Cumber? At—"

"Didn't he lose at Pezar? At Cumber?" He made as if to spit, instead slammed a fist on the table so hard it shuddered. "Rodrigo's a worthless sod."

Rust asked mildly, "What would you he did?"

"Fight to free us!" In a fit of anger, Jahl swept his table clear. His drained bottle smashed into shards, to the barkeep's disgust. "I buy whiskey instead of bread. Why not? In a week I'll sell a chair, and have naught in my hut but straw. Then we'll starve, Lenna and I. Would a true king let Stryx rot?"

"Faugh!" I kicked an empty stool; it skittered across the planks. "Were he here, would you aid him? No, you'd drink yourselves senseless. Tell me there's one of you who'd fight with his king."

Rustin grabbed at my arm, but I evaded him. Hands on hips, I waited.

Most looked to the floor. At length Jahl muttered, "I would. But I have only a dull hatchet, and a knife. No sword."

My tone dripped contempt. "One, out of a dozen!"

"And I!" A scrawny, sallow man shook off his woman's arm, got unsteadily to his feet.

Jahl snorted, "Why don't you join the Lady?"

"She's not the king!"

"I would." A hook-nosed fellow, sitting alone. "If he wanted a boat. I'm no use at much else."

"Garst . . ." The barkeep looked past me. "You say you saw him. What's he like?"

"Impetuous. Foolish at times. Noble. He strives to be worthy. And astoundingly brave."

The keeper said slowly, "You describe one you know."

In the air, a static, as before lightning strikes.

Rust said, "I do."

One of the women got up, casually scratched herself, wandered about.

Without turning I said, "Stop her."

Jatho caught her waist just as she reached the door.

I asked, "Would any others aid the king?"

A sailor cried, "Jahl, they're informers." Sharp, hooked knives appeared from nowhere. "In the bay with them." A gesture, of throats slit.

"We're not," I said. I met Rust's eye, seeking forgiveness.

Our necks were well in the noose, and I'd given him no chance to gainsay my cast of the die.

"Who, then?" They'd circled us, all of them, even the drunken woman, who wielded a huge nicked butcher knife.

"I'm the one you seek." I fished in my bag. They tensed, but I brought out a cloth, unwrapped it, set the coronet on my head. Slowly, I unknotted the bandage, let it fall. I eyed the sailor. "I'm that worthless sod. Rodrigo."

The effect was extraordinary. The sailor who'd spoken so disparagingly let his knife clatter to the planks. Slowly, he approached me, searched my face. A whisper. "The Lady was right. You came for us."

I stifled a sigh. When I died, would I too be retained as myth? In the dusty gray cave, would I know it?

The slattern with the butcher knife cackled. "It's a trap. The scar's painted on."

I snapped, "Finger it! You have our leave."

Contemptuously, she did. Broken-nailed fingers swept across my cheek. Her eyes changed. "Real." No more than a mumble. She backed away. "Dunno. Not only boy in Stryx with scar—"

I pulled out my chair, sat. "Take the coronet."

"Can't." She made a sign warding off demons.

"I order it."

Rust said urgently, "She's armed, she'll—"

Deliberately, I turned my chair to present my back. "Take it, woman. Know you gold?" I tensed, lest she abruptly end my pretensions.

In a moment, fingers at my brow. The gentle weight of the coronet lifted.

Her tone was grudging. "It's real."

"Show the others. If you'd have me as king, crown me."

Rust said angrily, "What mummery is—"

"Shush, my lord. I'm not king without them; I learned that at Pezar while you were . . . in a time of dream."

Stolidly, I waited my fate.

After a time, the coronet settled on my locks. I exhaled, not knowing how long I'd held breath.

Jatho said, with a note of apology, "What about this one?" He held yet the woman who'd sought to leave.

"Innkeeper?"

"She meant to turn us in. There's reward."

"For me?"

"No doubt. But also for seditious talk. She'd have had a silver for each of us." His voice grew hard. "Wouldn't you, slut!"

"No!"

"Kill her!" Jahl.

I said, "Not yet. Have you a cellar?" In a quarter candle, she was tied below.

"Now what?" They gathered round.

I stifled a yawn; it must be near morn. "Who has boats?"

"I." The hook-nosed sailor.

"And I." A brawny beard, calculating eyes. "And . . ." He looked about. "Two others."

"We'll need more." I stretched. "To coat your keels, do you not use pitch?"

"What else?" A touch of scorn, as any adroit to a novice.

"You've a storehouse for it, is there not? South of town?"

"Kandar has one."

"With barrels?"

"Must have twenty or so."

"Ahhh." For the first time in hours, the knot in my shoulders eased. "This is what we'll do."

THIRTY-THREE

IN THE STIFLING warehouse, I dozed on Rustin's shoulder. Outside, it was bright day, and we must need wait until night. Along with Pardos and Jatho, we were but four; I'd argued Rust into sending our other men back to Groenfil, that he know our plan and not fret at our absence. I hoped they'd thread their way through Sarazon's patrols; if caught and put to torture, they might reveal all.

Yet, were we not at risk simply sitting among the barrels of thick black pitch? A dozen—no, by now it would be more—Caled fisherfolk knew our whereabouts, and my rank. Who could say they wouldn't succumb to the lure of Sarazon's silver? Of course I'd made them grandiose promises—no greater, they said, than the Lady of the Hill—of silver, gold, remission of taxes unto the third generation. But Sarazon's coin could be spent, mine only contemplated.

"Sleep, my prince. You've done what you might."

"Are you angry, Rust?"

"I . . . know not what I think." He patted my knee. "We'll speak of it anon."

"It occurred so fast . . . no time to consult you . . ." I rubbed an itch on my collarbone. "Please, I know you take offense."

"Ahh, Roddy." His soft fingers caressed my locks. "You're a noble soul."

"Despite Mar?" Like an aching tooth, I couldn't let it be.

"I didn't say a *perfect* soul." Rust hesitated, lost in thought. "In your . . . other life? The one without me . . . did you use your Power for ill? Tell truth."

I contemplated. "I think not, sir. I vexed Jestrel the silversmith, but not as you saw it. Only to learn truth."

"But when I bound you at Verein . . ."

"I evaded you in my oath. Rust, I hate Mar beyond words. If that makes me foul, so I am."

Cool fingers flitted across my scar. "You've reason for hate; I only hoped you'd defer. Yet, am I sure you erred? Word spreads; across Caledon, men will know not to cross the king. Perhaps that is meet. Rest a bit."

On the bench across the way, Pardos stared glassily at my boots, sword across his knees. When did he sleep? Jatho, at least, had no such problem. Head back, he snored lightly. A seasoned soldier, he took ease when he might.

"ARE YOU WELL?" In the sliver of moon's light, Rust's expression was anxious.

Gulping, I nodded. I was well. I merely craved death.

On the thwart, Jahl chuckled softly. "No swell. Not even a ripple."

I'll have your head! I managed not to say it. To divert myself—not that I truly cared—I whispered, "Where are the others?"

"Look about, King."

"Call him 'sire.' " Rust's tone was disapproving.

Ignoring him, Jahl thrust his chin to the side. "Sarnut's scull is an oar's length to port." His tone took on a cajoling note. "Better if you open your eyes."

Better if I leave my stomach ashore. I swallowed air, fighting the urge to spew my dinner of bread and cheese over the side.

We were twenty-two of us, in ill-kept longboats and barques. The stench of fish pervaded every timber. My boots, my cloak, my leggings . . . if I survived the night I'd burn them all. I'd visit a ritemaster and seal a yearning-jar, never to see a fish again.

Rustin leaned back, hands clasped behind his neck, and gave a contented sigh, having no inkling he'd just become my foe for life.

"Is the lamp still lit?" Anything to bestir him to discomfort.

A fisher cautiously lifted an edge of the cloth. "Aye, my lord." Carefully, he replaced the cover. Rust hadn't moved.

I asked, "Which way does the wind blow?"

Jahl said, "Toward shore."

"That's good, isn't it?"

"It means if we cut anchors, the Norland ships will drift inward."

It had seemed such a simple scheme. Our new comrades gathered dilapidated fishing vessels—what other kind had they?—loaded each with barrels of pitch and ropes. In darkest night, we launched our tiny fleet from the breakwater south of Stryx.

The fisherfolk objected to the risk, of course. But I argued that they had not the use of their vessels; the Norland fleet crowded them out. If Hriskil won, it might ever be so. And if I was victorious, I'd reimburse any loss. They grumbled and muttered into their bowls, but a village consensus had formed in my favor.

So, we'd set out. But no one had told me how despotically the direction of wind controls direction of sail. As the breeze was pressing toward shore, we'd be forced to beat about so as not to be driven onto the rocks before we reached the mouth of the bay. Jahl said it was quicker to row, and so we'd taken turns, except that, as hard as I'd tried, I couldn't seem to keep rhythm with my thwartmate. The old fisher didn't seem to mind; his tone was affable enough as he bid me take a seat in the bow. I just wished he hadn't winked to his companion. And at least the rowing had shifted my thoughts from the constant roll and swell.

"You'll spend the rest of your life ashore." As usual, Rust had read my thoughts.

"Yes!"

"A pity, my prince. A sail in fresh wind, under the stars . . . a delightful roll; it feels like a hammock under—"

"Stop it!"

"My lords, voices carry over water." Jahl spoke barely above a whisper. "The bay's just past that rocky arm." Instantly, we were silent.

Only a sliver of moon rode the heavens, but our eyes were well-accustomed to dark. I looked about while our oars dipped over and again into the water with a barely audible slap.

In moments my stomach was forgotten.

Hriskil had sent so many ships to Caledon that a score clustered at the mouth of the bay, unable to anchor within. Ketches, yawls, trading barques, brigantines, what have you. One mast, two, three on the larger vessels.

Jahl breathed, "Where do we start?"

"What say *you*?" In this circumstance, he was journeyman, I the apprentice.

"That two-master. Broad enough the wind will take her once she's cut."

I looked to Rust. He nodded. So did I.

Jahl shipped oars, waited until Sarnut's timeworn barque drew near. Jahl pointed to a fat brigantine just inside the harbor mouth. "Remember to wait!"

"Aye!" Sarnut hoisted a blackened sail; I flinched as rope creaked through pulleys.

Jahl whispered instructions to each of our boats as they neared.

Too soon, it was our turn. I licked dry lips as we glided to the fat two-master. Ours was a small craft, barely more than a longboat, our mast well below the deck of the stout Norland cargo vessel.

One of Jahl's fishers slipped to the bow, gently fended us off with his palms. On the ship above, crewmen surely slept, perhaps on deck. We were demons in the night, visiting on them every seaman's nightmare.

As the Norlander's stern nets drew past, Jahl's man seized them; in a moment we were stilled alongside. Another crewman hefted a barrel, handed it to Jahl, who passed it to Rust. From Rust, to me. I caught my breath; it was weightier than it looked, and oozed pitch that stuck to my hands. I passed it to the fisher in the bow. With great care, he tied it with thoroughly wet ropes to the netting.

He breathed, "Are they ready?"

I turned to Jahl. "Are they ready?"

"Hold." Ever so carefully, so as not to make a splash, he and his companion backed their oars until Jahl could peer around the side of the two-master.

Eons passed. I fidgeted and fretted, 'til Rust's hand fell on my knee.

At last, Jahl nodded. A stroke or two of the oars, and we glided back in. Someone passed the fisher our lamp; Rust was ready with a pitch-soused torch. He held it to the flame; it sputtered and caught. Instantly, the fisher thrust it at the pitch oozing from the barrel.

"Now!"

As fire rose up the side of the barrel, the crewman drew his knife, sawed at the anchor ropes. It seemed to take forever, but they parted.

"Away!" Jahl's whisper was sharp. It seemed to echo in the
breeze. Already, flames licked at the Norland hull. The fisher
plunged our torch into the bay, dousing it. From the two-
master, the sweetish smell of resin alight.

With all their might our rowers hauled on their oars; our
darkened boat shot into the night. Jahl made past the next vessel, aiming for a yawl just inside the bay.

Behind us, the two-master drifted slowly shoreward. Fire
crawled along the deck. In moments it was aflame, a signal to
our compatriots. In moments, other lights flared, each from a
burning ship.

We raced across the still water. In a moment our rowers reversed oars; we glided almost to a full stop under an aged barque that rode far lower than the two-master.

"Barrel!" Willing hands passed it on.

"Wait!" Jahl stood; I gripped the thwart, praying we
wouldn't capsize. "Make ready a torch!" He threaded his way
to the bow, whispered a command. Together, he and the fisher
lifted the barrel over their heads, heaved it over the barque's
rail. It fell with a thud. From the barque, shouts. Rust lit a
torch. Jahl grabbed it, hauled himself over the Norlander's
side. A moment later he threw himself seaward, caught himself on a rope, lowered himself more gently to our bottom, so
as not to smash through our thin hull. "Go!"

Rust leaped into the rower's seat Jahl had vacated. They put
their backs into it, not a moment too soon. A mustachioed
sailor peered over the rail, brandishing a scimitar. Behind him,
the Norland deck blazed.

We rowed as if imps snapped at our heels. Suddenly I cried,
"We forgot the anchor!"

"No need!" Jahl's white teeth gleamed in the pale moon's
light. "They'll sail to shore." Even as he spoke, the barque's
anchor rope slid into the sea; someone had slashed it. A sail
flew into the spars. Soon they had headway, but too late.
Flames tongued the canvas. In a moment the barque was an
inferno. Flailing figures leaped into the sea. One was ablaze.

Three more barrels. We made for a brigantine, the heaviest
vessel in the bay. By now the whole Norland fleet was wak-
ened. Around us, ships hauled anchor, raised sail. Men peered
over rails. Sculls from burning ships careened about, adding
to the confusion. Our longboat was dark, our lantern covered,

but we surely cast a silhouette against the flames. I peered over my shoulder. Two ships, one fully ablaze, the other smoldering, blocked the neck of the inlet.

"Hold us off!"

Too late. Our prow smashed into the brigantine's ample side netting. Our boat shuddered and was still. Would we sink? I probed the planks. No water. Thank Lord of Nature.

Deftly, Jahl entangled a barrel in the web of the Norlander's net. He sought and found a torch. Overhead, a face. Frantic shouts. Two men brandished daggers. Three.

Jahl reversed his torch, smashed the top of the barrel, slammed the flaming end within. Rust and his companion arched their backs in a mighty tug at oars. Jahl caught his balance. A dagger whirled through the air, landed at his boot. He bent, plucked it out, flung it back.

Flames leaped up the side of the brig.

"The anchor!" Jahl's eyes glinted. "If this one drifts . . ."

We rowed to the stern. The overhang sheltered us from eyes above. I snatched out my dagger, reached to the rope.

No rope, a chain. I gaped, and cursed.

Jahl snapped, "On deck, they'll have an axe!"

"I'll go." Rust clambered to the stern.

"No!"

"He's fisher, not fighter, Roddy. Stand clear."

Numbly, I did. I ought go along. Rust had sword. Mine was tucked safely in the bow of the boat. Still . . .

Rustin leaned into the net, caught hold, scrambled up.

On the broad deck above, screams, orders, calls. A sail fluttered.

Rustin disappeared over the rail.

Not again. I couldn't lose him again. Numbly, I reached for the net.

The chain shuddered.

"Modre ko!" *Kill him!*

The chain slithered into the sea. Rust darted over the side, scrambled down. His flank dripped red. He dropped heavily into the boat. Jahl hauled at the oars. We shot from the stern.

"Rustin!" My cry was agonized.

"A scratch." He pawed at his jerkin. "Well, a bit more, but—"

I tore off my cloak, pressed it hard to his side. He winced. "Live, my lord!"

"I intend to." He leaned back, with gritted teeth. "They were passing buckets, but they'll lose her."

"Two more barrels." Jahl.

I glanced about. Everywhere, sails burned. Not twenty paces before us, a ketch had hoisted all her sail and slammed into a yawl. Her prow skewered the smaller vessel. Masts tumbled. Behind us, on the brigantine, fire leaped to the skies.

From the sea, cries of distress.

"Rust, are you . . ."

"Do it!"

Jahl picked a fat, elderly vessel, beribboned with spars.

In the water, a head loomed. "Sal noas!" *Save us!* Desperate fingers gripped our rail. The sailor's body acted as anchor, slowing us, turning us about. I seized a spare oar, raised it high, smashed it down. His skull split. Slowly, the body sank. I swirled the reddened oar in the salt sea before setting it in the bottom of the boat. Rust watched without expression. We rowed on.

Above us, men dashed about the deck. A sail was in place; the ship began to gain way. Jahl and his companion bent to their oars. I scrambled to our prow. We neared their stern. I stretched, couldn't reach. Behind me, Jahl panted from exertion. Our prow wavered in the one-master's wake. I leaned far out over water. My fingers brushed the netting. Again. I had it. I hauled us in.

"Hold tight!" Jahl abandoned his oar, scampered forward, tied us expertly to the fleeing Norlander.

From a passing ship, in the Norland tongue, "They're at you!" Frantic fingers pointed our way. Then they were gone. In the confusion, no one noticed. Jahl heaved up the barrel, set it on his shoulder, launched himself. He climbed precariously up the netting. Perhaps he'd decided he was fighter after all.

Vexed, but with admiration, I snarled, "Madman!" I made ready the torch. Carefully, Jahl set the barrel on the Norlander's thick, flat rail. He reached down for the torch, lit the oozing pitch, slammed both palms into the barrel's side. It toppled onto the Norland deck. As Jahl scrambled down I cut the rope binding us to the Norlander. Our eyes met. We grinned.

Our two fishers rowed madly. One's oar slipped, dousing Rustin with a bucketful of salt spray. His head rocked back.

His knuckles were white on the thwarts. I shuddered, feeling the sting on my own ribs.

"One more barrel." Jahl.

"No!" I waved. "Look at them." A score of ships were alight. More, far more; we'd sent five boats, each with five barrels. And fleeing Norland ships had beached themselves, tearing masts from their hulls. Others drifted; some came about madly in an effort to reach open seas. Even as I watched two collided, in a jumble of fallen rigging. Half a dozen ships lay low in the water; one half-sunken vessel tore the bottom out of an unseeing comrade racing to safety. Twenty alight? More like a hundred.

"No," I said again. "Put us ashore."

Jahl growled, "We agreed . . . at Stoneshore village . . ." We'd agreed to rendezvous at the warehouse south of town.

Rustin groaned. He clamped shut his lips.

I snarled, "Look you!" Though the inlet was blocked, a handful of ships bore down on it, as if they might smash through their disabled companions. "We won't get through. Row for shore."

"They'll kill—"

Rust was hurt, and I'd had enough. "Throw the barrel over, and the torches. We're Norland folk saving ourselves. Be quick!" I got cautiously to my feet, peered about. "Over there, nearest the Keep." It was the last place they'd look for Caled raiders.

"If they ask—"

"I'll speak!"

Reluctantly, Jahl muttered to his seatmate, and the pair rowed for shore.

We were a small enough craft to avoid the ships blundering about the bay. It wasn't long before we neared the rocky breakwater that barred the Keep. A dismasted Norland barque blocked part of the breakwater. The rocky arm swarmed with men, some armed with swords, others bearing bows. Torches sputtered. Men ran about shouting orders. I crouched in the bow.

Our rowers reversed oars. We glided to a halt. I cupped hands. "Ayut noas!" *Help us!* Frantically I beckoned to gawking troops. "Grab the rope! He's hurt!" Softly, "Rust, don't speak. You men, carry him ashore when they—"

"I can walk."

"Carry him; they'll make way for wounded." Clutching the bag that held my coronet, I threw the rope to a soldier. He strained, holding us tight to the rocks. "Now! To the Keep!" I spoke Norlandic, but jabbed my finger at the parapet. To the soldier, "How many Caledi?"

"Swarms! They raid from the castle! And look! Three score ships attack!"

I snorted. Imps of night and confusion were our allies. "Lift him gently! Over the side!" *Lord of Nature, I was speaking Caled.* The soldier was as overwrought as I; he didn't seem to notice. Our four fishers hosted Rustin, carried him onto shore. I gripped my sword, ready to rip it from its sheath at the first outcry.

"Roddy . . ." Rust caught my arm in a fierce grip. "Your cheek!"

My palm flew to hide the scar. "Stand clear! You men, this way!" This time, I spoke Norl. I shoved aside bystanders. "Hurry!" I dropped my voice. "Rust, forgive me." I pawed at his flank. He gasped. My hand came away bloody. I wiped it on my cheek, and again.

I led my crew to the joinder of the breakwater with the coast road. The Keep was but fifty paces distant. The postern was still open, but guarded by a dozen hard men. Pikes bristled; swords were unsheathed. Above, on the wall, flickering torches cast shadows on scores of bow and swordsmen.

I growled, "Empty, my bollocks."

Rust muttered. "Why there? It'll be swarming with—"

"Where else would a Norl officer go? Be quiet!"

Rustin lay supine in the clasped arms of my four fishers. We trudged to the gate. I marshalled ill-remembered words. Hurt, wound, help, save, surgeon—

A huge hand clasped my shoulder, whirled me around. "Voe hae vos?" *Where do you go?* Beady eyes, a bushy beard.

I almost dropped my wrapped bundle. Then, "Coth?" I tried to smile, fought not to cover my cheek. "He's hurt. The surgeons . . ."

Coth's eyes flicked to Rust's blood-soaked jerkin. "Faranga Caledi!" A bellow, to the portal guards. "Let them in!" Our fishers inched forward; with a curse, Coth thrust them aside, lifted Rust into his blacksmith arms. "Make way!"

I hauled Jahl after. "Be quick!"

We trailed Coth into the Keep. He stalked to what once had been Llewelyn and Joenne's kitchen. "Surgeon!" His roar echoed across the cobbles. He kicked open the door. The room was empty. He laid Rustin on a table. Instantly, I bent over Rust as if to examine him. "You fainted!" My lips barely moved. His eyes promptly shut.

I looked up to Coth, "Are there no other wounded?"

"A few. Burned men—" A gesture, knife across throat. "—save them agony. I'll skin the first Caled I meet!" His eyes swept across our fishers, who, ignorant of the Norl tongue, stood unafraid.

I said quickly, "They're ours."

"I know. Surgeon!" Scurrying steps. A curtain parted. A lanky boy peered out. Coth snapped, "Help my friend!"

The boy disappeared behind the cloth. Coth slapped Rust's knee in comradely salute.

"Thank you." I nodded, almost a bow, as a burly Norlander threw open the curtain. He wore a smock stained red.

"This one too, he's hurt his face again." Coth felt for his sword, made sure it was in his scabbard. "Fare thee well." He extended knuckles, to rap with mine. Jahl and his crew watched openmouthed as he stalked out.

The surgeon bent over Rustin, unbelted his sheath, cut off his jerkin, peered at the bloody flesh. I gritted my teeth. He called for water; the boy scurried in with a wooden bucket. The surgeon thrust me aside, splashed it over Rust's torso. I flinched. Rust's breath caught, but he kept his eyes closed. The surgeon touched the wound gently. "Not deep. Long cut." He placed his ear to Rust's chest. A nod of approval. "Must be from loss of blood. He'll need be sewn or—" A word that meant nothing to me, but his hands explained. "Bound. Tight."

"Bind him." I had a horror of sewing, made no less so by the ghostly memory of my injury. I felt for the cloth I'd used earlier on my cheek, quietly tied myself while the surgeon's eyes were elsewhere.

Peering at Rust, he seemed dubious. "Sewing would—"

Outside, a commotion. A Norlandic sailor peered in. "Ayut ko!" *Help him.*

The surgeon peered outside. "Bring him in!" He swept

clear another table, returned to Rustin, darted behind the curtain, brought back long strips of torn cloth. Behind us, sailors dragged in a sallow man with a shattered arm. The boy ran back, emerged with a saw.

Jahl and I helped support Rust while the surgeon wrapped his torso several times around. "Inside, there's bedding. What about you?" He reached to my bandage.

I tried to sound modest. "Later."

He turned immediately to the other table. We carried Rustin into the chamber beyond, one I knew well from days past. We set him down on cushions. From the next room, a moan.

Cautiously Rust opened his eyes. "I told you it was a scratch."

A scream.

I said, "Lie quiet; they'll hear—"

"Oh!" His eyes flitted from mural to portico. It was his boyhood home. His expression clouded. "Can we not—elsewhere—"

I'd never know what possessed me. I bent and kissed his forehead. "Be silent, sir. I beg thee." Jahl and his crew saw it all. I felt the rising warmth of my blush.

Rust's eyes filled. Abruptly he turned to the wall. His fingers sought mine.

THIRTY-FOUR

SOMEWHERE, A COCK crowed. Wearily, I stretched.

The airy chamber in which we'd romped as boys was crowded with wounded, moaning men. I'd guarded our corner, speaking as few words as possible.

Rust, awake, lay still and rigid. Twice, I'd brought him water; dutifully, he'd drained the cup.

The sadness in his eyes caused me profound unease.

Of our sailors, only Jahl remained. His crewmen were gone. Hours earlier, while night still prevailed, I'd whispered my plan and escorted them to the postern gate, now firmly shut. I snapped orders in Norl, bid the guard open, sent them on their way. As if entitled, they trudged along the coast road, heads down, to the nearest avenue into the town. There, they merged into shadows, to wend their way toward their half-abandoned fishing village. But Jahl, fearing interrogation and arrest, had chosen the illusion of my protection.

Once, during the long night, I'd stepped outside to stretch and take fresh air. The Keep was, after all, not heavily manned. What few guards there were clustered at the southern wall, eyes toward Stryx. The northern wall, past the breakwater, was unlikely to face attack.

Our raid had been a wild success, and I ought to be elated. Dozens of ships were wrecked, or near so; sailors drowned and burned, the harbor near blocked. Why, then, was I near tears? Exhaustion, perhaps, and the sight of Rustin's scored flesh. Fleeing to the Keep had been no inspiration; Rustin's gloom became mine. It was his father's treason troubled him. What, finally, was I to do about Llewelyn?

I snorted. Judgment on Rustin's parent was premature. Any moment I might be unmasked and slaughtered; even were we to escape I could boast no army, no refuge, no hopes. Yet, we'd had, finally, an unmistakable victory, one that would at least check Hriskil's thrust. No doubt Sarazon would call for reinforcements and fall back on Stryx to secure his position.

That might relieve Groenfil and Soushire, or at least prevent Hriskil from augmenting his force there.

So, then, why did my eyes sting?

What I sought in Rustin wasn't corporal. I was steadied by his resolve, his justice . . . his love of my soul, even before my crowning, when no others could see my worth. Yet, when the crimson stain oozed down his flank, my heart near sundered. Were he child of my flesh, I could feel no greater pain. Was this love? Would I feel so for Tresa, were she mine? What feel I now? She was gone to me, most likely dead or made a Norland soldier's bawd. Did my heart sting?

Yes, but less so. Was it distance eased the pain? Anavar too was distant. I gritted my teeth, knowing he was too proud to surrender Verein. By now, he was dead. Whom did I mourn with dampened cheeks? Tresa? Anavar? Rustin?

I crouched anew by the bed.

SLOWLY, WITH DAYLIGHT, the Norland foe restored order. The gate was thrown open; night fears had passed. I yearned to survey the harbor, but didn't dare.

A Norland officer passed through the Keep, seeking names, sending men to their regiments. My command of their tongue wouldn't bear close scrutiny; thrusting aside my revulsion, I painted my bandage in a dead man's blood, feigned unconsciousness. Jahl managed not to be seen. When the officer had gone, I allowed myself to waken.

Rustin regarded me quietly. "What now, my prince?"

I whispered, "You're regent; what say you?"

"I defer to my liege." Grunting, he pulled himself to sit. "Oh, that smarts. By what stratagem will we leave the Keep?"

"I'll decide at the time." Unparalleled arrogance, I realized too late, but he merely nodded as if he understood.

Jahl looked uneasy. "You don't *know*?" He kept his voice low.

"One never knows. One seizes the chance." It didn't reassure him. "It's true even of Hriskil," I said. "Kings know no more than churls."

"Oh? Then by what right do you rule?"

I bristled, opened my mouth to deliver a stinging rebuke, realized I had none. "I don't know."

Rustin smiled. "You ought be a counselor, Jahl."

Outside, the clatter of hooves. I peered past the portico. A
rider flung himself off his mount, ran to the dwelling's
guest-gate.

After a time, the heat of day permeated the room. Brushing
away flies, I dozed.

More riders. The sound of distant horns.

"Roddy!" Rust was careful not to be overheard, though the
chamber now held only a few grievously wounded, and ourselves. "Something's amiss."

"What?"

He shrugged. "I don't speak Norlandic."

Rubbing my eyes, I got to my feet, wandered outside.

Clumps of soldiers stood about. Listening, I edged toward
a squad of guards.

Wild rumors flew, as they had during the night. Verein had
not surrendered; Sarazon's thousands were in retreat. A fierce
Caled army had fallen on his caravans; the road from Stryx to
the hills was a deathtrap. Caledon had a great navy, hiding just
south of the harbor; tonight it would disgorge untold thousands. Sarazon would abandon the city.

I trudged back inside. "The usual nonsense."

"More." Rust sat, head back against the wall, eyes shut.
"They're worried, I don't need their speech to know that. And
too many riders come in haste. Dispatches, I'll warrant."

"This is their headquarters. Of course riders—"

"Can he walk?" The surgeon. Lord of Nature, if he'd heard
us speaking Caled . . .

I struggled to assemble my Norl speech. "If not, we can
carry—"

The surgeon said gruffly, "Get him to his regiment. They'll
have wagons."

"What . . . why . . ."

"We march to the hills." He turned, examined the stump of
a hapless sailor's leg. "We join Hriskil."

"You mean Sarazon."

"Hriskil, at the siege of Groenfil."

I managed, "All of us?"

"Yes!"

"And the Keep?"

"All of us!" His face set in stone, the surgeon stomped
off.

Hurriedly, I translated for Rustin and Jahl. I added, "We've got to get out. The fewer here, the more they'll notice—"

Rust said, "My room." When I was a boy, we'd slept there the night when I was too tired to ride up the hill. It annoyed Mother, but perhaps she knew I must have a friend. I knew well Rustin's room, a small chamber at the end of a corridor on the second floor. He reminded me, "The door has a bar."

"If they torch the Keep—"

"They won't; they'll want it on their return. And there's a window to the roof."

Moments after, we supported Rustin, one on a side. We slipped through the disorder of men and officers gathering supplies, bringing horses for their officers, loading wagons, assembling in squads. It helped that we knew our way about. No one guarded the servants' stair; we hurried up, found Rust's chamber abandoned. It was made up for an officer: desk and chairs crowded the unassuming bed; a leather map was nailed to the wall.

Safe within, we barred the door.

"Now what?" Jahl.

"We wait."

"My boat is smashed." His tone was accusing.

"How know you?"

He pointed to the window. From this level we had view over the wall, to the breakwater. He spoke truth; our fragile vessel was stove in.

Hurriedly, I closed the shutters. To mollify him, "You'll have the best boat in Stryx."

"How?"

"Jahl, we've no time for—I'll buy it."

He snorted. "When you visit my hut?" Apparently intimacy bred scorn; gone was the awe at my rank that had prompted him to adhere to my cause.

I said, "When all is done, climb the hill just past the wall. Come to audience. Choose a justice day; the great hall is open to all my subjects. I'll see you're rewarded."

Jahl rolled his eyes. "When all is done . . ."

Rustin's eyes grew hard; his mouth opened for some scathing remark. I held up a palm. "Jahl, in the alehouse, was it not you who set this coronet on my brow?" A reluctant nod. I said gently, "I am not king without you. You have done great service, for which I am humbly grateful. Why do you chide me?"

He swallowed. "Pardon, King." Then, his tone forlorn, "It was my only boat."

My voice was soft. "We too mourn. Caledon is our only realm."

From his bed, Rust's eyes studied my features.

An hour passed, and another. Ever so cautiously, I inched open the shutter, peered through the crack. A squadron of pikemen in the courtyard awaited their officer, who conferred, on horseback, with another. At length, he gave signal, and they set off. They marched through the gate, made their way down the coast road. No doubt they meant to turn east on the Seacross Road we ourselves had traversed, and make their way to Sarazon's column.

In haste, there assembled a train of milk-carts, high-sided drayer's wagons, flatbeds, every sort of wagon one might find. They creaked beneath the weight of corn sacks, wineskins, flour, household goods, piles of furs, sturdy chests, leather cured but not yet sewn.

I muttered, "They'll uproot the trees next."

One by one, the wagons lurched through the gate.

A flatbed wagon lumbered through the courtyard, pulled by a sturdy team of six drays. It was filled with wounded, lying on straw. Behind it rolled a cart, smaller, also near full. The surgeon's boy—he reminded me of Genard—scampered across the cobbles in chase, threw himself over the backboard, disappeared jouncing past the gate.

A few soldiers still walked the battlements, ill at ease, distracted. Some craned their necks to see the stables. I said softly, "The surgeon was right; they're all pulling out. But, why? If anything, Sarazon ought make himself snug in the Keep. Winter won't be that long coming."

Gingerly, Rust probed at his bandage. "Unless Hriskil assumes the war will be done. Jahl, help me to the chair." Together, they eased him from the rumpled bed. "Roddy, don't chew your lip: I'm half healed."

No more than a dozen soldiers were left on the parapet; they traded glances. Finally, one shrugged, descended the stairs three at a time, ran across the courtyard to the larder. The others raced after. I had no view, but needed none; the crash of a splintered door was view enough. In a while they emerged, bearing what bottles as they could carry. The last staggered under the weight of a cask. One found an unhitched mule cart and dragged it near; they set their booty within. Two pulled; two pushed the cart through the gate.

"Now." I rose. "Rust, can you walk?" Carrying his sheathed sword and my precious bundle, I unbarred the door.

"Certainly." Disdaining Jahl's arm, he rose to his feet. "Where?"

"Our horses are hidden in the Stoneshore warehouse." If the Norlanders hadn't burned or plundered the place. Too far, especially for Rust. I brightened. "The castle!" We had but to climb the hill.

"Lead on." But a half dozen steps left him clammy and pale. Still, he rebuffed my offered shoulder. "Don't coddle me. I said I'm well enough." His tone was short.

I shifted his sword to my left hand, drew my own. We tiptoed down the stairs.

The Keep was deserted. When we reached the portico Rustin stopped to lean on a pillar. "Jahl, the stable's past the kitchen, over there. See if they've left an animal."

"I'll go, my lord, but would they have dragged the cart if a horse were stabled?" He peered cautiously around the corner before setting forth.

I said, "Rust, we need climb the hill."

"What if I go upstairs, bar the door and wait? The castle is ours, ride down with a spare—"

"I can't leave you behind. You're hurt and can't fight." And I wouldn't lose him again, not for Caledon itself. "Looters and drunken troops abound."

"Nonsense. Every last Norlander has gone. Not a soul is—"

The clatter of hooves. A sprightly gray gelding cantered through the gate. His rider, a cavalryman bearing sword, spear and shield, looked worn and dusty. "Voe ordru?" *Where are the officers?*

Casually, I sheathed my sword, trudged across the cobbles. "Feran moni." *They flee to the hills.* Or was it *mona*? "I wait for Sarazon's dispatches. There's water in the well." I pantomimed a dipper.

"When did they go?"

"An hour." I caught his reins. "Qa vos dom?" *Who is your lord?*

"I'm Parth, I ride for—aiyee!" His jerkin caught in my grip; he toppled to the cobbles. He tore free. I leaped on him as he pulled loose his sword. We rolled in the mud and filth. I fastened a deathgrip on his wrist.

He was the stronger. I thrashed in frenzy, but he ended up on top. He twisted free his arm, raised the sword with both hands, point down, to skewer me to earth.

A blade flashed. My eyes screwed shut at the instant of death.

A breath. Mine. Incredulous, I opened my eyes.

The soldier sat atop me. His gaze flickered down, at the swordpoint protruding from his chest. Behind him, Jahl raised a foot, braced it against the man's spine, yanked free the sword.

A gout of blood from the soldier's lips.

Jahl raised high the sword. Down it plunged, cleaving the soldier's skull. I screamed. Blood and brains splattered my cheeks. Somehow, I thrashed free of the corpse, rolled aside.

Catching the gelding's reins, Jahl led him to Rust, handed him back his sword.

On my knees, I retched, tore off the bandage, now bespattered with more than blood, wiped the rest of my face. Shakily I got to my feet.

Jahl's face showed nothing. I nodded. He said, "A three-master. Trading as well as fishing rights."

"Done." He might have asked half Caledon, and I'd be hard-pressed to refuse it.

"We'd best go," Rust said.

"In a moment. Jahl, kneel."

"Why?"

"Roddy, if they see the corpse—"

"Because the king so said!"

Uncertainly, Jahl found a spot less filthy than the rest, got to his knees. I unsheathed my sword, touched his shoulders. Behind him, two townsmen peered through the postern, saw us, and disappeared. I said quickly, "As thou has greatly served thy king, I ennoble thee and name thee Baron Jahl of —what's the village name? Stoneshore. To your descendants, and all that. We'll do it right, in the castle. They've records, and . . ." I waved vaguely, and picked a mushy bit of brain from my hair. "Help Rustin mount. We're best gone."

*   *   *

I LED THE gelding up the winding Castle Way. Jahl—Baron Jahl, I must remember—kept hand on the pommel, watching that Rust didn't fall. Rustin had protested, of course—the king must ride, did I think him a weakling, he'd climbed the hill a thousand times, if he'd climbed it—until I said a few fierce words no youngsire ought utter to his guardian. At least it quieted him, perhaps to contemplate my penance.

Below us, a haze of smoke rose from the market and the houses behind Potsellers' Way. I hoped the town didn't burn, but there was naught I could do about it.

Stryx was strangely silent. In the harbor, a few ships worked their way past the wrecks at the mouth of the bay. A score of Norland sails remained, though not a shadow of what we'd seen the day past. The quay was void of sailors, though some worked feverishly setting masts in keels, stitching sails, fitting wood, mounting rigging.

Our gelding labored up the steep hill. At the trail that turned to Besiegers' Pond, where the road was flat, he balked and would have gone down the level footpath. I forced him onward. Rust swayed in the saddle. I said, "Need you rest, sir?"

"No, my prince. A bed, and broth." But his cut had opened; his bandage was damp with red.

"Soon."

"Roddy?"

"Aye, sir?"

"How did you know the Keep would serve us?"

"I couldn't see us wandering the town, with the garrison searching for Caleds. We must hide, and boldest was best."

At last, we walked the last winding, and the road opened to a narrow rocky plain before the walls. The gates were shut, and the wall bristled with guards, more than Stryx ought have.

I fished in my bag, removed my coronet. *It's I, Roddy, the wandering king who calls unbeknownst at castle gates. Usually they open; sometimes their bowmen take aim.* I cleared my throat. "Hail the wall. Open for—"

The gate flew open. A dozen men flew out. A score. A hundred.

"Stand clear!" A high-pitched voice, one I knew. "Lead the horse! Help them in!" Sensing the end of the journey, the tired gelding summoned will and trotted inside, guided by twenty hands. Rustin swayed, gripping the pommel.

Framed in the gates, an apparition. A slim figure, with auburn hair flowing from a crested helmet. A man's tunic under a shining breastplate. In her hand, a bejewelled sword.

Tresa of Cumber.

"Lady of the Hill!" Jahl fell to his knees. His cheeks were damp.

I said stupidly, "She's not the queen. Elena's dead."

"We've come, Lady. Late, but . . ."

"Take ease, good sir." Tresa's voice was gentling, as to a frightened mare. She strode toward me, her pace slowing. At the end, she attempted a womanly curtsy, chose instead to fall to her knees, as would a knight. Her clear voice rang out. "My lord King!" She proffered her sword. "Stryx is yours!"

"It always was." It was all I could think to say.

"For their sake . . ." Her voice could scarce be heard. "Let them attend . . ."

I summoned my wits. "Rise, my lady!" Gallantly, I offered a hand; it was flecked with dried blood; hastily I wiped it on my leggings. "In the name of Caledon, we greet you."

Together, arm in arm, we passed into Castle Stryx.

THIRTY-FIVE

RUSTIN, ATTENDED BY servants, limped off to bed. At the castle well I'd scrubbed hands and face, and, upon reflection, my hair. Now I stood dripping, waiting for a servant to fetch a cloth. Tresa's eyes sparkled, though she managed not to smile.

"Pieces of a Norlander . . . I dared not touch you with—" I dare not touch her at all. She'd fled me, and rightly. "What do you here?" My tone was more severe than I'd intended.

"I recruit for your cause." Judging by the crowded courtyard, she'd had no small success.

I stiffened. "Have we men to send to the Keep? They need not be warriors; the Norlanders are gone. But our folk will loot it . . . have they begun? Can you see?"

She cupped her hands. "Sir Willem!" He strode across the stones.

It was then I had my second surprise. A weathered face, no longer soft, presided over a body grown muscled. Willem of Alcazar, Mother's chamberlain, and now mine. A very proper bow. "My liege."

Automatically I bowed in acknowledgment. "I was . . . we're . . ."

"Roddy—his majesty—wants horsemen to occupy the Keep. Else there'll be looting."

Willem said, "I'll see to it. Koban! Trisk!" He issued crisp orders. To me, "The townsmen will be turned away, no more. They're starved and brutalized." How then might order be kept, when no authority was present? But, on reflection, I nodded consent. "And send to Stoneshore for Rustin's Orwal and my borrowed steed. Jahl will show where they're kept."

Willem waved past the wall, toward the harbor. "Magnificent. Did you send them?"

"I led them—that is, Rust did. I only went along to . . . Rustin took his wound cutting loose a brigantine."

His eyes were shrewd. "Whose idea?"

"Rust's." My response was so quick I'd no time to think. It

might not be truth, but in a way I couldn't explain, it was just.
I stepped back, took the measure of him. "You've hardened."

Willem's lips twitched in a brief smile. "Thank you."

"Why?"

"I thought long about your mother, Elena, and when we played as children. I imagined what she'd want, but Stryx had no warrior to hold its walls. I've always been . . ." He looked at his fingers, still soft. "I'm no great swordsman, but in these days, it's how I best serve."

"Thank you, my lord. There are wild rumors, you know. Twenty men hold Verein against Sarazon, Elena Queen is risen and is Lady of the Hill. Sarazon flees—"

"That's Tresa." A familiar bow of cousins, though they were not. "She's the Lady."

I gaped. "You've been bottled in the castle. How would they know—"

"Sarazon held Keep and town, yes." Tresa looked modest. "They didn't bother to send soldiers chasing up the hill for a washerwoman wandering about on a mule."

It made little sense, and I battled exhaustion and the aftermath of fear. "Speak plainly, else I'm off to tend Rustin!"

Willem held up a peaceable palm. "Tresa left Soushire weeks ago, shortly after you did. Stryx, of course was in Sarazon's hands. She threaded her way past Norland patrols to the village of Fort, where she left her steed in the innkeeper's hands—"

"He charged me outrageously!"

"—and procured a mule—"

"With nearly the last of my funds."

"—which she rode here."

I finally got a word in. "Past Sarazon's troops?"

"Not in my best clothes. My face was filthy. Whenever I came on company, I had a tendency to gabble—"

"Evidently."

"Roddy!"

I took deep breath. "Pardon, my lady." A stiff bow.

Willem said, "She rode right through Stryx, that first day. Pounded on the postern gate to the Keep, demanding entry. Grumbled and fussed when they refused. She led her mule along the Tradesman's Cut outside the Keep's walls, and up the hill, shaking her fist at the guards."

"Just that once," said Tresa. "Afterward, I judged the route too risky."

I waited, summoning patience. Their parchment would scroll at its own pace.

Willem said, "Once Tresa persuaded our gatekeepers she was a noblewoman, we had . . . well, quite a talk. She was, er, miffed that I didn't do more for your cause, and told me so in no uncertain terms. You were near destitute—was I hoarding your gold, and why?—and your army dissipated. Unless we took action *forthwith*, your cause was lost. I reminded her you'd stripped our walls months past, but it didn't serve. She would not be pacified."

Tresa said coolly, "Armies don't just appear. They're recruited."

I glanced up at the sun, down to the shadows. "Let me know if this mummery goes on 'til night. I'll send for candles."

"Rodrigo, you owe her regard and more." Willem's tone held rebuke.

It was he to whom Mother had sent me for chastisement. I colored. "Pray continue." I'd send for candles. And a bed.

"One day she slipped out, a washerwoman on her mule."

"But not past the Keep, you said. Where . . . how . . . ?"

Tresa smiled. "The trail past Besiegers' Pond. You showed it me once."

"Long past." I tried to imagine it. "And then to Fort . . ."

"To get my horse, and change into this." Her gesture took in her garb. "I went hamlet to hamlet, speaking of the king. The first night, I brought back six. We crept in late of the night."

"Churls?"

"But they learn. Willem set guardsmen to teach them, and brought out weapons from stores." Tresa hesitated. "I dared not use my name, for fear it get to Sarazon, and he bar my route. I called myself Lady of the Hill. The villagers, ah, seemed to enjoy the drama. Word spread."

Willem looked pleased, a proud grandsire. "The third day, two of our troops went along as guard. Volunteers, of course. That night she led home twenty, the next eve, twenty-five. One night, fifty."

"After a few days I found a peasant hut to hide my horse. I

needn't ride all the way to Fort. With the hours that earned, I began circling behind the castle to the fishing villages south of Stryx. I may have met your man."

"Baron Jahl?" My tone was cool. "Quite possibly."

"Roddy, she swelled our numbers by a thousand. The castle's well defended. Each day our guards are more proficient."

I gestured to her helmet, her breastplate. "Why all that?"

Tresa said tightly, "So they'd listen. As you pointed out at Soushire, *I'm only a woman.*"

I made my fists unknot. "Willem, might you leave us a moment?" I waited. Then, "I'd be a better king with my tongue cut out. I pray your forgiveness for such a boorish remark."

She studied me. Her eyes softened. "Granted, my liege."

"I owe you much, and thank you." My hand strayed to my scar, stayed to shield it. "I ought tend to Rustin." I stopped. "Do you know about . . . ?"

She smiled, and her visage lit. "One morning I awoke and knew he wasn't dead. Roddy, I'm so proud of you!"

"You . . . remember the other?"

"Your grace, your leadership. It was, and wasn't. What a noble sacrifice."

Resolutely, I faced a wild charging boar. "I sacrificed more. I intended . . . a Return . . . my scar . . . I meant to make myself fit for *you.*"

Abruptly, her eyes teared. "Why must you think you're not?" The hint of a curtsy, and she half-ran to the donjon.

Drying cloth in hand, I stared at her retreating form.

A judicious cough. Willem. "Well, my liege. Go mollify her."

I blinked. "She's loyal to Caledon, and I'm ever grateful, but look!" I rubbed my scar. "Surely she's repelled!"

"Roddy . . . my liege . . . pardon. At times I still see you as a boy. Know you how she presented herself to your vassals? The Lady of the Hill, consort to the king." Then, "Was she false?"

"Willem, I—I—" I gulped. "You can't imagine how I wanted it."

His tone was gentle. "Then go make it so."

"She won't . . . laugh? Scorn me?"

"No, lad." For a moment I imagined him Lord Groenfil, or Josip, my father. "Set right what's between you."

His blessing starched my resolve, all the way to the donjon doors. Once inside, I inquired where Rustin had been lodged. There'd be time for Tresa after.

I found him lounged on a cushion bed, watching a servant girl light a fire. His bandage was fresh changed. It seemed Willem had the castle well in hand.

Rustin followed my eyes to his ribs. "You ought have let him sew me."

"You'd have cried out in Caled."

"You're so sure?"

Behind us, the fire caught.

"I did, sir. It *hurts*."

"Well, no matter. In four days, I'll be as new. It was a scratch. Oh, shush. A *deep* scratch." Then, "Have you seen her yet?"

"Aye. We talked."

"And?"

"She rides all about Stryx. Instead of being gladdened, I insulted her." I grimaced. "What comes over me in her presence?"

The servant girl poured fresh water.

Rustin chuckled. "She has a fearsome way about her. That day she—"

I blurted, "I think if I ask nicely she'll have me again."

"—pulled my ear—"

"WHAT?"

We each stared, as if the other had gone mad. "Sir, you had a long ride, and lost blood . . ."

"Stop that at once!" He raised himself.

The girl glanced between us, as if gathering herself to flee.

I said cautiously, "You asked if I'd seen Tresa."

"I spoke of Nurse Hester, you dolt!"

I shook my head, sat in a daze. After a time, I began to chuckle, and soon couldn't stop laughing. Seeing me, Rustin joined, and clutched his ribs in pain.

When all was done, my gaiety vanished. "Rustin, in all these months, I've not thought once about our nurse."

"You've had much—"

"She raised me!" And now sat above, in the old nursery, her mind long wandered. "I think always of self."

"Go, then."

I threw open the door just as a page skidded to it, hand raised to knock. A quick bow. "Willem says—I mean, his respects, sire, and I'm to tell you we've word from Verein, and Groenfil's land."

Willem was in his usual office, in the wing that had once served Uncle Mar. "Come in, my liege. The falconer thought to check the dovecotes." He offered me tiny scraps of scrolled parchment; I left them for his reading. "From Groenfil's castle: Hriskil grows ever stronger. If we would aid them, we must hurry. And worse, Groenfil's sons had . . . a falling out. Franca stabbed his brother, Horst, who lies abed."

"The Rood again." May imps drown Hriskil in a lake of fire.

"From Verein," Willem said, "happier news. Anavar writes the Norlanders are repulsed. Sarazon's entire army withdraws toward Soushire and Groenfil."

"That's not possible." However valiant, Anavar defended Verein with but a score of men.

"What arrangement had you with Groenfil?"

"After the sailors joined us, Rust sent a man to the wood above Stryx, where Groenfil awaited us. If our raid succeeded, he was to fall on Sarazon's supply trains. The idea was to lure Sarazon down from the mountains."

Willem grinned. "In that, you failed. You meant to save the earldoms, and saved Stryx. I've sent riders up the Seacross Road. They need be cautious, not to blunder into Sarazon's retreating column. When they find Groenfil, they'll bring us word."

I grunted. "Send a courier to summon Anavar; I must learn what Power my young baron wields. I have need of it. Meantime, it seems I'll ride to Groenfil."

"If you denude our walls yet again, you'll command near a thousand, plus Groenfil's four hundred. Is it enough?"

"Enough to try. If Groenfil's holding falls, the earl will lose heart." And he'll lose his sons. Never forget that, Roddy.

Somberly, I made my way up the stairs. The nursery, Hester's old domain, was on the third floor, above Mother's chambers, which I'd never made my own. Perhaps it was that I encountered the queen so often in the cave, perhaps I merely felt too young. To lie in her chamber seemed the act of a usurper.

Hester's quarters were quite another matter; I'd slept there oft enough in my infancy, and in my youth on nights I fretted and was forlorn. Since earliest memory she'd bathed me, clothed me, bound my scrapes, dried my tears. After Mother died she smuggled Elryc out of Stryx and put up with my endless tantrums on the journey to her familial farm. When we parted roads, she boldly steered her ungainly wagon to Verein, to ferret out her baby Pytor's whereabouts. At Cumber, where I'd gone to be crowned, she reappeared, Pytor's corpse in her wagon, her wits unhinged.

Breathing hard from the stairs, I knocked softly. No answer. I knocked harder.

A harsh rasp. "Put the tea by the door. I'll fetch it anon."

"Yes, madam." I made my voice shrill, like a housemaid's.

A chair scraped. In a moment the door creaked open. "What raillery is—"

Warily, we regarded each other.

Hester's gray shawl was wrinkled but clean, frayed but serviceable. Her hair was wild, as if she gave it no thought. I could hardly say she'd aged; when I'd first laid eyes on her, she was older than the hills.

Her rheumy eye half-closed in a scowl. "What great overgrown boy is this?"

I found myself bowing, the respectful bow of youth to elder, one I'd never in my life afforded her. "Roddy, my lady. Have I leave?" My tone was uncertain; some tremor caught at my speech.

"Not Roddy; that clod would shoulder me aside to root for sweets in my larder." Whatever she may say, she was aware who stood before her, and we both knew so.

At the worn table I turned her chair. She trudged across the planks, eased herself into it. There was a bench opposite, but I wanted . . . what *did* I want? Awkward, a boy again in spirit, I glanced from bench to door to table to chair and . . .

Collapsed at her feet. Wondering if I too had lost my wits, I set my back to her, leaned against her knees, as had been my wont before I grew lanky and disdainful. "I've missed you, madam." I closed my eyes, yearning for a clawed hand on my shoulder, for a proffer of tea, for her acid disapproval of love, knowing they were forever lost.

For a while, I said nothing.

"It's few enough visitors climb the stair. One morn they'll find my corpse under the covers, and there'll be end to it." A sigh. "Since Elryc left, and Pytor . . ." A creak, as she shifted. "There's naught fills the chamber but dreams."

"When war's done, I'll visit every—"

"Child, see why Marta dawdles with my tea."

"Aye, madam." I jumped to my feet. By her fireplace there was no pot, no mugs. Was Hester properly tended? If not, I'd turn the castle over. I raced down the stairs, made my way to the kitchen, demanded tea and sweet pastries. They scurried about; it wasn't often the king played housemaid.

Scant moments later, I was back up the stair. I set the teapot in the embers, busied myself with a mug and the crushed leaves. When all was ready, I poured and resumed my place.

She sipped. "War's changed you, Roddy." Her voice was tart, as of old. "Or is it the coronet?"

"War, and . . ." How could I explain. "I've lost so many comrades. Uncle Raeth, and Imbar. Soldiers I sat at fire with, and held for the surgeons." No, that was a lost dream. "And Rustin too, for a time."

"For that, I pitied you."

"It wasn't so bad," I managed. "I tried to—it was lonely, but—really, I—"

A withered claw brushed my shoulder. "I've seen your tears. Set them free."

"It's not—he's back, I have no reason to—just hold me, Nurse." I rocked to and fro, bewildered at my misery.

"The road is exceeding narrow, young King, and hacked from a cliff. You guide your mount along its perilous way. Above you, sheer stone. Below—"

I twisted round. "Hester?" In a moment, her mind had flown.

"—below, a sheer drop to the rocks. So you go on, because there's no turning. Stop staring as if I'm daft!" Her sharp nails squeezed me in painful warning. "You go on, along that cliff road of life, until you slip off the edge. You can't turn back, no more than I!" Her clouded eyes near overflowed. "Oh, the Return works after its fashion, but even that Power can't bring you to what was."

I nestled my cheek on her bony, veined hand.

"No more than it can transport me to when you were a tot,

and Elena young and strong, to when I held you and rocked you and . . ." Silence.

I turned, to see damp cheeks, eyes staring to distance.

"Ah, Roddy, that's the way of it." A brisk pat. "Up, foolish boy, the floor is chill."

"Yes, Nurse." I slipped onto the bench, put chin on hands, studied her across the table. "If we can't go back, I'll make our road as smooth as it may be. You'll have tea, and a chambermaid all day, and—"

"Don't prattle. You come alone. What of her?"

"Who, Nurse?"

"That auburn-haired, starry-eyed beauty who moons for you. Oft enough she's climbed the stair alone; why not with you?"

"We quarreled." I blushed. "I'm about to seek her."

"So you hide beneath my skirts." She brushed them smooth, as if to thwart me. "Willem's a fool, to let her slip out the gate. One day they'll seize her."

"How know you . . ."

"Have I not eyes? Does not my window look down on the wall?"

"You miss little."

"I miss my boys. Where are they?"

I said gently, "Pytor's dead, madam."

"Yes, sometimes I know. Where's Elryc, that he doesn't dog your heels?"

"He's safe." I told her of the refuge Larissa of Soushire had provided.

Hester stiffened. "And so you left him?"

"We rode hard, and he began to sicken. Our lives were at hazard and—"

"Oaf!" Rising, she swept her mug to the floor, where it smashed on the planks. "Great blundering fool! Marta! MARTA!" She hobbled to the door. "Where's that lazy—"

"Hester, what would you?"

"A wagon, or failing that, a gentle mare. I'll hobble where you fear to tread."

I scurried to the door, barred the way. "Nurse, please! If I've done wrong, tell me—"

"Done wrong? You've killed your brother!"

"Heard you not a word I—"

"You rest on Larissa's oaths, you who wriggle through them like a mouse through a knothole! Have you *no* sense? Oh, my Elryc!" She snatched a cloak from the hook, her stick from its nook by the door. With its end, she prodded my ribs. "Out of the way!"

I held my ground. "Why would Larissa betray me?"

"Why would she not? What beyond that laughable oath secures her loyalty?"

"Groenfil's surety. They're fond of—beyond fond, I think they cohabit—"

"Knew you a whit about rutting, you'd not be so simple! Glare more, and I'll wipe your face clean!" Sharp-nailed, bent fingers hovered near my cheek.

An awful harridan, and I loved her. I swallowed. "Where ought I have sent him?"

"To me!"

"I could not; Stryx was in the hands of—"

"Sarazon, the monster. The terrifying brute who ran yowling into the night at first peril. For fear of him, you abandoned Elryc. Did you not swear to value your brother above your crown?"

"And I do still!"

"Then keep him by your side!"

"Aye, Madam!" Mother at her most imperious couldn't have cowed me more. With honeyed words, I coaxed and wheeled Hester out of her cloak, into her chair. I swept the shards of her mug, poured another, promised I'd send for Elryc the moment we knew the roads clear. At that, I'd have to keep a sharp eye on the stables; she was perfectly capable of commandeering a cart and setting out on her own.

"Is there anything else, Nurse?" I paused at the door.

A sigh. "Go to your woman." She snorted. "Lady of the Hill, indeed. Elena would pull her hair." But her tone was benign. Then, as I left, "Send up Pytor, it's time for his rest."

I CHANGED MY tunic before seeking Tresa; Hester had wilted the one I wore. I need not take Nurse's worries all that seriously; if Groenfil and Rustin were content, I ought be. But nonetheless, her fierce loyalty to Elena's sons warmed my heart.

Tresa herself let me in, leaving me to wonder if any servants at all attended her. She raised an eyebrow. "It took you long enough." A note of mischief in her tone.

"I know not what to say. It's our usual mode of discourse." I girded myself. "My lady, if I may inquire . . ." *Just say it, Roddy.* "When I asked your hand, it was with the promise this vile scar would be gone. I assumed you felt the same. But today . . . outside . . ." I licked my lips, not quite daring to repeat what I'd heard. "What say you of it?"

"That it matters not."

"Can you truly mean that?"

"Oh, Roddy, it hurts you so." She came to me, ran a gentle finger from eye to chin. Barely, I did not cringe. "I hate your disfigurement for what it makes you feel. But in no other way."

"But I . . . looking at it, can you . . . if I were fat and smelled of garlic, you'd find no attraction. As grotesque as I am, how can you not . . ."

"If I were scarred, you'd turn away?"

"I think so." I reddened. "You see, I'm callow and stupid. If I knew you not, I'd be repelled."

"But knowing me?"

I cried, "How can I not love you?"

"But surely I couldn't think the same. I'm only a woman."

I faced her, took a daring step closer. And another. "Don't toy with me. I toss and turn the night through, yearning for you. Almost I regretted saving Rust's life, for your loss. Always I've assumed that, thanks to Mar's work, you were beyond me."

"I called myself consort. Shall I cease?"

"No, my lady. Be my consort." I looked about, so muddled I feared looking foolish. I got down on my knees. "I beg you, Tresa, confirm you'll be my wife, damaged as I am." I managed to hold her gaze without flinching.

"Do get up! I said I'd have you as husband, not bondsman." Her eyes were merry. "Kiss me."

Our lips met. Arms around her, I closed my eyes, marveling in my fortune. Suddenly her tongue moved past mine. A tingle, and more. I squawked, broke free, propelled myself backwards until I slammed into the wall. "What—why did—*Tresa!*" I wiped my mouth.

"Yes, my liege?"

"That's not—no lady would—*where did you learn that?*"

Her look was demure. "Did it not please you?"

"No! Well, it startled—yes, but—stop laughing, I command it!"

"I don't . . . I'll try not to, but—there, I've stopped, you see? Have you never been kissed?"

"Not like that!" I twisted in an agony of embarrassment. "I've only groped one girl, a servant named Chela, and she was nearly the ruin of me. I've had to hold myself—oh, Lord of Nature, I must go. Your leave, Lady." But she caught my arm, whirled us around so she barred my way to the door. "You promised to stop laughing." My tone was accusing. Then, "Where did you learn such a thing?"

"In Cumber, there was a captain of the guard. We'd walk the parapet . . . are you appalled, my liege? Should I be as innocent as you? Then what, on our wedding night?"

Almost, I demanded, "Are you virgin?" but at the last moment came to my senses. I stumbled to a bench, put head in hands. I tried to picture our first night, but my mind shied away. What else might Tresa know, that I barely dreamed of? I'd have to ask Rustin, as a youngsire might his father. And if he too laughed, I'd need jump off the high tower.

"Here, my love." She bent to me. "Just a kiss. No surprise."

Again, her lips met mine.

THIRTY-SIX

TIGHTLY BOUND AND moving with caution, Rustin waited with me on the donjon steps to greet the savior of Verein.

Escorted by Groenfil and Danzik, Anavar pranced Edmund through the postern gate. In a signal honor, I raised my hands to applaud his arrival. My court followed suit. He bowed from the saddle, radiant and bursting with pride.

As soon as was seemly, I cornered Anavar by the stable, away from prying ears. Only Rustin was present, and Bollert, who rubbed and brushed Edmund. "Well? How'd you do it?"

Anavar's grin faded to something more wistful. "I didn't, sir."

"Sarazon panicked? A rabbit hopped out and alarmed him?"

"Not exactly." To Bollert, a grin, and one returned. "The Norlanders came at dawn. The field was thick with them. No parlay, no offer to spare lives. Against their thousands, we were lost. So . . . I called Bollert to the wall." Anavar clapped him on the shoulder. "It was he saved us!" The groomsman, patting Edmund's nose, leered a snaggletoothed grin and looked demented.

I blinked. "How?"

Anavar's eyes sparkled. "I had him race the length of the battlement, back and forth, waving and shouting so they'd look at him. 'Run away!' he yelled. 'Be afraid! Run!' They were befuddled; no one thought to look away. Each Norlander who heard turned and bolted to the ravine. After a time we let them come closer, for greater effect; besides, Bollert was winded. At the last moment he would pop out from behind an arrow slit and shriek; what soul wouldn't glance at that? 'Run! Feel terror! Begone!' All in hearing cast aside their ladders, dropped spears, ran as if demons gnawed at their heels. Oh, sir, could you have seen it!"

What nonsense was this? "None had presence of mind to loose a shaft at a screaming churl?"

"A few, but Bollert was stout of heart. And I followed close, with my shield. It took two arrows. The rest missed."

"But—you can't—he isn't—" I spluttered to a halt. "That's no way to war! Where's the honor? And Powers are for a royal house to wield. How dare you usurp—Rustin, don't tug at me, I know what I'm say—*all right!*" I twisted free, clenching my jaw.

"The king apologizes," said Rustin. "He's astounded by your feat. A touch dismayed, perhaps, that Bollert's power rivals his. But he'll get over it. Won't you, Roddy?"

"Yes, sir." Almost, I was sullen, but good sense burst through my petulance. "It's unheard of. I'm—" A deep breath. "You held Verein with twenty men." I shook my head at the marvel of it. Still, doubts assailed me. "It was your notion, Anavar? Entirely?"

Anavar said, "The night before you rode, did I not ask for Bollert?"

"That was before—" I gaped. "As soon as then, you conceived it?"

His shrug was modest.

"Well done, Anavar. You have my heartfelt thanks. Rust, shall we go? Imps and demons, don't glare so! If I've done wrong, say it!"

Holding his ribs, Rust made his way to the donjon. I threw up my hands.

"My lord?" Groenfil. "May I have word?"

"In a moment." To Anavar, "He's moody. Pain makes him more so."

Anavar said stiffly, "He thinks you ought to thank Bollert."

"Is that so?"

"As do I."

I tried to scowl him into submission, but he held firm. I sighed. "It's not meet. A bondsman *owes* his liege service. Why, just yesterday, a fisher from Stoneshore . . ." *And was made baron for it.*

No, not Bollert; he'd make a laughingstock of nobility. Still, Rust and Anavar were right. I was acting the Roddy of old, and found I wasn't proud of it. Resolutely, I turned my gaze to Bollert. The groomsman scuffled straw with his torn boot. I said, "Recall you the Warthen's Gate? You saved my cause, until the need was undone by Rustin's return."

My bondsman nodded.

"And now again. Thanks to you, Verein is saved. What would you, for reward?"

He shrugged. "Dunno, m'lord. A sly grin. "Sleep in donjon, 'steada stable."

An easy price. "Done." Then, reluctantly, "Bollert, you ask not enough. Confer with Anavar; he's skilled at wheedling boons from his lord. This eve, we'll settle."

I turned to Lord Groenfil. "Your raids went well?"

"Exceedingly." He permitted himself a wintry smile. "Jatho found us, and we watched from the hill. All was dark. Then a firefly, in the harbor. And another. Soon the bay was alight. Magnificent, Roddy." Groenfil stinted no praise; it made me feel shabby before Anavar and Bollert.

"My easternmost scouts reported Sarazon's haste to leave Verein. Meanwhile, two circles of their wagons camped on the road; our mounted scouts had left them unmolested. But if ever was our moment, it was now. Deep in night we sacked them, and left the trail to rest. Dawn came, and morn. By twelfth hour the Norland exodus from Stryx had begun."

"We saw it."

He was deep in recollection. "I made no attempt to block Seacross Road; instead, we crossed it north to south, crashing through the column from Stryx, pulling wagons over, spearing pikemen, putting anyone within reach to the sword, disappearing over the hill. Then, half a league east, the same, crossing south to north. And again." Some grim resolve kindled in his eyes. "I'd be there still, were not the horses utterly spent. To Bollert, "I heard, over Rodrigo's shoulder. You have courage. We thank you."

Bollert's eyes lit, and made me feel a miser. I said quickly to Groenfil, "You made camp . . . ?"

"A league up the road. Roddy, Willem told me about my castle."

"It was the Rood, my lord. Your sons were helpless before it."

Straw swirled in a sudden breeze. "No matter, if they spill each other's blood. I must go."

I said, "*We* must. As soon as I retrieve Elryc from Soushire."

"Today, my liege."

"Impossible. Elryc—"

"My sons! Would you my castle fell?"

Helplessly, I looked about. "It's near dusk."

"Time enough to join my men."

"Rustin's not well enough."

"Let him ride in a cart."

How was it I spoke of Groenfil's domain, and not Soushire? Inwardly, I sighed. I would ride to Elryc the moment Groenfil was comforted. Hester's warning should not be ignored; for all her temper, she was a canny old soul.

Meanwhile, Willem's new-found troops must need time to assemble; they were new at the soldier's game. "Ride ahead, my lord," I told Groenfil. "Harry the Norland stragglers. Anavar and I will organize the march and leave at dawn."

"You'll be two days behind us!"

"That is so." The wind gusted. I said evenly, "Govern your passion, my lord. It's always thus with troops afoot."

"If my sons die . . ."

He was my most faithful vassal, and I must give him more. "I'll ride ahead, to join you. Take a string of extra horses. Ebon—"

"And I." Anavar.

"—Ebon will be spent." To my baron, "Would you not hold Verein?"

"That danger's past. No Norlander who fled the field returned to face Bollert. Sarazon decamped rather than risk their mutiny."

"Very well." To Groenfil, "We ride at dawn and will meet you midday." As I started for the donjon Anavar called, "Wait, sir!"

"Now what?" I was less than gracious.

"Look what I found!"

"Gold?"

"You might say so." With great care, he eased a bundle from his saddlebag, began to unwrap it.

"I know you mean well, but give it directly to Willem. He needs to pay—" My voice trailed.

Anavar unwrapped the other half of the bundle, presented it to me with a flourish.

I sank to a round of baled hay. "Where did you get them?"

"I forced Verein's strongroom."

Odd. Knowing the value Mar placed on them, I thought he'd find a more cunning place to secrete the Vessels of the Still.

Oh, in a pinch, dirty water would do, in a cracked bowl, but stillsilver was better, and made the sight clearer. And the Vessels—the Chalice and Receptor that Mother had shown me in her strongroom, in my callow, foolish years—were the essence of my Power. I'd seen them but once, used them never. They ought augment my Power as stillsilver did water.

I ran my finger across the rim of the Receptor. Did I imagine the tingle? I shivered. "Thank you."

Anavar bowed.

"With all my heart, Anavar. You do me great service, over and again." Reverently, I covered the Chalice. A great peace descended. My eyes strayed to the groomsman Bollert, who watched raptly. He'd saved Verein, and given me entry to the Sands, that Rustin might live. Not once had he used his Power against me, when easily he might. I swallowed. "Come hither." I touched his shoulder, cautiously, as if he might bite. "Bollert, I slight you without thought. I know not why. Well, yes I do: you're lowborn, and I seem only to value nobles. It's a failing Rust hasn't knocked out of me. I pray pardon. Willingly I free you, though I ask that you stay with me. Would you?"

The boy's eyes shone. "Aye, m'lord!"

Anavar's posture eased. "Thank you, sir. He's grateful too, though he hasn't the words for it."

"Come, let us be gone, lest they dine without their liege."

RUSTIN'S EYES BLAZED. "You agreed *what*?"

"To ride at cockcrow. Groenfil's steadfast and true, and needs help." I glanced at Anavar, who sat on our bedside bench, but he offered no support.

"Roddy, what possesses you? Did we not wrestle with Hriskil before Groenfil's gates? Were we not repulsed?"

"Yes, but—"

"When we had far more men?"

"Aye." That force, or its remnant, now safeguarded Elryc and Lady Larissa at Soushire.

"Yet you convene a handful of unblooded men, churls a bare month ago, and hope for better? Are you addled?"

"We've had success and need follow it with another."

"Why?"

"That our adherents not lose heart."

"It's rash, headlong, and why I'm made regent."

Anavar stirred. "He's right, Lord Rustin. Think on it."

"Be silent!" To me, "I'd not overrule you before Groenfil, and you know it."

"Your pardon, sir." I made my voice meek.

"Go, Roddy. I love you, but you vex me."

I made a short bow, friend to friend. I swung open the door. Rust said sharply, "Not you, Anavar. Stay." It was like a slap. Disconsolate, I went to wander the courtyard. I was moody and tired, and when I saw Danzik sitting in the shade of a tower, I joined him.

The Norlander studied me. "You hasten the end."

"By chasing Sarazon?" We spoke Norl; I took care with my words.

"And Hriskil, when you should turn and run."

"Not today, *Guiat*. I've no patience for our play."

"I speak serious. Sarazon gives you Stryx, so you think he'll always flee."

"You think not?"

Danzik said, "A cornered wolf will turn and bite."

"Why warn me? Is that not your desire?"

He was silent a long while. "*Qay*. But you and El-e-rek like . . . hounds sleep in tent. Not want them wolf's dinner."

"Why, Danzik! Do you say you'll miss me?"

A reluctant grin. "*Quix iot*." *Perhaps a little.*

ANAVAR STAYED LONG with Rust, behind a barred door. After, when he emerged, he said as little as he might. When he was gone, I peered into our bedroom.

Rustin sat in a cushioned chair, squeezed wineskin in hand. His face was flushed. Seeing my raised eyebrow, he snapped, "Look to your own conduct, youngsire. Don't upbraid mine."

"Not a word did I—"

"Go to Tresa. Say your good-byes to Hester. Confer with Willem."

"But not you?"

He scoured the ire from his tone. "Not this eve, my prince. Not 'til we sleep."

"What troubles you, sir?"

"Nothing I'll speak of."

I dined, and cheered my nobles, and gave audience to Jahl of Stoneshore, that Willem might record his ennoblement. When I returned to my chamber, Rust was drowsy and disconsolate. He said only, "I'll stay in Stryx, to heal. Two days, or three."

"I approve."

"I order you, Roddy: risk not your life in foolish daring."

"I won't, Rust." I settled in bed.

Before dawn, a knock awakened me, and swiftly I dressed. The castle was a stirred anthill; cooks dipped ladles in huge vats of porridge, feeding men who shuffled past with their bowls. Outside, horses neighed, kicked at their traces, as our column was assembled.

At the stables, Anavar tugged at Edmund's bridle, walking him to the door.

I caught his arm. "What said you to Rustin?"

"He bade me not speak of it."

"I require it."

"No, sir, not today. Trust me in this." He held my eye.

Our party on horseback was small: Anavar, Danzik and I, and my bodyguards, led by Pardos. The men on foot would follow; our task was to overtake Groenfil by twelfth hour. We cantered out the gate, slowed to walk our mounts down the steep twisting road to the bay. The way through Stryx was long but ultimately faster; we had use of better, straighter roads than the trails bypassing the city.

We alternated canter and walk, resting our horses briefly where we might. In an hour or so we covered the league to Groenfil's camp of the night before, but the earl had roused his cavalry early, to press on to his domain. At least he'd had the courtesy to leave Jatho in the vacated camp, to urge us onward. And, in noteworthy kindness, he'd left us a dozen fresh horses. I transferred my gear, glad to give Ebon rest.

It was well past twelfth hour when we came upon Groenfil's outguard, mounted bowmen concealing themselves by the side of the road. They pointed the way; we spurred our tired mounts and soon found ourselves among the main body of his force. They were taking water from a stream.

Groenfil's bow was perfunctory. "Where are Willem's recruits?"

"Far behind," I said. "Why the shock and dismay? You knew it would be so."

"Time is short." He paced, thrusting Anavar from his path with a gesture of annoyance. "Hriskil's noose tightens. Sappers near the north wall, where the tower needs repair."

I asked, "How do you know this?"

"Scouts, on fast horses, half-killed." His tone was grim.

"By tomorrow our foot soldiers—"

"Tomorrow Hriskil will attack!" A gust twirled leaves from the willow. "Willem said Horst is sore hurt. Franca relies on him to direct the archers."

It was Franca who'd stabbed his brother, but I knew not to remind the earl.

Anavar's tone was soothing. "My lord, your sons have stood firm, have they not? One more day—"

"Horst took his wound three days past. That means Hriskil is rested from use of the Rood. Tomorrow, he'll wield it again." Groenfil ceased his pacing to face me. "Roddy, I must ride."

"I implore you, don't throw our force piecemeal into the fray."

He said forcefully, "I hazarded domain and castle, sons and all, knowing that unless you were saved, all I had was lost. In return, I ask leave to defend my domain."

Anavar said, "My lord, all the king wishes is that we gather our strength. With Willem's thousand—"

I knew not right, and had nobody to ask. Rustin was fretting in his bed, and Mother far distant in her cave. I might bid Groenfil wait, while I invoked the Still to consult Mother and my grandsires, but I'd squander use of the Power for no less than a day and a night, even for the shortest meet in the cave.

Groenfil wheeled on Anavar. "Youngsire, why must you insert yourself in my converse with the king? Is it affair of yours?"

Anavar struggled to make his tone meek. "I meant no offense, but can you not see it troubles the king when—"

"The Rood is fearsome. You care not that it destroys my sons."

I took deep breath. "No, my lords. Beleaguer not each other; you're allies in my cause, and I cherish you both."

Groenfil disregarded it. "What is your answer?"

"Your horsemen must wait for the men of Stryx."

His face was stone.

I said, "But we ourselves will ride the night through, a score of us, no more. At Groenfil Castle I will do battle with the Rood."

OF THE NIGHT'S ride, the less said, the better. I was saddle-sore, exhausted, frightened of the struggle to come. The horses were near spent, the hills ever steeper, the dark a miasma of terror.

When Groenfil inquired what place I sought, all I could tell him was a grove or wood where we might not be seen, near the plain from which rose the castle. I knew not the spot, hoped against hope we would find it.

Anavar reminded me I'd promised Rustin I'd not risk my life in foolish daring. An easy vow, but hard to preserve when my kingdom demanded daring and resolve. I comforted myself, saying that what seemed foolish in the planning appeared a stroke of genius if fortune smiled on the gamble. In retrospect, only those gambits that failed seemed foolish.

We'd long since left the main road; we were too near Hriskil and Sarazon to risk a stray encounter. As dark had fallen, of necessity our pace slowed. Now, we picked our way along a miserable overgrown trail, ducking low-hanging limbs that might pull us from our saddles.

Anavar spurred alongside. His voice was low. "I won't call you from your trance 'til battle's done. Or ought I?"

"I don't know. The cobra will be strong." I hesitated, then abandoned reserve. "I fear the cave, Anavar. I grow chill at the thought of it."

"If he—it—bests you, what then?"

"Perhaps it means death, though I think not."

"The Rood *is* fearsome. To counter it, you must know it is used, and in the learning, we're at each other's throats. Much is already lost."

"I know."

Anavar's tone was gloomy. "If only Hriskil had not the advantage."

In the eastern sky, stars began to fade. Cursing, I urged on my unfamiliar mount, leading Ebon by the reins tied to my pommel. Dutifully, Anavar followed. A muffled yelp marked where brambles caught his leg.

When I thought I could no longer bear it, the steep slopes gave way to rolling hills dotted with sleepy hamlets. Groenfil spurred to the head of the column, led us off the narrow trail. We climbed a hill, and another. Abruptly, we were on a wooded rise. Below lay the plain, and rising from it, Groenfil Castle. I caught my breath. Hriskil's main force was to the north, though the keep was enveloped, and siege maintained. His camp was astir, though no attack was in progress. Within the castle, torches moved about.

"Spread a blanket." My voice was a rasp. "Anavar, the Vessels."

"Aye, sir." He busied himself at the saddlebags.

I hugged myself. Truly, I dreaded the cave, and endless combat with the hooded viper. The Rood was wielded as it was fashioned to be, but the Still was a poor shield; its fit use was to consult my forebears, or, when occasion demanded, to worry a poor silversmith, or compel Genard to dance. As Anavar said, Hriskil had advantage. Always it would be so.

"Unless . . . do I dare?" I'd never used the Still in such a manner. I didn't even know if it was possible.

But I meant to find out.

"What, sir?" Anavar knelt, Receptor in hand.

"Pour."

"Not yet, sir; save your strength. Their army does not march."

I looked up. "Now."

THIRTY-SEVEN

ANAVAR STRIPPED OFF his cloak, settled it over my shoulders.

Groenfil paced, muttering to himself.

Pardos had drawn his sword, though no foe was remotely near. His men wielded bows, pikes and swords; a gallant but trifling defense if we were discovered. He and his band blocked my view of the plain. It mattered not. I would see with other eyes.

I set my palms across the Receptor.

With the words of encant, the wooded rise faded, as did the plain. The mist began to clear. The mouth of the cave loomed.

No. I planted myself, resisting.

For a moment, I was disoriented, as if waking from a blow on the skull. Some force, barely understood, urged me strongly to the firepit.

I turned my back, strode into mist.

Time passed, while I worked to master my craft.

Abruptly, I saw the plain. I squeezed shut my eyes, to focus on my work. The Still required close presence of the object, except . . . where was the Rood?

The plain grew clearer.

Like a lazy falcon, I rode a warm current of air over brush, campfires, pikemen, horses, tents. Norland troops waited, assembled in regiments; officers pointed to Groenfil's battlement.

There, *that* tent, the one with regal accoutrements. No matter. Were I blind I'd know it was the one.

Hriskil?

A groomsman held the reins of a fine black charger, combed, saddled, bridled, snorting.

Where is the king?

I sweated from the effort, but now I was in the spacious tent. Royal emerald trappings hung from the poles. Plush curtains apportioned it into chambers; one held the king's bed. The spare, soldierly furniture was in striking contrast to the effete luxury around it.

In the tall grass, officers led their troops to the field.

On the floor, exquisitely knit rugs dyed in emerald and black. How incongruous, for a savage who exulted in cruelty.

Hriskil sat in a rough-hewn chair, tying his sandal laces. A youth waited, holding breastplate and fur-lined cape.

Where is it? My eyes roved.

"They begin their march, sir."

Be still, Anavar!

Behind the king's patient attendant, a peculiarly shaped wooden chest: long, high, shallow. Burnished ash, dovetailed corners. Grunting with effort, I peered within.

Soft, luxurious cloth, binding something hard and harsh.

Hriskil glanced up, startled. After a moment, he finished his binding, slipped on the breastplate.

Take it, King, I panted. *Take up the Rood.*

Hriskil swung to the boy, grasped him, clubbed his temple with knotted fist. The boy reeled.

It wasn't he, demon's spawn!

Hriskil's eyes darted this way and that. He tore open the tent flap. The groomsman proffered his steed.

Take the Rood, King!

On Groenfil's wall, a shrill trumpet's blast.

RODRIGO?

Aye.

Hriskil dived into the tent, shoved aside the stunned youth, pulled open the chest, tore off the cloth.

A bejeweled cross, twisted, marked with runes.

His fingers stretched toward it.

I braced myself. *Oh, yes, King. Take it.*

Hriskil grasped the Rood. His fingers recoiled as from a flame. He clutched his wrist. Again, he reached for it, this time with caution.

I gritted my teeth.

His head whipped back, his teeth snapped shut. A tremor. In an instant it ended. Almost, he fell.

Wield it, brave King. Touch it anew.

From within the tent, a bellow. Half a dozen guards rushed in to attend their king. Hriskil roared. They cringed. An officer, braver than most, reached to the Rood.

His fingers touched.

He stroked it, looked in puzzlement to his king.

Hriskil spat a curse. He strode forward, took the Rood with both hands.

I hunched over my bowl, lips moving, forehead clammy.

Hriskil took two steps. Abruptly his back arched. His eyes bulged. The Rood clattered to the emerald carpet, skittered under a table. Sweat beaded the king's brow.

His guards converged, eased him to the bed. They laid the Rood near.

WHERE DO YOU HIDE, CALED REZ?

I paid no heed.

SON OF THE WHORE, BEARDLESS VIRGIN!

Take up the Rood, Norlander. Don't cower in your tent. Go forth with your Power!

WHAT DEMONRY IS THIS?

The Still of Caledon. Behold, and be afraid!

He seized a guard's throat: "Rodrigo is near; find and kill him!"

Outside, Hriskil's confident legions marched across the field. Behind them, horsemen made themselves ready. Archers paused in midfield, knelt with bows stretched. Pikemen took their places before them, a bristling wall of spears.

My heart pounded. I couldn't do this for long.

On Groenfil's wall, a frantic scramble to set rocks in place, heat the oil. Yeomen raced up parapet stairs with quivers packed full, distributing arrows to grim-faced archers. Soldiers gripped grappling rods to fend off ladders.

FIGHT AS A MAN, ROOD VERSUS STILL! I'LL CRUSH YOU TO DUST!

Mouth dry, muscles aching, I focused on the Rood.

PRETTY TENTBOY! KING WITHOUT SHAME!

Evermore, Hriskil, when you wield your power—

He leaped from the bed, snatched up the Rood. Almost, he wrapped his mind around it. A burst of malignant hate corroded my attention, sent me reeling toward the cave. With the dregs of my strength, I locked in struggle for the hard iron cross.

My strength ebbed. I concentrated my whole being.

He howled, dropped the cross. DEMON! NEXT TIME, THINK YOU I'LL LET YOU NEAR? I'LL SCOUR THE COUNTRYSIDE TO UNEARTH YOU. YOUR CHURLS

WILL DIE SCREAMING, YOUR LINE EXPUNGED!
CALEDON WILL BE MINE!

Outside, Norlanders trudged into battle. From the wall, the
first volleys loosed.

I settled in the emerald tent, while Hriskil ranted his impo-
tence.

"RODRIGO? MY LIEGE?" Anavar's voice.

Begone!

"Oh, don't, that hurts!" On my shoulder, the gentlest touch.
"Please, sir!"

I looked about. Of Hriskil, of the Rood, there was no sign.
Around me, walls billowed as servants hastily struck the tent.

Wearily, I withdrew from that far place of the Still. I peered
at Anavar. "What is come to pass?"

"The attack is . . ." He sought a word. ". . . abated." He gestured to the field below.

In good order, at their own pace, Hriskil's legions marched
from the field.

My tone was unbelieving. "A whole day is passed?"

"No, sir. Barely two hours."

A shadow. I looked up. Groenfil, a modicum of peace in his
eyes. He murmured, "My liege, what . . . how . . . ?"

"I denied Hriskil the Rood."

"But last time you contested with him, the battle waxed and
waned. At times he had us so vexed . . ."

Haltingly, I explained.

Groenfil knelt, peered into my eyes. "Can you do this
again?"

"Perhaps." Next time, Hriskil would be forewarned.

"Pray it is so." Briefly, the earl closed his eyes. "I'll see my
sons."

"The castle's still under siege."

"No, it's lifting. The Norlanders depart."

It was so. Swarms of attendants dismantled engines of siege
and dragged them from the field. "But, why?"

"I know not." He gave the hint of a smile. "Perhaps their
king's afrighted."

A FULL DAY and a half, before the last of Hriskil's hordes decamped, and we had entry to Groenfil Castle. Though I'd have

liked to ride to Soushire, that was impossible; the enemy host lay between us and Larissa.

During the enforced wait Groenfil summoned his four hundred horsemen, Danzik among them. The Norland chief was astounded. Hriskil gone? How could it be? Hriskil had vast superiority of numbers and ought win every battle. The Rood was never bested. He and Hriskil knew all about the Still, it was a petty Power, good for annoying vassals, divulging forebears' secrets. They'd long since discounted it.

I gazed upon the vacated field, letting a smile play upon my lips. Danzik muttered darkly, casting me perplexed glances.

A day's march behind our horsemen labored the yeomen and churls from Stryx. As they toiled up Seacross Road I held my breath lest Sarazon turn and maul them, but that cautious warrior was too intent on merging his force with Hriskil's. He met his master in the Southron hills, twixt Groenfil and Soushire. If the two Norland chiefs reproached each other for cities abandoned, I had no word of it.

Our entrance into Groenfil was a regal procession. The earl would have ceded me precedence as his liege, but I insisted he lead the triumphant march, with Anavar and me behind. After all, we were at his domain, delivered by his perseverance.

Once within the walls, Groenfil hurried to his son Horst's bedside, emerged a half hour later with at least some relief of spirit. Next he closeted himself with Franca. Winds swirled between wall and stables, blowing eddies in the courtyard. Afterwards, father and son wore thunderclouds. I remarked only that Groenfil ought to acknowledge the Rood had part in the brothers' estrangement, but the earl cut me short.

Two anxious, fretful days. While Groenfil rested his horses, he sent scouts to every hamlet of his dominion to assess what Hriskil had wrought. At last, our weary column from Stryx tramped in, having taken care to avoid the Norland force.

From the sparse chamber Groenfil assigned me, I wrote Rustin and Tresa, entrusting my scrolls to Groenfil's couriers. If I made light of my achievement in my missive to Rust, leaving the impression that the dash to Groenfil Castle had been the earl's idea, and that we'd been perfectly safe, and well hidden in a remote wood, my reticence could be attributed to natural modesty.

My scroll to Tresa proved more of a problem. Somehow, I

couldn't bring myself to salute her as "My dear betrothed," while "Lady Tresa of Cumber" seemed awkward and formal, though that was her title. By the time I'd discarded my third parchment Anavar was giggling openly—why I let him loll about my chamber, I didn't know—and I was hard pressed to turn aside my rancor.

In my contest with Hriskil I'd used the proper and powerful Vessels. Perhaps they further augmented my tendency to cruelty; time and again I found myself aghast at what I proposed. On the other hand, within a day of wielding the Still, I felt confident I might use it anew, should it be required. All in all, I preferred my true Vessels, and it was Anavar who'd unearthed them. So, I gritted my teeth and endured his raillery.

Our recruits from Stryx weren't used to a long march with heavy packs; we ought give them a day to recover. Larissa's keep was well defended; it would take Hriskil a week or more to mount a proper siege, and months or years to starve her out. A day didn't matter, yet I fretted and stewed as if Caledon were crumbling.

Upon reflection I found it remarkable how our fortunes had turned. I wished I could claim credit, but Sarazon had that honor, or perhaps Hriskil did, for appointing him. At Stryx harbor, Sarazon had squeezed his fleet as tight as feathers in a down cushion. That foolishness gave potency to our fireships.

I'd been fortunate, too, in countering the Rood. Almost, in our earlier encounter, the cobra had bested me. If I hadn't thought of preventing the Rood's use, rather than combatting it, Hriskil would still be encamped about Groenfil Castle.

Still, whatever the cause, my campaign was no longer quite hopeless. Yet—I cautioned myself, pacing my chamber— Hriskil commanded a force far larger, far better armed than mine, and was determined to grind Caledon under his heel. All we'd gained was a breathing space, and perhaps more will to fight on. The road still climbed uphill, our mount spent and struggling.

"To RODRIGO, KING of Caledon, from Rustin of the Keep, regent of Caledon, his guardian and ever friend: greetings.

"I am overjoyed at your tidings that Lord Groenfil's holding has been relieved and Hriskil is fled. You are entirely too

*modest depicting your part in Groenfil's deliverance; we will
have words on the matter directly.*

"*Yes, Hriskil will soon invest Soushire, but I remind you
that your force is too small to counter his army. My scratch
heals well, and I will set forth on the morrow, at a slow pace.
Expect me second-day hence, or third-day if I find riding
Orwal vexes my wound and must take to a wagon. On my arrival we will confer as to our best course.*

"*In the meanwhile, my liege, so as to protect you from your
own courage, I admonish you: do not depart Groenfil Castle.
I charge you with obedience to this my order. Hriskil cannot
commence a siege against Soushire in less than a week, and
may, in fact, turn west instead, to reclaim Stryx.*

"*Know, Rodrigo, that Rustin cherishes you, and his heart is
gladdened at our impending reunion.*"

"PLEASED?" TRYON STIRRED the chill embers. "Elena, did you
teach him nothing? For generations our line nurtured a mystery of the Still." He cracked a dry stick, hurled it into the fire.
"But your whelp trumpets its use. Silversmiths and stableboys
know its potency. And for what? That a bondsman's inno-
cence be proved, or a slight at table be avenged!"

I said meekly, "Neither wielding damaged us, grandsir."

Tryon said, "What of Hriskil, child? Pressure of the mind is
the most potent attribute of our Power, and only surprise allow
its use. That's why we hoard it. You revealed it in a mere skirmish."

"No." Mother. "Groenfil's his steadfast ally. If the earl left
him, his cause would be lost."

Tryon snapped, "What's Groenfil or any earldom, to Caledon itself? Varon, Cayil, speak I not truth? The boy ought
have waited until he'd maneuvered Hriskil and his entire force
into a grand battle to decide all. Then, only then, he might reveal—"

"Father, he couldn't know that. I never told him."

"Why not? Recall you, Elena, when the Warthen had mind
to break away, and you forced him to bind himself as vassal,
by oaths most severe? Think you that he'd have fallen into
your snare, knowing your resource? He'd have fortified himself behind Warthen's Gate, and the Sands wouldn't today be
Rodrigo's."

I cleared my throat. "Um, Grandsir? There's something I ought tell you."

ANAVAR AND TANNER helped me to the bed. I flopped on the cushions. The punishing sun of autumn afternoon stabbed my eyes.

"Where were you, sir?"

"In the cave." Gratefully, I gulped cool water from Anavar's cup. My tunic was soaked through; I'd need bathe before Rustin met me, and that would be soon. It was the third day since his letter.

"Rest, sir. You'll feel well anon. Did you take advice?"

I groaned. Once I'd told them about surrendering the Sands, my forebears' outrage was scathing. Varon's blast of fury hurled me from the firepit to fetch up against the wall. Cayil danced about, beside himself with waspish ire. Others whom I'd not known—one dressed all in furs—added voice to the rising chorus.

"They were . . . displeased that I freed the Warthen. That I confounded Hriskil and too soon denied him the Rood."

"You cried out. Almost I woke you."

"They say I'll pay great price."

"Don't fret so, sir. My father says bad news knows its time, and will—"

I put finger to his lips. "Let your father rest. Tanner, have them send hot water."

The bath was warm and soothing, and I emerged refreshed and in better spirit. After dinner, Anavar and I climbed a tower to peer into the dusk, in the hope we'd spot Rustin urging onward his faithful Orwal. We found no sign of him, or a column from Stryx, along the Southron Road. Well, he wouldn't be long. There was no one in the world I'd rather have near, though Tresa followed closely. Still, I wasn't fool enough to think Rust would overlook my disobedience in tackling Hriskil; he'd warned me so in his letter. "We'll have words on the matter directly." I felt a twinge of discomfort, and not a little resentment. I was near grown, and long crowned. Rust was regent, but in his absence, shouldn't I rely on my judgment?

We watched until the twinkling fires at peasant huts were all we could see. Later, I'd barely settled myself in bed when sandals clattered in the anteroom. An urgent knock: Tanner, bleary and tousled. "He's here, m'lord."

Heart soaring, I leaped out of bed, threw on my clothes, raced down the stair. In the courtyard, grooms led away half a score of horses. "Rust!" I threw myself at him.

Deftly, he fended me from his injured flank, returned my embrace. "My prince . . ."

"Our chamber's upstairs, I'll show you—how was your ride? Any bleeding? I worried so. Mother and Varon are furious about the Sands, I shouldn't have—" Too late, I heard my own prattle, cut it short. "We welcome thee, Lord Regent."

His eyes glinted with humor. "I thank thee. Has Groenfil meat and bread for a starving traveler?"

"Come, I'll order you a banquet. Tanner, see his baggage is put in our room."

After dinner, we closed the door behind us. With care, Rust stripped off his jerkin, massaged his scab. "Ahh, that's better. So, what have you to say for yourself?"

"About what?" I managed to sound innocent.

"About your wild jaunt to Groenfil. Did you not promise me you wouldn't risk your life?"

"In foolish daring."

"How many of you rode through the night to Groenfil?" He sat on the bed, grappled with a boot.

"I don't know, it was he who chose—twenty, Rust."

"It was Groenfil's idea?"

"He was anxious to go." That much was true, was it not? And so, ultimately, our ride had been Groenfil's idea. Under Rustin's cool inspection, I scratched an itch, looked casually out at the night, rubbed my hands. "Ask him, sir. He'd have thrown his horsemen into the battle, had I not dissuaded him."

"No doubt." Rust's tone was chilly. "If you loved me as I do you, you'd tell truth."

"I don't lie, it's—" I swallowed. Then, all in a rush, "It was my idea. Groenfil would have fought and lost; I knew not else how to preserve him."

"The rest of it, Roddy." He tossed aside his boot, tugged at the other.

"We were on a rise; with sharp eyes the Norlanders would see us. But we had view of the field; none could approach without our knowing. We were safe."

"And from behind?"

"We posted an outguard as best we could. We were only twenty, Rust."

"And my orders?"

I took bit between my teeth. "I disobeyed them."

"Not for the first time."

"No, sir."

"Why, I wonder, did you make me guardian and regent? Ahh." Contentedly, he tossed aside his boot, wriggled his toes.

"To restrain me."

"Which you resist."

"Not in personal matters. Look, I've fresh clothes, Anavar says they match. I washed my hair—"

"You're saying you're clean but disobedient?"

I couldn't restrain a smile. "I'm sorry, truly I am. But it was statecraft. Didn't you say I had an instinct?"

His voice had an edge. "What good statecraft if you're killed?"

"What good life if I'm dethroned?"

We glared. Finally he said, subdued, "Get ready for bed. There's no use in more speech."

We lay awake half the night.

THE NEXT MORN we met in conclave. I demanded that we take our army to Soushire. At best, we'd retrieve Elryc from danger. Even if we couldn't break through Hriskil's lines, our presence would make the Norland king cautious. If attacked we could fall back on Groenfil's land, and, should need arise, we could make our way to the safety of Stryx.

When all pros and cons were debated, Rust tented his fingertips, thought a moment or two. "Soushire."

THIRTY-EIGHT

DANZIK DISMOUNTED, STRETCHED his legs. "Do you tire of him?"

"Eh?" Cautiously, I held a tent peg while Bollert pounded it.

"Rustin." A sly smile. "Sa toda farang vos?"

I hissed.

From a recess of my mind, Genard's distant voice. *"M'lor', don't let him goad you. Why allow him the pleasure?"*

"Not for many months." I managed a grin. "We're too busy with your mother." I hesitated, but he mustn't cow me, or our lessons were done. "Why do you ask?"

"The look in his eyes." Danzik was serious now. "He thinks you'll send him away."

"Never. *Bollert!* You nearly took off my hand!"

"Sorry, m'lor'."

Danzik said stubbornly, "He thinks so."

"Impossible."

But that night, Rust was distant. As dusk fell, he sat by the fire nursing a wineskin, making clear I wasn't welcome. I retreated to my bed.

Presently, a knock at the tent pole. Anavar looked uneasy. "Sir, he wants—Lord Rustin demands you instruct me to speak of . . . private matters."

I roused myself on the cushion. "What nonsense this?"

"He wants me to tell him about you, in the time he was dead. And last week in Groenfil's Castle, before Rustin joined us. He ought ask you, I told him, but he says that as regent, he commands it on your behalf."

"Why?" I fell back, staring at a drop of wax oozing down the hour candle.

Anavar said hotly, "I won't say a word. He goes behind the king's back to—"

"Tell him what he would know."

"It's not meet!"

"Everything, youngsire! Whatever he asks."

Anavar looked stubborn, but said only, "Aye, my lord."

Hours later Rustin stumbled to bed, reeking of an alehouse. In the morn, he rode with Groenfil, not me.

At midday we gave men and horses rest. Rustin sought me, led me out of hearing, sat me under a beech's shade. He shared with me a loaf. "Tell me of Pezar." He grimaced. "When I was dead."

"That night, when I worked my Power, you knew all I—"

"Not all. You held back, I felt it. I would hear it all."

"It's nothing we ought—as you say, sir! I beg pardon!"

His fist unknotted. "Pray continue."

Unwilling, I dragged my thoughts to Hriskil, my challenge, my ride to his camp, the Norland death wagon that near unhinged us all. I knew not how long I spoke. Groenfil approached, but Rust waved him away. My words grated on.

At the end, my voice was dry and cracked. Rust got to his feet, patted me absently, wandered off as if he knew not the path.

I found Ebon, mounted him. Anavar eyed me; sharply I shook my head. I'd have no conversation about what had just passed.

Soon, we were on our way.

I RESOLVED, ON the weary trail, to ease Rustin's mind. I mapped my campaign; I'd begin with fowl. He particularly liked the legs and thighs, slow roasted. Tanner would help; I'd show him how to turn them slowly on a spit. Send him away? Outlandish nonsense. Whatever imp troubled my guardian, I'd oust. He deserved that from me, and more.

Our march was deliberate, unhurried; outriders probed ceaselessly for Hriskil's force.

Eons passed before we made camp for the night. Under a star-strewn sky I hurried to the cooktents, commandeered two fat chickens, plucked, dressed and ready. I sent Tanner to a nearby elm for deadwood, busied myself making a spit of two forked sticks dug carefully into the earth. A slim green bough of just the right size made a splendid spit; wet wood didn't burn, and wouldn't drop our succulent birds into the coals.

By moonlight Bollert helped erect our tent, and Rust sat before it, a reluctant smile twitching his lips. It wasn't so long ago that I tended to protest bitterly at a share of the camp's work; here was the king, cheerfully cooking dinner for his regent.

While I nursed the fowl, riders trotted to Groenfil's tent and left anon, dispatched on new errands. For the moment I ignored our scouts; the earl had matters well in hand. After a time, I left the birds, ferreted out a pair of wineskins, carefully watered the wine to half strength with chill water from the brook, presented the first to Rust.

His tone was suspicious. "What will you ask of me before night's end?"

"Nothing, sir."

"Hah. You've a scheme in mind. I've known you too long."

A rider cantered past, dismounted, ran into Groenfil's tent. To Rust, I pretended hurt I didn't feel. "May a ward not honor his guardian?"

"Too long, I say."

The browning chicken dripped fat into the coals, and the aroma near drove me mad. I swallowed drool. Anavar hurried by, knotting his cloak, despite the day's warmth. "You'd best hurry, sir." He pointed to the sky. Grim clouds scudded across the moon. Branches swayed in a rising wind.

I glanced at the fire. The bird needed half an hour, no more. But even as I calculated, the first drops fell. Curse this night! I'd had it planned down to the last—

Dust swirled. Hastily I put myself between the birds and the wind. "Rust, we'll need eat under canvas. Are both stools within?"

"Yes, but—" The tent flaps billowed.

I looked past him, the hair on my neck rising. The old elm's branches whipped back and forth. Clothing, leaves and blankets sailed across the camp. Horses neighed their fright. Men shouted to make themselves heard. A blast of light. A tremendous *crack*. Rain pelted us.

Rust was on his feet. "It's a freak storm! Inside!"

Dazed, I stared about. The camp was in havoc. The sky was ugly black. The wind was a gale that lashed men, beasts, brush and stone.

"*Roddy!*"

"What good's a tent in—" As if to underscore my words, the canvas strained as if a sail in Stryx harbor. For a moment, it strove with the ropes. The pegs gave way; with a crack they came loose, lashing at Rust. He flinched, but they were past, no damage done. The tent was a jumble. The top billowed, swayed and fell, a wounded beast. A keening filled the air as if Lord of Nature cried. Our precious hens fell into wet ash. I took a step to Rust, buffeted by strong winds. He clawed his way, got an arm around me. Together, we struggled through a torrent to the canopy of the elm. The lee offered shelter from the worst of the downpour. We huddled. A stallion thundered past, eyes wild.

Rustin shouted in my ear. "It's a seacoast storm. In summer, the winds gather . . ."

"Too strong! It came too fast!"

"Hriskil's revenge? Might the Rood—"

"Look, Rust!" Groenfil's tent flap whipped in the wind, but the tent itself stood unharmed, as if under a cunning bubble of glass.

A huge branch, abundant with leaves, careened across the camp. Its split and sharpened end embedded itself in canvas. I winced, hoping no poor soul had taken refuge within.

I risked a peek around the bole of the elm. Our camp was wreckage and chaos. The wind howled. I gathered my sodden cloak, took deep breath. I launched myself. A hand closed around my arm, hauled me back.

Rust shouted. "Are you mad?"

"Let me go, before his Power destroys us!"

Limbs, leaves, slats from a wagon flew past. A saddle, missing us by a hand's breadth, slammed into the trunk. The elm shuddered.

Desperately, I tore loose, galloped across the soggy field. I slipped on damp grass, fell into mud. A ragged sheet of canvas whipped past, just over my head, trailing ropes and pegs. I scrambled to my feet. Two steps. Five. A dozen. I slogged toward Groenfil's tent. I tore aside the flap, dived within.

In his tent, Groenfil sat at a plank table. His eyes flamed. The wind shrieked.

I shouted, "Control thy wrath!" I strode to the table, grasped his tunic, shook him. "Cease! I command you!"

Slowly, his eyes focused. Outside, the howl eased a trifle.

"Now, my lord! I will not say again!"

Groenfil shivered. In a moment the flap bucked and heaved

no more. Slowly, the tent grew still. Outside, in the silent air, cries and moans. Rain drummed on the canvas top.

Sloshing steps. Rustin, disheveled and dripping, peered in.

With strength I knew not, I hauled Groenfil from his seat. *"What is wrong, my lord?"*

With force, the earl removed my fingers from his tunic. His hand flitted to his sword; instantly Rust drew his dagger, but Groenfil laid his blade across the table, hilt extended.

"What is it?" My tone was hot.

Groenfil looked about, until his gaze fell. He stooped to pick up a scroll. I snatched it, tried to read, but my hands trembled, whether from fear or fury I could not say.

Gently, Rustin pried it from my grasp.

He sucked breath.

I snarled, "Demons take the lot of you! WHAT HAPPENED?"

Groenfil's tone was dull. "Larissa opened her gates to Hriskil."

A sharp blade churned my gut. *"Elryc's at Soushire!"* So would Tresa have been, had she not defied me.

"Aye. Lord Elryc is taken."

"That cannot be!" I hurled Groenfil's sword to the floor. "Hriskil had no time for siege. Larissa's walls are high and well defended—"

"He mounted no siege. Larissa surrendered, and made obeisance." Wearily, he unbuckled his dagger, let sheath and all drop. He bowed his head. "I submit."

"To?"

The earl's voice was chalk on slate. "I am surety." Almost, I'd forgotten. He'd pledged his life as surety against treachery by Larissa.

He said, "An hour after Hriskil rode in, Elryc was hustled out, tied on a mare. His boy behind."

I shot to my feet. "Where are they sent?"

"I know not."

"You, who know so much? You, with spies in all our camps? You, who so trusted Larissa that—"

"Roddy . . ."

"No, Rust, I'll have my say! Your life is forfeit, my lord earl, and gladly I'll take it! Guards!"

None answered. I stalked to the flap, threw it open.

The camp was utter shambles. Men wandered about, dazed and woebegone. "Pardos! Kadar!"

In his tent, Groenfil sat slumped, head in hands.

Rustin came up behind me, put hands on my shoulders.

I threw them off. "Not now. It is a time for rage!"

He waved at the demolished camp. "Look what Groenfil's ire accomplished."

I whirled, my eyes dangerous. "Lord Regent, we pray thee, bind us not. We are beyond fetter! Our brother, whom we love, is gone to his doom."

"Roddy, let's not be rash."

I wanted no restraint. "It's time for battle."

"Of course, you're furious. But the camp's in chaos, the men are exhausted. Tomorrow, we'll take counsel."

"Rust, they have Elryc. *Now's* when we must strike."

"How? We'll need send out scouts, determine where the Norlanders ride, find land that advantages us. Roddy, have patience."

"No!"

He took deep breath. "As regent, I insist."

"Do you? Then, I surrender the throne. But know you, I'll ride, even if alone!"

Rustin's face twisted. "Oh, Roddy."

"Sir, I must have my way in this."

After a reluctant moment, he nodded.

I stalked out of the tent. "You there! Have you your trumpet? Blow assembly! You! Take ten men, round up what horses you may. PARDOS! Groenfil is condemned; see he is held. Danzik! Help right that overturned wagon. *Nos ayut* with—with—LIFT THE IMP-CURSED WHEEL!"

Tanner, bedraggled, crawled out from a pile of brush. I snapped my fingers. "Find Bollert, help him reset tents. You! I'll have a list of wounded in the hour, or your head!" I strode through the devastated camp, barking orders. When I risked a glance behind, Rustin was hard at work, supervising the reloading of our battered wagons.

In an hour I had stock. By a miracle, none dead. Forty-one injured, two seriously; it might have been worse. Seventy horses missing; a catastrophe.

Two hours, and we were under way. Our pace was agonizingly slow. With heroic fortitude, I made no complaint. The men were groggy, hurt, bewildered. It was exploit enough that we were in motion.

If Hriskil gave siege to Stryx and took the castle, he'd never be dislodged; his force was too great.

The Norlands were beyond our grasp, the land too distant, our force too puny.

So Elryc would be conveyed to Stryx, or the Norlands.

I imagined Ghanz, the Norland capital, would be Hriskil's choice. It was his; he need mount no siege to reach it. For his journey he'd use the best road, the one we straddled. He would send escort, no doubt a substantial force.

We walked and rode, arms at the ready. In hours, perhaps less, we'd do battle.

To my right, Rustin rode in silence, his eyes averted. Before we left camp, he'd urged me not to squander my force in hopeless combat, much as I'd urged Groenfil a few days past. I gave no answer, my face stone. For the briefest moment, he bowed his head to my shoulder.

To my left, Groenfil, bereft of sword and dagger. My contempt was such I bothered not to bind him, nor ask parole.

Behind us, in the second row, Anavar, Danzik and Pardos. A strange alliance. Pardos would not be dissuaded that Danzik meant my death, at whatever moment he found opportune. Neither Pardos nor Anavar spoke a word of the Norland tongue; Danzik seemed not to mind, and communicated with expressions and gestures.

Anavar disregarded them both; my pain was his. I pretended I'd not seen his tears, at the news of Elryc. He deserved dignity, and more.

Groenfil stirred. "My liege, may I ask when?"

"At my pleasure." My voice was ice.

A nod.

I curled my lip. What right had the earl to mercy? He'd urged me to trust that foul, fat, twisted hag whose only thoughts were of Soushire and her belly. Thanks to Groenfil's perfidy, Elryc was lost.

Well, not his. Larissa's. He'd only warranted her loyalty. Yet, he knew her better than all; if he so misjudged her nature, no pity from me.

We rode half a league.

"Why, Groenfil?" My tone was a snarl.

"Sire?"

"Why'd she betray us?"

He said, "I know not." We labored up a hill. "From fear more than gain, I think."

"Fear of . . . ?"

"She, too, saw the slaughter on the Norland wagons at Pezar."

I cried, "You make excuses for her and ask compassion?"

"I asked nothing!"

"It's in your face!" I sounded a child.

Groenfil said quietly, "You, of all, ought not judge a man by his face."

My palm shot to my scar. *Demons chew his soul!*

I glanced at Rustin. He rode with head down, as if not to hear.

To Groenfil, I spat, "You were a fool. Your trust cost your life."

"Would you that I live without trust?"

We rode on.

Mother, I know what I do: I throw my force into hopeless battle, but one I wouldn't avoid for Caledon itself. I love Elryc, as I do Tresa and Rust. I'm sure hereafter I'll wear no crown; even if I retrieve my brother, in the work, Hriskil's multitude will cut us to pieces. But if there's a chance, one in a thousand, that I might sail with Elryc to exile, I am content. A few moments past I sent courier to Tresa and Willem, to flee Stryx at the first sign of incursion. Their lives signify more than the stone and mortar of my castle.

I'll hear your outrage, someday, in the cave. It was my lot to safeguard my realm, and I did not.

"Don't weep, my lord." Anavar, who'd come alongside.

"Be silent!"

"They count on your strength."

Not after this day. But I knew better than to say it.

WE RODE ALL the night, into morn. Our mounts were tired, but not spent; we'd kept them at the walk, that we not outdistance our yeomen.

The roadside environs were wooded, and high with brush. Going was slow, lest there be ambush; our scouts probed every hillock and gully. The birds above were strangely still.

My hackles rose, but we came on no foe. No matter; it wouldn't be long.

At dawn's rest I took Danzik aside, twisted my thoughts into Norlandic. "Soon, we'll meet your people . . ."

His face was stolid, unrevealing.

I said bluntly, "Will you take the occasion to leave us?" It was an honor I did him, not even to question whether he'd turn on us from within our midst.

"With no farewell?" Danzik seemed astonished.

I thought long. "Vestreth coa tern?" *You would see how it ends?* "This is the day we make an end. I'll fight until Elryc's freed, or I'm dead." I grimaced. "I know better than to think we'll win. So . . . farewell, Guiat." I raised a fist, to tap knuckles, as was their way. "Go to your people."

"And find your corpse after, with the scavengers?" He bristled. "I would myself SEE!"

"Consider. You ride in our second row." He'd be flung into battle, willing or no.

Danzik gave a reluctant nod. "Where you want I go?"

"To the rear, with the wagons. Or in the woods alongside the road."

"I'm no coward!" Danzik's roar could be heard all the way to Cumber.

"No, Guiat." I bent, in the short bow of familial respect. "Ride where you will."

We'd need to hurry. Before remounting I found Rustin, who stood absently rubbing Orwal's starred muzzle. "Rust . . ." A lump filled my throat. "My lord, my regent, my friend . . . have I said I love thee?" Not as he'd wish it, as bed-friends, but of all men living, I treasured no other.

He swallowed. "My prince, why say you this?"

"Because it's true." *And I may have no more chance. And I would die with conscience clear.* Briefly, I rested my forehead on his chest. "Would you come with me, sir?" There was one other I must address.

"MY LORD EARL . . ." I found the words hard. "I confess error."

Groenfil eyed me bleakly. "From that, I assume it is my time." He stood, drew tight his cloak. "Make your confession. Then do what you must." He hesitated. "Have you axe, if I may ask the boon?"

I said, "In Verein, Bayard prayed I joust with him for Margenthar's life. I refused; it was a barbaric custom, rightly discarded."

"What of it?"

"Likewise is our custom of surety of the person. I compounded my fault by weighing you as I might Larissa." I bowed, a deep bow of respect, youngsire to elder. "I renounce surety, once for all. I pray thy pardon."

Groenfil said, "Roddy, don't toy with me."

"I do not. You are absolved of your surety. If I survive this day, I'll seek out Lady Soushire for her misdeeds. I only ask—pardon my indelicacy—refrain from her company in my camp or presence."

"Don't lie with her, say you? I'd first hurl her from her donjon window!" A gust swirled the branches. "Oh, Rodrigo . . ." Groenfil's tone was forlorn.

"Pardos, return the earl his sword and lance." I mounted. "Onward; the Norlanders can't be far. Rust, why do you look at me oddly?"

WE FAST-MARCHED toward Tradesman's Fork, where one branch led to Soushire, while the other wound through hills and vales to emerge at the borders of Cumber. The latter was a roundabout track; Hriskil would not likely favor it, but if we held the cross, whichever road the Norlanders took they must contend with us. The road we wended was wide enough for perhaps six horses; to our left a rocky field climbed toward the horizon. On our right, the terrain dipped; below us now a wood, sometimes a stony pasture. The road itself rose and fell; the land was rumpled, like an unspread quilt.

The sun was well-risen. I was a touch annoyed with Anavar, who seemed moody at the attention I lavished on Groenfil, Danzik and Rust. Our cavalry led the column, and I was thinking of sending Anavar to ride with the yeomen. But my ire was a creature of the moment, that died unexpressed. My Eiberian was a friend too long to treat shabbily.

As we topped a rise, I said gently, "Anavar, know you that—"

"LOOK, SIR!"

Before us, the road dipped, and rose again. The far rise was thick with horsemen making their way slowly down the trail.

Rustin caught at my reins. "Back, my prince. Put yourself in the center of our column."

"But they have Elryc!" I reared in my saddle. "Surprise is our ally. Lances ready!" I raised mine, set it against the brace, looped my shield across the pommel. "Hornsman, be quick. Sound the attack!"

Rustin snapped, "Pardos, guard him!"

My bodyguard shouted commands. In a moment his mounted squad had Ebon surrounded.

The trumpet pealed. My stallion reared. "Go!" I dug in my heels. Ebon shouldered aside a guard's trembling mount. Snorting, he charged down the rutted road, but no faster than Pardos and his squad.

Rustin galloped after, a hoof ahead of Groenfil, Anavar and a dozen others. Beyond the dip in the road, Norland horse wheeled, caught in the mire of their mass.

I had just time to wonder whose mad cries of war echoed in my ears. Ebon found his stride. We sped toward the Norland host. Screaming, I aimed my lance at a Norlander's breast. I whipped Ebon's flank. *"For Caledon!"*

Around me, a clamor. "CALEDON!"

I risked a glance behind. Their fatigue forgotten, our cavalry thundered down the road. After them, our pikemen ran at full tilt, weapons at the ready.

Too late, a Norlander brought up his pike; my point caught him in the chest, hurled him to the dirt. His fall tore my pike from my grip. Ebon's momentum carried us deep into the Norland line. My sturdy mount plowed headfirst into a dusty sorrel stallion. The animal staggered and fell, crushing its thrashing rider beneath.

I reared in my saddle, whipped out my sword, slashed left and right while I fumbled to unloop my shield. Anavar came into view, his sword crimson, his eyes wild. A lunge, a jab. A Norlander shrieked. Then Pardos appeared, Groenfil, and a score more. The narrow road dissolved into a bloody, tight-jammed melee.

Slashing madly at horse and man alike, I dug my way into a twisting mass of tortured flesh. Elryc would be secured in the center of their march, I was sure of it. Once, standing on my stirrups, I caught a distant glimpse of tousled hair that might have been his.

Our savage attack had caught the Norlanders unprepared; they gave way or died. I pressed ever forward, guiding Ebon from the steep drop to the thickets below. My arm ached from wielding weighty steel. Sweat stung my eyes.

From the rear of the Norland line, the blare of trumpets.

A bearded foeman scrabbled in the mud, snatched up a fallen pike. Swinging it like a club, he smashed its blunt side into Anavar's ribs. With a cry the Eiberian toppled. I gouged Ebon's flanks. In an instant we stood over my dazed baron. Anavar shook his head, scrambled onto Edmund.

The bearded Norlander shifted grip, brandished his pike. I raised high my sword. He lunged. I yanked hard at my reins. Ebon heaved. The pike grew shorter. Ebon's knees buckled; he flung me over his head. I landed on one arm and a leg, but the road was slippery with mud and gore. I staggered, lost my balance. A second Norlander loomed, sword raised high. Rustin roared, hammered aside a foe in desperate attempt to reach me.

"Look at me!" Bollert tore down the muddy road, arms waving. "Leave 'im alone! Run away!" His eyes were fixed on the swordsman atop me. For a moment the Norlander's mouth worked. Abruptly, he bolted into the woods. Bollert spun around. "Run, all you! Leave king 'lone!"

Behind him, the pikeman wrenched free his weapon, firmed his grip.

I rasped, "Bollert—"

The boy turned. The pikeman charged. His point caught Bollert full in the chest, hurled him back, pinned him against a tree.

Rust reached me, glanced around, hauled me to my feet. "Are you hurt? Where's Pardos?"

Trumpets sounded.

I shook my head. "Not sure. Find Elryc."

"Roddy, look out!" From his saddle, Anavar pointed deeper within the Norland column. Whatever he saw was beyond me. A milling mass of men in desperate combat filled the road.

A rumble of hooves.

A squad of Norland horsemen burst through the throng. They hurled aside Norlander and Caled alike, swords raised high. Rustin yanked me back, threw himself before me, shield raised.

I tripped on a rock and tumbled down the hill. Brambles tore at my jerkin. My sword went flying. I rolled over and over, as a child playing in a hilly pasture. A gnarled old tree loomed.

A smash. White light.

The world faded.

"HE WAKES."

A cool compress soothed my temple.

I groaned.

"Gently!" The compress was snatched away. A new hand pressed it ever so softly onto my throbbing skull.

I squinted through half-opened eyes. Rustin's face was a mask of worry. Behind him, Anavar looked anguished. Danzik's thick fingers rested on his shoulder.

"Where's Elryc?" My voice was a croak.

Anavar and Rust exchanged glances.

I need not ask more.

Gripping Rust's wrist, I struggled to sit. "What's become of us?"

Rust wrapped his arm around my shoulders, eased me to a sitting position. "Do you recall their charge?"

Dimly, an echo of trumpets floated through my haze. "I heard the call."

"From their rear, Sarazon mounted a counterthrust. Five hundred cavalry. They smashed their own line and ours, and cleared the road."

Sarazon himself was among us? I thrust it aside. "The battle's theirs?"

"Not exactly." Rust examined my temple, decided to help me to my feet. Together, he and Anavar assisted me up the hill.

The road was a slaughterhouse. Dead men, gutted horses, overturned wagons, buzzing flies. The usual detritus of war.

I gulped. "What of our force?"

"Half are dead."

"Full half?" I turned away sickened. *No, King. It won't do. You must look.* "Bring Ebon." I would ride the length of the carnage.

"He's gone, my prince."

"Well, find him!" Ebon wouldn't have strayed far.

Rust's fingers drifted to my nape, and I knew. My knees went weak, and I fought an urge to settle into the mud. Ebon had been mine since . . . since Rustin had gifted me of him, in my unhappy youth. My eyes stung. Fiercely, I battled my sorrow. *It is not meet that thou weep for a horse, where men have died for thee.*

"Would you ride Edmund, sir?" Anavar's voice was soft. I managed a nod. He handed me my lost sword, and I struggled into the unfamiliar seat. Rustin and Danzik walked at either side, while I clung dazedly to the pommel.

Below, in the dirt, Norls and Caleds locked in final embrace.

The slaughter stretched to the rise, and beyond. Turning grimly to the stretch of the road we'd occupied, I paced Edmund, careful not to step on faithful men, ours and Hriskil's. Here and there among the multitude, a face that was familiar. Old Cobat, who'd complain about his stiff joints no more. Tondras of Kier, whom I'd known from Stryx.

At length, the bloodbath trailed off.

I turned Edmund, made for the Norland stretch of the road. Ebon lay a dozen paces into the slaughter, eyes glaring, teeth pulled back in a rictus of agony. They'd wrenched the pike from his belly. His entrails spewed. Gritting my teeth, I turned my head as Rustin knelt to secure my precious saddlebags.

Along the road, scores of Norlanders, as many Caleds. Torn, broken, gutted, decapitated, lopped.

Pardos lay face down in the mud, throat slashed. My breath came sharp. I swung down from the stirrups, staggered, righted myself. I knelt. *"Have peace, sir."* I wasn't sure if I'd spoken aloud. "Always, I'm impetuous. Your death was my doing." Gently, I closed his eyes. I made to climb back onto Edmund, but my legs were strangely weak. Danzik lifted me as a father would a tot, set me into the saddle.

I said to him, "You won."

"Think you so?" Holding my reins, Danzik led me down the abandoned road.

More bodies of Norls, a few Caleds. Across the road lay an older man, heavyset, by his dress obviously an officer. He'd been gutted by a sword. Around him, half a score of dead guards.

"Who?" I tried to sound as if I cared.

"Sarazon." Danzik gazed at the body with dour disapproval.

I blinked. I ought to feel joy. "Who did it?"

Rustin said, "After the Norland charge, Groenfil rallied our scattered horsemen. They came down that wooded hill, across the road."

"Where is he fallen?"

Rust looked startled. "The earl? He's not. He's gathered our men to form a rear guard, lest the Norlanders turn on us." A pause. "I think they won't. After Sarazon fell, they hacked their way through and were gone as fast as they might."

"They left us the field?" I marveled at it. We could call it a victory, were we so callow. "Did you see Elryc?"

"No, my prince. I was with you."

I twisted in the saddle. "Anavar?"

"No, sir. When you fell down the slope, we rushed to guard you. Even Danzik stood over you, sword in hand. If the thick brush hadn't hid us . . ." Anavar gulped. "No time to look for Prince Elryc."

"Faithless vassal!" From the saddle I aimed a cuff at him, barely missed. "Why died we here, if not for Elryc?"

"For you, sir." His gaze held mine.

At length, my shoulders slumped. "I pray pardon." It was a whisper.

We resumed our walk. As we returned to the midpoint of the battle I stopped short.

Bollert sat against a tree, a look of astonishment on his features. A spear pinned him to the trunk. I slid down from Edmund, lurched to Bollert's still form. "Ah, my poor peasant. My churl." My fingers flitted to his eyes, closed them. "You died for me, lad. Why? Our cause wasn't yours."

"He would be one of us." Rustin pried a dagger from the boy's lifeless hand.

"And I wouldn't allow it." I knelt. "Bollert, if you have forgiveness, if you hear . . ." I gave it up. I stared into anguished distance.

After a long while, I wiped my cheeks. "Let's find Groenfil."

"Hold a moment." Rust stayed me. "Roddy . . . you were right." His wave encompassed the battle, and the carnage.

"Was I?" It seemed not to matter.

Alone among my faithful, I trudged down the grim, muddy road. It twisted and turned, rose and fell. Wood and field, shade and sun.

Victory and defeat.

THIRTY-NINE

THE CAMPFIRE SIZZLED in raindrops' attack.

None of us spoke.

Anavar sipped his tea. I let my cup warm my hands. Groenfil, haggard and gray, drained his mug. Danzik watched, brooding.

I cleared my throat. "I say again: why not pursue them?"

Groenfil said, "They're sure to set scouts and guards. They won't be mauled twice."

"And now we're reduced to a bare five hundred." Anavar. "Even Elryc's guard outnumbers—"

"Yet they fear us." Had they not turned tail and abandoned the field?

Rustin stirred. "Another battle? Would you reduce us to bloody shreds?"

I tried to make my tone reasonable. "I would pursue them as long as Elrye's not locked in an impregnable fortress."

"They have your brother." His tone was gentle. "They mustn't gain you."

"I don't *want* the throne on those terms."

"Five hundred of us, Roddy. What can we accomplish?"

"What we might. Your caution does us no good, sir."

Rust shook his head. "Nonetheless, I can't allow it. We must preserve what's left of our force."

Someone threw fagots to encourage the flames. Perhaps I ought to sit at a chill distant fire, and heed mother. I gazed at Rustin, chewing my lip. In my stomach, a knot began to congeal. Abruptly, I lurched to my feet. "I would be alone, my lords." I stalked into the brush. Beyond, a stream chattered. With Pardos gone, there was none to bar my way. I clambered down mossy stones, and hunched on a rock above the brook, hugging my knees.

A long while passed, while I contemplated the unimaginable.

Presently, a sound above. I looked up, my eyes watery.

Rustin dropped down, crouched at my side, squeezed my knee. "My prince."

"Sir, I've been . . . thinking."

"So I see. What troubles you?"

I tried to speak, found myself without words, cast about in a vague gesture. After a moment, I tried again to summon my courage. "Rust, when I contended with the Rood outside Groenfil Castle, it was against your wishes."

"Yes. Though I'll grant that you confounded Hriskil and caused his retreat."

"And this morn, when we sought the Norlanders on the road, you opposed it."

He nodded.

"Though we near rescued Elryc, and killed Sarazon."

"Where do you lead, Roddy?"

"And tonight, when I would pursue Hriskil's column . . ."

A muscle pulsed in his jaw. "You risk yourself with abandon, my love. I can't bear to see it."

"Yes, that's so. But I *must* risk myself. Know you that?"

He pursed his lips. "I'll try to contain my fear for you."

My voice quavered. "It's more than that. In the days when you were dead . . ." But it was too cruel; I couldn't say it.

"Go on, my love." His tone was soft.

"I was noble, Rust! Truly I was!"

"I doubt it not."

"Don't you understand?" I pounded the mossy rock. "I was brave and clever. I was magnanimous to Jestrel, and on behalf of Caledon I watched the death wagon at Pezar. I redeemed myself with the troops, and—and—"

He steeled himself to meet my eye. "What of it?"

"I *was* noble, Rust! As I can't be with you!" There, it was said. Might Lord of Nature strike me dead; I deserved no less. I rushed on. "With your guidance I'm a boy, as always I was, when I need to be a man! Always, you would save me, from Norland swords, from my nobles' ire, from myself. Now I must save myself, or deserve no crown." Nor would I keep one, if Rustin's caution prevailed. That, I couldn't say to him, not for Caledon itself.

He threw a pebble in the rushing stream, and another. "Ah, Roddy." His tone was wistful. "I put aside our bed play because you wished it, and I imagined . . ." He blinked hard. "I consoled myself that I'd be your true friend, your right arm. I thought to ride with you, revel in my pride of you, see you at last triumphant. It wouldn't be long, I knew, until you reached man's estate. But not so—so soon, so—" Abruptly, he stared away, at a twisted tree.

"Oh, Rust."

"I rejoice."

"You weep."

"From gladness."

"Liar!"

"I don't—I ought be glad, whether or not I'm decent enough to feel joy. But I matter not. You are Caledon, and must have your way."

Sudden doubts assailed me. "Let's think on it, Rust. Stay a while. Perhaps if you gave up the regency . . ."

"No, I'll go." He brushed his cheeks. "We both know you're right. I had word from Anavar, from Groenfil, from your own lips. I tried hard not to understand." A sigh. "I'll always take pride in you. Now I'll see it from afar."

I cried, "I lost you once! How can I bear it again?"

"I cherish you not one whit less than before. It will always be so. There, my prince. Squeeze my hand. Aye. Tell me again of Pezar. Speak of great things."

THE MORNING SUN rode pale and fretful, to fade behind scudding clouds. Our camp was hushed, awaiting the summer storm. I sat awry on dew-damp grass, staring dully at the trail down which Orwal had trotted, bearing Rustin.

He hadn't looked back.

Was it not on Rustin that I'd spent my only chance at Return? Was it not for him that I'll pass my life a hideous creature?

Behind me, the rustle of cloth. At arm's length, Anavar sat cross-legged, his gaze fixed on his boots.

My fists knotted. *You will not take his place!*

But Anavar knew; oftimes, I'd made it all too clear.

I reached to my brow, toyed with the coronet Rustin had set upon my locks a few moments before leaving, when in ringing tones he'd resigned the regency of Caledon. In the moment before, I'd given him royal warrant, badly scrawled on crumpled parchment, to hold the Keep as Householder of

Stryx, for as long as he should live. Not long, he'd said, acknowledging for a moment what we all knew; that Hriskil had won.

The main Norland force was encamped in Soushire, looking anew, word had it, toward Groenfil. My earl reported the news in flat tone, eyes fixed on a point far behind me.

Groenfil Castle. As good a goal as any, now that saving Elryc was beyond us. Cumber was too far from our other duchies, important only to deny Hriskil the pass he already possessed.

I might retreat to Stryx, but then I'd seem to be following Rust. Besides, Willem and Tresa had matters there in hand; I must go elsewhere to rally Caledon, and to gnaw at Hriskil's heels.

To Groenfil, then.

Come, Roddy, you've moped enough. You've sharp blade in your sheath; when wretched night proves beyond bearing, you've means to make an end. Until then, be king.

I straightened, rubbed my aching spine. "Anavar, have I a horse?"

He started. "Aye, sir, there's more horses than Groenfil has men, after . . ."

I grunted. "Pack this in my saddlebag." I handed him the coronet. "And find Groenfil." I drew my cloak, as a gust brought more raindrops.

A few moments later the earl heard me out. "As you command, my liege."

I raised an eyebrow. "You're not pleased? Your sons—"

"Pleased I might die with them, in lieu of saving them?"

I was taken aback. "What was your hope?"

"That we might draw Hriskil elsewhere."

"Where?"

"To the demons' lake!" Groenfil's eyes glowed. "Don't look to me for wisdom. I'm not king."

I regarded him a long while. He asked no more than he deserved. Then, at last, "Prepare for march."

"To my castle?"

"No," I said. "To Soushire." I'd not remain king by fleeing my oppressor.

Why to Soushire, Anavar inquired.

Because Hriskil was there.

Danzik's eyes glinted with hard humor. Was that not reason to ride elsewhere?

Anavar asked: if a cohort of two thousand Norlanders broke our cavalry, why throw ourselves on a still larger force?

To free Caledon.

Had I a plan? Some scheme undivulged?

Of course, I said, and lapsed silent.

A plan. I ought have one.

IN MID-AFTERNOON, AS we rode down the muddy trail under dripping boughs, Anavar cleared his throat. "It seems to me that Hriskil holds the high terrain. Soushire is his, and with Cumber, the passes to Eiber. Groenfil's lands too, unless you're on hand to wield the Still against the Rood. Verein's wall is abandoned, Stryx barely defended. Our—excuse me, sir—*your* treasury is empty, the land in chaos. What shafts have we in our quiver?"

"Fear." I'd pondered for hours, to achieve the single reply.

"Sir?"

"Last fall we captured Danzik, Hriskil's most trusted lieutenant, when he was on the verge of seizing Stryx." Danzik scowled. I said, "I even sent him to his king, under parole. So Hriskil sees Danzik corrupted by Caled ways." Danzik's mien darkened. I added, "I'm the king he cannot kill. At Pezar, I taunted Hriskil in his own camp—"

Anavar reminded me, "That didn't happen." It was before the Return; in true life, Rustin had forbidden that I leave camp.

"Hriskil has ghost memory of it, as do we."

My young baron looked dubious.

I said firmly, "Then Sarazon took Stryx harbor. Yet we burned his fleet; it must be long before Hriskil can again assemble so many ships. He attacked Groenfil Castle, but I wouldn't let him lift the Rood. He was so unnerved that he fled."

Anavar began, "But still he—"

"By treachery Hriskil took Soushire, and Elryc. He sent my brother home to Ghanz with escort of two thousand. But we slew Sarazon. What thinks Hriskil now of the child king?"

Anavar was silent.

"He fears us," I answered myself. "And we'll use that fear."

"How, sir?"

"Ahh." That was the puzzle I sought to solve.

EARLY MORN, COLD and wet. We roused ourselves amid bleak mist. I took great care saddling and tacking my mount. She was an unpleasant beast, one I'd do well to replace at the first opportunity. Adjusting her tack was a trial; I'd finally tied her firmly between two trees.

A soggy day's march, but a short one. We'd be upon Soushire by noon.

Long before midday, we came on the first of Hriskil's patrols. Fifty men, well armed, but outnumbered ten to one. They turned tail, and I recalled our pursuers.

We slipped down from the brooding hills, the damp and dripping woods eerily silent. Beside the road we came on a clearing where a meadow sloped down into a vast sea of fog. Across the ocean, the uppermost ramparts of Soushire Castle loomed: remote, isolated islands founded in gray billows.

"We must wait." Groenfil had come alongside. "No battle can be fought—"

Some trick of wind scattered tufts of fog, and for an instant we glimpsed a wide plain crowded with tents, campfires, wagons, the paraphernalia of war. Hriskil's army. The king, though, and his lieutenants would no doubt be housed in the castle's most comfortable chambers.

"We must *not* wait." My tone brooked no refusal, even as swirling gray once more enveloped the enemy camp.

From where the road met the plain, it would be a long walk, or a few moments' canter, to the first of the mist-hidden tents. I dismounted.

Groenfil said dryly. "What, then? Sound the attack? Feel our way?"

"No." On the long, subdued ride, I'd devised my "plan." My lunacy. The last vain taunt of the child king. "Form for battle," I said. "Pikemen and archers, there, and here. Defend this rise. Groenfil, you have command. Assemble your horse behind the pikemen."

"What for?" He led, after all, a mere five hundred.

"To rescue me, if a moment comes. Anavar, my crown. Be

quick." As if lashed, the boy jumped to my saddlebag. "And the Vessels."

"Rodrigo, what do you?" Groenfil's voice was taut.

"I summon Hriskil." I brushed the dust from my rumpled clothes, knotted a cape over my shoulders, donned my bejeweled coronet.

"Sir, please!" If he'd dared, Anavar would have snatched the crown from my brow.

"They must be shown who I am. Danzik, where would you stand?"

"With you, Rez."

"No, you'll be cut down. There, in front of our pikes, you'll have unobstructed view." I hesitated. "Farewell, Guiat."

"Salut, Rez Caledi." An awkward bow, in the Caled manner.

Despite my pounding pulse, I smiled.

Into the mist, carrying my burden, I trudged across the fog-strewn field.

From time to time, as I neared, the mist disgorged me to the enemy. Men shouted alarms to their officers. Groomsmen raced with stallions of war; campfires were doused, cohorts assembled.

I strode across the sodden meadow, as to a damp picnic. Was Groenfil in place? I glanced over my shoulder, but all beyond five paces was obscured. Something solid clouted my ear; with a squawk I tumbled on my rump. I blinked. I'd walked into a thick sapling.

I got to my feet, rubbing furiously at my stinging ear.

Thirty paces before the first Norland tents, I sat cross-legged. The precious Receptor I balanced between my knees. I unstoppered the Chalice, poured shimmering stillsilver. Almost instantly, it stilled.

A deep breath, for composure, and I slid my palms across the bowl. I murmured the words of encant, and my Power burned through the mist.

Hriskil, slayer of children, where do you hide?

My questing thought roamed, found no response. Perhaps this day Hriskil had set aside his Rood. In that case I'd not find him unless he was within a few paces. Such was the way of the Still; only another Power could coax it beyond one's immediate presence.

Now, the tricky part. I took breath, focused my Power, raised my voice to a shout that might be heard in the tents. "Come forth, coward! Fight Rodrigo for Caledon!"

I waited a moment, hurled more jeers and taunts.

No response, of course. But my purpose was to expose his fear before his men. Yet, in truth, I judged him not so cowardly, but reasonably cautious. He had more to lose than I. And why had we armies, if not to do our fighting? Still, my example made poor contrast of his.

All the while, with the Still, I searched for a whiff of him. With the doubled vision I'd lately mastered, I probed within the tents while observing the Norlandic cavalry mounting, setting spears, preparing their charge.

Hriskil, you contemptible savage! Come out and play!

As before, nothing.

The mist disclosed a rank of Norland bowmen, and another line behind. Hundreds. I shivered. Ever since my wound had become infected at Pezar, I'd hated the deadly feathered barbs of war.

I forced my words into Norl. "Foolish men, who fight for Hriskil! He is nobody, nothing! He flees the child king! Is he worth your death?"

A whir; I did my best not to flinch. A hundred arrows, most loosed blind into the mist. A lucky pair landed within a handsbreadth, quivering hungrily in the sod.

"It takes more than arrows, children of the north! Take care lest you anger me!"

The thud of hooves. The Norland cavalry charged. One rider, braver than the rest, or on a faster mount, led by a half dozen paces. I was the target. I nursed my Power.

Fifteen paces. He loomed out of the gray.

Mother, help me in this. I'm not sure I—

Ten paces.

I unleashed my full fury. *Margenthar, Hriskil, Bouris, all that I hate, you are this man!* My eyes rose, met the foaming stallion's. The sorrel warhorse neighed shrilly, dug in his heels. The rider flew over its head, tumbled over and over in the grass.

He staggered to his feet.

I bent to the stillsilver.

The unhorsed rider screamed, slapped at himself, whirled about. He bolted toward the Norl camp.

I had just time to settle on another. As he raised arm to launch his spear, I struck him with all the rage I nursed. His spear went wide. He yanked his reins so hard his mount stumbled. They righted themselves, dashed toward the tents.

The brave Norland charge foundered. Riders deliberately steered wide, missed me by a full length or more. I bent anew to the Still.

They need not know I could challenge but one man at a time.

Uneasily, the horsemen withdrew, regrouped before their line of archers, who loosed over their heads.

A flock of barbs. I steeled myself, bent to the bowl. *Hriskil, where are—*

"Unh!" I rocked.

"RODRIGO!" Anavar's shrill cry.

My ribs oozed crimson anguish. I closed my eyes, whispered the encant, inwardly explored myself.

Behind me, half shrouded in mist, Groenfil raised an arm in signal.

Hold, my lords! It's not mortal.

Startled, Groenfil hesitated. His hand fell.

It hurt now, to draw deep breath, but I must. "Soa Rodrigo, qa han vos modrit!" *I am Rodrigo, whom you cannot kill!* I coughed, dreading the salt taste of blood, but none came to my lips. The arrow protruding from my ribs quivered with each breath.

Another volley. This time, all missed. It's not that easy, from afar, to hit a solitary target perched cross-legged on the grass.

"Think you I fear your shafts? Who loose at me, your mothers and sisters and children die! Even now, they wither!"

I bent to the stillsilver, ranging, searching for Hriskil.

The Norl cavalry formed a line; Groenfil their obvious mark.

Time, now. I set down the bowl, poured the silver back into the Chalice, stoppered it. I gritted my teeth, managed to stand without snagging the arrow on my cloak. As if red agony weren't ablossom, I began my walk toward the Norland tents.

"Roddy!" A distant wail.

I trudged onward. For this death I'd be remembered. Perhaps Caledon needed martyred hero more than king.

The urgent call of trumpets. Their bowmen, unsure at first, fell back. The Norl cavalry charged.

Groenfil would die now, or flee.

No. Summoned by urgent horns, the cavalry raced not to charge us, but to the Soushire gates.

I trudged toward the nearest white tent. One hand gripped the sack with my Vessels, the other clutched my leaking ribs.

As Norland trumpets called, their camp emptied. Men streamed ever more urgently toward the battlements of Soushire. They jostled each other in their haste to crowd through the gates.

Pikemen, archers, horse, even a cookwagon or two lumbered through the tall gate. Abruptly, the portal swung closed.

I came closer. The wall of Soushire resolved itself through mist. From its battlements, ten thousand peered through swirling fog, seeking a glimpse of Rodrigo, king of truncated Caledon, as he strode unopposed through the Norland camp.

Abruptly, I sat. I had little choice.

Wearily, my mind seeking some distant peace, I fished in the sack. Unstopper the Chalice. That's right, lad. Pour.

Let go your ribs. You need cover the Receptor. Oh, it hurts.

Roddy, take heed! Mother sounded cross. *Do what you must!*

And what is that, madam?

BE KING!

Is *that* the accumulated wisdom of Caledon? I coughed, and red fire bloomed. I hadn't much time. I peered at the field, to our defenseless rise, where my vassals fretted.

Lord Groenfil! Anavar of the Southern Reaches! I summon you . . . ten men, unarmed. No sword, no bow, no pike. Yourselves alone.

I raised my voice to the looming battlements. "Hriskil, timid mouse! A king awaits you!"

Perhaps the defenders heard. None deigned to respond.

Presently, the clop of hooves, invisible in the gray.

I sat still, waiting. At last they emerged.

Groenfil had divined my intent. Cloaked, scabbards bare, he and Anavar led ten soldiers in solemn procession. They rode at a stately walk, heads erect, deigning to glance to neither side. Through the Norland camp they made their way, oblivious of the billowing tents, the stacks of supplies, sheaves of arrows, equipage of war. Straight to me they rode, leading a riderless, prancing stallion.

Anavar leaped down; Groenfil dismounted more slowly, wrapped in dignity. Together, they bowed.

I swallowed. "I'll try to stand. No, don't help; they watch." Abandoning my Vessels, I lurched to my feet. "Sir, your shoulder."

Groenfil said urgently, "You can't mount with a shaft—"

"*Do* be quiet, there's a good fellow." I raised a leg. "Oh!" My face was pasty, but I sat astride my stallion. I straightened my coronet.

"Anavar, to the king's right. We slow walk to the rise, where our pikemen—" My tone had an edge. "Follow, my lords. To the wall."

Groenfil might have objected, if my command hadn't shocked him speechless. Anavar, bursting with pride, too young to heed his peril, gladly guided his mount alongside mine.

I murmured, "At the wall, we three in front, the rest behind."

We emerged from a row of tents. I led my mount to the lee of the wall, within easy bowshot. We came to a halt. Never had I seen a battlement so packed with defenders. My rough Norlandic echoed from the sturdy stones. "Hriskil! Come out or be dethroned!"

Anavar gasped. I paid no heed.

I raised myself in the saddle, that all see and hear. *"Go home, Hriskil, and I'll cede you Ghanz! Here, you will die."* I panted for breath, tried to conceal my distress. "You're no match for the Still. Flee while you can. Soldiers, your Hriskil is mean, petty and vain. His life is not worth yours. Sarazon knew this, and Danzik. Whom else must I destroy? GO

HOME!" I looked from eye to eye, as men bristling with arms jostled for view. I raised my voice to its full might. *"Norland king, I deny you Caledon!"*

To my cohort, softly, "Turn, one by one."

My spine crawled, expecting the shaft that would end it all. Head erect, I led our slow retreat into the mist.

FORTY

". . . LUCKY YOU'RE ALIVE!" Groenfil's eyes blazed as he bound my flank. An irate wind swirled through the fog, waving the branches of the tree under which I lay.

I forced open aching jaws, spat out the knotted cloth that had muffled my groans. "—told you it wasn't mortal."

"It may yet be. Lie back. Anavar, don't coddle him. I ought kick sense into his rump!" Groenfil's eyes darted about our makeshift camp, as if seeking a spot to chastise me.

"He's king!"

"And forgets it. Rodrigo, *what* was that about?"

Marveling, I let Anavar thrust a cushion behind my head. "Don't you see, my lord Earl? I meant to cede all, but again we won."

"*WON?* You're—what's the word, Danzik? *Graftig,* yes. Crazed."

"Think you so?" I tried not to let my doubt show. "Why am I alive?"

Groenfil growled, "My point exactly."

I said, "No, my lord. Consider it. Why?" A moment's pause, and I answered myself. "They feared to loose shafts on me."

"It's ill omen to slay a madman."

Anavar stirred. "My lord, Roddy's our king, and brave beyond all—"

"I called him lunatic, not coward!" Groenfil paced, threw up his hands, returned to glare at me. "Explain, sire, if you can."

"Water, I beg you." Someone poured; I gulped it down. Eventually, I was sated and had to find words. "Hriskil fears us now more than ever."

"Hah. That's why he holds Soushire while *we*—"

I snapped, "Holds it? He cowers behind its walls! Don't roll your eyes at me, Groenfil, why dare we camp here?"

"To staunch your blood, lest—"

I demanded, "But why *here*? It's an easy pursuit, but you know he'll send no riders this day."

"I've set outguards."

"How many?"

Groenfil shifted. "Enough. All right, only six, the men are tired. I ought post more."

"Not needed. You know as well as I."

"Well, the Norlanders are unnerved; who wouldn't be, with a mad king cavorting—"

"I didn't cavort." Wait. Wasn't I refuting the wrong charge? I pressed on. "I walked to the very foot of their walls. I showed no fear. Of *course* they're unnerved."

"Danzik, do you know enough Caled to follow? Tell him getting away with a daft escapade isn't the same as winning."

The Norlander was silent. After a moment we both turned from him.

I said, "Hriskil holds territory, that's all. Stones and gates. I have their spirits. You'll see."

Groenfil shook his head. "Sire, Lord of Nature knows I admire your courage. But you've won nothing except a wound. On that, nothing can change my mind."

"Time will tell." I lay back, riding out the throb of my ribs. "You were magnificent. Both of you." At that, Anavar flushed with pleasure.

Groenfil shrugged. "We followed your lead. But flattery moves me not. All you won—" From the edge of camp, an alarm. The earl bolted to his feet, drew his sword.

A perimeter guard galloped to our refuge under the tree, threw himself from his mount. "Sire! My lord!"

Groenfil snapped, "How many?"

He gaped. "Five, sir. Four guards, that is, and—and—"

"Spit it out!"

"Lady Soushire!"

Groenfil swung to me. His mouth worked. "How do you manage it? Is it the cursed Still?"

I said naught.

"Shall I bring her to you?"

Elryc's pale face swam before me, and faded. I said, "Hang her. I'll chat with her after." Resolutely, I turned my head.

WITH A WEARY sigh, I let Anavar cloak me. He drew the cloth across my bound ribs, in an effort to hide my wound.

I thrust it open. "What do we conceal? Every Norl on the wall saw my blood."

"She need not know how deep—"

"I walk. That tells her the gist of it."

Across the field, Larissa, surrounded by our guards, sat sidesaddle on her palfrey, her pudgy neck as yet unroped. Groenfil and Anavar had refused my orders, at first with arguments, then with mute stubbornness. "You don't mean it, Roddy." By the demons' lake, I did. She'd not leave the meadow alive, if I had say in the matter. But to pacify them, I must first grant her audience.

With distaste, I looked past the swaying grasses, the swirling leaves. Groenfil was restraining himself, but barely. Recollecting his gales of rage at Larissa's betrayal, I grimaced. We needed no more of that.

Taking care not to stumble and tear myself apart, I trudged across the field, Anavar and the ever-curious Danzik plodding at my side. I glared up at her, still mounted. "Well?"

Lady Soushire looked cross. "Where's Sergo?"

"Knotting a rope." My tone was sharp.

"Rodrigo, we haven't time for play. You left spoor that a blind man could follow. He'll be upon us."

"Who?" I knew full well her meaning.

"Hriskil. The enemy."

"Yours or mine?"

She frowned. "Ours."

"Odd, then, that he stretches his feet at your fire."

"What was I to do? You left me to siege!" She shifted in her fine-sewn leather saddle. "What thought you, Rodrigo, that I'd take on the whole Norland might, when you yourself fled?"

My mouth worked. "I've been afield without cease. We sought combat. We killed Sarazon. We bearded Hriskil at your very gate. What more would you?" My fists clenched. Here I sounded the supplicant, I who'd been mightily wronged. I clamped shut my jaw.

"I'd have you finish what you started. Make war!"

"Why, when disloyal vassals do Hriskil's work?" Our converse had gone impossibly awry. I wrenched it back on course. "Why came you here to your death?"

"Bah. You can't afford to execute me, and you know it."

"Do I, now?" I turned to Anavar. "Have ever you heard such affront?"

He didn't answer me directly. "Why not, madam?"

"You'd charge me with treason, Rodrigo? Then, I claim appeal to the king's council. Assemble the nobles, and we'll see if I'm condemned." She knew full well such a gathering was impossible in war. Worse, in council she'd play one side against another and soon have us at each other's throats, as had Uncle Mar. Her hand stayed my hot reply. "I know where Hriskil took Elryc."

My heart leaped. "Where?"

"Kill me and you'll never know."

My eyes burned into hers. After a time she shifted. "You're witness, Anavar, that I tell him freely. I gave not the king's brother to Hriskil. All under my roof were to have safe-conduct." To me, "Elryc's sent to Wayvere."

I frowned. "Where?"

Anavar said, "A seacoast town in Eiber, near the Norl border. At home, we call it Wyvern."

"Oh, that." It was said to be a low coarse place, but Tantroth's best harbor. The town from which he'd assembled his own invasion of Caledon, a year past, and now in Hriskil's hands. Why would Hriskil send my brother *there*? I turned suspiciously to Larissa. "How know you this?"

A small smile. "A lord ought know what is spoken of in her castle."

"And how came you to escape?"

"By your aid. When you—how should I say it—dissolved into the mist, there was much rushing about. Hriskil's lieutenant was all for chasing after you, but Hriskil forbade it. 'Not in fog,' he roared to his chieftains. 'Fog augments his Still.' "

"Does it, now?" My lips curled in a grim smile. I'd have to employ Hriskil's fear.

Larissa added offhandedly, "In the confusion, I slipped out."

"Just like that." I regarded her with deep skepticism.

"I'd, ah, made preparations." Lady Soushire sat straighter. "Hriskil went back on his word the very moment the gates were opened. If I stayed, soon or late he'd have me in chains." Of course. The Norland idea of *vade*, honor, was a good trick.

"Elryc captured, your sturdy, well-defended walls in Hriskil's hands . . . all for what? His promises? His gold?"

"I couldn't hold—"

I shouted, "You barely tried! Groenfil nearly died for your treason!" I brought my voice down. "Now is your time."

She said calmly, "Alive, I have value to you. Townsmen and churls will see: I know you and Hriskil, and choose you. And I'm proof of your mercy."

My mouth worked. "Anavar, take her from my sight. This instant, you clod! Lead her from camp!"

"Until . . . ?"

"Until—we'll—I need speak with Groenfil." And I fled.

"To my dearest friend and lord king, from his servant Rustin of Stryx, greetings.

"Words cannot convey how my heart swells at your exploit before the walls of Soushire. And yet I know full well I couldn't have countenanced it were I at your side. Truly, you've proven I need leave you, that you be a great king.

"Elryc's capture is outrage beyond bearing. I'm astounded you let Larissa live. By what honeyed words did she melt your heart?"

I set down the parchment, scowled into the middle distance. Not Lady Soushire's honeyed words, but the unspoken anguish of Lord Groenfil's eyes. And poor, shabby-souled Larissa was no villain, merely a grasping woman who could see not a whit past her immediate self-interest. Perhaps she'd even believed Hriskil's assurance her guests would go unmolested. Thank Lord of Nature Tresa had the sense to avoid Larissa's clutches, though at the time I'd reprimanded her for it. I sighed.

"Roddy, I fear your plan to remain afield seems sound. As Soushire's capture shows, battlements offer only an illusion of safety. Continue, then, to harry the Norland foe as best you may, but, I pray you, let Kadar guard you again, now Pardos is gone. If opportunity arises to turn the tide, I'm confident you'll seize it.

"Take heart, at least, that Keep and Castle are reunited. Behind the castle's stout walls above, Lady Tresa and Chancellor Willem continue to gather adherents, and I have no doubt whatsoever of their constancy to your cause. Meanwhile, the Keep will not fall whilst I live.

"I passed on to Lady Tresa the words you wished, and her heart seems lightened. I urge you, be gallant and open to her your soul. You'll both take benefit.

"My dear liege, I miss you so, I'm half crazed from it. I shouldn't write that—no, I will, for respect of the honesty between us, and for fear one or the other of us shall die with the truth unsaid. Rustin, your friend ever, awaits your next missive."

I carefully rolled the parchment, thrust it in my saddlebag. I'd write him again anon.

In the fortnight since I'd bearded Hriskil in Soushire, we'd roamed the hills, avoiding main roads, striking wearily at Hriskil's columns. As winter approached, our war was in danger of dissolving into mere bandit raids. It was with heavy heart that I set us plodding toward Verein and resupply.

Inexplicably, Larissa, Lady Soushire, had managed to attach herself to us. Well, it was explicable in that I vacillated about having her hanged, until she'd become again a fixture in our camp.

Four days we were on the road to Verein, where Lady Varess and Mar's son, Bayard, watched over denuded walls. They made no effort to deny us entry.

My bondsman Tanner went off with my mount. For a few moments I wandered about the courtyard, then followed to the stable. Tanner, stretching on his toes, made himself busy untacking and rubbing down my mare. I perched on a barrel while he refilled the water trough, laid a light blanket over the mare's back. A rough wooden bowl held a few carrots; idly I took a handful. One, at least, would go to my mare: gift, or bribe.

I kept a sharp eye, for Tanner's sake. I'd already noticed the mare had an evil temper—one was safe enough on her back, but afterward . . . She hadn't had a chunk of my shoulder, but it wasn't for lack of trying. I sighed. A far cry, this beast, from Ebon. But she had wonderful gaits and picked up the canter so eagerly she left the rest in the dust, so I was of a mind to overlook her peculiarities.

I paced. Verein was safety, of a sort, but our presence didn't *feel* right. How could I tarry here, while Elryc languished in captivity? Why Verein, and not Stryx, if I must abandon the field?

I wandered into the stall, but Tanner wasn't yet done. Idly, I reached through the slats to the adjoining stall and rubbed the neck of the shaggy black horse within. He whinnied, and nuzzled my fingers. He reminded me so of Ebon, I swallowed a lump. Smiling, I fed him a carrot. He munched contentedly, as was Ebon's wont.

Behind me, a neigh of fury. My mare reared up, hurling Tanner to the straw. Her eyes rolled back in her head. I snapped, "Tanner, out! Be quick!" My mare lashed out as the boy scrambled. Her heels barely missed Tanner's ribs.

Tanner hurtled into the alleyway. I slammed shut the gate, tied the rope. The mare careened about the stall, rearing, kicking, voicing her rage.

My voice was a whisper. "It was only a *carrot*!" How could a casual treat provoke such jealousy? Oh, Ebon, will I ever see your like?

Forlorn, I draped an arm about Tanner and walked him to the castle. My apparent unfairness in rewarding the shaggy mount who'd done no work, rather than my own charge, had driven the mare to frenzy. Must I take such care with my nobles as well, that they not betray me over trifles? Had I somehow been the instrument of Lady Soushire's disloyalty?

Later, from the battlements I looked about, my expression sour. I might as well have gone to Stryx; there, at least, I might mingle with Tresa and Rustin, and perhaps we could plot Elryc's release, or at least offer ransom. Still, even now, I might seek their counsel. The thought buzzed like a persistent fly at my trencher, one I couldn't wave away.

It was to escape it that I sallied forth.

FORTY-ONE

JUST PAST THE Verein crossroads, our column stumbled upon a small train of wagons, a mere forty Norlanders and guards, wending their way down to the coast. But, why? Hriskil had no outpost south of Stryx that we knew of, and the city was in Caled hands.

A whispered conference, on horseback, in our refuge among the trees. Even our mere hundreds heavily outnumbered the foe, and we sorely needed what provisions we might seize. Moreover, where were the wagons bound, and why? We had to know.

To take best advantage of our disparity, we committed nearly all our force. We were almost ideally situated. Groenfil's faithful horsemen would withdraw a furlong farther from the road, hurry ahead, creep back toward the trail and fall upon the wagons from a small rise that offered nearly ideal concealment in brush. I agreed, and made ready, but Groenfil and Kadar urged me to hold myself apart; there was no glory in a mere skirmish, yet I might be downed by a stray shaft. Reluctantly, that their minds be eased, I consented. Larissa was directed to remain with me; Groenfil's glance sealed with mine a pact: I'd stand sentry, lest she do some evil.

Kadar and a squad of horsemen kept vigil with me, though Anavar begged so piteously to be allowed the battle, I let him go. Even Danzik drifted off, though I knew he would raise no hand against his kinsmen.

Taking great care to make no sound, Groenfil led his horsemen farther into the wood, to loop beyond the first of the Norland wagons.

Near an hour passed. Nervously, I paced my mount. "What's keeping them?"

Kadar said, "The wagons make no haste. Groenfil must wait 'til they near, else his surprise fails."

Distant cries and alarms. The battle had begun.

I said, "Watch the road." It wouldn't be long before Groenfil sent a signalman that all was well.

A rumble rolled across the hills, as distant thunder. Rain would muddy the road, but not soon. The wagons would be ours. Surely they already were. Where was—

The thunder grew louder.

I glanced about.

Kadar licked his lips. "My liege—"

A trooper shouted, "The ridge!"

I wheeled. The ridge was dark with horsemen. Groenfil, returned so soon? And why was he on the far side of the road?

I took sharp breath. "Ride for your lives! No, down the road! Toward Groenfil!" My heels stabbed the mare's sturdy flanks.

Before I could plunge onto the road, it filled with Norland cavalry. I wheeled about, urged my perspiring mount up the hill. A branch loomed. I ducked it. Once past the woods, we'd have open meadow. With luck we'd—

Behind me, a desperate cry. I glanced over my shoulder. Bouton, Kadar's chief aide, was down, his foot caught in his stirrup. His frantic stallion dragged him over rock-strewn turf. I turned to urge the mare and caught a low limb in the forehead. Almost, I fell, but with desperate clutch of legs and arms caught myself. Salt blood gushed, blinding me.

"This way, Roddy!"

I reeled, wiping my brow.

"Give me your reins!"

I tried and toppled from the saddle.

Strong hands seized me, heaved me upward. I did what I could to help. My rescuer caught my left wrist, twisted it hard. I cried out. Someone clawed at my dagger.

"What are you—"

I was across the saddle of a huge bay. It pounded down the road.

"Where's Groenfil? Who—"

A fist clubbed the small of my back, driving the wind from my lungs.

My skull throbbed. I fought to gather my wits. A galvanic twist, and I might be free and slide to the earth. Better that than—

The rider reined in sharply. I wiped desperately at my eyes.

Two men jumped down on either side and pinned me. My right hand went behind my back to join my left, and leather lashed my wrists tight. Again I was thrown over the saddle. Before blood oozed again, I caught a glance of my surroundings.

Dozens of horsemen. Hundreds. Bearded Norsemen, in the garb of their country. I swallowed.

I was taken.

MY SKULL WAS splitting. I wished I were dead, and knew I soon would be. My body was sore from relentless pounding against the stiff saddle.

Our column dashed down the road. Where were we flying? Soushire? Verein? I knew not and had no vantage from which to peruse the terrain.

What of Groenfil, Anavar, Kadar? Were my liege men perished? Who would remember my demise? Bruised and aching, I twisted my bound wrists. *Ah, Mother. Someday you'll greet Hriskil, in the gray cave.* As will I.

The horsemen rode for hours, until the sky began to darken. My captors halted in a glade. Wagons waited, and a few dozen horses. Would we camp the night? A Norlander hauled me down, flung me on the turf. Hands bound, I could only glare and mutter curses.

Quickly, fresh horses were made ready. This time they set me upright on the saddle, but passed a rope under the horse's middle to bind my ankles. In bare moments, we again took to the road.

My escort was much reduced: hundreds of their riders had no fresh mounts and must perforce wait 'til morn. It mattered not, trussed as I was.

After a while, I recognized fords, farms, inns, and knew our road.

We were bound for Soushire.

THE CASTLE COURTYARD was bright lit by the flames of hundreds of torches. I tried to keep my face stolid. I knew what awaited me: torture, sport and death. I would try to give good account of myself.

Soldiers pointed to a high window, jostling each other. "Mor Rez!" *The king watches.* I raised my eyes. From the window of a tower room, a bushy beard. Smoldering eyes met mine.

Now, it would start.

But, no. They led me to a first-floor chamber that was entirely bare—four walls, an ironclad window and a stone floor—and barred the door.

By some act of kindness or negligence, my ropes were just loose enough not to numb my hands and destroy them. Not so loose I might escape, however. Certainly, I tried. At length, I crouched in the corner: it gave most respite to my aching shoulders.

Gradually, the clatter and murmur of the castle settled for the night. The glow outside my window faded, as torches were moved or extinguished.

A whisper. "Rust, be with me." I started, unaware I'd spoken. A swelling fear bit my heart and gnawed away. As the chamber grew darker, I licked dry lips, tried not to think of the morrow. One's worst thoughts have free rein in dark. It is a time for imps and demons.

A shadow flitted. Almost, I screamed. Did a demon seek me, or only a rat? Anavar once said his father claimed imps and their like were but phantasms, men's fears given construct. Let *him* meet one, bound in a dark chamber.

When morn came, and with it, my fate, I was almost glad. My relief enabled me to walk between my captors with firm step, arms still tied behind.

They took me to the courtyard. My eyes darted about, in search of the waiting axe. I saw none: it was to be something more grim. Despite my resolve, I shivered.

A saddled horse awaited. Two huge guardsmen hoisted me up. Their beards made them look much like Danzik. Almost, I wished for the solace his company. Hoa, Giat, vestre coa tern. *Today, Teacher, you'll see how it ends.*

Adjusting myself as best I could in the saddle, I turned to a guard. "Voe Hriskil?" *Where's Hriskil?*

He hawked, as if to spit.

I said quietly, "Kara vos morta." *It will buy your death.* He flinched, and swallowed. Inwardly, I exulted. To such petty victories was the king reduced.

The rider ahead hauled on my reins. We cantered through the open gate, along an unfamiliar trail that soon turned away from the fields surrounding the castle to meander through thick woods.

All too soon we emerged at a deep gully, at the bottom of which ran a swift stream. Halfway down, amidst the scraggly growth of brush, a clutch of some fifty Norlanders waited.

Was I to be stoned?

My captor slipped down from his mount, wound my reins about his hand, led my mount down the steep, rock-strewn path. Perhaps, if I jabbed the mare's flanks sharply enough, the Norlander's wrist would snap. I'd take some satisfaction in that.

I struggled to keep my balance. Who comprised my executioners?

One among them stood out. I blinked.

Hriskil.

Why ought I be astonished? He'd want to see my end, as I would his. Perhaps, in the cold of winter, he and Danzik would joke of it around the crackling fire.

As we neared, a dark shadow gaped through the brush. A cave.

They led me to its mouth. Hriskil gestured, and they hauled me down. I fought life into numbed legs.

Burly guards held my arms, as if I were still a danger, wrists trussed behind. Hriskil approached, his bushy eyes dark and serious. My stomach clenched. Would it be dagger, or stone?

"So, Caled," he said in his own tongue. He studied me, and perhaps learned what he sought. After a time, "I ought kill you at once, but you've earned worse. And you'll have it." A gesture, and they hauled me toward the cave.

"What are you—" My feet dragged. I forced my speech into Norl. "Qa iv dez vos?" *What do you to me?*

"Grot saj vos morta." *The cave will be your death.*

"But—" I had no time for more; they shoved and jostled me through the mouth. Inside, a rock-strewn floor, rough, uneven walls. Room to stand, beneath stalactites and a stony ceiling. Behind, a passage disappeared into dark.

I swallowed. With an effort, I faced the Norland throng and took deep breath. "*Mark this day, Hriskil. Never will you rule Caledon. Rodrigo King speaks.*"

The Norlander chuckled. "Is it the Still that tells you so?

I give you a cave, boy." He gestured, and men rushed up, bearing buckets, mortar and trowels. "I *do* rule, arrogant Caled whelp. Think of me, each day you starve. Think of me when you shrivel of thirst. Think of me as you slowly die."

"Thank your mother for spreading her legs. I forgot to." Not noble of me, but I was vexed.

"You've not been with my mother, nor any woman. And you never will." Hriskil turned. Over his shoulder, to a spearman, "Stab him if he tries to flee. In the gut." He stalked up the hill, mounted a splendid stallion. In a few moments, only his dust remained.

Wrists bound behind me, I sat slumped on a rounded boulder, while eager Norland churls walled me into the cave.

THE WALL THEY raised was no mere adornment, easily kicked through. It was thick and sturdy, and the building took them much of the day. As they finished, the light through the last, vanishing chinks was dim and forlorn. I stared intently until it was gone.

So, Roddy, they'd have you starve and thirst. How to defeat them? Charge the side of the cave and bash your head on the rocks? A better end, at least, than they'd arranged. But in the stupid lethargy of your terror, you failed to make note of where rocks were strewn on the floor. You'd more likely stumble and bash out your teeth on a stone, than make a decisive end.

What was that? I whirled. Was it my hair that brushed my ear, or something worse? But what animal could share my uninhabited cave? None.

What . . . being? What imp, what demon of the night? I blinked furiously, in utter dark. My fingers scrabbled helplessly at my bonds. If I could but see. Did a wickedly clawed, wart-encrusted finger reach out slowly, cruelly, to flay my cheek? I mewled, and shrank back on my rock throne. Feverishly, I muttered incants that had protected me as a child, racing through a dark courtyard to the beckoning safety of a torch.

Men's fears given construct, Father says. If imps are real, where go the bones of their dead?

Oh, shush, Anavar. You're not here. If only you were . . .

No, I don't mean that. If you live, may you have sanctuary and health. Remember that I tried to be valiant.

Damp paths trickled down my dust-caked cheeks. "If you must, demons, then take me quickly."

No response. Expecting sharp summons, I shivered.

Courage, my prince.

Courage. Oh, Rustin. Without demons, all I need fear is grim, inevitable death. Perhaps, if the cave is dry enough, some distant day they'll find my mummified semblance. But I'll be dead and unknowing.

No, I won't. I couldn't help a grim chuckle. My death will trade one cave for another. What would Mother think of that? Soon, perhaps, she'll tell me, before the cold fire where she sits with Grandsir and Varon.

Flexing my wrists, I settled back on my chill seat to await my end. It was hard not to fidget. *Idiot, no need to sit straight. Who watches?*

I slumped, and scratched an annoying itch at my rump. My fingers brushed the rocky stool. It was cold, hard, uneven. Soon, its outlines would be imprinted in my flesh. There, for example, that sharp spot, and that concavity.

I blinked again, seeing only the spots and jangles with which eyes deceive one, in dark.

Mother, how ought I prepare?

I'd ask her, if I could. But that required a bowl, and water. And my hands freed, to spread over the medium of encant.

Well, not a bowl, necessarily. Once, pacing a battlement—was it at Cumber?—I'd used a puddle of rainwater.

I sat a long while.

Then, feeling a fool, I stood, carefully turned, pressed my face to the rock that had a moment past been my seat. With lips and nose, I felt about.

Yes, there.

Piss wouldn't work; my breeches would deflect it, and I had no way to undo them.

So I spat.

And again. When my mouth was dry, I waited a while, summoned more saliva.

Cautiously, I eased my way back onto the seat, hunched backward as far as I could, opened my hands against the squeeze of the thong.

I whispered familiar words.

Must I shut my eyes, Mother? There seems no point, in absolute dark. Are you there? Hello? Why can't I see—

"Don't shout, Roddy." She sounded testy.

I blinked. "Where's your fire?" I might have seen faint shadows, but I had doubt.

Grandsire Tryon rumbled, "Use stillsilver, boy. The sight's clearer."

"I can't, sir."

With a sigh, he bestirred himself, threw fagots on the glowing embers. When the fire blazed high I looked about. It was their cave, not mine. Gray with dust, and a floor worn flat.

Mother scowled. "What's befallen you now? With what are you bound?"

"Thongs." Stammering as if ashamed, I blurted out my woes.

"So, then." Mother looked bleakly at her sire. "Our line is done."

Tryon stirred. "Not necessarily."

"He's lost Caledon."

"But has the Still."

She said, "What good that, when—"

"You, of all, should know."

They regarded each other. Mother's tone was doubtful. "He's still walled into a hill."

"But not yet dead. With life, there's—"

I snarled, "Look at me! Speak to ME!"

Tryon's tone grew hard. "Who dares—"

"Rodrigo, king of Caledon!" Almost, I clenched my fists, but remembered in time: I was in another cave, with palms spread over ooze. I made my tone peaceable. "You'll have plenty of time to berate me after."

From the corner, a familiar rumble. "What would you of us?"

"Oh, Father Varon, help me." My voice caught. "Now death is nigh, I fear it so."

"Yes . . ."

"The spirit that will sit among you . . . will it be me? Truly the *me* I know? My memories, my sense . . ." I knew not the words. "My sense of self?"

The great old king said simply, "It was so for me." As I struggled for relief, he added, "Why, though, look to death? Life is yet."

My laugh was near scornful. "For how long?"

"Long as may be. Free yourself. Find water."

"To what end?"

"What if they sent rescue, and you'd let yourself die? Life *is* hope, boy!"

"My hands are bound behind, sir. Free myself with what?"

"Surely there's an edged—"

"I'm in dark!" My voice was, perhaps, too shrill. I wasn't truly sure a clutch of waiting imps didn't share my prison.

"That, at least," said Tryon, "you can remedy."

A sudden, cruel stab of hope. "How?"

"Sit forward. Elena, make a place." Mother inched to the side. "Look about, Rodrigo."

I did. "Walls, a dark corner, the pile of sticks you—"

His voice was sharp. "Know you *nothing*, boy? Shut your eyes!"

In my walled cave, I did.

"Shut them *here*, dunce!"

Sitting beside Mother, I shut my eyes, looked about.

There, behind me, a stalactite loomed. I'd crack my skull if I took no care. Rounded rocks made my floor. In that alcove, split stones. A jagged edge.

Tryon snapped, "Look about, boy! Be quick. Memorize all you see. When you move from your cupped spit you'll be blind."

"I think under that slope, there's a sharp edge I might rub—"

"Is it the best you see?"

I cast my eyes from wall to wall. "I think so, Grandsir."

"When you're ready." His tone softened. "Look about. Be sure you can find your way back."

I shivered. Lord of Nature help me, if I wandered the cave, unable to find my puddle of spit before it dried. My mouth was so parched I doubted I could conjure more.

"Mind you don't fall." Mother, as if speaking to a child.

"Aye, madam." I traced a path to the jagged rock. I'd have to avoid that large round stone, and that rock pile there. Girding my courage I rose from my rocky seat.

All was black. There was no sound except for a crunch of pebbles under my feet. Step by cautious step I made my way across the cavern. The jagged rock should be a few steps ahead, under the slope.

Thunk!

I winced, crouching too late. Crouching, I duck-walked under the narrowing slope. I turned, to blunder rump-first toward the jagged rock. Where in the demons' lake—behind me, my hands scrabbled at cold stone. Not that one, too low.

That's too uneven, it couldn't . . .

No, too round.

Smaller than I remembered.

Not—*THERE!* I cried out for the joy of it. A rough, jagged edge. Well, not all that jagged. Not as sharp as it had looked across the—but something of an edge. And I had time. If I got so, on my knees . . . in utter dark, I worked my way into position.

Rub the thong, Roddy, not your flesh, else you'll be a bloody mess and still bound.

Grimacing, I set to work.

HOURS HAD PASSED. "Ah, Rustin, you berated my stubbornness. It's all I have. All that keeps me sawing away. Say something, Rust."

Anything, Rust.

My joints, beyond ache, were in some exquisite torment. My knees were raw and scratched. My wrists . . . on the whole, I'd avoided abrading my skin; each error had taught me more caution. But what magic bound the thrice-cursed thong? I'd rubbed steadily, 'til I thought I'd lose my mind. And the leather held.

I knew now just how to position my hands, clear of the stone. Half sobbing under my breath, I worked away at the endless, hopeless task.

"Will you remember me, Rust? Do you live still, or has the demon of the north taken your Keep? I doubt you'd surrender it, your mem—OUCH! Straighten your arm, Roddy. Memories of your father, I was saying." I panted for breath. ". . . too strong. You won't surrender, lest his treason be recalled."

Rub. *Hriskil, I hate you. Not you alone, every Norland churl who walks the earth.* Rasp. *Your mother, your line, your servants . . .* Scrape. *Your horse, your Rood . . .* Grind.

I stopped for breath, as I must every few moments.

Rage swelling, I sawed on. Grandsire, what do we accomplish? So I'll die hot and sweat-soaked, instead of cool and composed on my rough-hewn throne. What of it? Why do I—

My arm.

I stared stupidly, in pitch dark, as if I could see the wrist that had fallen to my side.

A sound, akin to a whimper.

Take no ease, Roddy. You're still doomed to slow death.

Feverishly, I gnawed at the remains of the thong, until my teeth ached, but each wrist was free. I licked at the ooze of blood; the lacerations couldn't be helped.

"Rustin, I did it!" Carefully, I worked my way clear of the sloped roof, stumbled across the floor, felt for my stone seat.

I knelt. Of course, the hole in the rock was bone dry. I tried to hawk a gob of spit. Nothing; my mouth was too dry. I doubted I could piss, or, in the dark, find the hole I'd filled. I felt for it, leaned over, resolutely stuck a finger in my throat, and gagged, bringing up weak bile. I spat it onto the rock, threw my palms over the sudden warmth. My lips moved.

"Ah, you're back." Mother. The cave wavered.

"Find water!" Tryon. "Be quick."

I asked weakly, "How?" The cave had looked dry when they'd sealed me in it.

"Show him." Father Varon's distant rumble.

"Sit here, lad." Unexpectedly, Tryon made space. I crouched. His rough hand flitted to my shoulder, gently guided me to my place. "Close your eyes, see the cave. Listen for a drip. Hold out your palms, so. Feel the water's call."

"How know you it's there?"

"I don't."

"And if not?"

"The sooner you'll die."

I threw my whole being into the search, hampered by ignorance, inexperience. What would water feel like, from afar? I licked dry lips. Already, thirst tormented me, and it was but the first day.

FORTY-TWO

I SCRABBLED IN the rear of the cave where I'd sensed dampness, hurling aside handfuls of small stones that I might crawl under the ledge. Had I led myself astray? How much energy was my frantic search consuming, that afterward I'd lament?

No matter. I was beyond frenzy, near madness. King of Caledon, wielder of the fabled Still, I was nonetheless a callow beardless youth whose voice still cracked in excitement. And I was walled into a black cave, for eternity.

I squeezed myself under the ledge, extended my arm. Surely it must be . . . right about . . . there.

It wasn't.

My arm outstretched to its fullest, I flung my hand about. Did Tryon toy with me?

Nothing.

Back to the seat, then, and its foul medium? Ask anew? Reach blindly about, until I saw what they'd have me see?

What was that?

I yanked out my finger, brushed it against my cheek.

It was wet.

Frantically, I squirmed as close to the ledge as I might, reached out again, cupped my hand palm upward.

Drip by slow drip, I let the droplets splash.

When my tight fingers had a spoonful of water, I eased it out, and lost my treasure.

Cursing mighty oaths, I struggled to cast aside loose rock. When at last the hole was enlarged, I squeezed under, held out my hand anew.

Eons later, I withdrew a precious iota of water, slurped it into my dry, cracked mouth. A long, impatient wait. Another handful.

And again.

How long I lay there, letting the precious drops fill my hand, I knew not. At length, I was, if not sated, eased.

What next?

I made my way back to the rock that had been my seat. I ought tell Tryon of my success.

No, there was time. Time was the one commodity I didn't lack.

The concavity I'd filled first with spit, then bile, wasn't all that deep. I felt about for a loose stone, found one that would do. With care, I positioned myself, made sure my fingertips were clear, and began to pound the basin.

After a time my forehead was damp with sweat. I blew out the dust and chips. Was the basin any deeper? Perhaps; it was hard to judge in dark. I crawled once more to the ledge.

"IT'S JUST A trickle. A drop at a time."

"Does it suffice?"

"Yes." My tone was reluctant. "Aye, Grandsir. If I don't move about and sweat." I stared moodily at the embers. "What about air?"

"If you're not panting, there's a source."

"An escape hole?" I could barely contain my eagerness.

"Have you seen such?"

I shook my head.

"Then I doubt you'll find it. Some caves go far." Tryon's tone was dreamy. "When I was a boy, the Warthen showed me a cave you might walk in for hours. He—"

"I could bash at the wall; there's enough small rocks for hammers. In time . . ."

Cayil, behind us, snickered. "You must think him a fool."

"Who?"

"Your Hriskil. As if he'd leave a cave unguarded, with his rival within. Faugh."

"But I *must* have out."

Tryon said gently, "I fear Cayil's right. The clap of your rock on stone will alert the guards Hriskil surely placed. He'll have no need to stint. You'll be met with spears and arrows, and die for naught."

I gulped. "What, then?"

"Wait for rescue." Tryon held up a hand to forestall me. "Fifty saw you immured, you say. Then a hundred more will know, and soon all Caledon. If your liege men love you, they'll make the attempt."

"Better I free myself than my vassals die in the effort!"

"Nobly said, but . . . impractical. You *can't* free yourself."

I sputtered, "Damn Hriskil to the lake! May his bones rot! May imps chew—"

"Yes!" From the corner, a rumble. "Gather the hate. Shape it, And . . ."

"Yes, Father Varon?"

"And wait."

OF THE TIME that followed, what is there to say?

Hours passed. And more.

Much more.

I crouched silently, as day and night entwined in black affliction that could only be endured. In Mother's cave I could see my own, and fixed in my memory every rock, every low spot, every twist that might trip my unsteady feet.

From time to time I grew thirsty and felt my way to the ledge, crawled beneath, stretched out my palm and took sustenance. Eventually I would crawl back to my rock, kneel with hands cupped, to commune with my forebears.

As venture succeeded venture to the ledge, I felt myself ever more lightheaded. My legs grew unsteady. After a time, I crawled all the way, rather than daring to stand.

Slowly, my stomach shrank to a hard knot. At first, I dreamed of roast fowl, dripping with juices, fresh eggs, hot steaming bread, tall mugs of beer, Uncle Raeth's dainty pastries. Eventually, in desperation, I quelled my self-torture. Now and then I chewed on my discarded thongs in hapless effort to relieve my misery.

I still urinated, in a far corner. After a while I produced no other waste. I cinched my belt rope ever tighter.

Sitting on a somewhat flat stone I'd dragged across the floor, I hunched for endless hours over my improvised vessel, my thoughts on Hriskil. In the far cave, Mother and Tryon edged away, as if troubled. But, rigidly courteous, I coaxed them back. They squatted at their fire, and helped me mold my Power.

The time came when I could barely crawl to the distant ledge. I drank long, knowing it was likely my last journey. With great care, I cupped my hands, waited an eternity, filled them with water, brought it down the well-memorized path to my basin. I slumped on my rocky stool, facing the mortared wall, and waited.

Rustin, it will be soon. I'm near spent.

Why is it you I seek for comfort? Why not Tresa, whom I yearned to wed?

You knew me long, my prince.

Aye, but not my lady. Would we have made a fair couple, do you think?

Silence.

If not for the Norland beast, I might have had answer.

I dozed, palms spread, swaying until I nearly fell. Wake, dolt! To sleep is end. Nurse the hatred that pervades you. Grandsir says to bet on the die that fate casts. Bet all: your Caleds will rescue you, or they will not. Your task is but to live.

Slumped over the vessel, I licked dry lips and impaled imagined Norland foes with pretended swords. With a cruel twist, I wrenched them free. I seized fiery brands, thrust them at wide staring eyes.

Die, all of you.

I was a wraith built of hatred.

Somewhere, a pebble clattered.

My lips twisted. Do you come for me, imps? I don't say I'm your match; I say only, lay claw on me, and I will teach you of the Still of Caledon.

More pebbles. The sound was from the cave's mouth.

I ought get up, feel my way, but for two reasons I did not.

If my palms left the basin, I would lose my Power.

And I couldn't force my body erect. I doubted I could crawl. I lay across the basin, my bony torso pressing my palms to the puddle of clear water. My head sagged.

You've won, Hriskil. I can wait no longer. If my spirit survives, I'll haunt you, I swear by—

Thunk.

My heart fluttered, beat more strongly.

Thumps and clatters.

A blast of searing light. I squeezed shut my eyes.

The shaft of fire grew brighter.

"Mother?" My lips barely moved. "Is it time? How do I make passage?"

"You live." Her voice was taut. "Harken."

The crash of rock. A shadow. Then, "Sa mord!" *He is dead.*

Yes, Rodrigo's dead. Only his thoughts remain.

Thoughts he's gathered for eons, unexpressed.

"Hae vestre!" Come see!

Thoughts he can no longer contain.

Mother's cave faded to naught.

So be it.

I forced open an eyelid.

They'd pounded out a doorway of sorts. Two Norls were in the cave. Behind, a half dozen peered eagerly through the opening. All had spears. Swords were drawn.

I bared my teeth. A bolt of pure hate escaped me.

The nearest Norl hissed, arched his back, dropped to the cave floor, cracking his skull.

The others gaped.

"Aiyee!" The second invader stiffened. He fell, convulsing.

"Bowmen!" A frantic cry.

Which of you is Hriskil?

Eyes shut, I searched past the opening to the slope beyond. One by one, methodically, I squeezed the souls I chanced upon.

Brave archers took a stance a hundred paces distant, across the stream. A few badly aimed shafts were loosed. In turn, each bowman stiffened, twitched, fell unmoving.

After a time, the frantic clatter of horses.

I let myself rove, choking off life where I found it.

Forever passed, and I fed on no more souls.

"RODDY." SOMEONE SHOOK me.

Let me sleep.

"Sleep ends all!" Mother's voice was sharp. "Now, King! Leave us."

Wearily, I forced open my eyes.

I lay slumped across my stone basin. My palms ached. I cast about, felt no one near. Slowly, reluctantly, I dragged stiff aching fingers from under my belly.

Mother's cave faded. I looked about my own cavern, unaccustomed to the sight of it.

The doorway framed a blaze of light, furlongs distant.

Life.

But too far ever to walk.

Crawl, then.

I thought to try, and toppled. A protruding stone drove air

from my lungs. I lay gasping. A faint echo of rage overwashed me. I would *not* die thus! Grimly, I inched my way to the door. The light grew ever brighter.

I heaved myself through, to day.

A dozen Norlanders lay dead among trampled brush. Weakly, I thrust aside twigs and branches, peered about. Below, the stream chuckled. On the far side, a lone tree. A pudgy body hung from a rope, abandoned even by crows.

Above was the road, but that was hopeless. I hadn't the strength, and never would.

I dragged myself to a staring, still Norlander. In his sheath, a dagger. He must be a horseman; he carried no pack with morsels of food that might revive me. With a feverish burst of energy, I thrust my hands into his clothing, searching for I knew not what.

Coins. A knotted cloth.

A flint.

I thought a long moment.

It would do.

I stretched unsteady fingers toward the brush, began to gather twigs and leaves.

"FEA HAE CERC, Rez?" *May I come near, King?*

I didn't bother to turn. "Qay." *Yes.*

Danzik edged closer. "Truly, you live." His voice was awed. "Qay."

As the Norlander studied me, his eyes widened. "Look at you, Rodrigo!" He pursed his lips. "Bones and no more." He unslung his pack. "I have rations."

My voice grated. "I've . . . eaten." Not much, but all I dared. A few bites and my stomach felt full to bursting. All the while, I struggled not to vomit.

"What found you—oh!" Danzik stared with dismay at the bloody haunch. He swallowed.

In the growing dusk, I met his gaze, unashamed. It had sustained life, and until Hriskil were dead, I must need live.

It was growing chill. With gaunt forearm, I nudged the last of my sticks into the fire. "How long was I . . . ?"

"Sixteen days."

I marveled. "That long." Then, "Why did they break through the wall?"

Danzik lumbered to his feet, gathered handfuls of brush, began feeding it to the greedy flames. "When you were taken, and your band dispersed, I rode to Norl camp at Soushire." He spoke slowly, clearly, that I might follow. "King greeted me, civilly enough. Asked if my pilgrimage was done. With your death, I told him."

A pause. We stared at crackling flames.

"You *were* dead, said Hriskil."

My smile was grim. "Soa Rez Caledi, qa han vos modrit." *I am the Caled king, whom you cannot kill.*

Danzik merely nodded. "Dicha Hriskil qa veztrez coa tern." *I told Hriskil I would see how it ends.* "Until seeing it, I was not done. He bade me unseal your crypt and look upon your rotting flesh. It had been half a month." After a time he added, "Hriskil asked me to bring back your head."

"Will you?" I shivered. It was growing chill.

"Han, Rez." He shook his head.

"They will, then." I gestured to the rise, and the Norland host who must wait beyond.

Danzik snorted. "They're long gone." He made himself busy. "I rode from Soushire with Sanchu's regiment of cavalry. Officers joked we'd find your corpse *hrutu*, dried, only skin and bones." His broad face darkened. "Not *kevhom*, to jeer at foe so brave. And—and—" He bit it off. Then, "Gallant." His eyes refused to meet mine. "Guards here told Sanchu that for many days there were no sounds from cave. But while they broke the wall, I waited across stream. Not sure why. Part, I didn't want to see you dead. And part . . . I not stupid-brave." The Norl word for *foolhardy.*

"Guards used hammers and steel to open cave. Sanchu's men helped. Suddenly, Norl kevhom began to fall. I grabbed reins, threw myself on saddle, rode as fast as mare go. Flanks bloody from whip."

We sat in silence.

"Everyone who stayed near cave died. Spearmen. Bowmen across stream. Sanchu himself. Did you know your Still so strong?"

"No. I . . . nursed it. Shaped it. I had a long while."

"A fearsome day. So sudden, from jokes to death. Above that rise, Sanchu's regiment was milling about. Few at a time, men lost their nerve. Suddenly, a dozen rode off. Rest raced after."

Then I'd live for a time. I shook my head at the marvel of it.

"I fled too," said Danzik, "a few hundred paces. But I turned back."

I said dryly, "To see how it ends."

"Qay." Abruptly Danzik rose and trudged down the slope to the stream, near the lone tree. In a moment he climbed back up with a skin of water. He crouched by my side, helped me drink of it. "This no place to stay. Morrow, they regain courage. Perhaps even this night, when Hriskil hears of it. He'll send whole army."

It mattered not. I hadn't the strength to climb the rise.

As if Danzik read my thoughts, he stooped, thrust his mighty arms under me, lifted me gently, like a babe. With stolid care, he waded across the stream to climb the far hill.

We passed under the tree, with its taut rope. Lady Soushire's empty eyesockets gazed past me to eternity.

I swallowed. "But who did . . . why?"

"Hriskil's orders, after she was captured. For slipping out of castle to join you."

DANZIK'S HORSE GRAZED patiently, reins tied to a branch. A half dozen other mounts wandered nearby. Their masters wouldn't need them. The Norlander gathered the reins of a gray gelding. He lifted me high, helped me into the saddle. I was too weak to be of much help.

"Where, Rez?"

My hand fell on his. "Danzik . . ." I hated to injure my cause, but I owed him much. "Guiat . . . this is beyond *vestrez coa tern*. You aid your king's foe."

A shamefaced look stole across his features. "Only in little things. I not fight Norls."

"Will Hriskil forgive it?"

"I don't know. Where, Rodrigo? I'd not want to be here at dawn."

"Who of my band lives?" I clung to the pommel, fighting a wave of dizziness.

"Most, I think. You waited apart, with your guards, while Anavar and Groenfil and all your riders attacked wagons.

Wagons were decoys. Not much of a fight there. When Caleds knew you were taken, too late." His eyes narrowed. "Trap was clever. Hriskil's way. Sacrifice drovers, but . . ." He shrugged. "War."

"I would not fight so."

"I know. Norl horsemen held off Groenfil while others took you east. Then they retreated north to lead your men off trail."

"Where were you?"

"With Groenfil, after fight. Anavar wanted to attack, attack, 'til you found, but Groenfil had older, cooler head. He decided to retreat near Stryx, and regroup. I left him."

I considered. "We'll go to Stryx, then. But surely your men guard every path."

"If not now, as soon as Hriskil hears." Danzik studied me. "You can't ride." He gathered a string of horses, tied their reins to his pommel, and mounted. He nudged his mare closer to my gelding. Before I knew it he swept me from my mount, set me in front of him on the generous seat, nudged his mare into a walk.

Stunned speechless, I almost struggled to loose myself. Then, surrendering, I leaned back, let my head loll against his chest.

Bushes, trees, brooks inched past. I had vague memories of a peasant's hut, and soup forced between my lips. A straw bed. More soup.

Two days came and went. Danzik fed me bread and apples and dried smoked meat from his pack. My interest in the world began to revive. I transferred to a mount of my own.

We rode slowly, often forsaking roads for hilly paths and goat trails.

Long before we reached Stryx, we blundered into one of Groenfil's outguards. Nearly, they skewered us. Danzik and I cried out, in Norl and Caled. Lord of Nature stayed their swords.

GROENFIL PACED, HIS eyes darting from me to Danzik, and back. Again, he shook his head. "An apparition. You cannot be else."

Anavar's voice was muffled. "He's real." His forehead nestled in the crook of my shoulder. His fingers still clutched the saddlebag he'd so proudly presented me, that contained my coronet and vessels. I'd thought it lost on my capture, but in the melee my mare had run off, and my gear was found intact.

Absently, I patted the young Eiberian's back, glad his tears had subsided. "Real enough." Thanks to Danzik, who'd helped me dismount in Groenfil's makeshift camp and calmly curled himself against a leafy elm to snooze, while around him astonished horsemen crowded to see the king returned from the dead.

Groenfil eyed my gaunt form. "Come, my liege. Sit."

"In a moment. Though, if you have any broth . . ."

"They've skinned a rabbit. Be patient."

My lips tightened. In recent days I'd learned patience, if nothing else. I rubbed my scar. "What know we of Caledon?"

The earl sighed. "Our way to Stryx is blocked. Hriskil's moved a portion of his army to the city. Rustin holds firm in the Keep. For now."

"What else?"

"From Cumber, no word, but Bouris is no friend of yours, and contests your revocation of his title. Verein's fallen; it had no garrison. My castle holds."

I asked, "What was your intent?"

"When we assumed you dead? To maneuver as best I might, so as to rejoin my sons. Now, command is yours. Anavar . . . ?"

"My lord?"

Groenfil's tone grew stiff. "Baron of the Southern Reaches, I pray thy pardon."

Anavar muttered, "Granted."

I raised an eyebrow. "What's this about?"

Groenfil flushed. "We had . . . harsh words. Anavar demanded—argued passionately—that we invade Soushire, free you from the cave. But a good portion of Hriskil's force was set in our path, against just such an eventuality. I would save you if I could, but not ride to suicide." A pause, then reluctantly, "Especially as I believed you dead."

I grunted. "You did right. No, Anavar." I stayed his protest. "Groenfil preserved what little army we had. Now we may act." Brave words, and hollow. To divert him, I added, "Is that rabbit cooked?"

"I'll see, Roddy. Er, sir! Sire." The boy rushed off.

Groenfil said, to a point in the distance, "The third day, I had him restrained, that he not rush off alone on a gallant death ride. I thought you would wish it so."

I managed, "Thank you."

"What path now, sire?"

I threw up my hands. In all Caledon, we had but two strong-points: Groenfil's castle and Stryx. Groenfil was besieged, and the enemy lay between us and Stryx. If we broke through to Stryx before Hriskil mounted a true siege, the yeomen Tresa and Willem had trained could reinforce our meager numbers. But where would men at arms be of most use? Did we not need to maintain Castle Stryx at all costs, as symbol of our defiance? And autumn was upon us. If Stryx held out until the first snows, the castle was ours 'til spring. Even the Norls couldn't maintain siege works in bitter winter.

Furthermore, we desperately needed resupply. An army couldn't live off the land and remain an effective fighting force.

What, then?

I knew not. In my weakened state, strategy was too much for me. That resolved it, did it not? "To Stryx," I said. "We'll consult Rust and Tresa. Hriskil may repulse us, I know. But I need their aid."

A short bow. "As you say, sire." He moved off.

"My lord?" Now it was I who hesitated. "Outside the cave—we saw . . . there was a tree. Danzik carried me . . ."

"Yes, Hriskil hanged Larissa." Groenfil's tone was flat. "Do you know, he had scribes make hundreds of copies of a broadsheet, and posted them at every cross for furlongs around. A crude drawing of a woman hanged and kind words for me. He was anxious I know."

"I'm sorry."

"It was like the wagons before Pezar. They think to weaken us by their barbarity."

"Do they?"

His eyes were bleak. "I mourn her, sire. Forgive me."

"Gladly. Even I couldn't find it in me to hate her."

"Yet you threatened what Hriskil accomplished."

"I'd like to think I'd have demurred, at the end." I waved it away. "To you, she was kind. You summoned her best."

He blinked rapidly, turned away. "Let us not speak of it."

*   *   *

ON THE ROAD to Stryx, Anavar was a constant shadow. Casting about for conversation I asked, "Is there word of Tantroth?"

"One courier from Eiber ferreted out our trail. The duke snaps at the Norlanders' heels, but Eiber Castle is beyond his grasp."

Danzik chuckled. "Always will be. Hriskil is too clever for his traps."

"Where might your king be now, Guiat?"

"When I ride with you, I know nothing more than you."

I pondered. "Hriskil will ride to Stryx, to direct the siege."

"Why?" Anavar.

"He can't afford to let it fail. He needs a great victory. Nobles and churls see us pique him over and again."

"Yet one by one he seizes your domains."

"I know, Anavar. He defeats us, but we maintain the illusion of defiance, and that's near as important as triumph on the field." Despite my bravado, I lapsed into gloomy silence as we plodded on, and ignored his attempts to draw me out.

As the afternoon drew to a close our weary column left one sheep path for another. Danzik squinted, and spurred to the trunk of a huge tree that held something white. He muttered an oath.

Lord Groenfil came up behind us. "More of Hriskil's taunts?" Danzik ignored my outstretched hand, thrust the sheet to Groenfil. The earl read in silence. His eyes briefly darted to mine. His lips tightened.

"Give it me!" Irked, I snatched it from his gloved fingers.

It was in Norl, beyond my ability. No, wait; the last half was in Caled.

My lips moved across the hand-inked page. *"TO THE ADHERENTS OF THE CATAMITE RODRIGO: Know that the boy Elryc, once prince, and last-but-one of the former House of Caledon, is recovered from his gelding, and pleasures his betters at the Inn of the Seven Maids in Wayvere."*

A dreadful cry, that startled the horses. My mouth worked. Anavar said, "Roddy, what—"

"Be assured the child Rodrigo will soon join his brother. Those who capture him will be granted six thousand golds of the Norland, and will be the first to bed the—"

ELRYC.

I stiffened, jabbed hard with my heels. Galvanized, the

mare reared. We plunged down the muddy road. I lashed her flanks. The trail flew past. A limb hung low. I ducked.

Behind me, the frantic clatter of hooves. A sob escaped me. I lay over my mare's neck, willing her onward, I cared not where.

Elryc!

ANAVAR AND TWO swift guardsmen on frothing mounts came up behind. One maneuvered past me, slowed his steed enough to block my way. Anavar snatched my reins. I gave a mighty tug, nearly unhorsing myself.

"Whoa, Edmund!" Anavar struggled to halt us both. "Roddy, why? Hold, horse! Go easy." After a struggle he had us at a walk.

I was beyond speech. Anavar got us turned, just as fifty horsemen thundered down on us, arms drawn. In a moment, Groenfil was among them, eyes blazing. "Where go you, sire?"

"Anywhere. To war. To death. You read it?"

"Yes." His tone was grim.

Danzik nosed his mare past Anavar, the better to hear.

I reared in my saddle. "Halt, you!"

"Rez?"

My smoldering eyes met his. "Norlander, leave my camp."

"Qa?"

"Now and forever!"

Danzik said firmly, "Caled, iv han dea tal cos." *I did not do this thing.*

"You are of the people who did."

A long pause. "Iot hom El-e-rek kevhom." *Little-man Elryc is a gentleman.* Then, forcefully, in Caled, "Hriskil should have not done this. I'll not go back."

"We fight your people."

"I'll try not fight." Then, as if in surrender, Danzik's shoulders slumped. "If I fight, then with Caled. Hriskil way has . . . han vade." *No honor.*

I let it be. "Anavar, is not Wayvere on the Eiber coast?"

"Aye, sir. It's a garrison town, seized by Hriskil when the war began."

Every moment of thought was agonizing delay. I marshalled my errant wits. "Baron Anavar, I place you in Lord Groenfil's care and custody."

"No!"

"Heed me. Until I return, or thirty days have passed and my fate is unknown. Groenfil, get word to Stryx Castle and the Keep. Do what you can to keep Hriskil's force busy."

"Where go you?"

"To Wayvere, of course. Where I ought have gone the day Larissa named the place."

The earl's tone was sharp. "To do what?"

My brother lay abused, scarred and mutilated. "Need you ask? Free Elryc, or die with him."

"Let us all—"

"Think you Hriskil's a fool? He's set traps, he'll watch the coast road. You've no more chance of reaching Wayvere than—"

Groenfil demanded, "How will you, then?"

"I'll seek Baron Jahl of Stoneshore."

"Who? Oh, the fisherman. Think you he could—"

"One ship, a drunken sailor set ashore? Yes."

"You're known. Your scar tells the world—"

"Dark dye. I'll go disguised as a trader from Chorr. I'll not look myself, and it will fade the scar too." The point wasn't to succeed, it was to try. Only then might I earn peace.

"Why you? If Elryc can be saved by one man in disguise, then any of us—"

"Elryc trusts me, and it's my oath to redeem. No, don't argue!"

Groenfil said stubbornly, "You can't go alone."

"Not alone." Danzik stirred. "I go."

"Then so do I!" Anavar. "It's my country; I know the land."

IT WAS NEAR a day before we were ready. Groenfil sent a yeoman to Seacross, where he found a leatherer, and came away with the brown dye that was so popular for saddles. The earl made me apply it not just to face and hands, but to my whole body. "If they have the clothes off me," I told him, "a bit of dye won't save me."

"I won't have Caledon lost by a rip in your breeches."

Reluctantly, I applied the foul-smelling paste to all my parts. None of us had a silver, but I caught a glimpse of myself in a polished sword, and grimaced. I looked ridiculous, or worse. Still, I studied my face. As I'd hoped, my scar stood out far less against dark skin than light.

Next, they cut my hair, over my fierce protest, but Groenfil was adamant. "If you must do this, Rodrigo, let it be done properly. Your wavy locks are familiar to all."

Eventually, our preparations were done, and our saddlebags bulged with food and drink. As we left our glade, Groenfil strode alongside, hand on my pommel, peppering me with advice. Stay away from inns. And the trails down to Stryx are unsafe. Norlanders abound. Jahl may be taken or turned. Be cautious in Wayvere; Eiberian ways are different from ours.

Gently, I placed my hand on his, on my pommel. "I'll take what care I might, dear my lord. I promise you."

He blinked. "A father's blessing, if you'll have it."

"With all my heart."

"Go now, my liege. Anavar, watch over him. He has sense, if he remembers to use it."

"Aye, sir."

"Danzik . . ." The earl forced his tongue around unaccustomed words. "Hae co domu nat." *Go with Lord of Nature.*

Danzik grinned. "And you, Caled lord."

WE PICKED OUR way toward the coast. My stomach was knotted with unease, but we encountered no worse than a clutch of churls from a nameless hamlet scything hay. They stopped their sweaty labor and stared as the three of us rode past. All eyes were on me. Fervently I hoped it was because they'd never seen a brownskin from Chorr, and not because they saw a familiar face.

We found Jahl of Stoneshore without incident. He told us the Norland army had occupied Stryx and its environs with casual contempt. They kept watch on castle and Keep lest our few defenders sally forth, but seemed to make no effort to organize attack or mount siege. Perhaps their only intent was to settle for the winter in comfortable quarters. Apparently they let the townsmen be, that their supply of wares and foodstuffs be uninterrupted. Patrols to outlying villages were few.

Jahl's barony was a shared secret among his taciturn fellow villagers. Months earlier, at Stryx Castle, I'd had Willem scrape together enough coin to replace Jahl's lost fishing boat—our promise of a tri-master was still unkept, though the ship Jahl purchased, an old Ukra barque, was considerably larger than the vessel we'd wrecked on the harbor rocks, and had a hold big enough for trading.

He wasn't overjoyed to see us. "Wayvere? A long sail." He rubbed his chin. "And death if we're caught."

"Most especially for me. Baron Jahl, I speak frankly: I've nowhere else to turn. Aid me, or I'm lost."

"What good is another mad escapade? Will Elryc redeem the kingdom?"

"No, only my oath, and my soul." I held his eye. "Then may I look again to Caledon."

"Hah. All is lost. Even I see it."

"It would seem so." But it no longer matters.

His tone was grudging. "Let me . . . ponder."

In the end, he agreed. He scraped together a few barrels of wine and other odds and ends, enough to pass for trade goods.

We crept out of the inlet at dawn. Jahl gave the harbor of Stryx wide berth. From the swaying deck, I squinted at the hazy outline of the castle, far distant. Tresa might even now be staring out a high window. Did she wonder of me, as I of her? Beside me, Danzik seemed as stolid as ever. Anavar, a hand on the rail, yawned prodigiously. I'd managed a good night's sleep, because the die was finally cast.

I might well die in the rescue of my brother. But if I succeeded . . . not only would I redeem my honor and save my poor mutilated brother, but I'd tweak Hriskil once again. Soon or late, my goads must have effect. He would blunder, in some unforeseen fashion, and drop his guard. Then, the sword of Caledon would plunge between his ribs.

We tacked up the coast. Jahl took amusement in setting the three of us at ropes. Once or twice I was almost sure he came about abruptly just to see the yard whistle over our heads as we ducked. Still, a king with his brains dashed out was no good to the realm, and I kept myself alert for a swinging spar. And it kept me too busy to be seasick.

All day we worked northward, against the prevailing wind.

By now we were far north of the Keep. Never had I seen the coast from the sea. I was landsman, not seaman, and would stay so. I asked Jahl, "How much farther?"

"The full day, with this wind."

"Will we land at night?"

"Just after dawn, we'll cause less notice. And the market will be open."

"But not the . . ." I made myself say it. ". . . the brothels."

"Hah," said Jahl. "Wyvern's a seaport. Do the brothels at Stryx ever close?"

A SMALL MISERABLE town, Wayvere, vexed with flies, its streets dusty and crabbed. Well, perhaps I ought not to be surprised. No king's castle dominated a hill above; no domain was ruled from its precincts. Long part of Tantroth's Eiber, it was ruled from afar. But still . . .

Jahl had gone ashore first and returned with a swarthy landsman who must be a local merchant. He was in the hold, inspecting our meager supply of goods.

Danzik had clumped down the plank as if he owned the town and shouldered through the squad of Norland soldiers who clustered on the wharf. I, on the other hand, dressed in near-rags, fresh dye applied, a packroll under my arm, clutched a bottle of stomach-churning spirits as I fought a drunken argument with Jahl, in which he threatened to sail without me if I wasn't back aboard by fourth hour past noon. Cursing him nonstop, I weaved my way past the amused Norl guards, but stopped abruptly. "Voe hoet sep virg?" *Where is the inn of the seven maids?* All the better that my accent was clumsy.

A guardsman scowled. "Why ask you?"

I sniggered. "Want to see the gelding." Danzik had worked with me for hours, to ensure I'd memorized the Norl words. I waved my bottle, offered the grizzled guard a swig, which he declined. "A prince, no less." I shook my head at the thought. "They won't believe it in Chorr."

His dubious eye strayed to my rags. "They say he's high-priced, brownskin."

I shrugged. "Just want a look."

He pointed to a row of shops. I lurched down the quay, careful not to glance back at the ship, nor to search ahead for Anavar, who, as an Eiberian, had stalked off the ship with near as much arrogance as Danzik. In this town, his accent would pass far better than my own.

I wandered past the stalls of potsellers, ropers, leatherers and winesellers. Anavar stood biting his lip, torn between two leather coin purses. "The stone building with the tree beside." His voice was a bare whisper. The inn was long and wide, no doubt built around a central courtyard. It had no windows in the outer walls. "Norlanders inside. Lots. Drinking."

"Did you see—"

"No." He shook his head, put down both purses, stalked off.

When next I found him, he'd bought a skin of wine and was pouring it down his gullet. I hoped it was well watered. "Easy, there. Did you see where they keep him?"

"Downstairs is a regular inn. Stables behind, see them? The brothel must be above."

I shifted my pack. "Where might I change?"

"Behind the potseller, if you're quick. Alley's deserted."

I asked, "Danzik?"

"Inside."

"Wait, then." I sidled around the stall, drifted into the alley.

In Stoneshore, I'd reasoned that a sailor in rags would attract the least attention disembarking, while a man of means would have the best chance of reaching Elryc. So, I quickly donned the decent leggings and jerkin I'd brought in my pack, and discarded my rags. I stuffed an ample coinpurse under my belt rope.

I edged alongside the potseller's shack; when the road was clear I popped out, strode arrogantly down the walk.

The inn smelled of stew and sweat. I stood just inside the door while my eyes adjusted to dark. Someone bumped my arm; I snarled, shrugged free. A barmaid muttered apology.

They don't know you, Roddy. Your hair's cropped, your skin is dark.

I found a bench, swept aside dirty mugs, took a seat. At the far end of my table, a cluster of Norland guards banged their glasses, laughing. I listened to the rise and fall of murmured speech. The soldiers spoke Norl, the locals Caled in their broad Eiberian accent. I'd best stay away from Caled. In Norl, as a foreigner, I was allowed my awkwardness of speech.

The fat innkeeper twisted his way past crowded tables. "Drink?"

I spoke my practiced Norl. "Is this where they have the boy?"

His eyes darted to the stairwell. "Upstairs, they have women. Boys too."

"*The* boy." My tone was harsh. "I've never had a prince. How much?"

"Two silvers."

I snorted. "I thought to rent him, not buy him." I mustn't be too eager.

"In advance."

I fished out my coinpurse, bent over it that he not see its contents. We'd had no idea what costs to expect, and I'd come prepared. I fished out two silvers, tossed them on the table.

The innkeeper gathered them up. "Have to wait."

"How long?"

"Hour, maybe more. Two ahead of you."

Almost, in that instant, he died. My blade was near my fingers. One thrust, and . . . Somehow, I managed an easy smile. "In that case, beer."

"We brew our own. Good stuff."

Across the room, a burly Norlander sat, his back to the wall, drinking and watching.

Danzik.

Our eyes crossed. Mine showed nothing. To my relief, neither did his.

Time crept past at snail's pace.

I felt eyes burn into my visage. Slowly, casually, I turned. Danzik watched. His gaze held worry. Slowly, with effort, I unclenched my fists, wrapped my fingers around my mug, stared moodily at the amber ale.

"Your turn." The innkeeper. He wiped his hands on his ample girth.

Heart pounding, I trudged up the stairs. A guard stopped me, took my dagger. I paused before the door, took deep breath, swung it open.

The room held a cushioned bed, a stand, a pitcher and ewer.

But not Elryc.

I rushed out to the hall. "What . . ."

"In a moment." The guard, sitting in a ledge at the far end of the hall, picked at his teeth with a sharpened twig. "He'll come."

The creak of a door. I whirled.

Silhouetted in the courtyard windows, an apparition moved down the hallway. Taller than I recalled, outlandishly garbed in short robe, silken scarf, sandals, sallow face painted in obscene travesty of a woman's.

I backed into the chamber, mouth working. Elryc, forgive me. Whatever I must do to earn—

The door swung open. "My lord, let me pleasure you." The tone was coaxing. Firmly, he closed the door. "I know all sorts . . . all . . ." He faltered, staring at my scar.

I gazed, speechless.

A whisper. "Roddy?"

"*GENARD?*" How could Elryc's stableboy vassal be—had they castrated *him* too?

We stared.

"Oh, m'lor!" He fumbled at his robe, threw it open. "Look what they did!" With a rush, he pinned me to the wall, and clung to me.

I managed to keep my voice low. "Where's Elryc?"

"Stables." Genard's eyes glistened. Awkwardly, I patted him.

Ah, my prince. A note of sadness.

Sorry, Rust. I know better. I put my arms about the wounded boy, drew him into a hug. "My poor Genard . . ."

It undid him.

Later, sitting on the bed, Genard whispered in my ear. "When Larissa let the Norlanders in, I was with Lor' Elryc. 'Which one's the prince?' 'I am,' I said quick, 'fore Elryc could. I tried to sound . . . er, haughty. Y' know, like a lord. I cocked a thumb at Elryc. '*That's* just my servant.' "

"Why?"

"Hadda protec' him. He's my lor'."

I swallowed.

" 'Take 'em both,' Norlander said. They rode us out, hands tied. They took us here." The boy paused, and his face twisted. "I said, mean as I could, I didn't want to share room with a mere *stableboy*. Tried to sound like you, m'lor', thought it would convince 'em. Guess it worked; they hauled Elryc out. I figured it'd give him best chance to run away, get help. But next day, they . . ." He drew silent.

"I understand."

He twisted his neck, to look me full in the eye. "No, you don't. They dragged me to that room at the far end of the hall. I saw the table, wasn't sure, but . . . they tried to put on a gag. The table had leg straps. 'I'm jus' Genard,' I cried. '*He's* the prince!' But they only spoke Norland, and I was so scared I forgot all the words we learned! Oh, King, I'd have given up my lord. I'd have let Prince Elryc be . . ."

"Of course."

"They got the gag on me, and it was too late." For a while, he could say no more.

I wondered how long they'd give us.

He wiped his cheeks. "I think Elryc's still in the stables."

"You never told them?"

"Too late to save myself. Might as well save Elryc."

Lord of Nature, is this my punishment for my beastly temper, my vicious disregard of human decencies? To meet this savaged boy, and know him my superior in all things?

Genard gripped my forearm with surprising strength. "M'lor', get Elryc out!"

"Yes, the both of you. Today. Tomorrow at the latest."

"Leave me." His tone changed. "I'd never be able to look at him."

"Don't be fool—"

His eyes blazed. "Don't you understan'? If not for the gag, I'd have done *anything*, said *anything* to get off the table!"

"Lower your voice." Then, "Genard, if I know one thing, if I'm a dunce in all else, I know you did no wrong. I'll be back with word of how we'll free you. But now I'd best go." I stood.

"Wait." Genard unknotted my jerkin, redid the thong a bit unevenly, mussed my hair.

Some contemptible part of me wanted to flinch.

We opened the door. "Thank you, m'lor'." And he was gone.

Dazed, I made my way down the stair.

FORTY-FOUR

DANZIK DRAINED HIS mug, sauntered behind me to the door.

Anavar crossed the street. "Is he—"

"It's not Elryc. Hire three horses. Meet me at the stable."

Danzik muttered, "Where is El-er-ek?"

"In the stables. They got him mixed up with Genard." I ambled toward the edge of town. Danzik followed.

Under the shade of a cluster of birches, I told the Norlander all. "I ought to see Elryc, make sure he's well, but . . . what if he blurts out my name? We need be prepared to flee the moment he sees us. We'll need to have Genard with us. I think there's a door from stable to courtyard; perhaps I could sneak into the brothel . . ."

"Easier to go back, ask for boy again."

"I'll lose surprise, and they'll take my dagger."

"How many guards?"

"Three."

Danzik grunted. "Three are no problem, you and I."

I gaped. "You'd fight?"

"Elryc's my friend. Genard is his."

"But how could . . ."

"I go up first, with girl. You come up, you whistle tune. I'll hear."

He made it seem so easy.

"We'd have to wait 'til the morrow. They'd never believe . . . twice in a day." I flushed.

Danzik grinned. "You're young enough."

My voice was tight. "Guiat, don't joke of this. I beg it."

"Did we not first learn with 'farang vos'?"

"Yes, but then my brother wasn't gelded, locked in a room and made to do it."

"He's not your brother."

My tone was somber. "He might as well be so."

Danzik studied me with new appraisal.

*   *   *

IN THE END, we decided not to wait another day. Let the guards judge me flesh-crazed; it mattered not.

Anavar returned, flushed and sweating, leading three worn horses. I took him aside. "Danzik and I will free Elryc. I've a task for you on which the kingdom depends."

His eyes lit. "What, sir?"

"Find Tantroth. Bid him meet us in the hills, at . . ." I cast about for a town we didn't know was in Norland hands. "Pineforest. In three days. Might you find spoor of Tantroth? Will peasants—"

"Oh, he's at Windcave, somewhere near. It's common knowledge in the town."

I gaped.

Anavar shrugged. "War talk is everywhere."

I threw up my hands. "I'd go to Windcave, but it won't be safe if they know Tantroth's near. The road will be crawling with Norls. So, it's Pineforest. Get word to the duke."

"You ought not put yourself in his hands."

"Oh, he's long past betrayal. If I'm wrong, I deserve not to be king. Take the fastest horse. Leave now. Tell him we'll use the road wherever possible. See he alerts his scouts."

"Yes, but—*sir, I want to help with Elryc!*" The boy braced himself.

"Elryc's the easy one; he's in the stable. It's Genard we need work at. I can't get him 'til night, and Tantroth must be told."

Complaining all the while, Anavar let himself be persuaded. He took the freshest horse and made his slow way toward the hills.

The inadequacy of my scheme soon forced its way to my attention. I said to Danzik, "Now what? We're standing on the street with horses we've nowhere to ride."

"Board them in the stable." He eyed the inn.

"And alert Elryc? It risks all."

"He's no fool."

"I—" A moment's confused thought. I knew of no better plan.

I handed a pair of reins to Danzik, walked my own spavined mount to the stable door. A bony old man was throwing straw in fly-infested stalls. He didn't bother to look up.

"Allo?" I spoke my own language with the most outlandish accent I could manage. "Will you board a horse?"

A grunt that might have been assent.

"For the day, then. Possibly 'til morn. Have your boy rub him down."

"Soan asta." *Mine too.* Danzik, behind me.

"Ho! Boy!" His voice was a rasp.

A patter of footsteps from the rear. Elryc appeared, gaunt, dressed in rags and torn sandals. "What—" He stopped dead.

He was unhurt. Relief left me faint. Brusquely, I thrust my reins into his hand. "Have him fed and watered. This man's mount too." I flicked my chin at Danzik. "We leave tonight, at tenth hour. See they're waiting in front of inn. Tenth hour, stableboy!" I skewered him with my gaze.

A gulp. "Aye." Elryc's eyes couldn't leave mine.

When we were out of earshot Danzik said, "Now they know we're together."

"Can't be helped. And it's only the old man who knows. I'll meet you at the inn this evening. You go up first. But for now, go back to the boat. Tell Jahl you'll need to leave just after tenth hour."

"At night, no wind for sail."

"Then he can row clear of the inlet."

"Whole town will be looking—"

"For me, not you. We ride to the hills. You don't. If you'd be my friend, go back to Stryx. Find Lord Groenfil. Seventh day hence, at dawn, he's to attack the garrison at Pezar from the rear."

He grunted. "Hriskil left many men there."

"I'll ride with Tantroth, from the north. We'll meet at the Pezar wall." I essayed a smile. Then we'll *vestre coa tern.*"

I SAT IN the din of the smoky brothel, waiting for dark.

Rustin, Lord Groenfil, any of my advisors would have deemed me mad. I should have found some hiding-hole until the last moment. Instead, here I sat, conspicuous by my appearance. I wiped my brow with my sleeve, found to my horror that sweat had loosened my dye. Inwardly, I shrugged. Better lurk in an inn crowded with noisy drunks than skulk about in the shadows, a dark stranger from Chorr.

I snagged a plate of stew, managed to get it down. Danzik was nowhere in sight. He wouldn't betray me, would he? No.

That, at least, I need not fear. But what if he'd been taken? For months he'd been my veritable shadow. Didn't his presence signal mine? What if guards who knew of my escape put two coins together?

As the sun was falling, Danzik trudged through the creaking door and lowered himself into a chair by the wall. As he sipped his beer his expression was calm, but his eyes never ceased to roam. I chewed on, mechanically. Lord of Nature knew when I'd eat again.

After a time, a pair of locals paused at the entranceway, letting their eyes adjust to the haze. Seeing me, one nudged the other. Together, they made their way to my table. "You from across the sea?"

"Chorr."

"You all so dark?"

"Mostly." How to be rid of them?

"Why are you in Eiber?"

Yes, Roddy, why? "I have trade goods on the ship. And wanted to see Hriskil, when he comes to Stryx."

A guffaw. "You'll have a long wait, brown man."

"How so?"

"He's in Ghanz. Rode as fast as his string of horses could take him. Day after Rodrigo burst out of the cave."

"How would you know?"

"Everyone knows. Sor! Hey, Sor!" He waved.

A Norlander with a curly black beard threaded his way across the room, scowling. "Qa dese?" I shank in my seat. Disaster loomed.

The Eiberian told Sor, "Tell him Hriskil's gone home." To me, "Sarazon sent Sor's regiment here ages ago. We think they're forgotten. He boards at my house; his men live in the barn."

The Norlander's eyes peered at my face. Bright-eyed, I sat, elbow on the plank, cheek on palm, hoping my scar was well and truly concealed. I wrestled my thoughts into Norl. "You mean I won't see king at Stryx?"

Sor's voice dropped. "Won't see him out of Ghanz, is my bet. The child's got him spooked."

"Coa?" *How?*

"A boy went into the cave, a dead man walked out." The Norl's eyes shifted, as if making sure we were unheard.

"Demons rode his shoulder. They killed Sanchu's whole brigade."

I said breathlessly, "Lord of Nature."

"Hriskil will win Caledon, no stopping that, but from afar. My bet, he won't set foot in kingdom 'til child Roddy's dead and his ashes scattered."

I said dryly, "That can't be long."

"No." Sor drained his mug. "Ah, wish I could be in Ghanz myself." He had a faraway look. "Even with the mess he's made of the wall."

"Mess?"

He waved it away. "Building, always building. Last year, it was new kitchens."

"I wonder—" Whatever I wondered, it vanished from my mind like a puff of smoke in wind. Danzik lumbered past, on his way to the stair. I turned back to my new cronies, my voice cracking with manic congeniality. "Drink with me." I shot to my feet, waved to the innkeeper.

Carelessly, I spilled coin. "Drinks my friends for," I said in atrocious Caled as I paid. "And . . ." I lowered my voice, "again, the boy. An extra hour this time."

His mouth widened slowly in a grin. "Enjoyed yourself?"

"How long wait?"

"Um, twelfth hour, I'd guess."

"Han." I shook my head, fished out a silver, slipped it into his hand. "Much sooner."

"Well . . . I'll see what I can do." He winked and sauntered off. After a moment, I saw him whisper to a barmaid, who hurried upstairs.

Now it was only a matter of time, and trying not to sweat through my jerkin. I dared not wipe my face, lest my hand come away browner, leaving white streaks.

Roddy, your brownskin disguise was a very bad idea.

My tablemates babbled on. At times I murmured a reply, or nodded.

A hand clapped my shoulder. Almost, I launched myself from my chair to cling from the low-hanging roof beams.

It was only the innkeeper. "It's time."

"Is it?" My voice cracked. I stumbled to my feet.

"Oh, brownskin, you're too drunk!" Sor chuckled. "What a pity, to pay so much, and be limp."

"Not too drunk." My mouth was dry. "Just . . ." Just frightened out of my wits. In moments I might get Genard killed, to say nothing of myself. And then, what escape for Elryc? I trudged to the stair.

Halfway up, I pursed my lips to whistle, and couldn't make a sound. Sweat oozed down my cheeks. I paused, in frantic, silent effort to pull myself together. Below, Sor's Eiberian cronies slapped their legs with glee.

I climbed the few remaining stairs, jauntily whistling the tune on which we'd settled. Well, perhaps not jauntily: what emerged was more a shrill squeak, barely audible over the commotion below. I stopped for breath, grinned in terror at the four brothel guards who crowded the corridor. Had I caught a shift change, or was the House of Caledon about to be extinguished? I asked the nearest fellow, "Heard this one? The Caleds sing it." I twittered away, a manic brown songbird perspiring like a waterfall.

The guard didn't bat an eye. "Your dagger."

I unbuckled the sheath, waved it uncertainly. "Take good care; my mother said never to part with it. If she knew I was here . . ." I smiled foolishly and broke into song once more.

Halfway down the corridor, a door swung open. Danzik stumped out, looking annoyed. "Damn girl's drunk," he said, in better Caled than I knew he had. "Who I see for another?"

"Marla, downstairs." The soldier who'd answered turned back to his companions.

"In there," my guard pointed. "Wait, your dagger."

"Of course." I pulled it from the sheath, frowned. "No, keep the whole thing. Is the boy ready?"

Danzik eased past the guards, stopped abruptly, frowning. "Problem, Norlander?"

"Han." His huge hands shot out. He grasped two guards by the neck, smashed them together with an ugly crack. I'd never seen a skull split like a soft melon, and cared never to see it again.

"What—" My guard gaped for the instant I needed to plunge my blade into his throat. His eyes bulged. His mouth worked. He thumped to the floor.

"Help!" A frantic squawk from the last guard. Danzik's massive fist smashed the bridge of his nose. The burly Norlander caught his fall. He dragged him, already dead, into an empty chamber. I stared in revulsion at the gory remains of the three guards. Their blood seeped among the planks. That galvanized me. I rushed into an empty chamber, tore off a sheet, frantically mopped the hall lest blood drip through the ceiling and rouse the inn. Danzik clumped out, picked up the second guard under the arms, dragged him into the dumping room. Just in time, I remembered to salvage my blade.

I ran down the hall, flung open the door.

Genard sat on the bed. Our eyes met, and held. "I didn't think you'd come, Roddy. Not truly."

"Have you street clothes?"

He shook his head.

"Danzik!" My voice was a hiss. "What can he wear?"

Danzik perused him. "Women's clothes. They won't expect—"

"Where can we—"

"My whore. She's tied to the bed. She said she has clothes in the room by the courtyard stair." Danzik was back in a moment, bearing a light robe and scarf, and sandals. They would do, but we need draw the scarf tight; Genard's hair was too short for a woman's.

The boy slipped into his robe. "Will I dress like this after?" His tone was morose.

I tried to smile as I poured water into the basin and soaped my face. "You're Genard, as ever you've been. This nightmare will ease."

"Will it?" His disbelief was clear.

I scrubbed at hands and face. To my joy, much of the brown dye oozed off with the soap.

Danzik growled, "What are you *doing*? They'll see who—"

"The brownskin from Chorr can't visit a boy and walk down with a woman, unremarked. Find me a cloak, and a hat."

He did. They altered my appearance somewhat.

"Danzik, to the ship. I'll greet you at Pezar. Leave now, so they don't associate you with this . . . atrocity. We'll be, oh, a quarter candle behind you; see Jahl sails the instant you're aboard."

"Qay." Danzik paused at the door. "Rez Caledi . . ."

"Yes?" My tone was impatient.

"You're a fit king. If I were Caled . . ." A sigh. "Salut."

My eyes stung. "Farewell, Guiat."

An hour candle burned on the sill. I couldn't bear to watch; it burned too slow. Besides, if a customer came up the stair . . . or for that matter, down . . . I bade Genard wait in the bed-chamber, and stationed myself at the stairwell, gripping the guard's sword.

For once, fortune was with us; no one climbed the stairs, and the chamber doors remained shut. When I could stand it no longer, I poked my head into our bedchamber. "Now. Follow me down."

"If there's trouble, m'lor', take heed of yourself. I'll . . ." He swallowed.

I slipped the sword in my scabbard, and we began our journey down the stairs. The inn below was a miasma of smoke and sweat and fetid air, but no one seemed to mind. Sor glanced our way without interest, turned back to his friends.

The foot of the stairs was blocked by a handful of towns-men waiting to sit. We thrust our way through.

And then we were outside. A bedraggled stableboy leaned against the rail, three sets of reins dangling.

I had Elryc. For a moment, I was dizzy with relief. I threw off my cape. "Mount, quickly!" I took a closer look. "Elryc, these aren't the horses—"

"Of course not, you dolt! I took the best they had."

"But the old man . . ."

Elryc's voice was ragged. "He asked what I was doing. I ran him through with a pitchfork. He's lying under a pile of hay!"

"It's all right."

"No it *isn't*."

"A furlong south, there's a trail to the hills. We'll take it only as far as the edge of town. After that, we stick to fields and wood. Hurry." I led the way.

The door flew open. "There!" Half a dozen men poured out, soldiers among them. They raced toward us.

"Go!" I slapped Elryc's gray on the rump. He bolted. "Genard, follow!" I wheeled, raised high my sword. My heels dug into my stallion's flanks. My sword whirled, cleaved an arm from a shoulder. I jabbed, a second man fell. Fingers clawed at my stirrups; I yanked on the reins; my mount reared back. His hooves slammed down, and I was free. Men dived aside, or back through the door.

I spun my excited steed, goaded him with my heels. He sped down the dusty road, leaving behind the hue and cry. I leaned over his shoulder, almost in joy. He was so like Ebon . . .

Almost, I overshot the trail. I spotted it just in time, pulled gently on the reins. We galloped off toward the hills. My mount flew like a summer wind. In moments I caught up to Elryc and Genard.

We plunged into the undergrowth. All we need do was elude Hriskil's army, and find Tantroth's.

FORTY-FIVE

ELRYC EDGED CLOSER to the fire, and coughed. "—lots of reasons. I didn't know the way. I was safer in the stable, where no one imagined I was the prince. And Genard . . ." His eyes glistened. "How could I leave . . ."

I threw up my hands, defeated. "So you'd die for each other, and neither would live. Does that make sense?"

"Yes." Elryc's tone was stubborn.

"How?"

"Ask Rustin."

"Arghh." I tossed on more sticks, hoping the hollow in which we camped would swallow the sparks. "It's colder than I expected; autumn's on us." Winter would follow, and a surcease to war.

"I'm all right."

"You're freezin', m'lor'." Genard felt his forearm.

I said sourly, "We're not dressed for cold, and I was too stupid to bring a blanket." Elryc had only his rags, and Genard a woman's cotton robe. I padded to the far side of the firepit, began hunting rocks. In half an hour, using the flattest stones I could find, I'd made something of a low wall quite close to the coals, to reflect back the heat. Then, on our side, I made a broom of my foot and drew dry leaves into a pile near the firepit. We lay as close as we could without being singed.

Elryc asked Genard gently, "How did you stand it?"

A silence. Then, "One day gives on to another, m'lor'. You pretend you're home, at the stables in Stryx. You pretend they're horses, not men. Don't make me talk of it."

"Never."

I lay under stars, knowing I'd been brave in the rescue, but not near so brave as Genard.

THREE HOURS OF cold, hungry ride brought us to the outskirts of a village. I bade my brother hide in the woods, and Genard watch over him. Elryc was coughing more frequently, and looked pale.

I rode boldly to the first house I saw. "Have you children?"

The yeoman owner was feeding chickens. "Why ask you?"

"Half-grown boys, so high?"

"Yes, but . . ."

I fished in my coinpurse, picked out a silver. "Warm clothes for two boys, and boots. I'll buy them, or kill you for them. Choose." I drew my sword.

In moments the transaction was done. The silver I'd tossed him was worth ten times the shabby clothes, and we both knew it. I was lucky he was richer than his neighbors, a man whose tykes had spare breeches and shoes. I said, "Blankets too."

"I've only our own."

"Buy more."

Grudgingly, he parted with two woolen blankets. "We've only two beds, sire, theirs and mine." Abruptly, with a look of horror, he clapped a hand over his mouth.

I said gently, "The scar?"

"And the brother snatched from the alehouse, the stableboy missing . . . that's two boys." Eyes on my sword, he made a sign, as one might make on his deathbed.

"How many eggs have you?"

He looked startled. "Today? Six."

I said, "Would you boil them for a king?"

"Will you . . . let me live?"

I smiled. "A fair trade. Done."

I followed him to his hearth. "Your boys?"

"Prenticed to the miller." He fetched a pot, poured water from a bucket, added a log to the embers. One by one, he settled in the eggs.

"Wife?"

His tone went bleak. "Wasted away. Dead these nine months."

"Someday, if all goes well—honestly, I can't say it will—bring your boys to Stryx. I'll set them to honorable service."

He brightened. "You'd do that, sire?"

"For fresh eggs? You could have asked my crown." I frowned. My coronet was somewhere in a saddlebag with my other sparse treasures, in Groenfil's keeping.

When we were done, I swore him to silence, galloped off.

I threw the clothes at Genard and Elryc. "Dress! Hurry, we haven't a moment!" The instant they were clothed, I swung back on my saddle. "Ride for your lives!"

"Roddy, what happened?" Elryc urged his mount to a canter.

"I was recognized. Perhaps he's true; he swore so, but who would not, with a sword at his throat? No roads today. Oh. Here!" I handed my brother a warm egg, careful not to drop it as we rode. "And for you, Genard."

It was rough going, and would have been worse but for the jug of well-water the yeoman had thrust at me on leaving. We refilled it at every stream and passed it around among us.

Later, when we stopped to rest, Genard and Elryc swapped clothes until each wore garb something akin to their own size. Elryc's boots were too large, but it couldn't be helped; I tore cloth from the rags he'd once worn, and stuffed them into the toes.

That night, wrapped in two blankets, we slept like kings.

In my case, it was only fit.

WE MADE OUR way into the hills. I dimly recalled the general location of Pineforest. Twice I sent Genard into villages to buy bread at the inn. We'd acquired mugs now too, a clay pot, and tea to steep.

Genard looked the boy he was, though sallow and withdrawn. I couldn't ride into a village; as my one attempt had proved, my scar would proclaim my identity. Genard's features weren't commonly known, like mine or my brother's. Moreover, I sought to give him a task of valor; he'd been moody and disconsolate all our journey. And in the quiet of he night, he wept.

Valor he certainly showed on one occasion: he rode back from an inn with two roast fowl. Our eager expressions made even him smile, but soon he turned morose again and withdrew when I tried to engage him.

Elryc's chest pained him, and he was oft distant.

That night, as we huddled in a clearing under our blankets, I stared at the starry sky, pondering.

Poor Elryc. He'd been terrified by his ordeal, as well he might. His nature was not bellicose; killing the old stableman would long trouble him. When I probed, he didn't care to speak of it. Perhaps Genard would be able to ease his mind.

Ah, Genard. He was a miserable shadow of himself.

I wrapped my blanket tighter. Even a stableboy had hopes for the future, and Genard was more, a liege man to a prince. No doubt Genard's dreams had been of manhood, wife, children.

No longer. Somehow, he'd have to bear it. That and the mockery behind his back. And also . . .

I sat upright.

What he'd endured . . . How does one absorb the venom of such memories?

One cannot. Already, he'd begun to draw away from Elryc, into his pain, his misery, his hate.

"No!" I threw off the covers. "We've lost men enough!" Once I'd despised him, mistreated him, and jeered. Now, my throat ached for the stableboy of Stryx.

"Elryc!" I shook him awake. "Take the blanket. Leave us alone for a time."

"What do you?"

"I would aid your liege man."

My brother rubbed his eyes. "Don't hurt him."

I gave him a reassuring pat. In a moment, Genard and I were alone. The stableboy regarded me warily.

I set down a mug and poured water.

"What do you?" His tone was wary.

"I wield my Power. I need see you within."

"No! ELRYC, HELP!" Genard scrambled to his feet.

"What do you fear?" My tone was gentle.

"You. The Still. That day in Stryx, you oozed inside me, made me dance like a fool! I felt your spite."

I poured. "This is different." I hoped it was so. I set my palms over the mug. I shut my eyes. In a moment the night became clear. My lips moved.

"King!" A wail of anguish.

Gritting my teeth, I slipped within.

A door thrown open. Fetters. The rough ride to Wayvere. A looming inn. The sparse room of their imprisonment. His haughty dismissal of the "stableboy" Elryc.

Genard paced the windowless chamber, ever more anxious, alone and abandoned. *Old Griswold, where are you now?*

Gladly I'd work in your stable at Stryx. "Get out! Roddy, don't see!" They hauled him from the room. He struggled, automatically at first, then with desperation. The gag. The straps.

"Please, king!" A whisper.

"I must know." I probed beyond.

"Let me bury it!"

Faces loomed.

The terrible knife.

Tell them I'm not Elryc! Bite through the gag!

Agony.

Blessed oblivion.

I fought fierce war, that my palms remain cupped.

"Enough, Roddy . . ." Genard's voice was broken.

"Not enough." *Mother, lend me strength, I beg thee.*

Long days of recovery while torn flesh knit. Pain, vast at first, receding in minute increments.

Then, sooner than they ought, they came for him.

Across the firepit, the desperate boy staggered to his feet. "No! This is mine! None must know!"

A bed. Grasping hands. Leering eyes.

"Lord of Nature, let me die!"

Shock. Amazement. Horror. Abasement beyond imagining.

Hugging himself, dancing brokenly on the cold grass, Genard wept.

I endured it all, every vile moment. My palms ached.

I knew no way to assuage his woe, except to dislodge it. And to dislodge it I must . . . absorb it. Take it unto myself.

In Jestrel, I had only looked, and learned. Tantroth, I'd commanded but a brief moment. To make Rustin understand his death, I'd given of myself. This was a realm beyond. I cast my nets, began gathering waves of pain, blotting the worst of the memories.

Genard wailed.

With grim determination I roamed his soul, absorbing his humiliation, the indignities, his degradation.

When at last I was done, Genard lay sniffling, arms and legs drawn in. His breathing was eased.

I wrenched my palms from the mug.

A pale moon rode overhead. Elryc watched wide-eyed from the edge of the grove.

My guts roiled. I leaned over an instant before I spewed my dinner.

I bore within me the unbearable.

I staggered to my feet, lurched out of camp. Abruptly, I rammed a young elm, so hard the bole shivered. My shoulder blazed in protest. I reared back, rammed it again. I howled. My throat was raw. I fell to my knees, thumped my head on the turf.

A calf at slaughter, I raised my eyes, let loose an inarticulate bellow. I began to pound the earth. My fists ached.

Insistent fingers tugged. "Come, Roddy. Don't scare me so. It's all right." Elryc tugged me back to camp. "Take ease, King. Tell me how to help."

"You . . ." I gasped. ". . . can't." I clung to him. At the firepit, I fell into a blanket. I lay unmoving deep into the night.

Genard's chest rose and fell in deep, peaceful sleep.

THE FOURTH DAY from Wayvere, we were most cautious, as Pineforest neared. We avoided even the slightest of trails, in case Anavar had been captured and our course divulged, but it worked our horses dreadfully. They'd had no fodder but grass—and apples from a farmer's tree—since Elryc had stolen them.

At evening, I struck flint for a campfire, while Genard tended the horses. I was wondering where to buy a bag of oats, when three archers, bows stretched, stepped from the trees and bade us disarm.

From Elryc, a cry of dismay. Genard glanced at his mare, as if contemplating a leap into the saddle. I said urgently, "No, don't." To the bowmen, "If you're Tantroth's, we're the ones you seek."

"And if not?"

"We'd already be dead."

Their leader grinned, and unnocked his arrow. "True enough."

I got to my feet. "Where is the duke?"

"Not near, but we'll show the way."

"And Anavar?"

"He partakes of my lord's hospitality."

Knowing Tantroth, that could be ominous, but I let it be. I'd know soon enough.

The archers led us a hundred paces, to where their horses were tethered. From there, we followed goat trails that in another season would revert to nature. It was a good two hours before we rode past vigilant sentries to a path that opened abruptly into a valley.

Below, wagons. Fire. Tents.

I clapped Elryc on the back. "*Now* you're rescued."

Elryc gave a weary smile and stifled a cough. "Will I ever feel safe, Roddy?"

My voice turned serious. "I pray so."

We rode into camp.

At the best of the tents, a flap opened. Duke Tantroth of Eiber emerged, cape drawn tight. His hair was grayer, his face more lined, his eyes desperately weary. Gravely, he held my bridle. "King of Caledon, welcome to my domain." A wry smile. "Such as it is."

"We thank you, my lord." I jumped down. "I'll sleep under a wagon if I must, but Elryc and Genard need a dry tent, warm soup, hot tea."

"Oh, even in straitened circumstances, we'll provide the king more than wagon planks for a roof." The edge left his tone. "Lord Elryc, are you . . . injured?" His question held unspoken volumes.

"My brother is unhurt." My voice was sharp.

"We heard rumors . . ."

"No doubt." Between us, some signal passed. Tantroth snapped his fingers at an aide. "Stew and bread for the boys. Is there mutton left? Set a haunch to roasting. Rodrigo and I will dine anon."

"*Sir!*" A familiar voice. Anavar sprinted across the camp to greet me.

"Ah. Our impetuous young baron." Tantroth's tone was dry. "You have quarrel with him?"

Anavar released me, my back sufficiently pounded.

"He still need be taught manners. I refrained, lest it irk you."

"My lord Duke, I'm tired, fretful and sad of the blood on my hands. I would not spar with you. Perhaps in the morn, I'll be lighter of spirit."

Tantroth walked me toward a tent. When we were alone, his voice dropped. "I meant not to vex you, Rodrigo."

"Why, my lord! That's an apology, if ever I heard one."

His lips twitched. "We all have our failings."

We settled in the spartan tent; it was furnished with two stools, a straw bed with torn blankets, nothing more. Tantroth looked me over. "You look ghastly, sire."

You don't look so good yourself, old fellow. "I'm not fully recovered."

"From?"

"There was a cave . . ." That was part of it. About Genard, I wouldn't speak.

"Yes, they claimed you were dead. Thereafter, when we met Hriskil's people, I gave no quarter, even to those captured. Perhaps, had I known . . . How long was it?"

"Sixteen days." Forever.

"You're all bones still, and there's an odd hue to your skin."

I smiled, and explained my disguise. Not all the dye had come off quite yet. Soon we got down to business. I asked, "What have you accomplished?"

"Not as much as I hoped. But we've kept them off balance." He hesitated. "It can't last. They have the towns. Without Eiber Castle, we've no place to winter."

"Would more troops help?"

"Need you ask?"

I said, "Groenfil will join you."

His ears perked up. "Where?"

"At Pezar. In . . ." I stopped to think. "Three days."

"The Norlanders hold Pezar."

I nodded. "We'll need help Groenfil through."

"March to the pass and mount an attack on the wall? Three days? You'll exhaust the men, sire. Even the horses will—"

"Dawn of the third day. Simultaneous attack from both sides."

He chewed his lip. "I suppose it can be done. We'll take heavy losses."

"Perhaps not." I knew of no other way to consolidate our force.

"We'll need march in a few hours. I'll give the orders." He left abruptly.

Later, sated with lamb, sleepy, I made ready for bed. Before

dousing the candle, I called for Elryc and Genard. To my
brother, I said, "In the morning, see you bathe nude at the
stream. Let the troops see you everyday."

He shifted with discomfort, being of that age. "Is it necessary?"

"Yes." Let them think I'd healed him with the Still; it added
to my aura. And as for you, Genard . . ." I gentled my tone. "I
salute your heroism, as does the prince. I pray you, let it be
unknown among the men."

Genard met my eyes. "I'll keep covered."

"If our yeomen see Elryc uncut, soon will townsmen hear
of it. Then Hriskil. His fear will augment."

"Does he fear us?"

I smiled. "Why should he not?"

AS TANTROTH HAD promised, it was a hard march to Pezar.
Even our light supply wagons were a strain on the lean and
hungry horses. Tantroth's was primarily a cavalry force, but
he'd gathered and maintained some infantry in his wander-
ings, and now numbered near two thousand. As we slipped
from hillock to dell, avoiding roads wherever possible, my admiration grew of his knowledge of the land. For years he must
have roamed his domain, memorizing every outcrop.

Two days and half the second night we tramped through the
hills, until at last he made temporary camp a mere stone's
throw from the Pezar pass. Men huddled around the slightest
of campfires, officers vigilant lest too high a blaze reveal our
force to the foe. Tantroth didn't bother to throw up the tents;
we all sat exhausted with the men. I saw to it Elryc had extra
blankets, and a plentitude of tea.

The night dragged on. Quietly, Tantroth made his dispositions. "You know," he muttered, "that we attack the defended
wall. It's Groenfil has the easy task, coming up behind." He
stared moodily into the embers. "If he's late . . . if he holds
back . . ."

"He won't."

"I'd not slaughter our men to no avail."

"I know." Then, "You're a fine commander, my lord."

He raised an eyebrow. "You've just learned so?"

I concealed a smile.

In morn, it was still dark when we scuffed out the embers, assembled near the trail.

I embraced my brother, clapped Anavar on the shoulder, found a kind word for Genard. I checked the cinches, adjusted my saddle, mounted my eager stallion. "Hold, boy." He snorted steam. "If you're to be mine, I'll need name you. What shall it be?"

He gave no answer.

"Racer? Grayboy? Warrior?"

Tantroth cantered past. "Pezar!" He pointed. Behind him, the rumble of hooves.

"Pezar!" I patted his flank. "You'll be Pezar, in honor of this day."

UNCLE RAETH'S WALL, from the Eiber side, was steep and forbidding. We had far fewer troops to throw at it than when we'd defended it from Hriskil. Now it was the Norlanders who manned its works, and we who trudged across the field, in the day's first light.

Tantroth—abetted by Anavar—urged me not to expose myself before the foe, but I argued, most reasonably, I thought, that my presence would hearten our men and dismay the Norlanders. Surely by now the barbarians thought me impossible to kill.

"Yes, but always you try to prove them wrong."

Be that as it might, I rode Pezar proudly, not quite in the first rank, but well forward of the center. My raised sword glinted in the sun, my voice was hoarse from encouraging our ranks. My shield, I left strapped, as virtually useless.

The Norland archers took aim.

"Lances set!"

I sheathed my sword, lifted my lance from its dangling scabbard, set it in the pocket near my pommel. Most of our men were dismounted, as they need be to assault a wall. We lancers would do our best to keep the foes' heads down while our men climbed.

The first volley whirred down among us. Some, not too many, fell.

In the distance, a commotion. I glanced back, but saw only our rows of marching men. I raised myself in the saddle. Did bowmen run along the parapet? Did eyes peer south, behind the wall?

Yes. I was sure of it. "CHARGE!" My shout echoed from the rock. I gouged Pezar's flanks. He bounded forward.

In moments I was below the wall. I leaped from the saddle, clung one-handed to an arrow slit, my lance waving. I dropped it, hauled myself up, rolled over the battlement. Norlanders gaped. I whipped out my sword. "CALEDON!" I lunged. A man went down.

Beside me, frantic Eiberians swarmed up the wall. Like a madman, I laid about, secure in the knowledge that whomever I hit must be a foe.

All about me now, the clang of steel, shouts of the enraged and wounded.

Suddenly, from the court beneath the wall, the thud of steps. I braced for new attack, but one face, I knew. "Kadar!" I spun to the battlement, shouted down to our troops, "Groenfil's among us!" It was all they needed to hear. Even the slowest among them quickened their pace. Soon the wall was awash with Caleds and Eiberians, and the Norland defenders were driven inexorably to the edge. One by one they plunged, and were hacked to pieces by aroused Caleds.

Now foemen threw away their arms, the quicker to hide themselves in the brush. On both sides of the wall, our men took up the grim hunt.

My two commanders tried to put a stop to the slaughter and eventually made their orders heard. The last of the Norls fled into the woods.

Road and field were strewn with enemy dead. Our losses were few, though none the less regrettable for that. Of prisoners, we had but a dozen; the battle had been fierce and quarter neither given nor asked.

Tantroth fell on the abandoned Norland stores and the few fresh horses left behind.

I walked the wall and came face-to-face with the earl. Groenfil seemed unutterably weary. His eyes were bleak.

I bowed, an extended bow of youth to elder. "Well met, my lord." My tone was exultant.

"Roddy." The hint of a smile. "I rejoice to see you. Elryc's safe?"

"And Genard. They're in camp."

Danzik climbed the stairs, stepping over blood and dis-membered bodies. His mouth was grim.

I said, "Danzik, hail. We thank thee for thy service."

A grunt. "Pretty words." But he essayed a small bow, in the Caled manner.

Groenfil cleared his throat, gestured to the man at his side. "You've met my son—"

"Horst, yes. Lord Tantroth!" I waved the duke near. "Do you know—"

"Save greetings for later." Horst's tone was harsh. "Leave the prisoners. Without pikes and bows, they're useless. Make haste: we must be off."

"Horst!" Groenfil was stiff with reproof.

The younger man ignored his father's rebuke. "Rodrigo, Caledon is lost. I join you from the ruins of Castle Groenfil, where my brother, Franca, lies dead. Our rear guard bleeds that we may stand here prattling. The Norlander cavalry pur-sued us from Groenfil to Cumber, from Cumber to the pass. They're scant hours behind."

"They're more than that." Groenfil protested. "Our guard slows them."

"Not so much more. A day at most. A day and a half."

My joy had vanished. "Very well. Tantroth, where ought we to camp?"

The old duke grunted. "A good day's march, if Norlanders are on our heels. I'd not have them sniff us out."

It was near noon. I sighed. "Gather the stores they aban-doned." We were desperate for resupply.

We halted briefly at our camp of the night before. We gath-ered our sick and wounded and put our wagons in train.

Danzik swung down from his mare. *"Iot hom!"* He lifted Elryc like a babe, enveloped him in a bear's hug. Elryc dan-gled, pleased and embarrassed.

We set out. Elryc basked in Danzik's attention, Anavar in mine. Groenfil looked tired and exceedingly worn. He chat-ted with Tantroth, when the duke wasn't spurring ahead to guide our march. Genard settled to a long sleep on a jounc-ing wagon and awoke much the better for it. For a time I drowsed in the saddle; I'd had too many nights under the stars. I woke abruptly when Groenfil handed me a scroll he'd brought.

I tore off the ribbon.

"To Rodrigo, king of Caledon, heartfelt greetings from his cousin and affianced, Tresa of Cumber, ensconced in Castle Stryx.

"Oh, Roddy, I miss you. What do men see in war? As long as need be, I'll play 'Lady of the Hill'; it dazzles and pleases our yeomen. But it's mummery, no more. 'The king's consort' . . . now, there's a station I relish, and would more so, were it already true."

Anavar, riding alongside, peered over my shoulder. I held the letter closer.

"I regret so to tell you old Nurse Hester died in sleep a week past. We buried her near your mother the queen; it seemed apt. She thought well of you, Roddy, though she was loath to admit it.

"The Norlanders occupy the town of Stryx. Rustin fortified the Keep with vigor and ingenuity and commands the greater part of our force, which we've crowded behind his walls for our mutual protection. But he dares not sally forth to battle, lest with his defeat the Keep be lost, and thus our castle above."

"Is it from Tresa? Is she well?"

"Yes, boy. Shush."

"In the past few days the Norlanders seem to have decided on a siege, drawing up catapults and engines of war. They haven't been brutal, as was Hriskil before Pezar. Asking little of the town, they haven't drawn its enmity as did Sarazon. I fear they'll have little trouble wintering in Stryx.

"Can you break the forthcoming siege? If so, will you winter with us? We might bundle, you and I, even if the restraints of your Power prohibit else. I imagine your gentle fingers caressing me and grow warm. Surely you won't lose the Still for a kiss, even one such as startled you when last we met.

"Oh, my King, my friend, my Rodrigo! I miss you more than words might reveal."

"What is it, Roddy? Why do you grin?"

"I must break off. Willem says the Norlanders infiltrate the lesser trails even as we speak. The courier who bears this may be the last.

"Love, affection and respect from the Mummer of the Hill, Tresa of Cumber."

OUR COLUMN STAGGERED into our new camp, the men utterly exhausted. Tantroth's troop had endured days of fast march capped by a short night and hard battle, then a full day's march after. Groenfil's horsemen were hardly in better shape.

Hours passed in a bustle of tent pegs, fodder, campfires and cookpots.

As soon as we were settled, we held council of war, in Tantroth's tent, the largest we had.

Danzik, admitted by courtesy, sat behind our circle, content to listen. Anavar and Elryc perched cross legged on the tattered carpet. Nearby was Kadar, once my bodyguard, present perhaps because he'd been among us so long.

Groenfil glanced to Horst. The young man folded his arms and glowered.

"Well," I said brightly. "How is it no one will speak?"

Groenfil turned to Tantroth, who shook his head.

With some apprehension, I studied the lot of them. "What ails you all?"

"They're afraid." Anavar.

"Of what?"

"Crushing your hopes."

A pulse throbbed in my jaw. "Go ahead. Crush them."

Silence.

"I'll do it, if none else dare." Horst. "Lord Rodrigo, few care to admit your cause is lost, but it's so. We hold not a single strongpoint in Caledon or Eiber save Stryx, and that's under siege."

"Go on." My voice was soft.

"While you were off rescuing your brother, mine died. Hriskil—no, he's gone to winter in Ghanz, but his army—pressed their siege. My father rode to our salvation a bare instant before we'd have capitulated. For a moment, he broke through, and some of us were saved." To the earl, a look of gratitude. "The Norland host from Soushire chased us through Caledon, and pursue us still."

"What else?"

"Verein's fallen. The Norlanders hold Soushire, and Lady Larissa is dead."

I said, "Verein's walls weren't man—"

"Cumber's in Norland hands—we had to skirt the castle—and Bouris's head is on a pike; he watched our passage, unseeing. The pursuing Norlanders have retaken Pezar, and we can't mount a successful attack from the north against the face of the wall. By your command, we're trapped in Eiber, where the foe holds Wyvern, Eiber Castle, Norpoint, Windcave, all the seacoast villages."

Horst's voice rode on, flinty and inexorable. "In Caledon . . . Searoad Cross, Warthens Gate Road, Fort, name the place and they hold it!"

"Stryx."

"They'll have it by the snows."

"How say you so?"

"They have all else. What has Stryx to resist them?"

My voice was hot. "Rustin of the Keep. Willem. Lady Tresa."

"They're valiant, I have no doubt, but undersupplied. My father says our treasury is exhausted—is that true, sire?"

Reluctantly, I nodded.

"—arms and stores are desperately short, and we've no base from which to resupply. Do you understand what that means, Rodrigo? An army can't march on dreams. We need—"

"Horst." Groenfil's tone was low. "He is your king. Speak with respect or—"

"King of what? Don't glare, Father, *someone* must say it. What does the House of Caledon yet rule?"

Groenfil snapped, "Me." Beyond the tent, wind whipped the branches. "And you, if you'd have peace between us."

Horst spat out the words. "Am I wrong in any particular?"

No one spoke.

Again Horst took up the cudgels. "I'll grant you, Rodrigo's struggled for his dreams. Struggled nobly. But dreams are cockleshell ships that smash on the rocks of fact. Here's a fact, my lord King: the army must eat. We've no food, and if we confiscate what little the peasants grow, they'll turn on us in an instant." He waited for rebuttal, but none came. I rested chin on hands.

"The horses are starved and failing," said Horst, "and in a month there'll not even be grass. We need oats, hay, barns. We need shelter beyond tents, the more so that we roam high hills. We need refill our quivers. We want smithies, armor, tack, saddles. More horses. We need replenish our numbers, but from where? Caledon, our base, is lost. Rodrigo, I wish it weren't I who must ask, but answer this: *where will we winter?* And in spring, when Hriskil ventures forth, *where will we flee?*"

I swallowed.

"In fact, even now, you've no retreat—"

I growled, "You've said enough. Who else would speak?"

Tantroth's tone was stubborn. "I want Eiber. I'll fight from the hills 'til it's mine."

I said gently, "Have you the strength to take Eiber Castle?"

"Well, if we—no." A bleak sigh. "No."

"How many men will you have left, by spring?"

"Some will stay."

A long silence.

"Groenfil?"

"I don't—it's not mine to choose whether . . ." The earl looked beyond me, to the canvas wall. "Sire, I've lost near all I love. It's not your fault Hriskil pounced. But my home is seized, Larissa hanged—yes, I loved her, how can I deny it?— my beloved Franca gutted in our muddy courtyard. Horst is all I have left, and I'll not lose him. I send him south. If he evades their patrols—"

"I won't go."

"Youngsire, don't dare defy me." It was said quietly, and silenced Horst utterly. "As for me, my liege, I've little left to lose. So if you'd fight, I'll follow."

I asked, "Have we a chance?"

"There's always—"

"Speak truth."

Groenfil brooded. "I see no chance."

"Anavar?"

"I'm of Caledon. I fight until my liege says nay."

Tantroth raised a sardonic eyebrow. "You're of Eiber, youngsire."

"No longer. I'm sworn to Rodrigo, and am content so."

I said, "None question your courage, not even my lord

Tantroth. You're privy counselor and baron. How advise you?"

His eyes glistened. "You want Caledon with all your heart. How can I advise other?"

My tone was forlorn. "You just did." After a moment, "Elryc?"

"You're a wonder, Roddy, know you so?" His boy's voice trembled. "With nothing but courage, you sent Hriskil fleeing home to Ghanz. In days to come, they'll tell of Rodrigo's War, over hearths in long winter nights. Your defense of Pezar, your march through the Sands. They'll speak of Rustin and Roddy, heroes of old."

"Elryc, don't—"

"I'm so proud I had a part, even a small one. But, Roddy . . . ?"

I steeled myself.

"With each battle, more die. Men we cherish. They die for you, for the idea of Caledon. If you rule nobly, after, their sacrifice is in part redeemed. But . . ." His voice quavered. "When it's all for naught, and we've already lost . . . how can we send more folk into the earth?"

I cried, "See you no hope?"

"Horst is unkind, he's angry for Franca. But what does he say that's untrue?"

"Can we not scavenge supplies, live off the land . . . ?"

"Can we, Roddy? You've tried."

I sat with head bowed. All waited, while my world melted to a grimy puddle. At length I stirred. "Very well. I'll do what I must. Send envoy—"

"Ask me, Rez."

"What?"

"*Pirda iv!*" Danzik's eyes smoldered.

I gulped. "Guiat, I ask thy counsel."

"Translate for these *barbati*. I speak Norl." He glared. *"Signit hom ke vos eo—"*

"The greatest man of your age . . ."

"Ve fro vos—"

"Sits before you . . ."

"And you bring him down like wolves!" Danzik stalked the tent in barely chained fury. "Hriskil is nothing before him. Cruel, greedy, unsubtle. Time and again, Rodrigo ties Hriskil in knots." Impatiently, he waited for me to catch up. "The Norls, I *know* them. They're ready to crumble. Hriskil inspires fear, not loyalty. But you've unnerved them. They—"

I shook my head. "Danzik . . ."

"*You* translate, Rez! *I* speak!" He hammered the tent pole, and nearly brought down the canvas.

"Qay, Guiat." Hurriedly, I did so.

Danzik said, "A few more victories . . ."

Horst snorted. "Escaping with our lives isn't victory."

"What more victory than that? War isn't about supplies, about numbers, else Hriskil would long since have conquered all; near every man he commands roams Caledon in search of Rodrigo!" The Norlander paced. "War about spirit, honor, the quest for men's souls. Fah, you people are nothing! I go home. *Vestra coa tern.*" *I've seen how it ends.*

I held up a palm to the babble. "I'll walk for a time, alone. You'll have my decision anon."

Outside the tent the night was chill. I set out aimlessly, clutching my chest as if to contain the sorrow. When I fell, I'd take so many into the abyss. What of brave Groenfil, stubborn Tantroth? How could they make peace with Hriskil, after the harm they'd done him? What of Anavar, displaced and homeless? Where might I send Elryc? Would Rustin yield, or go down in stubborn defeat, unwilling to yield though his liege had done so?

What of Tresa?

I swallowed. Almost, my hated virginity had worth, if I'd saved myself for her. But even if we escaped, how could I ask her to marry a penniless exile? She deserved more. Anyway, escape was most unlikely. The Norlanders from Soushire trailed us by only a day or so. When foemen from Eiber Castle came upon us, the two forces would seize us in a crab's pincers. We'd be done.

And what would befall Tresa when Stryx fell? If Hriskil sent Genard to a brothel, what fate for the Lady of the Hill?

Casually, I drew my blade, fingered its sharp edge. Why wait for capture, or death in hopeless battle? Why kill more men, to defend bare hills, sparse fields? The foe had all the towns, and would keep them.

"It's not so bad as that, m'lor'."

I whirled. Genard stood back a respectful dozen paces.

"How would you know?" I spoke without thought.

"I know." He eased closer. "Where do we walk?"

"Where my steps take me." I gentled my tone. "Is there ever a day that's worth the wait?"

"The day you came." He said it simply, without guile.

I resumed my wander. "Know you what we debate?"

"I can imagine."

"What say *you,* liege man of the prince?"

"I'll never . . ." he swallowed. ". . . be a man."

My hand shot out to squeeze his shoulder, but he shied away.

"When you used your Power . . . the hurt eased. Oh, Roddy, I don't know how you did it, but thank you!"

I dared not speak.

Genard's voice hardened. "*Now, make Hriskil pay! He's evil, Roddy. Think of the wagon in the Pezar field. You're good, and kind. Isn't it odd, I never used to think so, but you are.*" His fingers flitted to his loincloth. "I can live with this, if you put a stop to him. Else he'll mangle Elryc, and the sons of lords, and who will be left? Don't stop, King, while there's breath in your body!" His cheeks were damp.

In silence, we walked a while, and returned to the tent.

I FACED THE nobles of Caledon. "We thank you for your counsel." I was too overwrought to sit. I paced from flap to post, from post to wall. "Struggling on to defend Caledon through the winter is hopeless. As you say, we've no base, no supplies; our armies are disorganized, defeated, scattered. Cumber is fallen, Soushire and Groenfil, and Stryx not far behind. Our wishing otherwise will not make it so."

Anavar put head in hands.

I said heavily, "In a month, perhaps less, what's left of our strength will melt to naught."

Horst nodded in sour agreement.

Groenfil said heavily, "We concede?"

"No, my lords. We attack."

They stiffened, as if lightning coursed through them.

Tantroth said, "With Groenfil's new force, we have a chance. The Norlanders have strengthened Eiber Castle, but I know every nook, every cranny—"

"Not Eiber. Ghanz."

Every eye was on mine.

"The one border Hriskil can't defend: there's no natural barrier between Eiber and the Norlands. We can cross anywhere."

Horst said angrily, "They outnumber—"

"Near all their army occupies our land. Is it not so, Guiat? Hriskil cannot have much reserve. We'll all cross the border together. Tantroth, you'll torch every Norland village we meet. Burn it to the ground; leave not a timber. Ride day and night, spread fire without end. It will draw what troops Hriskil has, and instantly. My lord Groenfil, you and I, on our best horses, the four hundred strongest, dash the twenty leagues to Ghanz."

Horst cried out, "Why? A raid of four hundred may achieve surprise, but you can't hold the capital. They'll be on us."

"Not after we take Hriskil." I took deep breath and spoke into their astonished silence. "He's the head of the beast; strike it off and the beast collapses. They're already demoralized and looking for excuse. Why do you gape? Think you we ought fight defensive war 'til we're old and gray? No. I'll have done with it."

"But—"

"It's the last they'd expect of us." *And with good reason, Roddy.* "Still, I won't require it of you." I took deep breath. *"Now do we, King of Caledon, release you our peers from your oaths of fealty, and wish you well wheresoe'er you may go."*

Anavar shook his head, as if to halt folly.

"Now do we, Rodrigo, humbly ask our brothers, would you, of your free will, ride with us once more? Would you end the war our lands restored, our enemy expelled, our lives redeemed?"

FORTY-SIX

DANZIK RODE AT my side, silent a long while. Then, offhandedly, as if remarking on something inconsequential such as a
bird's plumage, "He constantly builds, you know. Palace is always in an uproar. New battlements going up, enclosing much
more land, but he's using stone from the old. Leaves gaps 'til
he's done."

"Yes, Guiat?"

He pursed his lips, patted his burdened mare for encouragement. "There's a terrace near his bedchamber . . . a low
wall surrounds it."

I listened, said nothing.

"He built trail from there to stables. His favorite route to
sneak out for ride."

"Hmmm."

"Or escape."

"Guiat, don't say more. You have to live with—"

"Treason? You made me Caled, day by day." He looked
sour. "I not traitor if you win. Patriot, then."

I looked at him with new appreciation.

Danzik gazed at the road ahead. "I could show you courtyard."

WE'D DIVIDED SUPPLIES and taken the best horses. For a week,
our four hundred camped shivering in Eiber's remotest hills,
while Tantroth's Eiberians did their work to lure out Hriskil's
minions. Now, dressed as Norls, armed to the teeth, we drove
our mounts ever deeper into the Norland. A day ahead lay
Ghanz, and the end of our quest.

We sent out no scouts. Danzik himself guided us. Groenfil
rode in silence, his son Horst at his side. Despite the young
man's proposals, he insisted on riding with his father, as
Anavar did with me. To my surprise, Genard demanded to
come too, which meant bringing Elryc. As we had no refuge
for him, I consented. He was well in the center of our column,
separated even from Genard.

Near Ghanz we met ten soldiers with a ramshackle cart creaking down the road toward Eiber. We'd never learn their mission; now they all lay dead alongside the trail. As planned, we ourselves would reach Ghanz before word of our invasion.

Once again, in the chill night air, we dismounted and walked our horses. We had sparse fodder and little to offer them save encouragement.

"How far now?" Anavar's voice was quiet.

"Three hours. Maybe four." Danzik.

Groenfil stirred. "Is it necessary we split ourselves?"

Trudging down the road, I looked to Danzik.

"How else," he said, "to drive Hriskil to courtyard and path to stable?"

Groenfil frowned. "I still say your party's too small. A hundred men more—"

Danzik stopped abruptly, grasped his pommel. "I told you, no room for many at gap. They'll be seen. Besides, you'll need every man to force gate."

I nodded. Even Danzik would go with Groenfil. Once inside, only Danzik, among us, knew the way to Hriskil's apartments.

I patted Pezar's neck and swung into the saddle. "Just a bit longer, boy." Thank Lord of Nature for that. Our mounts were worn near death.

MY PALMS WERE clammy as we cantered into the outskirts of Ghanz. We'd decided against any attempt at concealment; we were Norls riding home. But as we neared the palace, well after twelfth hour, I was glad of the dark that masked us.

Groenfil's men led their mounts into a farmer's field, as we'd arranged.

Danzik beckoned. "Hurry now." On foot, he led the few of us—Anavar, Genard, Kadar, myself, a handful of others—along the rebuilt outer wall. We passed through an unbuilt gap, came after a time to the inner wall. Parts stood strong, other stretches were knocked down in an orgy of reconstruction.

After what seemed like hours, but couldn't have been long, he pointed. "Hole in wall." I nodded. "Courtyard. Door in bricks, opens from inside. That path there goes to stables."

"Right." I touched fists, in the Norl style.

"Thank you."

"Salut, Rez." And he was gone.

Slowly, we worked our way to the courtyard.

"NO GUARDS, SIR!" Anavar reached over the half-finished wall. In his eyes, the fierce joy of a warrior. He hauled Genard over the broken stones to the level ground above, then the two reached down to aid my climb. Immediately, Genard hoisted his spiked club.

I'd insisted on leading our squadron, despite all objections. This was my last cast of the bones; I'd have revenge, or death. We were few, but we need be few, else we'd be seen flitting in the shadows.

To the distant clash of arms—Groenfil, hurling himself against the palace gates—we padded across the marble terrace. Columns of white stone glistened in the moonlight. We made for the wooden door beyond. Genard gripped his spiked club as if to throttle it. I shifted my sword from hand to hand, not daring to sheath it.

Abruptly, from within, the thud of running feet. Genard darted to the shadow of the palace wall. The door crashed open, knocking Anavar, behind it, to the deck. A dozen armed figures poured into the courtyard. "Ahia, ib Rez!" *This way, my King.*

Genard swung his club with all his might. A crack. A gush of blood. A Norlander went down, clutching his ruined leg. Our half dozen guardsmen leaped to the attack, but Hriskil's soldiers recovered quickly; in moments three of our men were rolling on the terrace, clutching wounds. I lunged with my sword, caught a courtier in the chest. Genard's club whirled anew. I spun about, blooded another guard.

Anavar leaped to his feet, brandishing his sword. A guard loomed. The boy ducked one blow, skittered back, evading another. Then, his shield set, he traded ferocious blows with the taller Norl.

Shrieking like a maddened brute, Genard lay about him with his wicked club. It tore flesh wherever it touched.

A helmeted figure lunged, his sword gleaming. Desperately, I twisted clear. Curses. A face I knew.

Hriskil. Two of his guards urged him to the broken steps.

I smashed the hilt of my sword into a Norlander's temple, clawed past the falling body, leaped onto the steps. I bared my teeth.

The Norl guards moved, each to a flank. Silent, a demon in the night, Genard raced up behind one, slammed his club between the man's shoulders. With a grunt, he went down. The embedded spikes tore the club from Genard's grasp.

Genard bent to retrieve it; a kick from Hriskil sent him flying. He jumped to his feet, stumbled on the bloody terrace.

I lunged with my sword, used the instant it brought me to draw my dagger. Kadar slipped on blood and crashed to the flagstones. As the guardsman raised his broadsword to finish him, I hurled the blade with all my might. It buried itself in the guard's chest. Coughing, he fell atop Kadar and was still.

Across the courtyard the remaining two guards drove Anavar into a corner. Frantically, he lunged and parried. Behind them, a lithe figure leaped on a guard's shoulders, wrapped itself around him, bit down on his neck. The man shrieked. He cavorted in desperate agony. Genard held on, remorseless.

Hriskil gripped his sword. His eyes never left mine. "Kenna vos sa mord." *Better you were dead.*

I raised my sword, as if in salute.

Instantly he lashed out, catching the corner of my shield. It tore from my grasp. A stab of pain in my left wrist. Was it broken? No time to know.

We lunged and parried, steel clashing in the night.

In the far corner, a howl of agony. I didn't dare look.

I drove forward. Catlike, Hriskil jumped back. He trod on a dead guard, stumbled. Violating all my training at arms, I lunged, sword high over my head. The blade sliced down. He raised his sword just in time to parry. My blow shattered his blade.

My sword whirled again. Hriskil skittered aside, jumped to his feet.

I risked a glance. Anavar battled a lone guardsman. Hriskil remained. I. And Genard, scuttling past to retrieve his club.

A gasp. Anavar withdrew his bloody sword. The guard clutched his opened guts. He fell heavily.

Warily, Hriskil retreated.

Genard rushed past, swiping with his club. Hriskil skipped out of the way. Genard took up station at the door to the palace.

Anavar ran to guard the broken wall. "We have him!" His tone was joyous. "Hurry, my lord!"

Hriskil threw himself at a fallen guard, tugged at his sword. I bore down; he retreated without the weapon.

The Norland king spun to the door. Genard raised his club. Hriskil hurled the remnant of his broken sword; it slashed Genard's calf. The boy yelped but held his ground. "Kill 'im, Roddy!"

Hriskil strode to the wall, and Anavar. I followed, girding myself to stab him through.

Hriskil ducked, scooped up a jagged stone. He whirled. I threw up my shield.

He spun again, hurled the rock with all his might. It caught Anavar full in the forehead. The boy toppled without a sound. His sword clattered.

Hriskil lunged at it. I stamped on the sword. The point of my blade hovered at his throat. Slowly, I backed him to the cold marble wall.

"Kill 'im, Roddy!" Genard danced, heedless of the blood trickling down his leg. "Do it, King!"

Hriskil's eyes met mine, unafraid.

"Tura pare," I said in his savage tongue. *Face the wall.* My razor-sharp steel caressed his jugular.

Almost with contempt, he did so.

"Genard, bind him."

The boy hobbled over, glanced about, unknotted his coin purse, tore loose the leather thong. While the edge of my sword wavered not an iota, he bound Hriskil's wrists behind him.

I wrapped Genard's fingers around the hilt of my sword. "Kill him if there's need."

I ran to Anavar's still form.

Some time later, we met in the deserted throne room of Ghanz: Genard, my erstwhile bodyguard Kadar, the earl of Groenfil, and me. Genard's leg was bound, and he walked with a grimace, but his wound wasn't deep.

They'd carried Anavar to a cushioned chair and laid him across it.

His forehead had bled, but dried. He breathed slowly, steadily, shallowly. We pressed cool compress on the angry lump over his eyes. He did not stir.

Hriskil was held by two of my guards, with drawn blades. He ignored them, but his eyes darted back and forth ceaselessly, as if he awaited rescue.

Within an hour of his capture the remains of his force had melted into the hills. Some half of the populace of Ghanz was doing likewise. Groenfil, by common consent, assumed command of the city, and slowly brought the palace to life. Servants were found, ordered to provide food and drink. Groenfil's men established a guard over the open places and made the palace ours.

I wrote to Rustin, and to Tresa, exulting in our good fortune.

Then I slept.

I unearthed the White Fruit of Chorr, summoned Hriskil. Shackled, he stood defiant before me.

"Swallow this, lord King, or be executed." For what he'd done to Genard, would have done to Elryc, he deserved no less.

"Mordre ot, si careth." *Kill me, if you will.*

I had him led away.

FORTY-SEVEN

I HUDDLED IN my chosen chamber in Ghanz's chill palace. I lived not in King Hriskil's grand rooms, whose wide windows gave out on the central courtyard, nor in his vanished queen's perfumed soft chambers, whose reed carpets and muraled walls were wondrously gentle.

There was no splendor to my court. Had I, in Rust's retirement, become something of an ascetic? I drank wine sparingly, ate what was put before me, dealt as best I knew with the consolidation of our realms. Willem of Alcazar held Stryx Castle on my behalf. Tantroth was at last restored to his realm. Tresa was home in Cumber, seeing to its restoration. In far Verein, in a high chamber, Duke Margenthar gibbered and twitched, attended by his son, Bayard, and Lady Varess. I let them remain, though the land and castle were awarded to Anavar, who could make no use of it.

For days after our courtyard battle, Anavar had lain senseless while ritemasters and healers near suffocated him with their ministrations. For a time the orb of one eye was larger than it ought be, when his eyelids were pried open.

Anavar woke slowly, over a week's time, wasted and famished. Eagerly I fed him thick soups and soft foods, and slowly his strength returned, but not his essence.

It was as if he'd returned to childhood. His speech was simple, his thoughts unclouded, and his form, always youthful, showed no sign of growth.

Elryc and I journeyed once to the coast, to see our Norland villages. On our return we'd found Anavar curled in a closet, clutching an old cloth as if a mother's breast. He hadn't eaten or touched his bed since our departure.

From that time on, I kept him near. He slept in a corner of my chamber, rose when I did. As time passed he grew more alert. He fed himself, cleaned himself after defecation, walked where he was led. He could even ride, after a fashion, though a steed such as Edmund was beyond his means. He took great delight in following me about the city, on a dainty mare, content that I hold his reins.

On my next visit to the coast, he and Genard rode along and slept in my tent.

Elryc and I grew closer, and spoke seriously about the dangers to the kingdom and the brooding strength of the Ukra foe beyond our eastern border. Genard served my brother faithfully, and fretted when Elryc took to his bed with yet another ague. He seemed to recover, fell ill again. This time he did not arise. Genard held one hand, I the other, as we saw Elryc off to that distant land shrouded in dark.

I was besotted for five days, and no liege man dared come near. It took that long for Rustin to ride from the Keep, to coax me from utter despair. Three weeks he remained, and I clung to him as of old.

Eventually I roused myself, resumed care of Anavar and took pity on poor lost Genard. Daily, Elryc's erstwhile vassal helped me bathe Anavar in the marble tub in Hriskil's former chamber, a fixture too heavy to contemplate moving. It was a task I had a score of servants to perform, but Anavar was comforted by my touch, and I would give him what diversion I might. Every tenthday or so, I shaved the down from the Eiberian's cheeks with a honed blade. Trusting, he would sit perfectly still until I was done. Often Genard fingered his own hairless chin, knowing it would remain so, and I would give him a rough hug, find some game or task to soothe his melancholy.

In a year or so, when Genard grew older and perhaps more sedate, I would make him Master of the Horse of all Ghanz, and he'd have men and boys aplenty to do his bidding. For now, I taught him figuring, even the art of reading, though it gave me great amusement to see him knot his brow in fierce concentration over his letters. Then I would think of the frantic dance I'd set him to, after he'd mocked my own reading, and my mirth would fade.

Hriskil, former king of the Norland, lived.

I'd set his execution for midday, not long after he refused my mercy. He'd strode to the block unaided, contemptuous of his fetters. He'd stopped abruptly, stared at the headsman's axe before him, turned to me. "Flavo ke iv, Rez." *I will taste of it, King.*

"You're sure?"

He exhaled, and something of his proud bearing left him. "Qay."

I had him brought to the throne room, bound and hooded. All my courtiers were banished, the doors sealed. I uncovered his mouth, fed him the White Fruit, waited a few moments, unhooded his eyes. He gazed upon me and became forever mine. It was a month later that he placed the Norland crown on my brow, in the presence of my nobles assembled.

As for his army in Caledon, it melted with the snows. I offered amnesty to all who surrendered what they'd seized. That Hriskil himself fervently endorsed my offer surely helped persuade them. In weeks, Caledon's strongpoints were again ours.

Danzik grudgingly consented to become my principal advisor in Ghanz; he knew the nobles, he said, and would fend off their mischief. To him I was "Rez," as ever, and he "Guiat." He would *veztrez coa tern*.

My bondsman Tanner remained in my new household. I sent him to tutors, to make of him what they might. In the chill evenings, the business of state completed, I would sit with him while he pored over his slate, and Anavar played quietly in the corner.

Tanner delighted in my notice, and I did my best to explain what he couldn't fathom. When his attention wandered, as a boy's must, I punished him with a stroke or two of a thin willow switch I kept for the purpose, enough to sting, but lightly so he would grin after, knowing I was deliberately far more gentle than his dour tutors. We reached an accommodation, and it wasn't long before I had to steal surreptitious glances at his scrolls, to stay ahead of his learning.

Almost daily, couriers flew between Cumber and Ghanz. Heedless of the risk of betrayal, I poured out my heart to Tresa, and her return scrolls comforted me with wisdom and care.

I visited with Mother, and Grandsire Tryon. Varon was oft gone, to his far place.

"So, Roddy." Mother crouched beside me, before the chill fire. "Is this the last time?" Her fingers flitted to my shoulder.

"I think not, madam. But soon." Visit by visit, I was steeling myself for the inevitable. Yet someday I would return to the cave and await my successor.

"Is the woman coming to Ghanz?"

"After the sowing." Despite myself, I blushed. In some ways, I was still a boy.

As if reading my mind, she smiled. "You mastered yourself after all."

"My lust, Mother. But not my cruelty."

"Fah. You're kind to that Tanner rapscallion, you adopted Anavar, even Genard doesn't—"

"But not Hriskil."

"He deserves no kindness." She dismissed it.

But after, in my room, I couldn't do as much.

Hriskil, having tasted of the White Fruit, was utterly devoted to me. He straightened my chamber, brought me soft cushions, eagerly refilled my tankard.

When the cruelty came upon me, I would confine him to comfortable quarters and deny him the sight of me. After, when I relented, he would rush about, smoothing my room, most anxious to express his pent-up servitude.

When Genard was despondent, and I felt particularly cruel, I would lock Hriskil away a day or two, then summon him to a room where every cushion was fluffed, my mug brimming, the fire crackling, and every imaginable want fulfilled. Expressionless, I'd let him rush about in growing dismay, desperate to give me ease.

One such day, he began gnawing at his fist, weeping, until I relented and asked some trivial assistance. Thereafter, I tried not to trouble him again, yet found it a hard vow to keep.

And so winter thawed into spring.

Now I sit awaiting Tresa, and our marriage. Tanner has memorized a florid speech of welcome, one of many she must endure. Mother says I need not fear the marriage bed, that Tresa will guide me in my ignorance. I trust it will be so.

I long for Tresa's companionship, and what relief our bedding will provide me. And I yearn for an heir. I imagine drooling youngsters on my lap, giggling and squirming. The first of them will someday have Caledon, and if I have the say of it, will be virgin and true.

By the imps and demons, I will be a good father. I have practice, raising two damaged children who are beloved to me, and young Tanner as well.

Rustin will come for the wedding, with Zetra and Jocyln, the boy and girl who share his Keep. How they sort themselves out at night, I fear to ask. When Rust rides through the gate, I'll weep, and mope, and be jealous.

Yet, while he's here I'll show him Hriskil's villa I've had re-done in Rust's favorite colors, not an hour distant. The various bedchambers he and his retinue could share, however they choose. The fine stables for his horses. Perhaps, just perhaps, he'll see his way to staying in Ghanz, instead of at his father's gloomy Keep. Perhaps, now and then, I'll be able to ride Pezar to him, to pass a spring afternoon in the sunlight of his company.

Life, I've learned, is not an affair of joy. Elryc, Nurse Hester, Tursel, Anavar, Uncle Raeth . . . on each tide, it seems, a barque drifts from shore, filled with friends and comrades who've shared adventures past. It hoists sail and slides into the mist, never to return. Each day, new companions crowd aboard and grip the rail, their faces set to unknown lands, and you know that one day, whenever fated, you too shall stride aboard to take your place on deck.

My new palace is bleak, my retainers civil and distant, my thoughts remote.

Tresa writes that my mood will lighten, that I've seen too much in too few years. Regardless, when all is done, I'll have my Lady of the Hill, and in a way for which I can find no words, Rustin, regent of my soul, is never truly lost.

I've thrown myself into the Still time and again, consulting Mother, making my peace with my predecessors before it forever passes from my grasp. Yet once, idly, pondering the growing menace of the Ukras, I picked up Hriskil's bent and bejeweled Rood, and an odd tingle coursed through my fingers so that I nearly dropped it. That, I imagine, will bear exploring, in dreary winter afternoons that stretch before me.

Of an evening, Anavar at my feet, logs crackling in the hearth, my palms cupping a ewer of stillsilver, I've searched desperately for his lost soul. Once, my hands over the ewer, deep in a glade, an elusive fawn with Anavar's eyes dashed off into the wood. I raced after, and came within a mouse hair, but couldn't catch him. If only I could reach the creature, persuade it to eat from my hand. That night, I wept.

I'm determined to try again, this night. Outside the cave, I've practiced running, until in my half-life, I'm swift as a gazelle. And I've devised a snare, made from twisted vine. I'll catch it around his neck . . . I cannot, will not, accept that my loyal liege man, my young Baron Anavar is gone forever.

This night, and next, before Tresa's entourage arrives at my court in full panoply and I am distracted, I'll seek my lost Baron of the Southern Reaches.

I've little time. Tenthday, after the pomp and rituals of marriage, I will take Tresa into my bed, and lay down forever the Still of Caledon.